This Woman Forever

This Woman
Forever

#1 *NEW YORK TIMES* BESTSELLING AUTHOR

JODI ELLEN MALPAS

Entangled Publishing, LLC
644 Shrewsbury Commons Ave., STE 181
Shrewsbury, PA 17361
rights@entangledpublishing.com

Amara is an imprint of Entangled Publishing, LLC.

Visit our website at www.entangledpublishing.com.

Edited by Marion Archer
Proofed by Karen Lawson
Cover art and design by Hang Le
Stock art by Nadtochiy/Istock
Interior design by Britt Marczak

ISBN 978-1-64937-773-9

Manufactured in the United States of America

First Edition May 2024

10 9 8 7 6 5 4 3 2 1

AMARA
an imprint of Entangled Publishing LLC

ALSO BY JODI ELLEN MALPAS

For all of you This Man lovers…
Long live The Lord.

Chapter 1

I look down onto the docks, my hands braced against the balustrade. I can hear Ava and her mother in the kitchen chatting. Everyone else has left after what was a lovely evening on the terrace, a fine meal, a proposal. But Ava's parents are still here, and I might need to physically escort them out.

"Good view."

I look over my shoulder and find Joseph on the threshold of the terrace, hands in his pockets. "I can't say I ever really appreciated it before."

"Mind if I join you?"

I smile mildly to myself. "Sure." I can't claim to know Joseph particularly well, but I do know he's a man of few words and each one carries weight. I hear him approach and see him in my peripheral vision, joining me to look out across the city. The black sky is illuminated with windows of yellow lights. The moonlight is bouncing off the water. It really is spectacular.

"They're talking about dresses and décor," he says, rolling his eyes when I look at him. "Well, Elizabeth is doing most of the talking."

I laugh under my breath. I can imagine. But she's wasting her time. By tomorrow evening, everything will be in place. "Thanks for coming all this way."

"Thanks for hosting us."

"No problem," I answer, and a lingering silence falls, not particularly uncomfortable but definitely loud. So I break it. "Is something on your mind, Joseph?" I ask, and this time it's him laughing under his breath.

"Is it obvious?"

"Well, I know you didn't come out here to join me in a romantic moment to take in the view." I face him, showing him I'm ready to tackle whatever he's going to hit me with. "Please, speak freely."

He nods, mirroring me, looking back at the doors into the penthouse, where his wife and daughter are, before giving me his eyes. "Is Ava okay?"

I can't hide my recoil. I wasn't expecting *that* question. Can't they see she's fine? That I'm looking after her? Always will. "Is she okay?" I parrot, hoping he'll elaborate.

"She seems a little...distracted."

I can still hear Elizabeth rabbiting on about God knows what. *Distracted*. "I think she's a little overwhelmed," I say quietly.

"And pale."

I shoot my eyes to Joseph. What the hell do I say? Tell him she's ignoring all the signs that she's pregnant?

But *is* she pregnant? The doctor said she wasn't. He also said it may be too early to tell. There's a box full of pregnancy tests hidden in the laundry room that could answer the question once and for all. Or her imminent period will. I've done the mental math. She's due in a couple of weeks. Can I wait that long to know beyond doubt? Ava's insisting on condoms. She's also asked me outright what I've been doing with her pills. So she knows of my sins. Or, at least, that one.

And yet she still agreed to marry me. Fuck, I'm so fucking confused by all of these mixed messages. *Distracted*. Her father has noticed. "I'll keep an eye on her," I say quietly, wondering how I'll handle this. Delicately is that answer. Problem is, I'm Jesse Ward. Not exactly known for a soft approach. I do try, though. I fail, but I try. I can't fail this time. I clear my throat. "Do you have my number, Joseph?" I ask, pulling out my mobile, prompting him to get his. "I'm sure she's fine."

"I'm sure," he says, albeit with hesitance he can't hide.

Fuck, is he doubting *me*? Has Ava's brother been pouring poison in his ear? "I'll look after her," I say, not for the first time, trying to squash any lingering reservations Joseph may have about the man his daughter's marrying, regardless of the fact that he should be bursting with reservations. *Fuck it all to hell.* My perfect evening feels like it's slipping down the pan, Joseph's doubts unearthing my own. Has Ava changed her mind about marrying me? Did she say yes out of ease or embarrassment?

Joseph nods mildly, checking the doors to the penthouse again. He's got more to say. He just doesn't know how to say it without offending me. "The drink," he asks.

I fight with everything I have not to visibly tense. "I don't drink."

"But you did."

Fuck Matt, and fuck Ava's brother. "I have in the past, yes."

"And now you don't?"

"It doesn't agree with me," I say, feeling like a complete tool. "I mean…" I exhale, raking a hand through my hair, wincing at the feel of the tender, damaged skin on my back rubbing against my shirt. "I don't know what you want me to say, Joseph. Some people can drink and get a buzz. I don't like the effect alcohol has on me, so I don't drink it."

"Because Matt—"

"Told you I'm a raving alcoholic, I know." I look out at the view again, struggling with this conversation, and really struggling not to tell Ava's father where to go. Can't do that. Besides, I like the guy, and everything coming at me now is a lot less than what I would throw if I was in his shoes. Will I ever be in his shoes? I flinch, squeezing my eyes shut, seeing Rosy in the haze of my regrets. Except she's not a toddler. She's a young woman. Reminding me I had a chance to be in Joseph's shoes.

And I blew it. *Killed her.*

"He also told you I beat him up," I say. "I didn't, but I won't lie and say I'm glad I abstained. He's a piece of work, and I won't have him forcing himself on Ava or trying to sabotage what we have." I'm yet to figure out where the hell Matt got that information from. A raving alcoholic? I laugh under my breath.

"I agree with you there. I never did like him." He obviously has good sense. *I like you even more now, Joseph.* His hand appears on the balustrade, his fat fingers wrapping around the metal. "Are you going to give me your number or not?"

I frown, looking down at my mobile in my hand as Joseph holds his up. That's the end of the conversation. And I'm so good with that. I give him my number and he dials me so I can save his. "We'd better go inside." I nod to the doors. "It's getting chilly." And it sounds like Ava needs saving from her mother.

"One more thing," Joseph says, stalling me. I look back. "The wedding."

"What about it?"

"Well." He shifts a little, looking uncomfortable, and everything inside me cools. "I'd like to contribute."

"What?" Oh God. "Jesus, no, Joseph, that's really not necessary." I laugh, uncomfortable. "It's taken care of." I can't take his money.

"I'm afraid I'm going to have to insist, Jesse. She's my little girl. My *only* girl. It's traditional for the father to pay for the wedding, but I realize you both probably have elaborate plans that will exceed any budget I could offer, so perhaps you'll graciously accept my proposal to take care of the bar bill." His eyebrows rise, and I smile.

"That's very kind of you, Joseph. I will very graciously accept." I hold out my hand and he takes it, shaking. "Thank you."

He waves me off. "Last thing."

Oh? What now?

"Let's just keep this arrangement to ourselves, okay? Man to man."

I laugh and slap his shoulder, holding my palm there as we wander into the penthouse. "Fine by me," I agree, knowing Ava won't be at all comfortable with her father using some of their retirement fund to pay for the bar at our wedding. The Manor's not cheap, and neither are the drinks. Not that Joseph will know the prices. I'll ensure he gets an invoice that's substantially lower, probably closer to wholesale price, if only to ensure his pride is kept intact. Besides, family gets a ninety percent discount.

We find Ava and Elizabeth on the couch, both with glasses of wine in their hands. Ava's hardly touched hers. Why? I eye it as I approach.

"Ah, here they are," Elizabeth sings, patting the cushion beside her for Joseph to take.

I pull my trousers up at my knees and lower next to Ava. Joseph is right. She's looking a bit peaky. "Are you all right?" I ask, getting a quick, unconvincing nod as she sips her wine. She wouldn't drink if she knew she was pregnant. Would she? Not that she's really drinking. More dipping her tongue.

"Are *you*?" she counters, eyes on me, watching for my reaction to her question.

"Yes." I smile, pushing away the conversation I had with John earlier this evening, and of which Ava caught the tail end of. Or, at least, caught my expression, which I'm sure was full of dread. To know that not only has Sarah made overt attempts to convince me I shouldn't be with Ava but has also been manipulating and orchestrating events to make Ava run from me? And nearly succeeded? I'm fuming. "I'm fine," I say, taking Ava's knee and squeezing. "What have you been talking about with your mother?" I see it in Ava immediately. Trepidation.

"Oh, we've been talking about all the things," Elizabeth chimes, as I study Ava's face, searching for any hint of excitement. "Guest lists, the cake, the menu, what season is best to get married." Elizabeth takes a mouthful of wine. "I do love a winter wedding, but this manor hotel of yours sounds like it has the most fabulous grounds, so I thought a summer wedding. That gives us just over a year to make all the arrangements, if you decide on next summer, of course. Plenty of time, I think. I'm not sure why people wait two years, to be honest with you." She laughs. "We should set a date to go dress shopping, darling." She gasps, placing her wine down on the side table and grabbing her mobile. I feel Ava getting tenser and tenser beside me. "It's Aunty Angela's birthday in July. Maybe we could make it a day out. Dress shopping for you, outfits for us, a bridesmaid's dress for Kate." She frowns. "Wait, you *are* having Kate as a bridesmaid, aren't you?" Ava nods jerkily. "I thought you must. Have you asked her yet?" Another gasp. "And best man? Who will be the best man? Sam? He seemed like a nice young man." She goes back to the screen of her phone. "So, Aunty Angela's birthday is the twelfth. That's a Monday, so perhaps we could do the tenth. The Saturday. Oh, we'll do Harvey Nics. Champagne for breakfast, lunch, and dinner." She chuckles and reclaims her wine, taking another sip before placing it back down. "I'll text her now and tell her to put it in her diary."

I glance at Joseph, who looks as exhausted as I feel after Elizabeth's verbal sprint, his chest rising slowly with his patience-gathering inhale. "Please, please, please let me," Ava whispers from beside me, obviously detecting my intention to delicately trample all over Elizabeth's grand plans. Ava's been in here for a whole half hour with her mother since everyone else left, and she's not broken the news yet? I have no faith she will now I'm sitting next to her. "Let me get you a beer, Dad," she blurts, high-pitched, diving up from the couch and hurrying off to the kitchen.

I watch her go, one eye narrowed as I rise to standing. "And more wine, Elizabeth?" I ask, eyes still on Ava's back until she disappears from view. I don't want either of them to have another drink. I'd really love for them to leave, actually, so Ava can make good on her previous intention to force me upstairs and rip my clothes off. Where's that need gone? An hour ago she was practically wrestling me toward the bedroom. It was painful denying her. Agony. But I'm not unreasonable. I would never disrespect her father like that. So what's changed since I not so subtly told Ava our wedding will be in two weeks and she very willingly agreed?

I snarl to myself. I know what. She's had too long out of my arms to overthink it. So I must get my hands back on her and reinforce the deal.

"Yes, please," Elizabeth says, handing me her glass. I leave the soon-to-be in-laws and go to the kitchen, finding Ava bent over the counter, her head in her hands. I look at her arse. Raise my brows.

Then quickly pull my lurid thoughts back into line. There will be no brutal fucking until it's answered—without dispute—if she's pregnant or not. "What's up, baby?" I ask, placing Elizabeth's wine glass down on the counter and taking her hips, doing myself no favors when I rub my groin into her arse. I quickly wrench myself away and pull Ava up to face me. I hate the despair I find. Joseph's observations, the distraction and pasty complexion. It's worry. She's pensive, listening to her mother's plans, and feeling quite sick about what her reaction might be to the news that we're getting married a lot sooner than Elizabeth imagined.

"What's up?" She laughs but quickly loses all humor, not that it was real humor. I don't tell her sarcasm doesn't suit her. Something tells me she won't appreciate it. "Did you hear her?" she asks, pointing past me.

"Yes, I heard her." The whole fucking borough of Tower Hamlets probably heard her.

Ava groans, breaking out of my hold and going to the fridge, pulling out a beer for her father. "She's going to freak out." The beer hisses when she opens it and overflows onto her feet. "Fucking hell," she breathes, looking down at her soaked toes. "Fucking, *fucking* hell."

My teeth grate, but like I refrained from telling her to mind her sarcasm, I refrain from telling her to watch her mouth. Delicately does it. Today has been a lot. For everyone. I step in, take her hips, lift her, and carry her to the counter to sit her on it. I remove the beer from her hands and slip off her heels.

She's silent as I dry the floor with a towel, before starting on her feet. Watching me. "What's the matter with you?" she asks, suspicious.

"Me?" I ask over a laugh.

"Yes, you. I just turned the air blue with my bad language and you've got nothing to say about it?"

I cock a sardonic eyebrow. "I have plenty to say about it. In fact, I'd like to fuck some sense into you right now but, unfortunately for me, we have guests." I finish drying her foot and lift it to my mouth, biting gently on the end of her middle toe. Her chest dips, her fingers clawing the edge of the counter. So I suck it into my mouth, relishing the sparkle in her eyes. That's better.

"Our guests will be leaving soon," she whispers. "So perhaps then you could fuck that sense into me."

She's goading me. Trying to get a fuck out of me rather than some easy, gentle lovemaking. "Perhaps," I muse, dropping her foot and moving in, un-clawing her fingers and guiding her hand to my hair. She tugs gently, and I smile. "Until then, we have some facts to share with your mother." I slam a kiss on her lips and swallow her groan of despair.

"I want to tell them," she argues.

"When?"

"I'll call her when they're home."

I laugh under my breath, pulling her down off the counter. "Sure. Like you were going to tell Patrick about me? Like you were going to tell him you can't work for Mikael Van Der Haus anymore?" The mention of his name has Ava's eyes dropping like rocks to my chest and *my* jaw tightening. The guy in the footage at the bar from the night Ava was drugged. He had all the credentials, looked just like Van Der Haus. I just need Jay to give me something clearer. More concrete. Then I can kill the fucker. "Come," I say, leading Ava out of the kitchen.

"Jesse, please," she pleads, but doesn't put up any physical resistance. "I don't want to ruin the day."

"It won't be ruined, because your mother will accept that this is what *we* want to do."

"What do you want to do?" Elizabeth asks, looking at my spare hand, frowning when she doesn't find any wine.

I stop Ava in front of them and look down at her. I can tell we're going to get nowhere if I leave this to my wife-to-be, so I take the lead. We're getting married in two weeks. Less than two weeks, actually. Twelve days. We haven't got time to pussyfoot around Ava's mother. "We're not getting married next summer," I say, feeling Ava move closer into my side, almost behind me. Hiding.

"Oh?" Elizabeth says. "The following summer then. I suppose that will give us more time, but we should still get your dress sorted, darling. I've texted Aunty Angela. She's so happy for you!" Going back to her mobile, Elizabeth scans the screen. "She's got no plans for Saturday July tenth, so it's a date."

"That's a bit late," I say.

"For a dress? No, no. Eighteen months seems reasonable." Elizabeth flicks across her phone. "This site has some wonderful dresses, Ava. I'll send you the link."

"We'll need it a bit sooner," I go on, as Ava slinks farther behind my back.

"What?" Elizabeth doesn't look up from her phone, but Joseph is watching Ava and me standing in front of them, curious. "Oh, Ava, white or ivory?" Elizabeth bangs on. "Pearls, diamantes?" She gasps, hand on her chest. "Veil? Oh, you must let your great aunty Glenda make it. She made mine *and* your aunty Angela's."

"We're getting married a week on Saturday, Elizabeth," I say clearly, waiting for it. Joseph sinks deeper down into the couch, obviously waiting for it, too, and Ava tenses behind me.

Elizabeth eyes lift, but her head remains low. "What?"

"A week Saturday," I affirm. "At The Manor."

"Don't be ridiculous," she says, laughing. "Who organizes a wedding in less than two weeks?"

"Me."

Her face falls, probably because she's comprehended how serious I am. "But half of your guest list will probably have plans already at such short notice."

I shrug. "This wedding is for us. Not for our guests." I'd happily whisk Ava off to a foreign land tonight if I could, but I can't. You need licenses, papers from whatever country you're marrying in, blah, blah, blah. So The Manor it is. I just need a license to hold ceremonies. I smile. I know just the man.

"But…" Elizabeth slowly gets to her feet. "But…but…"

"But…" I say.

"But…"

"Elizabeth," Joseph murmurs quietly, with soft warning.

"I won't hear of it," she snaps. "No. I won't allow it. For Christ's sake, people will think…" She gasps.

"I'm not pregnant before you start," Ava grates, pulling my interested eyes back to where she remains half-hidden behind me, avoiding the shit flying. She's not? Says who, the doctor, Ava, or an actual test?

"Then why the rush?" Elizabeth cries. "We have to give people notice. I have to find my outfit! No. No, you absolutely cannot get married next Saturday."

I feel Ava deflate behind me, and she looks up at me, as if to say… see? Yes. I see. I see that her mother is a pain in my fucking arse. Ava exhales heavily, defeated, and leaves the room, walking to the kitchen. Of course, I follow, rather than giving Elizabeth a deserved trample and upsetting the situation further.

She's pouring a glass of wine when I enter, and I don't miss the slight hesitation as she raises it to her mouth before her lips straighten and she swigs. "And that is why I wanted to tell her over the phone," she says, resting the glass down and facing me. "And I can't even blame her for being dramatic because…" She laughs. "I've known you two months! How could anyone possibly know they want to be with someone forever within two months?"

"I knew in two minutes," I say quietly, winning her eyes. Guilt. I see it on her. "Don't tell me you're changing your mind."

"Of course I'm not."

"You agreed a week on Saturday."

She sighs. "I know."

Well, this is wonderful. "You could at least *pretend* to be excited, Ava," I grumble, passing her and going to the fridge, yanking it open and pulling out a jar of my faithful. I unscrew the lid and focus on the digging some out—anything to soothe my injured state.

I don't get a chance to get my finger into my mouth, though. My wrist is seized and held still, and Ava takes the jar from my other hand and puts it on the counter. She looks at me with sorry eyes. "Forgive me?"

I pout. "Do you want to marry me?"

"Yes."

"Then let's do it, baby."

She nods and directs my finger to her mouth, slipping it past her lips. I inhale. What the fuck is she doing to me?

"You hate peanut butter," I whisper, my voice low and husky, my dick twitching. She sucks, licks, circles the tip with her tongue, then pulls it out slowly on an erection-provoking pop.

"But I love *you*," she whispers, swallowing. "*Need* you."

I back her up into the nearest wall, ready to ravish her, take what I've been desperate for all evening and what Ava has tempted me with. I kiss her cheek. "I'll take care of everything," I whisper, kissing her other cheek. "All you need to worry about is your dress." I move my lips to her forehead.

"Everything?"

"Every little thing," I assure her, dotting kisses down the bridge of her nose. I won't have her overwhelmed or stressed. She just needs to show up and say I do. "Even the honeymoon."

"Wait." She puts her hands into my chest and pushes me back a little. "I can't go on a honeymoon. Not straight away. I've already had too many days off work, and I've got to get Ruth Quinn's contract wrapped up." She grimaces. It sounds like this Ruth Quinn is a belly ache. But at least she's not Van Der Haus. "Please, just give me a few weeks before you book something."

My shoulders drop. I suppose this is compromise. "Fine. Don't ever tell me I'm unreasonable," I mutter, moving back in and resuming our closeness, now placing my lips on her mouth. "Can we get rid of your parents now?"

She laughs, and it's dick-twinging stuff. God help me. But my growing erection droops when I hear my soon-to-be father-in-law clear his throat. I cry on the inside, and Ava cringes as we face him. Elizabeth is silent by his side. A scorned child. "You mother has something to say." He nudges Elizabeth. "Don't you, dear?"

"I'm sorry," she gushes, coming to us and muscling me out the way to get to her daughter. "It was a bit of a shock, that's all." She squeezes Ava to her chest, and I grit my teeth, seeing her shoulders jump up, trying to deal with her mother's hands all over the lashes on her back. Lashes that never should have touched her skin. "Forgive me."

"Forgiven," Ava says quickly.

I breathe out when Elizabeth releases her, and Joseph gives me a nod which I return, a silent thank-you. "So your father and I had a little chat," she says, looking between us. "We're going to stay for a few days."

I choke on nothing, trying to disguise it as a cough.

What?

Stay? In London?

"There's so much to plan and to arrange," she goes on.

"It's all under control," I pipe up quickly.

"Maybe, Jesse, but there's one thing you can't do."

"Is there?" I ask, scratching through my head for what that could be. "What?"

"Buy her dress." Elizabeth goes to the fridge and opens the wine. "We'll go tomorrow. I'll call Aunty Angela. You call Kate."

"Mum," Ava breathes. "I'm working tomorrow."

"Working?" She pours as I get the beer from the counter and hand it to Joseph. "But you have a dress to find, Ava." She sips. "And what if it needs to be altered?"

"Zoe will take care of it," I say, laughing when Joseph picks up my open jar of peanut butter and grimaces at it.

"Will she?"

"Yes." She's the only woman I know who can make a dress happen with such notice. And she owes me for nearly bankrupting me last Friday. "I'll message her"—I take the jar from Joseph and put it back in the fridge, then tap out a message—"see what she's got tomorrow."

"I have to work tomorrow," Ava protests, lowering to a stool. I can see it. The gravity of it all overcoming her. "And what about my hair? And nails? And lashes. Should I have lashes?" She looks at her mother. "Do I need lashes?"

"That's it," Elizabeth says. "We're definitely staying, no arguments." She necks her wine and refills. "I'll never find anything in Newquay for such a special occasion, so I'll take myself shopping tomorrow while you're at work. Hopefully this Zoe can see us after you're finished." She huffs her disappointment. "Who has time to work when there's a wedding to plan?"

Finally, something we both agree on. I purse my lips and glance at Ava with high, agreeable eyebrows, and she, true to form, rolls her eyes and sticks her tongue out. "But I'm not organizing, am I?" she retorts, smug. "You must stay here," she says, returning her attention to her mother.

What?

Is she being spiteful?

"But we have a hotel, darling," Elizabeth says, laughing a little. I can see it in her eyes as she casts them around the surrounding luxury. She wants to stay.

"No, no, you must stay here." Ava stands, looking at me. "They should stay, shouldn't they?"

What can I say?

No?

Fuck off, I refuse to share your daughter with you?

I sigh, and it's really fucking deep. I can hear myself. Luckily, no one else can. I know at some point in our relationship I've suggested Ava's parents could stay, but I can't say with complete honestly I meant it. I was appeasing Ava when she was finding excuses for me *not* to meet them.

And now they're here. Our guests. Our *overnight* guests.

Great. For how many nights exactly?

I send a prayer to the dress gods that my testing mother-in-law finds one really fucking fast. "Yeah," I breathe. "Yeah, they should stay." In the room farthest away from ours. My phone dings. "Zoe can do five o'clock tomorrow."

"I'll leave work early," Ava says, biting at the corner of her lip through her smile. She leans up and kisses my cheek. "Thank you."

"You're welcome, baby." I take her in a hug and look over her head to her parents. "There are a few things I need to run by my wife-to-be," I say, cupping the back of Ava's head. "Excuse us." I start walking backward, bringing Ava with me, still tucked into my chest. "Make yourself at home."

I get us out of the kitchen and rush Ava up the stairs. To hell with abstaining while her parents are around. When I made that vow, I thought they'd be here for dinner, not for a city break.

I get Ava into our room and shut the door. "Strip," I order as I shrug off my jacket. "Now."

"I can't believe you did that," she says, pulling her dress up her legs.

"Really?" I ask on a laugh, making her working hands falter. "You really can't believe I did that?" I kick off my shoes and dip to remove my socks before unbuttoning my shirt.

"Dumbest thing I've ever said," she muses to herself, resuming her strip, which, frankly, is a bit fucking slow.

I get my shirt off, my trousers, my boxers, all at lightning speed, and help Ava finish, dragging her knickers down her legs. I remain crouched before her, staring at her flat stomach. *Pregnant.*

Until she reaches under my arms and pulls me back to standing, taking hold of my cock. I suck in air. Something tells me she's trying to distract me. "It really is the dumbest thing you've ever said," I say quietly, staring into her dark eyes. "And do you know what your wisest words will ever be?" I ask, cupping her between her legs.

"What?" she asks on a hitch of breath.

I kiss her neck, suck, before working my way down to her boob and refreshing my mark. I'd love to be a fly on the wall when she explains *that* to her mother on their shopping trip tomorrow. "The wisest thing you'll ever say, baby, is…" I slip a finger into her, looking up and relishing the ecstasy coating her face. "… *I do.*"

"Yes," she whispers, holding my shoulders as I work her. "And now you can fuck me." She takes my biceps and walks me to the bed, trying to push me down. *No.* I spin us and, rather than pushing her front forward onto the bed, I ease her down to her back, scanning every inch of her perfect, tight body as I do. I don't miss her flinch as her raw flesh comes into contact with the sheets. There will be no fucking. But her damaged back won't be damaged for long, therefore my reason to be gentle will be gone too.

But perhaps by then, when she's my wife, we'll have had some breakthroughs.

Perhaps by then, she'll finally admit what we both know.

Chapter 2

Ava and Elizabeth leave the penthouse together the next morning at eight on the dot, and Joseph leaves shortly after to visit some old friends. So once Cathy has finished clearing up the breakfast things, I send her on her way, leaving me alone to start making plans. My first job is to call Larry Hanna, a counsellor who plays at The Manor from time to time, although I haven't seen him for *some* time. Mind you, I haven't seen much since I met Ava.

"Ward," he says, his voice deep and suggestive of his age and background. Aristocracy. "How the devil are you?"

"Sober," I grunt, and he laughs. "I need some help."

"With?"

"A wedding venue license."

There's a small pause. "For The Manor?"

"Yes, for The Manor. Don't worry, The Manor is still The Manor." *For now.* "I'm getting married, and I'd like to have the ceremony and reception there."

"At your sex club?"

My shoulders drop.

"And you're getting married? To whom?" A gasp. "Oh, the young little interior designer? I've heard about her."

"I bet," I mutter. "Her name is Ava."

"Ava. Nice. And what does the whip-wielding, hard-hearted bitch make of this?"

I sink on the stool, reminded that Sarah is a big something I need to deal with. "Larry, can we get back to the matter at hand, please?" I need to remember this man has something I need.

"I can put you in touch with the right department. They'll have you complete some forms, make an application fee, and then they'll send an inspector to look at the space and ensure it meets regulations. They can only approve one area for ceremonies, not the entire venue. Then they'll take it to the councilors meeting, usually held on the last Friday of the month, and a decision will be made."

"That sounds quite long-winded."

"From start to finish, usually three to six months."

I baulk. "Months? Larry, I need it to happen much quicker than that."

"How quick?"

"Within the next week."

He laughs, and the rich, baritone sound irritates the shit out of me.

"I'll wave your membership fees for a year," I say flatly, and his laughter stops in a second.

"That's bribery."

"I don't believe any money is passing hands. I'll make it two years if you find me a registrar too. Call me." I hang up and get to ordering Ava's wedding present—the big one *and* the little one, a car and a watch—and then sort a new bed for our suite at The Manor. And, actually, I email some decorators too. One for The Manor's extension, and one for my office. In half an hour, both are lined up. I'm winning this morning.

Next.

I smile, looking down at my list of things to do. My smile falls. *Fucking hell.* "Wedding planner," I say, pulling my laptop close and hitting up Google. The list is endless, and I figure the ones at the top are likely to be the best and most popular, so I start there. Yes, that might mean they're also fully booked, but I'll make this well worth their while. Besides, half the job is done for them—venue, registrar, dress. I even know a baker and a florist. So, really, they'll be more of a coordinator. A very well-paid coordinator.

The first answers, and I ramp up my charm to top level, getting up from my stool and wandering. "Hi, Tessa, my name's Jesse Ward." God damn it, this would be much easier in person. I could flash my smile and biceps. "I'm looking for a wedding planner."

"I'm afraid I'm fully booked for the next three years."

I laugh. "Fucking hell." She must be *really* good. And exactly what I need. "We're getting married a week on Saturday."

Now it's her laughing.

"It's twelve days' work," I go on, not deterred. "For one hundred grand." And she shuts up. "There's no budget," I add.

"I think I might be able to figure something out."

I bet you can, Tessa. "Great. My wife to-be will be home this evening. That work?"

"Absolutely."

"Perfect. I'll send you our address." I hang up and go to my list, crossing out everything on it—it's now Tessa's list—and leave only two more things. I dial John, my stomach doing a little flip.

"Is she there?" I ask.

"She's here."

I nod and breathe out. "I'm on my way."

I sit outside The Manor for an eternity, staring up at the building that's been my life for the best part of twenty years, feeling...I don't know. Weird? I can't put my finger on it. Empty? Detached? Abs—

My phone rings, and I recoil at the dash display. Coral? I laugh sardonically. Seriously?

I reject the call and get out, heading up the steps, opening the door and listening. It's not busy—standard for this time of day. Swallowing, I walk on, vigilant, watching every door, waiting for her to appear. I find John first, coming out of my office, his wraparounds unusually sitting on his bald, shiny head. "All right?" I ask as I approach.

"She's not good."

I look at my office door. "Is she in there?"

"Yes, she's in there."

"What have you said?"

"I've said you're marrying Ava."

"And what did she say?"

"Nothing. She cried."

"Have you told her I know she used your phone to text Ava?"

"I haven't said anything." *Except that I'm marrying Ava.* He lightly pats my shoulder as he passes. "I'm around if you need me."

"Thanks," I say quietly as he wanders away, leaving me to fend for myself, putting his shades back into place.

I face the door.

Take in air.

Reach for the handle.

It's times like these I miss the drink most. Pushing my way in, I find her at my desk leaning over a file, a tissue in her grasp. She looks up, blinks, and sniffs, pulling a smile from nowhere. The last time I was with her, she was thrashing me with her whip. The last time I saw her, I had succumbed to her for the *second* time in my life. And each time I have yielded to Sarah, whether it be to her body or her whip, the aftermath has been excruciating. She's toxic. I've always known it, but when it was only me that she poisoned, it didn't matter. *I* didn't matter. I deserved everything, even if I knew deep down Sarah was in love with me. But now Sarah's venom is affecting Ava. She's trying to destroy our love. And I can't have that.

I clear my throat and motion to my chair, making Sarah get up. She puts herself on the other side of my desk as I lower, avoiding her eyes. "How's your back?" she asks, shocking me.

I lift stunned eyes to hers. "My back looks like I relented to your fucked-up fantasies and let you at me with your whip."

She shrugs. "Better than getting drunk."

I grit my teeth. How? How can she still sit there and be so vindictive after what she's done? Because she's Sarah. And it's an act. "How's your neck?" I retort, observing she's opted for a high-necked halter-type bustier to cover the scattering of bruises left behind after Ava had her by the throat.

"I'll live," she muses, crossing one leg over the other.

"You sent Ava a message from John's phone telling her to come here so she could see you thrashing me," I say, wondering how the hell she ever thought she'd get away with it. And I also wonder if she even cares that she hasn't. Does she think I'd stand for that level of betrayal? Because if she can do that, what else is she capable of?

"What?" she says, laughing. "Don't be ridiculous."

"Ridiculous?" I counter. "No, Sarah. Ridiculous is you thinking I could ever love you."

She recoils.

"After everything you've done, you honestly still think I could love you?" I lean forward. "I'm marrying Ava. And you need to leave." I get up, and her wide eyes lift with me.

"What?"

"Leave, Sarah. There's nothing here for you. There never has been, because my heart has *never* been open to you." I head for the door.

"Jesse, wait." I feel her hand on my arm, and I roll my elbow back, getting her off me, my skin burning under her touch. "I didn't do anything. You're wrong."

"And you lie?" I say on an angry whisper. "After everything, all the shit you've caused, the damage you've done, you don't even fucking own it?"

"Don't do this, Jesse, please."

"This is all you, Sarah." I wince, knowing that's a stretch. I gave her the rope to hang herself. I gave her the opportunity to fuck me over. So this is on me too. *Fuck.* I pull the door open.

"She can't make you happy!"

I swing around and stalk toward her, raging, and she backs up until she's virtually lying on my desk. "She already fucking does!" I bellow. "My heart beats for that woman, Sarah. What the fuck don't you understand about that?" I withdraw, heaving, as Sarah cowers on the desk. "Admit it," I demand. "Admit what you've done, Sarah. Own your fucking truths."

"Like you have?" she asks quietly. "How much is there for her still to know, Jesse?"

"Are you threatening me?"

"No," she blurts. "No, I love you. But will Ava if she knows the extent of our darkness?"

"Ava knows everything she needs to know."

"And when you fucked Freya and Nala in here?"

"She knows." Not *who*, that doesn't matter, but she knows.

Sarah can't hide her shock. "You told her?"

"She knew because she knows *me*, Sarah. Like she also knows we"—I wave a finger between us—"fucked once."

Her face is not a picture I want to remember. Hurt. Anger. *Realization.*

"But she doesn't know about Rosie and Rebecca?" she asks quietly. "Or Jake?"

I shake my head. "And she won't. You've done enough damage, Sarah. Let me have this peace."

Her face falls, and she looks at the carpet. "Please."

"No. You can't be in my life anymore. I don't *want* you in my life anymore. I hate you, Sarah. I hate you with a vengeance because you tried to take the one woman I've ever loved away from me." I turn and walk out, shutting the door behind me, nodding at John as I pass. He turns with me, flanking me. He say's nothing, but he's there. Always there by my side.

And this time, all the way to my car.

He opens the door for me, and I slip in, starting the engine. I look up at him. "I told her I hate her, John, and I meant it. I want...*need* her gone."

He nods, understanding. His loyalty is something I have never doubted, even when he's called me a motherfucker. *Deserved on some occasions.* But this man has been by my side unconditionally for years. Longer than anyone else.

"I need you next to me on my wedding day."

He reaches up to his glasses and removes them, giving me his eyes. "Where else would I be?"

I swallow the lump in my throat, nodding, as John shuts the door.

I pull away calmly.

Where else would I be?

And wipe my cheek with the back of my hand.

Chapter 3

Ava's parents finally left on Wednesday evening after shopping success. Can't say I was sorry to see Elizabeth leave. The woman exhausts me. But I will grin and bear her going forward, and only trample mildly. We're just establishing the boundaries. I'm managing her expectations. Building a bond. It's love/hate all the way. For both of us. But as I know she is of me, I'm fond of her. How could I not be? She's irritatingly endearing. And Joseph? Top bloke.

The next ten days seem to drag for years. Ava's been at work every day, and I've been busy. So fucking busy. But it's still dragged. I knew Sarah was the scaffolding of my business, but I truly didn't appreciate how much. I'm dealing with things I never knew needed dealing with, finding paperwork for things I didn't know existed, but it seems Sarah had her own unique system of filing shit, and as a departing gift, she didn't leave a key to what that system is. She also upended every filing cabinet in my office and the storage cupboard. I'm a little lost, to be honest. Drowning in emails and masses of paperwork, navigating the accounts system blindly. Requests from my accountant for invoices, quarter end accounts for the VAT return, employee documents, and statements have overwhelmed me. John has tried his best to support me but, like me, he's dumbfounded. If we ever needed anything, we asked Sarah. Sarah knew where everything was kept, filed, who needed what and when. I've not heard from her, but it's been difficult not to think about her when every fucker I see asks where she is. And Ava? She wanted details of Sarah's eviction from The Manor. Naturally, I was selective with the information I shared. She's gone. The end. Let's move on.

It's now *finally* Friday. The Manor has been cleared of any evidence that may point to the happenings, the communal room door has been locked and bolted, and Tessa has been flying around all day getting everything in place. Ava's parents have arrived, along with her charming brother, family, friends, and some people I don't even fucking know. I'm pretty sure Elizabeth went back to Newquay and rounded up the locals to bring to her daughter's wedding.

Everyone is here.

Except my fucking bride.

I look down at my Rolex, grumbling to myself. It's that Ruth woman again, I just know it. She's demanding, exhausting. I slide my phone off my desk and dial Ava, getting up and stretching my quads.

"Where the hell are you?" I grumble when she answers, wandering to the door and pulling it open.

"I couldn't fit my outfit in the back of my car without it getting all creased. Zoe's having it delivered."

I smile. Her outfit. And fitting anything in her car won't be a problem soon. That reminds me. I need to chase up the dealership on Ava's wedding present.

I wander through the summer room that's set up with rows of chairs and stand at the end of the aisle, looking to where I'll be waiting for her. We made it. Fucking hell, we actually made it. "How long will you be?"

"Nearly there."

"I'm hardly going to get any time with you this evening."

"But you've got the rest of my life," she muses, making me grin so wide.

"Just hurry up, will you?" I snap. "Your mother's swanning around like lady of the fucking manor throwing out orders. She wouldn't even let me in my own fucking suite earlier."

Ava laughs. I don't know why. Her mother's driving me nuts. "You're not allowed in my room."

I frown. "It's our room."

"Not tonight. Tonight it's *my* room."

"What are you talking about?"

"It's tradition for us to spend the night apart."

Say what? "Ava, come on," I implore. "You've been working non-stop, you won't give me a honeymoon—"

"I will give you a honeymoon just as soon as I've caught up with work."

I grimace. If she worked for herself, she could be more in control of work commitments.

"Jesse!" My shoulders shoot up when Elizabeth's shrill shriek of my name hits my back.

I snarl at the beautiful bouquet of flowers at the end of the aisle.

"Your mother's found me again," I hiss, and Ava chuckles. "Hurry up." I hang up, slap on a smile, and face Elizabeth. "Hey."

"You shouldn't be in here," she says, taking my elbow and guiding me out.

"Why?" I ask, looking back.

"It's bad luck."

"Stop making shit up, Elizabeth," I say, laughing. "How else do you expect me to get to my office?"

"You go through the spa."

"How do you know that?"

She shrugs, and I breathe in my patience. "We need your help."

"With what?"

"The cake."

"Kate's taking care of the cake."

"But where is it going?" she asks, leading me into the bar.

"I really don't give a shit where the cake goes," I say, looking at my watch again, jolting when she smacks my arm. I smile through gritted teeth. "In that corner," I say, pointing, pulling my phone out and texting Ava.

"What?" Her face bunches. "Don't be silly. No one will see it." She goes to another corner and assesses. I click send on my message.

It's a good thing I adore you or your mother would be squashed.

"It should go here," Elizabeth says. "Agreed?"

"Wherever you want it to go, Elizabeth." I smile, reading Ava's reply.

Keep your trampling under control, Ward.

I REALLY love you.

I REALLY know.

I back out of the room, bumping into Kate. "All right?" I ask, noting, not for the first time recently, her lack of sparkle.

"I'm fine," she says, carrying a bunch of calla lilies to the bar.

"You sure about that?" I ask, but I get no answer. She's definitely off, and something tells me Ava's brother is the cause. And, again, not for the first time recently, I ask myself how much Sam knows. Because if he does, he's not letting on, and I definitely don't want to be the one to share the news of Kate's and Dan's *history*. Especially since there's clearly unfinished business. I'm also wondering if it's why Dan's stuck around.

I still for a moment. *Wait.* Was Ava texting and driving? Because that's not acceptable. I go back to my phone, but just as I'm about to call her—not text—I hear the crunch of wheels on gravel. I back up, looking out of the open door. I see her Mini.

"Oh, the bride's arrived," Elizabeth sings, passing me, going to greet her daughter.

I don't think so.

I rush past her, hearing her shocked gasp, and pull Ava out of the car, hauling her gently up onto my shoulder.

"Whoa!" she yelps. "Jesse, what the hell are you doing?"

I'm getting my fix before some fucker robs you from me.

"Jesse Ward!" Elizabeth shrieks, tottering alongside me as I haul Ava into The Manor. "For Christ's sake, put her down."

"Nope." I take the stairs two at a time.

"But she has guests to welcome!"

"I'm sure you'll manage, Elizabeth," I call back.

"God damn you, Jesse Ward!"

I smile as Ava chuckles, not fighting me as I carry her around the gallery landing and take us into my suite. I hear the echo of Ava's mother's scornful voice hit the wood of the door as it closes, and I lower Ava to her feet. "How's your back?" I ask, taking her hands.

"Better. Yours?"

"Better." I ease her down to the carpet and spread myself all over her, settling, breathing easy, but I refrain from resting all of my weight on her stomach. "We made it," I whisper.

"We made it," she breathes, smiling, and it's fucking dazzling. She's happy. She *wants* to marry me. How could I have doubted that?

"Don't make me sleep away from you tonight," I beg. It'll feel like my limbs have been cut off. I won't get a wink of sleep, and Ava won't have me cuddling her all night. Wrong. *So* wrong.

"It's one night," she says. "It's bad luck. I don't want any bad luck."

I sigh, burying my face in her neck. *Compromise.* One night in exchange for thousands. "Fine. But I get you until midnight."

At that very moment, there's a knock at the door before it swings open. I don't look up. The horrified gasp tells me who it is. "Please, you two, won't you leave each other alone for just a few minutes?"

"Fuck off," I whisper into Ava's skin.

"We're coming," she says, chuckling.

"Are we?"

"Yes." Ava wriggles, trying to move me, and I grunt, rolling onto my back. Elizabeth stands over me, her face a picture of disapproval. Could give a fuck. But I absolutely do not. She helps Ava to her feet while I remain on my back, moody.

"Get up," Elizabeth says, offering her hands.

"I'm just going to stay here."

"Why?"

"Well, because this is where I'm sleeping tonight."

She swings a horrified look Ava's way, and Ava rolls her eyes. "He's not sleeping in here tonight, Mum," she says. "He's winding you up." Ava tilts her head, giving warning eyes. "Stop it."

"No." I force myself to my feet and let Elizabeth direct me out of the room. "I liked you when I met you," I say to her.

"I was just thinking the same about you," she retorts. "Out." I'm thrust into the corridor, just as Zoe appears with one end of a huge dress bag draped over her arms, the other end held up by John.

Fuck me, that's some dress. My stomach does a cartwheel.

"My dress," Ava breathes, biting her lip as she joins me outside the suite, her face subtly thrilled. My God, what is *the dress* like?

"Quick, in here," Elizabeth sings, opening the door wider and hurrying John and Zoe in. Then she grabs her daughter, and hauls her into the room with her.

And shuts the door in my face.

I snarl at the wood.

Chapter 4

I don't know how many times I've circled my office this morning. I left our suite at one minute to midnight when Elizabeth practically dragged me out. I made sure she knew I wasn't happy. Joseph told me to humor her. I asked Joseph how he lives with her. He laughed.

As anticipated, I didn't sleep at all, and I can really feel it. I couldn't even go to her at dawn and get my fix. She's mere meters away, upstairs in our suite getting ready to marry me, but it's been more than ten hours since I've seen her. Touched her. Fuck me, this is torture. I'm trying so hard to be respectful of her parents' traditional beliefs. And struggling. I'm tense, agitated, and even *I* know it's all very unreasonable.

We made it.

But still not communicating as well as we should.

My head falls back, and I look up at the ceiling, trying to find some calming thoughts. It's not working. I have serious issues.

Glancing down, I begrudgingly note it's only five minutes since I last checked the time. "For fuck's sake." I pull at my hair, like I'm trying to yank some reason into my stressed-out mind. What if Elizabeth's talked Ava out of marrying me? What if she's pointed out my age or the short time that we've known each other?

I snort.

Become very still.

What if Ava's confessed my pill-stealing sins to her mother and Elizabeth's talked some sense into her?

"Fucking hell." I pick up my pace and make another circuit of my office. I'm going to make myself fucking dizzy.

Too late, bro.

"Oh, you're here."

Always.

I raise my brows to myself, thinking. "I don't suppose you've been upstairs—"

And spied on your young bride?

"Fuck off."

You wish.

A knock at the door makes me jump. "What?" I bark, collapsing back in my chair, my arse hitting the seat hard. Then my forehead hits the desk.

Again and again and again.

"Stupid motherfucker." John laughs, pulling my face up. He shuts the door and strides over to my desk, amusement plaguing his face as he scans my T-shirt-clad torso. "Been running?"

"Might have." At five when I got the first glimpse of dawn.

"Nervous?"

"I'm not nervous," I scoff, picking up a pen and twiddling it between my fingers in a very nervous way. Not nervous for the reasons John thinks, anyway. "I'm impatient."

John smiles, a rare, all-white, piss-taking smile. "What's eating you?"

"Nothing's fucking eating me."

He starts laughing hard. It's a deep, rumbling, house-shaking sound, something even rarer than the smiles. I'm a fucking joke. "Jesse, get a grip. How many hours' sleep have you had? You look like shit."

"I feel it," I grumble, chucking the pen across the desk and swiping my palms over my scratchy face. "I didn't sleep."

"At all?"

I reveal my face to John and he starts nodding thoughtfully. "I would've slept just fine, had I not been dragged away from my wife by her delightful mother." I lean back in my chair and toss my feet onto my desk, closing my eyes and dragging air into my lungs. My damn heart is clattering, threatening to beat its way from my heaving chest. "Fucking pain in the arse."

"She's her mother. As much as I know you'd like to, you can't keep your girl from her mother."

"I know," I say, and doesn't that suck. I wish I could make everyone disappear, taking Ava away from anything that interferes with our private world of happiness and constant contact. I might just do that. Paradise springs to mind, but I quickly disregard it given the potential of what might find me there. "What time is it?"

"Just gone ten," John says, as his phone starts shouting from his inside pocket. He pulls it out as he stands and answers with a grunt on his way to the door. "On my way."

"Who?"

"Nothing for you to worry about."

I'm not comforted. "You checked up on Sarah?"

He stops and turns questioning eyes onto me. "She's not taking my calls."

I nod, damning myself for caring. She's done nothing but cause me pain and misery. *And yet.* That's what fucks with my head. Why do I care? *And. Yet.* Sarah has been a constant in my life for years, so to suddenly become invisible is…weird. But it was the right decision. For me. For Ava. Even for Sarah.

Enough, Ward. It's your wedding day. Stay focused.

I pull my laptop over when it dings and see a message from the dealership. I reply, telling them to have Ava's wedding present delivered to Lusso. "What time is it?" I ask again, despite having my own watch on. *And* a laptop in front of me.

"Just gone ten."

I sigh, pushing my laptop away and brushing a hand down my face.

"Bit different to last time, eh?"

I look at John. He was there but not invited. Hovering on the edge of the church grounds with Uncle Carmichael watching as I went through the motions, my moves robotic, my words emotionless, my body soulless.

My heart beats faster and has me rising to my feet, more agitated than ever before. "You mean because I actually want to marry this woman?" I ask as I make my way toward the door, deciding another run is my only option with Elizabeth keeping guard of Ava. I march past John and jog down the corridor.

"Calm down," John calls. His tone has taken on an edge of concern.

"I'm fine." I break out into a full sprint before I reach the entrance to The Manor and resist the urge to glance up the stairs as I do. I hear the shout of our wedding planner calling after me, but I keep up my pace, my legs going like pistons as I hit the gravel driveway.

Run.

Just…run.

The sun is warm on my face, the countryside air fresh, but my damn mind is still racing, and now it's also flooded with painful reminders of my past. Carmichael. Drink. Lauren…A beautiful little blond-haired girl.

Why haven't you told her about me, Daddy?

I skid to a stop in front of a tree, breathless—and not because of the run. "It's hurts," I say to thin air and the rustling trees.

And you're scared she'll think you won't be a good dad?

I take in air, my lungs burning. And that.

I pull back my fist in temper. "Fuck," I roar, just managing to refrain from burying my hand in the trunk of the tree. My forehead meets the bark instead, the backs of my eyes pricking with old tears.

Breathe. Breathe. Breathe.

You can never have happiness. You don't deserve happiness.

"No, no, no," I whisper, turning on the spot, taking in the grounds surrounding me. Beautiful grounds. Miles of perfect greenery. The Manor, majestic and handsome, the hub of pleasure for hundreds.

And the beginning of my end.

I rest back against the tree, needing the support, and close my eyes, trying to chase away the memories.

"Maybe ease off on the alcohol, Jesse," Uncle Carmichael says. "There's no fun to be had when you wake up the next morning and can't remember a damn thing." He rubs my shoulder as I rub my sore head. "Appreciate what it can offer but respect it. It would be all too easy to succumb to the addiction of sex and alcohol."

Fuck.

I sprint off, passing many cars driving up to The Manor, some staff who crane their necks as I run in the opposite direction, not even acknowledging them with a raised hand or nod. I'm focused firmly forward, chasing away unwanted thoughts, my legs carrying me so fast I can't feel them. I zigzag from one side of the driveway to the other, trying to lengthen the journey that will take me to the gates, the gravel crushing harshly under my pounding feet.

A car horn starts a chorus of short and long honks in the distance, and I force my eyes up to see Sam's Porsche headed toward me. I don't slow down, but he does, until he comes to a stop in front of me.

"My man." He whacks his car into reverse and slams his foot on the accelerator to flank me. "Doing a runner?" he asks, flicking his eyes between me and the rearview mirror.

"Don't be fucking stupid," I pant, maintaining my speed. *I'm trying to chase away the remaining demons.* "Ava's being guarded so I'm having to find other means of distraction from—"

"Your nerves?"

"I'm not fucking nervous." I should just go into full-blown trample all over Elizabeth's prim arse. I thought I could do this, to pacify Ava and her need to pacify her mother. But, fuck me, I feel like my heart is ready to explode. Or stop. "Kate's here," I say, taking my eye off the road for the first time to look at Sam. I'm glad I did. I definitely detected a fleeting wave of caution. "Everything all right?"

"Not really," he admits for the first time, my cheeky mate's constant smile nowhere in sight. "She's here but not here."

"Have you asked her what's up?" I feel like shit. Guilty. I know exactly what's up, and I feel like I should tell him.

"Nope," he says, blowing out his cheeks.

"Why?" *Because he's afraid of what she might say?*

"She's a woman. Who the fuck knows what goes on in their heads."

I laugh through my fitful breaths. "Talk to her."

"Maybe. Catch you later." He slams on his brakes, kicking up a cloud of dust, before screeching off toward The Manor.

I reach the end of the driveway and take a hard right, intending on completing three full laps of the grounds—anything to kill some fucking time. I pull off my T-shirt and toss it to the ground carelessly. Maybe I'll sleep for the final hour of this torturous wait.

I glance down at my watch. I'm in a fucking time warp.

Abstain. Abstain. Abstain.

I can't.

I've tried. I've tried so fucking hard.

I need to see her.

All I can hear is Elizabeth's ear-piercing voice in my head trying to convince Ava to wait a while before committing to me. It's driving me fucking insane.

I pelt up the steps to the entrance, nearly knocking Mario from his feet as I barge through the doors. "Mamma mia!" He staggers back, shouting obscenities in both Italian and English as I take the stairs three at a time.

"Sorry," I call, flying around the gallery landing until I land at the door to our suite.

I go to grab the handle, but quickly consider the response I'll receive from her mother if I burst in. I need to play my cards right. So I tap as gently as I can, which isn't very gently at all.

"Just a minute," Elizabeth calls. I sag slightly with the confirmation of her presence, just as the door swings open and her eyes immediately bulge. And then she shrieks, making me stagger back a little.

"Fucking hell, Elizabeth." I cover my ears as she yells some panicked words, then slams the door in my face.

My arms drop, and so does my jaw. "What the fuck?" I take the handle and push all my weight against it, knowing she'll be shoved up against the other side to hinder my attempts to gain entry.

"Open the door, Elizabeth," I call through the wood, giving her a fair warning, so that if I force entry, it's entirely her fault if she lands on her arse.

"Jesse, you and I are going to fall out if you don't do as you're told."

Oh please. "We won't fall out, *Mum*," I say, not helping my cause. But still. She's impossible. "…if you let me in." I smile, picturing her sour face. She's really quite wonderful, but she'd be even more wonderful if she lost the incessant need to interfere and block me from her daughter.

"Jesse Ward, you do not get to call me *mum* when I'm only nine years older than you," she huffs, telling me she clearly thinks my age is an issue. It makes me nudge against the door harder. "Now go. You'll be seeing her in half an hour."

"Ava," I yell. If she hears I'm here, she won't be able to resist seeing me. I just know it. Fuck tradition.

"Jesse, no!" Elizabeth yells, her strength quite surprising as she keeps me at bay. "Oh no, it's bad luck. Have you no respect for tradition, you stubborn man?"

"Let me in, Elizabeth."

"No," she retorts, short and sharp. If there was any question as to where my beautiful girl's stubbornness comes from, then I'd wonder no more. "He is not…oh!…Jesse Ward!"

I'm firm but careful as I overcome her hold of the door and push into the suite, immediately scanning the space and finding Ava. The world stops turning for a moment as I drink her in, like I'm looking at her for the first time all over again.

"Well," Elizabeth huffs. "Ava, tell him to leave."

Ava's eyes meet mine, and a silent understanding passes between us. She knows what I need. "It's fine, Mum. Just give us five minutes."

I smile on the inside, trying to keep hold of the last piece of respect I have for Elizabeth, which is currently stopping me from ravaging Ava.

Kate moves in. "Come on, Elizabeth. Just a few minutes won't hurt."

"It's tradition." She's squawking again as she's guided past me, her eyes catching sight of the mark on my pec. "What's that bruise on his chest?"

My shoulders relax as I hear the door close, but I'm too busy losing myself in Ava's dark eyes to check if we're really alone. Her gaze drifts all over my sweaty body, almost as if she's reminding herself of every plane, muscle, and ripple, before her stare meets mine again. I have a far better reminder in mind.

"I don't want to take my eyes away from your face," I whisper, my cock starting to pulse relentlessly, imagining the lace I know I'll see if I cast my gaze downward. Fuck me, confirmation is likely to make my shorts blow off.

"No?"

"There'll be lace if I do, won't there?"

She nods.

"White lace?"

"Ivory."

Oh Jesus, *fucking* Christ. "And you're taller, so you've got heels on."

She still says nothing, just confirming with subtle nods.

I try my damn hardest, reminding myself that we're getting married in a matter of minutes, and she's all beautified and stunning. But I can't hold back anymore and…

Fuck…ing…hell.

I take a deep breath, allowing my eyes to fall down her body. Lace. Lots and lots of lace.

"You just trampled my mother." I can hear pure, raw lust in her voice, and she surprises me when she starts toward me, getting right up close, despite my sweaty chest in close proximity of her flawless lace.

"She was in my way." I speak down to her, watching as her brown eyes home in on my lips.

"This is bad luck. You're not supposed to see me before our wedding."

"Stop me." I can't help myself, not when she's this close, not ever. I rest my mouth on hers, keeping my body away from any other contact. Otherwise, it'll be game over. "I've missed you." *Pined for you. Lost my mind over you.* Standard.

"It's been twelve hours."

"Too long." I lazily lick her lips, loving her moan and her hands flying up to my biceps, but hating the taste of lingering alcohol. "You've had a drink."

"Just a sip." She doesn't lie, which surprises me. "We shouldn't be doing this."

"You can't look like this and say things like that, Ava." I push for a full-on kiss, knowing she won't deny me. And she doesn't. Our tongues meet and fall into a perfect rhythm of rolling, retreating, and pecking, each one of us making our satisfaction known with continuous moans and whimpers.

"Jesse, we're going to be late for our wedding."

"Don't tell me to stop kissing you, Ava." I nibble my way across her bottom lip and tug gently. "Never tell me to stop kissing you." I fall to my knees, taking Ava with me, and spend some quiet time just feeling her, wondering how the fucking hell a screwed-up twat like me could be blessed with such a wonderful woman. I'm so incredibly happy, but terrified at the same time. There's still so much for her to know, and I'm a fool to think that getting her down the aisle at lightning speed will eradicate her need to be cognizant with my past.

My eyes pass slowly across her flat stomach, but she doesn't notice this time. She knows I've stolen her pills, that I've been underhanded and deceitful…and she's still here. That has to stand for something, doesn't it? Then why the fucking hell won't she talk about it? And what will I say when she finally plucks up the courage to face it head-on? How will I explain? I hardly know what the hell I'm doing from one minute to the next. And sometimes…it just happens, no thoughts, no reasoning. Just instinct. Will she understand?

I find her eyes and cry on the inside for the woman I've fallen so deeply in love with and, again, I wonder how she can feel so intensely for me too. I'm past grateful, but still perplexed by it. "Are you ready to do this?" I ask.

Her beautiful brow furrows completely. "Are you asking me if I still want to marry you?"

"No, you don't get a choice. I'm just asking if you're ready."

"And what if I say no?" She's playing with me, her small smile confirming it.

"You won't."

"Then why ask?"

My shoulders jump. "You're nervous. I don't want you to be nervous." That's a ridiculous request after my morning zooming around The Manor's grounds.

"Jesse, I'm nervous because of *where* I'm getting married."

My contentment at having contact diminishes at the reminder of her reservations. I've gone to the end of the earth to ensure The Manor is watertight. I've banished members. Compensated them for the inconvenience of our upcoming nuptials. She knows all of this. Not even a fucking rhino is getting in the communal room. *But Elizabeth could.* "Ava, everything has been taken care of. I said not to worry, so you shouldn't. End of story."

"I can't believe you convinced me to do this." She sounds defeated, doubtful, her head dropping and breaking our eye contact.

Her words and actions sting. I want her to have faith in me, never doubt me, which is an absurd wish, given my actions and behavior since I found her. I quickly direct her face to mine again, desperate to see her, and desperate for her to see *me*. To see how much I love her. It's my only weapon.

"Hey. Stop it now," I order softly.

"I'm sorry."

"Ava, baby, I want you to cherish today, not get your knickers in a twist over something that's never going to happen. It's *never* going to happen. They'll never know, I promise."

I can see my words have had the desired effect because she visibly eases up, looking slightly guilty, which makes me feel like total shit. She has nothing to feel guilty about. I know how crazy this whole situation is. "Okay," she says assertively, trustingly.

I've done nothing to deserve that trust.

Leaving her on the floor, I go to the chest of drawers and find a towel before going back to kneel in front of her. I soak up some of the perspiration from my face and hair with a quick swipe, then lay the towel across my sweaty chest.

"Come here." I hold my arms open and love her lack of hesitance as she climbs into my chest and settles on my lap. "Better?" I squeeze her tight, my body relaxing with her.

"Much better. I love you, My Lord."

I laugh, happiness sailing through my tired body, bringing it back to life. "I thought I was your god."

"You're that too."

Everything. I'm everything to her. So I need to stop doubting myself. "And you are my temptress. Or you could be my Lady of The Manor."

She's quickly pushing herself away from me, outraged. "I am not being the Lady of the Sex Manor."

Or...*this* manor. I chuckle and bring her back to my chest, my hands on a feeling frenzy, my nose pulling in deep inhales of her sweet scent. "Whatever you want, my lady."

"Just lady will do," she breathes, and follows it up with, "I'm so in love with you."

"I know you are, Ava." My guilt swells.

"I need to get ready. I'm getting married, you know."

I'm smiling again. "You are? Who's the lucky bastard?"

She removes herself again, watching me closely. "He's a challenging, neurotic control freak." Her little palm strokes my scratchy face. "He's so handsome." Her low voice is setting off the ache in my groin again. "This man stops me breathing when he touches me and fucks me until I'm delirious."

I resist telling her off for cursing, actually keen for her to continue telling me what she loves so much about me. Nothing will beat it, except her kissing me, which she does, starting on my chin before making her way to my lips.

"I can't wait to marry him. You should probably go so I'm not keeping him waiting."

"What would this man say if he caught you kissing another man?"

I feel her smile. "Oh, he'd probably castrate the guy, then offer burial or cremation—that sort of thing."

I feign shock. "He sounds possessive. I don't think I want to take him on."

"You really don't. He'll trample all over you." Her gorgeous shoulders shrug, making me laugh delightedly. She knows me so well. "Happy?" she asks.

"No, I'm shitting myself." I take her with me when I fall to my back. "But I'm feeling brave. Kiss me."

She doesn't leave me waiting. It's a wise move. I'm desperate for her and still seriously having to have a stern word with myself not to tear her lace off. Ava's quickly all over me, demonstrating just how irresistible she finds me, and I am all for it, lapping up her attention. Letting it settle me. Settle *us*.

"Jesse Ward, get your sweaty body off my daughter!"

I roll my eyes at the familiar shriek, while Ava blesses my ears with her giggling, still smothering my face with her lips. I don't stop her. Her mother can wait.

"Ava, you'll smell. Get up! Tessa, help me out here, will you?"

Ava's nails dig into my biceps as her mother tries to pry her away from me. She's not giving up easily, my defiant little temptress. I grin like a fool.

"Mum," she yells over her laugh, wrestling her hands away. "Stop it! I'll get up."

"Get up then. You're getting married in half an hour, your hair is a mess, and you've broken an ancient tradition, rolling around on the floor with your husband-to-be. Tessa, tell her."

Our frightening wedding planner steps forward and flashes me a disapproving look, mixed with a little lust. For me. Yes, as soon as we were face to face, I wielded my looks as well as my cash. No apologies. It worked. "Yes, come on, Ava," Tessa says.

Ava finally relents on a grumble, lifting and leaving me sprawled on my back across the floor.

"Oh, look at you." Elizabeth starts to poke and prod my girl while Ava looks down at me, her brown eyes sparkling, her lush lips curved mischievously. I lift up to my elbows, wanting a better view. "You're a pair of children." Then Elizabeth's eyes harden, all for me, actually making me wilt slightly. "Out."

"All right." I give in before I completely obliterate my relationship with my soon-to-be mother-in-law, smiling when I see Ava flashing a warning look at our wedding planner, who's got her eyes on me. It's the chest. She's not seen my chest in the various meetings we've had. I fucking love how possessive my bride is.

"I'll take care of the groom," Tessa declares, shooing me toward the door. "Jesse, come on."

Something catches my eye. Or, more to the point, something *doesn't*. "Wait." My hand brushes the hollow of Ava's throat. "Where's your diamond?"

"Shit." Her panic is clear, her hand feeling all over her bare chest where the diamond once rested neatly. "Shit, shit, shit. Mum!"

I would have accepted the first curse, but *four*? "Ava, please, watch your mouth."

"Don't panic." Elizabeth is on her knees in a second, feeling around the carpet while my eyes dart, looking for the diamond.

"Here it is." Tessa retrieves it and dangles it in the air, looking pleased with herself.

I take it more harshly than I mean to, snatching it from her grasp. "Turn around," I order, and Ava pivots quickly, letting me secure it firmly around her neck. "There." I can't help a final taste of her skin, my hips pushing forward automatically. *Shit.* I shouldn't have done that. I'm a fucking glutton for punishment.

"That'll teach you for frolicking on the floor," Elizabeth snaps. "Now, out." I'm seized, but I think better of trampling her further, grinning when Ava cheekily curtseys and waves. Twenty minutes—I have twenty minutes to shower, shave, dress, and head down to the summer room to wait for my girl.

This episode served its purpose. My heart is steady once again.

I'm pushed out the door before it's slammed behind me, and I wander around the landing, smiling like an idiot. Entering my designated suite, I hear my mobile ringing. I'm still smiling as I pick up my phone off the unit.

But my beam falls immediately when I see who's calling me.

Reject, that's what I should do, but I also don't want to antagonize her, especially today. I stall for a few seconds, gritting my teeth. Why? God damn it, I thought we'd established where we both stood. Mistakenly, it seems. "Fuck's sake." I stab at the connect button. "Coral."

"I didn't think you'd answer."

"Then why call?" I sound curt, and I shouldn't care. But I can't risk her delusional arse turning up and upsetting Ava. I take a deep breath and head for the bathroom.

"It's not too late, you know."

Oh my God, I don't think I've ever known a woman to clutch at straws so tightly. Except, of course…Sarah.

I don't know how many times I can say the same thing with different words. "Coral, please, I beg you, move on." I flick on the shower.

"I can't."

My eyes roll, my mind unable to compute such tenacity. It's embarrassing.

"Can I stay at The Manor?" she asks.

I still, staring at the water pouring down into the shower tray. "What?"

"I have nowhere to go, Jesse."

"Your parents. You said you could go to your parents when they're back."

"I can't face them."

That's her bad luck. I almost start laughing. *Almost.* "Not a chance. Fucking hell, Coral, have you lost your fucking mind?" She knows where I stand.

"But you said you would help me."

"I have helped you. I put you up in a hotel for more nights than we agreed. You're on your own." I grind the words out slowly, yanking a towel from the shelf. "I told you, I'm marrying Ava."

"Yes, today, I know."

I'm still again. Yes, I've told her, but I never said *when* or *where*. "From whom?"

"I heard Sarah's left too."

"You sure are keeping good tabs on me."

"I know you have feelings for me, Jesse. Why are you lying to yourself?"

Feelings? Yes, actually, I do. I fucking despise her. She's deluded. And, worryingly, given everything I've been through in my past life, I'm beginning to wonder if Coral is slightly unstable, because not in anyone's world would they be rejected so many times and still believe it's love. "Listen to me." I'm so tired of going over the same old shit.

Over and over again. I'm starting to shake, my earlier contented state obliterated. "There's a woman in a room just down the hall who has my heart. She owns me, Coral. She consumes every ounce of my thinking space, even when I have your whining voice in my ear. There's not a person on God's green fucking earth who will ever sever or influence what I feel for her, least of all *you*." I take a deep breath. "I don't see you, Coral. I see no one, except her, and I'm twenty minutes away from making it official in the eyes of God. The only thing that'll separate us is death, do you hear me?"

She says nothing, but I hear a low weeping sound. *And now she cries.* From spiteful to pitiful. I can't even feel guilty. I feel nothing for her. I hang up. I don't have time for this, and I certainly won't be keeping Ava waiting.

I shower and shave in fifteen minutes flat, then throw on my suit and head for the door.

But I think of something.

And smile.

I grab some handcuffs, check myself in the mirror once more, and leave the room, bumping into John directly outside.

"What's up?" he asks immediately.

"Nothing." I'm not wasting any more time or energy on Coral. Not today. Not ever. I look up and down his suited form. "Fancy."

"Fuck off." He shifts on the spot, highly uncomfortable. Not because of the suit—he's always in suits—but because of his role today. "Are you ready or what?" He turns and stalks off, yanking in the sides of his suit jacket.

"Have you got the rings?" I ask, tailing him.

"Yes."

"And the registrar is here?"

"Yes."

"And the guests?"

"All in their seats."

"The music?"

"Sorted."

"The—"

John stops abruptly, and I crash into his back, making him jolt forward on a grunt. "Everything is fucking done," he grates.

I raise my brows. Someone's tense. "Nervous?"

"Oh fuck off," he snaps, getting his big body moving again, taking the stairs. I follow behind him on a smile, straightening my tie. "And why the fuck have you got a pair of handcuffs?"

I quickly slip them into my pocket, not answering him. He doesn't need an answer, he's merely trying to distract me from the fact that the big scary fucker is shitting bricks.

When we reach the bottom of the stairs, I follow John into the bar. Drew and Sam both have a Scotch in their grasps, and I'm more than surprised when John holds his hand up for Mario to pour him one. Fuck, he's *really* nervous. John absolutely never drinks. I watch all three men gasp their appreciation and slam their glasses down.

"My man," Sam sings, slapping my shoulder and taking in my new three-piece. "Fancy."

John lets out a rare, rumbling laugh and points to his glass for Mario to pour another. Drew gives me a curious look, and I shrug. This is new to me too. "Are you ready?" Sam asks.

"Yep." I fiddle with my tie again.

"No nerves?" Drew asks.

"None at all." Get me down that aisle right now. "Ask him," I say, nodding to the back of John's gleaming bald head.

"Don't ask me," he warns in reply, not taking his attention off his second Scotch.

"There you are!" Tessa seizes me from behind and hauls me out of the bar. "Come on, boys," she yells back before looking me up and down. "How many have you had?" she asks, pushing me on. "The last thing we need is a drunk groom."

"You have no idea." I laugh, hearing John cough. "I've not touched a drop," I assure her, looking up the stairs when I hear a door open. The door to my suite? "Is she ready?"

"She's ready."

"And she's okay?"

"What's up?" Tessa asks, flipping me a sideways smirk. "Worried you'll get jilted at the altar?"

I snort. "Don't be fucking ridiculous." But I immediately break out in a sweat, looking back over my shoulder to the stairs. "Who's she with?"

"Her father." Tessa tugs me on, stopping at the summer room doors and facing me, brushing down the front of my suit. I eye her, stepping back, out of her reach. "You had a bit of lint."

I hold up my hands. "I also have hands to remove it myself."

She blushes and turns her attention to Kate, starting to faff with her dress instead, as if to make a point that she wasn't singling me out to be felt up. The boys join us, and I watch as Sam moves in on Kate, smiling at her, taking her in.

"You look incredible," he says, moving a stray lock of her red hair off her face. I frown when Kate shies away from his touch and then sways a little. Is she drunk?

"Now, then." Tessa opens the doors to the summer room and ushers us inside, leaving Kate behind.

"Everything okay?" I ask Sam as we wander down the aisle, all eyes on me.

"Yeah." He lowers onto a seat, and I look at Drew. He shakes his head mildly, his way of telling me he's noticed something's not right too. I haven't got time to wonder whether I should be sharing the news of Kate's history with Drew. Not today.

Joining John, I take a deep breath. "Ready?" I ask him, laughing on the inside. Anyone would think it's *him* getting married.

"I'm ready."

"You sure?"

He slowly turns his eyes onto me. No shades. "I'm fucking ready, you irritating motherfucker."

I smile at him, nodding mildly. "You're a good man, John Johnson."

His smile is barely hidden. "Fuck off."

I laugh but flinch when I hear Elizabeth approaching behind me, throwing out her hellos to all of the guests, lapping up the attention. I stare forward, gritting my teeth. She's going to fucking kill me when I handcuff myself to her daughter.

Don't care.

I swing around, all smiles. "Here she is, my beautiful mother-in-law."

She half-smiles, half scowls, giving me her cheek to kiss. "Not yet, Jesse Ward. Not yet."

"Any minute, *Mum*."

"Behave."

"No." I look past her, seeing Tessa closing the summer room doors. "How is she?"

"Having a moment," she says casually, going to her chair. My back straightens. A moment? What does she mean, a moment? "A moment?"

"With her father."

I breathe out, and John chuckles beside me. "Worried she'll change her mind?"

Yes. "No." Music suddenly filters through the speakers, and my lungs inflate with my deep inhale. "Oh fuck," I breathe, suddenly *very* nervous, my eyes on the doors into the summer room.

"Jesse."

I hear the distant calling of my name.

"Jesse?"

I can't respond, eyes still on the door.

"Jesse?"

This is it. This is the moment I've been praying for. Dreaming for. The moment I never thought could be mine.

"Jesse?"

She'll be my wife. A wife I've asked for. A wife I love deeply. A marriage I could only dream of. A love reciprocated, a best friend, a soul mate, my absolute fucking world.

Ava.

"Jesse, for fuck's sake," John grumbles, taking my arm and pulling. I'm suddenly walking backward, and I frown, seeing I've somehow made it halfway down the aisle. The magnet. As ever, it's powerful.

Leading me.

I jerk out of my daze, looking at John. "I think she's pregnant," I say quietly without thinking, and he recoils, his chest expanding.

"What?"

I blink rapidly, looking at the doors when they open.

And I see her.

Like a fucking angel, light radiating around her.

Lace.

"Jesus fucking Christ," I whisper, the words getting caught in my throat. "Jesus *fucking* Christ."

John moves in close to my side. "She's pregnant?" he says quietly.

"Yes. No." I shake my head, shake the daze away. "I don't know." I focus on Ava, straightening my shoulders and linking my hands, trying to look as perfect as a man should look while waiting at the end of the aisle.

Then she looks up.

And the world stops turning. Her chest starts to pump. She looks as nervous as I suddenly feel, and I know there is only one thing that can cure us both.

Contact.

I start toward her, making Ava stop in her tracks and the congregation gasp. I pay no attention, my eyes on my prize, and when I'm directly before her, I smooth my hand down her face, taking her in. I see all anxiety leave her, feel my own nerves melt away, and she pushes into my touch, her lips curving ever so slightly. Dipping, I get closer, hearing Elizabeth huff her disapproval. She's in for a bigger shock than me meeting Ava halfway up the aisle.

"Give me your hand," I order quietly as I dip into my pocket. The moment her dainty fingers brush my palm, I flip the cuff over her wrist and secure myself to her, smiling at the feel of her wide eyes on me.

Joseph laughs under his breath, relinquishing his hold and joining his distraught wife, and I watch Ava as she assesses the crowd. I don't. All of my attention is on her.

Did she expect anything less?

"What are you doing?" she whispers, smiling nervously.

I kiss the nerves away before moving my mouth to her ear. "You look so fuckable."

She coughs over her surprise. "Jesse, people are waiting."

"Then they'll wait." I take my time, kissing her, making sure everyone here knows I will never conform to expectations, especially Ava's mother's expectations. "I really, really, *really* like this dress." I've never seen so much lace. It's apt, but it's also a massive fucking problem. I'd love to rip it off, turn her around, and march her back upstairs.

But first...

I grunt lightly when I feel her hand slip into my hair, holding it, her smile glorious. "Mr. Ward, you're keeping *me* waiting."

Shame on me. "Are you ready to love, honor, and obey me?"

"Yes." No hesitation. I should laugh out loud. Obey? Sure, in the bedroom. Outside of it? That'll be the day. "Marry me now," she demands.

I find her eyes and absorb the love drowning them. "Let's get married, my beautiful girl." I take her hand and walk us to the registrar, unable to take my eyes off her, in complete awe.

Mine.

Chapter 5

I never anticipated *not* enjoying my wedding day. To be honest, I didn't consider all the things that come with actually getting married, I only thought about the significance of it. Husband. Wife. And all of the natural progressions that come with those titles. Dealing with a wedding planner, in-laws, guests, photographs, and endless other things has made my day painful. I just want Ava—all to myself. I've flexed on what I've wanted, pacified Elizabeth, had official photographs when I'd rather catch my own—natural, unposed Ava being Ava in real life— chatted to people I don't even fucking know, and silently observed the tension between Ava's brother and Kate. It's been far from my favorite day spent with Ava, because despite being handcuffed to her, I've spent absolutely no time with her.

After reluctantly being pulled around and positioned for photographs, I'm forced to free her so she can have some individual shots. I'm not happy, but I use the opportunity to get my own photos, clicking away, catching her between poses, natural. Beautiful. I lower my mobile and then my eyes to her tummy as she turns her body to the left, almost looking over her shoulder at the camera.

Yes? No? I don't fucking know. And it's driving me insane. I know she's not had a period, and I know it's due any day. When the fuck will we actually talk about this? But talking will inevitably lead to the admission that I've taken her pills. Am I ready to confess what we both know? Confirm what she fears? I blow out my cheeks, raking a hand through my hair. I don't know what the fuck I was thinking, and now as I stand here looking at my *wife*, I feel more ashamed than ever before. I tried to trap her when I absolutely didn't need to. She loves me.

I see Elizabeth and Tessa moving in on Ava, ready to claim her for the next duty. No. Not again.

I hurry over and muscle past them, handcuffing Ava to me again before Elizabeth can take advantage of the fact that she's free. Scooping her up, raising my brows at my wife's amusement, I carry her back into The Manor with Elizabeth chasing my heels demanding compliance.

"You need to learn to share," I call back, taking the stairs two at a time, Ava bouncing in my arms. I push my way into our suite, shoulder the door shut, get her on the bed, and crowd her. "Quiet time." *Finally.* I kiss her gently and burrow into her neck, smelling her sweet perfume.

"You want to snuggle?" she asks, cluing me in on where she thought this was going. Or hoping. *Fucking.*

"I do," I breathe across her skin. "I want to snuggle with my wife. Are you going to deny me?"

"No."

"Good," I grunt. "Our marriage is getting off to the best start, then."

She sighs, accepting, and lets me have my moment with her beneath me, every part of us touching. It should be peaceful. It's not. My mind won't shut the fuck up.

I feel her chest expand with an inhale, and I hold my breath, waiting for her words. Is this the moment she'll be brave? "Will you do something for me?" she asks, a definite tinge of anxiety in her voice.

She shouldn't be anxious. We've got this. We're a team.

"Anything," I whisper across the skin of her neck. She pulls me from my hiding place, looking directly into my eyes. "What do you want, baby?" *I'll do anything.*

"Can you please resist talking to Patrick about Mikael?" she asks quietly. I have to hold back my dismay. *That's* what she's been thinking about? Her boss? Her job? While I've been lying here contemplating life-changing stuff, worrying about how Ava will deal with this, how I will ever justify my actions, she's been considering her career? Well, doesn't that put things into perspective for me? My patience is wearing thin. I appreciate I'm the cause of this situation—and note how I call it a situation, not a mess—and Ava didn't ask for this, but…my God, are we going to tiptoe around it forever? Jesus Christ, a baby *might* be arriving. What will we do, pretend it's not here?

"I agreed not to visit Patrick if you spoke with him," I mutter. Fucking *work.* "And I don't believe you have." This is what Ava does. Tells me—and probably herself—that she's going to deal with things. And doesn't.

"Give me until Monday," she says, her voice pleading. "I'll talk to him on Monday."

She shouldn't be going to work on Monday. We should be going on a honeymoon. Finding out if she's *pregnant.* "Monday," I agree as she gazes at me with grateful eyes. Will she have braved opening up to me by Monday too? "I mean it, Ava. You've got till Monday. Then I'm stepping in."

She nods, assertive. "Okay."

Why the fuck is work the first thing on her fucking mind? "Monday," I mutter and put my face back in her neck. "And when do I get to take you away?"

"I did warn you if you wanted to marry me so quickly, there would be no honeymoon for a while. You accepted that, remember?"

How could I forget? "So when am I going to get my wife all to myself?" Today has been a chore. I need peace, quiet, space, and Ava. "When am I going to be able to love her?"

"You always love me. When I'm not working, I'm with you. And you text and call me often enough, so I'm technically connected to you all day, anyway."

I don't agree. "I want you to give up," I say, testing those waters again. "Be a lady of leisure."

She laughs under her breath. "How would I be a lady of leisure if I'm permanently nailed to you?"

"Okay," I whisper, resorting to my usual tried and tested tactics, grinding myself into her, smiling when she stiffens. "Be a lady of pleasure, then." Just look at her cheeks, instantly flushed.

"Ward." She's breathless, her hands holding my upper arms. "You are *not* taking me now." Oh, please. Not a few moments ago she was surprised I wanted to snuggle. Now she's going to be all coy? "Anyway, we should get downstairs before my mum comes in search of us."

Let her. I don't mind giving her an eyeful of my arse as I take Ava from behind. Gently, of course. I do know, however, Ava will. "Your mother is a pain in the fucking arse."

She laughs, loud and in disbelief. "Don't wind her up, then."

Wind her up? My trampling has been very mild. I don't mind dialing it up if necessary. "She needs to accept who has the power," I mumble as I get us up, reattaching the cuffs.

"You're touching me," she says tiredly. "Of course you have the power." I grin when she tries and fails to take her hand from mine before I can secure her to me. *Too slow, baby. Way too slow.*

"I'm sorry," I muse, thoughtful, casual, jiggling our joined wrists.

"Who has the power?"

"You can have the power for today," she mutters.

"You're being very reasonable." I'm suspicious. And still really fucking horny. I dip and steal another kiss, plunging my tongue deeply. "Hmmm, you taste delicious, Mrs. Ward." Even more delicious now she's my wife. And the sound of her name? Perfect. "Ready?"

"Yes," she says on a breathy whisper, giving me all of the signs. But rather than take her and indulge her, I find my untamable curiosity overpowering my untamable desire, and my hand lifts without instruction, laying on her tummy. She jerks but doesn't move away. I inhale. She's letting me feel her. What does that mean?

Flexing my fingers, I circle my touch, breathing in, searching my mind for the right words, a way to break the screaming silence. Is she?

I don't get the chance to ask. Ava moves away and my hand falls, but my eyes remain on her lace-covered stomach, silently begging her to speak to me. Trust me. Believe me when I tell her I did it for us.

"Come on, then," she chirps, happy. And I'm astounded as I watch her walk to the door. Or try to. I remain where I am, and she's pulled to a stop on a hiss, our arms extended between us.

Enough. This is madness. "Are we going to talk about this, Ava?" I ask, trying and failing not to sound short.

"Talk about what?" She's not looking at me, so she can't see my astounded face.

"You know what."

I study her persona, her eyes still avoiding me as she searches for… what? Courage? Words? Anger, happiness? What the hell does she want to happen right now, because ignoring it isn't an option anymore. I've given her time. I've waited for her to come to me, confide in me, confront me, whatever it is she needs to do. She's taken none of the opportunities.

"Ava, we—"

The door flies open, Elizabeth appearing, and I sag on the spot as she looks between us, oblivious to the screaming tension. "Can I ask why you two didn't just run off somewhere to get married?" she asks. That's a good fucking question. I honestly don't know what I was thinking when I decided we were having a big wedding. Perhaps I was appeasing Ava's unspoken romantic notion of a fairy tale. Perhaps I wanted everyone to see us wed. Who the fuck knows. "You have guests downstairs," she rants on. "Dinner is being served, and I'm thoroughly fed up running around trying to control you."

Then don't, I say to myself, because there will be ructions if I retaliate. I'm in no mood for Elizabeth right now.

"We're coming," Ava says, trying to get me moving.

I remain static. "We'll be a few minutes, Elizabeth." This is being dealt with *now*.

"No," Ava counters, her jaw rolling. "We're coming." She tilts her head, her eyes becoming glassy. She's upset, acknowledging the situation without actually acknowledging it. It's something, I suppose, but it still doesn't answer the fucking question, does it? The fact is, she should be pissy with me whether I succeeded or not. She's asked me outright if I was taking her pills and sounded quite chilled about it. I denied it, obviously. What can I say? I was caught off guard, unprepared. She's forced condoms on me since. But now I'm ready, prepared. And now she's avoiding talking about it. The mixed signals are driving me round the bend. "Please," Ava mouths, and I growl to myself, raking a hand through my hair in frustration. *God damn it.*

At least we've broken the ice. At least there's a conversation to pick up on.

When I finally get her alone again.

I let Ava lead us on, but I drag my feet, keeping one step behind her, watching the back of her head as her mother marches ahead, quietly condemning me for pulling the bride away from the guests. And isn't that my fucking point? She's *my* bride. Not theirs, not hers, not his. *Mine*.

"This way," Elizabeth says, short and sharp, as if I don't know my way around my own manor. "The starters have already been served."

When we reach the entrance to the summer room, I slow, tugging Ava to a stop. She stills and takes a moment—and probably a breath—before she faces me. She's smiling. It's a fucking insult. "What?" she says, looking back into the summer room, trying to move me onward.

"What?" I parrot. I can't believe how ridiculous she's being.

"Come on, people are waiting."

"Let them wait."

"Jesse," she grates, having the nerve to sound impatient. I'm about to yell my frustration when Tessa swoops in and manhandles us to the top table.

"Sit," she demands, pushing me down into the chair. Ava looks at the cuffs. She can forget it.

She must soon come to terms with the fact she's going nowhere because she picks up her fork with her free hand and starts poking at her food. I watch her, knowing she knows my eyes are on her, but she doesn't look at me. Can't face me. You could cut the atmosphere with a blunt knife. I sigh quietly, trying to talk myself round before what's supposed to be the best day of my life goes completely down the shitter. "Av—"

Her aunty Angela approaches, killing my fix-it speech, kissing Ava's cheek and rubbing her shoulders from behind, laughing when Ava says something, lifting her handcuffed wrist. Then Drew comes over. Then Sam. Then…someone else; I don't know who. Just one more person taking time that belongs to me.

I gaze around the room and resent every single person here, and once again wonder what the fuck I was thinking getting caught up in this ostentatious affair, when there's only one thing that really matters.

Us.

And we're at odds. On our wedding day, we're at odds. I reach for Ava's empty wine glass and move it farther into the table, farther away from her. She doesn't glare at me or scorn me. I smell the beautiful dinner that's put in front of me. No appetite. I take in the guests enjoying themselves, see their mouths moving, their gestures in slow motion.

Inhaling, I turn my attention to Ava. My wife. She's facing away from me.

But I don't see the rich, dark, glossy hair I love tumbling down her back.

I blink and frown, running my eyes down the long length of blond, straight hair. Slim shoulders. The puffy sleeves of her dress. *What?*

Confused, I get up from my chair, noticing my wrist is free. I look around the room. Not the summer room of my manor, but the village hall where I grew up. Stepping away from the table, I take the few short steps to the mirror hanging on a nearby wall. I get closer and closer, until I can see myself clearly.

It's me.

Twenty years ago.

Barely a man. I turn my arms over in front of me. Peek down my trousers to my shoes. The suit is too big. Borrowed from her father.

"Jesse?"

I inhale sharply and swing around, stepping back and slamming into the wall, knocking the mirror. I jump when it crashes to the floor and shatters into a million pieces.

"Oh no," she says lightly, walking across the glass, the shards crunching under the soles of her low heels. "Seven years of bad luck."

A particularly large, jagged piece of glass lies at my feet. I see my face in it as I look down. And suddenly, another face appears.

Lauren's.

"No," I whisper, moving away. But I get nowhere. She's still within touching distance. Within damaging distance. "No, no, no."

"Husband," she says, her hand lying on her belly, smiling in satisfaction.

"You trapped me," I breathe, my head spinning, my legs moving but taking me nowhere.

"It isn't considered trapped if you want to be here."

"You don't get to decide where I want to be."

"Yes, I do." She smiles, and it makes me want to slap it off her face. "Because I'm your wife, and this is your child."

I look past her, seeing the world whizzing by, as if I'm stuck in a tunnel and everything is moving except me. Carmichael and John are standing on the sidelines. Reaching for me.

But unable to reach me.

"Help," I whisper. "Help me."

A loud smash knocks me back into the present, and I look to see a guest—I don't know who—picking up their broken wine glass as a server rushes in to help. I blink, looking down my body. I'm sitting down. My suit is expensive and pale gray. My wrist is decorated with a Rolex and a handcuff. I dart my gaze to the woman next to me, coughing over a relieved whimper when I find dark hair. *Lace.* Her wrist secured to mine.

"Jesus," I whisper, dragging the back of my hand across my brow, feeling the sweat. Dripping. The dinner plate isn't in front of me anymore, a dessert is instead. Still no appetite. But I could really use a drink.

"Good luck, Jesse."

I follow the voice to Ava's father, startling when everyone in the room laughs and cheers. What the fuck's going on? Ava looks tearful. I find John. His forehead is a map of concern as he silently asks me what the fuck is wrong with me through his hard stare. I shake my head, reading the room, and laugh with them. I need a cold shower. I grab my water and gulp it back, setting my empty glass down and looking at Ava. She's given me her eyes now. Oblivious to the nightmare I just relived. This shouldn't be happening, not ever, but especially not today. And I can't help but think that my uncertainty is the reason for my past creeping into this monumental occasion. Ava and I need to have a conversation, and the more she avoids it, the more I sense she's hiding the facts from me. And the more I worry, because to hide something is to be ashamed of it. To *not* want anyone to see it. And I know that more than anyone in the room.

I need her to know there's nothing to be afraid of. I'm here, always here, and I am worthy of her faith. I deserve her trust. She should depend on me, lean on me, and everything will work out in the end.

I remove my arse from the chair and get on my knees before her, making sure she's facing me, my hands holding hers, our eyes glued. "Ava, my beautiful girl," I say quietly, seeing her glance around the room briefly. "All mine," I reiterate, reminding her that all of these people won't stop me. Never. I reach up and kiss her. "I don't need to stand up and declare to everyone here how much I love you," I say, not loudly, but loud enough. "I'm not interested in satisfying anyone of that." I squeeze her hands, and she bites her lip, definitely to suppress her sob. "Except you." I don't know how this has happened, what I was thinking when I took those pills, but something way out of my control was guiding me, and I couldn't have stopped it if I tried. And now we're here on our wedding day, not talking, doubting too many things. "You've taken me completely, baby," I go on softly. "You've swallowed me up and drowned me in your beauty and spirit." *Made me do crazy things, say crazy things, see crazy things.* "You know I can't function without you. You've made my life as beautiful as you are. You've made me want to live a worthy existence—a life with you. All I need is you. To look at you. To listen to you. To feel you." I move my hands to her thighs and apply pressure, reinforcing my words, not taking my eyes off hers. She's weeping now. So fucking emotional. "To love you," I finish softly. It's all I'm here for now. To love this woman forever and beyond. *Purpose.* "I need you to let me do all of those things, Ava." My voice cracks. "I need you to let me look after you forever." I try to smile and fail, hoping she reads between the lines. If I have her, I'm a better man. If I have her, there can be only light. If I have her, my past will heal and rest.

Hope.

She nods, snivels, tries so hard to smile. "I know."

So let me.

I stand and pull her up for a cuddle, hugging her fiercely and feeling her cling to me with what cannot be mistaken as anything but love. And love always wins.

I'm immune to the riotous applause, could not give two shits what anyone makes of this. So long as Ava is reminded.

"Jesse Ward." Elizabeth muscles in on our moment, and I sigh. "I love you," she says, surprising me. "But please remove those handcuffs from my daughter."

And there it is. "Not going to happen, Elizabeth."

She quickly moves out of my space, allowing Kate to attack. I catch her, definitely feeling her wobble as she rains praise all over me. I pull her out of my chest, frowning down at her, as Ava's hauled away. And we're back to sharing each other again, our arms at full length between us. "Are you okay, Kate?" I ask.

"Sure," she chirps, pushing her palms into my chest and getting away. Escaping. I seek Sam out. He's laughing with Drew and John.

Ava catches my eye, her gaze begging me to rescue her. She doesn't have to ask twice. I pull her to me and start leading her away, throwing warning looks everywhere.

"Ava," Dan calls.

I stop before the handcuffs cut into either of our wrists, watching as he approaches, flicking his eyes between us. There's no love lost between Ava's brother and me. He's made it clear he doesn't like me. I would have made it clear the feeling's mutual if I wasn't worried about upsetting my wife. Or clearer. He's a cock. I don't trust him.

Getting a little hot, my temper bubbling, I watch as Ava looks down at our wrists. *Fuck*. I have one option. Release her. Two options if I want to cause Ava more stress by butting heads with her bull of a brother and, of course, I absolutely *don't* want to cause Ava more stress. So, and it pains me, I reach into my pocket and get the key, freeing her.

Giving her up to her brother.

I flick a cold stare onto Dan as Ava rubs at her wrist, silent, obviously shocked that I've freed her. "Go." I hold Dan's eyes, making sure he knows I'm not doing this for any other reason than keeping Ava happy, as she drops a pacifying kiss on my cheek. It's entirely dickish, but I feel out Ava's arse, holding it, pushing her into me. I've stroked Dan's ego for weeks. Initially, I hoped I could smooth over the cracks, maybe even get us to the point of tolerating each other. It hasn't worked.

I give Ava my attention, another sign. She's my priority. If he upsets her, there will be no holding me back. "Don't be long." I break away and stride off, taking in valuable air, hoping to keep the urge to annihilate Dan at bay.

"All right?" John asks, falling into stride next to me as I head into the bar.

I smile across at him. It's an effort. "Good speech," I say for the sake of it, unable to comment further. I didn't hear a word, but I know John. It would have been short, simple, and lacking detail.

"Thanks," he grunts back, lifting his phone when it rings. I catch sight of the screen, stopping abruptly at the bar entrance.

"My man!" Sam calls from his stool, forcing me to hold a hand up, telling him I'll be a minute.

"Sarah?" I ask, pointing at John's mobile as he rejects her call. "I thought you said you couldn't reach her."

"I couldn't," he growls. "True to Sarah's impeccable timing, she chose today to surface." He looks left and right.

"Don't worry," I assure him. "Ava's with her brother."

"I didn't want to tell you. Especially today."

"Is she okay?"

He laughs. There's no humor. "Is Sarah *ever* okay?"

Good point. But…"I'll take that as a no."

"Take it as you will. She's drunk. Slurring, talking nonsense."

"Nonsense like…"

He sighs, placing one of his enormous hands over his forehead, gathering patience. "It's your wedding day, Jesse. This does not deserve your attention or concern. Let me deal with it." He strides off, leaving no room for me to accept or, perhaps, not. I hate the woman with a passion. Truly. For what she's said, what she's done. But, fuck me, that doesn't seem to stop my conscience from worrying about her.

"God damn it," I mutter, joining Sam and Drew at the bar. I watch as they both neck their Scotches and listen as they gasp their appreciation. "A water, please, Mario," I grumble, perching on a stool next to them, feeling the urge of many guests wanting to come and congratulate me. I hope my semi-scowling expression warns them off.

"Okay?" Drew asks, and I laugh sardonically.

Isn't it something that all I keep getting asked is if I'm okay? On my wedding day. Suffice to say, it isn't panning out how I hoped. "Fine." I look at the bar entrance, wondering what Ava's brother is saying. Wonderful things, I expect. Singing my praises. Wishing us well. Telling Ava how happy he is for her. What's his fucking problem, anyway? From the moment he opened his mouth to me, he's been hostile. I should find Ava's ex and thank him for stirring shit. With my fist. Again.

"What gives, man?" Sam rests his arse on the next stool. "This is supposed to be the happiest day of your life."

If it was just Ava and me in our bubble, it would be. Unfortunately, I have to share her with the world. "How's work?" I say, trying to distract myself. Sam leans back on his stool, making way for Drew, because why the fuck would I ask Sam that question? He's not done a day's work in his life, except in the rooms of my manor.

"I'm glad to see you didn't invite the prick of an estate agent," Drew says flatly.

"He's still rubbing you up the wrong way?" I ask.

"I'm not bothered."

Both Sam and I laugh, and Drew scowls. "Not bothered?" I ask. "Strange. Your constant twisted face whenever he's brought up says otherwise."

"He's insignificant."

"Tell that to your bottom line."

"Fuck off."

"Just let me know if cash flow is an issue and I'll pause your membership." I smile round the rim of my glass.

"Fuck...off," he grates, motioning for another drink.

"God, you're uptight," Sam teases.

"Jesse could change that." Drew looks past me to the staircase that leads to the top floors of The Manor.

"Forget it," I say quickly, as Sam chuckles. "Besides, there's no one here you'd want to drag up and bless with your filth."

"I don't know," Sam chimes. "Isn't Ava's work friend invited this evening?"

"Victoria?" Drew asks. "Seriously. Mention a dildo to that woman, she'll spray you with disinfectant and have you committed to an asylum."

I laugh loudly.

"There's Kate, though," Drew adds casually.

Sam stills, his body solid. Oh no. It's not often you see Sam Kelt scowling. It seems Kate can fix that. "Drew," I warn slowly, seeing the fucker smirk.

"Where is she, anyway?" he asks.

I don't bother trying to hold Sam back. Drew's being a dick. He deserves a whack. So I sit back and let Sam at him, watching as he gets up in our mate's face, fisting his suit jacket. "I don't want to hear her name come out of your mouth again," he hisses. "Do you hear me?"

Drew smiles. "You're in love with her."

My eyes widen. *Fuck*. He went there?

Sam's grip of Drew's suit loosens. He glowers. "Don't be fucking ridiculous." He thrusts him away.

"Totally ridiculous," Drew breathes, swiping his drink up and wandering off.

Sam takes his seat. "Where's Ava?"

And my time being distracted is up. I look toward the entrance of the bar again while taking a sip of my water, back to wondering what her brother is saying. "With Dan," I muse.

"Prickly fucker," Sam mutters. "Don't know what I've ever done to him."

I clear my throat, not looking at Sam. *You fucked his ex.* "Don't take it personally. He's frosty with me too."

"Obviously loving his life," Sam says. "Didn't Ava say he was living the dream in Australia?" he asks, and I nod.

"How are you and Kate?" I'm very keen to get off Dan. I look at my watch. How long has it been?

"I don't know," he says, frowning into his tumbler. "Like I said, it feels like she's here but not. But I'm no expert in reading women's minds, only their bodies." He gets up and slaps my shoulder. "Go find your bride, mate. You should be with her."

I watch him stroll off, his words sinking in. I should be with my bride. "Yes, I should," I say to myself, finishing my water and taking my mate's advice.

I walk with purpose, a message for anyone intending on intercepting me not to, and head for the gardens at the rear of The Manor. I wander down the lawn, past the tennis courts, hands in my pockets, a handcuff dangling and chinking with each step I take. When I reach the bottom, I stop, listening, scanning the trees before me. I hear Dan yell, I can't make out exactly what, but I definitely heard Kate's name. Frankly, I couldn't give a fuck what they're talking about. I do, however, give plenty of fucks that he's yelling at my wife. I take a few more careful steps, listening.

"He's good for her," I hear Ava say, her voice tight. *Sam.* She's talking about Sam, and if I wasn't getting so worked up, that would warm my heart. Sam deserves some stability in his life. A constant, other than me and Drew. Someone to go home to. Problem is, I'm not sure Kate's that woman, especially given what I know about her history with Dan, the amount of alcohol Kate has sunk today, and the fact I've not seen her with Sam. Not once.

I pass through two ancient oak trees and see them facing each other. I can't see Ava's face—her back is to me—but I can see Dan's and he looks pissed off. I laugh on the inside. He's not even experienced pissed off. But he's about to see it.

"You need to leave this exactly where it is," Ava snaps firmly. She tries to walk away, and Dan stops her by grabbing her arm.

"What if I don't want to?"

Oh, he did not. "Get your fucking hands off her," I grate, my jaw rolling, my fists balling.

"It's fine," Ava says, pulling herself free of her brother's hold. I disagree. It is *not* fine. "We're done."

"She's my sister," Dan fires, as Ava fidgets uncomfortably. Did he actually just move toward me?

"She's my *wife*," I snarl. That title trumps all others.

Dan laughs. Whether that be with nerves or pure mockery, I don't know. But he'll pay for it. I'm done stroking this prick's ego. Brother or not, he's a fucking cunt. I move forward and stop when something meets my arm.

Ava's hand.

I tear my rabid stare off Dan and find her begging me with her eyes. She's done that so many times today. Silently begged me. I feel her hand seize mine and squeeze. "Let's go."

Fuck. I know deep down I can't lay a finger on her brother. So, reluctantly, I relent and do what's right, backing off. Because if I let loose on Dan, Ava will be distraught. And that's a good enough reason to let the fucker off the hook.

I turn and walk away, taking Ava with me, demanding her hand. I re-cuff us. "Don't ask me to remove them again."

"I won't," she says easily. "Throw away the key."

With pleasure. She wouldn't be able to go to work. Leave my side. Runaway when I pick up the conversation we need to finish. "Wishing you'd have stayed nailed to me?"

"Yes." She looks at me with a soft but certain gaze. "Don't free me again."

I smile. It's soft like her words, but definitely not certain. "Would you like a drink?"

"I'd love a drink."

Wait. Does she think I mean a *drink*? Because I don't. Water, tea, perhaps a coffee. This might be a trigger for another disagreement, and I'm done with disagreements. But she's not having a drink. I sigh and pull her into my side, pushing my face into her hair. "I won't stand for it, Ava," I say. "Even if he's your brother."

"I know." I hear the dread in her voice, feel it in her body language. She doesn't think her brother will back down.

We'll see.

Even more people have arrived by the time I get Ava back into the bar, and we battle our way through the crowds, being attacked with kisses and squeezed with hugs. *Jesus.* How long do we need to stay at our wedding? I'm done with people.

I give Mario a nod as we near, and he swiftly has a glass of water on the bar. I get Ava on a stool, the water in her hand, and turn away, getting my own water before she can throw any defiance, protests, or sass my way. When I see Tessa marching over, I wonder whether braving Ava's inevitable disbelief over my choice of drink for her is a better option.

I'm blasted back with a thorough telling off from our wedding planner for being missing in action again, unavailable to cut the cake. What I want to tell her is that I didn't hire her and pay obscene amounts to be nagged—I have a wife to do that now. But instead I say, "It's fine," glugging back some water.

Then Ava is quickly on my case. "Don't you want to cut the cake? Kate went out of her way to make it at such short notice."

"Then let's not ruin it." I appease her, smiling, fiddling with her necklace as she exhales an over-the-top sigh.

"You're impossible."

I roll my eyes to myself and roll them harder when Tessa appears again. "I've spoken to Elizabeth." She has? Great. "We're cutting the cake and having the first dance shortly, so don't be disappearing on me again." And with that, she's gone, and rather than following her and relieving her of her duties, because I'm attached, literally, I realign my attention on what matters today.

Ava.

She looks as fresh and glorious as she did when she stepped into the summer room. Perhaps her cheeks are little pinker. And her hair a little wilder. Beautiful. But I know, like me, she's done with the day. And that fucking sucks. I wanted our wedding to be incredible for her. Unforgettable. "You okay, baby?" I ask, framing the side of her face with my hand. She doesn't nuzzle into it, and that's a first.

"Yes," she more or less sighs. "Fine."

"You don't look fine." Fuck her brother. "I said I wanted you to enjoy today." I think I jinxed us when I said that. Totally. It's been a bizarre mixture of exhilarating and tiresome.

"I'm fine," she repeats, this time shorter, looking at her glass on a shake of her head before drinking. What? Does she think alcohol will make her feel better? No. Alcohol masks things. Alcohol hurts. She needs to trust me on that.

It's all I can do not to groan my despair when I spot Ava's boss approaching with a woman in a wild, tight outfit. Animal print. Hideous. I face the bar and breathe in the patience I know I'm going to need as Ava elbows me in the side. "Here's Patrick," she whispers. "You said Monday, remember?"

"Yes, Ava," I drone. "Just till Monday, though."

I wince when Peterson screeches some sickly pet name for my wife, crowding her. Ava's shoulders are hunched, her smile tight. "Mr. Ward."

"Please, it's Jesse." I take his offered hand. "Thank you for coming."

"Oh. Jesse." Yes, let's get on first name terms, because when my wife doesn't follow through on her promise to advise Peterson of her intention to withdraw from working with Van Der Haus—and I have a nasty feeling she won't—I want to be able to talk to him man to man and have his respect. So I will grin and bear him for as long as this takes. I pray it's not too long "This is Irene."

"Nice to meet you," she purrs.

I blast her back with my smile. It's forced. "And you." I've changed my mind. I'm done already. "Please, the bar staff will see to you." *Translated: fuck off.*

But Peterson and his wife don't get the message, both of them moving in closer. I know what Peterson is thinking. He's thinking there are a lot of rooms in my manor and eventually all of them will need renovations.

"Thank you." Irene's arm brushes with mine. "This hotel is just wonderful."

She should be taking in this wonderful hotel if she finds it so wonderful. But no. She's taking in *me*. Until Ava pipes up.

"Hello, Irene," she says, edging closer to me. *Trample mode activated.* "How are you?"

"Delightful. Ava, you look stunning."

My wife blinks her surprise, and I motion past Peterson to the end of the bar where Mario has poured champagne into dozens of flutes. "Help yourself," I say, and he promptly pulls his wife away.

"Interesting woman," I mumble. Terrifying. Gaudy. Really fucking loud.

"She makes Patrick's life miserable."

"I can imagine." That will *never* happen with us.

Ava moves on her stool, looking past me. "Here's John."

I turn, my water halfway to my mouth, but it pauses at my lips when I register his expression. I've known this man for twenty plus years. I know when he's happy, even if he's grimacing. I know when he's amused, even when his lips are straight. I know when he's pissed, even when I can't see his eyes. And I know when he's stressed, even though there is not one crease on his smooth face.

He's definitely stressed.

Fuck.

"A word, Jesse."

A word? Shit, what's happened? I currently have Ava handcuffed to me, and I know she will kick up a royal stink if, after everything I've said, I uncuff us.

I stare at John, begging him to help me out on how to handle this. He stares back. He can't help me. *Fuck.* Then he discreetly tilts his head, twitchy, indicating the entrance.

Jesus, is Sarah here? The last thing I want is her walking into the bar. That thought has me reaching into my pocket swiftly and taking the key to the cuffs. It doesn't meet the lock. Ava wrenches her arm away, cutting into both of our skins. I grit my teeth.

"What are you doing?" she asks, snappy and high-pitched.

I don't look at her. Don't want to see the questions in her eyes. "John wants a quick word." I need to handle whatever needs to be handled and get us both the fuck out of here before our wedding day is well and truly ruined.

Too late, brother.

"Oh, no." Ava laughs. "You don't get to release me when it suits you." She gives our wrists an extra, assertive yank. "No way, Ward."

"Ava," I say softly, trying to get the key in the lock. "I'll be back shortly."

"No," she yells, and I flinch, glancing around, seeing a few people looking this way. *Yeah, happy couple right here.* "Where are you going?" she asks me before repeating her question to John. "Where is he going?"

"S'all good, girl," he says, as soft as I've ever heard him.

"No." She shakes her head, her lips straight, her face furious. Can I blame her? "It's not all *fucking* good."

"Watch your mouth," I whisper on a hiss, getting closer to her, trying to conceal her fury from the room, as well as soak up any more bad language she might throw my way. "I'll be a few minutes." Less if I can help it. "You'll stay fucking put, Ava." I hate to take on a stern tone with her, but whatever's waiting for me, I really don't need Ava coming to find it.

She gazes at me, hurt, and it fucking kills me. I look away from her silent form, releasing her, and leave hastily. I spot Elizabeth looking my way, her eyes questioning, so I give her a little nod, maybe to tell her everything is fine, maybe to tell her to step in and go to Ava. I don't know. My head is spinning.

"What's going on?" I ask as John and I stride away side by side, through the summer room where the band's started playing.

"Coral."

I shoot my shocked eyes his way. "Coral?" Surely not?

"She was at the gates. I managed to keep her out until evening guests started arriving."

"Fuck."

"Indeed. I took her to your office. It was that or have her find you in the bar."

I reach up to my collar and yank it loose. "I thought it was Sarah."

John laughs. "No. I think she's too drunk to even walk, let alone get herself here."

Should I be grateful?

"Hey, man," Sam calls as we breach the entrance to the corridor to the office. "Where are you going?"

"Just a small issue to be sorted."

"Oh fuck," he mumbles.

The female population is in mourning.

I frown at thin air. Hilarious, Jake.

"Have you seen Kate?" Sam asks.

"No." I carry on to my office. "Try the bar." Although I don't recall seeing her in there. In fact, I haven't seen her for a while. Passed out?

I stop outside my office door and take a few precious moments that I really don't have to cool my temper. "Is she drunk?" I ask.

"No."

I've dealt with Coral falling all over the place, and I've dealt with her falling apart. I can't decide which is the lesser of two evils. A deep breath. The time I've taken, *and* the air, hasn't lessened the pressure building in my head. Today? She chooses today to turn up *again*? What is it I said on the phone exactly that translated to an invite? *Fuck it.*

John's phone rings, and I look at him as he glances down at the screen. He doesn't have to say a word. "Take it," I say. "I've got this."

He backs away, and I face the door again.

You shouldn't go in there.

"What am I supposed to do, let her go roaming around my wedding looking for me?" I rest my head on the wood. "Fuck, Jake, how can I make it any clearer to her?"

Don't be mad, don't be nice. Just be together. Be calm.

So, basically, the exact opposite to what instinct tells me to do. I push my way into my office and shut the door. "Coral," I say coolly, walking straight to my desk and resting my arse on the edge, arms crossed. Protective. She's on the couch, comfortable, one leg crossed over the other revealing too much of her thigh from where her skirt's hitched up. *Tactical.*

Her eyes fall to my wedding ring. "You went through with it then?"

"Did I give you reason to believe I wouldn't?"

"I don't think you know what you're doing."

"I know what I'm doing."

"Do you?" she asks, standing. My God, if another woman tries to tell me what they *think* I need, I'll fly off the fucking handle.

"Don't come any closer to me, Coral," I warn. "The last time I saw you, I made it clear where I stand. Who I love." I told her on the fucking phone too. I put her up in a hotel for days, gave her money to try and get her back on her feet when her wanker ex-husband froze her accounts. Cut her phone off. My thoughts stall. "Your phone was reconnected."

"What?"

"You said it was cut off when you turned up on the night of the anniversary party."

"It was."

"But you texted me later that night."

"I had it reconnected."

"How?" I ask, hostile. "You didn't have any money."

"I…" She blinks, looking away, obviously trying to think up an excuse. She lied? Fed me a load of bullshit to make me feel sorry for her? Fucking hell, the boys were right. I've been played for a fucking fool. "You're going to leave now, Coral," I say firmly, seeing no point calling her out, making her answer to me. Explain herself. Because it doesn't matter. *She* doesn't matter. "And I'm going to sit down here and take a few moments to myself"—take a moment to compose myself—"before I go out and rejoin my *wife*." I go to the couch and lower, making my point.

"Jesse," she breathes, moving toward me. Oh, no. I hold up a hand, and she stops.

"Don't you remember that night?"

"What fucking night?" I ask. I've fucked her more than once, and I can't remember one encounter in any detail. Because I was pissed.

"The first night. How—"

"Coral, seriously. Enough. Whatever you thought I felt, whatever you imagined happened between us, you're wrong." There's a competition happening with an award up for the woman with the thickest skin. I think Coral might be edging out in front.

"Where's Ava?" she asks.

My shoulders lift, tense. It's a simple question but it somehow feels like a threat. "Leave," I order through a tight jaw. "And I swear, Coral, if I see you around here again, I will call the police and have a restraining order slapped on you, do you hear me?"

"But, Jesse, please, listen to me."

My head goes into my hands. My God, what will it take for her to hear me? The sofa beneath my arse moves, and I look up to see she's sat down at the other end. "What are you doing?" I sigh.

"I need you to hear me."

"No, Coral," I say calmly. "You need to hear *m*—"

The door swings open, and my heart jumps into my throat when I see Ava on the threshold of my office, her eyes bouncing from each end of the couch constantly, taking in the scene. *No. Oh fuck, no.*

I stare at her like a clueless fool, scratching through my mind for some instructions.

Get up! Go to her!

But the second my muscles finally listen to my head, Ava backs out and pulls the door shut.

"Oh, there she is," Coral muses.

I blink, turning my eyes slowly her way. She's resting back on the couch, relaxed. I stand, unable to control my shakes, and bend, forcing her back farther. "Get the fuck out of my manor and my life," I seethe, looking her up and down on a contemptuous sneer. "You pathetic leech." She can't hide her hurt. Good. Fucking hate me. *Please, just fucking hate me and leave me the hell alone.* "You'd better be gone when I get back." I stalk to the door and yank it open, finding John on the other side. "Get her out of here," I order, passing him and jogging down the corridor. I scan the summer room, try to see through the crowds of people who have taken to the dance floor, searching for an explosion of white. Nothing. I pass through, shrugging people off, smiling tightly, trying to get to the bar. No Ava. Sam looks up, as does Drew. "Have you seen Ava?" I ask.

"No." Sam frowns. "I can't find Kate either. Maybe they're together."

Drew laughs lightly. "Seriously. You can't find your wife and you can't find your girlfriend?"

"She's not my girlfriend," Sam breathes.

"Of course."

"Coral turned up," I say, backing out of the bar and looking up and down the foyer.

"Coral?" Drew blurts.

"Yes, Coral. Ava walked in on me talking to her in my office."

"Talking about what?"

"Nothing, Drew," I snap. "That's the fucking point. There's nothing between us, never has been." And even though Ava knows that, she has every right to be upset about me leaving her—on our fucking wedding day—to appease an ex-fuck who won't fuck off. Ava was right. I shouldn't have uncuffed us. Fucking Coral.

I leave the boys and hurry upstairs to our suite, bursting in and scanning the space, checking the bathroom, before dashing back downstairs. Where the hell is she? I look at the door onto the driveway. Has she left? I'm a bag of nerves as I walk slowly to the doors, pushing out of them. I find Kate sitting on the steps nursing a cigarette and a glass of water. She peers back at me as she exhales. Her face is blotchy. Her eyes puffy. "Everything okay?" I ask, trying to sound concerned while scanning the driveway for Ava.

"Perfect," she says, smiling.

Fuck it. I can't just ignore the fact she's been crying. "Sam's looking for you."

She turns back away from me. "I'll be back inside soon."

I haven't got time for this. "I don't know what's going on with Ava's brother, but—"

She swings around. "What's Ava said?"

"Nothing. Just that there's history." I look back over my shoulder into The Manor. "Look, Kate, Sam's a good guy. Don't fuck him around, okay?"

She doesn't answer. It's hardly reassuring.

I sigh. "Have you seen Ava?"

A shake of her head.

"You're looking for Ava?" Pete approaches, coming up the steps, an empty tray of champagne flutes lying across his palm. "I saw her leave out the glass doors at the back."

"Thanks, Pete." I don't go back through The Manor but instead take the steps down to the driveway and circle round the side, jogging past the garages. I see a speck of white in the distance and breathe out my relief, crossing the lawn to the woodland at the bottom of the gardens.

She's sitting on a trunk, and as I get closer, I hear her quiet, suppressed sobs. "Fuck," I whisper, mentally beating myself up. I made my wife cry on her wedding day. What kind of arsehole am I?

Her shoulder blades pull in. She's sensed me close by.

"I know you're there," she says.

"I know you do." I circle the trunk and lower my arse next to her. She won't look at me, but watches my hands playing nervously. How do I fix *this* mess? Pull it back?

"Isn't it funny," she says quietly, "how we're so in touch with each other, yet you sit here now and you don't know what to say to me."

I sigh and move closer, touching her leg, at a loss for what to say.

"So he touches me," she whispers, looking down at my hand.

"He loves you," I reply quietly. "He wishes he could eliminate the past that's hurting you."

"Then why did you see her?" she asks, looking at me. I hate the glaze of affliction in her eyes. "On our wedding day, when you vowed to have me by your side all day, why did you desert me to see her?"

Because I'm an idiot. I should have been transparent with Ava and taken her with me to send Coral on her way. *United.* Fuck, why the hell do I always make the wrong choice? "I couldn't leave her at the gates with guests arriving, Ava." I'm not passing the blame to John. I would have done what he did.

"So tell her to go away."

"And cause a scene?"

She bites at her lip, thinking. "What did she want?" She's asking questions she knows the answers to. "Did she know we were getting married today?"

Except that one. "Yes, she knew."

"And she still came?" she asks, shocked, perhaps now comprehending the determination of these women. "Was she hoping to stop it?" She's almost laughing. Yes, laugh, because it's fucking laughable. "Was she going to barge through the summer room doors and declare that we shouldn't be joined in holy matrimony?"

Truth is, I wouldn't put it past Coral. "I don't know, Ava."

"When did you speak to her?"

"She's been calling and turning up at The Manor." Do I mention the call this morning? Be specific? "I've told her repeatedly I'm not helping her. I've told her there are no feelings. I'm not sure what else I can do, Ava."

"What's your definition of an affair?" she fires quickly, catching me off guard.

"What do you mean?" Jesus, we're not here again, are we? We've been over this. Ava thinks I had an affair with Coral, I think I didn't. But I'm not about to devalue her views or feelings on this. I have no right.

"I mean, she's in love with you, and you've said it was only sex. It was obviously more to her."

"Baby, I've told you before, just sex." She has to hear me. "They always wanted more, but I never gave them any reason to expect it. *Never.*" But no matter how cold I was, no matter how detached, they always came back.

She looks away, hurt. "I don't want you to see her again."

"I won't." She ordered it, and I will listen. "I've no need to." God, she looks so tired. I can relate. If only she would relent and allow me to take her on a holiday. Take us away.

"I've had enough of my wedding. I'd like to leave."

"Ava," I beg softly. "Look at me."

She shakes her head. "Don't start making demands when I'm feeling like this."

She's not the only one feeling defeated. But, again, how can I whine about how tired I am? All the shit that's gone down today is because of me. "Perhaps you didn't hear me right," I say harshly, frustrated with everything. Especially myself. "I said, *look* at me."

She turns a bored expression my way. "What?"

I get on my knees and put myself in front of her. "I've fucked up," I say gently. "I'm so sorry, I was trying to keep her away from you." I search her eyes, begging her to understand. There was nothing underhanded about seeing Coral. It was all simply an effort to protect her. "I panicked and thought I could talk some sense into her. I didn't want her kicking up a stink on your special day."

"It's your special day too. You should've just told me."

And I really wish I had, but what's done is done. I move in and give her a hug. "I know. Let me make it up to you. What do you want me do, baby? Name it."

"Just take me to bed."

The best answer. *Escape.* We're both done for the day. "Deal." I get us up and give her a long, soft kiss, and I thank everything that she responds, syphoning off the calm she needs from the man who causes all of the chaos in her life. "We'll make friends properly later." I dip and sweep her off her feet, and she drops her heavy head onto my shoulder as I walk us back to The Manor. Exhausted. And yet despite her tears, she still looks…glorious. *I didn't ruin her beautiful face at least.*

I look up at all of the illuminated windows of my manor, see the bodies on the ground floor in the windows. I don't know if there's ever been a time in the history of this place when it's stood empty, not a single person in any of the rooms. Imagine how quiet it would be if it was just me and Ava living here. The lord and his lady. I smile.

It drops the moment I step into the summer room and spot Elizabeth gunning for me.

Oh, here we go.

"You've not cut the cake and you need to have your first dance," she snaps, outraged. "Tell me, are we having a wedding?"

I only needed Ava to say *I do.* "I'm taking Ava upstairs." I keep up my pace. "She's tired."

"But it's only ten o'clock," Elizabeth cries, flanking me. "What about your guests?"

What about them? "There's a bar, band, and plenty to eat, Elizabeth." And if they want to be adventurous, at this stage, I'd happily open the communal room to keep them entertained. "I'm sure they'll survive."

"Ava, please," she begs, deciding she's getting nowhere with me. "Talk some sense into him."

Ava's hands fall onto my cheeks, and my feet slow but don't stop, my forehead heavy as I look at her. Her face. "A little longer," she says, and I slow to a stop. "We can give her longer."

Can we? Haven't we given enough of our time to others today? "You're tired." *I'm* tired. Fucking knackered, in fact. "Let me take you to bed, baby."

She smiles a little, nuzzling into my face. "Dance with me." I'm a goner. "Let's dance." Dance. It's my next favorite thing to sex with Ava. I get to hold her close. Black out the world and just dance.

So I reverse my steps and carry Ava to the dance floor, hearing Elizabeth breathe out her relief. Everyone steps aside, giving the floor to us. Just us.

I put my wife down and go to the band. "Now?" the lead singer asks, and I nod. "The same track?"

"Please." It's perfect, now more than ever. I watch him set it up and, as soon as the intro of *Chasing Cars* starts, I smile to myself, facing her. She's all on her own in the middle of the floor. A beacon of pure, beautiful light. If I join her, will I cast a shadow over that light again? My feet won't move to take me to her. A sign? Her eyes sparkle, but tears are the cause. Emotional. So fucking emotional. At this point, given what the day has brought, I can't conclude it's hormones.

I walk into her body and hold her close, starting to move us slowly. The peace is instant. But my guilt is untamable. "I'm sorry, baby. I'm sorry I left you earlier."

"Let's leave it there."

"The harder I try not to hurt you, the more I do." I swallow down the ball in my throat, damning myself to hell. "I'm hopeless." *Fucking hopeless.*

"Be quiet."

I sigh, trying to smile at her order. "Okay. But I'm still sorry." I cup the back of her head and exhale my contentment. "I can't wait to crawl into bed with you."

"Me neither." Her fingers claw into my shoulders. "Tomorrow, we stay in bed all day."

"We need to go home first," I remind her, sensing her disappointment when she goes heavier against me.

"We go home first thing in the morning, then."

"We do, after we've soaked in the bath and had breakfast with your parents."

There are a few beats of silence, both of us contemplative. "I wish you'd have taken me away," she whispers. "Somewhere quiet, just us."

My heart sinks. How I wish I could change how we did this. "I wish I had too," I admit. "But I bet your mother would've had something to say about it." And isn't the reason we're not going on a honeymoon anytime soon because Ava can't take the time off?

I can feel her leaning in to me more every second I turn us on the spot. "Mrs. Ward, are you falling asleep on me?" She hums as others start to join us on the floor. "I love you," I whisper. "I love you so fucking much."

"I know." She finds it in herself to drag her head off my shoulder, giving me her mouth, and I read her message, kissing her as I lift her from her feet. "Mr. Ward," she mumbles, sleepy, her lips still on my mouth. "You're drawing attention."

"Fuck them. Wherever, whenever, baby. You know that. Let me see those eyes."

She looks at me, curious and drowsy, and with the mildest of smiles on her face. "Why do you always demand to see them?"

That's easy. "Because when I look into them," I say, doing it right now—staring into their dark beauty—"I know for sure that you're real."

"I'm real," she assures me, the bridge of her nose scrunching.

"I'm so glad." Because I hate to think where my life would be now if she wasn't. "I didn't tell you how beautiful you look." I kiss her, literally holding her up now, still moving us both. "I thought it, but my beautiful girl renders me stupid every time I lay my eyes on her. It's like I'm looking at her for the first time all over again." *She's so fucking magnificent.* "You keep my heart beating, baby," I say quietly. "And it will only ever beat for you. Understand?"

"Just for me." She feels through my hair, hardly able to keep her eyes open. "I need you to take me to bed."

"Will my delightful mother-in-law allow that?"

"I don't care. I just want you to myself. Take me to bed."

"Deal." I place her down and steal a quick kiss. "You don't have to ask me twice, Mrs. Ward." Fuck, that sounds so good. I might sacrifice my preferred *lady* for her official title.

"I just did."

She did? "That's your fucking mother's fault." I scan the room for Elizabeth as I turn Ava around and move her onward by her shoulders, bracing myself for her intervention.

"Oh, look at Clive and Cathy," Ava says as I follow her pointed hand to our resident concierge and my housekeeper. The rascal. He's had his eye on Cathy from the moment she returned from Ireland. I chuckle as they move awkwardly in a circle, but my amusement dies the second I see Dan across the floor, his attention on Kate and Sam. *Fucking hell.* I'm happy to see Sam and Kate together for the first time today, naturally, but Dan's face? I glance at Ava to see if she's noticed them, or even felt the atmosphere, because it's thick.

"It doesn't look like history to me," I muse, dipping to scoop Ava up, hoping that'll get us out of here quicker than Ava's feet seem to want to carry her.

But then I hear something, and I still, half bent, listening. *Oh no.* Now? The DJ chooses *now*?

"Hello, Justin," Ava says as I straighten up to full height. The beat starts to sink into my body. Fuck, she's tired.

Tell your body that, Ward.

Lovestoned has always been a favorite, but since the night when I looked into Ava's eyes on that dance floor and saw what I knew was love, and then she told me—drunk or not—it's *the* favorite. And as I look at her now—now that she's my wife—I just know it's hers too.

And I must dance with her.

Must.

Relive that night and smile because look where we are now. Married. Joined. Never to be separated. Let's finish the day on a high.

I fix my crumpled suit, my shoulders jigging. "Oh, Mrs. Ward," I muse, seeing some life trickle back into her at the prospect of her husband showing the world how to dance. "I'm about to tear that floor up." I pull her back onto the dance floor and put us in the center, removing my jacket and tossing it aside as Ava laughs. That sight alone, her face, her happiness, is enough for me to keep her up for a little longer. Justin is just a bonus.

This is how she will remember our day.

"Woohoo!" Kate yells, the change in direction of music seeming to sober her up *and* make her smile. Her arms go up in the air, Sam laughs, and I check Dan's whereabout discreetly, seeing him still on the edge of the dance floor, but now Joseph is with him. Talking some sense into him?

I refocus on Ava, happy to see her awake, and move in, crouching to get her closer. "Ready to reenact one of my favorite nights with you?" I ask, dotting kisses all over her face in time to the music, feeling my groin grind into her.

"My mother's watching," she says around a grin.

"And?" I take her hand and twirl her, watching her beautiful wedding gown fan, before pulling her back into my chest.

"And she might keel over if she sees you dry-humping me on the dance floor."

I laugh. "My amazing dancing will distract her." I spin her again and smile at the sound of her laugh filling my ears.

She crashes back into me. "Then she's in for a treat."

My eyebrows rise. "And you?"

She lifts up on her toes and nibbles at my chin. "I think I need reminding that my husband has talents outside of the bedroom."

I'm laughing again, my head falling back, giving her access to my neck. "Fucking hell, woman," I say, dropping my eyes and pushing my lips to her forehead. "I fucking love you."

"I know. Now dance with me."

So I give her what she wants and hope it redeems me for making too many bad decisions on her big day. I'd wanted to make our wedding unforgettable—and possibly have for the wrong reasons—but I *am* Jesse Ward, after all. A fucked-up arsehole who somehow managed to get the most beautiful, special woman in the world to marry me.

Chapter 6

"We need to consummate our vows," she says sleepily when I've finally got her upstairs.

Who is she trying to kid? She's good for nothing, as proven when she requested me to carry her, out of necessity rather than simply because she loves me carrying her everywhere. I mean, I'm tempted, always tempted, but as I've explained to her endlessly, I'd prefer complete cognizance when we're intimate. "Baby," I say softly, appeasing her. "You're too tired. We'll consummate in the morning." And every other morning for the rest of our lives together. I encourage her from my chest and look down at her sleepy face. Yes, she's knackered. God love her.

She relents, falling forward, back into my chest. I don't let her, just wanting to look at her this closely for a while, take in every inch of her, not that I need my mind refreshing. Just…well, I could look at her continuously, especially when she looks so peaceful. "What?" she asks.

"Tell me you love me."

"I love you."

"Tell me—"

"I *need* you."

"You'll never know how happy that makes me," I say around a smile.

"I *do* know," she counters as I drop a light kiss on her bare lips.

"I want you naked and spread all over me." *Snuggles.* "Let me get this dress off." It's almost a crime to remove it from her body since it's obviously been made for her. But ….*naked.*

When I've turned her in my arms, her chin drops to her chest and my eyes cross at the number of buttons that greet me, all tiny, all very close together. I frown at my fingers. This is going to be fiddly. I make a start, struggling with the first one, but once I have a few undone, it becomes easier. "What's happening with your brother and Kate?" I ask quietly. Like I said to Kate, I don't want Sam to be messed around. It's taken a lot for him to admit he's catching feelings, albeit in his own weird way.

"I don't know," Ava replies quietly, thoughtfully, telling me she's worried too. But is she telling me everything?

"Either you've learnt to control your bad habit," I say, watching and waiting for her fingers to move into her hair. "Or you're telling me the truth."

"I'm telling the truth."

I finish the last button, ease the lace off her shoulders, and draw the dress down her body for her to step out of, wondering how the hell she's managed to carry it around with her all day. It weighs a fucking ton. I'm hit with the vision of her bodice, and I swallow, quickly looking away and searching for somewhere to put the dress, seeing a hanger on the back of the door. I fiddle with the loops to get them on.

"I think seeing each other has sparked memories, that's all," she says from behind me.

"Memories?" I go back to her and get to work on her underwear.

"They were bad for each other. You know Kate, and Dan isn't the most tolerant man on the planet. They clashed terribly. It was best for them both when Dan left."

I inwardly laugh to myself. I know Kate, yes. Firecracker. And I don't know Dan very well, but I know I don't like him. "But now he's back."

"Yes," she breathes, sounding flat and defeated. "But he'll be gone soon."

What can I say? Good? Ava's brother is an interference I really don't want around. A punch-up waiting to happen.

"What about Kate and Sam?" she asks.

"I've told you, that's none of our business."

"But she's a member of The Manor. Why did you allow that?"

"It's not my job to ask potential members why they want to join. I check for criminal records, medical issues, and financials." Or Sarah did. I frown, wondering where I might start with that when we get any new member applications. "If they can pay, they're clean, and have no serious offences, they're in. I don't run therapy sessions to delve into their reasons, Ava." Shit, will John know how to deal with new member requests?

"Members could screw anything between visits to The Manor and catch something," she grumbles. "Or be arrested for violence. How would you know?"

"Because they're required to undertake monthly tests, and I obtain regular reports. They are not issues that can be completely prevented, but it's controlled as best we can. There is no penetrative sex without condoms, and their honesty and disclosure form part of their agreement. These people are respected members of society, Ava." Well, some. Many are plain wankers.

"Who love having kinky sex with strangers and weird contraptions."

"None of my business." It's just my…livelihood? I frown again as I remove her corset. Ava's my livelihood now. The Manor is just…there.

I place my lips on her shoulder, kissing her gently, because she's precious. Delicate. I feel her body expand on an inhale. "She's going to get hurt."

"What makes you think that?" I ask, tugging her against me. In all honesty, I think the chances of Kate getting hurt is less with Sam than with Ava's brother.

"I know she likes him."

"And I know Sam likes her," I reply quietly, pressing my body into her, doing myself no favors, goading my cock.

But her reaction to my touch? Magic. "Then why can't they date like any normal couple?" she asks on a wispy breath.

"None of our business," I murmur, trying to talk my dick down. It's no good. Ava's awake, I can feel every tingle on her skin, my dick is stirring, and there's no chance of it resting until it's satisfied. I'm about to turn her and worship her, but she beats me to it and spins fast, thrusting into my chest, forcing my backward steps to the bed. She looks determined. Who am I to argue? Besides, we haven't had sex today. *Criminal.*

"This marriage is getting consummated," she declares as I land on my back. She's soon sitting on me. "Mr. Ward, I'm taking the power. Any objections?"

My smile could short-circuit The Manor. Taking the power? Oh, lady, you are welcome to it. "Knock yourself out, baby." Then I scowl. "But please watch your mouth."

"Mouth," she retorts huskily, pulling me up to her by my tie. Jesus, she soon got over her tiredness. *Horny.* I'm here for it. "Who has the power?" she asks.

"It looks like you do for now." I'm slightly alarmed by her purpose. "Don't get used to it."

She slams her mouth on mine, eating me alive, and I fall back to the bed, taking Ava with me, letting her at me, cupping her arse, squeezing and stroking, moving to her hips, her back, her neck, and back down again.

"Damn you, woman."

"You don't want me?"

"Don't ask stupid fucking questions." I shudder, her mouth working around my ear, and all I can think is…get inside her. I'm not up for being teased, and that's what Ava does when she takes the power. She torments me, gets the most satisfaction from turning me into a desperate wreck. I think I'll lose my mind.

I lift my upper body ready to take her onto her back but barely get an inch off the mattress before I'm flat again. "Oh no, Ward," she pants, one eyebrow hitched cheekily. I'm immediately worried. I can't manhandle her, can't be too rough with her, I just…can't.

She takes my hand.

I take a breath. What is she—

I inhale when I realize her plan, my muscles tensing, stopping her from lifting my wrist to the headboard, the cuff still dangling around my wrist. She firms up her hold, tugging, fighting my resistance, as I try so hard to shake off the instant anxiety creeping into me, remembering the last time we were here—Ava with cuffs, me at her mercy. She left me defenseless and alone on the bed. It wasn't nice. My reaction was quite extreme, admittedly, but way past my control.

I breathe in, going against everything I am and know, letting her take my hand to the headboard. I have to prove I'm working on myself. It's just one hand. But…"You won't leave this time." I hear the metal meet the wood, and my arm jerks in response. "Promise you won't leave me this time."

"If you promise you won't get mad."

I clench my eyes closed, taking in air, as she secures me. And I fucking let her. Because something's just occurred to me…

If I'm handcuffed to the bed, I can't fuck her hard, and she can't protest that because *she* restrained *me*.

"Don't get mad with me," she whispers.

"Kiss me." Distract me. Take me. Love me.

"But I'm in charge."

"Jesus, baby, don't make this harder than it already is." I pull her down with my free hand and kiss her with purpose as she unravels my tie and unbuttons my shirt. Then her hands are on my chest. Her pussy rubbing me in the perfect place. My mouth works harder, my dick throbbing, my arm naturally fighting the restraint.

She abandons our kiss.

Fuck.

Don't yell.

Let her have this. It's been weeks of me taking it slow and gentle, and Ava trying to push it harder and faster. Weeks of her wanting to demand why I'm dialing back the ferociousness but daring not, because that will lead to a conversation she seems hell-bent on avoiding.

I hold my breath and look up at the ceiling, broken, rough whimpers coming fast as she works her lips all over my torso. I'm so tense, I'm aching everywhere. Her face is hovering over my fly. *Oh Jesus.*

And with one brief dash of contact, I jolt and hiss, seeing a smug, satisfied smile stretching across her face. What the hell is she up to? Do I care? The pressure is building. I feel frenzied. All control I have kept for the past few weeks is slipping. And that's okay because I have limited movement.

She finds her way into my trousers as I reach for the back of her head, working through the silky strands, resting my head back on a sigh as she takes my dick in her hold. I thought I was prepared for the contact. The heat. The sensations.

Nope.

"Fuck, Ava," I groan, twitching and jerking. "Fucking hell." She peeks up at me, and I both love and hate the satisfaction on her face. "Mouth," I growl. "Now." She needs to cool the burn, sate the need. I narrow one warning eye on her as she slowly crawls back up my body.

"You want me to take you in my mouth?" she asks, low and huskily, dragging things out.

"Do it."

"Who has the power, Jesse?" she asks, kissing and biting around my mouth.

"You do, baby," I assure her. "Mouth."

Thank God, she's had enough of playing with me and floats back down my body, taking me deeply into her mouth. "Oh fuck. Oh Jesus,

Ava. Your mouth is amazing."

"Good?"

"Too good." I relax for the first time since she cuffed me, shuddering as tingles glide through my body. "I knew I married you for a reason."

A little warning bite from Ava, a long inhale from me. "All the way?" she asks,

"Do it."

The incredible feel of her warm mouth sliding down my shaft sends me dizzy, my body melting into the bed, my hips flexing upward, encouraging her. Fuck me, that feels out of this world.

Hot.

Wet.

Then the oddest sound emanates through the room, my dick is suddenly cold, and Ava jumps up.

I jerk, knocked from my euphoria, and blink, dazed, just catching the back of Ava before she disappears into the bathroom, coughing and choking. "Ava?" I say, my voice hoarse. "Ava, baby, what's up?"

I hear the most incredibly violent hacking. Panic finds me. "Ava," I yell, looking up at the headboard. *Trapped.* She's choking, and I'm fucking stuck here. I yank at the cuffs, hissing through the pain. "Ava!" I still, listening, hearing all kinds of horrific noises. "Jesus, Ava." I yank my arm. "Fucking hell," I roar, gritting my teeth, sure my shoulder is about to pop out of the socket. "Ava!" Why the fuck isn't she answering? Because she can't. *Choking.*

I hear the creaking of wood above my head, look up and see a slat bowing. Another yank, and it cracks. *Mind over matter.* I growl and wrench my arm down, firing a few fucks, and the wood gives, splintering, and with one more bellow and pull, the headboard surrenders, and my hand drops to the mattress limply. "Fuck," I hiss, brushing away the remnants of wood from around me with my good hand, shaking some life into my dead one. I jump up and hurry to the bathroom, bowling in and taking in the scene—Ava slumped on the floor, sweating profusely, as white as a sheet. My brain takes its time figuring out what I'm looking at, how I should deal with it.

Then her eyes widen and she flings her arms out, catching the toilet.

And throws up.

The smell hits me like a bat to my face.

"Jesus, baby," I whisper, moving in behind her and crouching, taking her hair and holding it up while she convulses, unable to catch her breath between retches. And, of course, all I can think about is why she's throwing up.

"I'm fine."

"Clearly." Will she finally relent and have the conversation we need to have? "Let me look at you," I say, dropping to my arse and turning her to face me, my hand still numb. She looks wiped out. Clammy, pasty, exhausted.

"Still want to fuck me?"

"Ava, please."

"I'm sorry."

"Lady, you'll kill me off, I swear." I make a vain attempt to pick some wet strands off her sweaty cheek. "You okay?"

"No," she admits. "I feel sick."

I welcome her into my chest when she puts herself there. Hiding? "Why do you think that is?" I ask, nibbling my lip, feeling her limp, lifeless body become hard against me.

The silence stretches. It's so fucking uncomfortable. "Take me to bed," she eventually mumbles, her tone begging me to leave it there. "Please."

I look up to the ceiling, forcing some patience forward. She's maddening. "You are the most frustrating woman on the fucking planet," I tell her as I get us both to our feet. "You want to brush your teeth?"

"Please." She pouts, looking small and frail.

"Everything will be fine," I say softly, feeling at her face, making sure she's looking at me. Is that what she needs to hear? Reassurance?

"Okay." She smiles, that's small and weak too, then her eyes widen and she seizes my hand. "Jesse, what have you done?"

I stare down at my wrist as she inspects the damage. More war wounds. More pain. I take the cuffs off and drop them to the floor. "You keep my heart beating, baby, but you can also make it fucking stop." And she does, a little each day. "You said you couldn't live without me, didn't you?"

"Yes."

"Then stop trying to kill me off." I pluck the toothbrush out of the holder and squeeze some paste onto it.

"You're such a drama queen."

"There is nothing dramatic about being worried when my wife throws up after I've just thrust my cock in her mouth."

She suddenly comes to life, falling apart laughing. Literally. I'm forced to take her elbow to stop her toppling over. She finds this funny? I can't say we're on the same wavelength right now, although it's nice to see her laughing.

I wait for Ava to pull herself together, chuckling over her apologies. Rubbing at her eyes, I wonder what's going through her head right now. Does she think I've forgotten why we're in here? She dials her giggles back. "It is quite funny, though."

Is it? "I'm glad you find it amusing," I grumble. "Open your mouth." I give her teeth a brush, her face a wash, and take her back to bed before anything else can go wrong on our special day.

And that's what hurts. For me, I can't think of a better way to end our wedding day than finding out we're expecting. Just forget about how it came to be for a second and think about our future.

"In you get," I order, scanning the bed one last time for any pieces of splintered wood. Deflating a little, I start to strip.

"I can't believe I'm spending my first night as your wife in one of your torture chambers." She looks around the room, which is probably just as well because she doesn't see me rolling my eyes.

"No one has slept in that bed, Ava."

"They've not?"

Why does she look so surprised? Did she honestly think I'd be cool making a marital bed out of one of the places I used to fuck? "No one has been in this room since I cornered you." I raise my brows. *Take that, Mrs. Ward.* "And the bed is new." What a waste of fucking money it was. And, actually, subpar in the quality department. I'm not sure I'd get away with returning it, though.

"Really?"

"Really."

"Why?"

"Because I'm not having you in a bed that others have"—she knows exactly why, for Christ's sake—"frequented."

She appears to snuggle deeper. "And no one has been in this room since me?"

"Only me," I say, nodding to her body. "Get your underwear off, I want you naked."

"Did you sit in here quietly and think about me?" She fails to keep her grin in check as she wriggles out of her knickers.

Oh, if she only knew. I drop my boxers and wander over to the chest of drawers, pulling one open and plucking out her bra. "More than you know."

"That's my bra," she gasps, her eyes following it through the air as I toss it onto the cabinet.

I get into bed with her, and she's all over me like a rash immediately. "Comfy?" I whisper, following the path of her hands as they travel my chest, hearing her hum her answer. "How do you feel?"

"I'm fine."

My sigh collides with Ava's, and I pull her closer, hug her harder. "She's fine." If I could only make her see that she really will be fine. Because I've got her. Always. "Go to sleep, my beautiful girl."

And maybe in the morning she'll see the light.

The hope.

Maybe.

Her eyes are getting heavy, her lips parting. It's been a long day. Certainly unforgettable. For the right reasons? Not really. And, worryingly, I'm not all that confident about tomorrow, because I'm not willing to let another day pass without us finding out if my wife is expecting our first baby.

Our first.

Ava's first.

Not my first.

My throat becomes thick, my hold of Ava naturally tightening. "I'm not replacing you," I whisper, staring at the sheet covering our bodies.

Then what are you doing, Daddy?

"Searching for redemption, my darling."

You don't need redeeming.

"Oh, but I do." I smile, swallowing over a lump. "I wish I still had you."

Uncle Jake's looking after me.

I feel a tear fall, and I release one arm from around Ava and roughly wipe at my eyes. "That's good," I muse, smiling through my trembling lips. "Do you think I'm crazy?"

Sometimes.

I laugh under my breath, feeling Ava stir in my arms. I watch her relax on a sigh. "Do you think I've—"

Fucked this up?

I blink, jolt, scowl at nothing before me. "Watch your damn mouth." I look around the room, coming into myself a little. I swear, I hear her laughing. Is this my thing now? Talking to dead people? I still, quiet, waiting for her to come back at me. Wishing she would. "Jesus Christ," I breathe, shaking my head to myself. I'm certifiably fucking loopy.

I ease Ava off me and gently break away, settling her on the sheets, getting up and going to the bathroom. I go straight to the mirror. Stare at myself. Question myself.

Worry for myself.

But I'll be okay. *We'll* be okay.

I hope.

"Fucking hell." I cup my face with my palms and scrub them down my cheeks. *Crazy.*

I use the toilet, wash my hands, and pad back to the bed, stalling halfway across the room when someone knocks on the door gently. Given I'm naked, I look around the room for my boxers. I find them on the floor by the bed and quickly get into them, checking Ava. She's out for the count.

I pull the door open a fraction.

Recoil when I see who's calling.

I look over my shoulder to Ava before slipping out and pulling the door shut behind me. "What can I do for you?" I ask, my tone unfriendly. He can't expect anything else.

He sways a bit, and I fear the worst. A flying fist, a yell, a threat. So when he says, "I haven't given you a chance to prove yourself." I find myself taking a wary step back.

I want to laugh, but instead I cough, disguising it. "Prove myself? What, to you?"

"Yeah."

"There's only one person in this world I need to prove myself to, and it isn't you, Dan."

He shrugs, pouting, rolling back on his heels. "And you've proved yourself, have you?"

I frown. "Did you come here to pick another fight, because it's been a really fucking long day, and I haven't the energy." *But come back in the morning when I'm dressed, fresh, and all our guests have left The Manor. I'll happily fuck you up then.*

"I just want her to be happy."

"Does she seem unhappy?"

"Yes, actually."

As much as it pains me, this arrogant prick is my wife's brother and—*ouch*—he's known her a hell of a lot longer than I have. But as deeply? I don't think so. I think Dan's too wrapped up in his own world to know exactly what's going on in anyone else's, including his sister's. He's just acting out. Letting his ego out to play. "Let me assure you of a thing or two," I say, my hand clenching the doorknob. It's that or Dan's throat. Can't do that. "My wife is perfectly happy." A man does not need another man—brother or not—asking him if he can make his wife happy.

I'm surprised when Dan nods, albeit mildly. "Okay."

The fuck?

"I think it's time for me to crash." He backs up, slowly but surely, glancing around the gallery landing. "This really is a nice place you have here."

"Thanks."

"Must be worth a few quid."

"A few."

He smiles. "Good talking, Jesse."

Was it? He turns and wanders off. "Safe travels back to Australia," I call quietly.

"Oh, Mum obviously hasn't mentioned it," he says, looking over his shoulder.

"Mentioned what?"

"I'm staying in London." He smiles brightly and takes the stairs, again slowly but surely, and not because he's under the influence. It's because he's relishing the shock I'm trying and failing to hide. He isn't here to apologize at all. He's here to piss me off. "So we'll be seeing much more of each other."

"Anything in particular influencing that decision?" I ask. Like… Kate?

"No, just fancied a change of scenery."

Right. Sure. What the fuck isn't he telling me? "You need to fix things with your sister," I say, forcing a smile. I'll take Dan's arsehole behavior all day long. Will I let Ava? No.

I back into the room and shut the door. Brilliant. I get the pleasure for a little longer.

There's something not right, something Dan's not telling us.

But what?

And do I care? No. But Ava will, which means Dan's now my problem too.

Chapter 7

We woke up, we bathed, we talked, I tried and failed to get her to skive off work tomorrow, and Ava shirked yet another prompt from me to get some things off her chest.

But that's the last time. When we're out of here, alone, I'm ending this ridiculous stalemate. We're married. We live together. Adore each other.

The moment I step into the restaurant holding Ava's hand, I spot Dan. He doesn't notice me—he's too busy watching Kate, who looks— God forgive me—like she's been dug up. Sam, however, who's sitting next to her, looks suspiciously chirpy.

And where the fuck is Drew?

I'm about to pull my phone from my pocket to text him, but the room erupts into applause, and I look around to see all attention on us. The bride and groom.

Shit.

I quickly get back to husband duties and pick Ava up, carrying her through the tables to where her parents are sitting, putting her down on a chair.

"Darling," Elizabeth says as I lower to my seat, her volume too high for this time of day. I check Sam and Kate, nod my good morning. "What a wonderful day it was," she goes on. At least she's not still banging on about the cake not being cut. "Despite a certain difficult man."

Is she talking about me? A quick check across the table gives me my answer. It's really quite something that she calls *me* difficult. The woman is draining. "Good morning, Elizabeth," I say on a smile meant to dazzle her. And it does. Her nose wrinkles and she goes back to her coffee. "How are you, Joseph?"

"Very well," he says. "Did you two enjoy your day?"

That's debatable. "We did, thank you. Are you being looked after?"

"Too well." He laughs. I'm not sure how to take it. Amused by the hospitality? He should be here when The Manor is actually operating for its intended purpose. "We'll be hitting the road after breakfast, so

I'll take this opportunity to thank you for your hospitality." Joseph nods, and I smile on the inside as I pluck a slice of toast out of the rack in the middle of the table. "It really was a special day."

"Is Dan going back with you?" Ava asks, pulling my interested eyes her way briefly. I had wondered last night after I shut the door on my visitor if he had mentioned to Ava that he was staying in London. Obviously not. I pick up a knife and scrape a sliver of butter off the knob.

"Oh, no," Elizabeth says on cue. "Hasn't he told you?"

Here we go. Do I look surprised? Happy? I put the toast in Ava's hand, and she looks at me on a frown. I can't tell if it's because of the toast or because of her mother's words. "Told me what?" She takes a nibble of the toast as I discreetly look over to Dan. He's back to watching Kate, and as I check Kate to assess her persona, I catch her looking at him too. She quickly diverts her eyes back to the table. I shift, uncomfortable. Something's going on, and I don't like it.

"He's staying in London for a while," Elizabeth says casually, faffing over Joseph's plate.

"He's what?" Ava blurts. She doesn't sound pleased about that. Interesting. If I was a betting man, I would have put my money on Ava being thrilled if she was told her beloved older brother wasn't going back to Australia. So...what the hell has happened?

"Staying in London, darling," Elizabeth repeats, wiping her hands on a napkin.

"Why? I thought he has the surf school to expand and work on." Ava puts the toast she's barely touched down. Oh no. I retrieve it and set it back in her hand. She hardly ate yesterday, and what she *did* eat came up. We are not getting into bad eating habits, especially if she's pregnant. Ava's once again frowning. And, once again, I don't know if it's the toast or the news.

"He says there's no rush," Elizabeth goes on, happy. "And I'm not complaining." Yes, because she's blind to the fact that her son's a cunt. I smile up at Pete as he lays some drinks down, and Ava abandons her toast *again* in favor of her cappuccino.

"Eat," I order gently, putting the toast back in her grasp.

"I don't want the fucking toast," she barks, making me jump and clang the cutlery on the table.

"Ava," I say, my shock obvious, as she stares at me, wide-eyed and a little shocked herself. Good. It tells me she realizes she's being unreasonable. I'm just trying to make sure she has something in her tummy after she emptied what she ate yesterday in the toilet. "Mouth." I cast a quick look over to Elizabeth and Joseph, relieved to see they're stunned too. But unlike them, I now know the toast isn't the issue. It's Dan and his plans.

Ava stands, her fire eyes on her brother. "Where are you going?" I ask, dumping my napkin on the table and rising. "Ava, sit down."

She inhales, her jaw rolling, anger rampant. Oh Jesus, is she thinking at all? What is she going to do, cause a scene right here in front of everyone? What the hell has happened?

"Sit down and eat your breakfast, Jesse," she orders shortly.

Say what? I take hold of her wrist as she moves away from the table, stopping her. "Excuse me?" I ask in disbelief. She's definitely pregnant. Has to be. Her emotions are all over the fucking place.

She turns a steely stare my way, and I withdraw. "I said, sit down and eat your breakfast."

Oh, she means business. I throw a snarl Dan's way, since this is his fucking fault. "Yes, I thought you did." Then I sit, pull Ava down to her chair, and fill her hand with the damn fucking toast. "Ava, this isn't the time or the place for you to start throwing your weight around," I whisper close to her ear. And because I'm an arsehole—and maybe because I'm truly worried she'll kick off and cause a shitstorm that obviously needs a more delicate approach, which is ironic coming from me, I know—I call on my power, breathing in her ear. "And have a little respect in front of your parents." I find her leg under the table and skate a *delicate* palm up her thigh. She's a statue in her chair in an instant. "I like this dress." My finger tickles the edge of her knickers, and her thighs clamp together over my hand. I kiss her lobe, pulling back a fraction to see her cup shaking as she takes it to her mouth.

Done.

I free her of my touch, lifting my brows when she peeks out the corner of her eye at me.

"Jesse is right, Ava," Joseph says. "You should watch your language."

"Yes, it's not very ladylike," Elizabeth adds.

I try not to smile. "Thank you, Joseph," I say, casting a look Ava's way, hitting her knee with mine, smiling when she scowls into her drink and returns the favor.

"So when are you two honeymooning?"

Ah, yes, onto something more constructive and useful right now. "When my wife says so. When will that be, lady?"

She takes the biggest bite of her toast while staring me down, talking around her mouthful. "When I have time. I've got a lot to sort out at work." She chews, swallows, and smiles sweetly. "My husband knows that." *Don't I just.* God, I love and loathe her sass. Love it more. "What are you grinning at?" she asks.

I'm grinning? Better than snarling. "You."

"What about me?"

Where do I start? "Everything about you," I muse, my eyes on her lips. *Your smart mouth.* "Your beauty." *Your sass.* "Your spirit." *Your incessant need to rile me.* "Your need to drive me insanely crazy." I know I drive her nuts too. *Made for each other.* Her eyes sparkle, her smile impish as I play with her necklace, just to touch her. To be close. "And the fact you're mine."

She breathes out, exasperated by my fussing. But loving it too.

"Oh, Joseph, do you remember being that much in love?"

I laugh, as does Joseph. I'm certain no man has felt the way I feel about Ava. "No," Joseph says, confirming my thoughts. "I don't. Come on, I want to get on the road. I'll use the bathroom and get our cases," he says, standing.

Joseph leaves and Ava goes back to looking between her friend and brother. She's not telling me something. "You've noticed it too?" I ask, subtly hinting that I'm aware of the atmosphere.

"Yes, but I've been warned to mind my own business."

About Kate and Sam, yes, but we're not talking about Kate and Sam, and we all know what will happen if I step in and make sure Dan knows how I feel about any interference. "You have, but I didn't say you couldn't tell your brother to back off."

Ava looks at me in horror as Elizabeth excuses herself. I stand, polite, feeling my wife's eyes lift with me, and nod when Elizabeth declares she'll be back.

"You want me to warn my brother off?" Ava asks the moment her mother is out of earshot.

I need to be honest. As does Ava. She won't let me talk to Dan, because she knows damn well I won't hold back. She also knows her brother won't take too kindly to being told what to do by the family's new golden boy. But…"I think he needs to be told. I don't want to upset you by doing it myself, so perhaps you should have a word with him." Appeal to his reasonable side, if he has one.

"I'll speak to him." She looks at her toast, grimaces, and places it back down. The thought of talking to her brother has obviously put her off her breakfast. "And before you start"—a halting hand comes up—"I'm not hungry."

"You need to eat, baby," I say softly.

Her hand stops mine reaching forward. "I'm not hungry," she says again. "Can we go home now?"

What am I going to do? Make a scene over toast when I've just spent the best part of breakfast ensuring Ava doesn't make a scene herself? "We can go home now." I stand and pull her up. "Come on." I take her shoulders and push her toward the door. "I need to find John."

"I haven't seen him this morning."

No, so where is he? "You say your goodbyes, I'll meet you out front."

"Okay."

I leave Ava at Sam and Kate's table, heading through the summer room, calling John on my way. "Where are you?" I ask when he answers. I push my way into my office.

"Here." He's at my desk, and he looks like he's had no sleep whatsoever. His shades are hanging under his chin. His tie loose. His suit crumpled.

"Have you been to bed?"

He lifts his eyes but not his head.

"What's going on?" I ask, closing the door, my heart climbing into my throat. "Is it Sarah?"

He stands, going to the fridge and getting a bottle of water. "She turned up here."

My jaw loses all control, dropping. "What?" Coral *and* Sarah? Jesus Christ, I'd be divorced if Ava knew.

"You were in bed. *Everyone* was in bed."

In a bit of a daze, I walk to the chair and drop into it. "Drunk?"

"Smashed."

"More than drink?"

He shrugs, unscrewing the cap of his water and glugging it back.

"Fuck," I hiss, rubbing at my forehead. I take no pleasure from the state Sarah's clearly in. None at all. "What did you do? Shit, John, you should have called me."

He turns, his eyebrows slowly creeping up his forehead. *Okay, yes, stupid suggestion.* "I put her in my car and drove her home."

"She let you?"

"She was hardly in any fit state to fight me off."

"Wait, how did she get here?"

Another slow rise of his brows.

"She drove?" I balk at him. "Fucking hell." Is she out of her mind? I pause that thought and rewind. Stupid fucking question. "She could be dead."

"Hmmm." John's thoughtful as he finishes his drink and tosses the bottle in the bin. "I'm going to check up on her."

What can I say or do? Offer to help? We both know that can't happen, and not only because my new wife will undoubtedly tip the edge if she found out I was dealing with *another* woman from my past on our wedding weekend. My intervention would also mislead Sarah into thinking I care. Fuck, I do care, we all know it. But I can't be involved anymore. I can't.

I drop my head in my hands. "Shit."

"Don't worry, I've got this."

"You shouldn't have to deal with this, John. She needs to pull herself together." I wince. *Harsh.*

A knock at the door sounds and Sam pokes his head round. "Ava's looking for you."

I sigh, standing. "I'm coming."

"Meet me round the back," Sam says to John, before he disappears. I look at John in question.

"He's following me to Sarah's in my car. I need to drive hers."

"Her car's out front?" I ask, alarmed. If Ava sees that, I'm toast. I let out a stupid bark of laughter.

"No, it's around the back."

"Right, yes, good." Of course he'd have it covered. Protect me. I frown at the carpet. "What do you think of Ava's brother?"

"I think he's a prick."

"Don't hold back, will you?"

"Whenever have I minced my words?" *Very true.* "Besides, you think he's a prick too."

"Is it that obvious?"

"Yes."

"Do you think Ava sees it?"

He smiles, but only mildly. "That girl sees more than you give her credit for." Is that code for *tell her everything*? "Any news on Van Der Haus?"

"Nothing." That's it. The wedding is over and real life is back. All I need is Freja to rock on up and make it a clean sweep of irrational, deluded females. John grabs his shades off the table and walks away. "I'll wait until you've left."

"John," I call, stopping him at the door. He turns, slipping his glasses on. "Thanks."

"No problem." He picks up his steps.

"John," I call, making him stop again, this time on a sigh. He doesn't turn around this time. "I think this is the first conversation we've ever had when you've not called me a motherfucker."

"Motherfucker," he mumbles, pulling the door open and exiting as I laugh lightly under my breath. I pull my phone out, thinking, wondering where Van Der Haus is and when he might strike. Because he will strike. It's a given. Or perhaps he's retreated after his failed attempt to drug my wife. I spin my mobile, slipping a hand in my pocket and walking in slow circles. Van Der Haus is a monumental arsehole, but a criminal? I chew my lip and dial someone with no hope they'll answer. Not after I threatened to make such a mess of him. And they don't. *Fuck.*

The door opens and Ava appears. "There you are," she breathes, ushering me to her with an impatient hand. "Mum and Dad are waiting to leave. They want to say goodbye. Come on."

I pull a smile from nowhere and go to her, pocketing my phone and sweeping her up into my arms. She squeals, then laughs, arms around my neck. "Anything you say, wife." I wrinkle my nose when she wrinkles hers, rubbing them together as I walk out with her draped across my arms.

"Why are you lying?" she asks, her eyes set firmly on me.

Lying.

There's only so long I'll get away with telling myself my lies are lies of omission. "I love you," I say, like that's the answer for all things.

"I know." She rests her head on my shoulder as I walk on.

"Oh, put her down," Elizabeth says, exasperated, as I walk down the steps. I'm not sorry to see her go. She's all right in small doses, and I've had too many big doses these past few weeks.

"Did you just roll your eyes?" Ava asks.

"Yes."

"You're asking for it."

Another roll as I place her down and sacrifice her one last time to others. Ava moves in on Joseph first, throwing her arms around him as Elizabeth claims me. "Look after her," she says quietly. It's an insult. "And promise you'll visit us soon."

"I will," I say, to the latter demand, not the first. "But your daughter has to take some time off work first." And if she does, I'm even willing to share her with her parents for a few hours before I take her on our honeymoon, whenever that may be. When the fuck will that be?

Elizabeth surrenders my shoulders for Ava's, and I take Joseph's hand when he offers it. "Safe journey," I say.

"Thanks for everything." He quickly checks where Ava is. She's buried in the crook of Elizabeth's neck. Then Joseph releases me and replaces his hand with an envelope, slapping the back of my hand with his spare.

"What's this?" I ask, looking down at the bulging package.

"For the bar," he says. "I said I wanted to cover the bar bill for the day."

"Joseph, really—"

"Don't," he orders, as sternly as I've known Joseph to talk. "I won't take no for an answer."

"I've not even raised an invoice." Funny. I don't know how. Sarah does.

"I'm sure that'll cover it, but let me know if not."

I back down, because who the fuck am I to stop him from spoiling his daughter, even if she's unaware. "She won't like it," I say for the sake of it.

"Which is why she won't know."

Many might ask what the point is if she doesn't know. The point is, Joseph feels like he's done her well. It doesn't matter that she doesn't know. He's there without needing the praise or credit, and that is a commendable quality. I hold the envelope up, nodding my thanks, before slipping it into my back pocket. I hope I can make the same gestures for *my* kids. The pang of pain isn't avoidable as I look at Ava. Will she ever fucking accept it? And the money Joseph just gave me? That's starting our kid's trust fund.

"Elizabeth," he calls, forcing mother and daughter apart.

"I'm coming." She rubs Ava's cheek, slips into the car, then they drive off, Elizabeth waving out of the window as they go.

I see Dan. Ava sees Dan. Then she walks to the Aston. "You're not going to say goodbye to your brother?"

"No." She gets in and shuts the door.

And that's that.

I look across to him as I round the car. He's glowering. Fuck me, what's his problem? I feel like he's got my card marked. What's worrying is my card is a fucking mess of marks already, and I really don't need Ava's brother digging to find those marks.

Chapter 8

I pass through the glass doors of Lusso with Ava in my arms, feeling her smile on my cheek. Isn't that what any man wants? A happy wife? But there's this awful underlying tension lingering, and I absolutely can't go into another week with it hanging over us. Get her inside, sit her down, and talk. It's all that's been on my mind since I pulled away from The Manor. I'll have to speak my truths, I know that. I'll have to explain my reasoning, show her my vulnerability, I know that. She's pregnant. She has to be. Everything points to it—the emotions, the vomiting, the tiredness.

We've been through so much, I *know* we can get through th—

I stop abruptly halfway across the marble floor, my head emptying when my eyes and brain register someone behind the desk. Someone who definitely isn't my usual old, round concierge. *Who the fuck is this?*

He looks up at me as he talks on the phone, and I take him in. All tall, good-looking, *young* inch of him. Jesus Christ, is this the new concierge? My eyes naturally narrow as he looks back at me with a wary gaze. *Yes, be wary, kid.* Be *very* wary. I feel my chest expand of its own volition and my grip of Ava tightens. He definitely takes a step back, despite the meters of marble between us. How old is he? Mid-twenties?

His stare finally moves from me.

Onto my wife.

My beautiful, sexy, mid-twenties wife.

I'll dig his eyes out with a spoon.

"Where's Clive?" I ask shortly, feeling Ava wriggling in my arms, trying to remove herself from my hold. Absolutely not. "Stay where you are, lady."

She laughs a little but does as she's told. For once. Did I miss the funny part? "You're behaving like a caveman," she whispers.

I have nothing to say to that. So I double down on my knob-ish, arrogant behavior. "Shut up, Ava," I say, making her eyebrows arch in disbelief. She looks like she's going to slap me. I hope she waits until we're in private. "Clive?" I ask again, returning my scowling face to my issue. Where the fuck is the old goat who's been bleeding me dry of cash since

I moved in? I like the old boy. We have an understanding. An agreement.

His call now ended, the imposter walks out from behind the desk, and I instinctively peek out the corner of my eye to Ava. Is she checking him out? With a poorly concealed grin on her face?

"I'll be working alongside Clive, sir," he says. I flip my wife a scowl she can't appreciate because she's too busy taking in the new concierge. "I was supposed to start my new position some time ago. Personal reasons delayed the commencement of my employment here." Personal? What, like he had to finish school? "I'm Casey, sir." He comes at me with his hand offered. "I look forward to assisting you with anything you may...well"—he smiles, awkward—"need assistance with."

There is nothing in this world that this kid could help me with.

The kid that looks about the same age as your wife?

"Mr. Ward," I tell him, ignoring Ava trying to get herself on her feet again and ignoring the new concierge's hand, because mine are currently busy locking down their hold. I hear her huff. She can huff all she likes. This pubescent thing has the hots for my wife. It's written all over his face.

"Nice to meet you, Casey," Ava says, chirpy and upbeat. Oh? So she's happy? I see her hand come up in front of us. I step back. I didn't tell my feet to move. They just...did. I can feel her incredulous stare on my profile. I hope she's thinking about how handsome her husband is as she drills holes into me. How talented he is in the bedroom. How much he loves her. How—

Ava's suddenly out of my arms and in front of the concierge, giving him her hand. *Take it, you die, kid.* Stupid fuck takes it. "Welcome to *Lusso*," she chirps.

"Thank you, Ava," he says, flicking a wary look my way. I narrow my eyes further. Ava? That's very bold. I'm about to give him a lesson in appropriate ways to address residents, but he goes on. "Nice to meet you too. You're in the penthouse?"

"Yes," Ava says. "That's us."

Us. Husband and wife. *Possessive* husband and wife.

"Maintenance called to say your new front door has arrived from Italy," he says.

"That's great, thank you."

Am I supposed to just stand here like a spare part while my wife and the concierge have a nice old natter? "Have maintenance fit it without delay," I snap.

"Already done, sir." He dangles a pair of keys, and I snatch them, chucking him my car keys before claiming my wife and escorting her to the elevator. "Bring the cases up," I order as I hit the call button, peeking down at Ava. She's amused. Good for her. I'm not. And is she forgetting that she is quite the pro at this trampling business too?

The doors open, I get Ava inside, and I don't wait for them to close before I pounce. She was expecting this. Probably hoping for this. I love nothing more than showing my wife who has the power. "He fancies you," I whisper, pressing my body into hers, feeling her torso sink with her inhale. Isn't that just wonderful? No matter how much she anticipates me, calls for me, braces herself for me, she can never control her reactions.

"You think everyone fancies me."

"That's because they do," I whisper, hearing the doors close as I fight my compulsion to push her to her knees and make her apologize for laughing at me. Can't do that, she might throw up, and I absolutely need us connected on a physical level right now. We haven't had sex for nearly thirty-six hours. We'll talk after. "But you're mine." I kiss her harder than I mean to, and she welcomes my force with a telling, whimpering moan *and* by grabbing me, pulling me closer.

"I'm yours," she vows, going at me, starved.

"You don't need to reassure me." I slip my hand under her dress and, I swear, feel her throbbing against my palm as her tongue hardens, fighting with mine. Everything hard. I push my finger into her knickers. Inhale at the hot, wet feel of her flesh. "Wet." So fucking drenched, just like that. One kiss, one touch, she's mine. "Just for me. Understand?"

"I understand," she gasps, her walls sucking me in deeper. "More."

Breaking our kiss, I lean into her, watching her eyes darken by the second. I pull my finger out and add another, my lips parting as I push them into her, and she breathes in, staring into my eyes. "Like that?" I whisper, watching her taking it, struggling to keep her head up, struggling to speak. "Like that, Ava?"

"Just like that."

Fuck, I could watch her all day as I fuck her with my fingers. "Or would you prefer my cock slamming into you?" Passion and possessiveness are ruling me. I can't stop this, the familiar feelings of power overcoming me, the need inside to prove to Ava *and* myself that I can be the best lover, take her to the clouds, keep her addiction alive and feed it. She swallows as I massage her, her hands moving to my jeans as her gaze drops. Lusty, heavy eyes. Eyes that are so expressive. Eyes that remind me of the first time she succumbed to our chemistry. I saw it back then. The struggle she was having to resist me.

We stare at each other as she undoes my fly and slides her hand into my boxers, claiming me. I bite down on my teeth. "You haven't answered my question."

"I want this," she whispers, rubbing over my shaft slowly. "I want you inside me."

My groan is suppressed as I pick her up, and she wraps every limb around me. "I knew you were a sensible girl." I can feel the pressure inside building as I carry her out of the elevator and get us inside.

Straight up the stairs.

Straight into the bedroom.

"You make me a desperate fucking mess, Ava." Straight on the bed.

Her dress off, my T-shirt off, my shoes, jeans, boxers all off.

All while she watches, her chest pumping.

Knickers, off.

Bra, off.

The pressure builds, my dick weeps, and I cast my eyes down her naked body, breathing out my awe. She sits up, pulling me to stand between her open thighs, and kisses my stomach as I comb through her hair with my fingers. Just her lips on my skin. *Calm.* I take the moment while she's adoring my stomach with her mouth to watch her. *Stillness.* I look down at her.

My wife. I keep saying it, thinking it.

Can I believe it?

I don't think I ever will.

To love her, make her smile, take care of her, protect her.

Complete.

She peeks up at me, her hands all over my torso, and pecks her way up to my neck. I close my eyes as she directs me to her mouth, helping her to climb onto me, accepting her kiss, devouring her mouth slowly and firmly. I take her into the bathroom, the place where she first surrendered to me, and step over the chaise, lowering. "We need to make friends," I whisper, seeing her brief smile before I bring our mouths together again. "No one will ever stop me taking you, Ava." I don't even know what I'm saying—just speaking, throwing out declarations, making sure Ava knows who she belongs to.

"Good."

I hiss when she tugs on my hair, my cock aching from being so hard for so long. I circle the girth, grunting, the pressure around the base easing the painful throb a little. But not much. A bead of sweat trickles down my temple. I breathe out, searching for restraint before I give in to what she wants, what she's been trying to get out of me for weeks.

To fuck her hard and fast, without apology.

Can't.

Releasing her mouth, I pull back, smiling on the inside at her mumble of displeasure. "My girl wants it hard." But I can bring her round to slow and intense. Always do. It's never any less overwhelming when we take our time. Love each other. Watch each other.

I ease her down, feeling her resistance.

"Jesse," she gasps, shaking in my hold, fighting me.

Condom.

Really?

"Ava," I breathe harshly, pleading. "I'm taking you now, and you're not going to stop me with trivial fucking requests." I tug a little harder, and the moment I have her mouth, I feel her soften, and the moment the tip of my weeping dick brushes her pussy, I feel her complete surrender. The friction could kill me, skin on skin for the first time in weeks, no condom, and no fierce refusal from Ava. My mind bends, the pleasure and sensations too intense for me to consider why now she's allowing this. Because we're married? Because she's accepted the situation? *I don't know.*

Her legs wrapped around my hips, she forces her boobs to my chest, moaning constantly, appreciating what we've both been missing for so long.

"Oh Jesus, fucking perfect," I mumble, overcome, trying to focus on kissing her and absorbing her. I close my eyes and soak up the pleasure, feel her mouth on my neck, her nails in my arms, her sweat on my tongue as I lick the small void on her collarbone.

"Move." Her hoarse whisper heats my flesh where her mouth rests. "Please move."

"In time, baby." I need to take a moment and reel myself in. "Just let me feel you for a moment." I help her hands to my neck, my breathing becoming more labored, and I've not even attempted movement yet. I skim the curves of her hips, brush the back of my hand over each nipple, then stroke down and circle her waist, holding her, making sure she doesn't move before I'm ready. Jesus, I'm struggling on every level, trying to control the deep throb in my dick, trying to control my breathing, trying to control my urge to let loose and sate us. I blow out my cheeks, grit my teeth, and slowly lift her, making sure I have a firm hold to control our moves. She follows my lead, calmly breaking away from her hiding place in my shoulder and gently feeling my chest.

"Don't try to tell me it doesn't feel right," I mumble drowsily, feeling drugged but high. "Don't try to tell me this isn't how we're supposed to be." Nothing between us, whether that be a some*one* or some*thing*. I grind her onto me slowly, watching her sustaining the unthinkable pleasure. "Not ever."

"Don't come inside me," she croaks.

"Don't tell me what to do with your body, Ava." I moan the words, my eyes on her parted lips, wet and inviting. "Kiss me," I demand, now growling, my body taking over.

My head is forced back by the hardness of her kiss. She can't get close enough, her torso pressed hard into my chest. Losing her mind. So I must keep mine.

I manipulate all the moves, lifting her, lowering her, grinding up into her.

"You feel so good," she says, breathless. "Jesse, fuck me."

"Mouth." *No.* "Just like this." I knew it was coming. *No.* "We stay just like this." I'm clenching my teeth again, resisting her demand. I'm outnumbered. Everything is demanding I release my restraint—my cock, my body, Ava. But my head is telling me no. *Careful.*

"Why are you being so gentle with me?" she asks, sinking her face into my neck, trying to break me down, kissing me, biting, licking my flesh. She's succeeding. I have to take a moment and a few more breaths.

"Sleepy sex," I whisper.

"I don't want sleepy sex." Her teeth sink into my neck. "Fuck me, Jesse," she demands huskily, circling her tongue, catching me by surprise and lifting, slamming down quickly before I can stop her.

"Mouth, Ava," I breathe, sounding drunk, my cock lunging inside her. "Jesus." I'm losing it. My control is slipping. The tingles are getting too intense. The pressure too much.

I feel her lift again, and I'm powerless to stop her, my dick absorbing the incredible feeling of her walls stroking it. "Yes," she yells, dropping back down.

My vision becomes blurred. "Ava," I bark, clamping down on her hips. "No, damn it." I can't fuck her like a madman, slam into her, throw her around, pound her hard, knowing of her delicate condition. I'm not making any sense. She's always delicate. But while she's keeping our baby safe inside her, I can't. It feels so...wrong.

Ava locks down every muscle around me, holds me tighter, gasps to match mine. We're so wet. Inside and out. Slippery. Inside and out. "Stop treating me like glass," she says quietly, the edge of pleading so loud.

"You are glass to me, baby." I swallow. "Delicate."

"But I'm not breakable. I wasn't two weeks ago, and I'm not now." She moves, and I fight to hold her in place, worried to face her. Ava wins. She'll always win. "Hard," she says, calmly. "I need you hard."

She needs me. But..."Sleepy."

"Why?"

I subtly breathe in. She wants to talk now? When I'm balls deep inside her, ready to detonate, and she wants to talk *now*? Or does she simply want me to confess? It makes no sense to me. She *knows*. "Because I don't want to hurt you." It's the truth.

"You won't," she grates.

I sigh, dropping my eyes, thinking. It's impossible to think straight when my body is demanding relief.

She moves too fast for me to stop her, rising and falling onto my lap on a yell laced with frustration. I cough over my shock. "Fuck!" I'm back to fighting my compulsion, fighting my body's instinct to feed Ava's want. "Fucking hell, Ava, no."

"Do it," she hisses, holding my jaw as she kisses me hard, moving her lips to my cheek. "Own me."

I shake my head, despite my tongue leaving my mouth and entering hers, returning her kiss. She rises and falls onto me again. "Fuck!"

"It feels good, doesn't it?" she says, hypnotizing me, breaking me down. "Tell me it feels good."

"Jesus, Ava. Please," I beg. "Don't."

Bang.

"Hmmm," she hums, holding my face, kissing me, rubbing her cheek against mine, licking the sweat trailing down my temple. "You taste good." My mind blanks. My body wins. "I need you," she whispers, driving down.

I roar at the ceiling, willing my dick to calm down.

It's a battle I can't win.

She's finally broken me.

Just like I broke her all those months ago.

I take her waist, my lip curling, and smash her down onto my lap. She was expecting it. But it doesn't stop her eyes from widening or her yell of surprise at the deepness. I'm so fucking hard, so fucking pent-up. Her fault. "Like that?" I yell.

"Yes!"

Her scream only adds to the pressure.

How loud do you think you'll scream—

I stand, flashbacks of Ava standing before me in her little red dress on the launch night of Lusso, looking at me like she wanted me, but acting like she didn't.

I get her against the wall. "You want it hard, baby?" I growl.

"Fuck me." Her screamed order bounces off the walls and pistons my hips into action.

"Stop swearing." I pound into her, choking on every drive, watching her throw her head around, pulling my hair, holding on for dear life. "Better?" I ask. She's lost the ability to talk, only scream. "You wanted it, Ava. Is that fucking better?"

She blinks, her eyes becoming heavy.

"Answer the fucking question," I yell.

"Harder!"

"Fuck." I gulp back some air, banging into her fast, out of my mind with her, all control lost, and focus on reaching the peak of pleasure. No condom. Her cries are constant, her fingernails scratching at my back. I can no longer see straight. I can only hear her muffled cries and my distorted bawls. It's mad, frenzied, out-of-control fucking, and

I can't stop it. Her walls clench hard around me, trying to slow my moves. She's coming, her body solid, her eyes rolling with her head. "I'm not done yet, Ava."

She gasps, climaxing, softening, my sweaty hands gripping her under her thighs, my hips going faster.

Claim the pleasure.

Let it bend me.

Let it put me on my arse.

I blink, chasing my release, looking into Ava's eyes, feeling her body hardening again. Fuck me, she's come down and is on her way back up again, her eyes looking panicked, as if she's not sure she can deal with the intensity so close off the back of her last orgasm. She's got no choice. She seeks comfort in my mouth, smashing our lips together as hard as I'm pounding into her. My tongue battles with hers. *Come on, come on.* The sweat pours from my body. *Come on, come on.* My hands begin to slip on the backs of her legs. *Come on!*

"Yes," she yells, giving up my mouth, slamming her head against the wall. "Oh God!"

"Eyes," I demand when she looks up at the ceiling.

She takes in air and does as she's bid, looking at me, clawing her hands in my hair harshly. Like she's mad. She's mad with me? I stop moving. Take a moment to let the burn cool, take a breath, clear my vision and my hearing.

I see her.

Wet.

Breathless.

Fit for nothing.

I slip out slowly, swallowing, watching her, feeling her stiffen.

Bracing herself.

A small voice at the back of my head is telling me I'll regret this. It's not loud enough. I slam into her fast, forcing her into the wall.

She cries out.

I repeat.

She stares at me, searching my eyes.

Then she holds on tighter.

I go again, never taking my eyes off her, as she goads me, takes what I'm giving because what else can she do? She started this. *I* will finish it. "Hard enough for you, Ava?"

"Yes," she yells with conviction, no holding back. So neither will I.

I slam into her over and over, her screams fueling me, her body now limp. Over and over, I chase the end, feeling it teasing me, the pressure stuck, waiting to burst out, needing just a little more encouragement while holding me in that constant, divine state of torture. "Come on," I grate, dripping wet, adjusting my hands on her thighs, trying in vain to hold on. "Come on!"

Fuck.

I'm losing my grip, my pace, the pressure subsiding. I pull her away from the wall and take her into the bedroom, my mind as frenzied as my body. I throw her onto the bed and flip her onto her knees. The moment I have her arse in my sights, I'm back to where I need to be, on the cusp.

I slide into her on a frenzied yell, dropping my head back, gathering myself but unable to stop my body from doing what it needs to do.

"Jesse," she yells.

I blink and look down at her, seeing her hands bunched in the sheets. "You wanted it, Ava," I grate.

Bang.

Bang.

Bang.

"Don't fucking complain." What, it's too hard for her now? She's had enough of what she's been begging for?

"Harder," she counters, pushing back onto me.

I bark her name in warning, holding her still, watching as her arms begin to shake where they're braced into the mattress. Here comes number three. And along with a few more smashes of our bodies, it's the push I need to carry me over the edge.

She screams, her throat hoarse, I bellow, the sound animalistic, and I explode, harder than I've ever known myself to come in my life. I can't see. I'm struggling to breathe. My body is shaking as I spill myself into her, dropping to the bed on top of her, crushing her to the mattress.

Beat.

In more than one way.

"Thank you."

And she thanks me for fucking her like an animal. Thanks me for losing my control.

I slowly peel myself away from her, staring down at her delicate body. And then down at my big, powerful frame. I'm shaking. She can sustain my force, my dominance, my needs.

But a baby?

Fuck.

Ava's body is rolling as she gasps for oxygen.

Oxygen that our child needs.

And I've stolen it.

I shake my head, my thoughts all over the place. I took what I needed. Lost my reason. Lost my mind.

And the guilt that's just slammed into me hurts. It hurts so bad.

I'm not gasping for air anymore because I'm depleted.

I'm panting because…remorse.

I get up and walk on unstable legs to the bathroom, my head in my hands. How did I allow that to happen? The relief was short-lived, as I always knew it would be, which is why I've abstained. *Fuck.*

I sit on the edge of the bath, looking at my hands, turning them over as they tremble. She asked me why I wanted soft and slow. I didn't answer. I could have. I *should* have. "God damn it," I breathe. God damn me. God damn *us*.

Enough.

I can't go through this again. The guilt stings. I hurt Rosie, and I'll be dead before I knowingly hurt any other child I'm blessed with. And I'm pissed off. Pissed off Ava's made me lose my control when she knows damn well how hard I've fought to keep it. When she knows why I'm treating her with care.

I stalk to the door, ready to face this head-on before I blow up, every inch of my body rolling with my stressed breathing. She's on the end of the bed, her arms hugging her knees.

She looks as guilty as I feel.

Good. I'm not alone.

What the fuck were we thinking?

"I've been taking your pills," I say quickly, struggling to get the words out, not because I'm reluctant to say it—this ends now—but because my jaw is ticking harder with each second that passes.

I detect only a slight widening of her eyes. Like…shock? Surely not. Her shoulders lift a fraction, making her sit up straight. But that's all I get.

"I said," I grate, wondering why the fuck she's staring at me so blankly. "I've been taking your pills." I think I just need a reaction now. Something. *Anything.*

I can hear my own breathing. Feel my own shakes. But from Ava? Nothing.

"Ava," I yell, stepping forward. "For fuck's sake, woman, I've been taking your fucking pills." My palms slide onto my head and rest there. *Come on, give me something.* Let's talk about this. Get it off our chests. "I ne—"

She moves so fast, she's a blur, and I back up as she flies at me, stopping directly in front of me. I stare down at her, searching her eyes, seeing anger, fire, and disbelief.

Which just makes me feel nothing but disbelief too. She didn't click? But she asked me outright. What the fu—?

Her hand collides with my face, snapping my head to the side, jarring my neck. The burn is instant and intense, the sound ear-piercing, and I blink, shocked, keeping my head and eyes low, not wanting to see the rage in her. Rage I deserve.

But I must face my wrongs and my fears. I don't know what I expected from this conversation, but the blinding anger pouring from her was not it. I've never seen her like this. I slowly, cautiously, lift my head, and the moment I see her eyes, I know another is coming. She doesn't know what to do, what to say, so she's lashing out. She doesn't want to hurt me. She's not that kind of human.

I lift my hand quickly and catch her flying palm just before it meets my already flaming cheek, but she wrenches herself free and comes at me with both hands, this time balled, hitting me over and over on my chest, pound after pound as she screams and yells.

And I stare at her, taking it, shocked to my core.

I really have made her crazy. Turned her from a level-headed young woman into a deranged, irrational female.

Irrational? Brother, you've decided her future. Trapped her.

But how can she be trapped if she wants to be with me?

I don't know how long I stand in the middle of our bedroom, naked, being hit repeatedly. My upper body is numb.

Ava eventually gasps, pushing both fists into my pecs, her head coming to meet my chest. She's drained. I'm about to pull her in for a hug, hold her, apologize, when she thrusts me away and bursts into tears, trembling.

I'm back to staring again. Back to being shocked. I prefer being used as a punchbag than seeing Ava cry.

"Why?" she screams at me, arms flailing.

"You were ignoring it, Ava," I say calmly, staying exactly where I am, respecting her need for space. "I need you to acknowledge this." And she's refused. "I needed to spike a reaction from you." But this? This, I never anticipated.

"I don't mean why you've told me," she yells, sniveling, roughly wiping her runny nose. "I knew! I mean why the fuck did you do it?"

Why? Isn't it obvious? It's not justified, I realize that, but she knows me. She knows how intense my feelings are for her. She knows I will do anything to keep her. But still, again, nothing can justify it. "You make me crazy." I gulp, swallowing the lump in my throat. "You make me do crazy shit, Ava."

"So it's *my* fault?" she asks, outraged. "My pills started going missing only days after you took me."

Took her? She makes it sound like I kidnapped her. That she didn't want me. But I can't challenge her. I have to let her vent, let her say her piece, and take it like a man.

Her red-rimmed eyes pour with tears. I can't watch. "I know," I whisper, staggering back a step when she charges into me and roughly yanks my face to hers. She looks psychotic. It's as if I've dislodged a blockage to her brain that was stopping her from considering exactly what's happened.

"You don't get to evade your reasons for this," she hisses in my face. "You've taken it upon yourself to dictate my life." Her fingers apply pressure on my face, and it hurts. Everything hurts in this moment. "I don't want a fucking baby," she screams. And that hurts the most. She doesn't want kids? "This is my body! You don't get to make these decisions for me. Tell me why the fucking hell you did this to me!"

She needs me to say it? "Because I wanted to keep you forever." That's my truth.

Her hold on my face loosens. "You *wanted* to trap me." She steps away, appearing and sounding calm all of a sudden. But I feel her energy as well as I feel my heart beat for her.

"Yes." I look at my bare feet, ashamed. Always. But it didn't stop me when I was hiding her pills. Not the first time, and not the last time.

"Because you knew I'd run when I found out about your business and your drinking problem."

"Yes." *Like you might run now. Like you might run when you find out about my true life before you walked into my office. When you find out I'm the reason everyone I've ever loved is dead.*

"But I came back after I found out about The Manor and the alcohol problem," she says, still calm, still even. Getting everything into place. Trying to understand. I have a horrible feeling in my gut that nothing I say will make a difference. "Yet you still took my pills when I replaced them."

"You didn't know about my history then."

"I do now."

I flinch. "I know."

"Stop saying you know," she cries, gesturing wildly with her hands.

"What do you want me to say?" I ask without looking at her. I'll say anything. And then I realize I haven't even apologized. Will it make a difference? Or begged, I've not begged for her forgiveness. "I'm…" I look up, seeing her disappear into the dressing room.

I hurry over, my heart crawling up my throat. Why would she go into the dressing room? I stop in the doorway, seeing her yanking some jeans on. *What?* Oh my God, no. She's not— "What are you doing?" I ask, my eyes watching her every move as she dresses. Then she gets a bag. "Ava?" I say, my words airy and weak. I go to her, taking the bag. "What the hell are you doing? You're not leaving me."

"I need some space," she says with no emotion at all, snatching the bag back and starting to pack it fast and messily.

Space. "Space for what?" I grab her arm, my panic ruling me. "Ava, please."

She wrenches herself away, and my heart splits. She's leaving me? "Please what?" she asks coldly as she takes her anger out on her clothes.

"Please, Ava," I beg. "Don't go." What will I do without her? What will happen? How will I cope?

"I'm going." She pushes past me, and I reach to grab her again, to stop her, but I'm so worried she'll fight me and injure herself. She's not thinking straight. I follow her to the bathroom, searching for the words I need to save this, to save us. I'm coming up blank. My fear is too strong. I can see nothing past it.

She stuffs some toiletries into her bag.

"Ava, let's talk about this."

"Talk?" She turns abruptly, her eyes still wild, her persona still so volatile.

"Please."

"What is there to talk about?" she asks. "You've done the most underhanded thing possible. Nothing you could say will make me understand this. You do not get to make these decisions. You do not get to control me to this extent. This is my life!"

Nothing I can say will help? But she's not even given me a chance. "But you knew I was taking them," I whisper.

"Yes, I did!" she cries, obviously not quite believing it. I'm stumped. I know I've done wrong, but I also knew she knew, and I took the fact that she knew and hadn't left me as a good thing. How could I have got it so wrong? "But perhaps because of all the other shit you've landed on me since I've met you," she goes on, breathless. "I didn't consider how fucked up this really is. This is *really* fucked up, Jesse, and you've got no redeeming reason. Wanting to keep me isn't good enough. That's not a decision you get to make on your own. What about me?" She gets up in my face, making me retreat. "What about what I want?"

"But I love you," I say quietly, pathetically. I never thought about what Ava wants. I only thought about what could save me. Her. A baby. A family.

A wife, happiness, forgiveness, mercy.

If anything, I saw all the signs that she *didn't* want kids. And I ignored them. I convinced myself she'd accept this because she loves me.

What have I done?

Ava rubs at her eyes, pushes her hair off her face, sniffs, and storms away.

"Ava?" I call, going after her, getting a flurry of flashbacks invading my mind. The last time I chased her through the penthouse. Or tried to. I could hardly walk, the vodka fucking me over. I can't go back to those places. *No.* "Ava, stay, please, I'll do anything." I race down the stairs, two at a time, forced to hold my limp dick against my thigh as I go. I look up as I reach the bottom, seeing her hand on the doorknob ready to open it. I pick up my pace, wondering what the fuck I'm going to do when I get to her. Force her back upstairs? Manhandle her? Yes, I've done it before, but this is different. There is absolutely no element of fun here, which has always seen me through those moments of conflict. This is serious. *More* than serious. She's leaving me.

I skid to a stop, just as Ava faces me, the door open. "You'll do anything?" she asks, her face painfully stoic.

"Yes." *Shut the door, please shut the door.* "You know that."

"Then you'll give me some space." She backs out, the door closes, and I stare at the wood, shocked into stillness.

And that's where I stay, a frozen form of a broken man, for an age. She's gone.

"Gone," I whisper, instantly numb. But in so much fucking pain. I push a hand through my hair, my eyes burning, remaining on the door. The sound of my phone ringing in the distance is what eventually pulls me from my inertness. I don't rush to answer it, letting it ring off. It won't be Ava. I drag my heavy gaze across the penthouse, listening to the screaming silence, seeing the empty space. "What now?" I ask myself. I look down at my naked body and rub roughly at my eyes.

Vodka.

"No," I grate, angry, the devil on my shoulder reminding me of what will fix this.

Not vodka, Daddy.

I gasp, staggering to a nearby wall and placing a palm onto the plaster to hold myself up, my head hanging. "Not vodka," I say, listening to the angel on my other shoulder. My baby girl. My *dead* baby girl. I sniff, my lip curling, turning and facing the wide-open space. "Never again, do you hear me?" I bellow, physically smacking at my shoulder, like I can squash that devil. "It will never happen again!" I swipe a hand out and knock a vase off the cabinet, sending it flying across the room. It bounces off the floor twice before finally succumbing to the impact and smashing to pieces. The sound kills the quiet, kills the noise in my head. I savor it, hope the shards hitting the floor echoing around me never stops.

Then it does.

Vodka.

I exhale, try to breathe long, deep, controlled breaths.

Ava.

Raking a hand through my hair, I pad around the glass, watching carefully as I place each foot down, going upstairs. I get my phone, seeing a missed call from John. I can't even find the will to try and sound okay. I'll call him back when I can.

Give me space.

I drop my arse to the end of the bed, my elbows to my knees, and dial her, not bothering to lift my mobile to my ear. The silence means I can hear it ringing perfectly well. Voicemail. I hang up, try again. Ringing. Voicemail. Again. The same. I swallow, opening up my messages. Ava's the last person I've texted.

I REALLY love you

I REALLY know

I feel my lip wobble as I type out a message, struggling to see the screen through my hazy vision.

Give me space.

I throw my phone aside on a gruff, frustrated bawl and get up, getting some shorts on and slipping my feet into some flip-flops, refusing to look at Ava's parts of the dressing room, then I grab my phone and head downstairs. I look at the mess before me. This is what I will do. Clean up my mess before I start with the mess that I've made of my life. I put on some music—*Chasing Cars*, because I need to be punished more—and rootle through the laundry room until I find a broom and a dustpan. I take my time, no longer holding back the tears. I feel empty. A shell. Just going through the motions.

I stamp on the bin and empty the dustpan for the last time, taking it back to the laundry room and shoving it on the shelf. Then I go to the fridge. Open it. Scan the shelves. Close the door. I put myself on a stool. Stare at my mobile. I drag it over and dial her again. No answer. So I open my messages and click send on the one I typed out earlier.

I can't be without you, Ava

Dragging myself to the couch, I drop to my arse and stare out of the glass at London. Holding my phone.

And that's where I stay until the gray sky disappears and blackness replaces it.

She doesn't call or reply.

My bones creak when I eventually stand. I head upstairs, slow, weary, pull on a sweatshirt, and head out, grabbing my keys from the concierge as I pass. Sam calls me as I'm pulling out the gates of Lusso. I could ignore it, but after shirking John's call, I'm at risk of raising alarm bells and one of them calling Ava.

"All right?" I answer, hearing myself. Low.

I'm not the only one. "Been better," Sam replies. "I think Kate and I and done."

Why aren't I surprised? I don't have any energy to spare right now, but I can promise I'll rip Dan a new arsehole if he's got anything to do with this. "What's happened?"

"Good fucking question," he says over an exhale, sounding beat. "Apparently it really was just a bit of fun to her."

"What?"

"And now she's had her fun, she's done."

I narrow an eye on the illuminated road ahead. That's bullshit. She caught feelings, so did Sam. What the fuck do I say? *Fucking Dan.*

"Has Ava said anything?" he asks before I've had a chance to figure out if I should talk and what I should say.

I breathe out. I like Kate. I do not like how she's handling this. And I am a fine one to talk. "I think she and Ava's brother were a thing once."

"You think?"

"I know." Silence. I cringe. "I didn't mention it before because you and Kate seemed okay."

He laughs. "No wonder the prick was hostile."

"Don't feel singled out. He's a dickhead with me too."

"I think something happened at your wedding between them."

"Have you asked Kate?"

"What's the point? We're over. Are you driving?"

"Just popping to the shop." Since when do I pop to the shop? "We're out of milk." What the fuck am I saying?

"So what do I do now?" he asks.

He's asking *me*? Jesus fucking Christ, I'm hardly an ambassador for doing the right thing. Besides, he just said they're done. *Clearly.* "Give her space," I say quietly, my grip of the steering wheel getting tighter. "Give her space and let her figure out what she needs to figure out." *And how long will Ava take to figure it out?*

"So just wait while she decides if she wants me or him?" He snorts his disgust.

Is that an advantage for me? There's no other man in the frame, no competition. But *every* man is competition. I don't think Kate wants Dan. Who would, he's a bellend. "If you have feelings, yes. Give her space. You can't force someone to be with you." I clench my eyes closed briefly, discreetly sniffing. Something I've proven. Again.

"I hear you," he says. "I'm sorry, you don't need my life dramas forced on you a day after your wedding. It was a great day. How's married life?"

I brace my arms against the wheel, forcing my back into the leather. "Great. Listen, I just pulled up at the store."

"Sure. What are your plans this week?"

Trying to convince my wife of one day not to divorce me. "This and that," I muse.

"When are you going on your honeymoon?"

"Ava's got some work stuff to sort out."

"Have you spoken to Drew?"

"No, he left the wedding without saying goodbye."

"I'll call him. Speak later." Sam hangs up, and I exhale, my cheeks ballooning, my sweat real. It's only a matter of time before everyone finds out Ava's left me. I smack the steering wheel hard, wincing on impact, seeing the aftermath of my encounter with the handcuffs glowing in the shadows.

Deserved. All the pain, deserved.

Ava, however, didn't ask for any of this.

And I'm so fucking sorry.

I drive aimlessly, reliving my regrets, the guilt and pain increasing, until I pull into Kate's street. I see Ava's Mini parked outside by Kate's van. It's a mild relief. I knew she'd be here. I drive past slowly, looking up at the windows, seeing the lights all on. She'll be in there telling Kate…everything.

I don't pull over or even think about calling or knocking on the door.

Give her space.

How much, and for how long?

Because I feel like I'm slowly dying.

Chapter 9

I went home, didn't sleep, ran at four, put a suit on at six, left Lusso at six thirty, got to Kate's twenty minutes later.

I park at the end of the road and wait, wondering if she'll go to work. Can she face it? Put on a brave face? Or will she tell everyone it's over? I check my watch repeatedly, every minute, in between watching the front of Kate's house. I nearly lose my breath when she appears, seeing her for the first time since she walked out on me. It's not even been twenty-four hours, but it feels like years already. I watch as she rummages in her bag as she walks down the path. Searching for her keys? How I'd love to get out, go to her, offer to take her to work. Fear of rejection is stopping me. *Space*. It doesn't matter that I'm mere meters away. She thinks I'm listening to her, respecting her wishes, and I have to give her that. It's hard when I can see how drained she looks. Stunning as always, but the underlying turmoil beneath her makeup is so clear to me. I'm surprised when she walks straight past her car. She's heading for the Tube station.

Getting out of my Aston, I follow her, taking a small comfort from having her close enough to see, even if I can't go to her. I keep a safe distance, holding back when I need to, boarding the next carriage on the Tube and watching her through the glass. She finds a seat and pulls her phone out, just staring at the screen. Thinking about calling me? Replying to my message?

She eventually puts it back in her bag and stands, staggering when the train jolts, starting to slow. My heart jumps into my throat as her arm shoots up and grabs the rail above her head, a man nearby reaching for her arm to steady her. It physically hurts.

Ava smiles her thanks, moving past him, and as soon as the tube stops at Green Park and the doors open, she steps off. I follow her with the sea of commuters, my eyes nailed to the back of her head. She reaches the top of the steps on Piccadilly and stops, so I pull back, waiting with bated breath for her to turn around and see me. Has she sensed I'm near?

But she doesn't turn around. She just stands there while people dodge her motionless form. Worried, I pick up my feet, but she gets moving before I make it to her, crossing the road outside The Ritz and walking up Berkley Street to the square. The closer she gets to her office, the unrest inside me worsens. It's going to be hours before I get to look at her again.

She turns onto Bruton Street. My pace increases. I've got to talk to her. I skirt around the masses of people, hurrying to the corner. I see her in the distance, close to the Rococo Union office. I won't make it to her before she gets there, and I know I can't turn up at her workplace. It'll raise too many questions neither of us want to answer. I'm of sound enough mind to realize that. I can't put her in that position, and it won't help my cause. So in desperation, I call out to her, stepping into the road to circle round a group of students. "Ava!"

Beep!

My yell gets drowned out by the horn, and I jump, startled as screeching tires blend into the sound. "Shit," I gasp, just as a black cab skids to a stop. I look down at the bumper touching my knees.

"What the fuck are you playing at, mate?" the cabbie yells out of the window, waving his fist. "Get out the fucking road!"

I blink, stepping back. "Sorry," I murmur, looking up to see the door of Rococo Union closing. Shaken, I rake a hand through my hair. I double-check for traffic before crossing, standing on the other side and watching as Ava settles at her desk.

Ready for work.

Ready to distract herself from me.

I breathe out my weariness, drop my eyes to my feet, stuff my hands in my pockets, and make my way back to the tube.

• • •

A new Jaguar is blocking the gates when I pull off the main road to The Manor, forcing me to a stop. "The fuck," I breathe, getting out. I pace to the driver's side and find the car empty. The door's locked. Who the hell abandons a car in front of gates that are obviously in use?

"Oh, morning."

Swinging around, I find a suited bloke appearing from the lane. "Morning," I say cautiously.

He smiles, motioning to the gates. "Nice place, eh?"

"Yeah," I reply, taking him in. He's got salesman written all over him. "Visiting?" I ask.

"I'm trying to get in touch with the owner."

"Why?"

"Because I want to buy it."

I'm jarred, my one step back cautious and slow. "It's not for sale."

He tosses his keys, nodding. "Everything's for sale. The owner, his name's Jesse Ward, right?"

"Right," I breathe.

"Do you know him?"

"Yeah, I know him."

"Great." His mobile appears. "Mind sharing his number?"

"Yes, I mind."

His eyes lift from the screen of his phone, his smile now milder. "Maybe I could leave you my card instead," he says. "To pass on." He dips into his trouser pocket and pulls out a gold embossed card. "I'd be very grateful."

I nod, eyes on him, as I accept, and he gets in his car and drives off.

OWEN CUTLER

That's it. Just a name. The Manor for sale? I huff and slip the card into the inside pocket of my jacket, returning to my Aston. What's the fucking point of having a business card if it only tells people your name? "Idiot," I mutter as I drive past the trees, pulling in around the fountain.

"I didn't expect to see you today, Mr. Ward," Pete says as I pass through the hallway. "Congratulations again."

I smile lamely and increase my pace before anyone can find me and thrust their well wishes on me. The summer room is back to normal, no signs that a wedding happening here this past weekend. I swallow, feeling at my chest as I push my way into my office. I find John at the desk. He looks up, a pile of paperwork in his hand. "What are you doing here?" he asks.

"Ava's at work. What do you expect me to do?" I close the door and wander over. "What are you doing?"

"Trying to find the contract for the CCTV system."

"Ask Sar—" I stop as John looks up at me tiredly. "Shit," I breathe. It's going to take some getting used to. "Why do you need it?"

"To check the warranty on the cameras. Two more went down."

"Great." I sit on the edge of my desk as John places the paperwork down. I can see the questions coming. "How's Sarah?" I ask.

"I took her car back and posted the keys."

"You didn't see her?"

"Spoke to her. She wasn't talking much sense. I think the hangover was kicking in."

I tilt my head. "What was she saying?"

"That she can't live without you." He eyes me, his face serious, and I shrink. "That she's lost, that death would be better than living without you and this place."

"She was still drunk." I'm awkward as I reach for my laptop and pull it closer, getting my email account up. Now there's a way to get my attention. I can't play that game.

"Probably. Now what's up with you?"

I laugh to myself. Aside from the guilt trip he's just sent me on? "Nothing."

"What's up?"

"Nothing's up, John," I say, tapping with too much force at my keyboard. I see an email from the dealership reminding me I need to pay for the car before they deliver it. Stupid me. I'll ask Sarah to—

Fuck.

"Tell me what's going on, motherfucker."

I slam my laptop shut and stand abruptly. "Nothing is fucking up, John," I yell, storming out. It takes everything in me not to put my fist in every wall I pass as I stalk through The Manor. *Everything.*

I go upstairs and walk into my suite. Look around. Back out again, heading past the stained-glass window into the new, unfinished wing. I stand on the threshold of the room I showed Ava on our first meeting. I see her standing in her lovely navy pencil dress looking like a deer in the headlights.

I was the headlights.

I see her on the floor sketching, looking like the wind had been taken out of her sails.

I stole that wind.

The last time she was here was just last week. A few days before our wedding. She stood in here and pinned her drawings to the wall, showed me the material she had in mind for the curtains, the soft furnishings, the lighting. We were making progress.

Now, like my marriage and my life, limbo.

I walk to the wall and pluck one of the drawings down, looking over it.

"Are you going to talk or am I going to beat it out of you?"

I glance over my shoulder and find John filling the doorway. "We've had words," I say, at a loss. I can't tell him what I've done. I can't tell him Ava's walked out on me.

He laughs under his breath, wandering in and joining me by the wall, looking over the drawing in my hand. "What about?"

"Something trivial." I put the picture back on the wall, pressing into the Blu-Tack. "You know Ava and me," I say robotically. "It's fiery. We'll be friends again later."

I see him nodding mildly in my peripheral vision, humming. "You said you thought she was pregnant."

I stare at the drawing. He spared me the interrogation on my wedding day. The time has come. "Still do."

"It's—"

"I don't want to talk about it, John." Don't want to face my reality. And yet here I am, staring it in the face.

Loss.

He releases a sigh only a body like John's is capable of releasing. "The end of month accounts need sending to the accountants."

I look at him. "Have Sa—" His eyebrows rise. "Fucking hell."

"I've tried to sort the files." A shake of his head confirms he's failed.

"I suppose I asked for it," I say, knowing this is Sarah's way of proving that I, indeed, cannot live without her. Or, at least, The Manor can't. "I'll take a look."

John nods and leaves, pulling out his phone. Checking on Sarah. I go to the window and look out across the green landscape. I can't stand this. The hollowness, the uncertainty. How much space, and for how long?

I try calling Ava again and get ignored. So I try Kate, desperate to get some reassurance. But Kate doesn't answer either and that only heightens my worries, because Kate has always had my back, even when I've put a foot out of line. Which means Ava's told her best friend what

I've done. I've lost an ally.

I'm alone.

The excruciating sense of helplessness feels horribly familiar. I feel like I'm on the verge of losing everything.

Which will leave me a shell of a man all over again.

• • •

I tried to sort the files. I lasted five minutes before I tossed them aside and gave up, unable to concentrate. I sat in silence for twenty minutes, my mind circling, before I headed up to our suite. But it's not always been ours. It was mine. The old me. Hence, the new bed for our wedding day. Biting my lip, I go back through to the extension and pull Ava's drawings off the wall, snapping a picture with my phone and heading back down to my office. Maybe I'm being optimistic, but what else can I be? I attach the drawings to an email and get them over to the decorators. It's something to do. Hope to cling on to. My wife doesn't want to see me, and I can't face telling my closest what's happened.

Fuck, I miss her. I growl, fisting a hand full of hair, tugging. "What the fuck am I meant to do?" I yell, frustrated, snatching up my keys and heading out. I'll beg, grovel, get on my knees. Whatever it takes. I'm going crazy, my mind circling, thinking of every scenario, best and worst. The worst is edging out in front. I feel sick.

Drew is getting out of his Merc when I emerge into the sunshine, slipping my shades on, more to hide my red-rimmed eyes than protect them from the sun. "What are you doing here?" I ask, looking at my watch.

He slams the door and passes me. "You were shut all weekend."

"And where did you disappear to on Saturday?" He was there one minute, gone the next. I don't get an answer, just a dismissive wave of his hand over his head. "No one's here yet," I call. What's he going to do? Play on his own? I hear the sound of an engine and look up. A red Jaguar swings into a space and Natasha steps out.

She looks me up and down. "I don't think marriage suits you, Jesse."

"Oh fuck off," I snap, getting in my car and speeding away.

Chapter 10

I drive down Bruton Street, seeing Ava sitting at her…what the fuck is that? It's definitely not her desk. A paste table?

I don't have time to figure it out before I'm past the office. I look up at my rearview mirror, noting traffic behind me. "Shit." Scanning for a space, I find nothing, resorting to parking in a car park off Arlington Street and walking back to her office.

The café I've used before when I've waited for her is just up the street—it's better than loitering outside her office—so I trudge up, pulling out a chair and sitting. I order a water and a sandwich that I won't eat, looking down at my watch. I've got quite a few hours before she finishes. Not that it matters. I have nowhere else to be. Nothing else to do. Only hope. Pray.

By late afternoon, I've had six waters, the sandwich I ordered is stale, and I'm in desperate need of a piss but dare not leave the table in case I miss Ava leaving. But I'm at risk of embarrassing myself if I don't get to the men's soon. I wave the waitress over who looks at my untouched sandwich as she has each time I've ordered another drink.

"Another water?" she asks.

"No, actually, I need the men's."

"I can't imagine why."

I give her a tired look.

"Through the back on the left." She motions to the sandwich. "Are you ever going to eat that."

"No."

"Is something wrong with it?"

"No."

Poor thing looks perplexed. I dip into my pocket for my wallet, pulling out two twenties. I hold them up. "That's too much, sir," she says, plucking one of the twenties from my fingers. "I'll get your change."

"No," I call as she walks off, stopping her. I flash the other twenty. "Spare me sixty seconds and you can have this one too."

She looks alarmed for a moment. "Sir, I'm flattered, and don't get me wrong, you're really hot and all, but how old are you? Like…forty?

Because I'm seventeen and that's all kinds of wrong."

I stare at her, dumfounded. She thinks I'm offering her money for… what? A date? Jesus, does she think I've been sitting here all day to admire her? "Whoa," I say, laughing nervously, my hand up. I point to my ring finger. "I'm married."

"That doesn't always matter."

"Well, it matters to me," I snap. "And I'm thirty-fucking-eight, okay?"

She recoils. "Okay."

I push the twenty into her hand. "I want you to watch that door over there and come and tell me if a dark-haired woman comes out before I'm back." Listen to me. What the hell do I sound like?

The young waitress looks at me alarmed, like I'm some kind of fucking stalker. *Nearly right, love. Nearly.* "It's my wife," I say, pointing to my ring again.

"Sure," she mumbles quietly, pocketing my cash.

No, I'm not having this. If she's taking my money, she's taking my word. "It's my wife," I repeat, my head tilted. "Her name's Ava. She's twenty-six. Sh—"

"Twenty-six?"

"Oh, forget it," I mutter, stalking off before I embarrass myself further and piss myself. She already thinks I'm a fucking dinosaur. Let's not make her believe I'm an incontinent one. "Sixty seconds," I call.

"After all the water you've drank?"

"Just watch the fucking door." I rush to the men's and make fast work of relieving myself, shuddering. Jesus, I've held it too long.

Bang, bang, bang.

I jump, looking back at the door that's vibrating on its hinges with the constant thumps. "Dude, she's come out."

Fuck!

I quickly put myself away, wash my hands with not nearly enough time and no soap, and hurry out, throwing a thanks over my shoulder as I jog down the street, seeing Ava turn onto Berkeley Square. "Fuck it."

I catch up with her, slowing when I'm just a few paces behind. I check my watch. It's too early for her to finish. A meeting? And with whom? Naturally, my mind goes to Van Der Haus. Surely she wouldn't.

I dial her. She doesn't even get her phone out. I see the Tube station nearing and try her again, willing her to give me a chance and talk to me. I don't want to confront her on the street, and I don't want her to know I've not respected her demand for space. Okay, so I've called her a few times, but given my usual response to situations in the past when she's walked away from me, I think I'm doing quite well. Is she going to ignore my calls forever? Will I never be given the chance to express my remorse and spill my apologies? The thought angers me. I accept it's unreasonable, but it's been twenty-four hours now since she walked out on me. She's not told me where she's staying, how she is, what happens next.

This is just typical of Ava. Ignore the problem. Walk away. When will she start dealing with things head-on? We haven't got time to waste on arguing. I, more than anyone, know life's too short.

Enough.

I jog past Ava and jump in front of her, and she startles, inhaling her shock. "What are you doing?" she snaps.

Could be me, but she doesn't look too pleased to see me. *Fuck.* Even at our worst she's always struggled to hide her desire, even when just looking at me. Not today. What the fuck? "You wouldn't answer your phone," I say, studying her curiously as she shifts on the spot, more uncomfortable than I've ever seen her. "Maybe you didn't hear it."

"You were following me?"

She's surprised? Does she know who she married? I scowl at myself. "Where are you going?" I ask, moving into her.

She moves away. "A client."

"I'll take you."

"I've told you," she says over a sigh, "I need space, Jesse."

"How much space and for how long?" *Touch her.* "I married you on Saturday and you left me on Sunday." My hand reaches for her of its own volition, sliding down her arm to her hand, holding it. And there it is. Shortness of breath, a shiver, a swallow. But I can't just depend on that, and I know she'll fight it with all she has to make her point. "I'm struggling, Ava," I whisper, watching my fingers entwine with hers, seeing our rings sparkle together. She's not taken it off. I look up to gage her expression, thankful to see she's not displaying the same, cold blankness she left me with last night. She doesn't like to see me struggle. I know she doesn't. She's gone to extreme lengths to make sure I know she can't stand the thought of me being hurt. Well, I'm hurting now, and she can fix it. "Without you, I'm really struggling."

Her eyes close, hiding from the broken man before her, and her body shakes, fighting the magnet drawing her closer. "I really need to go." She turns, and her hand slips out of mine.

"Baby, please," I call to her back. "I'll do anything. Please, don't leave me." She stops, and I feel my hope lift. "Let me at least drive you," I say. Baby steps. "I don't want you on the train." *Falling over, hurting yourself, having other men saving you.* "Just ten minutes, that's all I'm asking for."

Ava slowly turns to face me. "It'll be quicker on the tube."

"But I *want* to take you."

"We won't make it in time with the…" She frowns, and I hitch a brow. We absolutely will make it in time. No question. Her shoulders drop. "Where's your car?"

She's softening. *Thank you.* I push my chances a little more, tentatively reaching for her hand and lacing our fingers, waiting for her to retract, bracing myself for the disappointment. She watches as we come together. I definitely catch her subtly gulping. It feels so good to hold her hand.

I gently tug her, encouraging her on, watching her as we walk side by side to the car park. *Silence.* It's so fucking uncomfortable, but still better than being alone. I get my keys and finally but reluctantly let go of her hand when we get to the car, opening the door for her. I bend, ready to put her seatbelt on, but withdraw, remembering myself. Too much? *I don't know.*

"Where am I going?" I put on some music, anticipating the further stretch of silence ahead of us, filling it while I figure out what to say and how to say it.

"Luxemburg Gardens, Hammersmith," she replies quietly, not looking at me.

"Okay."

I can smell regret on her. Sense her hopelessness. It's…I can't put my finger on it. Odd. There's no anger, and I know she should be angry at me. She's so withdrawn. Sad.

Done?

I swallow, returning my attention to the road when the traffic starts moving again. I know I've fucked up, I know she has every right to be like this with me, but I have a funny feeling in my gut, and I'm terrified it's because this really is the end.

No.

I can't accept that.

Constantly splitting my attention between the road and Ava, I will her to speak up, while I continue to search for the right words and the miles tick down. I'm pulling into Luxemburg Gardens far sooner than I'd hoped. "Here will do," she says, unclipping her belt before the car's stopped. "Thank you."

"You're welcome." My mind remains blank as I watch her get out of the car, and panic inevitably sets in. *Fuck, fuck, fuck.* "Will you have dinner with me tonight?" I blurt quickly, seeing her freeze on the curb, the door half closed.

"You just asked for ten minutes," she says calmly. "And I gave them to you. You said nothing." The door closes, and I stare at the steering wheel, even blanker, my forehead bunched. *Ouch.* Maybe I didn't speak in the car, but I told her how badly I'm struggling. If that's not a plea for her mercy, then I don't know what is.

And said with such spite.

Fuck.

I look up at the rearview mirror, my heart lifting when I see she's stopped walking away from the car. I hold my breath, wondering if she's realized how harsh that was. Hoping she regrets it and is coming back to let me talk. But she doesn't come back. She goes into her bag, rummaging for ages instead. As a man who is familiar with his wife's handbags, I can attest they're packed full of various shit, so if she's looking for something, it's no wonder she's struggling to find it.

If she's looking for something.

I squint, slipping my car into *Drive*. I quickly check the road in front and pull away, my eyes back on the mirror. She's stopped searching through her bag. Then she looks over her shoulder. Making sure I'm leaving?

What the fuck is going on?

I slow down, checking the road again before going back to the mirror. She's walking past all the houses. Why wouldn't she have me stop directly outside her client's house?

That feeling in my gut has just worsened.

I pull into the next available space at the end of the road and hop out of my Aston, jogging down the street on the other side, slowing when I see her in the distance. She takes a left, then a right, and before I know it, we're outside a newbuild. Definitely not a residential property. Ava pushes her way through the glass doors, just as I spot the sign. Medical Center? My mouth hangs open as realization slams into me. "Her period didn't come," I breathe.

And she's doing this without me?

What the fuck is she trying to do? I should be beside her, holding her hand, sharing every minute of this. Is this her way of punishing me?

Pissed off, I yank the door open and walk through the corridor to the large reception area, finding Ava's sitting on a row of chairs in the middle of the room, flipping through a magazine. Her knee's jumping. She's nervous. I go to the chair next to her and lower, talking myself down from kicking off. This isn't fair. To push me out, it's not fair.

She doesn't look up from the magazine she's reading. Doesn't notice I'm here. I'm not sure what that means. Immune to me now? *Or something massive is on her mind.*

Every time the little buzzer thingy sounds behind the counter, I wait for Ava's name to be announced. What am I going to do? Muscle my way into the room when she's called? Yes. She'd fucking notice me then.

I turn my head when I hear what I'm sure is a small chuckle.

She's laughing?

"Something funny?" I grate, incensed.

She slams the magazine shut, stills for a moment, as if wondering whether she heard right, before she swings her eyes my way, shocked. She should try being in my shoes right now. "You followed me?"

Yes, I fucking followed you, because I know you, and I knew something wasn't right. "You're a rubbish liar, baby. Are you going to tell me why you're at the doctor's and why you lied to me about it?" I cock my head, covering her knee with my palm. I can't see it jumping now, but I can certainly feel it.

"Just a checkup." She rids her hands of the magazine and tries to rid her knee of my hold. I don't let her.

"A checkup?" Does she think I was born yesterday?

"Yes," she says through her teeth.

For fuck's sake. If anything needs *checking*, it's her head.

And mine. "Don't you think we should we doing this together?"

She looks at me, stunned, and fights against my hold of her knee again. I let her win this time, but only because I think I might need my hand to block her swing at me. "Like the decision you made to try and get me knocked up?" she asks. "Did we do *that* together?"

Knocked up? She's my wife. My wife will not be *knocked up*, she will be…I don't know. Something I haven't got the capacity to think of right now, something more romantic. "No." I bite at my lip, holding back from yelling at her for pushing me out and…I withdraw, my thoughts stalling. Did she say *try*? *Try* to get her knocked up? So her period came? Then why is she here? I stare at my knees, my head spinning. Is she? Isn't she? She's been so emotional. Throwing up, for Christ's sake. She has to be.

"You can't even look at me, can you?" she snaps, the anger that was missing earlier now here with a vengeance. I *would* look at her if I was sure she wouldn't kill me with her glare. "You know what you've done is wrong." *Yes, I know. But worse fucking things have happened, trust me.* "I pray to God I'm not pregnant, Jesse, because I wouldn't inflict the shit you put me through on my worst enemy, let alone my baby."

I jolt like I've been stabbed. And, again, trust me, I fucking know what that feels like. Her nostrils are flaring, her cheeks pulsing from the force of her bite, emotions getting the better of her. Of both of us. "I know you're pregnant," I say, as calmly as I can. "And I know how it'll be."

"Oh?" She's laughing again. "How's that, then?"

"Perfect," I say quietly, reaching for her cheek, finding her eyes and making sure she sees the sincerity in mine. I don't want to fight, and I know she doesn't really want to either. She's lashing out. Being hurtful. This isn't Ava. *This is what I've made her.*

I wince those thoughts away as her body softens and she stares into my eyes, searching for reassurance. I'll give it to her, all day long.

"Ava O'Shea," the receptionist calls, snapping us out of our moment. *O'Shea?*

Ava shoots up, and I follow. "Don't you dare," she snaps. "Sit." I have never heard such anger in her tone, and I take notice, slowly lowering my arse back to the plastic obediently. She walks off, and I glance around the waiting room, seeing a few people looking this way, eyebrows high. Yes. I'm in the doghouse. Yes, my tail's between my legs.

I grimace and stand, going to the reception desk and placing both palms on the wood. "It's Ward," I say.

"Pardon?"

"It's Ava Ward, not Ava O'Shea."

"Oh?" She taps a few keys on the computer. I don't know why the fuck I'm standing here like a pillock telling the receptionist this. I realize Ava won't have registered her married name yet. I'm just killing time, doing a bit of housekeeping, in an attempt to stop myself from storming into the doctor's office.

"We got married on Saturday."

"Oh, well if you tell Ava to email us, we can get that changed for her."

"Can't you do it now?"

"We need it in writing, sir. From Miss O'Shea."

I huff and go back to the chair, checking my watch. Five minutes. I slump forward, staring down at my shoes.

Ten minutes pass.

Fifteen minutes.

How long do these things take? Ava tells the doctor she's probably expecting, the doctor checks, and that's it.

Right?

I crane my head to look down the corridor, drumming my fingers on my knees. I hear a door open. Freeze. Ava appears, and she looks awful. Fucking *awful*. I'm up like a rocket, racing to her. "Ava, what's the matter?" She props herself against the wall, and I dip, seeing her face is damp. "Jesus, Ava."

She stares at me, her eyes watery, her breathing a little fast. What is this? A panic attack?

I don't have a chance to ask. She's off, running across the hallway and falling through the doors of the ladies'. I'm in quick pursuit, there in a heartbeat, rubbing her back and scooping her hair back as she throws her guts up. *Again.*

She tries to talk but each time she's stopped by another retch. "Shhhh," I hush, looking back when the door opens. A middle-aged, blond lady takes in the scene, definitely frowning at me.

"Oh dear, should I get you some water?"

"Please," I say, shuffling in closer to Ava, moving her hair to my other hand and pulling off some tissue. "Are you done?"

"I don't know." She sounds far from done, like she's choking.

"It's okay, we can stay." I get as comfortable as a six-foot-three-inch bloke can get in a toilet cubicle crouching. Really *un*comfortable. "Are you okay?"

"I'm fine."

I roll my eyes. Of course she is.

The door opens behind me again, the lady appearing with some water. A doctor? I tilt my head in question, silently asking her what's wrong with my wife. Of course, she doesn't entertain me. "Can I get you anything?" she asks.

"It's good, thank you. I've got her."

She nods, that frown back, and leaves the ladies'.

"Here," I say, putting the water in front of Ava, helping her take some. "Take as long as you need." As long as she needs is a few sips and about thirty seconds. It's not long enough.

"I'm good." She takes some tissue from my hand and sniffs as I rise.

"Here." She lets me help her up and also lets me fix her hair. I'm grateful. "Do you want some more water?"

She nods, accepting the glass and going to the sink, getting some fresh water and rinsing her mouth and generally doing what I just did—fixing her hair. It feels like a ploy to waste some time, and I know it is when her hands pause and she looks at me.

"Let me take you home," I beg.

"Jesse, I'm fine," she breathes. "Really."

She's maddening. She's not fine, and I think I might blow my stack if she says it one more time. "Let me look after you," I whisper, feeling at her cheek, watching her in the reflection trying her damnedest not to sink into my touch. She's made her point. I get it. We need to move on.

"I'm okay." She breaks away from me and picks up her bag.

"You're not okay, Ava," I grate, feeling my patience disappearing.

"Something hasn't agreed with me, that's all."

I stare at her, absolutely staggered. Is she for real? "For fuck's sake, lady," I breathe. "You're at the fucking doctor's surgery, so don't tell me you're fine." I'm at a fucking loss. I have to turn away from her, my temper threatening, my hair getting a punishing yank. I should be yanking Ava's head out of the fucking hole she's got it buried in.

"I'm not pregnant," she says, sounding...upset?

"What?" I ask, facing her.

"I've had it confirmed, Jesse."

What is the pain in my chest? "Then why are you throwing up all over the place?"

"I have a sickness bug. You failed. My period came."

My eyes naturally drop to the skirt of her dress. I don't understand. She's not pregnant? "I'm not happy about this." A bug? Where has she caught a bug? And what the fuck is it? Is it dangerous? Because this sickness thing is violent. "I'm taking you home where I can keep an eye on you." And maybe get a second opinion. Does she need meds? A jab? I grab her hand, and she immediately yanks it back, her face a picture of disgust.

"You're never happy with me," she says, struggling to get her words out, her face still damp, her skin still pale. "I'm always doing something to upset you. Have you thought that perhaps you would be *less* not happy without me around?"

What the fuck? "No." What is she saying? I'd be dead if it wasn't for Ava. *Literally.* "I'm worried, that's all."

"Well, don't be," she snaps. "I'm fine." She turns and walks out, leaving me, not for the first time today, stunned into silence and stillness. Doesn't she want me to look after her?

That makes me redundant. Not required.

Ouch.

But is she serious? Does she really believe I'm never happy *with* her? All I want is her. She's my world. That's why I married her. That's why I do every crazy thing. *Less* not happy without her around? I can't believe she would say that. Whether rashly or not, in spite or not.

Ouch, ouch, ouch.

I eventually convince my legs to work and go after her, following her out of the building to the attached pharmacy, but I don't go inside, leaving Ava to herself for a moment, hoping, maybe, she'll take stock and come out feeling a bit more reasonable. So she's got some medication for this bug?

Not pregnant?

Fuck me, I really am broken. She might be dead set against having kids now, but she might change her mind in the future. And I'll be useless to her.

Not that any of this matters. She hates me right now.

I laugh under my breath and start pacing, feeling a stressed sweat developing. This is too much. Maybe it's me who needs to see a doctor. Broken? Pickled. "Shit," I breathe, turning on my Grensons and marching back, peeking inside as I pass the window. She's sitting, waiting, her knee bouncing again. Still nervous. Up and down I go, having a heated discussion with myself, analyzing the situation, Ava's persona, our marriage, my mental state. My conclusions aren't reassuring.

I hear the door open, and she appears. Eyes me. "What's that?" I ask, motioning to the paper bag in her hand.

She comes up close. Definitely not for a kiss. "Backup pills," she says reproachfully. "Now we know I'm *not* pregnant; I want to stay that way."

The sting is real. She doesn't need pills, because I've clearly done myself some irreparable damage with years of drinking and mistreating myself. Another reason not to want me. *Fuck.*

She pivots and walks away, and the hollowness intensifies, my heart thumping with panic while slowing at the same time. "You're not coming home, are you?" I call, my words as broken as I feel.

She doesn't answer.

It's a no.

Does that really mean she's completely done with me?

Chapter 11

I don't remember my walk from the chemist to my car. I don't remember the drive from Hammersmith to Lusso. I vaguely recall texting Kate to ask if Ava's there, just to make sure. I got a thumbs up. Nothing more. I can't blame her for giving me the cold shoulder and, really, she didn't even owe me that thumbs up.

I watch my feet as I stride through the foyer to the elevator, hearing the new kid greet me. I think I hear him ask me where my wife is. I don't answer. I get in and stare at the reflection in the mirror, but not the reflection of myself. I stare at the empty space next to me. Where she usually is. Beside me.

The doors open, I find my key, and let myself in. Cathy's getting her coat on when I enter, her face a picture of happiness.

And then...not.

"Boy?" she says, a million questions in her voice as I close the door and wander past, going straight to the stairs.

"See you tomorrow, Cathy," I murmur to thin air in front of me.

"I made a lasagna," she calls.

"Thank you." My body feels so heavy. So slow. *Shutting down.*

"Where's Ava, boy?"

I don't answer. Can't. Entering the bedroom, I slowly cast my eyes around the vast space as I kick my shoes off. *Empty.* I leave my clothes on and collapse on the bed, grabbing her pillow and snuggling into it. *Lonely.*

I probably shouldn't be alone, but the thought of facing anyone? Besides, loneliness isn't measured by how busy your life is with people. It's measured by love. I never quite understood how someone can be surrounded by others but feel so incredibly lonely. Their head full of noise, but their life still so empty. And solitude is only heightened when you've experienced something that's enriched your life. Something that makes you smile. Gives you purpose and feel your heart beat strongly.

But it can be taken away.

Gone.

And it doesn't matter what people say, what they do, what you do yourself to conquer it, there's only one thing that will.

Peace.

Contentment.

Ava is those things for me, and she knows it.

And yet, she left me after less than one day of marriage.

I know I look terrible—my skin sallow, my eyes dull, my body heavy. I don't need John to tell me. I'm empty.

Three funerals in two weeks. Carmichael first—a massive affair, the church packed—but I was the only member of his family there. The rest of the congregation? Friends, lovers, members. All of them admired him. Respected him. It wasn't a funeral. It was a celebration of life. My parents couldn't even bring themselves to be there for me.

Rebecca's was next.

Now Rosie. My girl's funeral isn't a celebration of life because she barely had a life.

As I stand at the front of the church staring at my daughter's little coffin, all I can hear past the sobbing and the priest talking is my own voice constantly asking...why?

Why, why, why, why, why?

I feel Sarah's hand rest on my bicep and swallow, subtly shrugging it off. "Don't," *I say flatly, knowing Lauren is nearby. Knowing she'll be focused on me, not on the coffin that has our dead little girl inside.*

"Just trying to be here for you," *Sarah says quietly.*

I don't counter, there's little point. The priest's stopped talking, and it takes me a moment to realize there's someone else up in front of the congregation now. Our eyes meet as she pulls out a piece of paper. Hers turning onto Sarah beside me. Crazy eyes. Sarah shouldn't have come. I told her not to come. She's a red flag.

I look down at my feet and close my eyes. "My husband and I would like to thank you for coming," *Lauren says. Her husband. It takes me a moment to remember that was me. The divorce completed months ago.*

Sarah breathes out her disbelief.

"We feel so blessed for the time we had with our little girl," *Lauren goes on.* "She will never be replaced, but one day the pain of losing her will be soothed by another child."

I jolt.

"Oh my God," *Sarah whispers.*

Lauren's eyes fall onto me. "I know her father feels the same, and I know this loss will only bring us closer together."

I hear John clear his throat, and I notice Lauren's parents out of the corner of my eye. Alan looks at me, refusing to show his concern. I shake my head mildly, making sure he knows she's not speaking for me.

"You need to be careful," John says quietly as Lauren rambles on, telling the few people here how we've got through these first few difficult weeks because of each other. I've hugged her, of course, I'm not a fucking monster, but she must have felt my reluctance. She must have noticed the lack of warmth.

John's right. I need to be careful.

"I love my husband," Lauren goes on, putting emphasis on that one word. Husband. I'm barely a man. We're twenty-one years old. Lauren's talking like we've been happily married for years—close, tight, madly in love. A family. "Only he can ease my pain." She looks at me, her eyes burning my skin.

I can't listen to this. See this. I step out of the row and go to Rosie's coffin, placing both palms on the glossy wood, staring at the plaque.

ROSIE AMALIE WARD

1993 – 1996

My heart turns in my chest, my throat clogs. Lauren's stopped talking, stopped trying to convince the world that we're solid, in love... together. At least, she's stopped talking. She'll never stop trying to convince everyone. Scary thing is, I think she's convinced herself. I swallow as I dip, pushing my lips to the wood. "Goodnight, my baby girl," I whisper, pushing off and walking out of the church, roughly wiping at my eyes. I see my parents in the back row.

I don't stop.

Despite hearing my mum calling me.

I'm done with this life.

The hurt, pain, regret, guilt.

Done.

Ring, ring, ring.

I blink my eyes open and stare at the ceiling for a few moments, trying to come round. Trying to push the dreams away. "Fucking hell," I whisper, swiping a palm down my rough cheek as I lift my arse off the bed. I reach into my pocket and pull out my phone, grimacing at the dozens of missed calls. John, Sam, Drew. Four voicemails. I listen to John asking where the hell I am. I listen to Sam ask me why the fuck Ava's at Kate's. I listen to Drew demand I call him.

And then my sister's voice comes down the line, catching me off guard. "Hey," she says tentatively, as every muscle I possess hardens. "I hope you listen to this." My mind demands I cut the message off. I don't. "We're leaving for Seville at the end of the week," she goes on. "I'd so love it if you would come. Dad's not been great lately, and I worry you'll regret it if you don't make amends. They're getting old, Jesse. Just…think about it. I love you."

I push myself up and sit on the edge of the bed, staring down at my phone, my thumbs moving instinctively.

I love you too. I'm sorry I can't be there, but send me pictures, okay?

I drop my mobile on the sheets without clicking send, burying my head in my hands. I can't go to a place where people are waiting to remind me of all my wrongs. I'm too busy trying to fix the fuck-ups in my present. Amalie is stuck in the middle. She didn't ask for any of this. She's lost two brothers, and through my own misery and self-loathing, I somehow missed that along the way. So, for the first time in years, I show Amalie the love she absolutely deserves.

I snatch my phone up and click send while holding my breath, exhaling as I rise, feeling hot. I shrug out of my shirt and head downstairs, hovering over Ava's name, ready to dial her. But I refrain, typing out a message.

Good night. I miss you.

But I don't send it. I said I'll do anything. So space it is.

I sigh, rounding the corner into the kitchen.

And walk right into something. I jump back on a crash of my heart. "Fuck!"

John pulls his shades down his nose and looks over them at me, his eyes traveling up and down my half-naked body. "Evening."

"What are you doing here?" I snap defensively.

"Cathy was worried."

"I'm fine."

"Where's Ava?"

"In bed."

"Liar," Sam says, appearing behind him. "I just drove past Kate's and saw her letting herself in. What's going on?"

"And I thought I was the stalker around here," I grumble, pushing past them. "Driving past Kate's?"

Sam tosses me a dark look as I flick the coffee machine on, then off again when I register the time. "What the hell are you doing here?"

"There you are," Drew says, stopping at the door and taking in the kitchen. "Where's Ava?"

"Oh, for fuck's sake." I look to the heavens for help, knowing I'm asking in vain. They're all here, they know Ava's not—thanks, Sam—and I know I've got some explaining to do. "She left me, okay?" I throw the words out and watch as each and every one of them step back, alarmed. "She walked out on me, and I don't know if I can convince her to come back." I go to the fridge and yank it open, snatching a jar of Sun-Pat off the shelf. I turn and try to unscrew the lid, gritting my teeth, straining to move it. "And where the fuck did you disappear to on Saturday?" I bark at Drew.

"Home."

"Sorry, wasn't my wedding day exciting enough for you?" I strain harder, feeling the veins in my temple bulging. *Give me my peanut butter!*

Drew rolls his eyes, coming at me. "Shut up bitching." He takes the jar and pops it open with ease, handing it over on a sarcastic smile.

I snarl and swipe it back, tossing the lid on the counter and ramming a finger in. "Now you all know I'm alive, you can fuck off." I shove my finger in my mouth, thinking John looks like he wants to take this jar and put it somewhere painful. Sideways.

"Sit down," he grunts, taking off his shades.

"Oh, you're in for it now." Drew takes a front-row seat and joins his hands on the marble. "I've sacrificed a night of pleasure and pain for this, big man, so make it messy."

"It's a big enough mess without anyone else's help," I say, dropping to a stool and casting my vice aside. It didn't even take the edge off my anxiety. Can't stomach Cathy's lasagna. "I've fucked up." I drop my head in my hands.

"Has she found out?" Sam asks. "About Jake. About—"

"No." I can't believe I'm sharing this. "I did something stupid." I give the room my face so they can see my remorse.

"What?" John asks, taking a seat, along with Sam. "What the hell have you done now?"

"I took Ava's pills." I say it quickly before I can bottle it and watch as every man at the table slowly leans back on their stools. Silence. It's fucking awful.

"You tried to get her pregnant?" Drew asks, while John and Sam stare at me, obviously wondering if when I say *pills*, I mean what they think I mean.

"I thought it would cement our relationship," I mumble pathetically. "Stop her worrying about my devotion when she saw how happy I'd be."

Sam coughs, Drew shakes his head, and John just carries on with his staring. His silence is the worst.

"I just wanted Ava to—"

"Have no say in the matter?" Sam asks. "Fuck me, Jesse, are you hearing yourself?"

"Yeah, Jesse, I've got to say, this is leaping the line." Drew blows out his cheeks. He's not a man easily shocked, so I'm achieving something. "What the hell were you thinking?"

"That's the point," I grate. "I clearly wasn't really fucking thinking, was I? All I know is she made me feel incredible and I desperately needed to keep that going."

"You don't feel so incredible now, do you?" Drew asks, laughing, but it's a laugh of disbelief. "Fucking hell."

"So she found out?" Sam asks. "How?"

"Because she's not stupid, unlike me." I look at John again. He's still staring, still quiet. "Will you please talk?"

He stands, pulling in his suit jacket, and then he walks right out of my kitchen without a word, all three of us watching him go.

"John," I call, getting up and going after him. "John, wait."

I'll take a punch, a mouthful, anything, but his silence is unbearable. I make it to the door as he's walking out of it. "John, come on."

He turns, and I back up, seeing the threat in his eyes, but the man can move fast when he wants to, and he wants to now. I'm naked from the waist up, so he has nothing to grab and use to thrust me up against the wall, so he resorts to a good old, very effective, shove in my chest, sending me crashing back against the plaster. The back of my head bounces off it, making me grit my teeth and ride the pain. *I can't go back at him*. He's up in my face, savage, and I'm seriously regretting wishing for something more than his unbearable silence. His nostrils flare, his eyes wide and crazy. "You took away a woman's right to be safe. To choose." He's physically shaking, and I know it's to hold back the punch that I thoroughly deserve. "It's fucking despicable. I'm done with you, you motherfucking bastard." Turning, he leaves, slamming the door.

And I stare at the wood, frozen, my heart cracking some more.

Shocked.

Done with me? What, for today? Or forever?

"He'll calm down," Drew says quietly, coming to me, doing something very unlike Drew, placing a hand on my shoulder and massaging. "This crazy has got to stop, Jesse."

"I know." I peel my back from the wall and go to the couch. "It already stopped. I know I was fucking stupid and selfish." I look at my two mates and smile mildly. "You don't have to hang around. I'm not going to make a grab for the vodka."

Sam laughs, going to the TV cabinet and collecting the remote control before dropping to the other end of the couch. "I've got nowhere to be." He clicks the button to reveal the TV and turns it on.

"Me neither." Drew takes his suit jacket off and drapes it neatly over the back of the couch before he puts himself in the middle of us.

"I thought you'd be heading to The Manor."

"Changed my mind. Wanna watch a film?"

"Notting Hill?" Sam asks, flicking through the channels.

"No." Drew grimaces. "Something less lovey-dovey. I don't want you two girls crying on me."

"Fatal Attraction?" Sam offers.

Drew snorts, and as inappropriate as it is, I find myself laughing lightly. In all the years I've known these two, we have *never* sat down and just watched a movie together. This is…weird. But I'll take it. *Better than wallowing and torturing myself alone*. "Go on," I say. "It might make me feel better about myself."

Sam chuckles and puts the movie on, and we settle in, but my mind doesn't stray far from Ava and how I can fix things, as well as how I can fix things with John.

If I can.

Chapter 12

The boys were gone by midnight. I went to bed, tried to sleep, gave up at four, pulled on my shorts, and ran to Kate's. I took a breather outside. Ran back to Lusso.

I showered, dressed, and left before Cathy arrived. The new concierge lifted his head as I passed but didn't speak.

I drove to Kate's, parked, and waited for Ava. She left at just gone eight, today in her car. She looked drained. I made sure I stayed well back as I followed her to her office. She parked at the NCP off Berkeley Square, and I parked in the next street, then waited for her to emerge before following her to Rococo Union. Then I took myself to the café and sat outside, settling in for the day. My new waitress friend faltered when she spotted me before handing me a menu and bringing me a water. I ordered a sandwich at ten and tried a bite. It wasn't unpleasant, but my stomach refused to accept it. Is Ava eating? Looking after herself? At eleven, the decorators called me to let me know they'd started and proceeded to fire a load of questions about the designs. I told them to follow the drawings. Down to every tiny detail, just follow the drawings. At eleven-thirty, I'm reminded I *still* haven't paid for Ava's wedding present when the dealership emails me again. And at noon, Rolex calls to tell me her other wedding gift is ready.

Every time the doors to Ava's office opens, I sit up straight. Every single one of her colleagues leave and return during the morning. Then at three, she walks out. I jump up and throw a twenty on the table, following.

She goes into the car park, so I rush to collect my car and wait for her to pull out. She drives to an address in Lansdowne Crescent and goes inside a house. A client? I park down the street, my eyes lasers on the front door, and after two hours, she's driving back to Kate's, looking exhausted. And she hasn't contacted me once.

Wednesday is much the same as Tuesday, except Ava looks even more tired when she emerges from Kate's. Had I not been so stupid, I could have saved her from all this. How can she think I'm better off without her? This is excruciating. Seeing her…but remaining so far away. I stopped off at Rolex after following her back to Kate's. Forced a smile when the staff made a big, elaborate affair of handing over Ava's new watch. I paid on my credit card and left, unable to even force a smile.

Ava doesn't leave the office on Thursday, so my day is even more boring, exhausting, and uneventful. I now know my waitress's name—Bianca—and she hasn't called the cops on me yet, so that's a win. I also had two bites of my sandwich today. The decorators I hired for The Manor are nearly complete, which is the only surprise of my day. They're extremely quick, perhaps because of the exorbitant amount I'm paying them.

Dan, the sleazy fucker, was leaving Kate's when I followed Ava home. I know Sam hasn't heard from her because he's been at The Manor—trying to move on, as he put it. And yet he's not ventured into the rooms and he's been driving by Kate's. Has he seen Dan there? I don't know what Kate's thinking.

Today I brave going to The Manor to face John, but before I do, and perhaps to build up my courage, I head upstairs to the extension to check our new suite. I forget how to breathe for a few seconds when I enter. Incredible. It's everything she created. *Finally*. Down to every detail, they've nailed it. And my heart becomes even more heavy.

"Alright, mate," the electrician says, his cockney accent thick, a screwdriver held in his mouth as he fiddles with a light switch. "Some place this, eh?" He nods to the St. Andrews cross, grinning. "Someone's gonna 'ave some fun, eh?"

"Yeah," I back out, wondering as I head downstairs if Ava will ever see it. I can't consider that. It hurts too much. *Hope*. I have to hope.

John looks up from my desk when I enter. Then down again. I put myself in the chair opposite him, fiddling with nothing on my knee. It's clear he's not going to break the ice. I've never gone so long without speaking to him. "How are you?" I ask.

"Fine," he grunts. "How are you?"

"Fine."

Silence falls again, and I chew my lip, waiting for divine inspiration.

"I'm giving her space like she asked for," I go on. What am I hoping for? Praise? Affirmation?

"I know how hard that must be for you."

Does he? I'm not sure anyone knows how much pain I'm in right now. How lost I feel. More silence. John's glasses are going to melt off his face soon. "Ask me," I say, seeing the questions swirling.

"You said you thought she was pregnant."

"I did."

"And she's not?"

I shake my head. "She went to the doctor's on Monday."

"And you know that because…?"

"I followed her there."

"Space?"

I shrug. "No one's perfect."

"Fucking hell," John breathes, rubbing his forehead. "I don't know what to do with you anymore." But he's not done? "And she found out you've been stealing her pills?"

I nod, the shame ever present. "I truly regret it."

"Why? Because you failed to get her pregnant?"

"No, because I didn't consider Ava in any of my backward thinking, only myself. What I needed. What would settle me. I'm a selfish fuck, and I deserve everything coming to me."

John sighs, not saying whether he agrees or not. "The dealership's been emailing you." He motions to the laptop with a limp finger. "You bought a new car?"

"A wedding present for Ava." I pull over my laptop. "I need to transfer some money to them." I go to my bank's website and frown at the screen. "Any idea how to do this?" I ask, clicking through various options.

"No. Sarah dealt with the online banking."

I sigh. Of course she did. It's become glaringly obvious that Sarah did most things around here, and John and I are up Shit's Creek. "I'll call my personal bank manager," I say, scrolling through my mobile for Juliette's number and dialing. She doesn't answer. Why would she? She hates me. "God damn it." I hang up and check the email from the dealership for a number, calling them instead. "Hi, Jesse Ward. Cameron please." I'm placed on hold and use the time to try and figure out the online banking. "Fuck it," I curse, at a loss.

"Mr. Ward, good to hear from you."

Yeah, I bet. He must have been wondering if I've bailed on the purchase. "Cameron, hi. I'm sorting the transfer today. When can you deliver?"

"If the money lands today, we can get it to you by close of play."

"Thanks. I'll be in touch." I toss my phone down and get up close and personal with the screen, clicking a *login* button. It asks me for a customer number, password, the first, second, and tenth digits of my security code, *and* to have my card reader ready. "My God," I murmur, swiping up my phone and calling Juliette Cook again. No answer *again*. "Bollocks."

I persist, calling her on repeat until she finally answers on a tired, "Hello, Mr. Ward."

"Juliette, how lovely to hear your voice." I only know John's rolled his eyes because of the few creases that appear on his usually smooth forehead. "I need to transfer a payment to the Range Rover dealership."

"BACS or CHAPS."

"Pardon me?"

"How soon does the money need to be there?"

"Today."

"You need CHAPS."

"Great. I'll take CHAPS."

She laughs. "No, Mr. Ward, you have to log on to your accounts and create a CHAPS payment."

"I'm looking at the screen now."

"Okay," she says slowly, hesitantly. "Type in your customer number."

"What's my customer number?"

"You don't know your customer number?"

"No." I pull my phone down a bit, looking at John. "Do you know my customer number?"

"For fuck's sake," John breathes. "No. Sarah knows your customer number."

Sarah knows everything. I expect the security digits, the password, and card details are also all logged in her brain. *God damn it.* "Juliette," I say, nice as pie. "I'd be grateful if you could walk me through this."

"Mr. Ward, I'm afraid you need your banking credentials to create a CHAPS payment."

My jaw rolls. "You're being difficult."

"I'm not." She laughs. "I can't make payments for you."

"Look, I'm sorry Steve joined my manor. I'm sorry he—"

"We're trying again."

I freeze. "What?"

"He asked to see me a few weeks ago, and I agreed. He's no longer a member and we're trying to make our marriage work."

"That's great." I'm stumped. Is that why he didn't answer my call? "Would you do me a favor?"

"Mr. Ward, I can't make a pay—"

"No, no, something else. Will you get Steve to give me a call? Not about anything sex related," I quickly explain, feeling John's exasperated look on me. "It's about work. His work. I need his help."

"I'll let him know."

"And the payment?"

"You need your banking details."

I growl under my breath. "Fine." I hang up, smashing the lid of my laptop down. "Awkward, bitter cow."

John laughs. This isn't funny. I'm a multi-millionaire, and I can't access any of my money, only my credit card and current account, and I'm quite sure I can't pay for a car on a card. "How's Sarah?" I ask, not liking it when John's writing hand pauses.

He puts the pen down and levels me with a serious look. "She's in the hospital."

I sit back in my chair, an odd ripple of dread moving through me. "What?"

"She tried to kill herself."

Air catches at the back of my throat as I stare at John. His face is impassive, like he just told me something inconsequential. "She what?" She threatened it, but...

"I checked up on her Monday night. She didn't answer. I had to break in. I found her on the kitchen floor, wrists slashed, dozens of empty pill pots around her." He goes back to the pad he's writing on. "I didn't tell you because you've got enough on your plate."

And because he didn't want me to feel guilty. I feel *so* guilty. Fuck, what have I done? "What hospital?" I ask, standing.

He looks up at me. "No."

I turn and walk out, dialing Sarah, and she answers after just one ring. "What hospital are you at?"

Silence. Surprise?

"Answer the question, Sarah."

"The Royal London," she says, sounding as meek as I've ever heard her sound. "They've discharged me. I'm waiting for a taxi."

"Cancel it. I'm on my way." I hang up, looking back at John stomping after me. "She's been discharged."

"Then I should go."

"*I'm* going."

"For fuck's sake," John mutters, reluctantly backing down, holding up a bunch of keys. Sarah's. "You'll need these. Call me."

I reverse my steps and take them, my emotions all over the fucking place. Guilt, hurt, anger.

Drew's coming up the steps as I'm leaving. "Where are you going?" he asks as I pass.

"Did you know Sarah's in the hospital?" I question, trying and failing not to sound accusing. His silence speaks volumes. "And no one thought to tell me?"

"You've got enough on your plate," Sam says, appearing on the steps with John.

"No, I fucking haven't," I yell. "Because my wife's walked out on me, and I'm not allowed to even *try* and win her back so, actually, I've got fuck-all on my plate to deal with because I'm giving her fucking space!" I get in my car and wheel-spin off, blinking back the anger, because of all the emotions, that one's the most potent. For someone who supposedly loves me, Sarah doesn't half know how to stick the fucking knife in.

Fucking woman.

I have enough deaths on my conscience.

• • •

It takes me a moment to realize it's Sarah sitting on the wall outside the hospital. She looks small, pale, and weak. Drained. I've never seen her be anything but perfectly made up, tits out, shoulders back. A salacious smirk stretching her red painted lips. Today, she's the polar opposite—her blond hair scraped back, her chest covered with a fleece hoodie, her shoulders hunched in. The sleeves are pulled over her hands. Hiding the bandages.

I get out and walk to the wall, stopping nearly toe to toe with her. Her head is low, and I can see the effort it takes for her to lift it and look up at me. This is not the Sarah I've known for years. She didn't even look this pitiful when she lost her daughter. I wince away that thought, feeling more guilt.

She blinks, her blue eyes glassy. "You didn't have to come," she says quietly.

I press my lips together and crouch to relieve her of the strain to look up at me. Just fucking look at her. "I did," I reply softly, knowing I could be making things so much worse, but I'm unable to stop myself from caring. Her bare, dry lips tremble as she tries to hold back her tears. I'm at a fucking loss, unsure how to navigate these murky waters. I know I won't be increasing my chances of making amends with Ava if I help Sarah try to get back on her feet, but I don't think I can turn my back on her. Not even after everything she's done. I didn't want this. I never knew it might come to this.

I reach for her arm, pushing back the material of her sleeve to reveal a bandage. "Sarah," I breathe in despair. "What have you done to yourself?" A tear drops onto her cuff and soaks into the material.

"I'm sorry," she murmurs, her voice croaky, as she pulls down the sleeves again, holding them in place with her fingers, pinning them to her palms.

"Come on," I say, cupping her elbow and taking her weight, helping her stand, feeling her exhaustion. "Let's get you home."

I walk her slowly to my car and get her in, putting her bag in the boot. The drive is long and silent, and it's only when I pull up outside her flat that I realize I've never been inside. Feeling inevitably on edge, I get her out and walk her slowly up the steps, letting us in with the keys John gave me.

I'm sure I can thank John that the blood and pills have been cleaned up. But it's desolate. It's the only word that comes to mind when I get her inside, settling her on the couch. "I'll make tea." I go to the kitchen and search for mugs. I find one in a cupboard with one plate, one bowl, and one glass. "Jesus," I whisper, getting it down and going to the drawers, pulling one open after the other. All empty except for the bare minimum utensils and a few knives and forks. I lift the kettle off the stand. Empty. I go to the fridge and pull it open. There's a pint of milk. Out of date.

I close the door and look around the room. It's a shell. Soulless and cold. This is simply an address.

Breathing out, I rub my hands down my cheeks. This was like my apartment, my life before Ava. I knew Sarah's life was me and The Manor, but this has knocked me.

I had sex and drink.

Sarah had her whip and The Manor.

Now I have purpose, and Sarah has nothing.

Because I took it away.

I give up on the tea and get the glass, filling it with water and taking it to her. I sit on the chair opposite, unable to stop myself from taking in this room too. Bare minimal furniture. No photos on the walls, nothing lying around—no books, blankets, or cushions. It screams loneliness.

Solitude.

I have never, not once, thought about Sarah's life before she met Carmichael. Her family. Did she have any? Does she now? I quickly pull my wondering into line. I can't go there. Especially not now.

"How's Ava?" she asks.

"Let's not talk about Ava," I say, feeling I need to keep her separate to this.

She nods, looking down into the glass. "She looked beautiful," she says. "On your wedding day."

I can't look at her, the shell of a woman before me, taking me into unknown territory. "Sarah, I don't know what to do," I admit.

"You must miss me," she says, shocking me as I glance at her, full of caution. "I mean around The Manor," she goes on. "Doing things. Working."

I laugh, uncomfortable. "Yeah, kind of. I needed to pay for something earlier. Couldn't."

"Why?"

"Well, because your brain stores all the information I needed to log into my accounts."

She quickly grabs her phone and swipes, handing it to me. "Here."

I look down at the screen and see the banking app open. She still has access to my accounts? Of course she does. Fucking hell, how stupid can I be? She could have cleaned me out and disappeared. I'm not sure if I should be more uncomfortable that she hasn't. That's she's still here. *After trying to take her own life.* I eye her warily and take her mobile. I still have no idea what I'm looking at or what information to input. I shake my head and hand it back, slightly embarrassed.

"You could send me the details and I'll make sure the money is sent."

Shame on me, I take her up on her offer, forwarding the email from the dealership. She doesn't ask any questions, just goes right ahead and sends the hundred grand in a few short, very easy minutes. "Done." She smiles mildly. "You also have a meeting with Niles on Monday."

"What for?"

"The new stock is being delivered."

"Right." New stock. New stock for my sex club. "Thanks."

Hope seems to pour into her eyes as she looks up at me, and it makes my wariness double. "I could apologize to Ava," she says.

"What?"

"For how I've been. What I've done. I could—"

"What have you done?" I ask softly.

Sarah's eyes drop to her lap, and a few beats of silence fills the room before she breaks it. "I texted her from John's phone to get her to come to The Manor," she says quietly. "So she could see me." A swallow. "With you." *Intimate.* Not sex, but it's the next best thing for Sarah. Her whip goes hand in hand with sex. "I told her ex-boyfriend you're an alcoholic and that Ava mentioned him often."

"You told my wife's ex that she talked about him often?" She fed him?

Sarah nods. "I know I can never have you, but I didn't want to lose you either."

I close my eyes and breathe calmly. "You could have destroyed something amazing for me." Even though, in the end, it could be *my* actions that do the most damage.

"I know, and I'm so sorry. It's only because of how much I care for you."

I'm sorry too. I fucking hate what Sarah's version of *caring for me* has done to my life. And yet here I am, amid my own turmoil and fears, making sure she's okay. Because, God damn me, I care.

Five days ago, Ava said she loved me. Married me, for fuck's sake.

Said she wanted me as hers forever. Now? She hasn't called me. I've given her space. I'm sorry I've done that. The last time I sent *her* away, when I was drunk and repulsively emotionally abusive, she came back. She wanted to know I was okay.

She cared.

Now? She's not reaching out to me, not worried for me. I could be lost in vodka for all she knows. Doesn't she care about that? I wince at the sharp pain in my heart. My wife doesn't care anymore. So where does that leave me?

A key sliding into the lock on the front door pulls both of our attention there, and John walks in, looking tense and worried, obviously by what he might find. I didn't call him. He looks between us. "I have to go," I say, standing, feeling anger rising. Not because of Sarah, but because of Ava's silence. *She doesn't care.*

I walk to the door, and John moves out of my way, letting me pass. I stop on the threshold, looking back at Sarah. "Don't ever do anything like that again, do you hear me?" It's a low blow, but I know she'll listen because now she knows I actually *care*. I just hope she doesn't push me for more than my concern.

I leave and drop into the seat of my car, staring at the steering wheel, my fists balling, sending a shooting pain up the arm of my damaged fist. I look down at the fading blemishes and bruises. The fist that I damaged breaking free of a headboard to get to my wife because I thought she was choking. Because I *care*.

Taking my anger out on my Aston, I pull away fast.

My wife doesn't care anymore.

She doesn't care.

What the hell am I supposed to do with that?

Chapter 13

Friday is a slow torture. I follow my usual routine: run, shower, dress, drive to Kate's, follow Ava to work, sit in the café, wait.

But today I'm restraining anger too, trying and failing to push back the hurt. I got home last night and stewed. Walked circles around our empty penthouse, revisiting every moment that's led me to now. I scrolled through the endless photos of Ava trying to convince myself I've got it wrong. She *has* to care.

But she obviously doesn't.

Because if she did, I wouldn't be without her right now.

Ava leaves the office at one o'clock and walks to the nearest Starbucks, getting a coffee—cappuccino, no chocolate, no sugar. She drinks it on her way back. She leaves work at six, and I follow her to Kate's and sit outside, contemplating knocking the door. Confronting her. She's hiding, and I'm enabling her to. She can't expect this space for much longer.

I'm about to get out of my car and knock the door when I see Kate pull up. I breathe out my disbelief when Dan gets out her van too. What the hell? I take my hand off the handle and rest back in my seat, my plan obliterated. I can't storm Kate's flat with Ava's brother there. It will be carnage. Does he know Ava's living there? Does he know she's left me?

I clench my fist and push it into the steering wheel, starting the engine and pulling away before I give in to the urge to throw my weight around. My phone rings before I've made it out of Kate's street, and I stare at the unknown number. Unknown as in, there's no name assigned to it. But I know who it is.

"Jesse Ward," I say calmly, feeling anything but.

"Why's my sister at Kate's again?" he asks. No friendly hello, or how ya doin' from my shiny new brother-in-law. *Standard*. My arms straighten against the wheel, my jaw rolling.

"Why the fuck are *you* at Kate's?" I counter. I need to bang some fucking heads together around here. Mine and Ava's included.

"That's none of your business."

"Likewise." I hang up before I fire some abuse and give my wife another reason not to take me back. Not that she fucking wants me or *cares*.

"Fuck," I yell, hitting the steering wheel repeatedly. I've had enough. We're going to dinner, and we're going to talk this out. She's had her space. If she doesn't know by now if she'll forgive me, I think that's my answer. Not that I'll accept it, obviously. But I need to know when to pull out the big guns.

• • •

I get back to Lusso, shower, change into some dark jeans and a white shirt, brogues on, and head straight back out. Determined. I stride through the lobby, my laser focus directed straight ahead, a clear sign to the hot, new, young concierge not to bother talking to me.

He doesn't.

Sam calls me when I'm on my way back to Kate's and, naturally, I wonder if he's done another drive-by and seen Dan there. "Hey," I say, tentative.

"Coffee?" he asks. Coffee to discuss what Dan's doing at Kate's?

"I'm taking Ava out to dinner," I say surely.

"Oh, that's good."

"She doesn't know."

"Oh, for fuck's sake," he breathes. "So you're just going to show up?"

"Yep."

"Good luck," he quips. "How's Sarah?"

She cares. "Broken." I frown at my phone when I see an incoming call. "I've got to go, Jay's calling me." I hang up and take Jay's call. "Have you finally found some more CCTV footage for me?" That's one mystery still in need of clearing up. Who drugged Ava? Which also reminds me, Steve hasn't called. Did Juliette even tell him? I huff. Probably not.

"No, it's a dead end."

"For fuck's sake, Jay. So I'll never know who drugged my wife?"

"Wife?"

"We got married last Saturday."

He laughs. "Congratulations."

"Thanks," I mutter.

"Then I'm even more surprised to see her here," he goes on. "Did someone get you some chill pills for a wedding gift?"

My foot slams on the brakes just off Kate's street. "She's there?"

"Yes, she's here."

"At the bar?"

"That's what I said."

"On a Friday night?"

"Why don't you know this?"

My head swells, the pressure getting too much. She's out on the town? Drinking? Flirting? I'm killing time, annihilating myself over and over, and she's gone out drinking? What is she doing, celebrating being single again? I pull my hands off the wheel and stare at them shaking.

"Ward?" Jay says, definitely wary.

"I'm on my way."

"Hey, listen, I don't want any trouble."

"No trouble," I assure him. *Only anarchy.* I drop the call and it immediately rings again.

"What did Jay want?" Sam asks.

"Ava's out."

Silence.

"I'm going to the bar."

"No, Jesse. No, no, no."

"Yes, yes, yes."

"Fuck it!" There's a few bangs and crashes. "Wait for me outside," he demands. "Do you hear me? Do *not* go into that bar without me."

I snort, hang up, and put my foot down.

• • •

Jay looks like he's one domestic argument away from quitting. His big body fills the doorway, his arms crossed over his chest, his eyes warning me as I approach. I know I'm not getting in this bar unless I can demonstrate complete composure, so I drag a smile from somewhere deep. I'm certain it's got a psychotic edge. *She doesn't care.* I laugh under my breath. We'll see.

I reject yet another of Sam's crisis calls and slip my phone into my back pocket. "Evening," I say calmly.

"Evening," he replies, just as calmly.

"Good night?"

"Quiet," he says. "And by quiet, I mean there's been no trouble." His eyebrows lift. "Just how I like it."

"Long may it continue." *Still calm.* I haven't a clue how I'm managing it.

"Don't make me wrestle you out of here, Ward."

"No drama," I muse, laughing at my nerve. I can't promise Jay that at all. I feel volatile. Unhinged. I pass him and stop just shy of the next door that'll take me into the bar, breathing in some air and calm. The plan is simple.

Find out if she cares.

I feel someone brush past me, and I look to my right when a lady's voice apologizes. Her eyes light up. It's not an opportunity I'll pass up, so I dig deep and unearth the smile that has always sent women weak at the knees, blasting her back with it. "No problem." I look her up and down briefly, taking in the red dress, just enough for her to read into it. Her friends stop chatting behind her. It's been a while since I've silenced a crowd of women with my smile. Or noticed that I have.

Casting my eyes across the group, I watch as each and every one of the women—all younger than me, I must add—breathe in their awe. I feel for my wedding ring with my thumb, spinning it, like a subliminal apology to my wife for what's about to go down.

If she cares.

"Have a good night," I say, walking backward slowly, giving them all a bit longer to take me in, before I turn and stride toward the bar.

I feel Ava before I see her, the left side of my body burning from her stare. *Yes, here I am, baby.* I briefly flick my gaze her way, seeing her at the bar with her friends. Looking perfect. Her dress on the ridiculous side of short. A glass of wine in her hand.

So she's not only making the most of being single, she's making the most of *not* being pregnant. It's a double kick in the gut.

Breathe.

I drag my eyes away, edging through the congestion at the bar. "Water," I say, my eyes landing on the optics on the back wall. How easy it would be to go down that rabbit hole. Chase away the pain. Escape. I swallow, ripping my eyes away, focusing on the barman getting my water.

A hand rests on my arm. It's not Ava's, there are no flames inside. Red nails. Dark hair. Darker than Ava's. Her skin's paler. Her eyes not as big. Her lips not at rosy. Her red dress more on the respectable side of short.

"What's your name?" I ask automatically, turning into her a fraction.

"Selina." She eyes the water being passed across the bar to me, obviously waiting for me to offer her a drink.

I look over my shoulder, just catching Ava with her glass to her mouth. *Defiance.* Doing all the things she knows will trigger me. I take my water and turn, leaning back against the bar, ignoring my new friend. Watching my wife.

She heads to the dance floor, and my eyes narrow, studying her, seeing her and Kate close, talking. Yelling? Then Ava is suddenly on her way back to the bar, ordering another drink. It's hardly landed on the bar before she swipes it up and necks it.

Breathe.

So she *does* care?

"You didn't tell me your name." The woman beside me is doing her best to project confidence and sex. *The red dress.* I look down at it and see Ava on the launch night of Lusso. See the dress on the bathroom floor after I removed it.

She's back on the dance floor when I look up, arms raised, her body flowing to the deep beat. Various men in her orbit are watching her. Vultures circling the meat.

Breathe.

Necking my water, I walk away from the woman at the bar, blocking out the men, focusing on my wife. There's one way to find out how over me she is.

I move in behind her, seeing her moves slow as she registers my presence. *Affected.* It's the answer I need, but I don't stop there. Pulling her back to my front, I dip, latching onto her neck, feeling my heart kick for the first time in days. Yes, it beats, but it still fucking hurts.

Her backside pushes into my groin, my dick loads, and my senses are saturated by her in every way. Doesn't care? Then why is she positioning her head so I can get my mouth on her throat? Doesn't care? Then why is her body vibrating with need against me? Doesn't care? Then why the fuck is she forcing every inch of her body into mine?

Doesn't fucking care?

Like fuck she doesn't care. So please, for the love of God, tell me why she's been acting like she doesn't. Tell me why she's left me alone for days.

I stroke down her arm to her hand and clench it, leading her off the dance floor. My wife is about to get a stark reminder that she'll never get over me.

I go straight for the accessible toilet and get Ava inside, acknowledging Jay's warning before I shut the door and get to the business of reminding my wife who she's married to and how passionate he is about making sure they *stay* married.

I push her against the wall, studying her as she breathes heavily up at the ceiling. I smile on the inside.

Mine.

And no amount of fight from her will prove otherwise. We both know it, as well as we both know I am irrevocably hers. I take her jaw and direct her face down, my need for her starting to get the better of me, every inch of me anticipating her. I release her face, my stare telling her not to look away. She obeys, eyes on me, as I seize her wrists and push them to the wall, my face close to hers, feeling her hot breath hitting my skin as I lean into her. I take her lip between my teeth and clamp down lightly, tasting her for the first time in too long. Her whimpers are drowned out by the loud music engulfing the small space.

She tries to kiss me.

No.

I dodge her mouth and wait until she's retreated before I put my face close to hers again, my gaze penetrating. Desperate eyes. Desperate body.

Desperate.

"Kiss me," she demands as I push her farther into the wall with my body and take my lips teasingly close to hers. She heaves against me, her heart thudding against mine, her eyes on my mouth.

Just a teasing brush.

She lunges to capture me.

No.

"Kiss me," she orders through her teeth.

Not today, lady. Today I'll fuck her until she remembers who the *fuck* she belongs to and where the *fuck* she lives. I move both of her wrists into one hand and stroke up her body until I have her neck in my hold. Her pulse pushes into my fingertips. I breathe in her face.

My cock pounds in my jeans.

But I will maintain control. I will *not* have her believe I don't know what I'm doing right now. Her whimpers become more desperate by the second, and my satisfaction gets stronger. As always, I just have to get her in my hands to prove my point. She's not fighting me off. She's not protesting. I see her intention as her body rolls, her mouth coming at me. I move my head and slam my lips on her chest, pulling her dress down to get to the sweet spot, sucking, making sure the small bruise is revived before I turn her and push her front forward into the wall, separating her thighs with my knee, placing her palms against the tiles. She cries out. I don't need to tell her what to do. I release her hands and they remain exactly where I put them as I dip and pull her dress up, taking in her arse, smelling her desire, as I undo my fly and pull out my dick. She won't need much prep. It's a good job, because I'm in no mood for accommodating her.

And to make my point, I strike her with a stinger of a slap across her right cheek when she sticks her arse out.

That's for leaving me.

"Fuck!" she yells, earning herself another on the other cheek.

That's for pretending you don't care.

"Jesse!"

Now it's time to scream, baby.

I get into position and guide myself to her pussy, slamming in fast. She yells, I grunt, and the room spins.

Maintain control.

Easier said than done when you're balls deep in your wife after being deprived for five days. *Fuck.* Goodbye, control. I can't hold back. Don't *want* to. I thunder into her, watching as her hands grapple at the wall, her head thrashing, hearing her scream to high heaven. I pull her head away from the tiles by her neck, worried she'll bang it in her delirious state, turning her face outward. Her eyes are drowsy. Her lips are parted. The blood in my cock starts to thump, my release looming. I have to kiss her. I can't kiss her.

Fuck.

I slam my mouth on hers, tackle her tongue, moan, pump, sweat.

No.

I stop, panting, my shaft buzzing as I widen my stance, grip her hips hard, check her head, and start slamming her arse into my groin, my head falling back, my mind shutting down, just taking the pleasure. Taking it all.

Her body tightens, her yells become broken. I blow out air, chasing my release. Beads of sweat trickle down my temple, and I reach up to wipe them away.

Fuck.

I pull out and spin her, lifting her to my body and getting straight back inside her, leaning into her against the wall as I pump, clumsily kissing and licking her throat, tasting the sweat. Madness. Utter madness. But also inevitable after so long without her.

She shudders, screams, and I tip the edge, exploding around her, feeling her muscles clenching my cock as I come inside her. I'm out of control, out of my body, twitching, spasms shaking me, my knees quivering. Yes, the pressure has subsided, but the anger? No. That remains. She's on a night out, in a dress she knows I would never approve of, and she's drinking. All the things I hate. Leaving me wasn't enough?

I sniff, pulling out of her neck.

She looks at me, gasping in my face, her hands going to my hair and hauling me onto her mouth.

And now she wants a loving kiss? What, does she feel worthless?

I get her off me, propping her against the wall, refusing to look at her as I sweep a hand across her pussy, collecting our desire and wiping it across her chest next to her refreshed bruise. She's watching, confused, as I tuck myself away.

And then I walk out, taking a few breaths outside the door. Ava doesn't want to be that woman to me. Drunk, easy, wearing a short dress. And she doesn't want me to be that man. The man I once was. Lost in a bottle of vodka, no self-respect, fucking anything with a pulse. If our little encounter in the restroom is what it takes to remind her, then so be it. But still, it takes everything in me to resist going back to her and doing it all over again, but this time gently. Lovingly.

No.

I walk down the corridor just as Sam steams into the club, out of breath. He stops, looks me up and down, probably to check for blood. "I'm fine," I say, going back into the bar.

"Have you seen her?" he calls over the music.

"Yes, I've seen her."

"And?"

I wave for another water. "And...we cleared a few things up."

The woman in the red dress appears again, coming in close to me, and Sam recoils, looking her up and down as she virtually sticks herself to my side. I pick up my water with one hand and, because I'm not done proving to my wife that she *does* actually fucking care, I put the woman's arse in my other.

Sam's eyes widen. "What the fuck are you doing?" he asks.

I could never explain, and I could never expect anyone to possibly understand. Not that I have time to even begin fathoming how to defend my actions. I feel a force, like a whirlwind, and Ava bursts through the crowds, the sexual flush gone, an angry one in its place.

"Oh, Jesus," Sam breathes, moving back, getting out of the way, revealing Drew as he does. When the fuck did he arrive?

Ava looks pretty fucking lethal as she swipes the glass from my hand and drinks it. Checking if it's vodka. Did she hope it was because *that* would explain why I just fucked her coldly like I've fucked every other woman in my life? I can only conclude it angers her that it's only water when she smashes it on the floor before getting up in my victim's face, screaming a clear and dangerous, "Fuck off." I release my hand from the woman's arse. No more action is required. The woman in the red dress retreats, leaving me at the mercy of my wife. I'm grateful. It's time to get some things off our chests.

"What the fuck are you doing?" she yells.

Oh, and here she is. The woman who definitely cares.

I try to hide my smug smile. A little.

"Answer me!"

When she's screaming at me? No. *Stew. Fucking stew, just like I've stewed since you walked out on me.*

I turn away, ordering more water and advising the staff there's some glass on the floor, looking over my shoulder when I hear Drew release a despairing curse. Sam catches my eye, looking…what's that look on him? Pissy? I turn back toward them, wondering what's going on. Then I see Ava's brother and it all makes sense.

"What the fuck is he doing here?" I say, spotting Kate hurrying to the dance floor.

"I don't know," Drew answers, his head batting back and forth between everyone, while Sam sneers at Ava's brother. "I'm sensing some couple's therapy is on the cards."

"You dick," I mutter, as Dan spots me. I hold back my snarl. Only just. He makes his way over, determined. *Here we go*. I haven't got time for this. Where the hell is my wife? I push off the bar. Scan the crowds.

Nearly bite my fucking tongue off.

"What the hell?" I whisper, seeing her hauling some tall, dark-haired dude into her body. Then onto her mouth.

I double over to try and stem the pain in my stomach, my eyes on the floor, my body heaving. Did I just see my wife kissing another man? Nausea grabs me, and I look up, hoping I imagined it.

I didn't.

I slowly unbend my body, standing up tall, watching as she virtually eats the bloke alive.

What. The. Fuck?

"No, Jesse," Drew yells, practically circling my waist with his arms to hold me back.

I'm like the Hulk, my whole body expanding, the red mist not creeping up on me, but attacking.

I can't stop it.

And no one can stop *me*.

I steam through the people before me, enraged, and grab him, hauling him off my wife and launching him halfway across the dance floor with a right hook that's loaded with a week's worth of anger and frustration. How the fuck it doesn't knock him out cold, I don't know. Trust my wife to pick the one man in this bar who's as tall and built as me. *Tactical.*

The brave bastard comes back at me, taking me off my feet and slamming me onto the hard floor. I grunt, winded, blinking, feeling disorientated. *This fucker has just kissed my wife.* I roar and fling myself up, going back at him, cracking his bloody nose again before getting him up against the wall and finishing him off, sinking a knee into his stomach.

It ends the brawl, and he folds to the floor, coughing, his face a mess, and I sniff, wiping my nose, trying to control my shakes. Another epic fail. I need to leave before I kill someone.

I turn to find Ava but get tackled from the side and shoved through the crowds. "I fucking told you, Ward," Jay seethes.

"I need my wife, Jay." I search around me, seeing Sam, Kate, Dan. No Ava.

"I'll bring her out."

I spot her standing on the edge of the dance floor, her face a picture of shock. She's shocked? What the fucking hell did she expect me to do? Fall to my knees and beg her not to kiss another man? "Fuck you, Jay." I fight him off and bowl through the building crowd, grabbing Ava. "Get your fucking arse outside." Of course she struggles, yelling and kicking.

"Out," Jay roars, fighting me as I fight with Ava. All out of patience—I can't imagine why—he shoves me aside with force and seizes Ava. "I'll carry her out if you remove your stubborn fucking arse."

"Fine," I snap, happy to let Jay take the punches, my face throbbing as I follow him out of the bar, watching Ava going loopy in his arms. *Crazy.* Her dress is riding up her thighs, her boobs not far from spilling out. Jay's struggling to contain her, his hands slipping across her torso. "Keep your fucking hands exactly where they are," I warn.

"Get the hell off me," Ava screams, bucking and turning in Jay's grasp as he walks her out calmly.

"Ward, how the fuck do you put up with this?"

I laugh dementedly on the inside when Ava looks at me in shock. "She drives me fucking crazy." I overtake Jay, wincing at my achy jaw. "Be careful with her."

The cool air hits me when I make it outside, and I'm surprised when Jay gives me a civil and calm goodbye. I think he must feel sorry for me. I feel sorry for me too. And Ava, because I'm about to lose my baggage in a really unpleasant way. My mood doesn't improve when everyone piles out of the bar. Including Dan.

"Fuck off," I bellow. "All of you." I am not airing our dirty laundry in front of everyone, especially not her brother.

"You think I'm leaving her with you?" Dan says on a snort of disbelief.

Did that prick just fucking challenge me? With a shitty tone, a sarcastic laugh, and by physically coming at me? I lift a foot, clench my fists, suck back air...and place my foot back down.

Calm. Give me calm.

Taking Ava's arm, I make my point in a way that doesn't involve caving her brother's face in. "You don't mind if I take my *wife* home, do you?"

"Yes, actually." Another step forward. Everyone needs to pray for Dan. "I do."

"Dan," Ava says on a rush, not fighting my hold. "It's fine. I'm fine. Just go. All of you, please, just go."

Everyone remains static—the only thing moving on any of them is their eyes. Even Drew and Sam. I know Sam wouldn't mind ripping Dan a new arsehole, but I can see he's concerned that I'll go further.

"What the fuck do you think I'm going to do?" I bellow. "This woman is my fucking life." I feel Ava jump in my hold, and Kate backs up. Dan, though? He flinches, although tries to hide it, but the steely fucker remains in place. I need to calm the hell down, the temperature of my blood feeling like it could burn its way through my flesh and have me bleeding out.

Ava pulls herself from my grip, breathing heavily, looking around the group. She doesn't know what to do. So she takes the wine in Kate's hand and knocks it back, grabs her purse, and faces me, her expression challenging. Every time I think she's pushed all the buttons I have, she goes and finds another. I can't talk. Can't yell. So I give her a dark look I pray she takes notice of.

She doesn't. "Don't bother following me," she seethes, matching my look as she storms off, giving me a little shove as she does. I can't work out who's fuming more right now.

I touched another woman's arse.

She kissed another man.

Definitely me.

She just has to go one better.

The look Ava just hit me with, I pass on to her brother behind me, as well as everyone else. *Leave us alone.*

I go after Ava. She's so obviously trying to walk in a straight line as she marches away. How much alcohol has she had? *Too much.* I frown as she moves closer to the curb, her heels wobbling. The headlights of a car make me shield my eyes, putting black dots in my vision.

Jake! Jake, get out of the road! Jake!

Bang!

His limp body catapults into the air.

And lands yards away.

No. Please, no.

I flinch, coming back into my body with a violent jolt. *Jesus Christ.* I move fast, grabbing Ava and putting her on my shoulder where she's safe. "Don't step out into the fucking road, you stupid woman."

"Fucking hell, Jesse, put me down."

"No." Not on her fucking life, because, clearly, she doesn't have as much respect for it as I do.

"Jesse," she cries. "You're hurting me."

Hurting? *I'm* hurting *her*?

I put her down and check every inch of her. "You're hurt?" I ask. "Where?" Wait, did she roll her ankle? Did I catch her somewhere when I picked her up?

"Just there," she yells on a broken sob, smacking her hand on her chest.

Oh. Her heart?

"Join the fucking club, Ava," I roar, thumping mine too, forcing her to take a few backward steps. I reach for her, missing when she turns and stomps off, this time less wobbly. The emotions are sobering her up. I fucking hate the sight of my wife drunk. Hate that we have only ever rowed when she's been under the influence.

"The car is this way," I call, going after her but halting when she abruptly stops. Then she turns slowly and comes back toward me. "I don't like your dress," I mutter when she's passing me.

"I do."

"And why is that?"

"Because I knew you wouldn't," she screams, right in my face as she swings around. I hate that I know her so well. She's predictable but completely unpredictable.

"You're right!" I fucking hate it, and I hate us right now. This is *not* how it's supposed to be, not after getting married. Not ever.

"Good," she huffs. "Is that the only reason you're pissed, or is it because I'm drunk, or is it because I kissed another man?"

Oh, hold me back. "All of the above," I hiss. "But kissing another man gets the fucking gold."

"You had your hand on another woman's arse!"

"I know!" But a kiss?

"Why?" she snaps. "Getting bored of keeping it for just one woman?"

I recoil, injured. What the hell is she saying? "You fucking asked for it, woman."

"Me?" she gasps. "How?"

"You left me," I yell, trembling. "You promised you would never leave me." She broke a promise. She left me. She came out on a Friday night wearing a scrap of material as a dress, drank in excess, flirted, and kissed another fucking man. Don't tell me her transgressions aren't topping mine.

Blinking, looking surprised, Ava takes a brief few moments to breathe. "You shouldn't have taken it upon yourself to decide my future." She walks on, back to wobbling again. John's already schooled me on this. I denied a woman her choice. What I did was wrong. But, she's not pregnant, and it's a relief given how fucking drunk she is right now.

"For fuck's sake," I whisper, looking at the heavens. How did we get here? "You're a fucking pain in the arse." I catch up and pick her up, and this time she doesn't fight me. "And I was thinking about *our* future."

"Put me down."

"I'm not putting you down, lady." I stride to the car, feeling her becoming heavy and limp in my arms. Out of fight.

I get her in the passenger seat and secure her belt. "This fucking dress is fucking ridiculous." *And it's going to meet my scissors as soon as we're home.*

Starting the engine, I pull out and turn onto the main street, seeing Kate still outside the bar with Dan, a good few meters between them. The atmosphere between them looks as thick as it feels in my car. Kate's arms are folded over her chest, her body language not looking good for Dan. But Sam's nowhere to be seen.

I check Ava, tapping the steering wheel, wondering what to say. I'm not sure anything will benefit the situation. She's not thinking straight. There's a man back there nursing a bruised body and a bruised ego to prove it. I grimace at the state of my shirt.

One for the bin.

I drive calmly, wondering if she'll speak. Condemn me. Yell at me some more, hit me. The bright lights of a billboard shine into the car when I come to a stop at some lights, and I press my palms into the wheel, bracing my arms, taking in a long breath. "I love you, Ava," I say to the world outside my car. "With my fucking heart and soul, I love you so much." I press my lips together, facing her. She's staring out of the window. "Will you ever understand how much?"

She doesn't answer, so I gingerly reach for her face, turning her toward me.

Her eyes are closed. Too much drink. Too much drama.

"No," I answer for her, sighing. "You couldn't possibly." A horn sounds behind me, prompting me to pull off, the lights now green. "I don't know what tonight was all about," I go on, talking to myself. "But it was below the belt."

Worse than you stealing her pills?

"Oh." I laugh. "You chose *now* to join the party?" I ask. "Where have you and your shitty sense of humor been the last week while I've been alone?"

Observing from afar.

"How good of you."

"What the hell are you talking about?" Ava slurs.

I flinch and look across the car, finding drunken eyes squinting at me. "Never mind," I mutter. "Go to sleep."

"I'm not tired."

I roll my eyes, silently asking my dear brother how to deal with *this*.

Are you kidding? I died before I had the pleasure of a dramatic female to contend with. Thank God.

I laugh but quickly stop, checking Ava. She's closed her eyes again. "Not tired?" I ask. "No, but totally shitfaced." Returning my attention to the road, I frown. *Thank God.* "Are you saying I should walk away?"

Did you hear me say that?

I hum, smiling a little. "She's a handful, isn't she?"

Yeah, bro. And you're two handfuls.

"She kissed another man."

You fucked her like she was just another lady of The Manor.

I wince.

Stole her pills.

Another wince.

Felt another woman's arse.

"Okay, enough."

"No, actually, *I've* had enough," Ava mumbles, coming alive again.

I sigh. "Go to sleep."

"I'm not fucking tired."

"Okay." She's fighting to keep her heavy eyes open. "You're a case, Mrs. Ward."

"Well, you're a *nut*case."

I hear Jake rolling around on heaven's floor, laughing his tits off. *She's got spirit, bro.*

I laugh with him and relax back in my seat.

You've not been out on your bike recently. Are you forgetting about me?

"Never."

Wish I could ride with you, Jesse.

I smile sadly. He never got to experience the thrill. "Me too, Jake."

I don't hear from my brother for the rest of the journey. But I *hear* him.

Don't waste a moment.

. . .

I'm glad to see Clive back at his spot behind his desk. Not so glad that I'm once again carrying Ava into Lusso because she's in no fit state to walk. His shock is clear, and I definitely sense disappointment. Yes, she's in a shocking state. Yes, I'm disappointed too. Clive and I share the same values.

He grabs something off the counter and comes at me, holding whatever he's picked up out. It takes a moment for the penny to drop.

Keys. Keys for Ava's nice, new, sparkly car. Not that she deserves it.

"It was delivered earlier," he says. "Very nice indeed."

"Thanks, Clive." I hold my hand out under Ava's legs, accepting them. He offers to help, but I politely decline. I get Ava inside the elevator and look down her body as the doors slide closed. "Fucking dress is ridiculous."

"I can walk." She springs to life in my arms, wriggling like a manic worm.

I seriously doubt she can, but I'm done arguing. Exhausted. So I place her on her feet and watch her, hands braced ready to catch her, as she pulls at her dress. She can pull to her heart's content. It will never cover enough of her.

As soon as the elevator opens, she takes measured, careful strides to the door, me following. "So stubborn," I mumble. "Defiant. Difficult." She ignores me, going into her bag and pulling out the keys, guiding the right one to the lock. I exhale heavily as she fiddles and faffs, trying to get it in. We'll be here all fucking night. "Let me." I brace myself for her rejection, taking her hand and helping. I get no thanks. And now she'll go upstairs and put herself in the wrong bed.

I follow one of her heels as it gets kicked across the floor, then the other, before she paces away, taking the stairs as I throw my keys on the side table and put the ones for her new car in the drawer. Her body sways as I go after her, putting myself a few steps behind, palms up ready to stop her falling. It's a miracle, but she makes it to the top upright. And as predicted, she turns right instead of left and goes to the last bedroom. The one farthest away from the master suite. From me. "You never disappoint, darling," I say sardonically, following. The door slams in my face, forcing me to take a minute and a few deep breaths. *No more arguing.*

Letting myself into the guest room on an exhale of exasperation, I find she's spread-eagled on the bed, unconscious again. I walk to the edge and stand over her, shaking my head. I've been here, drunk, sparko, fully dressed—mostly not—many times. It didn't feel good on me. It doesn't feel good on my wife. But she's home, and my heart is beating calmly rather than limping along in dull thuds. I don't know what tomorrow will bring but she's here, and it's a start.

I begin to get her out of her dress, negotiating her limp, unresponsive form, peeling the nonexistent material from her body. "Let's get rid of that."

"Aaarrre youuuuu g…g…going to cuuuut it tooo piec…iec…ieces?"

I laugh in disbelief at the state of her. "No." I'm done annihilating things today. "I might not be talking to you, lady." I heave and grunt as I wrestle her to the side of the bed, getting my arms under her back and legs. "But I want to be not talking to you in *our* bed." Where I've *not* slept for five fucking nights all alone.

She slumps into my shoulder on a sleepy, drunken sigh, her legs dangling as I walk her back to the master suite. I place her down and watch, half amused, half staggered, when she flops down, conked out. I get out of my blood-stained shirt. "We're having a serious conversation on acceptable levels of retaliation," I say to her useless form. "There will be no shouting either." I kick my shoes off and reach down to pull off my socks. "We need a holiday." Slipping my hand into my pocket, I pull my phone out and place it on the bedside table. "No arguments on that either." Getting out of my trousers, I crawl up the bed, my nose wrinkling at the stench of wine. "Come here." I tug her close, feeling her body pushing closer to me. Instinct. And to have her back in my arms, whether she's talking to me or not, feels like the best kind of reprieve.

I look down at her head. "Ava?"

She mumbles a croaky, "What?"

"You make me crazy, lady."

"Crazy in love?"

I smile mildly, planting my face in her hair and breathing her into me. Breathing life into me. "That too." I don't know how a woman can make me crazy but calm me at the same time. Honestly, I just don't know. "So fucking crazy in love." I feel her become heavy again, leaning on me. "Let's not do this week again," I whisper. "Promise me."

Of course, she doesn't reply, and when my phone rings, I scramble to shut it up, answering on a hushed. "Hello?"

"Still alive?" Sam asks.

"Yeah."

"And Ava?"

"Alive, although I'm sure she's going to feel dead in the morning." Her hangover isn't going to be pretty. "Where are you?"

"At The Manor."

Do I ask if Kate's with him?

"Alone," he adds, as if reading my mind.

"Oh." So he's getting on with his life, is he? I've heard it before. "Listen, mate, I think Dan's just fucking with her head." Ava's brother strikes me as the kind of man who doesn't like losing.

"Yeah, and I'm done with her fucking with mine." Hence, he's at The Manor *alone*. But will he play? I check my phone when another call comes in. "John's calling me. Mind if I take it?"

"Sure, talk tomorrow."

"Okay." I hang up and answer. "John?"

"Where are you?"

"With Ava."

There's a slight, surprised pause. "We need to talk."

My back naturally straightens, and I check Ava. If she was awake, she'd hear every word down the line. But she's not. "About…"

"Having Sarah back at The Manor."

I blow out my cheeks. "John, so much has happened."

"And she's not entirely to blame."

I raise my eyebrows but don't counter. Because he's right. Ava still doesn't know all of me. All of who I am. If she did, I wouldn't be so fucking worried about what Sarah will spill. "I'm not sure I can make that happen, John."

"I can't find shit, Jesse."

"What are you looking for?" Like I'd be able to tell him.

"Contracts, medical records. I've had all the paperwork out."

"There must have been a system."

"If there was, only Sarah knew it. Ava's not unreasonable. Will you just talk to her?"

I look down at my wife. Not unreasonable? I don't know if I can agree. "I'll come over on Sunday. We'll talk." Now is not the time to talk to Ava about Sarah. Neither is tomorrow. Or…ever.

"Okay."

I chew my lip a little. "How is she?"

"A shell."

I'm wincing all over the place tonight. A shell because her purpose has been taken away, and I'm the only one who can give it back to her. Problem is, I'm not sure Sarah has the strength to only accept what I'm willing to give and not try to take more. I can't risk her succeeding in her attempts to break me and Ava. Or has she finally learned her lesson? Finally accepted there never was and never can be anything between us? And what really confuses me is the fact that John is looking past his understandable anger at me to call about getting Sarah reinstated at The Manor. Can or should I even consider that? "I'll see you Sunday."

He cuts the call and I drop my phone to the bed.

"Who was that?" Ava mumbles, pushing her face into my chest.

"John."

"Is he mad at me?"

"He's mad with both of us, baby."

"Me too," she whispers. "I'm sorry for kissing another man."

"And I'm sorry for fucking you like you were just another lady of The Manor."

"I'm *the* Lady of The Manor," she slurs. "And you're the Lord."

I can't smile. I want to be *her* Lord. Not *the* Lord.

Chapter 14

I work my way through at least half a jar as I listen to the whir of the appliances in our otherwise silent kitchen, while staring at the missed call from Ava's brother. I won't call him back. He saw and heard way more than I'm comfortable with, and I'm too exhausted to take him on this morning. I have more important things to do. Like fix my marriage. It's been tumultuous and we're only a week in.

I screw the lid back on and pop the jar in the fridge, reading a message from Jay as I get a glass down.

You and your wife (if you're still married) are barred.

I chuckle sardonically, sending him a thumbs up—fine by me—as I fill the glass and empty a sachet of Alka Seltzer into it, listening to it fizz before giving it a quick stir. I take it up to Ava, perching on the edge of the bed and taking a few moments to appreciate the quiet before I wake her. Before I take her on.

"I love you," I whisper, reaching for her face and pushing back some strands of hair. She murmurs sleepily, her closed eyes squinting. My own head bangs in sympathy, but if she's going to be reckless with alcohol, she must face the consequences. As must I, apparently. She's going to be good for nothing today, feeling sorry for herself. Perhaps that's a good thing. No one wants to argue when their head feels like it could fall off.

She gingerly opens her eyes, obviously preparing for her head to explode. "Drink." I hold out the glass, and she grunts, throwing me a disgruntled look before turning her back on me.

"Leave me alone."

I laugh. It's the only way forward. Laugh or bite and take us back at square one when we were tearing strips off each other. "Hey, come here." I pull her across the bed with little effort and put her on my lap. "Drink," I order more sternly, tipping the glass at her lips. "All of it."

She does as she's told—it's a novelty—before she falls into my bare chest in a heap.

"How bad is it?"

"Bad."

Yeah, I can smell it. I rid my hand of the glass and move up the bed, resting back against the headboard.

"I'm sorry," she whispers, making me peek down at her head in surprise. "...ish."

I smile into her hair. "Me too." That's it. We're both sorry. It's a good start. But now she's back where she should be—and I'm not consumed by the fact that she walked out on me, that I was alone, feeling hopeless and lost—I have space in my mind to feel sad about what led us here. I'm absolutely gutted she's not pregnant. *Gutted.* It's an added layer of worry and something I need to look into. *I'm...broken.*

The silence stretches, Ava's breathing shifting frequently from deep to shallow. She's clammy and a little shaky. It's not nice. "What are you thinking?" I ask.

"I'm thinking we can't go on like this. It's not good for you."

Me? I'm fine. Probably infertile, but I'm fine. Ava, however, is becoming irrational. Reactive. "I don't care about me."

"What are we going to do?"

That's a good question. I am *fully* aware that our relationship is volatile. I know my insecurities are a contributing factor to that. Problem is, I'm a man who has lost everything I've ever loved, and now I have Ava, I've become quite...attached to her. No man loves harder than a man who needs it returned. Or a man who's hiding endless pain. I don't want to be that broken man for Ava, but it's clear that by trying to be strong and dependable, I've become unbalanced.

I get Ava onto her back and lie on top of her, snuggling between her boobs. "I don't know," I whisper, kissing the center of her chest. "But I do know how much I love you."

"Why did you do it?" she asks quietly, making me pause, breathing her skin in. Why? Because I was desperate. Five days without her felt like I relived the past twenty years in slow motion, except without the usual distractions from my misery.

I look up at her, hating the hurt I see in her eyes. "Because I love you. Everything is because I love you." My craziness, my protectiveness, my extreme...everything.

"You treat me like a slapper," she says with a frown. *Oh?* She's talking about last night? Not the fact I stole her pills? "Fuck me in the toilet of a bar with no words," she goes on. "And then walk out to go and feel up another woman?" The frown's turned into a mild scowl. It's warranted. Because I fucked her like she meant nothing. I didn't mean to. I only meant to prove that no matter how hard she tries, she will always gravitate toward me. Respond to me. *Need* me. "Did you do *that* because you love me?"

"I was trying to prove a point." And it backfired. All I've done is make her feel cheap and forced an epic retaliation. "And watch your mouth," I grumble.

"No, Jesse," she retorts. "You were trying to be a wanker." *Ouch.* She wriggles, trying to free herself, and panic grabs me. She's going to leave again? Not over the pills, but over me fucking her? "I need a shower," she says as I beg her with sorry eyes not to go. I'm given an expectant glare in return. I'll stop her this time, I swear. Hopefully not with force.

Reluctantly, I move off her, holding my breath as she gets up, wondering which way she'll go.

The bathroom.

She closes the door, and I exhale my relief, hearing the tap run, followed soon after by the shower.

Make it right.

"How?"

Patience.

Hmmm. It's not one of my finest qualities. I get up and go to the door, pushing it open gently, seeing her under the spray. I could go back at her. Point out all her misdemeanors. But I won't.

Grovel.

I push off my boxers and step into the stall, putting my front to her back, reaching round to claim the sponge. "Let me," I say, stroking across her wet tummy. I apply pressure, encouraging her to face me, and drop to my knees, starting to look after her.

Quiet. Patient.

And she lets me, because she knows I need this element of our relationship and also because, despite her fierce independence, she likes me taking care of her. I feel everything inside of me settle and silently thank her for giving me what I need in our chaos. Does she get that from me? Does she ever settle when I care for her? Does this bring her calm throughout her storm?

I can hear her mind racing. Hear the endless questions. *Possibly not.* "Where have you been since Monday?" she asks, and I smile at her thigh as I swipe the sponge across her skin.

"In hell," I whisper, watching the water wash away the suds. "You left me, Ava."

"Where were you?"

"I was trying to give you space." I continue with my task, cleaning her, taking my time, savoring it, making up for the days I've lost. "I realize how I am with you," I whisper. "And I wish I could stop myself, I really do." God, I've tried. I've had endless conversations with myself over it. Listened to the people I love, those who are alive *and* those who are not. "But I can't."

"Where were you, Jesse?"

I'm about to answer her with another half answer, but then it clicks *what* she's actually asking me. *The fuck?* She thinks I betrayed her again? Got blind drunk and fucked someone else?

Never.

"Following you," I say quietly, reluctantly. But I'd rather she knows that truth—knowing I didn't actually respect her request for space—than think I was lost in booze and women. "Everywhere."

"For four whole days?"

Four whole days. Is that all it was? It felt like forty years. "My only comfort was seeing how lost you were too," I say, looking up at her surprised face. Does she believe me? I get her on the floor with me, my hands all over her face, my lips unable to hold back from kissing her. She breathes my breath into her deeply, holding my wrists. "We're not conventional, baby," I say. "But we're special. What we have is really special. You belong to me, and I belong to you. It just is. It's not natural for us to be apart, Ava."

"We drive each other crazy." Her eyes scan mine, looking for me to confirm it. I don't need to. "It's not healthy."

It's healthier than the alternative. "Not healthy would be my life without you in it." I just had four days of not healthy. Not a fan. I pull her close, crowding her with my arms. "This is where you're supposed to be. Right here, always with me." In my arms, on my mouth, a constant on my mind. "Don't ever kiss another man again, Ava," I say quietly. "They'll be locking me away for a long time."

"You need to stop with the crazy shit," she orders, looking at me while she feels my face. I'd say her kissing a stranger is crazy. But I know it could be argued that my crazy pushed her to that crazy. So I keep my mouth shut, hoping we can now move forward and spend the rest of the weekend making up for lost time.

"And you need to stop with the defiant shit." I steal a kiss, smiling when she scoffs.

"Never." Her arms come around my shoulders, her legs straddling my thighs.

And there is that first dash of contact. I inhale, feeling her heat on me as I snake an arm around her hips and lift her, while she kisses me wildly, obviously keen to get on with making up for that time too.

"I've missed you," she mumbles, her tongue frantic in my mouth. It's my undoing.

"Lower," I order softly, holding myself upright, my cock singing for her, my lungs expanding as she slides down, her shoulders high, her body solid until I'm buried balls deep and shaking madly. "Fuck," I whisper, tearing my mouth from hers and burying my face in her hot neck. She flexes her hips. "Fuck, fuck, fuck." Then pulls my face back out, scanning my eyes, my face, before taking my mouth again, her arms braced on my shoulders, her hips rolling.

And it's beautiful.

But I'm so surprised she doesn't demand a condom. Not that it matters, since she's restocked on pills. And I'm apparently infertile. Has she concluded I must be? Is she reassured by that? Is that why she's here? Being reasonable? She's okay because she didn't want kids. She's okay even though I'm so fucking sad I'll never get to share the ultimate with her. Devasted. But I'd be even more devasted if I didn't have Ava.

She moans as I move her on my lap, lifting and lowering her slowly, working us both up steadily and slowly. No rush. It's fucking exquisite. The friction, the pace, her mouth worshipping mine, her boobs slipping all over my chest, the hot water raining down on us. Her pussy clenching me. "Ava," I mumble, preparing her, telling her, feeling the blood racing through my body to my dick.

"Yes," she breathes, tugging at my lip with her teeth. "God, yes."

I grunt, lifting my arse from my heels, holding hers with one hand, the back of her head with my other. The calm becomes frantic, mouths, bodies, and heartbeats. I pull back and look at her, seeing the excited sparkle in her dark eyes. She pushes her forehead to mine, fists my hair. "I love you," she whispers. My hips jerk, my control lost, the muscles in my thighs burning as I tackle her mouth again and kiss us to the finish line, bucking on a grunt as I come. Ava hardens our kiss more, every inch of her becoming stiff, the walls of her pussy sucking me deeper as she climaxes on a whimper. The shakes set in, my lungs are screaming, and my arse collapses back to my heels.

"Welcome home, baby," I say, spent, hearing her long, exhausted exhale as she settles in my neck, clinging to me. We're home. "You need to eat."

"I'm not hungry."

I pull back, one eye narrowed. "You need to eat," I reiterate.

The corner of her lip quirks. "I said, I'm not hungry."

Oh, I see. So this is how it's going to be, huh? "You'll eat."

"I'm not hungry." Her challenging eyes feed the energy charging through me. *And* my softening dick.

"If you don't eat," I say quietly, loading my voice with threat, "I'll have to find a way to make you."

"Oh?" Her eyes fall to my lips. "And how will you do that?"

Temptress. I get to my feet, turn off the shower, Ava still in my arms, and walk our soaking wet bodies to the bed, slipping out of her and throwing her down. She squeals, landing on the mattress, her wet body glistening. My dick twitches as I start slowly working it back to full hardness. She bites her lip, watching. "Will you eat?"

"No."

"Does someone need some sense fucking into them?"

"Maybe," she purrs around a small grin, looking me up and down.

"Then let me help you out." I grab her ankles and spin her onto her front, slapping her wet arse. Her scream blends with the stinging sound as I blanket her body with mine and move her hair aside, forcing her head back so I can kiss her, kneeing her thighs apart and sliding into her on a satisfied groan. "Oh, baby, this weekend is going to be fun."

She cries out, my hips fire into action, and the sound of our wet bodies slapping together fills the bedroom.

Along with Ava's constant screams.

Chapter 15

It's Sunday. We made it another day but, to be fair, we've not left Lusso. We're always safe in Lusso. I slide a plate of toast onto the island, looking up when she appears at the door. Naked. Hair a wavy, damp mess. Her bruise is nice and fresh. Her eyes are still sparkling. I've had her twice already this morning. Still not done.

I look her up and down as she returns the favor. "Eat," I order, sucking some butter off the end of my finger.

She looks at the toast. "I don't think I'm hungry."

Oh, we're doing this again, are we? It's how most of yesterday was spent. Ava saying no to any trivial thing, and me enforcing a yes. I narrow my eyes, chewing my lip. *Game on.* I stroll over slowly, seeing her body tighten with each step I take until she's breathless with anticipation, her head tilted back to look up at me. I lick my fingers under her watchful, needy eyes, and slip them between her thighs. Now *this* is what I expected marriage to be like. Sex on tap, my wife constantly desperate and not too far away from me. I raise interested eyebrows when Ava grabs my forearms on a sharp hitch of breath. "You want me again, baby?" I ask, pushing into her. Her eyes close. My dick recharges. "I think someone needs a reminder." I drive into her a few times, then withdraw and bend her over the island. Her palms slap the marble. Her boobs squish into the cold top. I dip and kiss her back. "Ready?"

"I can't remember."

I smile and slam into her on a yell. "Are you going to eat, baby?"

"No."

Oh, how she plays me. And how I enjoy playing with her...for the next hour.

I stare at the top shelf of the fridge, frowning. None in the cupboard, none in the fridge. How? How the hell has this happened? I roll my shoulder, wincing at the sting her fingernails have left behind. Turns out my wife needed a Retribution Fuck after her Reminder Fuck. Not because she's been utterly unreasonable this past week. But because, according to Ava, she should be punished for refusing to eat. *Insatiable.*

I'm here for it. So I handcuffed her to the bed and fucked her like a madman. I don't even feel guilty that her throat must be sore. *A bit like my muscles.* I feel like I need a good stretch. Maybe I'll go in the gym later.

In the meantime, where the fuck is my peanut butter? I'm not panicking. Maybe just a little. This has never happened.

If you can kick drink, you can kick this bad habit too.

I snort to myself. It's not a bad habit. I like peanut butter, that's all. "And so did you," I remind him. Although crunchy rather than smooth. *Yuck.* I cough, disgusted, searching again in vain. "Damn it," I mutter, turning away from the fridge. Ava's on the other side of the island, her smile wide and amused. "What are you grinning at?" It looks like she wants to earn herself another fuck of some description. I'm not complaining.

"Why the compulsion for peanut butter?" she asks, her delight at my mild meltdown obvious.

"I like it," I answer, feeling a bit defensive.

"You *like* it?" Her face looks like it's about to split.

"Yes," I grumble. "I like it." Smooth. Only smooth.

Freak.

"You're in a bit of a pickle," she muses casually, "considering you just *like* it."

"I'm not in a pickle. It's no big deal." I can take it or leave it.

Liar.

"Okay," Ava says easily. She doesn't believe me. Do I care?

I roll my eyes to myself and go to her. I might bend her over the island again. It's been over an hour since I had her handcuffed to the bed. But all forms of fuckings are forgotten when I cop a load of what she's wearing on her bottom half. Or what she *isn't* wearing. "What the hell are they?"

"Shorts."

I beg to differ. They are *not* shorts. "You mean knickers?"

"No," she says slowly. "I mean *shorts.* If they were knickers, they'd look like this." She wrenches them up her thighs a bit more, and I very nearly choke on my tongue. Her smooth, tan, firm thighs. Around my waist. Gripping me.

"Ava, come on, be reasonable."

"Jesse," she breathes. "I've told you, if you want long skirts and roll-neck jumpers, go find someone your own age."

I recoil, offended, as Ava pulls the offending shorts back into place and ties her laces. "I might go for a swim at The Manor."

"In a bikini?" I ask, looking across the kitchen for my phone. I'll call John. Have him close the spa.

"No, in a snowsuit." She chuckles, mocking me. "Of course in a bikini."

Whenever has Ava wanted to go for a swim at The Manor? I suppose I should be grateful she's even coming. But then again, Sarah's not there. Which is why I have to be there today as promised. We're in a fucking mess.

"You're doing this on purpose, aren't you?"

"I'd like to go for a swim."

"I'd like to strangle you." I feel like she's constantly testing me. Setting the standard going forward. I look down her incredible body on a pout. *My eyes only.* "Why do you do this to me?"

"Because you're an unreasonable arse and you need to loosen up." She flips me an accusing look, which is fucking rich. Her level of unreasonableness has been off the charts recently, but since we've only just got back on track, I won't risk derailing us again by challenging her. "You may be an old man," she goes on, and I roll my eyes, "but I'm only twenty-six. Stop acting like a caveman." *Only if you stop being so fucking defiant.* "What'll happen if we go on a beach holiday?"

It's a nonissue, because if we go on a beach holiday, the beach will be private. "I thought we could go skiing. I'll show you how good I am at *very* extreme sports."

Her smile lights up the room and my life, and I catch her in my arms as she launches herself at me, carrying her out of the kitchen. "You smell luscious," she says into my skin, hugging me hard.

I'm sure I saw a jar of Sun-Pat in the fridge in my office. "You *feel* naked," I grumble, squeezing her arse cheek. I grab my keys off the side.

"You *look* edible."

I stall by the mirror, smiling at myself. I look complete. That's how I look with Ava clinging to my front. "You *taste* divine," I whisper, turning my face into her neck and biting.

"You *sound* sexy," she whispers, pushing onto my hips. I growl, she laughs, and I walk on, looking forward to getting this done with and returning home so I can resume this easy bliss. And fuck her some more.

I feel the new concierge's eyes follow us through the lobby as I carry Ava, my palms spread over her arse cheeks in an attempt to cover them. "Morning, Casey," she sings, breaking out of my neck.

"Morning, Ava. Morning Mr. Ward."

"Mrs. Ward," I grunt.

"Lighten up," Ava says over a laugh.

"No." I open the door of my Aston and get her inside, pulling her belt round. "Those shorts, Ava," I sigh. They take Daisy Duke's to a whole new level.

She pushes me out of the car and pulls the door closed.

Insolent.

But today, I'm feeling amenable. Loved up. Relaxed.

And punishment fucks are so much more fun than arguing.

. . .

John meets us outside The Manor, and I definitely catch his interested look as I lead Ava inside. Yes, her shorts are non-existent. No, I've not put my foot down. We've only just made friends. Which reminds me… are John and I okay now? We've not really…talked about it. About anything. I look at him flanking me, see him peek out the corner of his eye, even through his shades. I think we're good. "Ava would like to go swimming," I say, and he smiles. He already knows this because I texted him in preparation.

"You do, girl?"

"It's hot out there," Ava says, all too casually, making me look down at her in disbelief. It's not *hot*. It's warm. Definitely not warm enough to warrant her outfit. But, in the name of peace and tranquility, I will keep my mouth zipped. Because, unlike my wife, I can be reasonable.

I hurry her through The Manor and check the fridge as soon as we get to my office, mentally cheering when I find what I hoped I would. I pull it out and dive right in, taking a seat opposite John, casting my eye across the piles of strewn papers. What the hell has he been doing with it all? "What's happening?" The first dip is the best, and I hum, satisfied.

"Camera four went down," he replies.

"Another one? How many is that?"

"Four. I've managed to fix three of them, albeit they're temporary fixes, but the camera around the side by the garages needs more than my limited tech and DIY skills."

I roll my eyes. Not long until the new system is installed. "Thanks for trying."

"An engineer was due Friday." He pulls out his phone. "I'll chase them up."

"The contract states a twenty-four-hour window for call-outs."

"I know." He gets up and wanders away, and I find Ava still by the door, distracted.

"Baby," I say, snapping her back into the room. "You okay?"

"Yes, fine." She shakes herself back to life and comes to the desk, sitting. "Daydreaming, sorry."

"What about?"

"Nothing. Just watching you settle now that you have your peanut butter."

I'm settled because she's with me. The peanut butter helps, I suppose. "Want some?"

"No." She grimaces as I fix the lid. "How's Sam?"

Hmmm, what should I say? Ava hasn't mentioned her brother being at Kate's. "Shit. He won't talk about it. How's Kate?"

"Not good."

"What do you know?" Did Kate open up to Ava? "Why did she end it?"

"Because of this place, I suppose. It's probably for the best." We all know it's got nothing to do with this place and everything to do with her brother. What the hell did he want yesterday? I didn't return his call and he didn't follow up.

I look at John by the window on his phone. We have a lot to discuss. I've just added Sam to the list. All stuff I can't talk about in front of Ava. "Do you want to swim or stay with me?" Shame on me, I'm using a bit of reverse psychology. She thinks I'd rather her *not* take option one.

"What are you going to do?" she asks.

The paperwork on my desk calls for me. "*This* is what I'll be doing."

"Why don't you employ someone else?"

Yes, just like that. Jesus, I own this place and even I don't know what I'm looking at on my desk right now. How the hell can I expect someone else to come on in and get us straight? "Ava," I say on a sigh. "It's not that straight forward in this line of work. You have to know someone, trust them." It's only ever been John, Sarah, and me. "I can't just call the job center and ask them to send along someone who can type." My God, where the hell *will* I start?

"I could help," she says.

I glance up, hopeful. "You would?" She'd do that for me? I inhale subtly. Work for me instead of Peterson? She'd be here with me every day. In more appropriate clothes, obviously.

Ava frowns and picks up a piece of paper. "An hour here and there, I suppose."

I laugh on the inside. It needs a lot more than an hour here and there. Sarah was always working, and when she wasn't working in the evening, she was whipping. I watch as Ava frowns, craning my neck to see what she's looking at. A bank statement. Her eyes are nearly popping out of her head.

I smile when she looks up at me in disbelief. "We're very rich, Mrs. Ward." And what she's looking at is just a fraction.

"Fucking hell."

"Ava—"

"I'm sorry, but…" Her eyes drag slowly across the sheet. "This sort of stuff shouldn't be lying on your desk, Jesse."

It wasn't until John started looking for something.

"Wait—" Her eyes widen. "Did Sarah look after your finances?"

Sarah looked after everything, which meant I didn't need to know an awful lot, and isn't that obvious now. "Yes." I won't try to fool her. I was good for nothing but drinking and fucking before Ava walked into my life. And after? Well, I was too infatuated by her to pay much attention.

"Do you have any idea where your money is?" she asks. *Yes, it's in a bank held hostage by a scorned wife of Steve Cook.* "How much there is?" she goes on, eyes back and forth between me and the bank statement.

"Yes," I say, showing her the paper. She's shocked enough as it is.

I won't share the other statements, wherever they are. She'll pass out. "I have this much"—*and quite a few million more*—"and it's in this bank." *Where I hold a few more accounts, both business and personal.*

"You have just one account?" she asks. "What about business accounts, savings, pensions?"

One doesn't need to worry about savings and pensions when one owns properties worth in excess of forty million, but one still has them because Sarah took care of it. Again, I'll hold back on that. So I mutter, "I don't know," and hope we move on.

Ava's face tells me I'm hoping in vain. "She did everything?" she asks. "All of your accounts?"

"Not anymore." *As you can see from the state of my desk.* And Ava's clear aversion tells me John's head is in the clouds. There's no way Sarah can come back here. Not if I want to stay married. "But you'll help?" Because I can't imagine the alternative.

Ava shakes her head, looking across the chaos again as she collects a stack of papers and starts sorting through them. "Yes, I'll help."

My heart swells. She'll help. We'll make an incredible husband and wife team. A force. This could be the start of something amazing, and as an added bonus, she's with me all the time. I smile, but it falls when her sorting hands pause and she looks up, something coming to her. "I said I'd help, that's all," she says. "A few hours here and there, Jesse."

"But it's the perfect solution." She could be our in-house interior designer too. There are dozens of rooms in The Manor. By the time she'd worked her way through the building, it would be time to start again.

"For you," she splutters, tossing the stack of papers back on my desk as if they've caught fire in her hands. "The perfect solution for you. I have a career." *Don't remind me.* "I am *not* giving it up to come here every day and file paperwork."

Do you want to take a minute to think about it?

"And anyway." She gets up, and I scowl at the pathetic excuse for a pair of shorts before giving her my annoyed eyes. Anyway, *what?* "I don't know how to lash a whip, so I think I'm a little under qualified."

My jaw hits my lap. *Why?* Why does she need to be so fucking spiteful? "That was a little childish, don't you think?"

She looks away, obviously ashamed. It's a relief. "I'm sorry," she murmurs. "I didn't mean it."

Then why fucking say it? And people around here think *I'm* impulsive and shoot from the hip? I scoff. At least my mouth's under control, which is more than I can say for my wife's. And now she won't look at me.

"They'll be an hour," John says, looking between us. "And before I forget, we've had a further three memberships cancelled."

Before he forgets? "Three?"

"Three. All female," he says as he leaves.

Whose idea was it to come here? My mood has fallen into the gutter, and this place seriously spikes some undesirable behavior from Ava. I rest my elbows on my desk and sigh into my hands. I'm there all of five seconds before I'm out again, being pushed into the back of the chair by Ava. Oh? She sits on the edge of the desk and motions to the mess. "I'll sort all of this out." She feels guilty. Is it terrible that I'm secretly happy about that? "But you need to get someone on this. It's a full-time job."

And there's one woman who can solve that problem. A woman that needs The Manor as much as The Manor needs her. Everyone's happy. Except my wife, I expect. "I know." I lift her feet to my knees. What the hell am I going to do? "Go for a swim," I order. I need to talk to John. "I'll make a start on this, okay?"

"Okay," she says quietly, but she makes no attempt to move, watching me, her mind obviously spinning.

"Go on, beautiful girl," I say quietly. "Spit it out."

"They're withdrawing their memberships because you're no longer available to fu—" Her lips press together, and my eyebrows raise. "To have sex with," she finishes.

"It would seem so, wouldn't it? I can see this pleases my wife."

"What's the ratio of men to women?'" Her curiosity is getting the better of her again.

"Members?"

She nods.

"Seventy thirty." Last time I asked, anyway.

She can't hide her surprise, and do I detect a little worry? Surely not. "Well, you might have to turn The Manor into a gay club," she quips around a smile, and I laugh. We have many gay men and women, a few bisexuals too. Ava's just not encountered them playing yet. Maybe never will, because I know she can't face the communal room again.

"Go take a swim," I order, getting her down from the desk and sending her on her way. The door is hardly closed behind her before it's open again, John striding in.

"So you're friends again?" he asks.

"Yes, we're friends. What about us? Are *we* friends?"

He huffs, going to the window and gazing out. "You understand what you did, right?"

"Yes." There's no way I'd be rolling my eyes right now if John was facing me. "I understand."

"And you understand that it was wrong?"

"Yes," I grate.

"And you should be grateful you didn't succeed, because that kind of life-changing decision should be made as a team, right?"

"Right."

"So what's wrong with you then?" he asks, facing me.

I twitch in my seat, uncomfortable. *Where the fuck would I start?* "What do you mean, what's wrong with me?"

"Well, apart from the fact that you're an irrational, neurotic, unreasonable, selfish prick."

"Not a motherfucker?"

He takes off his shades. "Are you shooting blanks?"

I cough, insulted. "Don't hold back, will you, *mate*."

"You should get yourself checked out."

"Yeah, I know." That'll be something to look forward to. *Fucking hell.* "God, you sure do know how to bring me back down to earth."

"Well, here's something else for you to consider." He nods at the mess of papers on the desk.

I'll sort all of this out. But you need to get someone on this. It's a full-time job.

Ava wasn't wrong. If only there was a wise way to straddle Ava's concerns...and Sarah's mental health. I can't have another death on my conscience. "Fuck," I breathe, clenching my eyes closed in dread. "John, I feel cornered."

"I know." He backs up and opens the office door, and there she is.

Sarah.

I jump up, instantly stressed, and hurry over, pulling her in and checking the corridor. Jesus fucking Christ, I only just got my wife back. I close the door and look between John and Sarah in disbelief.

"I only came because he made me," she says, sheepish, flicking John a look I'm sure he wouldn't appreciate. "I'm not feeling much like being rejected at the moment."

If John forced her here, it's because he was worried. My gaze drops to her wrists. They're covered by a long-sleeved blouse. In all the years I've known Sarah, I have never seen her in a long-sleeved *anything*.

"I know you don't want me here," she says, going to the couch and lowering.

"If I don't want you here, it's because your actions made me feel like that. Made Ava feel like that." I look at the door, praying to all the gods that Ava doesn't come back to my office. *Christ, John.* But life is life, and I have to remember that. After all, Ava has given life to me. And, again, I can't be responsible for the loss of another. *Fucking hell.* I give John a look to suggest he better have my back if Ava walks in, and he nods, reading my warning well.

Moving across to the couch, I lower, my eyes constantly bouncing between Sarah, John, and the door. "How are you feeling?"

She stalls, resting back, regarding me with an expression I've not seen on Sarah often. Wariness. "I'm okay."

"Okay?" I parrot, laughing. "If you were okay, Sarah, John would not have brought you here and risked a situation where my wife might leave me..." I only just bite my tongue before adding "again." John brushes his finger across his top lip, quietly observing. "I don't know what to do," I admit out loud. I feel like I'm in a catch twenty-two situation. Save Sarah, destroy Ava and me. Make sure Ava and I are okay, destroy Sarah. Obviously, Ava comes first, but it's not as easy as that, unfortunately.

Sarah sits forward on the couch, her eyes briefly going to John. I look at him too, seeing him giving her a small, encouraging nod. God damn him. But I can't call him out, be mad at him. Just like me, he doesn't want any harm to come to Sarah.

I wait for her to go on, my hands joined, my fingers twiddling nervously. It's so much easier to hate her when she's being a heartless bitch. Problem is, it's a defense mechanism. Always has been. Sarah uses her bitchy streak to shield her from being hurt. She hasn't got the energy required to uphold that front right now. "Jesse." She's hesitant, gathering courage. "I'm lost," she says, her bottom lip definitely quivering. Shit, she can't cry on me. "Please, I beg you, let me back in."

John's interested stare is on my profile, I can feel it. But he's remaining respectfully quiet. Letting us talk. Except, I'm not talking. Just sweating. I press my fingertips into my forehead and sigh, trying to rub away the stress. "Sarah, you tried to destroy my relationship. And worse than that, you never once considered that by doing that, you would have destroyed me."

"I know, and I'm so sorry."

"And now you sit here begging me to give you the opportunity to do it all over again?"

"I won't," she rushes to say. "I give you my word. I'll stay out of your relationship, I swear it."

I laugh. I feel like I've heard this before. "I don't know whether I can risk it." I don't look a John. I don't need to. I can feel his concern. Poor guy is caught in the middle. It feels like only ever one of us—me or Sarah—can be okay. "And I could never ask Ava to accept your return to The Manor."

"Let me talk to her."

"No," I say, horrified. "Never talk to Ava."

"Jesse, please."

I can't stand her pleading. "Sarah, stop," I order, getting up and going to the fridge, grabbing a bottle of water. "I can't give you what you need."

"I need my job, Jesse, and you can give me that."

My bottle of water stops at my lips as I regard her. Then John. He remains silent. Then my eyes move to my desk. I can't see the top for all of the paperwork. Sarah notices my direction of sight and gets up, walking over, gathering up all of the papers. "John needs the surveillance contract," she says, fingering through the stack. "It's here." She pulls out a sheet and holds it up. "All of the medical assessments are in alphabetical order by surnames rather than date order like the invoices." I feel my tense shoulders lowering. "You need me," she whispers.

Such powerful words.

But not in the context Sarah needs them to be. My damn gaze falls to her wrists again, a bandage poking out from beneath the sleeve. *Fuck.* I didn't mean to kill any of the people who have died because of my bad choices and judgment. Knowing my next words could be the cause for her harm? I swig my drink. But I'll be signing my divorce papers if I agree to this. And therefore, causing myself harm. And Ava. "I'm sorry, I just can't," I say, hearing my regret. I hope Sarah does too. "I'm going." I leave the office and close the door, falling against the nearest wall and resting my forehead on it.

"All right?"

"Dandy," I quip, considering Sam as he approaches. "You?"

"Dandy. I was going to use the sauna but the spa's closed."

"Since when do you use the spa?" I ask, facing him.

"Since now."

Or...I eye him, thinking. "Have you been active since you and Kate split up?"

A steel wall shoots up. "We weren't *together.*"

"Have you been active?"

His jaw rolls. It's the answer I need. No. And why would that be? "Go home, Sam," I say over a sigh.

"I'm taking him for a beer." Drew appears, holding Sam's shoulder and massaging into it. "Coming?"

My phone rings, and I pull it out. "I'll catch up with you soon," I say to the boys, turning and taking the call as I leave them, too curious to let it ring off. "Jesse Ward," I say formally.

"Dan O'Shea," he replies dryly.

I push my way into the spa and head into the ladies' changing rooms. "What can I do for you, Dan?"

"Are you free anytime soon?"

I pass the lockers. "Why?"

"To talk."

"About what?"

"Things."

"What *things*?" I'm not interested. I'm sure he senses it.

"Various *things*."

Which tells me it's more than just my wife. Kate? Sam? I'm now interested. Sam's the lowest I've ever seen him. "What's the situation with you and Kate?" I ask.

"Is that any of your business?"

I smile. There's my answer. If he was still fucking Kate, he wouldn't hold back telling me. "No, but neither is my marriage any of yours."

"She's my sister."

"I know, because you keep banging on about it. So am I to assume you want to meet with me to discuss her well-being? Whether I'm looking after her?"

He sighs. "When are you free?"

There's my answer again. He doesn't want to talk about Ava, and he can't want to talk about Kate with me. Unless he wants me to talk to Ava on his behalf, therefore make an ally out of me. Seems a stretch after how well we've kicked things off. "Tomorrow?" I expect Ava will insist on going to work, and I'll need something to do. I better start filling my days. "Come over to The Manor. Say, two." I hang up, spinning my mobile in my grasp. What the fuck is his game, I wonder, as I go to the pool entrance and pop my head around the door. Sarah, Sam, and Dan are forgotten in a heartbeat when I see my wife, the water calm around her as she swims, her hair piled high, the ripples reflecting off the glass surrounding her, making it look like serene, calming disco lights dancing around the pool hall.

Back to cloud nine.

I smile and take a picture, then back up and head into the men's changing room, stripping down and leaving my clothes in a pile on the bench before going to my locker on the end and getting my shorts out, itching to get in that pool with Ava. I can count on one hand how many times I've been in my own pool. I've never been sober enough.

I wander out and the very second I step onto the tiles, she stops swimming and looks for me. I go to the edge and dive in, swimming under water, seeing her legs paddling calmly to keep her above the surface. Not for long. I reach forward and wrap a palm around her ankle, pulling her under, engulfing her body with my arms and her mouth with mine, fighting around the water to kiss her for as long as my ballooning lungs will allow before pushing off the bottom and breaking the surface, grabbing air. She clings to me as I tread water, smiling like a loon.

"You closed the pool, didn't you?" she says, a little breathless, her hands on my face.

"I don't know what you're talking about." I guide her arms around and help her onto my back. "It's never busy at this time of day." Ava onboard, I start swimming to the edge.

"I don't believe you. You couldn't stand the thought of me in a bikini and others seeing it. Admit I'm right."

Never. I maneuver her to my front and push her into the side of the pool, feeling her semi-nakedness pressed into me. Her smile is knowing. "I love the thought of you in a bikini." And the feel of her.

"But for your eyes only?" she asks coyly.

"I've told you before, Ava," I whisper, scanning her face, her sparkly eyes. "I don't share you with anyone or anything, not even their eyes." *But their lips when she's got the hump with me?* "Just for my touch," I say hoarsely, studying her as she sustains the burn of our skin together. "Just for my eyes." My fingers meet the heat of her flesh and stroke softly, before I push them inside. "Just for my pleasure, baby. I know you understand me, don't you?"

"I do," she exhales her words, stiffening, loosening, over and over.

"Good. Kiss me."

She's all mine in a second, and I am all hers, my fingers pulling free and my hands moving to her hips as I adore her mouth for the longest time until I can no longer hold back. I pull her bikini bottoms aside, lower the waist of my shorts and drive into her, loving the echo of her moans bouncing off the glass around us. I watch her between drives, treasure the feel of her hands grappling at my back, adore the glistening of her skin as she climbs to her release.

And once again this weekend, she doesn't demand protection. *This. It's bliss.* This is what married life is meant to be like. Feeling vulnerable but safe. Feeling sated but still—always—wanting more.

Mine.

"Jesus," I whisper, on the cusp, and on only a few more swivels and thrusts, I come calmly with her, feeling her trembles melt into mine, the water starting to sizzle around us.

"Hmmm," she hums as I pant against her neck, feeling her twitch against me. "I like swimming with you."

My palms cup her cheeks, my lips pushing onto hers. "Time to go home. I need to feed you."

"I'm not hungry," she says, her nose wrinkling playfully.

"How so when you're such a glutton?"

"You're cute."

"I know." Another kiss before I slip out and pull my shorts into place, turning her around and lifting her onto the edge, going under the water to do so. I emerge and push myself out of the pool. It's Monday tomorrow. The start of another working week. *Please, God, don't make it too stressful.* "What's in your diary this week?" I ask, getting us both to our feet and curling an arm around her wet body, leading her back to the changing rooms.

"This and that."

"A honeymoon by any chance?" I ask, looking down at her.

"Jesse," she breathes.

I pull her into my side and kiss her head, holding her hand where it's lying on my chest. "I know," I breathe, dejected. "You're busy."

"Maybe when I've got Ruth Quinn out of my hair." She sounds dejected now too.

"The client?"

She hums non-committedly, and I look down at her.

"Okay?" I ask.

"Yeah, she's just a bit…"

"What?"

"Demanding."

"So's your husband, but you find it easy to take no notice of him."

She slaps me lightly, but neither of us laugh. We both know we need a break from London. If only I could hurry the Ruth Quinn project along. But I know my wife, and the way I'd like to help would never be accepted.

Chapter 16

I don't drag Ava out of bed the next morning to go for a run. I don't tie her to the bed and refuse to let her go to the office. I woke her up, smiled when she demanded sleepy sex, and smiled harder when I told her the time.

Sleepy sex was forgotten.

She leapt up and darted into the bathroom in a panic, leaving me to get dressed. It doesn't make any sense to me why she wants to live by someone else's schedule. If she worked for herself, we could have all the sleepy morning sex in the world. Not to mention, no more challenging customers. What Ava said about her difficult client stuck with me overnight. I finally slept more than forty minutes—*Ava was beside me again*—but I considered how Ava reacted to Ruth Quinn's demanding nature. She seemed deflated. Exhausted by her. Yes, I'm self-aware and know I'm demanding, but only with Ava because she's my world. I don't want to exhaust her. Deflate her. My conclusion after ruminating for a while? I have to work on myself. But in the same vein, Ava doesn't have to deal with demanding clients if she doesn't want to. Why on earth would she want to? I don't understand it.

I pull on a white shirt and my navy suit, grumbling my way through my task, before collecting my grey suit off the back of the chair and emptying the pockets, ready for Cathy to take it to the dry cleaners. I feel around in the inside pocket and pull out a card on a frown.

OWEN CUTLER

I laugh under my breath and slip it into my pocket, intent of throwing it in the bin when I make it down to the kitchen. The Manor's not for sale.

I'm not looking forward to the day ahead. But definitely still curious about what Dan could want. I need to try calling Steve Cook again too, since his wife clearly hasn't passed on the message, see what he can find out about Mikael Van Der Haus. Check if he's got a record, and I should find a way to check in Denmark too. So, yes, lots to look forward to today. I huff to myself as I fasten my belt. This routine really doesn't work for me. How can I remedy this?

I head downstairs pondering that, tucking my shirt in as I go. If I could just get Ava away from London for a while, somewhere hot and relaxing, somewhere we can both chill out, then maybe I could use my powers of persuasion and convince her she'd be better off working for herself. I won't mention it would work better for me too, which is exactly what she'll conclude—that my suggestion isn't purely selfless. I'll reframe it. She's an amazing designer. She's working herself to the bone, dealing with exacting people like this Ruth Quinn, all to line the pockets of Patrick Peterson. What's worse, she doesn't need the money. She doesn't need to work. But being the reasonable man that I am, I can appreciate why she wants to.

Kind of.

I walk into the kitchen, all smiles, but it falls when I find the space empty. "Cathy?" I call, going to the laundry room and poking my head around the door. No Cathy. Odd. I check my Rolex as I wander back out, collecting my keys off the table by the door and slipping the ones for Ava's wedding present out of the drawer beneath. Something red invades my vision coming down the stairs, still in a fluster. Just look at her. She's thrown herself together in record time and looks exquisite. I pout to myself. "I'll take you." *Down to your new car so you can drive yourself to work, just as you always insist you want to.*

"Where's Cathy?" she asks, doing a terrible job of resisting an ogle of my suited form.

I pull at my lapels, standing taller. "I don't know. It's not like her to be late." Now to her gift. *Finally.* "You got everything?"

"I have." She comes without fuss, gripping my hand firmly, and I look back, having my own ogle. She looks gorgeous. God damn work. Who's going to get to appreciate her today? The difficult client? Will Van Der Haus rear his ugly head?

I hum to myself, stepping into the lift and hitting the button for the ground floor as Ava releases my hand and rootles through her bag. I hear her car keys jangle, but I know she's not looking for those because I just told her I'm taking her. Her new supply of pills? I crane my neck to see and retract it again when she looks up.

"What?" she asks.

"Nothing." Didn't I read somewhere that it takes a week for the contraceptive pill to get into a woman's system? And yet she's not demanded I wear a condom all weekend. Again, has she, like me, concluded I'm infertile? I add a call to a fertility doctor to the list of amazing things I need to do today.

As soon as the elevator opens, the mystery of my missing housekeeper is solved. Cathy and Clive are chitchatting, laughing. Since when has Clive laughed, except when he's rinsing me dry? I narrow an eye on him as I pass, mentally telling him to watch his back.

"That would explain," Ava muses as we pass.

"They're just talking." I can't let my mind go to those places. I saw them at our wedding. Close. Dancing. I shudder.

"They look very friendly."

I think Clive wants more than *friendly*.

"Oh," Cathy sings, happy. "I was just on my way up."

"No problem." I narrow *both* eyes now as Clive watches me pull Ava past. "I'm out of peanut butter," I mutter, a little reminder to Clive that Cathy is here for me, not him.

"There's a whole box of it in the cupboard, my boy," Cathy snaps, disgruntled. Is there? Which one, because I looked in all of them? "Do you think I'd let that run dry?"

"It should be in the fridge, not the cupboard," I say under my breath, knowing what's good for me.

I hear Ava chuckling. "Don't be so moody. They're only talking."

Sure. Friendly talking. I huff my thoughts and put on my Ray-Bans when we break out into the sunshine, inhaling the fresh air. It's going to be a good day. *Please be a good day.*

"It's not right," I say. Cathy's always been prompt. Clive's obviously a bad influence.

"Oh, she might be inviting him up when we're not there," Ava says seriously, her hand plunging into her bag again. What the hell is she looking for because, clearly, she can't find it? And I *definitely* didn't take anything. *This time.* "I did notice the sheets in the spare room were a little"—she hums, pouting—"ruffled."

"Ava," I splutter. Is she serious? "Don't."

"Stop being ageist."

"I'm not." Anyway, enough about the housekeeper and the concierge. I want to give her my gift. I feel in my pocket for the keys, excited.

"What are you smirking at?" she asks, finally giving up on whatever she's searching for.

"I bought you a present," I declare, pulling my glasses off as I move in, nuzzling her cheek before offering my mouth.

"You have?" she asks, wary as she pecks my lips. "What?"

"Turn around."

She withdraws on an unsure, questioning face and slowly turns away from me. I pull the keys out and hold them over her shoulder. She doesn't say a word, not for quite some time. Has she realized? I jangle the keys. "Over there," I say. You can't miss it. It's sparkling.

"You mean that spaceship?" she finally asks.

Spaceship? Okay, it's very new and very sleek, but I wouldn't go as far as to call it a spaceship. And she didn't sound too thrilled. "You don't like it?" I ask, my excitement sinking.

There's a moment's hesitation. Just a moment. "I like my Mini."

"It's not safe." I round her as I roll my eyes and hate the semi-scowl I find. How can she not like it? "This is safer."

She gapes at me. What's so surprising? "Jesse, that's a man's car—a John car." She points at it, looking again. "It's fucking huge."

I flinch. "Ava, watch your fucking mouth." *So fucking uncalled for.* "I got it in white. That's a lady's color. Come on, I'll show you." She'll come round when she sees how much effort I've gone to, but she remains unmoving, forcing me to hold her shoulders and walk her to her new car. "Look," I say, pulling the driver's door open and smiling at the pristine interior. I take a hit of the smell. *Lovely.* My DBS hasn't smelt new for a while. Perhaps I should fix that. I hum to myself, thinking I might pay a visit to the dealership this week.

I find Ava again. She's staring at the Range Rover, silent, taking it in. "I don't know what to say," she breathes. "You could've just bought me a watch or a necklace or something."

I've already bought her a watch and a necklace. "Jump in." I can't wait for her to see the personal touches.

But her body is suddenly unmoving, her eyes on the headrests. She's spotted it. I grin, chuffed with how it's turned out. I might get the Aston dealership to do the same on my new car.

"I am not driving this!" she cries, and I jump, my contentment going down the pan. She looks utterly disgusted. Why the hell wouldn't she drive it? It's lovely, bespoke, and, more importantly, it's safe.

"You fucking are." I put all of my thought and energy into this gift, thought she'd love having her new name stitched into the leather headrest, but nooooo. Not my wife. My difficult, unreasonable wife.

"I am not." She snorts, constantly scrutinizing the car. "Jesse, it's way too big for me."

"It's safe." I lift her in and put her behind the wheel. "Look." I release the internal computer and touch the screen. "Everything you'll need," I say, navigating the screen to my favorite track and playing. I turn up the volume and Ava looks at me in disbelief. Yes, thoughtful, I know. "I've loaded all of your favorite music. You can think of me."

She stares at me for a few moments, just stares. "I think of you every time you call and I hear that track," she says. That's sweet. But it's still not enough.

I frown when she slips out, looking determined in her stance. I'm so fucking confused. Who wouldn't love a Range Rover bought for them? "I want your car," she declares. "You can have this."

"Me?" She wants *me* to drive it? "But it's a bit…" How do I put it? "…girly." If it was meant for a man, it would be any other color except white. Hence, I got white.

"It is," Ava retorts shortly. "And I know your game, Ward." She comes at me with her finger, jabbing me in the chest. What's my game? "The only reason you want me to drive this thing is because it's enormous and there's less chance of injury if I crash. Prettying it up isn't going to convince me." She's making it sound like I'm trying to hoodwink her. Didn't she hear me put emphasis on the fact that it's safe? She throws the Range Rover a filthy look before marching away, leaving me standing by the car like a dickhead, wondering what the fuck a man has to do to make his wife happy?

Tell her some truths.

"Oh, do fuck off," I mutter. "My lack of sharing isn't an issue, because she doesn't know there's anything left to share."

No, but she might understand why you've bought this beast of a car for her.

"I bought it because I thought—mistakenly, it seems—that she might appreciate it."

Oh, please.

"Fuck off." I sigh but pout when my vision is invaded by Ava's arse swaying like a pendulum in that fetching red dress as she storms off toward her Mini. That arse. *Yum*. She gets in, and I wander over to my Aston, getting comfy, leaning on it. Perhaps I should get in the boot, because shit is going to fly very soon when she realizes she's going nowhere.

I look back when I hear someone coming out of Lusso.

"Everything all right, Mr. Ward?" Clive asks, watching Ava pulling out of her space and driving to the gates. They remain closed as she approaches them. "Oh, perhaps her remote control has run out of batteries. I'll get the gates for her."

"Don't do that, Clive," I say, smiling when I hear Ava's angry yell blend with the sound of her car braking. She gets out, heaving, furious.

"Planning on going somewhere?" I ask cockily.

"Oh, fuck off." She swipes her bag from the seat as I twitch, and marches to the other gate. Oh, no. I break out in a run and intercept her escape, picking her up and taking her back to the Range Rover.

"Will you watch your fucking mouth?" I snap, putting her inside and belting her up. I snatch her keys from her hand and start separating them, putting her pink key to the penthouse on her new set. "Why do you have to defy me on absolutely everything?"

"Because you're an unreasonable arse. Why can't you take me to work?"

Oh, *now* she wants me to take her? "I'm already late for a meeting because my wife won't do as she's told." I'm not late. But I do have things to do before I head to The Manor to meet Niles. I haul her onto my mouth and kiss her hard. "Anyone would think you're after a retribution fuck.'"

"I'm not."

Why does she lie to me? And try to resist me? I move in, teasing her mouth open with my tongue, expecting her to be defiant for the sake of it, so when she opens up to me and matches my heat and pace, I'm surprised. But not complaining. Never. "You taste delicious, baby," I hum. "What time are you finishing work?"

"Six," she gasps.

"Come straight to The Manor and bring your files so we can finalize the orders for the new rooms." She's in for another surprise. I can't wait to show her *our* new room. Holding a finger up for her to see, I slowly take it to the control on the window, like…look. *This is how to operate the windows.* I let it down, close the door, and lean in. She's so indignant. "I love you."

"I know." She starts the car, scanning the dashboard. She'll get to grips with it soon enough and never look back.

"Have you spoken to Patrick yet?" I ask, knowing the answer, of course. She only woke up half an hour ago. I'm just reminding her.

"Move my car," she orders shortly, evading my question.

"I'll take that as a no." I grin to myself. "You'll speak to him today."

"Move my car."

"Anything you want, lady."

She takes the steering wheel and looks around the interior. "Where the hell am I going to park this thing?"

That *thing* practically parks itself. It has sensors everywhere. I take her in as I back away, thinking how dainty she is behind the wheel. "Enjoy," I murmur, going to her Mini and parking it in a visitor's space.

Slipping into my Aston, I drive out, waving my goodbye. I'm too far away to see her expression, but I know she's glowering.

I call my friend at the florist as soon as I'm out of the gates. "Mr. Ward," she sings, thrilled to hear from me. "You've been married for over a week and not sent your wife any flowers. Shame on you."

I cringe. "Let's fix that," I say. "How quickly can you get some across to her office?"

"Ten minutes."

"Make it twenty. I have something I want you to take with the flowers."

"Ohh, what?"

"You'll see."

• • •

My second call of the day goes to Steve Cook. I get no answer. Still. Juliette definitely hasn't passed on my message. I can't blame her. But he also didn't pick up the first time I tried him, or call me back. Again, I can't blame him. He probably thinks I want to slice him open after what he did to Ava. I do. But…he could help me. My third call is to a fertility clinic. I *need* to know.

Ava doesn't—at least not for now.

And if you're a jaffa, will you keep that from her too?

"Does it matter?" I ask thin air. "She obviously doesn't want kids." Maybe that's a conversation we should have. Not now off the back of the recent traumas, but definitely a conversation for the future. Or maybe not, depending on the results of these tests.

"Good morning, Harley Street Fertility Clinic, how can I help you?"

I'm cringing already. "Yes, hi, how would one go about getting tested?"

"I assume you mean sperm tests, sir?"

"Yeah, that."

"We would book an appointment for you to discuss the issue with a consultant and they would advise a plan of action."

"Great. Good."

"We have availability on Friday if that suits. Around one o'clock with Dr. Richie."

"Perfect."

"Let me take some details."

The call takes the rest of the drive to Berkley Square, and I'm absolutely astounded by the number of *initial* questions I have to answer in order to get the appointment. I'm not looking forward to the other questions on the day, which will no doubt include being interrogated on my lifestyle. "See you Friday," I say, seeing a white Range Rover pass, driving shockingly slowly. I chuckle as I slip into a space and get out, crossing the road to the florist and sliding the box onto the counter.

"May I?" she asks, and I wave in prompt for her to help herself. She opens the box and gasps. "Wow."

"Don't lose it, will you?" I say on a mild smile as I dip into my pocket, putting some notes on the counter before backing up.

Florist girl chews the corner of her lip. "I don't suppose you have any friends looking for a younger woman?"

"You cheeky sod. How old do you think I am?"

"Older than your wife."

"I think I might find another florist."

"No, you won't. I'm too prompt for you." She slips the box under the counter, cocking her head. "What should the card say?"

"No card today. Just the flowers and the box." I dip my chin, leveling her with a playful look. "With the watch inside."

"That'll be extra."

I laugh under my breath and leave, frowning as Ava's white Range Rover passes the shop. Is she driving around in circles? I check the time. "Someone's going to be late." Maybe she'll be fired. I hum, slipping my hands into my pockets and crossing the road. Of course, I wouldn't want her to be fired because she'd be upset. But I'd cheer her up. Set her up in business. Make sure she's got everything she needs to be a roaring success. Like an assistant, for example, who would take the pressure off and deal with all the admin work, which would free up some of Ava's time. Less stress, less pressure. And, of course, the less stressed and pressured my wife is, all the better for me too.

Her new Range Rover rounds the corner and I slip into my car, starting it and pulling out, following her. I just catch the back end as she pulls into an underground car park. Guaranteed, she was trying to find a space on the street so she didn't have to tackle the restricted maneuvering spaces in one of London's tight car parks. I chuckle. She'll be fine. Like I said, sensors everywhere.

I indicate and take a left at the bottom of the road, putting my foot down.

But slam down on my brakes when someone on the pavement catches my eye. "What the fuck?" I murmur, turning in my seat to watch her walking up the street. I frown, rubbing at my eyes, opening again and looking in my rearview mirror for her. She crosses the road, her arm in the air. No.

Getting out of my car, I pace after her, my legs breaking into an urgent jog, then into a full-on run, my eyes set on the woman in the road. "Lau…" I fade off, my legs slowing, like my mind and body are telling me to rein myself in, reminding me of the last time I thought I saw her. I grabbed some poor strange woman, gave her the shock of her life. It wasn't Lauren.

She gets into a cab, and it drives off as I stand in the middle of the road watching. My racing heart bangs in my chest, making me rub at it, my scar tingling. What the hell is going on? I back up, eyes on the cab, pulling out my phone and getting Google up. And I wonder, what the hell do I intend on googling? I squint at the screen. Where she went was never divulged, and I didn't care as long as she was out of my life. The police weren't involved, and her family agreed to get her help.

I reach up to my forehead and wipe it, backing up, watching the cab take a corner. I need to find her parents and check she's still locked up, because I feel like I'm losing my fucking mind.

. . .

My drive to The Manor is spent constantly shifting in my seat, checking the surroundings around me, and pushing back my nightmare past. When I pull up, John is getting out of his Range Rover. I stalk past him and go to my office, opening up my laptop, my fingers hovering over the keys. I can't remember their address, and if I did, would they still live there?

"What's up?" John asks.

Should I mention it? I've told Sarah about these episodes, but not John. He'll be sending me to an asylum to join Lauren. "Nothing," I say, retracting my hands from my laptop.

"Niles is here."

"Right."

"Shall I see him in?"

"Yeah." I look across my desk. The mess. "Is the camera fixed?"

"They sorted three first thing this morning. The one by the garages needs replacing, but they don't appear to be in a rush since we're switching security providers."

"Of course," I murmur.

"So did she like it?" John asks.

"What?"

"Her new car. Did she like it?"

"Loves it," I say quietly, every inch of me tingling. Am I losing my mind? "John, I—"

A knock at the door cuts me off and Niles falls into the office, literally, a box being juggled in his arms. He gets his balance, saving the box from toppling, and glances around, obviously looking for someone.

"She's not here," John says flatly, relieving him of the box and setting it on the table between the couches, slipping his shades up onto his forehead.

"Who's not here?" Niles asks.

John rolls his eyes and dips inside the box. "So these are the Ferraris of the sex toy world, huh?" He pulls out a glass butt plug.

"Indeed," Niles says. "The lorry will be here shortly."

"Lorry?"

"With the larger pieces." He dips into the box too and pulls out a gold-handled crop and whips the table. "Spanking benches, love chairs."

Sex, drink, hedonism, women, play, desire, pleasure, dominants, dominatrixes.

Am I losing my mind?

Always.

I get up. "I'm just going to..." I point to the door as John cocks his head. "I just need—" I look out of the window, to the grounds of my manor. "Some fresh air," I say, walking out of my office in a bit of a daze. I pass through the summer room, looking around the vast space, at the couches set out, at the curtains draped at the windows, the doors lining one wall. The tennis courts. The glass house with the pool.

The rooms upstairs, the communal room.

It's all always been here, but I feel like I'm looking at it differently. The flowers in the vase on the table are being replaced as I pass. Not callas. Stepping outside, I breathe in deep and take the steps, stopping at the bottom and casting my eyes around the vast estate. It's so beautiful. But so wasted. No one enjoys the grounds of The Manor, only what the inside rooms offer. I approach the fountain, laughing under my breath when I notice a cherub is holding his less-than impressive dick. The irony. I circle the stone piece, counting another five chubby angels. All holding their dicks. And never have I noticed that the water comes from their cocks. This isn't irony. This is Uncle Carmichael.

Backing away, I turn and walk. I don't run. I just walk. I walk every inch of the grounds, taking in every tiny thing. I see things I've never noticed before. Trellising up one side of a wall, roses climbing it. A stone pot carved with fleurs-de-lis that's had a few cigarettes stubbed out in it. Some steppingstones through a nearby flowerbed.

I carry on back to the front of The Manor, starting down the tree-lined driveway, the gravel crunching beneath my dress shoes. When I make it to the first two elm trees, one on either side of the driveway, I turn and look up at The Manor. The bay windows, the bay trees lining the face of the building, the huge limestone bricks that make up the structure. The glossy black front door, the gold knocker that never gets knocked. It sparkles. Who polishes that every day?

I continue, passing under the trees, being sporadically hit with bullets of sunlight through the branches, until I make it to the closed gates. Taking hold of two bars, I look through onto the country road outside. How many times have I passed through these gates? Entered my haven?

Except, it's not my haven anymore.

I think for a few moments before reaching into my pocket and pulling out the gold embossed business card. Spinning my mobile in my grasp, I start walking back to The Manor, punching in the phone number.

Do it, brother. Do it.

But no matter how hard I try to press down on the dial icon, something is stopping me. Guilt? I wish I could be done with guilt.

The trees above rustle as I walk on, and I squint when a bolt of light shoots through a gap. I shield my eyes, lifting an arm, blinking back the black dots as I slow to a stop. The moment I can see clearly again, I see something else new. A bench. It's set back between two trees halfway down the driveway, tufts of grass climbing up the wooden legs. I let out a short, sharp huff, turning my body toward it. How have I gone so many years not seeing things that are right under my nose?

Wandering over, I lower to the old wood, running my palms over the flaky surface. It could do with a sand and paint. I smile to myself, resting back, taking a moment. Listening to the nature I've never heard before, birds tweeting, squirrels doing acrobats through the branches, the odd fox screaming in the distance. Here at The Manor, I've only ever heard moans of pleasure, seductive laughs, small talk. I look at the card again, tapping it on my knee.

Talk to John.

I get up and pace back to The Manor, pausing at the door for a second to admire the sparkly gold knob. I can see my face it in before I encase it with my hand and push my way inside. I notice the landscape pictures on the walls mounted in heavy, chunky gold frames and move closer. They're not random landscapes. They're of the grounds of The Manor. I laugh under my breath. Carmichael's way of getting members to appreciate the exterior while being on the inside? The only way these pictures would be appreciated is if they were hung on the ceiling of the communal room. I turn, admiring the staircase that sweeps elegantly up to the first floor. The round table in the center on the entrance hall that I've only ever seen a vase of flowers on.

John appears from the summer room. Stops. Looks me up and down. "Drink?" I ask, motioning to the bar. His raised brows are warranted as he follows me in and perches on a stool. I round the bar, getting us a water each.

"Have you thought anymore about Sarah?" he asks, wrapping his sausage fingers around the glass when I slide it across to him.

Not really. I've had other things on my mind. "You mean since I said a clear *no* to her yesterday?" I remain on the other side of the bar, lifting an eye to look at him. "You heard that, right?"

"I heard."

But he's still hoping. "I don't know if my marriage will sustain it, John."

He nods, thoughtful. "She's sorry, you know that."

"Yeah, I know that." Whether that be because she's lost everything or not, I don't know. "She wanted to see Ava. Apologize."

"If anyone needs to talk to Ava about this, it's you."

"Oh, I know," I say, taking some water. "But we're just back on track, John, and I'm not sure I want to rock the boat." I pull out the card and slide it onto the bar.

John looks down at it. "What's that?"

"A card."

"I can see it's a card." He pushes the tip of his index finger into the cardboard and drags it towards him, removing his shades with the other hand, reading it, silent. Then he exhales and pushes it back.

"Well?" I ask.

"Well, what?"

"He said he wanted to buy The Manor."

"I know.

I stand up straight. "What do you mean, you know?"

"I mean what I say, and I said, I know. He manages the property acquisitions for a luxury leisure company."

"Wh—" I snap my mouth shut as John dips his chin, drumming his fingers on the bar. "You saw him loitering too?"

"I saw him," John confirms.

"And what did you say?"

"I said the owner was unobtainable at that moment in time, because he was."

"Where was he?"

"Barricaded in his office drinking and fucking his way out of a happy ever after."

I inhale, the sting real. "You didn't tell me?" That was weeks ago.

"Because you've been trying to get back on track since, and I didn't want to hurt that little brain of yours more."

I huff. Cheeky fucker. My brain in fine. *Not pickled.* It's my reproductive system that's the problem. "What do you think?"

"I think you should talk to them."

I cough over my surprise. "You do?"

"Yeah, I do." He smiles and it's not a smile you see on John much. Mild. Knowing. "You've outgrown The Manor, Jesse. It no longer serves a purpose for you."

"But Carmichael." I round the bar and lower to a stool, my legs struggling to hold me up.

"What about him?"

"Well, it was *his* life."

"And he's dead, Jesse." He shrugs his colossal shoulders. "You're not dead."

"But what would *you* do if there was no manor?"

"Me?" He smiles, and it's precious. "I'd have a fucking life beyond worrying about you, motherfucker."

I laugh, but my throat closes up too. *Shit.* Are we actually having this conversation? "So we talk to them?"

"Sure," he says, easy as that. "Hear what they have to say. It can't hurt."

"Can't it?" I ask, feeling a stab of pain in my gut. Oddly, The Manor ruined my life. It also saved it, and the deep attachment, no matter how much I have resented it lately, will be hard to let go of.

John stands, and my eyes lift to accommodate him. "I'm not going to mention Jake or Rosie again," he says quietly. "You know my position. You know I think you should share that part of your life with your wife." A tilt of his head, and I look away. "It's your call, but I think you're making a mistake." His hand lands on my shoulder and rubs. "Let me know what you decide to do about Owen Cutler." He nods at the card on the bar before he leaves, and I pick it up and stare at it as I sit in silence alone.

No Manor.

The glass turns slowly in my grasp on the bar, the water crystal clear as I keep my focus on it, watching the small ripples. Could I really let it go? Give it up?

Jesus, no, what am I thinking? I laugh out loud, shaking my head and that crazy thought away. My mobile brings me back down to earth, and I smile when I see who's calling me, even if I'm more than surprised. "Ava?"

"The gates won't open," she cries, and my heart instantly drops into my stomach at the sound of her distress. What gates? Where the hell is she?

"Hey, calm down," I order, getting up from the stool, my feet moving without me telling them to, instinct taking me out of the bar. "Where are you?"

"I'm at the gates," she yells, hysterical. "I've been pressing the button, but no one's opening them."

She's here?

I'm out on the steps of The Manor looking down the driveway before I know it, even though the gates aren't visible from here. "Ava, stop it." I feel in my pocket for my keys. "You're worrying me." My mind starts to race with reasons for her distress. Has Van Der Haus shown up? Coral, Freja, Sarah? My heart misses a beat. The woman I saw this morning? I take the steps down to the gravel in a few panicked leaps. Was it really her? *Fucking hell.*

"I need you," she whispers on a ragged breath, forcing me to a stunned stop. "Jesse," she sobs. "I need you."

Panic chokes me, my legs breaking out into a sprint to my car as I fumble with the fob. "Pull down the sun visor, baby," I say, breathless with worry. "There're two buttons." I get the door open and fall behind the wheel. "One for the gates to Lusso, the other for The Manor gates." Slamming the Aston into gear, I pull off, tossing my phone on the passenger seat when it connects to Bluetooth. "Ava?" I say when I get no reply. "Ava, talk to me?" I can hear noises, banging and...sobbing. *Jesus Christ.* "Ava?" The steering wheel in one hand, my other raking through my hair, I race toward the gates. "Ava, please, talk to me." A stressed sweat dampens my forehead, her cries so loud I can hear them over the roar of my engine. "I'm coming, baby." I see her Range Rover in the distance, coming at me at speed. The brakes screech, she skids to a stop, and I watch in horror as she dives out of the car and runs toward my Aston. What the fucking hell has happened?

I slam my foot on the brakes and get out, using the top of the door as leverage to push off, sprinting to her, adrenaline feeding my urgency. Her body collides with mine, my arms pulling her in, holding her, hugging her hard. "Jesus, Ava."

"I'm sorry," she sobs, hardly able to talk through her shakes, her arms clinging to me tightly, grappling at my back, as if she wants to crawl into me.

"What's happened?"

"Nothing," she breathes into my collar. "I just needed to see you."

I stare down at the ground in disbelief. "Fucking hell, Ava." I try to wrestle her out of my body, but her hold is fierce. Unmoving. "Please, explain," I beg, my mind spinning with endless reasons for her state, none of them particularly pleasant. "Ava?"

"Can we go home?" she asks, her words broken over her constant jerks.

She needs me. *Just* needs me. I know this woman inside out. Yes, I know she needs me, but this? "No," I grate. "Not until you tell me why the fuck you're in such a state." I use brute force to pry her hold away from my back, putting her at arm's distance and checking her over. For what? Wounds? "What's going on?" Anger is overtaking my worry.

Her body convulses when she lets out a gasped sob, her eyes releasing a steady stream of tears down her cheeks. "I'm pregnant."

Something enters by body so fast, some kind of force, I jolt violently.

"I lied to you," she sobs quietly, following it up with an apology.

"What?" I whisper, stepping back. No. She's *not* pregnant. The doctor confirmed it. She's *not* pregnant. I'm shooting blanks. She went out and got absolutely obliterated on Friday night. Kissed another man! I've fucked her hard and wildly since. *So* hard and wild.

She *can't* be pregnant.

"You make me so"—her breathing's shaky, strained—"mad." She can't even look at me, her gaze directed at her feet. Disgrace is oozing off her. "You make me mad, and then you make me so happy."

I make her mad? I make her mad, so she lied to me? And I can't even feel any shame for my thought process, because my lies have always been to make her happy. This lie? She told it to intentionally make me sad. She told this lie in a mean fit of revenge. "I didn't know what to do," she whispers.

"Fuck," I blurt in disbelief, holding my head with both hands, staring at her wilting frame. "Ava, are you trying to get me sectioned?" I have to look away from her, can't bear to see her looking so pitiful. I also can't bear the cold, hard fact that she's been so deceitful about something she absolutely knows I want and need. "Are you fucking with my mind, because I really don't need this, lady." I laugh. It's a cold laugh. Or...wait. Has she just found out? Was it a faulty test at the doctor's office? Did she do another? Maybe she *didn't* lie to me. "I've just gotten my head around you *not* being pregnant, and now you are?"

"I always have been."

My God. No. How could she? I don't even know what to say. She's pregnant, always has been? I knew it. I fucking *knew* it! "When were you going to tell me?" I ask, staring at the woman I love, unable to convince myself to comfort her.

"When I accepted it."

So she's accepted it? Does that mean she's happy about it? Fuck, my head feels like it's going to fall off. "We're having a baby?" I whisper. I think I'm in shock, because nothing in me is moving except my lips, emotion clogging my throat. Is this another chance? Is this really happening?

Yes, Daddy. I'm happy for you. The universe had other plans for me.

My weak knees give up on me, folding, taking me down to the gravel, and Ava is suddenly in front of me, her watery eyes scanning mine as she pulls me into her body and hugs me.

Life.

More life than I ever dreamed I was worthy of having again.

Ava's. Our child's.

And mine.

I lift my dead arms and hold her, squeezing my eyes closed,

squeezing all of the tears out. This is my weakest moment. From now, I'm nothing but strength.

"I'm so sorry," she sobs against my neck, her tears trickling down my skin past the collar of my shirt, as I silently stare at the gates of The Manor past her.

And hold onto her tighter.

Another chance.

Another life.

Chapter 17

The ride home is silent. I expect if I was even remotely with it, I'd sense it's uncomfortable, but I'm not. Nowhere close. I never once considered how I would actually feel to have it confirmed Ava's carrying my child. Our child. Not really. I think I probably imagined, but never truly considered the reality of it. And hearing her say the words *I'm pregnant*? It's like a deluge of emotions have drowned me—every emotion imaginable. The most prolific?

Disbelief.

I'm confused when we walk in and find Cathy. Then my mind reboots, and I remember it's early afternoon. Ava should be at work. I should be killing time waiting for six o'clock when I can follow her back to our bubble. But today, we're here, and I honestly can't remember anything before her heartbreaking call. I shake my head and look down at my hands. My keys and Ava's bag in one, Ava's hand in the other.

I release my hold of her, feeling her look up at me, and set my keys on the table.

"Is everything okay?" Cathy asks, the caution in her tone screaming. I must look like I've seen a ghost. I feel oddly vacant, like I'm not sure how I'm supposed to react, feel, or be, all the emotions swirling around, mixing things up. I look at Ava's bag in my grasp again, frowning as I pass it to her. "Boy?" Cathy prompts.

"Everything is fine," I reply, though I know it doesn't appear so, and despite not being able to look at Ava, I know she won't seem okay either. "Ava's not feeling too well." My hand lifts of its own volition and encourages her toward the stairs. I need a moment alone. I never dreamt I would ever feel like that when Ava's around me. Never alone.

She resists my light push into her back, her worried eyes looking back at me as she accepts her bag. "Are you coming?" she asks, but I still can't look at her. I'm scared about what I'll see. My wife. A liar. She knowingly set out to hurt me. It just doesn't compute.

"I'll be up in a minute," I say, my throat rough and quiet. "Go." She's hesitant and unsure, but she slowly walks away, having a brief moment with Cathy. I don't know what to say. All I can hear is my inner mind telling me this isn't true. That I've heard things. That Ava's not pregnant, that she's going to scream at me at any moment that she hates me, that I want a baby more than I want her. I know that's crossed her mind before. I know she's wondered why I stole her pills.

And I know I should give her some context and work hard to make her see I've not done this on a whim.

I frown to myself as she takes the stairs, constantly looking back at me.

"Jesse, for the love of God," Cathy says. "Will you please speak?"

Blinking, I give Cathy my eyes. She recoils. "I'm fine," I say robotically. "Really."

"Well, you don't look it, boy." She comes to me, placing a palm on my forehead. "You said Ava was unwell. It's you who looks it."

I take her hand and force a smile. "I'm okay."

Her old face wrinkles, looking doubtful. "I put your peanut butter in the fridge."

"Take the rest of the day off."

She nods, but it's reluctant, unfastening her apron and going to the kitchen as I slip our keys onto the table by the door. She appears moments later with her carpet bag. "Are you sure, boy? I could stay. Cook for you and Ava."

"I've got it." I put an arm around her shoulders and walk her to the door. "We'll see you in the morning."

"Okay. Okay, boy." She reaches up with her lips to kiss my cheek, making me dip so she can reach. "Be well, now."

I see her out and face the penthouse. What the fuck is going on in my head? I just don't know what to say to Ava. I realize I asked for this. But the process from then to now, everything that has happened in between, it's got me good. She left me because I took her pills. And now I realize, she left me because I had achieved what I set out to do.

Secure our future. Or, as Ava would say, trap her.

But does she feel trapped now? And is that why she left? She got drunk, knowing she was carrying our baby. *Unacceptable.* But she was at a loss. I've been there. Am hardly in a position to judge.

Fuck.

I cover my face with my hands and drag them down, exhaling, my mind bending.

What should I do?

Scream, shout, yell?

No.

I call Peterson and tell him Ava's come home because she's unwell, hanging up before he can think to question me, then I take the stairs slowly and enter the bedroom. She's sitting on the bed, looking lost and nervous. It's exactly how I feel myself. Lost for words and nervous about how this is going to pan out. So I will do what I need to do to bring us both together and put us back in our bubble. She's carrying our baby. She's holding our future within her. Everything up to this point doesn't matter. She's always been precious to me—my redeemer and my ruin. Now she's beyond that. She is literally holding my life in her hands.

I go into the bathroom and take a moment to look around the space where we first came together. How far gone is she? How many weeks? I turn on the tap and pour some bath soak in, taking extra towels off the shelf and putting them on the warmer before placing the sponge on the side of the enormous tub. Will we need to move? Getting a pram and all other kinds of baby paraphernalia up to the penthouse daily will be a pain. I sweep my hand under the tap, testing the water. Too cold. I adjust the tap, making it warmer. She'll have to start taking it easy. No more ten-hour work days. I whip up the water to stimulate more bubbles. And what will people think? The wedding was just over a week ago. I laugh to myself. I couldn't give two fucks, but I give endless fucks that Ava *will* care. Her mother, her father, her brother. What about outside space? We'll need a garden with a child.

I still, staring at the frothing water. The Manor. So much outside space, a whole fucking park on the grounds. And yet still wasted. I reach into my inside pocket and pull out my phone, punching a text out to John.

Let's meet them and talk.

Breathing in, I bite down on my lip, feeling my whole universe pivoting again. I felt the same way the day Ava O'Shea walked into my office. "Fuck." I delete the message. She's in the next room, alone, unsure, and I'm in here trying to wrap my head around something I wanted all along. I turn off the tap and go back into the bedroom, my heart breaking when she looks up at me. She's holding her breath.

Pensive, unsure. So fucking guilty.

Easing her to her feet, I silently undress her, smiling mildly at the watch on her wrist as I remove it, then her necklace, finishing with her underwear. I dip, pick her up, and take her to the tub, lowering her in slowly. "Is the water okay?" I remain fully dressed outside the tub, removing my jacket, and rolling up my sleeves under her watchful, confused eyes.

"It's fine." She studies me as I wet a sponge and start washing her.

"Aren't you getting in?" she asks.

"Let me look after you." I can't get in. I don't know what I'm supposed to be doing right now, so I'm just following my instinct. Looking after her.

And, apparently, Ava isn't okay with that. She turns in the water, feeling at my blank face, cupping my cheeks. "I need you closer than this." They're the golden words. "Please."

I can see so much remorse in her brown eyes. So much worry. She can't possibly think I'd leave her. *Like she left me.* I look at the sponge in my hand. At my fist wrapped around it, my wedding ring shining. How long has she been pregnant? Have I caused any damage pounding into her like a jack hammer? I sigh. Did I honestly think this would settle me, because I can feel anxiety creeping in.

Get closer to her.

The sponge hits the water with a wet slap as I rise and unbutton my shirt. Has Ava done any damage with her Friday night escapades? I drop the white material to the bathroom floor and bend, removing my shoes. I, more than anyone, know how fragile life is. This little person growing inside of my wife is depending on us to protect them. Fucking, drinking. I push my trousers off with my boxers, feeling Ava watching me go through the motions.

Shifting forward to make space for me behind her, she watches as I lower into the water and settles when I encase her with my arms, pulling her back to my chest. I don't get the overwhelming rush of calm by having her attached to me like I normally do. My heartbeats don't get stronger. It's fucking odd, as if a higher power won't allow me to absorb this news or truly grasp what is happening right now.

Ava settles for only a few seconds before she's moving again, breaking away and putting herself on my lap. Facing me. Facing *this*.

It's a gesture to assure me she's not burying her head anymore. Her hands feel for mine, our fingers threading and feeling, my mind a mash-up of absolutely nothing and absolutely everything.

"Why did you lie to me, Ava?" I ask, studying my wedding ring as she slowly spins it.

"I was scared," she whispers, peeking up at me. "I'm *still* scared."

"Of me," I say quietly. "You're scared of me." I can't blame her. I'm scared of me too.

"I'm scared of how you'll be." Her voice has become strong but remains soft. She doesn't know it, but I appreciate her honesty. It's not often Ava speaks her truths unless forced to.

"You mean even more crazy?"

She nods mildly, her chest expanding. Taking in courage? "It wasn't even definite, and you were treating me like a priceless object."

That's because she *is* priceless. But there's more to it. I narrow my eyes on our joined hands, wondering. "You also think I might love our child more than you," I say, feeling her reaction through her body and nothing else.

"Would you?" Her question is laced with uncertainty, and it breaks my heart. Why wouldn't she think that? After everything I've done to get us to this point, of course that thought would linger. I'm a thirty-eight-year-old man who, prior to Ava, had one priority.

Me. Only me.

Because I'd lost everyone I loved. I didn't look after myself. Didn't care for myself. Hated myself.

But as Ava's husband? I'm a work in progress, granted, but I'm better with Ava. It's fact. And my best years were as Rosie's daddy. I have this amazing opportunity to have my own family. A unit for me to care for, provide for, love. Of course I'm going to be protective of it. Passionate. But for Ava to think I could love something more than her? Crazy. She's the crux of the goodness in me. The reason for me to breathe, and the whole reason for me to love again. She's my fucking hero.

Reaching for her hand, I bring it to my chest and place it in the center. "Do you feel that?" I ask, smiling gently as she watches with interest and curiosity. "It was made to love you, Ava." Her eyes blink a few times, her throat pulsing with a swallow. *Don't cry, baby. I'm barely holding it together.* But I have to say this. I need her to know my love is *not* conditional. That if she could never give me kids, it wouldn't change how I feel about her. I'd be devasted, of course, but as I've thought before, Ava's my beginning and my end. Whatever comes in between is simply part of the journey. This is about love. Peace. "For too long it was useless, redundant, not required." *Dead*. "Now it's gone into overdrive," I whisper, smiling softly when her lip starts to wobble. She's hearing me. Listening. Understanding. "It swells with happiness when I look at you." I push her palm into my chest harder. "It splinters with pain when we fight." She looks as overwhelmed as I feel right now. "And it beats wildly when I make love to you," I add, now squeezing her hand. "Maybe I go overboard with my love, but that's never going to change. I'll love you this fiercely until the day I die, baby. Children or not."

Her shoulders fold in, her torso shrinking with an exhale. "I never want to be without your fierce love."

Well, that's handy, because it's endless. I pull her close, as close as I can get her. Her watery eyes dart across my face. I've seen need in my wife before. But now? It's powerful. "You won't be. I'll never stop loving you hard. It'll only get harder because every day that passes with you is another day of memories with you. Memories I'll treasure, not memories I want to forget. My mind is being filled with beautiful images of us, and they are replacing a history that lingers. They're chasing away my past, Ava. I need them. I need *you*."

"You have me." She's half swooning, half taken aback, her touch on my shoulders gentle but firm.

"Don't ever leave me again." I don't mean for it to come out as an order, and yet it does. So I soften my demand with a kiss. "It hurt so badly." I'm hauled up, her strength surprising, my big body wrapped in her dainty arms tightly.

"I'm crazy in love with you," she whispers in my ear, making me smile. "Fiercely too. That's never going to stop, not ever." These are the words I needed to hear from Ava ever since she walked out on me—*on our marriage*—hours after we said vows. I can taste her forgiveness. I can taste our forever. Her lips on my ear makes my body shudder and my dick finally join the moment. *Down, boy.* "End of," she adds.

End of. She's so cute. "Good." I find her mouth and kiss her deeply for the first time in what feels like years. "My heart is swelling," I mumble as I lay us back down, Ava sprawled all over me, her breasts slipping over my skin. With all my might, I try to push the blood back, not wanting this to turn sexual, if only to prove that we can communicate without sex, even if neither of us are talking right now. It's perfect. Utterly perfect.

I open my eyes, maintaining my tongue's soft strokes through her mouth, wanting to see just how lost she is. So lost, completely in this kiss as I trace light hands across her back, humming my contentment, nipping at her lip before plunging into her mouth again.

And we go until my tongue aches and my cock aches harder. "Let me bathe you," I whisper, slowing my mouth, Ava following my pace until our kiss comes to a natural stop.

"But I'm comfy," she grumbles, burrowing deep into my neck.

"We can be comfy in bed, and you can fall asleep in my arms where you're supposed to be." Let's keep up this closeness.

"It's not even mid-af—" She stills against me for a brief second before she's flying up in a panic. "I've not gone back to work," she blurts, reality crashing into her.

For Christ's sake. Work? She thinks of work *now*? I take her wrist and pull her back down. "I've taken care of it," I say. "Unravel your knickers, lady."

"When?" It's not fair, but it bugs the shit out of me that my wife is answerable to another man. And I don't care how chauvinistic that makes me sound.

"When I brought you home." I put her between my legs and start soaking the sponge and squeezing it across her back. Would she agree to let me do this every day? Bathe her and wash her? Do all the things for her? Her tummy will grow, her mobility will suffer. I remember when Mum was expecting Amalie. Jake and I were only six, but I remember it vividly. She struggled, first with sickness—the reason for Ava's aversion to my dick in her mouth recently is now confirmed beyond all doubt—her ankles got puffy, she was *so* tired, and getting up and down the stairs became a two-person job. She's going to *really* need me. And I can't wait.

"What did you tell him?" she asks, calm and accepting.

"That you're ill." But he'll soon have the truth.

"He'll be sacking me soon." Ava's head hangs heavily. Her words were without the despondency I would have expected. Is she now considering the merits of working for herself too? I can only hope. The seed was planted long ago. I thought it was dead in the ground, but perhaps...

I chew on my lip, discarding the sponge. Can she still be Little Miss Independent when she's carrying our baby? Because surely I have some say in where my baby goes. Somehow, I don't think Ava will agree, even after today when she's been openly passionate about needing me. Which, come to think of it, is why? Why now, after all these weeks, has Ava come to her senses, opened up, and confessed she's pregnant? What happened to instigate such an emotional confession? I don't know, but whatever it was, I'm grateful. "Come on," I say, sure I might rub her away with this sponge if I wash her anymore. I stand up and reach under her arms, lifting her to her feet and stepping out. She has a small ironic smile on her face as I pick her up and place her on the bath mat, quickly wrapping her in a towel. I ignore the smile. I can feel the cause between my legs, growing, yelling for some attention. It's not happening yet, but when it does, it will be gentle. And another cause for a debate. I have a feeling there will be many discussions in the coming weeks while we navigate exactly how this is going to work. How we get through this pregnancy without me suffering a cardiac arrest or Ava killing me in frustration. But she can't kill me. She needs me. I roll my eyes to myself. *She needs me.* Maybe today, but as soon as I make a...request, that need will vanish and defiance will bounce back. It's going to be fun.

But first, I need to do something.

It's been a roller coaster, and I feel like it's just slowed down long enough for me to take a breath and brace myself for the loops on the horizon. I lift Ava onto the counter and peck her lips. "Stay there."

"Where are you going?" she calls, her frown following me out of the room.

"Just wait." I shudder, chills catching my wet skin as I hurry across the bedroom and enter the dressing room. I scratch around in drawers and behind clothes. Nothing. Where the hell are they? I moved them to here a couple of weeks ago. Definitely. Cathy found them in the laundry room, so I moved them to a cupboard in the kitchen, then moved them to the dressing room. "Ah." I go to the end wardrobe where my suits hang and get on my knees, feeling at the back. "Bingo." I pull out the paper bag and go back to the bathroom.

"What's that?" Ava asks, eyeing the bag cautiously. I'm nervous. How can I explain what I need her to do?

I gnaw on my lip, opening the bag and holding it out for her to look, and she reluctantly peeks inside. "You don't believe me?" she blurts, injured, holding her towel closer protectively.

I knew she'd draw the most negative conclusion. It's a habit of hers. "Of course I do." But she's done one test. Just one. And I didn't see it. Forgive me, but the past few weeks have been a seesaw of *is she? isn't she?* and after everything, I'm feeling like I want to see it for myself. *Need* to.

"Then why do you have a paper bag with…" She takes it and upends it, sending the boxes falling into the sink. She then proceeds to count them while I watch on. I could have told her how many are there. Sixteen. "Why do you have eight pregnancy tests?" she asks.

I lift my shoulders on a half-hearted shrug and push the box she's holding aside. "There are two in a box."

"Sixteen?"

"Sometimes they don't work properly." I've heard stories before, women who have had false positives and false negatives. Again, I'm taking no chances. I'll also be arranging a scan tomorrow. "They're just backups." I get one out and hold it up. "You have to pee on this bit here," I say, pointing to the end. "Look."

"I did one at the doctor's, Jesse," she moans, exasperated. "I know how they work. Why won't you take my word for it?"

"I do take your word for it," I assure her. The pregnancy test's word, however, I don't trust, which is ironic because my wife is the one in this situation who's been misleading.

And you haven't?

I still, holding back my scowl. I should have known Jake would have something to say during this conversation.

Fuck off.

No.

"I need to see it for myself," I say to Ava's indignant face. She can't protest and she knows it, but rather than tell her what she knows and risk her sass coming out to play, I give her a cute smile and wide, hopeful eyes.

"How long have you had these?" she asks, softening.

Yeah, not telling her that. Her open palm hovers between us, and I grin at it.

"Give," she orders.

I'm thrilled. Delighted. The dynamics are going exactly the right way already. She huffs and puffs about it, but she slips off the vanity unit and goes to the toilet. I throw a towel around my waist.

"Some privacy, please?" she says.

Absolutely not. I know her body on the deepest level. It's about to go deeper, so she'd better get used to it. "I'm staying."

"I'm not peeing on a stick in front of you. No way, Ward."

Yes, way, and to demonstrate how passionate I am about her peeing on the stick while I'm in the room, I sit myself on the floor. "Move me." I cock a cocky brow and don't bother covering myself when the towel slips open.

"I'll use another bathroom." She moves past me, and I reach for her ankle, stopping her. "Jesse," she yelps, trying and failing to walk on, my impressive, *heavy* frame hanging on to her.

"Humor me, baby," I plead. "Please."

Ava looks back, sighs, and sags. "Can you at least turn around?"

Is she shy? "No." I stand and pull my towel away. Ava blinks, her attention captured and, hopefully, she's distracted from her issue, which isn't even an issue. I fucked her up the arse the second time I fucked her, for the love of God, which happened to be on the same day I fucked her for the very first time. And *now* she's shy?

Let the battle commence. "Does this make you feel better?" I ask, arms out, showcasing myself for my wife to enjoy. And she really enjoys.

"No." She sighs dreamily, head tilted. "That just distracts me."

Mission accomplished. Now let's get on with this. I want to celebrate. Tell the world.

Tell Ava about me?

My eyes narrow without telling them to. For someone who supposedly wants me to be happy, Jake ain't half trying his best to piss all over my bonfire.

"You wield that physique unfairly," Ava grumbles, trying and failing to hide the lust in her eyes. I'm here for it, but before we get to celebration sex, we have sticks to pee on.

"Of course I do," I reply on a cheeky smile, eyeing her towel-covered body. "It's one of my best assets." I grab Ava's towel and whip it away, inhaling my appreciation. Fuck me, it gets me every time. Made for me. All of it. Every handful, curve, and dip. "It comes a close second to this one." And soon all of *this one* will be growing. More to love. More for me to take care of. I bet she can't wait. "Just perfect."

"You won't say that when I'm fat and swollen." Pouting, she peeks down at her perfect body. "And if you say there will be more of me to love, I might divorce you." Her towel is quickly missing from my hands and covering my best asset again. *Really*?

"Don't say the word *divorce*." I walk her to the toilet and position her ready to sit. "If it makes you feel better, I'll eat for two too." Two jars of peanut butter a day instead of one.

"Promise you won't leave me when I'm unable to reach your cock with my mouth because my belly is in the way."

Laughter rises and bursts out loudly. "I promise, baby," I say around my amusement. We'll find a way, and hopefully Ava gets past this aversion she's developed recently to my dick being in her mouth. "Now, let's pee on some sticks."

She shifts the towel and sits, and I grin as I crouch, her playfully narrowed eyes following me down. "Do you want to stick your hand in the loo again?" she asks around a smile. "I could mark you officially."

Another bark of laughter erupts and makes me lose my balance, my arse hitting the floor with a thud. She's on fire with the humor, and it's fucking wonderful. My muscles are mush, hampering my attempts to get up. "Ava, baby." I chuckle, planting my hands onto the floor, fighting my way up. "I love you so fucking much." I hear the steady flow of her peeing, her hand between her legs. So romantic. I lean up and kiss away her wrinkled, mortified face.

"There," she declares, pulling her hand out from between her legs and holding the stick up. I quickly take it, not fazed in the least, and reach for another, putting it in her hand. "What?" she asks.

"I told you"—I ignore her questioning face—"sometimes they don't work." I push the stick toward her, hoping she's not completely empty. "Quick."

She groans, exasperated, but does as she's bid, her face straining to squeeze out more pee. She hands it over, and I hand her another. "Jesse." She laughs. "Come on."

"One more," I say, helping her along, removing the cap.

"For God's sake." She whips it from my hand and gets to work as I pop the caps back on the others, wondering if I can squeeze another out of her. By the sound of her dripping pee and her pink cheeks from the strain, I'm thinking not. "That's it," she says, watching me, probably concluding—correctly—what I'm thinking. Okay, I'll flex, since she's flexing too. I'll save the other tests for another time. She gives me test number three and wipes herself, and I go to the vanity unit and lay each one next to each other, tweaking them, making sure they're level and straight. My eyes run across each one over and over again, as I pout, watching carefully. How long does this take? How accurate is it? Scan. I should sort out a scan. I'll do that tomorrow. How many weeks are we? A book. I need a book that's going to help me help Ava. I'll order one. And a midwife. We should see a midwife. Maybe I'll hire one full-time.

How long do these damn tests take to show a result?

I scan them again, bent over, watching closely for any change in the little window.

"Are you okay there?" Ava asks.

"I think they're broken." I register her next to me, looking at me, not the tests. She'd better drink some water. "We should do some more." I move about an inch before my arm jars, Ava pulling me back.

"It's been thirty seconds," she says over an amused chuckle. Seconds? It feels like I've been bent over this unit for an hour. "Here, wash your hands." She guides my hands under the tap, turning it on and rubbing at them. I keep my eyes on the tests. Is that a letter I can see? I crane my neck, scowling when I note it's a shadow.

"It's been longer than that." For fuck's sake, they're definitely broken. "Much longer."

"No, it hasn't. Stop being neurotic." She releases me and mirrors my bent frame, and I look out the corner of my eye, well aware she's making fun of me.

She grins. It's beautiful. She's about to have it confirmed beyond all doubt that she is carrying my child, and she's grinning. I don't know what's changed, but I'm fucking grateful. "I'm not neurotic."

"Of course you're not." Her dark hair falls over her shoulders, skimming her nipples. How the hell am I still standing here and not carrying her to the bed?

"Are you taking the piss out of me, lady?"

"Not at all." Her lips twitch. "My Lord."

She's got that right. Her Lord, her God, her everything.

What the fuck is wrong with these tests?

This is ridiculous. If she's pregnant, the baby will be here before these fucking tests tell us she's on her way. I inhale subtly. *She?* Would I get the privilege of having a little girl again? Would I—

My thoughts pause when I notice a change in the window of the first test. I lean in more, blink my eyes so I don't have to blink them again anytime soon. Is that a P?

I feel every muscle and limb stiffen, my lungs inflating, my breath held. Is that an R? I quickly check the other two tests. More letters. *Fucking hell.* I stare, my eyes burning, not daring to blink, as a whole word slowly forms before my eyes.

Pregnant.

I snap my eyes to the second.

Pregnant.

My heart bucks, and I quickly check the last test.

Pregnant.

Jesus.

Pregnant, pregnant, pregnant.

We're pregnant.

My whole body starts to shake, and I absolutely cannot control it. *Pregnant.* Swallowing, struggling for air, I turn my wide eyes onto Ava. She's still bent over too. Smiling mildly, watching me process what I'm seeing.

Pregnant.

"Hi, Daddy," she breathes, her lip definitely wobbling. Like my body. *Daddy.*

"Fuck…me." I asked for this. Prayed for this. Manipulated everything for this to happen. And now it has? "I can't breathe." Or stand. My legs fail me, and I crumble to the floor, breathless, full of so many more emotions, I'm not sure where to start sorting them out.

"Are you okay?" Ava's quiet, unsure question wakes me from my trance, and I look at her. I don't see just Ava, though. I see…my family. I see a second chance. I see an opportunity to make right what went so horribly wrong.

I see the chance to make Rosie proud. But it fucking kills me that my little girl won't be here to see me return to the man she made me before I lost myself.

The emotions suddenly unravel and overpower me, and my eyes well, a mixture of pure elation and sadness devastating me, but for Ava, I must be happy. Stable. *Fucking hell.* I smile through my grief and get up before she sees my tears, grabbing her and hauling her into my body, hiding my face in her neck, holding her tightly.

"What's the matter with you?" she gasps, taken aback, as I walk into the bedroom and put her on the bed, removing her towel—skin on skin, I need skin on skin—and laying myself on her lower body, my face level with her stomach. Fuck, I can't get ahold of these fucking tears.

Understandable, Daddy.

You've got this, bro.

Shit.

I stare down at Ava's stomach, marveling at the wonder of life growing. Life created by me. It's hard to accept, hard to swallow, when I've spent years thinking I'm only capable of *taking* life. Ruining it. I gaze up at my wife—how fucking lucky I am to call her that—and am greeted by a mixture of contentment and concern. "I love you," I say softly. I'm not only speaking to Ava. I'm speaking to Rosie. To Jake. "*So* much."

We know.

Ava's hands work through my wet hair, her body settling. "I know."

I have to kiss her stomach. Feel it. And, God, it feels incredible. It's a new addition to my need list. This. Every day. "And I love you too." My baby who I'm yet to meet. I kiss my way all over Ava's belly, excited that with each day her tummy grows, it'll need another kiss to cover it in kisses. I might need to quit work. I'm not sure she'll appreciate me following her around with my mouth attached to her, fetching everything she needs fetching, carrying everything she needs carrying, including her. Driving her, feeding her. The list of responsibilities is endless.

I work my mouth over Ava's boobs until my face is level with hers and I'm once again taking in this beautiful, sassy young woman and trying to comprehend that she is mine. "I'll try to be better," I say as she smiles up at me. "With you, I mean. I'll try not to smother you and make you crazy."

"I like you smothering me."

Oh good. So my lips stuck to her all day will be fine? Following her around doing all the things so she doesn't have to will be fine?

"It's the unreasonableness that we need to work on," she adds.

Can my lips stuck to her be considered unreasonable?

"Give me specifics." Because I need to know my limits. I don't want to argue. I want pure bliss. Constantly. So Ava needs to be straight with me, and I need to listen. I don't want to stress her out. Definitely not.

This might be harder than I think.

"You want to know exactly what drives me crazy?" she asks. She's holding on to a laugh. She's laughing because I need it spelled out?

Well, she just said she likes me smothering her. I don't know what the line is between acceptable and unacceptable, so she needs to elaborate. I can't promise I'll accept without question, but I need to have a measure so negotiations can commence. "Yes, tell me. I can't try to control it if I don't know exactly what bothers you." I push my lips to hers before she can laugh at me.

"You treated me too gently," she says, and I still, hitching a brow at her. She noticed that? *Idiot.* Of course she noticed that. "When you thought I was pregnant, you stopped being fierce in the bedroom, and I didn't like it. I want my dominant Jesse back."

"What the hell have I done to you?"

"You're addictive." She shrugs, nonchalant. "And lately I've been having Jesse withdrawal."

Oh? "I've taken you hard lately."

"Yes, but only when you thought I *wasn't* pregnant, and when you thought I was, I had to provoke you into it. I want shock and awe."

Fucking hell. How much shock and how much awe? Because I'm pretty sure her body can't sustain the levels we're used to. Besides, we have plenty of different degrees of fucking. Not all need to be hard. In fact, since I met Ava, I've become rather fond of the more...placid sex. "Don't you like sleepy sex?" She *always* demands it.

My cheeks are suddenly squished in her hands, her smile small and fond. "You won't hurt it, you know."

"It?" I parrot. "Let's get one thing straight, lady. We will *not* be calling my baby 'it'."

"It's hardly a baby at the moment."

It is definitely a baby. *Our* baby. "What is it, then?"

"Well." She pouts, thinking, and it's adorable even if I don't agree. "It's probably more like a peanut."

A peanut? Well, we all know peanuts are one of my most favorite things. That's that settled then. Ava's smile falls. Realization hits.

"Oh no, Ward." She chuckles.

"What?" I give our peanut a little nuzzle with my nose. "It's perfect."

"I am not referring to our baby as *peanut*, end of."

So defiant. It's time for some convincing. Eyeing her hip, I move in, seizing it and massaging teasingly, making her buck and yell. "Stop!" she gasps.

What the fuck am I doing? My clenched fingers are mere inches from her fragile tummy. "Shit." I release her quickly and rub the area, and Ava yells, throwing me a furious scowl.

"What are you doing?" she asks, and for a moment I think she's pissy because I just practically squeezed our peanut to death. Fucking hell, I can't be trusted with life at all.

But then I realize. She's not angry because of that. This is what she's talking about. Acceptable levels of fretting and fussing.

Oh.

"See," she says, arms thrown up in disbelief. "*That* is what I mean." *Yes, darling, I just this second figured that out.* "If you don't reinstate some of your normal behavior soon, I'll be moving to my mum and dad's for the rest of this pregnancy."

I blink, stunned. Is she threatening to leave me again? Ten minutes after we've just found out we're pregnant? What the fuck is she on? Other than hormones, I mean.

"I mean it, Ward," she barks, furious. "All of the fierceness, the rough, the countdowns, and fuckings of various degrees, I want them back." She gathers breath. She's not done? "And I want them now."

Yes, I hear you, because you're fucking shouting. And now she's breathless. Stressed. Don't tell me that's good for the baby. And don't tell me I'm the cause. Fuck, this is going to be a tricky ship to captain.

"Calmed down yet?"

She snorts, in disbelief, I think. I should release a few snorts myself, because she's fucking unbelievable. She wants me to fuck her. All this because she wants me to ram my big cock into her begging pussy. I grin on the inside. *Oh, how you crave me, lady.* I love it. But she's going to have to control herself for a while, and I'm going to have to get creative if I'm going to keep my wife happy and my baby safe.

"That depends on whether any of this is sinking into this thick skull of yours." She pulls my hair.

"Ouch." I chuckle, both at her and at me. Look at us. Listen to us. We're fucking perfect.

I roll over to my back and put my wily wife's legs on either side of my hips, getting us comfortable, me against the pillows, Ava against my thighs. Soon, like this, I'll be able to stick my tongue out and lick her tummy. Can't wait.

I consider her fresh, young face, and I wonder how I can ever love her more. But I know I can, because each day that passes, she gives me more. Teaches me more. "Do you remember when I found you at the bar, when I showed you how to dance?" I ask.

She settles into my legs, laying her hands over mine on her knees. "That was the night I realized I'd fallen in love with you."

"I know because you told me." It was so fucking frustrating, but it was the way it was supposed to be. It was how our story was supposed to be told. "You were drunk, but you still said it." And I will never forget that moment. Or her face.

Because I took a picture.

"Hmm," she hums, stroking over my hands, casual. "Must have been the dancing."

"I know." And the body contact, the feel of me against her, the fact she missed me terribly. "I'm good."

"You're arrogant."

She loves my arrogance, even if it's a front as wide as the Atlantic. "It would seem that I'm a little brighter than my beautiful wife." I slide my hands down her legs to her ankles, smiling at her deep intake of breath to sustain my soft strokes.

"You're *really* arrogant."

"No." I shake my head. "Not this time. This time, I'm just honest."

She cocks her head, and I smile at her curiosity. "You see," I go on, killing that curiosity. "I realized that I was in love with you before then." *Way* before then. In fact, I think if I really consider the events from the day she walked into my office and my life, I fell in love with her on the spot.

"Does that make you cleverer than me?" she asks.

"Yes, it does." Because self-awareness wins. Listening to your heart wins, and considering mine was pretty much dead, I'm winning. "The whole time you were running, I was so frustrated. I was thinking there must've been something wrong with you." Like…was she blind? Could she not see me? "You know, because you wouldn't submit to me."

Why does she look so pleased with herself, like she's achieved what no woman has achieved by resisting me? But as I knew it wouldn't, her self-control didn't last long. "Like the others did," she asks, and I nod. "It was only because I knew I'd get hurt. Even though I didn't know you, it was obvious you"—her lips straighten, her eyes scanning mine—"were experienced."

Isn't it interesting? She's talking about sex. I'm talking about love.

I skate my hands up the backs of her legs. I think we're breaking records. This is the longest time we've been naked without being asleep and *haven't* had sex. And I'm good with it. Not that I'd say no. "When I left you for those four days—"

"Don't." Her contentment falls, sadness dropping into her eyes, and I feel terrible. But I need her to hear this. "Please don't talk about that."

"Just let me explain something," I beg. "It's important." I release her legs and get her closer. So close, she could blink and her lashes would brush mine. "I was so confused by what I was feeling," I explain. "It took that time away from you to piece together exactly what it was. I couldn't work out why I was behaving like a madman. I really did think I was going fucking crazy, Ava." Turns out, I realized I was in love. And that explained everything. Because to me, to love is to lose. And I couldn't lose again. My heart wouldn't take it.

Ava stares at me, struck. I get it. I was struck for days after she walked into my office and my life.

"I spent days three and four reliving every single moment with you," I explain. Day one and two were spent getting over one of the worst hangovers I've ever had, and not only because of the drink. "I replayed them repeatedly until I was torturing myself, so I came to find you. Then you fucking ran again."

She looks apologetic, and she has no reason to. This is on me. I know that. Accept that. And I've paid for that. "Ava, the night you told me you loved me, everything became so fucking clear, but at the same time it was a massive blur." Still is. And the guilt was unbearable. "I wanted you to love me, but I knew you didn't really know me. I knew there was stuff that would make you run again, but I also knew that I belonged to you, and it scared me to fucking death to think that once you started unravelling it all, you'd be off again." Justification. I seem to be a master at it. And I'm still playing that game. Justifying why I've not told her about Rosie or Jake. Yes, there's shame. But there's also so much fucking pain. As strong as it's always been. I don't know if I can face saying the words out loud. Don't know if I can face Ava's reaction. Or sustain the doubt my past might cast. "I couldn't risk it, not after it took me so long to find you." I take a gulp of courage and say what we both know but haven't really discussed. Because she left me just as I feared. "I took your pills that night." And many times after that. But she doesn't need confirmation of what came after in that department. Because…she knows. And right now, her face, blank but soft, tells me she understands that level of crazy.

I kiss her, because I just have to. Kiss her endlessly. "I sat there all night and watched you sleeping, and all I thought about was every reason for you *not* to want me." It was one of the longest nights of my life. "I knew it was wrong to take them, but I saw it as collateral. That's how desperate I was."

She's smiling. I have no clue why, but I'm grateful. "So you don't want a baby?" she asks. "You just want to keep me?"

Why is she asking such stupid questions? I look at her. Like *really* look at her. She's pure bliss. My dark-haired, dark-eyed, olive-skinned piece of heaven, wrapped up in a banging body with a side of sass and a huge heart. A heart, thank God, that's kind and a mind that's understanding. Her perfect nose wrinkles, her eyes willing me on, her lip curving at the corner. *Go on, baby. Smile for me.* And it breaks, her eyes bursting with happiness that I could never measure. She loves that I love her so hard.

"I want everything in the world with you, baby," I whisper, returning her smile. A smile only Ava can draw from me. "And I want it all yesterday."

She nods, albeit mildly. "Thank you for my watch," she says quietly. I know she's not only thanking me for that. And for me, the watch is not just a symbol of how much I love her. How much I want to give her, share with her. It's a symbol of time. And what I have left is all hers. And our peanut's.

"You're more than welcome." I press gently into Ava's lips, before I move in and kiss them like I adore her. Because I do. And now that we've talked, we'll *talk*.

I moan and roll us, getting Ava beneath me, and nudge her legs apart with my knees so she's wide open to me, my mouth still adoring her, her hands all over my back. "Going to ask me to wear a condom?" I mumble around her lips, moving across her cheek to her ear, feeling her hips lifting invitingly.

"Ha...ha," she practically moans, her hands slipping down to my arse and applying pressure.

"Do you want me inside you?"

"Don't ask stupid fucking questions."

"Mouth." I swivel, entering her slowly on a gush of air, instantly dizzy with pleasure, and Ava mumbles some incoherent words, probably curses, her short fingernails sinking into my flesh. "Fuck," I hiss, pulling back and looking down at her. "Give me those eyes."

She blinks them open, and the level of lust, need, want, and love staring back at me would put me on my arse if I was standing. "We're going to be okay," I whisper, starting a slow, steady pump of my hips, half expecting her to encourage something harder and faster. She doesn't. Because in this moment, soft, slow, and steady wins the race.

But Ava gets there first, coming on a shallow gasp, stiffening all over, pulling my throbbing dick deep with the contractions of her muscles.

Am I'm gone, gasping, my head hanging, coming with her.

I remain on my forearms, suspended over her, pulsing, until my shoulders ache from holding myself up. Her stroking hands have slowed on my arse. Her breathing has changed. *She's fallen asleep.* And this is how it should be for the rest of this pregnancy. No drama, no stress, no work pressure, just serenity. She looks so serene. Is it unreasonable to only want her to focus on this pregnancy and us? I wrinkle my nose and dip, gently kissing her cheek. Her eyes open. "Go back to sleep," I order, pulling out of her and smiling when she snuggles down. How I want to stay with her and cuddle. But somehow, even after such a deep conversation—a deep connection and sexual release—I'm not tired. I'm energized. Second chances do that. So I leave Ava to nap—I expect there will be plenty of those in the coming months—pull on some boxers, and head downstairs, collecting some peanut butter on my way to the couch and checking my phone, seeing endless notifications. And a missed call from her brother. I laugh under my breath as I dip and lick. Fuck, I forgot about him. This will be interesting in light of the news we've got to share. And that's exactly why I don't call him back. I can't promise I won't blurt out that Ava's pregnant, and I'm reasonable enough to know that *that* will get me a one-way ticket to the doghouse. So first I call the clinic and cancel my Friday appointment, grinning the whole time—I'm not broken—then I call John back, but before my thumb can dial, my phone rings and Dan's name flashes up on my screen. *Don't answer.*

"Fuck," I curse.

And answer.

Do not mention your peanut, bro.

I smile.

"Hi," Dan says when I give him nothing. "I came to your place today."

"Yeah, sorry about that, something came up." I settle back, taking another suck of my finger. "Why don't we cut out the meet and you just tell me what you want?" I can't help my hostility, but he's the one who set the tone for our relationship.

"I want to apologize."

My eyebrows shoot up so fast, they nearly leave my face and hit the ceiling. "What?" And what is he sorry for, I wonder, because the list is endless. Disrespecting me, disrespecting my wife, upsetting her on her wedding day, telling tales, bitching to Ava's parents, being hostile toward my friends…

"You're going to make me say it?"

"You haven't actually said it. You said you *wanted* to say it."

"I apologize."

He sounds about as sorry as I am. Not sorry. "For what?" I need to shut the fuck up and accept. Get him off my back, but then there's Kate. Sam. This guy has breezed back into town and caused a shitstorm at every turn. And *now* he's sorry? I'm not buying it.

"I was worried about my sister," he says.

And that was before this raging alcoholic barbarian got her pregnant. "And you're not worried now?"

"She obviously loves you."

I hum. *She's pregnant.*

"Look," he goes on. "I'd really like it if we could meet up."

What, for coffee and a chat? *She's pregnant.* I bite my tongue. It's fucking hard. Dan and I will never be best mates, so where the fuck is this going? "You want to meet up?" I'm so fucking curious. It feels like he's got something to share. As have I. *She's pregnant.*

"Yes."

"Right," I say slowly. "I'm a bit busy this week. I'll call you." I hang up and chomp on my lip, my mind racing for a minute before my phone's ringing again. "Ava's pregnant," I blurt to the room, needing to release the buildup of words before I answer to John. I'm not sure how I'm going to tell him. I know I'm in for a royal dressing down, and I'm not in the mood for that now. "Hi," I say when I answer.

"Alive?"

"Very much alive."

"Where did you go?"

"Just a small something to deal with."

"Ava's brother showed up."

"Did you let him in? Offer him tea? A tour?"

"No, but he was quite curious about the truckload of sex furniture that showed up."

"Oh fuck."

"It's fine," John says. "I diverted him."

"He just called me. I was supposed to meet him."

"What for?"

"Not a fucking clue. Something's not right."

John hums. "I saw that Owen guy hanging around the gates when I left earlier."

"Did you speak to him?"

"No, why would I?"

Doesn't hurt to talk to them. John's words. The silence stretches, me waiting for John to speak, John waiting for me. Except I'm not sure what's the right thing to say. "John?"

"Want to talk to him?"

I inhale, chewing my lip. "Doesn't hurt to talk, right?"

"Right."

Is John tired of The Manor and all the drama it brings too? "Do you want to start the process?"

"Sure, I'll start the process."

"Thanks."

"Are you here tomorrow?"

"Yeah. See you then." I hang up and sink down into the couch. "We're just talking," I say to the empty room.

"Who is?"

I look up and see Ava at the top of the stairs in her knickers and a T-shirt. "Nothing. No one." I get up and go to her, collecting her and attaching her to my front.

"I can walk, you know."

"I know," I reply, carrying her into the kitchen. I place her on the counter and dip, getting up close to her tummy. "Time to feed you."

"What about me?" she pipes up, injured.

"I suppose I ought to feed you too."

I get a smack on my bicep for my trouble, and I laugh, seizing her and kissing her hard. "Unravel your knickers, lady."

She holds my face and kisses me everywhere she can. "It's you who tangles them in the first place."

My phone chimes, and I reach for it, my eyebrows raising as I read John's message. Tomorrow at ten. Fuck, they're keen. My heart turns in my chest, and I try to push the feeling of guilt away. Just talking. It doesn't hurt to talk.

"What is it?" Ava asks.

Her concern snaps me back into line. "Nothing. Just John about a meeting tomorrow."

"So you're at work tomorrow?" she asks.

"Might be."

She smiles knowingly. "Do you know something, My Lord?"

"What?" I ask, my face bunched as she puts her lips all over it.

"I feel very lucky."

I open my eyes, surprised. This is interesting. I wait for her to elaborate, my curiosity raging. Her palms stroke across my chest, her head tilting in admiration from time to time, appearing in no rush to feed my interest. "Go on," I prompt, impatient.

"Sometimes you drive me crazy," she says quietly.

Ditto.

"Sometimes you make me want to scream."

Ditto.

"You're irrational, unreasonable, demanding."

Ditto, ditto, ditto.

"But more than that," she says, watching her fingertip draw a light line down the middle of my chest to the waistband of my boxer shorts. I inhale my anticipation as she peeks up at me. "You're passionate, adoring, protective, and possibly the sexiest man to ever walk the planet." *Possibly?* The cheek. Her hand slips past the material of my boxers and takes me in her grasp, and I blow out my cheeks, buzzing for friction. Buzzing for her. "And you're my husband."

"Yes, I am."

"What woman wouldn't want to be loved so fiercely?" She strokes down my length, and I'm a goner, cupping her pussy, massaging her as she massages me, and we stroke each other to orgasm, Ava moaning her release into my mouth as I come all over her hand, panting. She buries her face under my chin, kissing my throat. "And now you're my baby's daddy," she whispers, pulling me in for a hug. "And I know that any kid would be blessed to have you as their daddy."

The pain is very real.

And the peace and turmoil blending is suddenly unbearable.

Chapter 18

We spend the rest of the day between the bed and the couch. I wait on her hand and foot, let her initiate sex over and over, and each time, I sense her desire to take it up a notch...or ten. I resist, and Ava expresses her annoyance. I'm pretty sure vigorous sex should be avoided. In fact, I have endless questions about many things. So I ordered a book for next-day delivery. I have some catching up to do.

As the sun set and Ava dosed off, my mind rolled over the words she said.

Any kid would be blessed to have you as their daddy.

Naturally, that's left me wondering if Ava would be of the same opinion if she knew about my past. About Rosie. The twinge in my stomach prompts me to rest my hand there. Can I bring myself to talk about her? And, of course, Rosie leads to Lauren. The twinge returns. My mind reminds me of the various times I've thought I've seen her. *Thought.* I know my head's fucking with me, but for my own sanity and peace of mind, I've got to find out what happened to her.

I get up early and hit Google, trawling through the internet for Lauren's parents details, thinking I'll stop by. I can't imagine they'll be pleased to see me, but at the risk of my sanity. I find their small country estate on a map and the address comes back to me quickly. Not that it is of any use. I find a record on a property site detailing the sale. "Fuck." But I keep searching. The last record of his name is from a private practice, in Scotland of all places. I make a note of the number to call later, then hit the endless sites about pregnancy again, what to do, what not to do, what to eat, what not to eat. It's overwhelming to say the least, recommending other websites, books, classes. No mention of whether or not vigorous sex is okay. *Strangely.*

I look at the clock on the stove, my eyes burning from all the reading. It's too early to get Ava up, and she shouldn't be running anyway. Heading upstairs, I check on her in bed—out for the count—then get some shorts on and head down to the gym. The noise in my head forces me to flick on the TV, and I pull up a sports channel, watching the latest news coming in. Unfortunately, it does nothing to drown out the commotion in my mind.

Any kid would be blessed to have you as their daddy.

Or cursed.

I shake my head, increasing my pace, forcing my thoughts to better places. Where the fuck is Van Der Haus?

"Shit," I yell, smacking the button on the pad to take me to the next level, my legs like pistons. *Think of Ava. Think of our baby.*

I stare at the TV as I work my way through the members of The Manor. Is there a doctor? Someone I can convince with a smile—and a stack of cash—to tell Ava that pregnant women shouldn't work if they can help it? I huff. She'd see straight through me. Maybe we can compromise, agree she works from home for part of her week. I'm sure Peterson would be amenable. After I've flashed him some money too. This pregnancy could cost me a fortune. Doesn't matter, the pot of cash is as limitless as my love.

And there will be even more cash if I sell The Manor.

I laugh to myself, wiping my brow. I'll never sell it. I'm simply curious. It doesn't hurt to talk.

But why wouldn't you sell it?

The question jars me. Why *would* I?

Oh, no reason. Make sure you put a trampoline in the gardens for Ward Junior. Maybe one day he/she will bounce high enough to get a peek into the communal room window.

I smack the button to slow the pace a little when I cough, losing my footing for a second. Fucking hell. What a fucking comedian he is. "Go away," I mutter.

Don't say things you don't mean.

I smile and keep running, feeling the air around me heating, the familiar electric surge enlightening me of her presence. She rounds me and, good fucking morning, she's stark bollock naked.

I frown to myself, briefly looking around the gym.

Jake?

Ava lowers to the padded bench beneath the TV, her smile coy, as she drinks in my front and leans back on her hands, pushing her chest out, her open legs giving me a peek of her beautiful pussy. I swear my brother better have fucked off and gone to haunt someone else for a while.

Jake? You here?

I'm forced to slow the machine or fall flat on my face. Pulling the towel off the handle, I wipe my brow, leaning on the front of the machine, comfortable, giving my eyes a good fill of her. "Morning."

"Morning yourself," she says with a telling seductive edge to her quiet voice. "Why are you running in here?"

She knows exactly why I'm running in the gym rather than on the streets of London. "I fancied a change."

She hums, thoughtful. But she doesn't challenge me. "I don't remember falling asleep."

I do. I watched her eyes get heavier, felt her breathing change, and studied intently as she drifted off. "You went out like a light. I was happy to have you tucked into my side, so I let you be. You're sleeping for England, baby."

"What time is it?" she asks on a yawn, arms up, her torso becoming taut. My eyes cross. My dick yells and throbs.

"Morning!" Cathy's voice drifts into the gym, and Ava springs up from the bench.

"I'm naked!"

"So you are." Gloriously naked. I get off the machine and rub the towel through my hair. "Whatever will Cathy think?"

She whips the towel from my hand and assesses the small rectangle on a worried frown.

"I don't think that'll quite cover it."

"Help me," she whispers.

"Come here." I smile and open my arms, and she's attached to my front in a second, hiding in my neck. How long will it be before her stomach stops her arms from circling my neck?

I go to the door and look out, hearing Cathy in the kitchen. I call her to confirm it before nipping out and taking my naked, pregnant wife back upstairs. Those three words.

Naked. Pregnant. Wife.

My smile widens as I put her down and steal a kiss.

"What time is it?" she asks.

"Ten to eight." I nibble my lip, waiting for her to yell at me, although, to be fair, I lost track of time on the running machine this morning. But I can't say I would have woken her had I not lost track of time.

"Why didn't you wake me?" she moans as she disappears into the bathroom.

"You needed to sleep." It looks like it's back to work for Ava and back to killing time for me.

"Not for fifteen hours," she calls from the bathroom. I hear the shower start raining water and go to join her.

"You obviously *do* need it," I grumble, kicking off my trainers as Ava works at lightning speed, washing her hair and body and stepping out before my shorts hit the floor. Well, that's me redundant this morning. I follow her path past me, sighing as I get in the shower and take my time washing. "Fucking hate weekdays," I mumble, squeezing some shower gel into my palm and rubbing it everywhere. "She should be taking it easy. Sleeping. Eating." I rinse and step out, hearing the sound of her hairdryer. I brush my teeth, continuing to mumble my displeasure around my mouthful of paste. Maybe I can convince her to join me for lunch after my meeting with Owen Cutler.

As I walk into the bedroom, Ava's on her way out. Fuck me, she's moving fast this morning. I dress, squirt on some cologne, quickly pick a tie, and head downstairs, grabbing our keys off the table by the front door and pocketing them.

"I'll grab something at work," Ava says as I enter the kitchen.

"You'll eat," I retort firmly. She spins around, probably ready to argue with me, but she stumbles over her words, her delighted eyes taking me in as I fasten my tie. "She'll have a bagel, Cathy." I put Ava on a stool. I don't care if she's late, she's having breakfast. It's non-negotiable. "With eggs." Wait. Eggs? I saw them on a list of foods to avoid during my marathon trawl of the internet. "Actually, no eggs."

Ava snorts and slips off the stool, getting her bag on her shoulder. "Cathy, thank you," she says, directing a reproachful look my way. *What did I do?* "But I'll eat at work." She walks out, leaving me in the kitchen wondering what the fuck happened to the negotiations?

I blink, feeling Cathy looking at me. "She's pregnant," I say quietly.

Cathy gasps, and a second later she's got her hands over her face, her eyes wide. "Oh, Jesse."

I smile mildly. "We're thrilled," I say, seeing she's unsure how to react. Although you'd never know we're thrilled.

"Oh, how wonderful!"

The front door slams. What the fuck has gotten into her? It's the outside world. It doesn't agree with her. She goes from passive and obedient at home to a fucking nightmare in a heartbeat on the outside world.

"I'll see you later." I go after Ava and swing the door open, finding her by the elevator hitting the call button like she hates it. I widen my stance and slip my hands into my pockets, confused by this unexplained outburst. Will pregnancy bring on more sass, because we definitely don't need that?

"No eggs," she yells at the closed doors.

And it becomes clear. She's got the hump because she can't have eggs?

"You okay?" I ask calmly, hoping she'll syphon some off me and bring it down a notch or twenty. All over eggs?

"I can eat eggs," she shouts. I beg to differ. Just ask the World Wide Web. "What's the new code?"

"Excuse me?" If she asks nicely, I might share. But she doesn't look like she's in the mood for nice this morning. Fine by me. It just means she's going nowhere. Again, fine by me.

"You heard," she snaps, blindly hitting the keypad as she drills holes into me with her blazing glare.

"Yes, I heard." Is there any need for this? It's a complete overreaction. I'm not accepting it. "But I'm giving you a chance to retract that tone."

She momentarily looks taken aback. I don't know why. My wife needs to understand that if she's unreasonable, I will call her out. If she talks to me like I'm a petulant child, I will call her out.

Quickly gathering herself, she deflates with a sigh and comes to me. Oh good. She's seen reason. I don't want to leave on bad terms. I don't want us to leave each other at all, no surprises there.

Coming close, she leans up, and I dip, ready to catch her lips and her apology.

I can smell her breath. Her skin. Her...rage?

"Fuck...off," she whispers quietly.

I jerk like I've just stuck my fingers in a live socket. What the ever-loving fuck? My ears bleeding, I watch her march away, pushing through the door into the stairwell with a bang. "Over eggs?" I gasp, feeling at my stubble. Jesus, that's one small thing on a list I got fed up of reading. I know Ava won't read it, so it's down to me, which means it's also down to me to share the information I learn. "Pray for me," I say to myself, laughing under my breath when the elevator dings and the doors slide open.

Praying, bro.

I step inside and hope the thirteen flights Ava has to descend will be enough time for her to calm the fuck down. Clive looks up from his desk when I step out, his old face expressing his question before he asks it.

"No Mrs. Ward this morning, Mr. Ward?"

"She's taking the scenic route," I say, going to the stairwell door and waiting for her. I suppose this is one of the things she was talking about. Levels of smothering. Ava's a smart woman. She must know pregnant women can't eat eggs. She doesn't want the eggs. She just doesn't want me to tell her that she can't have the fucking eggs.

The second the door opens, I move forward and walk her back into the stairwell, getting her up against the closest wall. She's gasping for breath. Her cheeks are red. Her forehead's damp.

"You're not getting an apology fuck," she breathes, her look an endearing mix of lust and pure filth. Her heart isn't only hammering from overexertion now.

Close.

Contact.

"Mouth," I say calmly.

"No, you're not—" I cover her mouth with mine, slipping my tongue past her lips and sweeping wide, swallowing down her defiance, and she's with me, grabbing my suit, climbing me like a fucking tree. Oh, she's delightfully receptive. It makes her sulks laughable.

"Stubborn woman," I whisper, nibbling at her lobe. "Someone's gagging for it." And it won't hurt to remind her that no matter what, I can take her from zero to one hundred on the horny scale with one kiss and one touch. "Shall I make you scream in the stairwell, Ava?" I ask, smiling as she clings to me, silently begging me for it. Insatiable. Why does she fight it? I've got to admit, though. I do enjoy proving to her who has the power.

"Yes," she gasps.

My dick's screaming, begging me to put it in its favorite place, pleading for me to relieve it. I want to. I *really* want to. But long-term gains mean short-term sacrifices. So I detach my body from hers, mentally apologize to my cock, and leave her a panting, desperate mess propped against the wall. "Would love to," I say, my voice low, my hard stare fixed on her flushed form. "But I'm late."

Her realization is a beautiful thing to watch surface. Beautiful. "You bastard," she whispers, not trying to seduce me into giving her what she wants—what we both want—because she has a point to prove. But today, I win. A little win, but it's a win.

She swipes up her bag and pushes her way out of the stairwell, and I follow, smiling, adjusting my trousers as I watch her arse sway, her angry stomping feet giving it extra bounce.

She stops outside briefly before heading to her Mini. *Here we go again.*

She gets in, and I sigh, approaching and tapping the window as the engine roars to life. She takes the tip of her finger and presses a button with accuracy and a smile that would win any competition for sarcasm.

"Yes?" she says in a singsong voice.

"I'll take you to work." My voice is not a singsong voice. It's a *don't fuck with me* voice.

"No, thank you." More singsonging. I growl as the window rises and she very nearly runs over my toes as she zooms out of the parking space.

"For fuck's sake." But I smile, because my lovely, hormonal wife—please be fucking hormones—doesn't realize the remote fob has been removed from her car.

She stops at the gates, and I wait for the reverse lights to come on. They don't.

But the gates do start opening.

Huh? How the fu—?

I gasp, every muscle engaging to run after her. There's no way I'll make it. She whizzes out and drives off. Fuck it. "Clive!" I yell, storming back into the foyer. "What the fucking hell are you playing at?"

The old boy looks startled. Confused.

"You opened the gates!"

"Well, Mr. Ward, when a resident asks for the gates to be opened, it's my job to open them."

I slam my palms on his desk and lean over threateningly. "Ava's an exception."

"Oh. Okay, sir. Should I relay that to Casey?"

"No." I push my way off his desk and go to my car. "I'll tell him." I fall into my Aston and count all the ways in which she's defied me this morning. Endless. "Grrrrr," I growl, leaving Lusso, splitting my attention between the opening gates and my phone, searching for the number I need and dialing.

"Good morning, thank you for calling Tea and Two Sugars, this is Bianca speaking, how may I assist you?"

I laugh out loud. "That was very professional."

"Who's that?"

"It's Jesse Ward."

"Who's Jesse Ward?"

"That man from the café."

"There are a lot of men who come to the café."

Jesus. "Tall, suit, dark blond, green eyes."

"I don't look closely enough at my customers to note an eye color."

I grit my teeth. "Old, rich guy."

"Oh, Mr. Ward, how are you?"

"You're hard work, Bianca."

"Good morning to you."

"Good morning."

"What can I do for you, Mr. Ward?"

"Deliver my wife some breakfast, please."

"You mean the woman you've been stalking?"

"I'm allowed to stalk her because she's my wife." I roll my eyes, pulling out of the gates. "And she's pregnant."

"Oh, wow, congratulations."

I smile, chuffed. "Thanks."

"I'm afraid we don't deliver."

"It's across the road."

"Yes, but—"

"Two hundred."

"What?"

"I'll pay you two hundred pounds to make my wife some breakfast, no eggs, and deliver it all twenty yards across the road." I raise my brows at the lingering silence.

"I am more than happy to help, Mr. Ward."

"Thought you would be."

"Because, of course you are one of our best customers."

"Indeed."

"And we value our customers."

"Bianca?"

"Yes?"

"Shut up."

She laughs. "What's on the menu?"

I reel off my order. "And a Starbucks. Cappuccino, no chocolate."

"We're not a Starbucks, Mr. Ward."

"I know, but you can pop to the one down the street."

"What's wrong with my coffee?"

"Nothing."

"I haven't got—"

"Two fifty."

"Happy to help."

I shake my head. "Thanks. I'll drop the cash by soon." I hang up, checking the time. The surgery I noted down will be open. I take a breath and call, pressing one for reception when prompted. I'm then told I'm number ten in the queue. I wait, because what else will I do on my way to pay for my wife's breakfast?

I'm number one in the queue when I pull into Bruton Street. I snag a parking space at the top end of the street and take my phone off Bluetooth, walking down to the café with it at my ear. Bianca appears from the back, just as someone answers my call. I hold a hand up to her and take a seat at a nearby table. "Hi, yes, I was hoping to speak to Dr. Alan Pierce."

"Dr. Pierce?" The receptionist sounds confused. "I'm afraid we don't have a Dr. Pierce here."

"But it says online that he works at this practice. Or worked."

"Oh, I see. Well, I've only been here for eighteen months, so perhaps it was before me."

"Perhaps," I muse. "Could you ask someone who's been there longer?"

"Sure. I'll have the practice manager call you back."

"Thanks."

"Okay then, goodbye."

"You've not taken my name or number."

"Your number is on my screen. Ends in 674?"

"That's it."

"And your name?"

I don't want to give it in case it rings any bells with anyone. Like whom? I don't know, but I'm not taking any chances. I can't imagine Alan will want to hear from me. So I scratch around in my brain for a name. Any name. *Fuck.* "Norman," I blurt. "Norman Partridge." *What the fuck?*

"Got it." She hangs up, and I have absolutely no faith that anyone will call me back. "Norman fucking Partridge?" I question as Bianca approaches. I hand over the cash as promised.

"I just took it over," she says. "She looked surprised."

"You mean annoyed?" I reply over a laugh.

"Yes, and that. Are you smothering her?"

"Apparently," I mutter, leaving the cafe. "Thanks, Bianca."

"Anytime, Mr. Ward."

I bet. I give Ava's office front a wide berth—or as wide as I can while walking on the same street—and head to the florist.

The girl looks up when I push my way in, and then gets to work quickly. "When am I delivering?" she asks.

"You're not."

She blinks, surprised. "I'm not?"

"I'm delivering them myself today." I hand over some cash, my chest puffing out. "It's a special occasion."

"What's the occasion?"

"We're expecting."

"Expecting what?"

My shoulders drop. "A ba—"

"I'm playing with you, Mr. Ward."

"Oh. Okay." I grimace, giving her grabby hands. "Very funny. Give me the flowers."

She hands them over on a smirk, and I scowl lightly. "Congratulations, Mr. Ward. And have a good day."

"Yeah, you too," I say, pulling in my suit jacket and breathing deeply as I pace down the street, unconsciously checking the face of every blond woman I see. *Paranoid.*

I'm not expecting to be welcomed with open arms by my wife. The flowers are a bargaining chip. Lilies in exchange for acceptance. I'm not holding my breath that they'll work, but this is me listening to my wife. Flowers are an acceptable form of smothering, I'm sure of it. Couple that with storming her office, which I know to be unacceptable, I'm hoping I land somewhere in the middle.

Arriving at the Rococo Union office, I look through the glass. She's standing at her desk. Breakfast untouched. For God's sake.

I text her.

Are you eating your breakfast?

I watch as she looks down at her mobile. Did she just roll her eyes?

Yummy.

She's a gem.

I'm so glad our marriage is based on honesty.

Did you really just text that, bro?

I scowl, ignoring Jake, as I push my way through the door, and Ava stills for a moment before she looks up at me. She drops to her chair, exasperated. She should try being married to my wife. I nod my hellos to her colleagues as I walk to her desk and help myself to the chair on the other side.

"Eat." I place the flowers down, motioning to the paper bag.

"I'm not hungry, Jesse."

She might be if she knew how much that poxy roll cost me. Or it might make her a bit nauseous. Speaking of which…"Baby, you look pale."

"I feel rubbish," she breathes, shrinking in the chair. My God, what is she doing here? She doesn't want to be at work, feels terrible, but to prove her fucking point, whatever the fuck that is, she's forcing herself to endure the torture. Am I going to have to put my foot down? Pick her up and carry her out? Because I will.

I stand and round her chair, feeling at her forehead. I expect her to bat my fussing hands away. The fact that she doesn't only reinforces how drained she is. "You're hot."

"I know." She accepts my kiss on her cheek as I pull her hair off her face, checking over my shoulder for Peterson. His office door is open, his desk empty. Where is he?

"I hope you feel guilty," she mumbles.

Right now, I really do. But I can make her feel better. Look after her, if she'd only bloody let me. I lower to my haunches and turn her chair toward me, my face soft, my eyes softer. "Let me take you home."

"It'll pass," she says on a weak smile.

"You're impossible sometimes. Pregnancy is making you moody and even more defiant."

"I like keeping you on your toes."

Yes, I'm a fucking ballerina these days. "You mean you like keeping me crazy."

"That too."

I'm not going to win this one. And forcing anything work related isn't getting me any brownie points. So I'll have to endure her job until she relents to pregnancy. I truly hope Ava gets more happiness and fulfillment from being a mother, so much so, she wants to be a stay-at-home mum. Wouldn't that be wonderful? I'd be a stay-at-home dad too. We'll be stay-at-home parents. Not everyone is lucky enough to have that option. We do. Both of us present and undistracted by life to raise our baby. Be there constantly. It would be perfect. I rise and peck Ava's lips. "Please eat. It might make you feel better."

"Okay."

I shouldn't get too excited. Her acquiescence is probably because she feels too ill to argue. "Good girl." I turn her back toward her desk and pull the bacon bagel over.

She opens the bag and snaps it shut again, her shoulders jerking. "I don't think I can."

She has to. She needs food in her belly. I get the bagel out and set it in front of her, and she stares at it, bracing herself while I silently will her on, patiently waiting for her to brave a bite, and when she does, she chews forever, the effort obvious. "Can I just eat the bagel?" she asks.

"Yes," I sigh, pleased with her willingness. "Do you see how happy you make me when you do what you're told?"

She doesn't humor me, on a roll now, chomping her way through her breakfast. I can literally see the color rising into her cheeks with each bite. Don't tell me I don't know what's best for my pregnant wife. She knows I'm not leaving here until she's eaten, but I *will* leave here. That's my flex. We're figuring this out slowly but surely. "Happy?" she asks, even sounding better.

"Your color's back, so yes, I'm happy." Very happy indeed. I clear her desk so it's ready for her to work and lean in over her chair, forcing her back. "Thank you." A bit of gratitude doesn't hurt, and the smile that mirrors mine feeds my soul. "My work here is done." For now, anyway. I crush her smile with my lips and breathe her into me, setting myself up for the next fuck knows how many hours without her. "Now I'll leave my wife to work in peace."

"No, you won't," she says over a laugh.

"I might check in once or twice." And that would be perfectly reasonable given her condition.

She laughs harder. "No, you won't."

I'm taking her amusement as a sign of her acceptance. "I won't make a promise I can't keep." I quickly take a peek into Peterson's office again. "Is Patrick here?"

"No. He's in meetings all day."

Hmmm. Is she stalling the conversation she needs to have with him about Van Der Haus? I glance at my watch. "You've made me late."

"You make *yourself* late." I'm forced away from her desk. "Go."

"Feeling better?" I ask as I reverse my steps.

"I do." She admitted it? Wow. "Thank you." And gratitude too? Strike me down now.

I blast her back with a smile, kiss the air, and stride out, happy.

Perhaps a happy balance won't be so hard to find after all.

Chapter 19

I stop off at a pharmacy to pick up some folic acid for Ava, so I'm ten minutes late for my meeting with Owen Cutler, but it's not a problem because there's no one here, no cars, only Ava's Range Rover, where I left it by the gates, and John's car outside The Manor.

I stroll through the door and meet him in the hallway. "He's not here yet?" I ask, motioning back to the empty drive.

"He's running late."

"Incredible," I say in disbelief. He's stalked me for weeks and then doesn't even show up on time when I finally agree to see him. *Prick.* "How long?"

"He's rearranged for four."

"Four?" I look down at my watch like I need confirmation that that's six fucking hours away.

"Did you take Ava to work?" he asks.

"No, she wouldn't let me." I can see John's wondering how the hell she got to her office if she refused my ride and if he wasn't there to take her. So I enlighten him. "Her Mini." I scroll through Google on my phone for the number I need and dial. "Yeah, hi, I have a broken-down vehicle I need collecting from the NCP on Berkley Square and taking to St. Katherine Docks." John's head is shaking. I smile through straight lips and answer all the questions being fired at me by the man on the other end. I give my credit card details, my phone number, then thank them profusely for his help. "What?" I ask John when I've hung up. Stupid question, I know.

"If you're having her old car towed and her new one is here, how is she getting home?"

"I'll pick her up," I say, shrugging. His eyebrows lift. "Okay, *you'll* pick her up because she's less likely to rip your head off."

"I can't cope with you," he mutters, leaving me.

"Just wait until you find out we're pregnant," I say quietly. Although, apparently, not quietly enough.

John stops. *Oh shit.* Turns around. "What?"

"Nothing." I still haven't found the courage I need to tell John.

Might never. "I'm going to get Ava's Range Rover." I start the long walk down the drive, passing through the trees, smiling at the newly discovered bench. I take a pew, since I have six hours to kill, and text Ava.

How are you feeling?

Better.

And that's that. I contemplate calling her but go against my instinct and get on my way again, stalling getting behind the wheel of her Range Rover when I see someone looking through the gates. "Can I help you?" I call.

"Delivery for Jesse Ward," he says, holding up a package.

Ah, my pregnancy book. I jog over, give him a signature, and accept the package through the railings. "Thanks." I go to Ava's car, jumping in and throwing the package on the passenger seat, smiling at the stitching in the headrest. Maybe I'll have peanut's name stitched into the rear headrest. What will we call…it? I frown and start the engine, turning in the driveway and making my way back toward The Manor. Girl or boy? If it's a girl, she'll look like her mother. Will she have her sass too? "God help me," I breathe. If it's a boy, he'll look like me. I smile. God help the female population of his generation. I'll take him to football. Teach him everything I know. Well, not everything. Most things. Boy or girl? I know it's nice to be surprised, but I don't think I can wait. Will Ava want to find out? She's traditional, so I suppose not. Could I convince her? I laugh under my breath. Do bears shit in the woods?

I park Ava's Range Rover next to John's, grab my delivery and hop out, tossing her keys in my hand as I walk to my office. The piles of paperwork greet me. "Fucking hell," I breathe, ripping the package open and scanning the book. It's thick. Very thick. I puff out my cheeks and slip it into the top drawer of my desk, dragging my laptop over and staring at the screen like it can help me. Then before I know I've done it, the screen is filled with baby stores. I blink, stunned, and go for what I know, smiling when I find myself somewhere familiar. Harrods. My smile falls. Car seats, prams, cribs, sterilizers, baby carriers, monitors… "Organic nappies?" I blurt at the screen. Teats that are imitations of nipples? I scoff. "Never." I get up close and personal with the screen and click through a few pages. The endless equipment blows my mind.

I'll call Zoe. She'll make this a breeze.

"What are you doing?"

I reach for the lid of my laptop and snap it shut. "Nothing."

John's scowl is fierce as he reaches for my computer. I slowly pull it out of his way, swallowing, certain I look every shade of guilty. *Fuck it.*

"Open the laptop."

"No."

"Open the motherfucking laptop, motherfucker."

I sneer and shove it toward him, resting back in my chair and fixing a filthy look on my oldest friend as he lifts the lid and turns the screen. "Jesus fucking Christ," he murmurs, lifting his shades and his eyes to me. "Is this what I think it is?"

"Baby stuff?" I ask. "Yes, it's baby stuff, John."

"And why are you looking at baby stuff?"

"Why do you think I would be looking at baby stuff?"

John's always hidden his shock well. He's struggling today. Lowering to the chair, his mouth open, his gold tooth glimmers. "I'm just trying to figure out if it's possible for Ava to fall pregnant in the time you've been back together."

"We got back together on Friday, John." Although we hardly split up. "It's Tuesday."

"So your plan to trap her worked?"

"Why does everyone make it sound so immoral?"

"Because it is. And she's okay with this, considering the circumstances?"

"Yeah." I don't know what happened yesterday to make Ava come round, but I'm grateful. "She's happy."

"She's happy," he mimics quietly.

"And me. I'm happy too."

"I can tell."

"And it also means I'm not shooting blanks."

He rolls his eyes and rubs into his frown. "How far gone?"

"I don't know. I need to sort out a scan."

"Well...wait—"

"What?"

The map of lines across his head multiplies. "Is this why you've decided to talk to Owen Cutler?"

I look away, pulling open the drawer and getting my new pregnancy book out. "Doesn't hurt to talk, right?"

"Oh, for fuck's sake," John breathes, eyeing my new book.

"No one can say I'm not committed, eh?" I fan the pages, grinning.

He laughs at the irony, a deep, baritone laugh with absolutely no humor. John remembers as well as I do the moment I learned Lauren was pregnant. Dread. I obviously wouldn't have changed having Rosie for the world. But…had she not been born, she would never have been taken. And I wouldn't have become a shell of a man. I shake my head and those thoughts away. Or I try to. I would have been a shell. Rosie saved me from myself for a while. Until I let her down. I've been letting her down ever since too. I wince and feel at my chest.

"I suppose I should be congratulating you," John mumbles, sounding surprisingly genuine.

"Go on then."

"What?"

"Congratulate me." I smile mildly. "Uncle John."

"Moron."

"I prefer motherfucker."

"And have you thought about how to tell Sarah?"

"Kill the buzz, why don't you." I flick through the book, reading a few things here and there. Will she do something stupid again?

"I'm just asking."

"She doesn't need to know." I pluck a highlighter out of the pen pot and drag it across a few things I absolutely should remember. One being information on pregnant women flying. Bollocks. That's taken a honeymoon in the sun off the table.

"She definitely should know," John says. "You can't let her find that out from someone else."

I drop the pen and my head back. "It's none of her business." Suddenly parched, I get up and grab a bottle of water from the fridge, waiting for John to come back at me.

"I called the security company again. They aren't committing to an engineer visit to replace the camera," he says, pivoting the conversation completely. His way of agreeing to disagree. Fine by me.

"Convenient."

"Should I push or relent?"

"It's just the one camera still out?" I ask.

"Around the side by the garages."

It's a small mercy. At least it's not an internal one. "When's the new system being installed again?"

"Friday."

"Fuck them."

"Okay. You should cancel the direct debit."

"Have Sa—" *Fuck my life.* "I'll call the bank." Surely I don't need a million numbers and passwords to simply cancel a direct debit. "Could they show up to remove the equipment?"

"They'll be trespassing. Besides, the equipment is paid for. They can't remove it. It's the servicing agreement that's ongoing." John waves the contract that Sarah found when she was here on Sunday. "They're not fulfilling their end of the deal by actually servicing or replacing so we stop paying."

"Okay, good."

John puts his shades back on, looking across more paperwork. "I was looking for the site plans."

"What for?"

"The Manor. To check the boundaries."

"Why?"

"I don't fucking know," John grumbles. "Not that it matters because I can't fucking find them."

I press my lips together. Sarah would put her hands on the plans in a beat, just like she did the security contract. John looks up at me, thinking the same. "I can't, John," I say, getting up and walking to the window. "I value my marriage and my wife's feelings too much."

He sighs. "Ava's a reasonable woman."

I cough over my laugh. "She's also very hormonal right now. Let's reverse the situation, shall we?"

"What?"

"If Ava came to me and told me she'd continue working for Van Der Haus after what he attempted."

"You don't know beyond doubt that Van Der Haus did anything."

True, but he's after my woman and that's enough. "Still, I wouldn't have it, so I'm in no position to stand in Sarah's corner."

"Then we struggle on."

"We do." I head out.

"Where the fuck are you going?" John calls.

I stall, my hand on the doorknob. "Breakfast." I swing it open and go to the bar, snagging a menu. I don't think I've ever read the breakfast menu.

"Since when do you eat breakfast?" John joins me and sits on a stool, waving Pete for a coffee.

"Since today." It wouldn't be very reasonable of me to force-feed Ava and skip meals myself. "Isn't there any peanut butter on this menu?" I ask, unimpressed.

John chuckles, as if my favorite thing's absence from my own fucking menu is funny, and Pete's quick to pacify me. "Not on the menu," he says. "But we keep a stock."

"Why isn't it on the menu?"

"Well, sir, it's an acquired taste, you see."

"Is it?" I ask, as John's laughing increases. I can't even feel grateful for the therapeutic sound.

The fucker.

"An acquired taste...like you," John adds, and I slowly turn an evil glare his way.

"Fuck off."

"Now, now, kids." Drew, suited and booted, strolls into the bar.

"What are you doing here?" I ask.

"Meeting Sam for breakfast." He leans past John and claims the coffee Pete's just placed on the bar. "I think he's lovesick."

"No shit," I quip. "And you're going to make him feel better, are you?"

"How you wound me." Drew takes a sip of the coffee and grimaces. "What the fuck is this shit?"

"Black Americano," John growls, claiming the coffee. "Get your own, boy."

"What's eating him?" Drew asks, taking his stool as John leaves us.

"Me, I think."

"What did you do?"

"It's what I *won't* do," I reply, nodding a thanks to Pete when he slides a coffee and a jar of peanut butter onto the bar. Drew raises his brows in question. "Sarah," I answer. "He wants me to bring her back."

"Oohhh."

I laugh. I'm glad someone understands.

"Yeah," Drew breathes. "That's an easy no."

"Is it?" I grab my peanut butter in need of a hit.

"Is she all right?"

"No," I sigh. "Far from it, and it really fucking sucks that I'm the only person on this fucking planet who can fix that."

"By letting her back into The Manor?"

"By letting her back into The Manor," I mimic.

"And your life," Drew adds quietly.

"Exactly. I can't do it, especially not now."

Drew's smooth face wrinkles. "Especially not now, what?"

I chomp on my lip, trying to hold my tongue, trying to…not trying at all. "Especially now that Ava's pregnant."

This must be one of a handful of times that I've rendered Drew Davies speechless. His blue eyes blink rapidly, and then as if his brain has caught up and reminded him of a previous conversation we recently had, he gasps. "That's fucked up, Jesse."

Shame eats me alive. "I appreciate the circumstances aren't ideal, but—"

"Ideal?"

"What's ideal?" Sam asks, appearing at the bar, looking between us.

"Are you going to tell him, or am I?" Drew asks.

Fuck me, am I on trial? I motion to Drew with a limp hand on a tired breath. "Go for it, *Dad*."

"Ava's pregnant," he declares.

"Oh, my man, that's awe—" A frown hops onto Sam's forehead. "Wait." A recoil. "She's pregnant because you stole her pills." A gasp. "Fucking hell, Jesse."

I fold over the bar and bury my face in my palms.

"Yes, you hide from the judgments," Drew says. "As you should."

"I'm not proud," I mutter. "I realize I've done wrong."

"Do you?" Sam blurts. "Do you really?"

"I don't think he does," Drew pipes in.

I stare into my darkness.

"Me neither," Sam breathes.

That's it. Enough. "You're both barred," I bark, standing abruptly and marching out of the bar. "You can leave now."

"Wait, what?" Drew's chasing my heels instantly, Sam not far behind. "You can't bar us."

"Yeah, you can't bar us."

"I just did." I stalk through the summer room. "Shut the door on your way out."

"Jesse," Drew says on a nervous laugh. "Be reasonable."

"I'm not long off the back of a breakup, mate," Sam says, urgency in his tone. "Have some mercy, for God's sake, man."

John's still sifting through paperwork when I push my way into the office, looking for those boundary plans. Anyone would think he *wants* me to sell The Manor. He glances up at the three of us.

"He's barred us," Drew barks. "Talk some sense into him, John."

"There's no talking sense into that man." He returns to his task, unfazed by my two panicked mates.

I get myself some water and text Ava again.
How are you feeling?

Better.

I roll my eyes and tip the bottle to my lips. "If you two can find the plans John's looking for, I might reconsider." I point to the piles of paperwork. Four sets of hands are better than one.

"What do you think of this?" Drew asks John. "Really, what do you think?" He plonks himself on the couch, sitting forward, elbows on his knees, interested.

John looks over his shades. "What do I think about what?"

"Him," Drew practically screeches. "Stealing his girlfriend's pill—"

"She's my wife."

"She was your girlfriend when you stole them," he says, and I pipe down, in no position to retaliate.

"I think you're being rather judgmental," John muses, still fingering his way through endless paperwork, "considering you restrain women with chains."

"What?" Sam looks at Drew, stunned. "Chains? Since when?"

"Is anything around here confidential?" Drew barks, throwing his hands up.

"It's The Manor," John says to the papers in his hand. "Not a fucking STD clinic. Which reminds me"—he picks up more paperwork and waves it—"you two are a week late on your routine tests."

"Oh, then you're definitely barred," I say, lowering to the couch and crossing one leg over the other, all casual. "Maybe I'll reinstate you when you confirm you're clean."

"I didn't think I'd need tests if I was sticking to one woman," Sam mutters.

"But she's dumped you for Ava's tosser of a brother," Drew says, making everyone in the room flinch, including Sam. *Harsh.*

"And what about you?" I ask Drew, making him shoot a surprised look my way. "Why are you late?" Drew is *never* late with his tests. Absolutely never.

"Yeah, what about you?" Sam sings like a fucking brat.

"Fuck off," Drew spits, standing, outraged. "I've been…" He scowls. "Distracted."

"By what?"

"Just…it's…" He trips up all over his words, getting more and more worked up. "Things!" he barks, storming out, making a good job of slamming the door behind him. We all flinch at the sound.

"What's eating him?" John asks calmly.

"He's fine," Sam mutters, leaving too. "I suppose I ought to go get those tests." He stops at the door and grabs his dick, thrusting into his hand. "I've got some catching up to do."

He opens and slams too, and I look at John, eyebrows high. "Think I upset them?"

"Maybe." He returns to his search but we both look up again when the door swings open and both my mates stand on the threshold with dirty, confused frowns on their faces.

"What plans?" they ask in unison.

My bottle pauses halfway to my mouth. Do I say anything? Next to John, these two dipsticks are my best mates. I look at John. He dips his head, peeking at me. "The plans for The Manor," John says, probably thinking I won't. He's right. He knows me. And saying it out loud almost feels like admitting betrayal.

Both men walk calmly back into my office and sit on the couch opposite me. Both look concerned. "I have a meeting at four," I say, biting at my lip.

"With?" Drew asks quietly, reluctantly.

"An acquisitions manager for a leisure corporation."

Both men's eyes widen a fraction. "Why?" Sam asks, and I fidget, uncomfortable.

"To hear what they've got to say."

"Or offer," Drew adds.

"Look, it's just a fact-finding meeting, okay? He was sniffing around outside The Manor and gave me his card. I stuffed it in my pocket and thought no more of it."

Drew stands, his face irritated. "But you've since found out you've got your wife pregnant on the sly, and suddenly you're going to be a family man, so now you're gonna sell The Manor?" His voice gets higher the more he rants on. "You get a wife, a kid, a happily ever after, and what the fuck do we get? Booted out?"

I explode, shocking myself, shooting up from the couch in a deranged fit of fury. "Yes, I get a fucking happily ever after, Drew," I bellow, making him cower. "What's the problem, don't you think I deserve that?"

"Whoa," Sam says, coming to me, rubbing soothing circles into my back with his palm. "Let's all calm down, yeah?"

I shrug him off and get out of there before I sink my fist into one of my best mate's faces, nearly taking the door off its hinges when I slam it. "Wanker," I bark, going to the changing rooms and wrestling my way out of my suit. I pull on my shorts, a T-shirt, stuff my feet into my trainers, grab a racket and some balls, and fuck off to the tennis courts where I can take my anger out on an inanimate object rather than someone I love.

As I stomp my way moodily to the courts, I notice a few more things I haven't seen before. A bird table nestled amongst two huge rhododendrons. A gold sphere at the base of an apple tree trunk. Further proof that my eyes are wide open. That I'm seeing things for the first time in nearly two decades. I'm thinking clearly. Of course I should listen to any business offers. It's just a talk.

I let myself through the gate and start smacking balls over the net with force, until I'm out of balls and walking the length of the court to retrieve them and start again. I've done this five times when I see Drew and Sam walking down the cobbled path toward the courts. Both in gym gear. Both carrying rackets. I scuff my trainers on the grass, pouting down at them, swinging my racket as they let themselves in. Drew puts himself at the back, Sam comes to the net. They bend, rocking, swiveling their rackets.

Game. On.

I chuck a ball up and smack it with power.

Right at Drew's head.

He ducks, looking back as it hits the caging, before slowly turning his narrowed, piercing blues back onto me. "First serve," he grates, as Sam chuckles. I grin and toss another ball up, serving again. It hits the grass just inside the box and skims Drew's racket.

"Ace," I muse. "Fifteen love."

"Okay, no more Mr. Nice Guy," Drew says, bending, getting ready. "Let's do this."

"I'm ready," Sam sings.

Yeah, I'm ready too.

For anything.

It goes to five sets. "Match point," I yell, sweating like a beast, glancing at my Rolex. Fuck me, I've been running around this court for nearly five hours. I get low, anticipating Sam's serve. Low and deep. But he surprises me and goes high and wide. I break to my left, reaching and returning, skidding across the lawn before spinning on the spot and racing back to the center, just in time for Drew's return. The fucker goes short and low, tapping the ball so it lands just over the net. "Fuck," I curse, running to the net, reaching with my racket, aiming for a connection rather than skill, finesse, or accuracy. I hit the ball into the net.

"Deuce," Drew sings, wandering to the back line. I can only see the back of his head but I know the fucker is grinning.

I get ready, Sam serves, and I watch as the ball hits the chalk and sails past my shoulder.

"Ace!" Sam yells.

"Match point," Drew declares.

For fuck's sake.

Sam tosses the ball a few times, bounces it, his eyes squinting as I sway, wait, spin my racket. He throws it up, smacks it on a grunt, going safe, getting it a good few feet inside the line. "Pussy," I yell, returning it with an accurate backhand.

"Meow," Drew purrs, slicing the ball, the fucker going for the same shot.

"Fuck." I dive forward, hitting the ball with the edge of my racket. It pings, bounces off in the complete wrong direction, and hits the cage. "Shit."

"Game, set, and match to Sam and Kinky Drew," Sam sings, tossing his racket and spreading his legs, yelling to the heavens.

"Yeah, baby!" Drew runs at him, diving, wrapping his legs around Sam's torso, and Sam begins to bounce him up and down as he whoops and yells.

I laugh and collect up the balls. Two against one, for fuck's sake. And it took them five hours to beat me. "You're so humble," I quip.

Drew hops down from Sam's body and leaps the net, slinging his arm around my shoulders and getting me in a headlock. "You lost, Lord."

I roll my eyes, but I appreciate his backward apology. I throw my arm around him, and Sam comes in at my other side, joining the lineup. "I've not lost," I say, as we walk back to The Manor in a row. "I'm winning everyday right now." Except at tennis.

The boys flick fond smiles my way. I know I didn't exactly do this conventionally, but they know me. "She's happy?" Sam asks.

"Yeah, she's happy. Sick as a dog, but she's happy."

"I'm sorry for being a cunt," Drew murmurs quietly. "I know you need this." They didn't know Rosie. But they *know* Rosie. I smile, a little sad, a little happy, feeling them both squeeze me between them. "You know," Drew muses. "I never thought I would say this."

"What?"

"I'm too fucked to fuck."

I burst out laughing with Sam, sniffing back tears.

"And you?" I ask Sam.

"Never too fucked to fuck."

Maybe. But he's still too *smitten* to fuck, unable to let go. And given I've been the same since the first day I met Ava, I commiserate.

The power of a good woman.

Chapter 20

After showering, changing back into my suit, and texting Ava to check up on her, I join the boys in the bar. It's busy, members starting to arrive after a day's work to unwind. But Sam and Drew still haven't made their way upstairs. Sam, I'm not surprised. But Drew? He's never too fucked to fuck.

"Why are you still here?" I ask, sitting with them in the corner, casting my eyes around the bar, seeing numerous female members of The Manor looking this way. Wondering where my wife is? Hoping she's left me? Oh, their faces when they learn we're expecting.

"Just still here." Drew dismisses me quickly, knocking his beer back.

I look at Sam. He avoids my eyes. "What's going on?"

"Nothing," they both chime, Sam grinning like a prick, Drew through his teeth, making him look demented. I shake my head and stand when John walks in, looking down at my watch. Four o'clock. Owen Cutler appears behind him, taking in the bar. Suited. Booted. He means business. Let's find out when he's got to say.

"See you two chumps later," I say, leaving Sam and Drew.

"Wait," Drew blurts, forcing me to a stop. I face him, finding he's half standing. He checks himself and lowers, playing all casual. I'm not buying it. Especially when I glance at Sam and he avoids my interested look by swigging his beer too, peeking around the bar.

"Wait for what?" I ask, slipping my hands into my pockets.

"Well, it's a nice atmosphere. I don't know why you wouldn't have your meeting in here."

"Here in the bar?" I ask, taking another look around.

"Yeah." Drew shrugs. "Here in the bar."

"In front of many interested members?"

"They're not interested."

I raise my brows and jerk my head in indication, and the boys look, seeing some very interested members all with eyes on John and Owen. "You sure?"

Drew throws them all a filthy look. "Can I come?" he asks.

I laugh. "You want to come into my meeting?"

"Yeah, as a friend. Support. I'm a businessman, Jesse."

"You're an estate agent."

"Which makes me one of the best salesmen on the planet." He smiles. "I could sell condoms to a convent of nuns."

I laugh. "You're not coming in."

"That's not fair," he whines. "Why?"

Sam laughs, but it dries up when his mobile rings and he stares at the screen. "It's Kate," he murmurs, looking up at me. "What should I do?"

"Answer it," I say, and with those two words, he connects the call and wanders out of the bar, no longer interested in my meeting.

"Look," Drew says. "I just want to know if I need to go speak to Hux or not."

"Hux?" I gape at him.

"Well, where else do you expect me to get my kicks?"

"Hold your horses," I say, leaving them. "I'm just hearing what he's got to say."

"I'll be here when you're finished!" he yells at my back.

I flick a semi-friendly smile to Owen. "Afternoon," I say, and he stares at me, somewhere between realization and disbelief.

"You're Jesse Ward," he breathes.

"I'm Jesse Ward," I confirm. "My office is this way." I pass him and head toward the summer room. "So something came up earlier today?"

"I can explain."

I laugh. "Only my wife ever needs to explain to me."

"Oh, you're married?"

"Yeah, I'm married." I stop in my tracks and look back at him. "You sound surprised."

The guy was so together previously. Almost cocky. Now, he's in a bit of a fluster, looking between John and me, his mouth opening and closing like a goldfish. "I heard—"

"You heard?" Has he been asking around about me?

His shoulders drop, and his eyes roll. "It's just part of our background checks."

"And what did your background checks unveil?" Obviously shit background checks if they don't know I'm married.

"Not a lot, actually."

"I'm a private man." I tilt my head, feeling John studying me. A private man who put it around. A lot. But that was before Ava.

"That's quite obvious."

"I'm here to listen to what you've got to say, Owen. Nothing more."

"But you're not interested in selling?" he asks, almost coy.

"I don't need the money, if that's what you're getting at." Let's be clear on that.

"I figured." He smiles. "You have an Aston, a penthouse in central London, a villa in Marbella."

Obviously not private enough. Who's he been talking to? "Very good." I carry on to my office, leaving the door open and going to the couch, motioning to the one opposite and looking at John in instruction to sit next to me. Both men lower to their places. "So why are you late?" I ask.

"I went back to the CFO of Fairlands, my client, to get the go-ahead for a wider window for negotiations." Owen places his briefcase on the table in front of him and reaches forward, releasing the catches. The loud clicks fill my office.

"I'm not here to negotiate, Owen. I'm here to hear what you've got to say."

"Of course. You don't need the money."

I sigh and settle back, semi-scowling. "Let's get on with it."

"Five million."

John does a terrible job of hiding his cough. But not because he's surprised. He's insulted. I smile across to Owen, trying to conceal it with a light brush of my top lip with my index finger. "Owen," I say, his name a breathy sigh. "I make sixty times that in one year."

And like John can't hide his cough and I can't hide my smile, Owen can't hide his balk.

"Perhaps you should have requested the company accounts." Not that I would have sanctioned the release of them. So much for his background checks. I stand. "I think we're done."

"No, no, no, Mr. Ward, please." His hand comes up. "Ten."

"You double your offer in the space of sixty seconds?" I scoff, insulted. "Time to go, Owen." I check my watch and text Ava again.

"Fifteen," he breathes, beaten.

The cheeky fucker. I lower my phone, eyes narrowing in interest and nothing more. "Something tells me your commission depends on what price you can secure."

He looks guilty. I don't know why. He's a salesman.

"Let me educate you on a few things, Owen." I pull my trousers up at the knees and lower to the couch. "My uncle bought The Manor in 1989 for a cool two million." I glance at John. He's looking slightly reminiscent, almost sad. "He spent another two renovating the building and the grounds, not to mention the blood, sweat, and tears."

"It was three," John says, his voice flat and gruff.

"Three," I say. "That's five million. The property was valued at eleven on completion in 1990. My uncle was twenty-six at the time. It's not official, but I'm pretty sure that would have made him one of the youngest millionaires in the country at the time. The property and grounds are just a fraction of The Manor's worth. The running of this business brings me in a hell of a lot more a year. So, if I were to sell this grand, glorious old building, it would need to be a pretty fucking big carrot being dangled. Gold plated. The tastiest thing I've ever tried, and I've tried some tasty things in my time, if you get what I mean." God help me if Ava heard me say that. The only thing I'd be tasting is blood from my split lip. John clearing his throat confirms it. Owen looks like he's prepared for a donkey and got a racehorse. "Want to take time to regroup?" I ask.

He breathes out, the sound filling the room, and pulls out a folder from his briefcase. "Let's pull back on the money talk and have a chat about Fairlands." The folder slaps on the wood, and John and I both look at the photograph on the front of a pretty impressive golf course. "They have one other location in the north of the UK. Dozens across Europe. They want another in the south and this is perfect."

"I'm not much of a golfer." I pick up the file and have a browse.

"I've been thinking about it," John says. I look at him, surprised. "What's wrong with that?"

"Nothing," I say, going back to the glossy brochure. "Your bonsai trees might feel a bit neglected, though." I get a swift punch in my bicep, and I laugh. As does Owen. I glare at him. He pipes down. "Look, Owen, this is all very pretty, but why the hell am I going to sell The Manor for a fraction of what the business operating from it is worth?" He delayed our meeting by six hours just to insult me? "Now, if you will excuse me." I stand and walk out, uninterested in anything more he has to say. I'd rather sit in the bar with the boys and listen to their drivel.

Both Sam and Drew look surprised by my appearance, their beer bottles lowering. "That was quick," Drew says, looking behind me for Owen.

"Deal done," I say, smiling at Mario when he gets a water and hands it to Pete.

"Serious?" Sam asks.

"No." I don't fuck with them too much. "Waste of my time."

Both men deflate, Drew more than Sam. I check my watch and text Ava again. She's still feeling better. Did she have lunch?

"Oh, he's not gone?" Drew says.

I look up. John's at the door with Owen, his glasses off, his eyes telling me to go to him. I make a meal of getting up slowly, showing my inconvenience. "What?" I ask, approaching.

"I'll be in touch," Owen says, nodding, backing away.

"Right." I exhale my impatience, watching him looking around as he goes, taking in the many women throwing many sultry looks.

"I need you in the office," John says.

"What for?"

"We need to find the deeds to this place."

"Why?"

"Because when they come back with a more realistic, sweeter offer, and they will, trust me, you're going to have to provide proof of ownership." He turns and walks away. "Plus the accountant wants some information for your tax liabilities, you need to find your banking customer number, and somewhere in there are my pension details." He looks back, his bushy eyebrows appearing over his shades. "I'd ask Sarah, but—"

"So she looked after *your* paperwork too?" John should have details of his pension, that's standard.

"Get moving," he grunts, swerving my observation.

"I'm coming," I grate, signaling to the boys that I'm off. I stop at the door and look back at Sam. "All right?" I ask.

"I'm meeting her in an hour." He stands and pulls out his keys.

My smile is unstoppable. No point mentioning Dan, but I'm still curious why he wants to meet me. "Happy for you, mate."

"Me too," Sam says.

We both look at Drew as he passes his eyes between us both. "Me too," he breathes tiredly, then scans the bar for potential playmates.

I carry on with John and once again sigh at the paperwork when I enter my office. "Fucking hell," I murmur, going to my desk and flicking through a few pieces. "So you're thinking of retiring?" I ask, casual.

"I'm off."

"What?"

He taps the screen of his watch. "Your wife finishes work at six, am I right?"

"Oh, yeah." I think I'd rather face Ava's potential wrath than this paperwork.

"And where am I taking her?"

"Well, here," I grunt. "Since you're cracking your whip and putting me to work." I flinch. Whip. "God's speed."

He laughs under his breath, shaking the room. "And have you told her I'll be bringing her here?"

I glance up.

"Just preparing myself for what I'm walking into," he adds.

"I'll let her know." I can finally show her the new bedroom too…if I get through this mess.

"Good. You need last year's accounts and tax calculations too."

"What do they even look like?"

"Numbers. Very big numbers." The door closes, and I drop to the couch, exhausted by the mess. So I get up and head to our new suite to check it one last time before I show Ava.

I smile as I stand on the threshold, pleased with myself and the workmen. The lighting is moody, the soft furnishings pure luxury, the bed beautiful. I sit on the end and take a few quiet moments to myself, absorbing every detail. This room. It was the beginning of my new life.

My eyes fall to the wooden cross. Not a part of Ava's initial design, naturally, since she had no idea what would go on in this room. But a later addition.

She wants hard. Shock and awe. She can't have it. But there's a way round that.

Compromise.

The key to appease my wife is to blindside her. I smile and go to the music system, loading it, ready, before brushing a hand across the bedsheets, smoothing out the crinkles I've made. Then I head back downstairs, texting Ava on my way.

I'm still at The Manor. Come? We'll have steak.

She replies in a second, no argument. Because she knows Sarah isn't here.

On my way x

I enter my office and pout at the mess of papers. One call and it would be sorted. Can't do that.

After searching through one pile for half hour and then sifting through another for twenty minutes, finding nothing that looks like tax papers, accounts, or deeds, I'm close to losing the will to live. I need Ava. She offered to help sort this out. But will she be too tired after a day at work? Undoubtedly. I can't ask her to do extra work while she's carrying my baby.

I start transporting the piles to the floor—I need space to spread out.

Knock, knock.

"What?" I call, sounding irritable.

Drew's head pokes round the door. "Where's John?"

"Picking Ava up. Why?"

"No reason." He grins and backs out, and I follow him, wondering if there's some trouble I need to sort out.

"What's going on, Drew?" I ask his back as he hurries down the corridor to the summer room. He slows. Exhales. Looks back. "Steve Cook's here."

The burn inside is instant and very fucking real. *Cool it.* I asked him to call me, not pay a visit. Have him and his missus split up again? Has he been caught whipping young, naïve women without offering a safe word? And, come to think of it, does his wife even know about that?

"Is it wise to let him pass?" Drew asks.

"Probably not."

"Do you want me to join the meeting and hold you back if your fists decide to take off."

"Probably should."

"Okay." He nods, assessing me up and down, thumbing over his shoulder. "I'll go get him then."

"Okay."

"Stow those fists, Jesse."

I clench them and tuck them behind my back. "Got any cuffs?"

Drew smirks and leaves, and I put myself back in my office, flexing my fists, working away the tension. I also remind myself that I wanted to talk to Steve, that he could help me. Mikael Van Der Haus still hasn't reared his smarmy Danish head, and the longer he remains underground, the more certain I am it must have been him who drugged Ava. I just can't wrap my mind around such vindictiveness and desperation. His beef is with me, not my wife.

I sit on the couch and stand up again. Perch on the edge of my desk. Stand again. I settle for behind my desk. He'll have more of a chance to escape if I fly at him.

Or maybe not.

The door opens and Drew appears. I nod as he stands aside and lets Steve enter. "Jesse," he says, his lips pressed into a straight line, the usual cockiness nowhere in sight.

I swallow down the dormant anger hearing his voice spikes. "I'm surprised you're here."

"I'm surprised you haven't got me in a choke hold."

"Me too," I admit. But, again, given the severity of the situation—my wife was drugged—I'm willing to put my grievance aside.

Whips. Lashes. The marks all over Ava's back.

Drew closes the door and puts himself on the couch between my desk and Steve, who's remained by the door. Close enough to intercept if I let my restraint ping. Drew must be concerned—I know he'd rather be upstairs.

"I needed to apologize," Steve says.

"You mean apologize for whipping my wife until her skin broke and she was practically unconscious?" Just speaking those words has me fidgeting, the whole horrendous scene parading through my head again. I shake away the thoughts quickly before they take hold and Drew's forced to play kamikaze. "Does Juliette know about..."

He shakes his head, and with that gives me all the ammo I need... should I need it. "And I'd rather she didn't," he confirms.

"I need you to look into someone for me."

Steve doesn't hesitate. "Name?"

"Mikael Van Der Haus." I can feel Drew's uneasiness and flick him a look. I'm good. I've got this. He can leave. And he does, closing the door quietly behind him. "Danish," I go on. "Owns a development company." I write down Van Der Haus's name and his company name, wandering over to Steve and passing it to him. He looks caught between relief and wariness. "Call me if you dig anything up." Leave it transactional. I saw his face the night I carried Ava out of here covered in his whip marks. He was shocked, and something tells me his disbelief wasn't only due to my reaction. He wants to right his wrongs, so he'll do this. Plus, he doesn't want me to tell his wife about the depth of his debauched time while he frequented the rooms of my manor.

"Any background information?"

"Ava was drugged the night before…" I clear my throat. "The night before…" I don't need to finish. He knows. "One of the security team at the bar got some CCTV footage showing a man in the vicinity. It looks like Van Der Haus."

"Did you report this?"

"No, I don't want the police involved." Ironic, since I'm talking to a cop. Steve stares at me long and hard. He knows what's happening here. I will find Van Der Haus and deliver my own kind of justice, and Steve will let me.

"What's his connection to Ava?" he goes on, folding the piece of paper and slipping it into his pocket.

"He's a client. He's also the ex-husband of Freja Van Der Haus. She is…*was* a member."

"Freja?"

"Yeah, Freja."

"You…"

"Yes, I did." Say no more.

Steve nods in understanding and takes some backward steps to the door, almost as if he doesn't want to take his eyes off me in case I change my mind and lunge at him. "I really am remorseful, Jesse."

I know he's not here to grovel so he can worm his way back into The Manor. So he's sincere. Doesn't mean I'll ever forgive him. Or forget. "Thanks for stopping by." I turn and face the masses of paperwork I've moved onto the floor, hearing the door close.

I need to occupy my mind with something numbing and mundane before I go after him, drag him back, and pummel him. So I get on my knees and start sifting through the piles, setting aside any that look even remotely official. Which is a lot. "God damn you, Sarah," I whisper, my mind short-circuiting.

The door swings open, and Ava appears. And isn't she a sight for sore eyes.

She looks at the mess surrounding me and smiles. I think there's a tinge of guilt in there somewhere. "Hey."

"Here's my beautiful girl." I'm done playing office junior for the day. I cast aside the papers and get on my arse, ushering Ava into my arms. "Come here. I need you."

"Need me, or need me to sort all of this out for you?"

Would she? I mean, I'd silently hoped, and she did offer an hour here or there. She must see how lost I am. But she's tired. "Both."

Coming to me, she lowers between my spread thighs. I saw her brief look of alarm at the mess. I crowd her completely and get a long hit of her scent. "How are you feeling?"

"Better."

"Good, I don't like seeing you poorly."

"Then you shouldn't have been underhanded and knocked me up," she counters, the words loaded with sarcasm. I still smile though. "I saw Steve leaving," she goes on.

"Hmm." I don't want to talk about Cook. I want to show her our new room and then get us home.

"Did you offer burial or cremation?"

I knock her leg with mine as I suck on her lobe. "I offered him an olive branch, actually." Kind of. It was more blackmail, I suppose. "Sarcasm doesn't suit you, lady."

"What's made you so reasonable?"

"I'm always reasonable," I reply. "It is you, beautiful girl, who's the unreasonable one."

"What's so reasonable about having my car stolen?" There she goes again, making something sound as terrible as possible. I didn't have it stolen. I had it delivered back to Lusso so Ava didn't have to drive it there. Or here. Or wherever. "And how did you manage it without any key?"

"Tow truck. How was your day?"

She reaches for a piece of paper. "Productive," she says. "Shall we make a start?"

She definitely looks perkier. Full of color. Bright eyes. "Suppose so." She has no idea what she's getting herself into. It's fucking painful.

Ava gets to it, working quickly, glancing at papers, sorting them, tidying them, bundling them. She's a pro, and I am clearly redundant. So I leave her to it and go to my computer, doing something far more enjoyable.

Making a list of things for Zoe to source.

Car seats, strollers, cribs, sterilizers. What else? I scroll the pages, browsing. Blankets, clothes, nappies, baths, baby monitors…

It's fucking endless.

Ava appears at the foot of my desk, startling me, and I quickly shut my laptop and get up. "Dinner?"

Her expression is a beautiful blend of curiosity and amusement as she leans past me and flips the lid back up. *Bugger it.* I know she'll think it's too much too soon, but we have lots to get done. The nursery, the birth plan, buying every piece of baby equipment ever invented. "Just doing a bit of research."

I can't take her judgmental eyes on me anymore, so I look away. And then I'm suddenly warm and fuzzy everywhere, Ava hugging me. "I know you're excited," she says softly. "But could we hold off telling people?"

Ah.

Oops.

"I want to shout about it," I say. "Tell everyone."

"I know." She looks like she's struggling, as if she braced herself for this conversation. I thought she was happy. "But I'm a few weeks. It's bad luck. Women usually wait until their first scan, at least."

"When's the first scan?" I ask, ready to hit Google again. "I'll pay. We'll get one tomorrow."

She leans back and holds my forearms while I keep hold of her hips, smiling at her. She suits pregnancy already. "It's far too early for a scan," she tells me. How does she know? "And anyway, the hospital will do it."

What? Wait, she thinks we're waiting around for an invitation from a hospital to check everything is okay and how far she is officially? Nah. Not happening. "You are not having my baby in an NHS hospital." Because they don't accept drop-ins every day of the week just to check things over.

"I th—"

"No, Ava." Absolutely not. I will not be flexing on this particular wish. "This is not up for discussion. End of. Never, no way."

Looking rather alarmed, Ava shakes her head. "What do you think they'll do?"

Make us wait. But I don't say that because I'll be accused of being unreasonable. "I don't know, but I'm not giving them the chance." Now it's time to show Ava what I've been working on.

"You pay your taxes and so do I," she says on a laugh. "It's a privilege to have a National Health Service. You should be grateful."

"I am, it's wonderful, but we won't be utilizing it. End of."

"Neurotic."

I balk at her cheek. She's playing with me. She's cute. "...ish." I look down her body. "I like your dress." It'll be on the floor soon, but I like it.

"Thank you."

"I want to show you something." I lead her with a palm on her back through The Manor. "Come on." Up the stairs, around the landing, past the stained-glass window. "Here." I open the door and watch her face fall in astonishment as she steps into the room. I bite my lip, nervous, watching her take it all in.

"You did this?" she asks.

"I gave someone your drawing and told them to create it." I close the door. "Is it close?" It's identical, but Ava wasn't overseeing these works and it's been a while since she created those drawings.

"It is." She has another quick look. "When?"

"It doesn't matter when. What matters is if you like it."

"It's perfect," she breathes.

"It's ours."

"Ours?"

"No one has ever been in this room and no one ever will be. This is our room. If I'm working"—which is likely given Sarah's absence—"and you're with me, maybe you'll want a sleep or some rest."

"You mean when I have swollen ankles or exhaustion from carrying too much weight?" Her face becomes pensive, and I know why. She doesn't want our child here. She's been thinking about that—The Manor, my old lifestyle, the baby.

"I mean," I say softly, keen to explain myself. "If we need it, it will be here."

She nods, only very mildly, and takes it in some more. "Why is that in here?" she practically whispers, looking at the cross.

I smile. "Because I had it put in here."

"Why?"

"I think it might…help." I watch her chest start to pulse with her breathless anticipation.

"What do we need help with?"

"You want it hard," I say quietly, moving in on her. "And I'm not very comfortable with that when you're carrying my baby." I can't have this battle for the next…how long? Fuck me, we've been together a couple of months. Is she months or weeks? Yeah, not waiting for a routine scan. "So I thought carefully…" Shoes, gone; socks, gone; jacket, gone—all under Ava's watchful eyes. "And came up with the Compromise Fuck." I already love the Compromise Fuck, and Ava will too.

"I don't understand."

Is she being coy? I start on my shirt and tie, and her eyes drop down my front as I slowly expose it to her hungry gaze. "You will." I go to the sideboard and press play on the system, turning back to Ava when a slow, sensual beat joins us.

"What is this?" she breathes. I get close, absorbing the thrums of her body.

"This is Amber, *Sexual*." My skin buzzes. "*Afterlife*." Specifically chosen. "Appropriate, don't you think? It doesn't always have to be hard, Ava. I hold the power, no matter how I take you." I guide her to the cross. She lets me. "It's not the hard you love, anyway. It's me taking you so unapologetically."

"You'll never fuck any sense into me again?"

"Will you defy me again?" I ask around a mild smile.

"Probably."

"Then I've absolutely no doubt that I will, my temptress." But for now, we compromise with the Compromise Fuck. "If I want to fuck you hard and make you scream, I will. If I want to make love to you, Ava, and make you purr, I will." I lean in and kiss her softly, breathing in her exhale. "If I want to bind you on this cross, I will." I start removing her dress slowly, extending her torture, loving the anticipation staring back at me. Her eyes have clouded. It's stunning. Not dissimilar to the very first time when we were in this room together. Her, flustered. Me, enchanted. Wondering how I might convince this woman to have dinner with me. So I told her I liked her dress. Came on a little…strong. Watched her dash off, literally hearing her heart pounding.

Look at us now.

I help her step out of her dress, feeling her wobbles. She closes her eyes. Tightly. "And you are mine, so I'll do what I like with you." *Go on, baby. Tell me I'm wrong. Tell me I can't.* Of course, she doesn't because, right now, I have the power.

I start on her bra and stare at her breasts, but I resist kissing them, moving her hands to the manacles in turn and securing her. No fight. "Look at me, baby." I caress her face, using my spare hand to press into my dick, inhaling some control. I nearly lose it when she obeys, opening her eyes.

"Tell me you've never done this before," she whispers.

My hand on the back of her head, I pull her close. "Never." And I kiss her gently, reinforcing it, exploring her mouth slowly and lovingly, listening to her soft whimpers of pleasure over the music. I put my mouth all over her face, her ears, remind her to open her eyes when she closes them.

I move back. Take her in.

Swallow.

Fuck. I imagined this. Could never have anticipated the sheer, unbelievable sight of her spread on the wooden cross, naked, every inch of her screaming for me. The sexual energy is charged. She looks fucking incredible, and I *feel* it. The undying desire, the ceaseless adoration. From both of us.

She closes her eyes again, but before I order them open, I pull my phone out and take a picture of her bound on the cross, naked except for her lace knickers. Breathless. *Fuck.*

I remove my trousers as she opens her eyes again for me, and enjoy her silent observations of my body, smile on the inside when she finally starts to fight the shackles. She held out for longer than I expected. I whisper my encouragement, calm her when she insists she can't control her instinct to fight her bounds, wrap my palms around her balled fists when she tenses everywhere and cries out quietly. Her lips part, her body relaxes, her hands loosen. I drag my touch to her breasts, skim her nipples with the back of my hand, and then dip, taking one in my mouth. Her moan vibrates through her body, the metal of her restraints chinking. I worship her boobs, nip at her sensitive nipples, indulge myself completely. Lost. Consumed.

Peeking up, I see her panting down at me, gritting her teeth, dealing with the pressure around her nipple.

Sustaining it.

Sustaining *me*.

She's sending me a silent message, and I hear it loud and clear. I release her and lick life back into her boob. "My beautiful girl is learning to control it." I drag her knickers down her thighs. Kiss my way back up her body. Slide my fingers into her.

Her breath hitches.

"Shhhh. Soak it up, Ava. Feel every single bit of pleasure that I bless you with." I start fucking her gently with my fingers, smiling at the feeling of her gripping me, as I circle myself at the root and draw a few long strokes. Withdrawing my fingers, I start brushing the swollen, wet crown of my dick around her flesh, mixing our wetness, shaking violently. *Fucking hell.* I catch her mouth, and then our moans are mixing too.

"Are your arms okay?" I ask urgently.

"Yes."

"Are you ready for me to take you, Ava?" I ask. "Tell me you're ready."

"I'm ready." She gasps the words, her eyes clenching shut, her panting off the charts.

"Open your eyes for me, baby."

Her lids peel open, and as soon as I have her gaze, I slowly swivel my hips and drive deep and high into her. "Oh God."

"Jesus." My knees buckle as I crouch to pull her up by the backs of her thighs, my mind blanking. I pump slowly, allowing both of us the time to accept the pressure and pleasure. My mouth works her throat, licking away her sweat, nibbling at her flesh. "I set the pace and you follow."

She turns her head and finds my lips, and we kiss soft and slow, each plunge into her measured and deep, each grind firm, each withdrawal steady.

It's not long before I feel the telltale signs of my looming release, and Ava's legs around my waist start shifting. I claw my fingers into the backs of her thighs.

"You're going to come," she gasps.

"Not yet." Fuck, not yet. *Control it.* She watches me fighting to rein myself in, sweating like a beast, needing to stop moving, but the feeling is too good to stop. I'm no longer in control, and when she pushes her mouth onto mine and sweeps her tongue wide, I'm a goner.

Fuck. I hoist her up higher, and it's all it takes. I feel like I come out of my body and slam back into it again, Ava's scream of pleasure sounding miles away. She jerks violently against me, the shackles clanging as she fights them. I don't have it in me to tell her to stop before she marks herself. Each thrust is becoming hard, firm. My body knows where it needs to be and there's no stopping it.

"Jesus fucking Christ," I bark, looking at the ceiling as Ava buries her face in my neck. The pulse in my dick becomes a buzz, the sensitivity becoming unbearable. But I've got to release the pressure. She screams my name as I bang into her, and when she sinks her teeth into my shoulder, I tip the edge and freefall into a deep pit of pleasure, trembling, mumbling, my mind blank, my breathing shot.

Christ, I'm struggling to keep us upright, my body shaking as my orgasm rips through me with force.

"That was perfect," she pants as I drag my face from the crook of her neck and find a damp, flushed beauty staring back at me. I release her from the cross, content when she wraps every limb around me. I carry her to the bed and lay us down, both of us needing to catch our breath.

"Do you like our room?" I ask, a little wheezy, lost in her neck again, her hair tickling my nose.

"Are we going to have a cradle put in here?" she asks, dampening the serenity. "You know, for when we bring our baby to The Manor?"

There it is.

I push myself up and settle next to her, drawing circles across her belly. "Sarcasm doesn't suit you, lady."

"Just a question," she says quietly.

Yes, a loaded one. And it's definitely something we should talk about. That's a discussion for another day, though, and I can't help but wonder what she'd say if she knew I'd been in *talks* with a potential buyer. Even if it was a waste of my time. "You have a bump," I whisper, gliding my palm over the planes of her tummy, my eyes narrowing, assessing, definitely seeing a very slight rise on her usually flat stomach.

"Don't be stupid." Bless her, she looks offended. "I'm barely pregnant."

"I'm not being stupid. It's faint, but it's there." I drop a chaste kiss there, again looking forward to the day when I can spend ages working my way all over her rounded stomach with my lips. "I know this body, and I know it's changing."

She pouts down at my hand resting just south of her boobs. "Whatever you say, Jesse."

Smiling, I scoot down the bed and level my mouth with her belly. "See, peanut? Your mother's learning who has the power."

Her gasp is endearing. Her look fierce. "No *peanut*. Think of another name. You're not referring to our child as something disgusting that you obsess about and devour daily."

Disgusting? "I obsess about you. I also devour you daily." I move fast and sit astride her, securing her to the bed by her wrists, having a quick check for welts. She's good. "Let me call our baby peanut."

She grins. "Never."

Hmmm. "Sense fuck?"

"Yes, please."

Oh, how I love her voracious appetite for me. "Pregnancy's making you a monster," I say over a laugh. "Come on. My wife and peanut must be hungry."

"Your wife and *baby* are very hungry," she counters. And doesn't that sound amazing. *My wife and baby*.

I get her up and retrieve her knickers from the floor, bending to hold them at her feet, kissing my way up her legs, spending extra time on her tummy, until I'm at her face again. More kisses. Her bra. More kisses. Her dress. More kisses.

And once I'm done dressing and kissing Ava, I grab my boxers and step into them, pull my trousers and shirt on, and get my hands knocked away from the buttons when I start to fasten them. She wants to dress me? I hold my hands up in surrender and watch her with fascination as she takes her time putting me back together again.

Looking after me.

She's being attentive but playful. Loving, caring, compliant.

I'm content. So fucking content. So content, I refuse to allow anything to ruin this. I feel like we've moved into new territory. One that's absent of problems. I know many of those problems are still there, but I can't let them affect us. Affect Ava. Especially now.

When we're both decent, we go down to the bar to get some dinner. Mario is his usual cheerful self, he and Ava chatting while I scan the space, seeing who's here, who's not. Natasha catches my eye, her curved eyebrows arched to within an inch of their lives as she sips from a tall glass, observing me. I ignore her. She's a leach. And she'll be a squashed leach if she pushes Ava over the edge. What the hell is Drew doing getting his kicks from her? He's got the pick of The Manor.

"What would you like?" Mario asks as I take a stool next to Ava.

"Two waters. Just two waters please, Mario."

"I might like some wine with my dinner," Ava says.

I roll my eyes to myself and don't entertain the glare my wife currently has pinned on me. Wine? Did she forget she's pregnant? "You might do, but you're not having any." End of. "Two waters, Mario." I find Pete at the end of the bar. "Two steaks, Pete." Now I *know* I read rare meat is a no-no. "One medium, one well done. No blood, whatsoever." I'm erring on the side of caution.

"Urhh…yes, Mr. Ward," he replies, his astonishing waiter brain probably pulling the fact that Ava likes her steak medium from among all the other things he remembers about various clients he serves. "Salad and new potatoes?"

"Yes, just make sure one steak is thoroughly cooked."

Mario is back with our bottled water, looking as struck as poor Pete. If Ava wasn't here, I'd tell them our news, give them some context, but she is so I won't. Right now, they'll just have to deal with my uncharacteristically demanding self.

I save Mario the task and pour Ava some water, feeling her eyes still on my profile. But she's quiet. Accepting? Wait…"Is there egg in that salad dressing?" I ask Pete.

"I'm not sure. Should I check?"

"Yes, if there is, leave the salad with the well-cooked steak undressed."

"Okay, Mr. Ward."

I nod and mentally scan back through that endless list of foods to be wary of during pregnancy. Wait, coffee. Did I see coffee on the list? Jesus, I had coffee delivered to her office this morning. I must check about coffee. And cheese. Was it soft cheese or hard? Blue or Swiss? I groan, the pressure in my head getting too much.

"If you don't go to that kitchen, change my order, and get me a glass of wine, I'm one step closer to moving in with my parents for the rest of this pregnancy." She speaks so calmly, staring at the optics above the bar. I blink at her, startled. Is she for real? "You're not trampling my diet, Ward."

Wanna bet? I understand that this is all a bit of a shock—the pregnancy and all—and she's still trying to get her head around it, blah, blah, blah, but anything, and I mean *anything*, that puts her or our baby at risk is off the menu. Literally. "You've already gotten yourself pissed while you were pregnant," I hiss quietly, that fact—and grievance—finally falling out of my mouth. And I can tell it stings her.

"I was mad with you."

She was mad with me? A cop-out. "So you thought you would take it out on my baby?"

"You keep saying *my* baby. It's *ours*."

"That's what I meant," I grate.

"You're not worried about me, then?" she asks, her frown small but telling. *What?* "It's not *my* safety anymore?"

I'm stunned. Whenever have I given her any hint that her safety isn't at the top of my priority list? I can't deal with this kind of unreasonableness. She infuriates me. And we've talked about this. I told her, plain as day, eased her underlying fear that I might want a baby more than I want her. I'm about to state a bombardment of facts that will squash Ava's grievance when I catch the table of women nearby—Natasha included—looking this way. Fucking hell, what did they hear? Do I need to ask? Their faces are an irritating shade of shock.

But...do I give a single shit? No.

Back to my wife.

My unreasonable, stubborn wife.

"I…" Fuck it, I did say *my*. I didn't mean to, but I did. And how the hell is this *discussion* going to help either of us? God damn it. I'm guessing controlling meal choices is past Ava's limit of acceptable levels of smothering. But she absolutely *does* need to read up on a few things. She doesn't want wine. She just doesn't want me to tell her that she can't have it. And, actually, I fucking didn't.

I blink as Ava stares at me, her eyes clouded with emotion—frustration, hurt, disbelief. She's a grown woman, I get that. She's also smart. I'm playing this completely wrong. "Fucking hell." My hands go into my hair and pull, maybe to try and yank some reason out of me. When will I learn that my wife doesn't do well being dictated to. Outside the bedroom, at least. "Fucking, fuck, fuck, fuck."

"I mean it, Jesse," she goes on, like I haven't just mentally beaten myself up enough. I heard her. I *hear* her. And I see her remorse for doing what she did, even if she's not outwardly apologizing. I don't want to argue. I want to put that in the past and move forward. I face her, take her drink, and hold her hands tightly. "I'm sorry."

"You are?" Her eyes widen.

"I am. I'm sorry." We need to figure out a way to navigate this pregnancy together as a team, otherwise I'll be certified officially crazy by the time this baby arrives. "This is going to take some getting used to."

She laughs, and despite it being a sweet, comforting sound, I'm quite injured. This is no joke. "Jesse," she sighs. "This is hard enough to cope with, without dealing with an enhanced control freak. It's not something I planned or even considered." No shit. And *enhanced*? "I don't need you on my case, analyzing every move I make, monitoring everything that passes my lips. Please don't make this tougher than it already is." She gets up and moves into my chest. She thinks I need comforting. I do. "I want my baby to have a daddy," she whispers, smiling at my forlorn pout. "Please try to reduce the risk of a stress-induced heart attack by chilling out a little."

We all know chilling out isn't exactly my forte when it comes to anything relating to Ava. I need to stop *telling* and start *asking*. Or enlightening. Sharing the things I'm learning about pregnancy. I hum as Ava smothers my face with kisses. Pacifying me?

"I'll work on it, baby," I say. "I'm really trying"—kind of—"but can we at least compromise?"

"Compromise how?" she asks, the uncertainty in her voice clear. Okay. Let's see how this goes. I'll be gutted if she digs her heels in on this particular issue, because it's a massive no-no, and not only because her husband doesn't like her drinking under normal circumstances. I pull her out of my chest, scanning her eyes as she scans mine. "Please don't drink," I whisper softly, my voice undoubtedly as pleading as my eyes.

She visibly softens before me. "I won't." Smiling mildly at my obvious relief, she strokes though my messy hair. It's as I thought—she just doesn't like being *told*. "Go get me a medium cooked steak," she says, following it up with a kiss before sitting herself back down. "And I'd like that dressing on my salad."

I leave her at the bar and head to the kitchen, finding Pete. "So it's two medium steaks."

Poor Pete looks so lost. "Okay, Mr. Ward." He takes one step, and I reach for his arm, stopping him.

I look over my shoulder to the corridor that leads back to the entrance hall. She can't possibly hear me. "But make one closer to well-done, okay?"

His frown is epic. "So medium well-done?"

"Yeah, but we'll call it medium when it's served, okay?"

"Mr. Ward," Pete says, exasperated. "Is everything okay? You seem a bit .. strung."

I release a bark of laughter, dropping my hold. "I'm fine, Pete." I scrub a hand down my face. "Ava's pregnant."

"Oh, wow," he breathes. "Congratulations."

"A baby!"

I jump out of my skin as Mario shuffles past with a tray of clean glasses. "I see a bloom!" he sings, and I chuckle. "Marvelous news, Mr. Ward. Most marvelous."

"Thanks, Mario." No celebrating with the marvelous stuff, though.

I leave a stunned Pete to order us two steaks, one disguised as a medium, and head back to Ava, happy.

But my smile drops like a rock and I skid to a stop, my mouth gaping, when I encounter something in the entrance hall I really didn't expect.

Chapter 21

Sam and Kate are in a full-blown embrace, eating each other alive by the doors. Jesus Christ. "Get a room, you two," I call, disturbing them.

Sam turns a cunning smirk my way, and Kate—it's ridiculous—gets all flustered. "We were just about to, actually," he says, adjusting his groin area.

"What?"

"Is Ava here?" Kate asks, looking slightly apprehensive.

"Yeah, she's here." *And she's going to flip her lid when she sees you, Kate.*

"Great," she quips, looking up at Sam. He smiles his reassurance and circles his arm around her waist, walking her toward me.

"So," I say, waving a hand between them. "You two are..." Exclusive? Dating? Fucking? What?

Sam's grin widens, and Kate presses her lips together. Oh God, Ava's going to freak the fuck out.

I pick up my feet quickly to make it to Ava before they do. She's still at the bar when I get there, smiling. "Just remember," I say, glancing over my shoulder, "none of our business."

She looks confused. To be expected, I suppose. "What? What are you talking about?"

I cringe, hearing Sam's laugh behind me. Here we go. I don't know if she'll be shocked because Kate's not with Dan or if she's here with Sam. Obviously not for a regular date per se.

I know the second Ava's clocked them because her face falls. "What the hell?" She hops off her stool.

And I put her straight back on again.

"Ava." She's shocked. Emotional. Might have endless questions about her brother, among other things. But I'll have to hold her back for now.

For a moment I'm worried she's heard my thoughts because she glares at me in disbelief. "Who else have you told?"

Told about what? "I—" *Oh.* I flip a filthy look around the bar to whoever's opened their big mouth. Could be anyone, really. "A few."

"You've told everyone, haven't you?"

Pretty much. "I might have."

"Jesse," she sighs.

I jut out my lip, hoping she'll go easy on me. "Can we visit my in-laws this weekend?" I suppose they ought to know too.

"Well, yes." Ava laughs. She's finding me quite amusing today. Better than annoying. "We'd better before news travels and makes it to Cornwall before we do."

Look at her being all willing. We're both flexing. "You make me a very happy man, Mrs. Ward." I crowd her with my body and my mouth.

"That's because I'm letting you trample all over me at the moment."

"No, it's because you're beautiful, spirited, and all mine." I leave out stubborn, unreasonable, and possessive. I'm done arguing for the day.

Sam splits us up and takes Ava in, up and down. "I can tell," he says, and I suppress a cough, praying for him. "You've got that healthy glow about you."

"That's funny," Ava replies, removing herself from Sam's grasp and finding Kate. "Because I mostly feel like shit."

For the love of God. "Mouth, Ava." Especially now. I don't want our child hearing such terrible language. I frown as Ava claims Kate and leads her to a quiet corner, probably to wring her for information. Not gonna lie, I'm quite curious myself. I turn to Sam. "What gives?"

"Yes, I want to hear this too." Drew muscles in. Where the fuck did he come from? I look him up and down. "What?" he asks, smoothing a hand through his hair. "What are you looking at?"

"You have a hair out of place."

"Fuck off." He goes back to Sam. "What gives?"

"A fiery redhead gives—"

"Good head." Drew says.

I cough over my water, and Sam nearly knocks his teeth out when his beer bottle hits them. "Not cool, Drew," I say, ready to hold Sam back.

"I'm messing." His hands come up. "Sorry, habit."

"Well, break the fucking habit," Sam hisses. "Or I'll break your fucking legs."

Drew presses his lips together, hiding his knowing smile. He's thinking what I'm thinking. Sam's falling. Or he's already hit the deck.

"We're exclusive," Sam says.

"Like exclusive, exclusive?"

The poor, clueless twat frowns. "There's more than one kind of exclusive?"

The laugh that erupts from Drew is rare and infectious. "You prick."

"What?" Sam asks, looking a bit worried.

"Exclusive is exclusive," I clarify. "That's it."

"Oh. Good."

"So what the fuck are you doing here?" I ask.

"We can be exclusive here too, can't we?"

"Sure. You can be whatever you want to be. Just make sure it's clear to other members." I look at Drew, and he points to himself, like...*what, me?*

"Yes, you," I clarify for the sake of it.

"I like Kate, but—"

"But?" Sam asks, offended. "What's wrong with her?"

"Nothing's wrong with her." Drew chuckles. "She's just not my type."

Both Sam and I turn our full bodies into Drew and tilt our heads.

"I told you." He laughs. "Gagged and heartless." He looks past us to Natasha and the rest of the table. "I need some food and a fuck. And what the fuck's wrong with your wife?" Drew points to the corner where Ava dragged Kate. "She looks like she's been released from the Funny Farm."

He's right. Ava's slumped back in her chair, holding her belly, howling at the ceiling. Kate's grinning at her. Intrigued, I go over, but not before I capture a picture of my wife belly laughing. "Something funny?" I ask.

"No, nothing." Ava snorts, wipes her nose, snorts again, her body jigging up and down on random short bursts of laughter.

"Here's your dinner."

"Oh, I'm starving." She's virtually salivating as Pete places her steak down. It's a familiar look, except...well, I'm usually the steak. "Medium?" she asks before gobbling down a potato.

I look at Pete out the corner of my eye, eyebrows high. "Just to your liking, Ava," he says with the stupidest, toothy smile. I take my plate from his other hand. "Can I get you anything else, sir?"

"No, thanks, Pete."

"I'll leave you to eat," Kate's says, standing.

Ava points at Kate with her knife, the blade catching one of the spotlights above and blinding me.

I quickly lean back.

Feel something sink into my gut.

Pain.

I look down at the wooden handle hanging out of my stomach. What the fuck has she done?

"Do you want me dead, Lauren?" I ask, grabbing on to air urgently. But breathing hurts, the rise and fall of my chest making the pain flare. Blood pisses all over the couch. "Because you're too late."

The fuck?

My hand darts out, seizing Ava's wrist, pushing the knife down to the table. "Don't wave your knife around, Ava."

"Sorry," she says, almost in confusion. Like I'm overreacting.

"I'm sorry," Lauren blurts, her hands in her hair, the panic in her deranged eyes real. "Oh God, I'm sorry. I don't want you to die."

"Then why the fuck did you stab me?"

"I need you to love me," she screams. "Why can't you love me?"

I shake my head clear and take a second, looking around me. Where I am. Who I'm with. My stomach. It twinges. I wince, resting a hand on my scar over my shirt, frustrated that Lauren keeps slipping into my present and knocking me off-kilter. *Fuck off.*

"Good?" I ask Ava, picking at my own plate, suddenly not so hungry. *You have to eat, bro. Something other than peanut butter.*

My appetite has vanished, and I'm thankful when the boys join us, the conversation nice and easy, although Ava's too busy smashing her way through the steak to partake. And what's with Kate's permanent grin? I shake my head, bewildered, returning to my salad, picking at a few leaves. But then Ava starts coughing, her face turning bright red, her eyes watery. She's choking?

I jump up, hitting her back, probably harder than I should. "Fucking hell, woman." I check her face. Still red. And then she's gasps, deflating, and I deflate with her. "Slow down," I say, my heart going ten to the dozen. "It's not going to walk off your plate." *I made sure of that.*

She heaves and wheezes, hand on her chest. "I'm okay." She chuckles a little, like this is funny? "Went down the wrong way."

Don't tell me I'll have to *actually* feed her, as well as make wise food choices for her. "Here." I confiscate her cutlery and give her some water. "Drink."

"Thank you," she breathes, supping it back urgently. And then her cheeks balloon, a little dribbles from the corner, and I stand back, seeing what's coming. Water shoots far and wide, mostly all over the boys, who bolt up, while Kate remains on her arse, laughing it off.

"Fucking hell, Ava." I dab at her face, the table. "What the hell is wrong with you?" Has someone given her some laughing gas?

"I'm sorry. I'm so sorry." She chuckles, and finally, after a few more moments of jerking and snorting, settles down.

"Are you okay?"

"I'm sorry," she says again. "I don't know what's"—*laugh*—"wrong with me."

My eyes follow her hand as it collects her knife and fork and she starts calmly working her way through the rest of her dinner, oblivious to the concern around the table. At least from me and the boys. Kate's still fucking grinning. I cock my head at her. She shrugs.

"Is this what pregnancy does to women?" Sam asks, amused.

"It's better than mood swings," Kate adds.

I snort. *Fear not, Kate, we have those too.*

"Yeah, let me know when they start," Drew says. "I can handle being spat at, but I'm not up for a tongue-lashing."

Ava coughs again, and I'm about to go all Heimlich on her, but she pulls in a breath and continues calmly with her dinner until the plate is spotless.

"I take it you're done?"

She hums her satisfaction, sated, and collapses back. "That was heaven."

"Yeah, we can see." Drew looks at me in astonishment. I'm with him. I've never seen her tuck food away so ravenously. His phone rings on the table, and he swipes it up swiftly, making everyone at the table pause and look at him. "Sales call," he mutters, hitting the screen to reject the call before getting up and wandering across the bar toward Natasha.

"Say your goodbyes, lady," I order. It's been a long-arse day and I've shared her enough. "It's getting late." I give Sam a telling look that he completely ignores as Ava kisses each of them in farewell.

"Gathered yourself together now, Mrs. Ward?" I ask as I walk her out, amused.

"You knew, didn't you?" She peeks up at me, her cheeks still flushed from her laughing fit. Or could be our Compromise Fuck. Or a combination of both.

Knew? "About what?"

"About Kate, Sam, and Drew."

Oh, fuck me. Kate's told her? Is that what had her laughing hysterically and nearly choking on her dinner? "Is that what you were laughing about? She told you?"

"Yes. Why didn't *you* tell me?"

I laugh on the inside. "And give you something else to get your knickers in a twist over?"

"I wouldn't have," she says, indignant. We both know that's a load of crap. "Shall I take my giant snowball?"

I roll my eyes. "No, you're coming with me." I get her in, buckle her up, and get behind the wheel.

As I cruise down the driveway, I notice her hand on her stomach. *Protectiveness.* She's doing it without thinking. *Instinct.* I know she didn't plan for this. I know she doesn't need an *enhanced control freak*. But as I've told her so many times now that I have her in my life, I need a certain amount of control. Crave it. Feel stable with it.

I just wish she knew the true reasons behind my quirks.

But the problem remains...

I don't want her to doubt me as a husband.

Or a father.

Chapter 22

She fought it, but she drifted off on the way home. I carry her into Lusso, trying and failing to smile at the new concierge. "Mr. Ward," he says, hurrying out from behind his desk. "Let me call the elevator for you."

"Thanks." I hold back for him to access the keypad, but his finger stalls over the buttons. "Three, two, one, zero," I mutter. He looks back on a frown. He probably thinks that's the most uncreative code on the planet. How wrong he is. "Anytime today." I nod to my wife in my arms, currently clinging to my neck. I know she's awake now. She could walk. But I also know she loves me carting her around.

"Of course." He punches in the code and the doors slide open, then he holds the door until I'm in with Ava. "I'm on the nightshift until Clive arrives at nine, Mr. Ward, so anything you need, you know where to find me." He enters the code again and steps out, tipping his hat.

"Thanks." The doors close, and I look down at Ava. She's smiling, eyes closed. "I don't like him," I say, and she chuckles. "Bed?"

She nods, speech evading her, and continues clinging to me all the way up to the bedroom. I'm not surprised that she also lets me get her ready for bed, holding her arms out for me to join her once I've tucked her in. This is what she likes—me looking after her.

When it suits her.

"Snuggles," she murmurs, finding enough strength to reach up and grab the lapels of my suit jacket, hauling me down. I don't fight her. Why would I? I settle on top of her, my elbows on the mattress keeping me semi-suspended, my face in her neck, hers in mine. I try so hard to focus on the sound of her breathing, to stop anything else from infiltrating our calm. But as if a ticking timebomb is counting down, the tension inside seems to get worse. The pressure growing with my frustration. How does Lauren keeps muscling her way into my happiness? I can deal with my dead brother popping up unexpectedly from time to time. Welcome it, to an extent. And Rosie has a place in my forever. But my ex-wife? No. I escaped her once, and I feel like I'm trying to all over again. Moments of uncomfortable flashbacks, the smallest thing triggering. Like Ava pointing with a knife. Lauren has no place here—in my life, in my mind. It's fucking with my head, and isn't that obvious when I think I'm seeing her.

I squeeze my eyes closed and focus on calming my restless breathing, carefully lifting my body a fraction to check Ava. She's sleeping. I peel myself off her body, drop a light kiss on her forehead, and take myself downstairs. After fetching a glass of water, I go into my office, settle in my chair, then answer an email confirming the decorator on Friday, making sure he remembers he has an eight-hour window of opportunity. It shouldn't be a problem; it's just one wall.

Then I load some music and rest back in my chair, my fingers laced and resting on my chest, my eyes on the ceiling. I just need a moment to close my eyes and breathe, allow the music to settle deep and let my mind empty, making room for only the blessed things.

Rosie.

And she comes to me, blurring in and out of my mind's eye, every stage of her short life from birth to the day I watched Carmichael put her in his car and drive away from me.

The first bath I gave her, the first banana, jangling my keys trying to get her to walk to me, smiling when she'd collapse to her little butt, her nappy cushioning the impact.

Her grabby hands, her gummy smile, her dark blond hair flicking out at her nape. The first time I managed to get a hairclip to hold the fine strands out of her eyes. Her disgusted face when she yanked it out. How utterly edible she was, especially in her babygrows. How her little bowed legs stomped along when she started walking. How she looked when she fell asleep in my arms.

And how she only ever looked at me with love. No judgment. No scorn.

Her face, confused and innocent, as Carmichael carried her away from The Manor.

Carried her away from me.

Sarah flounces into my bedroom, not knocking as usual, and I drop my magazine to my lap and give her tired eyes. "Why are you looking so sorry for yourself?" she asks.

I don't entertain her. She doesn't care. I picked Rosie up this morning for the weekend. I got the usual looks of disapproval, the scathing words. I'll never harden to it. "I'm fine." I get up and check the monitor, seeing Rosie's still snoozing. She can have another fifteen minutes. We have a date with the ducks before dinner, bath, and bed.

I go to my bathroom, feeling Sarah's eyes on my naked back. "Where's Carmichael?" I call back, grabbing my toothbrush. I look at myself in the mirror...and clench my eyes closed when my face blurs into Jake's. I feel like he's always with me, but today he's really with me. No surprises there.

How the fuck has it been four years? Today was always going to be hard. I can only thank my lucky stars that I have Rosie to keep me busy. Happy. Fulfilled. But just for today and tomorrow. Then she leaves me. Then I'm kicking my heels until the next time I'm allowed to see her.

I scrub my teeth, which is easier said than done when they're trying to clench, noticing Sarah in the reflection, her shoulder resting on the doorjamb. "He's taken Rebecca to pick apples in the orchard."

I spit, rinse, and pass Sarah, giving her a wide berth. "I'm taking Rosie out for a few hours."

"Want some company?"

"No," I answer shortly. It's the only language Sarah understands. Curt. Abrupt. "Go find another man to hunt." I look over my shoulder on an unamused smirk as I pull my T-shirt down my chest.

"But I like hunting you." She approaches me, reaching for my arm. I grab her wrist before she can touch me, holding it, and she snaps her eyes up to mine. I shake my head.

"You'll lose the fight one day," she says quietly, moving her gaze to my lips.

"Never," I answer her. Sarah's an attractive girl, but she's my uncle's girlfriend. Their relationship isn't monogamous. I don't understand it, but I don't have to. I just need to make sure Sarah never wins the fight. I think I must be the only man to walk in The Manor who has resisted her. She's young, has a beautiful body, and she's quite talented with a crop.

A magnet for the male members.

But I'm not a member.

And given she's Carmichael's in my mind, I want nothing to do with her.

Her way is not what I want in a sexual partner.

Never will.

"Excuse me," I say, releasing her hand. She yanks it away, like she *was in control of her freedom. "Have a nice evening, Sarah."*

"I will," she sings as I leave her to go get my girl up.

I come back into my body on a gasp, a screeching noise piercing my ears. It takes me a moment to realize it's my mobile. I dip into my pocket and pull it out, laughing under my breath when Sarah's name glows up at me. God damn her. What if Ava wasn't asleep? What if Ava thought Sarah was calling me regularly? As much as I'm still angry at Sarah, I know being cut out of my life has crippled her. And my conscience won't allow me to reject the call. *Fucking conscience.* "Hi," I say softly.

"Hey."

How different she sounds to the Sarah everyone knows and *doesn't* love. "How are you feeling?"

"Good." She clears her throat. "Yeah, better, thank you."

I nod, silence falling down the line. I don't know why she's called me. Her job? Has John told her about the baby? "You?" she finally asks.

"Since when have we done small talk?"

She huffs. More silence. "I went to see Ava," she says.

I become rigid. "I told you to stay away from her." What the hell was she thinking? And why hasn't Ava mentioned it?

"I wanted her to see how sorry I am. I'm losing my mind, Jesse," she says quietly.

I close my eyes and rub into one of the sockets. "Ava's pregnant, Sarah," I whisper, waiting. I definitely hear a deep breath taken. This will hurt her.

"She's trapped you?" she blurts. "Oh my God, she's done exactly what Lauren did to you."

I laugh out loud. *Fucking hell.* "She didn't trap me, Sarah."

"I can't believe you let this happen."

"Sarah, she—"

"Are you some kind of idiot?"

"It's not like—"

"Jesse, you need—"

"I trapped *her*, Sarah." The silence that falls is unbearable. "It was me. *I* trapped *her*. I manipulated the whole fucking chain of events because I wanted her to be pregnant. I wanted to make it as hard as possible for her to run if she found out what I fuck-up I am. I stole her pills. I purposely put my dick in her repeatedly knowing she wasn't protected. This is on *me*. So rein in your fucking opinions, okay? You don't *know* me like you think you know me, Sarah, and you certainly don't know Ava." I feel my nostrils flare. "Only Ava really knows me. Because she's my *wife*. And soon she'll be the mother of my child."

"You're replacing her," she whispers.

I'm shaking. In fury. I am *not* fucking replacing my baby girl. "Do not contact me again." I slam down my phone, raging. *I'm not replacing her!* My hand shoots out, knocking a paperweight flying across the office.

"I'm not replacing you," I breathe. "Never."

I know, Daddy.

Chapter 23

I didn't sleep. Nowhere close. *I'm not replacing Rosie.* I hit the slow button and work my way down to a jog, grabbing the towel and wiping my face before laying it across my bare shoulders and wedging my palms into the handles, staring at nothing on the TV screen. Then I'm staring at something.

Ava.

My present. My future.

She looks peaky. Drained. Jesus, this morning sickness has got her good. "Oh baby." I take in her sorrowful face. "Crap?"

"Terrible."

That makes both of us. She'll still insist on going to work, though. I scoop her up, carrying her to the kitchen. "I was going to ask why you're not naked."

"Don't bother, I'll throw up on you."

Chuckling, I sit her on the counter. "You look beautiful."

"Don't lie to me, Ward." She pouts. "I look like shit."

"Ava," I whisper. She's clearly got enough energy to curse. "You need to eat."

Her cheeks balloon, an unattractive sound rumbling up from her stomach. I step back, genuinely worried she's actually going to throw up.

"I'm here," Cathy sings, the door closing in the distance. She appears at the door. "Morning." Then she takes us both in, Ava looking green, me looking worried. "Oh dear. Whatever is the matter?"

"Ava's not feeling too good."

"Oh, the dreaded morning sickness? It'll pass."

"Will it?" Ava asks, sounding truly hopeful, looking for reassurance as she sinks into my chest. "When?"

I look to Cathy, holding Ava, hugging her, fussing over her.

"It depends," she says, starting her usual faff around the kitchen. "Boy, girl, mum, dad. Some women have a few weeks of it, some struggle throughout the whole of their pregnancy."

Oh shit, that's not ideal.

"Oh God," Ava grumbles, clinging on to me weakly. "Don't say that."

"Ginger!"

I jump, jarring Ava from my chest. Ginger? Is she telling us ginger babies make morning sickness worse? "What?" Ava asks what we're both wanting to know.

"Ginger." Cathy dives into her bag and pulls out a pack of…biscuits? "You need ginger, dear. I came prepared." I'm shoved aside. I'm not injured. Cathy's just put one of those biscuits in Ava's hand, telling her to have one every morning, and she's started nibbling it without protest. It's a miracle. Let's see if she keeps it down. Ginger? Who would have thought. "It'll settle your stomach." Cathy pats Ava's cheek, her old nose wrinkling. "I'm so excited."

No shit. I claim my wife back and sit her on a stool, checking the biscuit. Half gone. This could be a gamechanger.

"The new boy gave me these," Cathy says, holding out some envelopes. "Cute little bugger, isn't he?"

Cuter than Clive? I hear Ava chuckle, life suddenly in her bones. Good for her. I take the envelopes on a scowl.

"He's very sweet," Ava says, as I work one of the envelopes open, still scowling.

They chat happily about the new concierge while Cathy makes breakfast and Ava works her way through her biscuit. I rest my arse on a stool and pull out a letter, seeing a few leaflets attached to the edge. At first I think it's junk mail. Then I see Ava's name. Or, at least, her old name. *O'Shea.* And her *old* address.

Where she lived with her ex.

Confused as fuck, I look at the front of the envelope. It's addressed to me. Not Ava. And it's marked private. Ava's next to me, talking happily, a little more color in her cheeks, as Cathy pushes a plate toward me. I smile my thanks, going back to the letter, reading. It's a scan appointment. I thought I told Ava I'd organize a private scan. But then I look at the date in the corner, mentally doing the math. This was sent a week ago. Last Monday, to be precise. Last Monday when I followed her to the surgery. Last Monday when she walked out of the doctor's office and threw up all over the bathroom. Last Monday when she told me she *wasn't* pregnant. That I'd failed.

A horrible coolness slithers through my veins as I read on, past the appointment date and time.

Options.

Will be discussed at the scan.

Termination last resort.

Consider adoption.

My stomach drops like a fucking rock as I turn the letter over and read the leaflets.

All on abortion.

"Eat your breakfast," Ava says, sliding my plate closer to me. I look at her, everything inside becoming heavy. Everything hurting. She searches my face, her chewing slowing. I can see her mouth moving. Can't hear a fucking word she's saying. She was going to let me believe she was *never* pregnant? Have an abortion and not tell me?

"What is that?" Ava asks, leaning in to see the envelope.

"Go upstairs." They're the only words I can find.

She withdraws. "Why?"

"Don't make me ask you again, Ava." I feel like a tightly coiled spring, an inferno burning me from the inside out. What the fuck is this crazy?

Not arguing, she slips down from the stool, looking tense and uncertain, and I don't have it in me to fix that. Cathy looks between us as Ava leaves, no questions asked. I have to take a moment to breathe some measured breaths. *Options. To be rid of my baby. Our* baby. She doesn't want this baby.

I could sit here for a year and find no control.

I get up and follow Ava upstairs, entering the bedroom. "What the fuck is this?" I ask, waving the letter and leaflets in her face, noting how she takes a step back, a step away from me. It's a good indication that I'm looking extremely volatile. I'm definitely feeling it.

"What is it?" she asks, her voice quiet.

I have to drop the letter, the damn thing burning my skin. Maybe this is a mistake. Maybe the letter was sent to Ava by mistake. "You were going to kill our baby?"

The instant fall of her face tells me my *maybes* were wasted hope. Her eyes drop to her feet. *Hiding.* My God, she was going to end this pregnancy? She was intending on killing our baby and letting me believe she was never pregnant?

My hands. I can't focus on them, they're shaking so much. "Answer me," I bellow. She flinches, letting out a small, suppressed whimper. "Ava, for fuck's sake." I hold the tops of her arms, dipping, getting my face level with hers. She turns her head away. "Damn it, look at me."

God help me, she continues to hide, silent, her body shaking along with her head. Shame's engulfing her. Disbelief's engulfing me. I take her face and turn it toward me, scanning every inch of it, wondering how the hell she could do this. My perfect wife. The woman who has literally given me life was going to take a part of it away from me.

Her eyes are full of tears, and they're quickly rolling down her cheeks. "I'm sorry," she whispers, sniffing.

She's sorry?

She's...*sorry*?

My eyes dart across her blotchy face, my mind willing me to wake up from this nightmare. "You've broken my fucking heart, Ava," I croak, releasing her and backing up. I can't look at her. Can't be near her.

I go to the dressing room, randomly grab some clothes, and walk out. And I walk fast, terrified I'll change my mind and go back to shake her. I don't use the elevator, needing to burn off the anger, so I take the stairs. My hands are trembling so much, it takes four attempts to enter the code correctly, and when I get to the bottom, I look at my hands. "Fuck." I throw my clothes in a pile on the floor and strip out of my running shorts, pulling on my jeans, a T-shirt, and stuffing my feet into some boots. I leave the stairwell, ignoring Casey as I pass, and break out of Lusso, going to my car, calling John on my way. "I need you to collect Ava and take her to work, no questions asked." I hang up before he can ask. Not that I think he would.

I get in my Aston, slam it into drive, and screech out of the car park. I narrowly miss the gates that are still opening as I exit, checking my watch. I hope for his sake he's not left for work yet because I absolutely *will* go to his office to release this unbridled rage.

• • •

I don't bother finding a parking space. I double park directly outside his flat and leap up the steps, hammering on the door repeatedly until some poor, elderly lady in a dressing gown answers. I pass her, leaping up more stairs to his flat and proceeding to smash my fist into that door too. The second I hear the latch release, I push my way in and grab the first thing within reach.

Matt's throat.

I slam him into the wall, my snarling face up in his sleepy one, and before he can even murmur a plea, my knee has come up and slammed into his stomach, waking him up. I don't ease up my hold so he can double over, keeping him pinned against the wall.

"You fucking psycho," he chokes, grappling with my hold of his throat.

Psycho? He's seen nothing. "You thought that was smart, did you?" I snarl through my words. "You thought you'd slither in and try to cause upset?" I draw my fist back and sink it into his face, making his head ricochet off the wall.

He barks his shock and pain, gasping. "Are you sure it's even yours?" he hisses, the sick fucker.

That's it.

Any slice of control I had is lost, and I absolutely batter the fucker, punching him until my fist physically can't take anymore, leaving him curled in a ball on the carpet, blood pouring from his nose, his eyes closed from the instant swelling. "Stay the fuck away from me and my wife." I leave before I kill him, getting in my car and hitting the steering wheel over and over before screeching off. I drive like a total fucking idiot, my emotions changing as much as the gears of my car, tears clouding my vision, then anger, my mind in utter chaos.

Unforgiveable.

It's unforgiveable, and that truly scares the shit out of me, because I didn't think there was anything in this world that could make me question my feelings for Ava. This, though? It's got me. And, worse, Ava will never know the level of betrayal I feel.

Because she still doesn't know I'm a father who lost his daughter.

• • •

Two hours driving around the countryside didn't cool me off either. John watches me pass him on the driveway, my car too fast over the gravel as I steer it around the side of The Manor. I get out and go straight to the garages, hitting my fob to open the doors and scanning the line of machines before me. I haven't needed to do this for a while. I pull down my helmet from the shelf. No leathers. No gloves.

Swinging my leg over the bike, I settle in the cushioned seat. "She didn't let me take her to work," John says.

I laugh on the inside. Of course she didn't.

"Jesse," he goes on, appearing before me.

"Not now."

"Then when?"

When I feel less likely to explode and destroy everything in my path. "Later." I reach up to get my helmet on, but John's hand on the front of my bike stalls me.

"What's going on?" he asks, concerned.

I stare at him, unable to speak the words. How could she? "I'm fine."

"Shut the fuck up, Jesse. Tell me before I drag you off this bike and kick it out of you."

"She was going to have an abortion."

His massive chest inflates from his shocked inhale.

"Yeah," I breathe. "I know."

"And the blood?" he asks, pointing to my fists.

I lift my hand, seeing smears across the knuckles. "Matt's face."

"What?"

"He sent me the letter Ava's doctor sent to his flat confirming her scan appointment and *options*."

"Shit."

"I need to ride." I push my helmet on and turn the key in the ignition, kicking the stand up and revving the engine as I hit the button on the fob for the gates, ensuring they're open by the time I get there. Ensuring I don't need to slow down. Stop. And they are. I fly through them, checking for oncoming traffic, and as soon as I'm on the main road, I open her up, flying through the gears until she's maxed out, my T-shirt stuck to me, the world whizzing past in a blur, wind rushing past, the noise mingling with the roar of the engine, diluting my thoughts. But not enough. Abortion? How could she? I'm at a loss, so fucking hurt.

Killing yourself isn't the answer, bro.

Then what is?

Compassion. You think she'd have even considered it if she knew about Rosie?

I slow a little and take a curve wide, seeing the road ahead is clear. I max her out again. It doesn't matter. She was going to take a life without a second thought for the aftermath. The guilt. The loss.

Is it the same thing?

"I don't fucking know!" I scream at the road.

Slow down, bro.

"It should have been me, Jake." My voice cracks, the road becoming blurry. "If it had been me, it would have *only* been me." But it wasn't only me. It was Jake, and that was a catalyst to many more lives being ruined.

Slow down.

Because of me.

Slow down, Jesse!

Jake, Rosie, Rebecca, Carmichael. Nearly Sarah too. All because of me.

Slow the fuck down, now!

I jerk, my fingers pulling at the brakes, and I skid to a stop by the side of the road, diving off my bike, leaving it to fall to the tarmac with a crash. I fumble with the strap under my chin, feeling suffocated, and yank my helmet off, gasping for air, struggling to breathe as I stagger to the verge. I collapse to the grass and fall to my back, looking up to the sky, my chest pumping hard.

Heaven.

Will I ever earn my way into that sacred place?

Will I ever see my loves again?

I don't want to see your ugly fucking face for a long fucking time, Jesse. Do you hear me?

"Watch your mouth," I murmur.

Fuck off. You have a job to do there. We're fine.

"We?"

Uncle Jake's looking after me, Daddy.

I cough over a sob, rolling onto my side, wanting to curl into a ball of shame and stem the pain. "That's good," I whisper. "Tell him thank you. Tell him I love him. And you, baby girl. I love you too."

Silence.

I wait, listen, holding my breath.

No voices.

I roll onto my back again, looking up at the clouds. "Did you hear me, Rosie?" I roughly wipe my eyes, sniff back my tears, listening, waiting.

"Shit, mate, are you all right?"

I lift my head and come face to face with a young lad in a Manchester United kit. I laugh under my breath, seeing Jake and me in the garden, him in red, me in blue. Fucking hell, our looks were the only similar thing about us.

Come on, you Reds.

I blink, seeing him dribbling the ball toward me, goading me as I widened my stance, holding my hands up, getting ready to save his shot. But the fucker nutmegs me.

Goal!

"Jesus Christ," I gasp, pushing myself to my feet. "I'm fine." I notice his little boy racer car on the roadside behind my bike, his hazard lights on.

"I thought you'd come off, mate," he says, flanking me to my bike, watching me stand it up. "That is one awesome machine."

I laugh under my breath, getting back on my awesome machine. "What's your name?"

"Bran."

"How old are you, Bran?"

"Seventeen."

Seventeen? Fuck, it feels like yesterday but also like an eternity ago. I look him up and down. He's just a boy. His whole life ahead of him. "New driver?" I ask.

His puny chest pushes out with pride. "Two months."

"Drive carefully, okay?"

Poor, confused thing frowns. "Yeah, okay." He trudges back to his car, constantly looking back at me, probably thinking I'm all kinds of weird. "See ya," he calls, opening his car door, just as another car goes sailing past, moving out onto the other side of the road to clear us.

My frown follows it down the road before it takes a curve and I lose sight of it.

"Fuck me," the kid blurts. "Did you see that?"

"Yeah, I saw it," I murmur, a chill enveloping me.

"I'll have a DB9 one day," he says, confident.

"That was a DBS," I call back, still staring at the road.

"How do you know?"

"Because it was mine." I blink and pull my phone out, seeing a few missed calls from John. *Fuck*.

I don't get the chance to call him back. He pulls up in his Range Rover behind the kid, and my apprehension is instant. "That was my car, wasn't it?" I say.

One sharp nod, and I just stare at him, because I don't know what else to do. "Who the fuck would steal my car?" I ask. "And how the hell did they get in and out of The Manor?"

"I don't know," John admits. "We need to call the police."

"Fuck that," I snort, putting my helmet on again, hearing John yelling at me. Distraction. Another opportunity to alleviate some of this pressure. I get on my bike and skid off, hearing Jake in my head warning me again. Unfortunately for him and John, I'm not feeling very receptive to advice today.

I yank at the throttle, hardly slowing for corners, dipping in low for them, my knees heating they're so close to brushing the road. "Where the fuck are you?" Every bend I take, I brace myself for my Aston to appear in the distance. It never does, and before I know it, I'm back in the city with too many turns in the road and options for the driver of my DBS to take.

I reluctantly call it quits when my bike yells it's in need of some fuel. Defeated and pissed off, I pull into a petrol station and fill her up, calling John as I do. "Not fucking cool, Jesse," he spits, angry.

"It's an Aston Martin, John. They should be impossible to steal."

"They're also one of the most stolen cars because they're one of the most desirable. Where the fuck are you?"

"The Shell station, Marylebone."

"Meet me at Lusso." He leaves no room for refusal, hanging up.

I sigh, watching every car passing as I fill the fuel tank on my bike. No Astons. Not one.

Trepidation settles deep in my gut.

Who the fuck was driving my car?

Chapter 24

I pull into the car park at Lusso and park, setting my helmet on the ground and perching on the seat of my bike, looking up at the face of the building. I need to call the police, the insurance company. I don't know where I'll find any of my documents. I breathe in some patience and call the Aston dealership, who put me through to their customer call center. I tell them my car's been stolen, they ask me if I have a crime reference. "I don't have a crime reference yet," I grate. "I just need you to tell me where my car is."

"Okay, let me see what we can find out," the lady says, sounding happy and passive. Both are inappropriate. "Can I take the vehicle registration?"

I inhale my patience and answer every question thrown at me, my responses getting shorter and sharper with each one I give. I don't have fucking time for this. "Last known location is Grantly Lane, in Surrey Hills."

I breathe out, starting to lose it. "That's my business address. What time?"

"An hour ago, sir."

"Well, it ain't there now."

"Oh?"

Fuck, I haven't got time for this shit. I hang up, squeezing my mobile in my hand, thinking. I unclench my hand then dial before I can second guess myself. "I need to speak to the practice manager."

"I'm afraid she's busy right now. Can I take a name and number and I'll have her call you back?"

"You told me that already and she hasn't called me back."

"Let me take your details again."

I take in air. Breathe. "Jesse Ward," I say, this time giving her my real name, thanking her for her help despite my ready-to-burst frustration.

John pulls up, slipping out of his Range Rover with two coffees. "Who was that?" he asks.

"A surgery in Aberdeen."

He passes me the caffeine. I could do with something stronger. "Why are you calling a surgery in Aberdeen?"

I don't hold back. I'm out of strength. "Because that's where Lauren's dad works or worked."

The falter in his expression is telling. "Is this something to do with you seeing her?" he asks, so normally. *Sarah*. Did she tell him? "Yes." John answers my silent question, and I scrub a hand down my face. It was probably part of Sarah's justification process, her reasons for needing to save me from my fate with Ava. *Ava's making me crazy*. No. My past is making me crazy.

I laugh to myself, sipping my coffee. "I know it wasn't her," I say. "One woman I fucking chased so I could be sure of it."

"But you needed to check?"

"It would settle me to know where she is, yes."

"Still locked up, I expect. But we'll find out for sure."

I nod, smiling my thanks. No judgments. John knows I've been straddling stable and unhinged for a while now. Like…since I met Ava. "The dealership said my car's at The Manor."

He snorts, and we both sit, silent for a while, until John breaks it. "Are you going to sort this shit out?"

"Which shit?" I ask on a smile.

"A car can be replaced," he says, as serious as John can be. Which is deadly serious. "A human can't."

I flinch, swallowing, staring at the concrete beneath my boots. So true. Ava doesn't know my truths…but does she really loathe the idea of being my child's mother so much that she'd destroy it? At least that explains why she was so distraught when she finally confessed she was pregnant. *Guilt*. She hadn't wanted me to know. And yes, I see the irony—she hid something from me. But it hurts. I just didn't see that coming. Not from Ava. "I feel let down, John," I admit, whether I have the right to feel that way or not. It's how I feel, and I can't help it.

"If she knew about Rosie, maybe things would have been different."

Maybe. Or maybe she would have run. Or, worse, gone through with it. I look at John, smiling through my tight lips. "Jake said the same thing this morning."

I expect him to whip out a straitjacket and bundle me into the back of his motor. But instead, surprising me, he chuckles. Like it's funny that I'm having merry old chitchats with my dead brother. I won't mention my daughter. Even I know that's pushing the boundaries of acceptable levels of crazy.

"You need to get in touch with the police," John says. "Sounds like the tracker's been deactivated."

"What about the CCTV?"

"I haven't checked yet. I jumped straight in my car when I heard yours roaring down the driveway. We know the camera by the garage is down, and your car was by the garage."

"But one of the other external cameras might shine some light."

He nods, sipping his coffee, quietly pensive. He's wondering too. Who would steal my car, because this sounds like more than a planned theft. It sounds like a vendetta. "I've got Cook looking into Van Der Haus."

"Thought you would," he replies, easy as that.

At the same time, both of our mobiles ring. Neither of us look particularly thrilled. I leave John to take his call while I connect mine, wandering away from him and my bike. "Yes?" I say in answer, sounding harder than I intended. Jake and John are right. Ava doesn't have any context. And bottom line, I trapped her. I realize she acted out of spite and anger. I realize she was trying to get some control back in her life. Still, it's a really fucking hard pill to swallow.

I expect an apology. A plea for understanding. I expect her to ask if we can talk, sort this out. I get none of that. "Nice drive?" she asks, her tone curt.

She's pissed with *me*? "What?"

"Are you having a nice drive?"

"Ava, what the fuck are you talking about?" I snap, irritation rising. "And when I send John to fetch you, get in his fucking car."

"I'm talking about you following me," she says, impatient.

"What?" Following her? Like a complete idiot, I circle on the spot, as if to remind myself I'm at Lusso and not following Ava. "Ava, I haven't got time for fucking riddles."

"I'm not talking in riddles, Jesse. Why the hell are you following me?"

"I'm not following you, Ava." I look to the heavens and take more caffeine.

"So I suppose there are hundreds of Aston Martins driving around London, and one just happens to be following me."

My coffee cup halts at my mouth, a rush of cold sweeping through my body. "You're driving?"

"Yes. I'm driving around in bloody circles, and you're following me. You'd make a shit detective."

"My car's following you?" I ask on a murmur, looking around the car park blankly, my mind struggling to absorb the information being given and what that could mean.

"Yes," she yells, angry.

"Ava, baby, I'm not driving my car," I say quietly. "I'm at *Lusso*."

She's silent for a few worrying moments. "But it's your car."

Realization slams into me with such force, I drop my coffee. My stolen car is following my wife? "Fuck!" I kick the cup away and stalk to my bike, my stomach dropping over and over, my throat clogged with apprehension. "John," I yell. The big guy looks over his shoulder, his phone still at his ear. His glasses are pulled off his face the second he registers my disposition.

"Jesse," Ava says. "What's going on?"

"My car's been stolen." I make it to my bike, hearing Ava talking but not hearing her, John pacing over in long, heavy strides. "My car's following Ava," I say, and he withdraws, his stoic face falling. "Where are you?" I ask Ava, as John goes straight to his phone and ends the call, heading to his car.

"I'm on the embankment," she says quietly. "Driving toward the city."

"John," I call. He looks back. "The embankment. City bound. Call her in two." John nods, gets in, and pulls away. Together. Calm. Collected. Makes one of us. "Baby, listen to me." I swing my leg over my bike. "Just keep driving, okay?"

"Okay," she whispers.

"I've got to put the phone down now." I stare at the handlebars of my bike, praying on anything I've ever believed in to watch over my wife and baby until I can get to them. *Beg.*

"I don't want you to." Her voice cracks, her fear thick. "Stay on the phone, please."

"Ava." I try to inhale some calm. "I've got to put the phone down.

John's going to call you as soon as I hang up. Put it on loudspeaker and place it in your lap so you can concentrate. Understand?"

Silence.

"Ava, baby. Tell me you understand."

"I understand."

I start the engine of my bike and hit the throttle, gripping hard to stop my shakes, taking a few needed deep breaths before I pull away. I see John in the distance, swerving in and out of traffic, running red lights, overtaking anything in his path. More than once, I'm forced onto the other side of the road, and more than once I feel something—a car, a bus, a moped—brush my arm or knee. The rushing air is hitting my eyes brutally, making me constantly squint and, as a consequence, hampers my vision. *Fuck*. I don't have a death wish. I'm not wearing a helmet, any leathers. One clip will have me coming off my bike and then I'll never make it to her. So when I finally catch up to John, I fall in line behind his Range Rover and follow his lead, using him as a barrier between the world and my bike. And he isn't fucking about, not slowing down for anyone or anything. We fly past Tower Bridge, London Bridge.

Closer.

And then John's brake lights come on and stay on, his Range Rover slowing down. I pull out and see the traffic has come to a standstill in the distance. No oncoming traffic too. People are getting out of their cars. "Fuck," I breathe, knowing all the signs of a car accident are in front of me. My heartbeats become painful, my breathing strained, as John moves onto the other side of the road and picks up speed again. And when his hazards start flashing but he doesn't slow, I pull out again.

And I see it. My Aston up ahead in the road. And not far away from it, Ava's Mini. The bonnet is crushed up against a metal barrier.

"My God." I feel the blood drain from my face, my eyes on her car, searching the inside from a distance. She's not in there? And then I see her standing in the middle of the road, motionless. Shocked. *Fuck*. The Aston screeches away, and John goes hell for leather after it.

The moment I'm near Ava, I slam on my brakes and hop off my bike as soon as it's slow enough, leaving it skidding away across the concrete. I run, feeling like it's taking an eternity to make it to her, the world slowing in every element. Her face is blank. I scan her body the closer I get, checking for marks, for grazes, anything. I reach her. Her empty eyes look up at me. There's nothing in them. Nothing—no fear, no anger, no grief, no emotion whatsoever. I feel her cheek, hoping my touch might shock her back to life. It doesn't. An ambulance pulls through the traffic up ahead, two police cars coming from the other direction. Endless cars around us damaged, buried in walls, streetlamps.

"Ava? Jesus, baby." I pull her close and try again to take in the carnage surrounding us. She feels heavy and limp. "Fucking hell," I whisper, losing myself in her hair for a brief moment. Escaping the madness.

She's alive.

She's okay.

What the fuck is going on?

As if hearing my question, my phone rings and I free one arm from Ava to take his call. "John?"

"Isn't it fucking typical that you would own one of the fastest commercial cars on the motherfucking *fucking* planet?" he snaps.

"Where are you?"

"Trying to keep up. How's the girl?"

I will Ava to snap out of her daze and hold me. Give me some sign that she's okay. "In shock I think."

At those words, she stirs, breaking away, and starts gazing around. More police, another ambulance. Her mind is finally processing what's happened. She's starting to shake.

"Don't stop until you've found out who's in my fucking car," I say to John, hearing his foreboding grunt before the line goes dead. "Look at me, baby," I order gently, encouraging her gaze away from the carnage to me. Her eyes are empty.

"Where's your helmet?" she murmurs on a frown.

"Fucking hell," I breathe, kissing her, squeezing her cheeks. *If she had just got in the fucking car with John.* "Why do you refuse to play ball?" I ask, smothering her. "I sent John to get you, Ava. Why didn't you let him take you to work?"

"Because I wanted to shred Matt," she says. I look down at her. She went to see him? "But you beat me to it."

"I was so angry, Ava," I say quietly. Matt had to take the brunt of my rage or I was likely to self-combust with the pressure needing out.

"I would never have seen it through," she says on a sob. "I wouldn't have killed our baby."

Thank. Fuck.

She has no idea how much I needed to hear that. No fucking idea. "Shhh." I do my best to comfort her, hold her, and this time she holds me back tightly, sobbing into my shoulder.

"Excuse me, sir." A copper approaches, taking us both in. "Is the young lady okay?"

"I don't know." I haven't checked her properly or closely. "Are you okay?" I feel at her arms, check her face again, her fingers, her wrists, even her dress for rips. Nothing.

"I'm fine," she says quietly, looking past the officer. "What about the other drivers?"

"Just a few cuts and bruises. You were all very lucky. Shall we get you checked over before we run through some questions?"

"I feel fine," Ava protests. "Honestly."

Dear God, help me. "I'm going to take that *fine* in my palm and slap you all over the arse with it."

"I'm fine," she reiterates, taking in her mangled Mini. The Mini she *shouldn't* have been driving.

"Ava, don't defy me on this, please," I say, taking on a begging tactic rather than a full force demand. She's delicate. Still in shock. "I have no problem pinning you down in the ambulance so they can confirm you're okay." I tilt my head and see her flick a nervous smile at the officer. "Are you going the easy way, or the hard way?" I ask.

"I'll go," she breathes, and that's the only reason I release her. "My bag."

I check she's stable on two feet before I let go of her. "I'll get it."

"My phone's on the floor," she calls after me. The closer I get to her Mini, the colder I feel. How differently this could have played out. It's chilling. I thought an attempt to drug her was low enough. This? I need to get us out of town for a while. Make a few calls, and maybe now actually get the police involved.

I retrieve Ava's bag and phone and hurry back to her, holding her hand as we're led through the crowds to the ambulance. I help her into the back.

"Sir," the copper says, armed with a notepad and pen. "While she's being taken care of, do you mind answering a few questions?"

Now? "Yes, I do." I snort, eyes on Ava as she looks down at me and the paramedic fiddling with a machine beyond. Blood pressure? Heart rate? "You'll have to wait." They should know she's expecting. I need to tell—

"Sir, I'd like to ask you a few questions."

I turn a death stare his way. Yeah, I'm sure. Problem is, answering his questions isn't a priority right now. Not to mention the fact that I have no fucking clue what to tell him. "My wife and child are in the back of that ambulance," I say, pointing blindly to Ava, seething. I expect I'll get told he has a job to do. Well, so do I. "The only way you're going to stop me from seeing to them is if I'm dead." There's a fucking time and a place for questions, and now isn't it. "So fucking shoot me."

He backs off, and I return my attention to my wife. She's standing just inside the ambulance doors while the paramedic continues to fart-arse around behind her. What, there's no rush because she's walking? What the hell does someone need to do to get a little urgency around here? I shake my head in despair, drop my eyes, take a breath, and have a quiet word with myself before I upset the medics as well as the—

I frown when a see a trickle of blood appear from beneath Ava's dress, and my eyes follow its path over her smooth skin down her leg. "Baby, you're cut," I whisper, running my fingertip through the trail.

She fists the material of her dress and shifts it up, looking down at her legs. "Where?" Her dress gets higher. Higher. No cut. I step back, looking at my finger covered in blood, understanding creeping up on me. I gaze up at Ava with worried eyes, hoping she'll diminish my fears.

Her face is blank.

No.

I act without thought, moving back into her, taking her dress and lifting it higher, trying to find the cut. *There has to be a cut.*

I lose my breath when I see the blood-stained lace of her knickers, my body locked tight.

"No," Ava yells distraught.

Her distress realigns me. "Oh, Jesus." I pull her dress into place and get into the back of the ambulance, hauling her into my body, feeling her vibrate against me. "Fucking hell, no." Surely God can't be this cruel. I clench my eyes closed, because I know He can be. And the familiar surge of grief hijacks me as I hold my wife, squeeze her, try to protect her from this injustice.

"Sir?" The paramedic looks at me with concern.

"Hospital," I demand, my vision hazy. "Now."

I sit Ava on the stretcher and put myself next to her, gritting my teeth when she retreats into my chest, her tears soaking through my T-shirt. "I'm sorry," she croaks.

"Shut up, Ava," I snap, angry, not with her, but with the fucking world. I pull her out of my T-shirt and find her eyes. I'm fucking crushed, even though I probably deserve this endless serving of grief. But Ava? She does not. And I have to ask myself now, when she's losing like I have lost before, if I can stay. My punishments are my own. Ava shouldn't have to face them. Knowing she will always be hunted by my horrid fate. Knowing she'll always suffer loss if I remain in her life.

Can I stay?

"Please," I beg her, as she sobs and shakes, apologizes over and over. "Just shut up." I try to wipe her tears away, but they're coming too fast. "I love you," I whisper, pushing my finger into her lip, trying to stop it wobbling. She swallows and curls into my side, making herself so small.

"Pregnant?" the paramedic asks.

"Yes," I answer, even if that's not the case now.

She nods and gives me a sympathetic smile, and I cuddle Ava that little bit closer, hearing her mumbled apologies. I can only hold her. Until the paramedic explains we can't leave until Ava's lying down on the bed. So I release her, watching as they ease her to her back. Watching her silently crying, her chest jumping.

How much more do I have to sacrifice before my dues are paid?

Chapter 25

I don't know what to do, how to act. Strong? Broken? Sad? The latter two are easy. But being strong? I've never faced grief with strength. *I've hidden. Fucked. Drank.* But now...*now* I have to be different.

I carried her to a private room because physical strength is something I could offer. I remained quiet while they checked Ava's obs. I lost myself in my palms a few times when the tears were at risk of escaping. I feel useless, propped in a chair, trying to comfort Ava while fighting to hold myself together.

Vodka.

The thought jars me.

The nurse lays a gown on the bed, says something—I don't know what—and leaves. It takes Ava to stand and start undressing for me to realize something is happening. She's changing? I watch her, see her slow, lethargic movements, not because she's in actual pain, but because she's in fucking agony mentally.

I have to hold her up in both senses. I can be strong. Emotionally and physically. Because that's what she needs from me right now. And because it isn't just about me anymore. I have Ava.

I get up to help, to feel useful. "I can manage." She doesn't look at me.

"You probably can, but it's my job and I'd like to keep it."

Her whole body shrinks, her chin trembling. "Thank you," she croaks as I remove her dress. Her chin drops to her chest, her eyes low. She doesn't want to look at me. Or can't.

I dip and nuzzle into her, forcing her face up. "Don't thank me for looking after you, Ava," I warn softly. "It's what I've been put on this earth to do. It's what keeps me here. Don't ever thank me for that."

"I've ruined everything," she whispers. "I've lost your dream."

My dream? Is it tragic that I feel like giving up on dreams? If you don't find your dreams, they can't be lost. If you have no faith, it can't be destroyed.

I sit her down on the bed and kneel in front of her, my hands clenching hers. "My dream is you, Ava. Day and night, just you. I can manage without anything, but never you. Not ever." Manage? Can I? Because my track record isn't exactly shining. This is a cruel blow. I'm not sure how either of us will navigate this or get over it, but Ava needs to know that she is my priority. "Don't look like this, please." So broken and heavy with guilt. So…hopeless. "Don't look like you think it's the end. It's never the end for us. Nothing will break us, Ava. Do you understand me?"

Her breath catches at the back of her throat, making her jerk as I caress her cheek, my tear-filled eyes staring into hers. I can understand her fear though. I stormed off, unsure I could ever forgive her, and yet now I'm professing my undying devotion. But it's true. I could never not love this woman. "We let these people tell us you're going to be okay, and then we go home to be together."

She nods jerkily, dislodging more tears.

"Tell me you love me," I order, desperate to bring something familiar and comforting to this whole horror scene.

"I need you," she sobs, hauling me into her and cuddling me hard.

She feels so fragile and weak in my arms. "I need you too." And I need her to let me look after her. "Let me get you into this gown."

The silence falls, but it's an oddly easy silence, yet at the same time, a really fucking hard one. I wipe the insides of her thighs with a cloth and slowly get her into the gown, letting the nurse know when we're ready. Even if we're not.

She enters, that sympathetic smile still on her face, and a doctor follows her in. I try so hard to stop it, but my body tightens, dread for what's to come gripping me. He nods at me as he sits on the side of the bed. "How are you feeling, Ava?"

What a stupid fucking question.

"Fine."

And an even stupider answer.

"I'm okay," she says again, sensing my despair, finding another word for *fine*. "Thank you."

"Okay." He looks across her gown-covered body. "No aches or pains, cuts or bruises?"

"No." She shakes her head, her hands fiddling wildly. "Nothing."

He reaches for the sheets and eases them down to below her stomach, and I shift in my chair, uncomfortable, bracing myself for the tragic news. "Let's see what's going on. Would you like to pull the gown up so I can feel your tummy?"

I can't sit here and watch this stranger poke and prod at my wife, all with the sole purpose of telling us we've lost something so fucking precious. *Always losing.* This is painful enough. I feel Ava studying me, pensive, and all I can do is wonder how I make this better. I can't even force a weak smile to try and reassure her. Fuck, I need some air. My lungs are burning with the effort to simply breathe. *Loser.* "I might step outside." I feel like a ticking time bomb.

"Don't you dare," Ava blurts, stopping my backward steps to the door. "Don't you dare leave me." Her jaw is between quivering and tightening, her eyes steely but watery.

She needs me.

Fuck. It's a lightning-bolt moment. I always wish for her vulnerability to shine through. But not like this. I pick up my feet and go to her, sitting and holding her hands with both of mine, my gaze low, my mind trying to block out the sounds of the doctor working.

"This will be a little chilly," he says.

And a lot fucking painful. I laugh sardonically on the inside. I should be fucking used to it. Immune to it. But no. The universe wants to carry on fucking me over. And because I'm now married to this young, bright beauty, she will be fucked over too.

I breathe in.

Breathe out.

Breathe in.

Breathe out.

In.

Out.

I hear clicks, turns, whooshes, *my* breathing, Ava's breathing. I notice her staring at the ceiling, her face painfully expressionless. My head drops heavily again, my hands squeezing tighter around hers. Time stands still for a while, my hearing heightened, the clock hands ticking in between the machinery and the thumps of my heartbeats. I blink my dry eyes, head still low, still clinging to her. Keeping me grounded.

I need a drink.

Vod—

"Everything is okay, Ava," the doctor says.

I frown, not daring to look up, scared I'm hearing things. It wouldn't be the first time. Hearing things, seeing things. Ava murmurs her confusion. I hear the doctor tell us light bleeding isn't unusual during the early stages.

Everything is okay? My wife and my baby are okay? I blink, feeling the tickle of a tear rolling down my cheek. Is this a dream?

Ava sucks in air sharply, and I realize it's a sound of pain. Then I realize I'm the one causing her pain, squeezing her hand to death. I quickly relax and look up in a state of utter shock. Our baby is okay.

She's not been taken.

Ava doesn't look all too present either. What the fuck is going on?

And is one of us going to ask for confirmation? Did Ava hear what was just said? My mouth opens and shuts. Ava's mouth opens and shuts.

I stand, but my legs wobble, so I sit back down. Then get straight back up. "Ava's still pregnant?" I murmur, staring at the doctor, watching his face so very closely, trying to read every slight move in his expression. He's smiling. That has to be a good thing. No doctor would smile if the situation was dire. "She's…she's…" I can't string a fucking sentence together. "There's…we're…" What am I trying to say?

"Yes." The doctor chuckles. That was definitely a chuckle. Smiling, chuckling. He's happy. But what am *I* feeling? Dazed. "Ava is still pregnant, Mr. Ward," he says cheerfully as he works on the machine. "Sit down, I'll show you."

Sit down? How do I sit down? I quickly check Ava's still on the bed. Because where else would she be? "I'll stand, if you don't mind," I mumble, my eyes on the screen, the mass of black fuzz and white blobs a total mess. "I need to feel my legs." I study the pulsing images, the dusty dots. "I don't see anything."

"There, look." The doctor points to the center to what looks like a really long, really dark tunnel. "Two perfect heartbeats."

Say *what* now? "My baby has two hearts?" Am I an absolute moron? Jake makes his presence known and starts laughing hysterically, and I scowl at the sarcastic fucker. Is this a joke? Two heartbeats? Two as in…one more than one heartbeat? One plus one equals two?

Two?

Two heartbeats equal two babies, and two babies equals twins.

What the ever-loving fuck?

"No, Mr. Ward." The doctor chuckles again. Anyone would think something amusing is going down. "Each of your babies has one heart, and both are beating just fine."

Stunned, my legs move without me telling them to, and I collide with something. I hope it's a chair because my knees have just given way and I'm freefalling. I grunt when my arse hits the seat. Now, I know I have been hearing things lately. Seeing things. Questioning... everything. So, just to be sure, for the avoidance of doubt, to absolutely eliminate any confusion..."I'm sorry, say that again," I order quietly.

"Mr. Ward," he says assertively. "Let me put this into plain English, if it will help."

"Please." It would help a great deal.

"Your wife is expecting twins."

"Oh fuck." *Twins.* "I had a feeling you were going to say that." Is this the universe telling me to start opening my mouth on a few things?

Yes, you fucker. Tell her about me.

"Watch your damn mouth," I breathe, looking at Ava, wondering what she's thinking. By her face, she's not thinking at all. She looks spaced out. "Baby—"

"About six weeks, I would say," the doctor muses.

Six weeks? I start mentally counting back through time. My God, all this time? All this fucking time I've been stressing, wondering if I'm broken, she's been pregnant? With fucking twins? And drinking. She's been drinking. My teeth grit.

"I'm sorry, that can't be right," Ava says as I watch her look between the screen and the doctor. "I've had a period within that time and was on the pill previous to that."

Yes, she had a period. Didn't she? When? My head feels like it could pop. "You had a period?" the doctor asks, getting a very sure, assertive, *yes,* from Ava. "That's not unusual. Let me do some measurements."

Measurements?

Yes, right. Measure the babies.

Plural.

Twins? How the fuck did this happen?

Need me to walk you through that, bro?

Ava's now lying back, eyes closed as the doctor does his thing. She's completely relaxed. I can feel her energy, and I honestly don't know what to make of it. She's not freaking out, which is ironic, because here's me freaking the fuck out.

I didn't bargain for this when I stole her pills.

Is this what they call karma?

I look between the screen and Ava, watching as she stares, rapt by the squirming blobs. And Jake continues to laugh his dead head off in heaven. This seesaw of emotions is too much. I started my day on cloud nine. Passion for breakfast, fury for brunch, terror for lunch, despair for dinner, and now complete and utter wonder for supper.

Twins?

You better be talking about me by the end of the day, brother, or I'll never talk to you again.

I huff. "Don't tempt me."

"Mr. Ward?"

"What?" I blurt, jarred from my moment. The doctor's smiling at me. Ava is half-smiling, half fascinated.

"Your babies." He holds a scrap of paper across the bed.

I accept on a mumbled thank you and stare down at the black and white image, hearing the doctor talking to Ava, but what he's saying I don't know. I'm...mesmerized. I tilt my head one way, then the other, studying the image.

"Are you ready?"

"What?" I murmur, eyes on the picture.

"Are you ready?"

We can go home? "Sure." I stand. How big should they be at six weeks? Big enough to see, I'm sure. I look at Ava. She's dressing. Her stomach is definitely a little rounder. Isn't it any wonder? *Twins.*

How many times have you got to say it before you believe it?

I don't think I will until they're actually here. What will we have? Two boys? Two girls? One of each?

"Let's go."

"What?" I tear my eyes from the picture and find Ava. She's smiling. She's happy. I'm unable to appreciate that in this moment.

"Thank you, Doctor," she says, taking my arm.

"Thank you, Doctor," I mimic, letting her lead me from the room.

The next thing I know, I'm outside in the fresh air and John is staring at me. I turn around and look at the hospital exit. She's been discharged. Because everything is all right.

"You okay?" he asks, pulling my attention back his way.

"What?" I reply.

He looks at Ava. She's still smiling.

"What's going on?" he asks.

"We just had some news," Ava goes on. We did? What news? What did I miss? "I'm expecting twins."

"What?" I blurt, and she laughs.

And John? He looks momentarily dazed. Then he explodes with laughter, joining my irritating *twin* brother. It's the kind of laugh on the big man that comes once in a blue moon. Today, apparently, is a blue moon. "Let's get you home." He chuckles over his words and opens the back door to his Range Rover.

I climb in and stare at the picture the whole way home while Ava rides up front with John. I vaguely hear them chatting. How lovely. Why the hell isn't she flipping her lid? She was mad enough when I trapped her with one baby. Delighted now because it's two? *Six weeks.*

I blink and look at the door when it opens.

We're home? I remember none of the journey. I heard none of the conversation. Ava looks at me, eternally amused, apparently, and reaches in to the car. I follow her hand to the clip of my seatbelt, releasing it. I slip out and Ava links arms with me. I look up and around.

"I'll call you," she says.

"Call who?" I ask.

"Me."

I look back and see John getting back in his Range Rover. "Oh, hey," I say. He shakes his head.

"We should talk when you're ready." He suddenly looks stressed. Why is he—

Oh fuck.

It all comes flooding back. My car. The accident. Multiple cars hit. Someone tried to hurt Ava. "Yeah," I murmur, checking her up and down. She's okay. We're all okay.

I let Ava walk me on, my eyes down again, studying the picture. All four of us are okay. Is it those two blurry blobs to the left of the tunnel? If I squint, they're a little clearer. Like peas.

"Sit."

"What?" I look up and see we're in our kitchen. A stool is in front of me. Dazed, I drop onto it and place the picture on the marble. I've seen one of these before. A scan picture. Except when my ex-wife had her first scan, she was over twelve weeks pregnant. And I could see Rosie as clear as I could see Lauren's intentions. Vividly. This scan picture isn't the same. And although I feel terrible for having such thoughts, I can't stop myself from having them. When I looked at Rosie's scan picture all those years ago, I felt cornered. Trapped. But when I look at this picture, I only feel an incredible sense of relief and freedom. I suddenly have three people to look after and protect. That's more than a full-time job. *Twins.* That's a full-time job for *both* of us. *Fuck…me.* They're safe and warm, cooking in their mummy's belly right now. But when they're here? She'll need me more than ever.

I feel something on my face—a hand—and it forces my eyes away from the picture. I frown when I see Ava has wet hair and has changed. She's showered and put on those ridiculous pants I bought her in Camden. The ones I remember thinking would pass as maternity pants. And now they are. *My God.*

"Are you going to speak anytime soon?" she asks, searching my eyes.

Speak? "I can't fucking breathe, Ava," I whisper. I'm absolutely gobsmacked.

Her smile is small and unsure. "I'm shocked too."

Shocked? She's never known shock. Maybe. Perhaps. I don't fucking know. I mean, I've delivered some corkers to this woman during our time together but, somehow, this just feels like a catalyst to a bigger picture that I one hundred percent know I don't want my wife to see.

I look at her, this young, uncomplicated, normal woman, who is now married to a man that practically stalked her and got her knocked up in a weird and wonderful plan to keep her forever. With twins, no less.

You always did do things in style, bro.

I hope she's ready for this. I also hope she remains upright, because I still can't feel my arms and legs, so catching her might be a challenge.

I take in air. Brace myself.

Do it, do it, do it, Jake chants. The fucker. But I smile, knowing he's enjoying this. Loving the notion that I am his entertainment.

And that he's looking after my little girl for me.

And he's right. Ava needs to know about him. She needs to understand my wonder and just how truly incredible this is. It was meant to be.

"I was a twin," I whisper, eyes on hers.

She drops me like I'm diseased. It's ironic. It stings. And she just stares at me, wide-eyed, her mouth hanging open in disbelief. She could throw a hissy fit. She could annihilate me for keeping this from her.

But she won't.

"My spirited girl is speechless," I whisper, slipping my hand around her neck. I'm out of my daze. I'm not over the shock, but I'm thinking clearly. This is the right moment, and I realize as I sit here preparing, not sharing Jake with Ava wasn't only about my fear of where that conversation might lead and Ava doubting me as a good man. It was also about simply talking about him. It was about revisiting a time in my life that I've spent most of my life trying to blank out.

It's the same with Lauren.

It's the same with Rosie.

"Have a bath with me." I stand and help her to her feet, and despite her clearly having showered already, she doesn't object. "I need to be with you." If I'm going to go there, I need to go there while I hold her in my arms. And the tub is our place.

I pick her up and carry her up to the bathroom, feeling her amazed eyes glued to my face as she seeks out my neck with her lips. It's her way of telling me she's not going anywhere. I need it.

I sit her by the sink and get the bath ready, running over where to begin. *How* to begin. I honestly don't know, so I'll let instinct lead. I start to strip her down as I kiss her, loading up with courage to talk about Jake. Her hands slip under my T-shirt, feeling me as her tongue rolls around mine. "Take it off. Please, take away everything between us."

She rips my T-shirt up my torso, urgent, and yanks my jeans open, everything becoming clumsy and rushed. Not because either of us need to get to sex, but because we need to get to intimacy in another way. I kick my jeans off, pull Ava down to her feet, kneeling as I pull her pants and knickers down, faltering for a moment, swallowing, briefly revisiting the moment I realized she hadn't cut herself.

The dread.

But we're okay now.

We're okay.

I rise, cast her knickers aside, and lift her to my body, looking up into her dark, alive eyes as she drops her mouth to mine, accommodating my silent demand. I step into the bath and lower to my knees, holding her under her ass. Her breath hitches, her boobs squishing to my chest. "Is the water okay?"

"Fine," she says between our deep kisses.

"Always fine."

"Always perfect if I have you."

That felt like a message. "You have me." I can't get her despair out of my head. At the hospital, her withdrawal. She thought no baby meant no *us*. I break our kiss and find her eyes. Her bare skin glistens. Her eyes search mine. Strands of her wet hair stick to her cheeks. "You do know that, don't you?" I ask.

"You married me, of course I know."

I find her ring and remove it, feeling her watching, confused. "Do you think this signifies my love for you?" I ask.

"Yes," she whispers, sounding like she's missing something. Because she is. The ring is just a fucking ring. I'd be lying if I didn't hope it served as a massive *back the fuck off* to any man. But still, it's just a ring. "Then we should get these diamonds removed," I whisper, "and have it re-encrusted with my heart." I smile down at her hand as I slip it back onto her finger, sighing to myself. It feels like I'm on a lifelong mission to try and convey to this woman how I feel. I'm sure I'll never succeed.

Her hand lies across my pec, and I consider the sparklers decorating her finger. Pretty. I'm not sure my heart would pack the same visual punch. "I like your heart exactly where it is," she declares, bending her upper body so her lips can reach my chest. She kisses me softly, looking up at me. I raise my brows. "I like how it swells when you look at me."

"Just for you, baby." I pull her up and kiss her hard, feeling blood dripping into places I don't want it to go right now. *Not now.* Now, I have to talk. "Let me bathe you." I steal one more kiss of her neck and start moving her away from me before we both deviate from the plan. "Turn around for me." Moving off my knees, I rest back against the tub and pull Ava to between my legs, getting us comfortable. She folds her body over and sighs, staring down into the water as I soak the sponge, squeezing it across her nape and watching the water run down her olive skin, over the kinks in her spine. Her silence is making me smile. I had expected a barrage of questions or impatience within a few seconds flat of declaring I was a twin. "Are you fine?" I ask.

"I'm okay."

I smile and shift in closer. "I'm a little worried about my defiant little temptress," I say into her ear, feeling her body light up.

"Why?"

"Because she's too quiet when there's information to be had." I lower back, taking Ava with me.

"If you want to tell me, you will."

How nonchalant she sounds. "I'm not sure I like what pregnancy is doing to my girl." I rest my palms on her tummy, covering it completely. How I wish I could do that forever. Be big enough to physically shield them from everything. "First of all, she's developed a phobia of my cock in her mouth." She gasps subtly as I thrust myself up into her arse. "And secondly, she's not blessing me with her forceful demands for intelligence."

"My Lord isn't blessing me with his wide range of expert fuckings, so we're even, aren't we?"

I let out a bark of laughter. "But she's still blessing me with her filthy mouth." I give her tickle spot a quick, warning squeeze and she jolts, sending water over the edge of the tub. And yet she still doesn't hit me with any questions. What the fuck is going on? It's easier to be questioned than to give a "talk." Where are the questions? I frown at the back of her head, willing her on. She's not going to ask—she's going to make me talk with no prompts. She's proving a point.

For fuck's sake. "His name was Jake," I say, my lips twisting as I wonder where to go next. Ava doesn't help me out. I scowl at her back. "You're doing this on purpose, aren't you?"

Silence.

God damn her.

"He idolized me," I go on, scratching around in my brain. Have I even started at the right place? Fuck it. "He wanted to be me." *The stupid fucking idiot.* "I'll never understand it." I knew this wouldn't be easy, but this hard? I'm getting nothing back, no questions, no encouragement. Jake's not even piping in to help me along, which I suppose I should be grateful for since my wife is naked in the bath with me. I turn Ava around, needing her eyes. "I can't do this on my own, baby," I whisper. "Help me."

Her expression falls, and she comes closer, nuzzling into me. "Were you not alike?"

I laugh under my breath, relaxing. This is better. "We were the furthest away from alike you could get," I say. "In looks *and* personality."

"He wasn't a god?"

My smile is wide as I stroke her wet back, my hands gliding up and down. "He was a genius." And kind, calm, handsome, smart, and considerate.

"How is that far away from you?"

"Jake had his brain to get him by. I had my looks and I used them, as you well know." I squint at the space above her head, holding her tighter. "Jake didn't use his brain. If he did, he wouldn't be dead." I swallow, blink, trying to chase away the inevitable flashbacks, feeling Ava's body stiffen against me. I can hear the question coming a mile off.

"How did he die?" she asks quietly, and everything about her tone and volume, along with her tense body, tells me she's wary of asking. That she's sensed something is…off.

"He got hit by a car." I spit the words out fast before I can swallow them back down and choke on them.

"How would that be not using his brain?"

"Because he was pissed when he staggered into the road."

Jake! Get out of the fucking road!

I wince, squeezing my eyes closed.

"Carmichael isn't the only reason you don't talk to your parents, is he?" she asks quietly.

"No." This is it. "The fact that I'm responsible for my brother's death is a major contributing factor. Carmichael and The Manor came after and kind of put the nail in the coffin."

"Jake was their favorite?" she asks.

"Jake was everything they wanted from a son. I wasn't. I tried to be. I studied, but it didn't come as naturally to me as it did to Jake." A bit like charming the knickers off women didn't come naturally to him. I always think we weren't alike in looks. It's not really true, we were identical, but there's something about how a man portrays themselves that affects their physical appearance. Jake wasn't confident like me. He wasn't cocky or rebellious.

He was perfect. Wholesomely handsome. A fucking brainbox.

"But he wanted to be like you?"

"He wanted the small piece of freedom I gained through being considered the one with the least potential. All of their attention was focused on Jake, the genius—the one they could be proud of. Jake would go to Oxford. Jake would make his first million before he was twenty-one. Jake would marry a well-bred English girl and breed well-spoken, polite, clever children. Except Jake didn't want any of that. He wanted to choose the direction of his own life and the tragic thing is, he would've chosen well on his own."

"So what happened?"

Fuck, am I really going there?

Don't stop now.

"There was a house party," I begin, my heart beating faster. "You know, full of drink, girls and...opportunities. We were coming up to our seventeenth, prepping for our finals, ready for the Oxford application. Of course, it was my idea."

"What?"

"To go out and be teenagers, get away from the constant grind of studying, and to stop trying to live up to our parents' expectations. I knew I'd pay for it, but I was prepared to face my parents' wrath. We were going to have a few drinks together, like brothers. I wanted to spend some time with him, like normal kids. It was just one night. I never expected to pay so severely." I tense all over when she moves. Looks at me with soulful, innocent eyes that have no comprehension of the guilt I've lived with.

"You got carried away?" she asks quietly.

"Me?" I ask. Of course she'd think that. "No." God, how I wish it was me who stepped into the road. "I'd had a few, but Jake was throwing back shots like he'd never drink again. I virtually carried him out of that house. Then it all came out." He didn't say it, but I heard him. "How much he hated the suffocation, that he didn't want to go to Oxford. We made a pact." I see his face in my mind's eye. The excitement. "We agreed to tell them together that we didn't want to do it anymore. We wanted to make our own decisions based on our dreams, not based on what would impress the snotty fuckers who my mum and dad socialized with. He wanted to race motorbikes, but that was considered uncouth and common. Reckless." Fuck, just talking about being reckless got Jake killed. Ironic. "I'd never seen him so happy at the thought of rebelling with me, doing what we wanted for once, not what we were told to do." I study her, fascinated by the veil of irritation that sinks into her face. "And then he walked out into the road."

"You can't be held responsible," she grates.

"I'm held responsible because I *am* responsible," I reply, holding her achingly beautiful, angry face. She's not angry *at* me. It's sweet that she'd try to make me feel better. Wasted but sweet. "I shouldn't have dragged Jake off the perfect path. The stupid idiot shouldn't have listened to me."

"It doesn't sound like you dragged him anywhere."

"He wouldn't be dead, Ava," I go on. "What if—"

"No, Jesse," she snaps, silencing me. "Don't think like that. Life is full of *what ifs*. What if your parents hadn't suffocated you?" She tilts her head. She wants an answer? "What if you stood up sooner and said enough?"

"What if I'd have played ball?" Did what I was told, tried harder in my studies. Jake would still be here.

"You would never have found me," she whispers, her words tight. "And I would never have found you."

I withdraw, taken aback by the raw emotion in her broken words and the stream of tears that roll down her cheeks. *Shit.* I can't hold it against her that she's said that. I've thought it myself numerous times, asked how it's fair that to find love and peace, I had to lose it first. I let my eyes drop to her tummy. And as much as it hurts, she's right. "Everything that's happened in my life has led me to you, Ava," I whisper, the agony in my words obvious. "It's taken forever, but I've finally found where I belong."

"With me and these two little people," she says, holding my hand on her tummy.

And what would I have done if she hadn't stumbled into my office? Where would I be? I pull her down to my chest, scanning her face, her eyes, her lips. "With you and those two little people. *Our* little people."

She smiles, small but sad. "What about Amalie?"

"Amalie would marry well and be a good wife and mother, and I believe she might have fulfilled her obligation." It's happening this weekend in Seville. "It said Dr. David, didn't it?"

"It did."

"There you are, then."

"And you started spending more time with Carmichael after Jake's death?"

"I did. Carmichael knew the score. He'd been through it himself with my granddad. Are you comfy?"

"Yes, I'm fine."

I smile. "It was a relief. I escaped the daily reminder that Jake wasn't with me anymore, and I distracted myself with jobs that my uncle gave me around The Manor. Are you sure you're comfy?"

"I'm bloody comfy," she gasps, exasperated, pinching my nipple.

I chuckle. "She's comfy."

"She is. What jobs did you do?"

"Everything. I'd collect the glasses in the bar, mow the lawns. My dad went through the roof, but I didn't let him stop me. Then they announced that we were moving to Spain."

"And you refused to go."

"Yes, I hadn't ventured into the rooms of The Manor at that point. I was still a manor virgin, but on my eighteenth birthday, Carmichael let me loose in the bar. Worst thing he could've done. I slipped right in. It came naturally. *Too* naturally." I look down when she moves, gazing up at me. She's taking it all quite well. "If simply being at The Manor took my mind away from my troubles, then being drunk and having sex at The Manor eliminated them completely."

"Escapism," she says, and I nod. "What did Carmichael think about all of this?"

"He thought it was a phase, that it would pass." *Pain.* "Then he went and died on me too."

"And your parents tried to make you sell The Manor." She whispers her words, hesitant, building the picture.

"Yeah," I breathe, and for the first time in as long as I can remember, I see my father's face. His fury when I calmly and confidently told him I wouldn't. I remember so vividly how I felt in that moment too.

Immovable. The Manor had quickly become a safe haven. The thought of losing that was…well, unthinkable. It was like losing Carmichael all over again. Jake too. Now, though? I inhale through that thought. Now, what? Would I feel differently? "They soon flew home from Spain at the news of my uncle's death," I say, robotic, my mind elsewhere. *Like on a golf resort.* "They found me, a younger version of the family black sheep, lording it up, drinking, and gorging on women." *Emancipation.* "I'd experienced freedom without them trying to mold me into suitable son material." *No pressure.* "I'd grown cocky and confident, and I was also extremely wealthy." *Approval.* Fucking hell. "I told them where to shove their ultimatum. The Manor was Carmichael's life, and then it became mine. End of." But not the end, apparently. The Manor. It's just a building. And yet so much more than bricks and mortar. And for the first time ever, now I've let my mind venture to potentially selling it, I consider what my parents were doing.

Trying to save me.

The thought comes from left field, shaking me. *Jesus Christ.* They were trying to save me. I shake my head, feeling a bit dazed and confused, and offer a small smile as Ava stares at me, taking it all in.

As I'm trying to take in my revelation too.

Her chest dips—a breath—and I breathe in too, waiting for what she will say as she braces herself. "Our children will be whoever they want to be." She slides up my body and licks my chin, nibbling. "As long as they don't want to be playboys."

I laugh to myself, clawing my fingers into her soft, peachy arse. And there it is. They can be whoever they want to be. So long as it doesn't involve The Manor. Isn't that how my parents thought? Was that love or was that continued judgment? *Rejection. Scorn.* Because what would I do if my children wanted to become a version of me in my past? I'd try to stop them. "Sarcasm doesn't suit you, lady," I whisper, swallowing.

"I think it does." Her breathy words in my ear sends bolts of pleasure directly into my dick, which is a welcome distraction from thoughts about my parents.

And I'm running with it. "You're right, it does." I push her up my body and pout at the bruise on her boob. "My mark is fading."

"Freshen it up, then," she teases. So I do as I'm bid—with pleasure—and suck her flesh into my mouth, smiling when she groans.

"Nice?"

"Hmmm."

Yeah, really nice. My tongue traces the edge of her areola, flicks across the stiff peak. She tastes phenomenal. "Ava," I mumble, feeling my dick begin to throb demandingly. *Down boy.* "I'm not sure how I feel about our babies taking to your breasts." I peck her gently and let her slip back down my body. Epic mistake. The friction of her sliding over my groin sends blood surging unmercifully. "Oh no, we can't. I won't, Ava." I try to get her off my lap, wary of the steely determination in her eyes. I'll never be able to say no. "And don't you dare kick into temptress mode, either." Christ, she's six weeks. I can't even bring myself to recall all of the brutal fuckings she's received in that time. But now especially, off the back of a car accident, there is no way I'm putting my dick in her. No.

"Cornwall," she says simply, and I still. She *didn't* just say that.

"You're not going anywhere." I leave her on her knees and stand. Look down at her. *Fuck.* Her eyes on my erection sparkle with want, her wet skin glistens. *Hot.* I need to get out of the tub. I engage my muscles and freeze when her dainty hand wraps around me, bolts of pleasure shooting through my wet body. "Fuck," I hiss. "You little fucking tormenter."

She strokes me, and my torso folds. "Are you going to walk away from me?" she whispers huskily.

"Ava, there's not a fucking chance on this planet I'm taking you."

"Sit down," she orders, her eyes resting on the edge of the tub. Oh? Is this her version of the Compromise Fuck? I'm all onboard, but...

The tip of her tongue licks my dripping cock. *Oh my God.* "Ava," I grate, my hips shaking from trying to keep them from thrusting into her mouth. "If you leave me hanging to throw up, I'll lose my fucking mind."

"I won't." She takes me slow and deep, looking up at me with round, excited eyes, encouraging me to sit on the edge of the tub, putting herself between my open thighs. She won't? I'm not so sure about that. I think it could send me to loony-land if she does.

She moves forward to take me, but I stop her, holding the tops of her arms and she peeks up at me in confusion. "If I'm sitting on this side, you're sitting on the other." I kiss her hard, catching her by surprise. *I'm keeping the power, baby.* "With your legs wide open."

Her inhale is endearing. Did she really think I'd sacrifice control? I lift her back to her feet and watch as she puts herself opposite me, my appreciative gaze taking in every inch of her perfect body as mine tingles, until I arrive at her eyes.

"Lick your fingers, Ava."

She obeys.

Slowly.

It's sexy as fuck. "Slide your hand down your front. Slowly."

Her mouth open, her eyes drowsy, she deliberately and leisurely slips her hand across her boobs and onto her stomach. "Slow enough for you?"

"Did I say talk?"

Her scowl is light, matching her intake of breath, as her touch moves farther down.

"Stop." I swallow, my eyes moving to between her thighs. "One finger, baby. Slowly slide one finger in." I watch closely as she follows my orders, her body responding beautifully. "Remember, that's mine." I look up. "So be gentle with it."

She exhales, visibly trying to keep control, her eyes closing.

"Eyes, Ava," I order, making them spring open. "Good girl." I circle myself. Inhale. "Taste."

She makes a meal of slipping her fingers into her mouth, moaning, sucking as I watch.

"Good?" I ask, starting to stroke myself as she laps at her fingers. "I'll take that as a yes." My dick buzzes, begging for more friction. "Fucking hell." She looks out of this world, her touch moving back to her pussy, massaging, her back bowing, her pleasure tangible. She's getting close, her focus on her own pleasure, her eyes heavy, her body stiffening to deal with the building orgasm.

"Damn it, Ava, look at me." I jerk, grit my teeth, squeeze myself to hold back shooting my load. "You're close, baby."

"Yes," she yelps, her hand working faster over her pussy.

"Oh Jesus, not yet. Control it."

"I can't." Her head drops back, her legs splashing in the water. "Oh God."

My thrusting fist picks up speed when I comprehend she's past the point of return. "Ava, fuck, control it."

This Woman Forever

"Jesse."

"Ava, you look fucking amazing." I move off the edge of the tub and drop into the water, and she sees my intent, moving her hand and spreading her legs wider, making space for my mouth. The moment my tongue slips into her wet heat, her hands find my hair and yank brutally while I suck her orgasm out of her, holding mine back, absorbing her shaking thighs either side of my head. She gasps, goes limp, shudders, and I pull her into the water. Kneeling opposite each other, I rest my cock in her heat. "My turn. Hold it against you," I order, letting her take over, moving my hands to her face and kissing her as she strokes me calmly. "Just keep it like that," I mumble around her lips. *Oh God.* "I could stay like this forever."

"I love you," she gasps, her words as urgent as her thrusting hand.

It's my undoing, and I come hard, kissing her through my release, the pressure releasing, my body unraveling.

"My work here is done," she whispers, breathless.

Her work will never be done, and neither will mine. Especially now. "You're a savage, lady." I lower my arse to my heels and pull her onto my lap, feeling her skin cooling. "The water's getting cold."

"A little," she says, unbothered.

"Let me clean you down." She fights my attempts to move her, sealing our fronts, clinging tighter. *Sealed. Connected. Always.* "I'll be quick. I don't want you catching a cold."

She finally relents, letting me take over, and I wash her down quickly, avoiding *certain* parts of the water. I grimace, laughing on the inside. I'm looking forward to cuddling up for the night, a weight lifted from my shoulders. "My lady's tired." It's been a long, draining day. "Snuggle?"

She's suddenly lost the ability to talk, her body heavy as I lift her out of the bath and dry us both down, Ava, once again, happy to let me take care of her.

Once she's in bed, I let her put herself where she wants to be, holding her close. Just a little nap. We can have a little daytime nap.

I sigh, melting into the bed *and* Ava's clinch. "I'll never love one more than the other," I say quietly, holding her tighter when she answers with a kiss and nothing more, dosing off in my arms. I smile at the ceiling, truly astonished by how much pregnancy is taking out of her already. Or how much I'm taking out of her with my constant bombshells. Maybe a bit of both.

I try to fall asleep too, try to shut down, but for all the will in the world, I can't find the land of nod. Is it my utter disbelief? Ava disproving my fears? I don't know. I feel so awake, so alert. We're having twins. We'll have *two* babies to love. We're so fucking lucky.

Except...

Someone somehow stole my car, and they tried to run Ava off the road. Who? Who the fuck is so twisted and warped they would do that? It takes revenge to another level. *Danger.*

I need to call John.

Ava's breathing is low and level, the kind of breathing she has when she's deep in sleep. I ease her away and edge off the bed, taking myself downstairs to get some water and have a few dips before I call John and start getting down to the not-so pleasant business of finding out who stole my fucking car and used it to attack my pregnant wife.

I'm mid-dip when the there's a knock at the front door, and I lift my head, my finger hanging out of my mouth. Who the fuck is that at this time of day? I get up and open the door to Sam. "My man, what the hell happened?" he asks, letting himself in.

Drew appears, looking me up and down. "You're naked."

"It's my home, I can be whatever the fuck I want to be." I frown at their backs as they go into the kitchen. "For fuck's sake," I mutter, closing the door and following. They're both at the island with a glass of water each when I arrive. "What?" I ask, looking between them, both sitting comfortably.

"*What?*" Sam asks in disbelief. "Where do you want me to start?"

"You spoke to John?" I ask, joining them.

"What the fuck?" Drew breathes. "Any ideas who it was?"

I raise a brow as I dip, and Drew shakes his head.

"You think Van Der Haus is a car thief?"

"I don't know, Drew," I admit, dropping my jar. "Maybe not him personally."

"So he paid someone to steal your car?" Sam chimes in.

"I don't know," I grate.

"Is Ava okay?"

"Yeah, she's fine. A little shaken." Wait. *How* much did John tell them? "Is that it?" I ask.

"What?" Both look at each other on a frown.

"Did John mention anything else?"

"Like what?"

"Like the fact Ava's expecting twins?" Stupid me, I say that just as Sam's taking a slurp of water. His cheeks balloon, and he sprays it far and wide. I don't mind, I'm naked, but Drew? He looks pristine, ready to make a trip to The Manor, I guess.

He dives up from his stool, arms held out at his sides, and looks down his front. "This is fucking cashmere, Sam, you prick!"

"Twins?" Sam squeaks, wiping his chin, eyes wide.

"Wait, twins?" Drew forgets his wardrobe drama and points piercing blue eyes full of shock my way. "Ava's pregnant with twins?"

I nod.

"Fuck," they breathe in unison.

I nod again.

"And…"

"I've told her about Jake," I tell them. "She knows about Jake." The absence of Rosie and Lauren from this conversation is screaming. "And that is that," I say, standing. "And you two girls are going to fuck off and leave me in peace." I go to them, hooking an arm around each of their elbows, trying to hoof them up off their stools.

Sam comes with ease.

Drew dives out of my way, looking down at my dick. "Don't ever try to manhandle me when you're naked ever again."

"Oh, you only like Sam touching you when you're naked, huh?"

Sam snickers. Drew's nostrils flare.

"Out," I say, pointing the way.

"Fine." Drew stomps off. "You won't need these." He holds something up above his head.

"What's that?"

"Keys to the Aston the dealership's lent you while yours is located. John put a call in."

I go after Drew, swiping them from his hand. *Must call John.* "Thanks."

"Fuck off."

"John sent this too," Sam says, and I turn and find him holding up my book on pregnancy. "Might want to swap it for one on twins." The book drops. "Fucking hell, man."

"Yeah, I know." I take the book. "You and Kate okay?"

"Yeah, we're good."

"Will you let her know I'm taking Ava away tomorrow?"

He looks surprisingly surprised. "Where are you going?"

"I don't know," I muse, hoping I can convince her to let me get us away from the fucking city for a few days while we figure out what the hell is going on.

I'm not holding my breath.

I close the door on the boys and get my mobile, calling John.

"Are you back in the land of the living?" he asks, his deep rumbling voice strangely comforting.

"It was a bit of a shock, eh?"

He laughs. "A bit. How do you feel about it?"

"Good," I say, knowing he knows it will have unearthed endless regrets and guilt in me. "I've told her about Jake."

Again, the absence of Rosie and Lauren's names in that sentence screams. "Okay," he says slowly. "How did she take it?"

"Well."

"I wouldn't expect anything less. Ava's a reasonable young woman. When she's not being driven crazy by her husband."

I scowl. "Ha. Ha." And is he trying to say something without saying it? Like…I bet she'd take the bombshell about your dead daughter and ex-wife well too. And I bet she'd be reasonable if you suggested Sarah returns to work. "Anything on the cameras?"

"I'm trying to access the backup recordings. Playback is on the blink."

Jesus, the new system can't come soon enough. "Let me know."

"I will. Listen, a police officer gave me his number when I went back to the scene. You'd already left with Ava in the ambulance. I said I'd get you to call him. He wants a statement from Ava."

My hackles rise. "They'll have to wait."

"This is serious. There were multiple cars involved. You can't deal with this on your own, Jesse."

"I know, John." I wish I could, though. I wish I could find the fucker and break every bone in his body. Whoever the fuck he is. Jail time just won't cut it.

"Your bike and Ava's car have been picked up by the police. They may need them for evidence, depending on how the investigation goes."

I blow out my cheeks. "Okay." He's right. This needs urgent attention. "Text me the officer's number. I'll call him now." I hang up, and my phone soon bleeps the arrival of a message. I hit the number, taking my phone to my ear.

"PC Gladstone."

"Yeah, Hi, my name's Jesse Ward. My wife was involved in the collision today near Tower Bridge."

"Mr. Ward, thanks for calling me."

"No problem." I lower to a stool and take a deep breath, fighting with my instinct to hold back information. I've dealt with the police before. I haven't much faith they can work at a pace I'll be comfortable with. Like really fucking fast. But I might know a man who will.

"Can I speak to your wife?"

"She's sleeping."

"Of course. Is she okay? Any injuries?"

"No, just shook up, as you can imagine. She's pregnant with twins. I'm sorry I was so short with you on the scene."

He breathes out. "Understandable. Would you get her to call me when she's feeling up to it?" He's not applying pressure, but I sense it. To John's point, there were several vehicles involved and a runaway Aston. I should mention the Aston. It'll look strange if one of the other witnesses mentions it and I don't.

"There was an Aston at the scene."

I hear the rustling of papers. PC Gladstone turning the pages of his notebook. "Yes, a black DBS."

"It's mine. It was stolen earlier today from my property outside of the city."

I hear his shock, even if he doesn't make a sound. *No, PC Gladstone, this isn't a simple case of reckless driving.* "Are you saying this is a personal vendetta?" he asks.

"I think so."

"Anyone spring to mind?"

I suppress my laugh. Where would I start? "No," I say quietly. "I called Aston Martin to get information on the location—it has a tracker—but they couldn't help me. Then I got a call from Ava asking me why I was following her. Obviously, my alarm bells went wild."

"Obviously," he parrots. "And you don't know of anyone who would want to hurt your wife?"

"No."

"Okay, well, we should definitely take a statement from you too. When's convenient?"

"I'll call you," I say.

"Thank you. And thanks for calling me. I'll wait to hear from you."

I hang up and lay my phone on the counter, mulling over too many things in my mind. But the loudest question?

Who?

Chapter 26

I fell asleep as soon as my head hit the pillow—I'm putting that down to mental exhaustion—and I don't come round until morning. But I don't open my eyes, too content with the feel of my hand on Ava's tummy and the feel of her light fingertips tracing every inch of my body. Inevitably, she works her way down to my scar and lingers. Thinking, I suppose. Reflecting on what she's learned.

"Have you finished feeling me up?" I ask, the old wound tingling.

"No," she whispers. "Just be still and silent."

"Anything you say, lady." I sigh and sink deeper into the sheets, happy to oblige and feed her monster.

Her breath tickles my lips. "Good boy."

"What if I want to be a bad boy?"

"You're talking," she says, making my lips tug, my eyes no longer willing to be deprived of her morning beauty. The vision of her wakes *everything* up, and I take her all in, scan every gorgeous inch of her smiling face, my sleepy eyes blinded by her perfection. "Morning," she whispers, her dark, lusty eyes locked with mine.

Oh, I can see what's coming a mile off. I move her onto her back, smiling at her breathy gasp of shock, and pin her to the bed, my body resting gently on hers. Now how am I going to handle this? I'm not an egomaniac, but I am a realist.

My dick is massive.

And I'm not sure how I feel putting it so close to my growing babies. Poor little things would be terrified if they saw that hurtling toward them. I'm also not sure how I feel about abstaining. Well, I do. Horrified. So, as I have in recent weeks, I'll be careful. Gentle. *Slow.* And Miss Insatiable will accept that. "Someone has sleepy sex on their mind," I whisper, having a brief nibble of her nose.

"No," she breathes happily. "I have Jesse Ward on my mind, which means I also have various degrees of fuckings on my mind."

It's as I thought. *Fucking.* "You're insatiable, my beautiful girl." I kiss her with conviction, hoping hard in that department quenches her greed. I'm a fool. "Watch your mouth."

She's quick to respond, her tongue invading, setting the pace. Or *her* pace. Oh no. I need to set the bar, take control, make sure she understands the limits. Hard fucking is off the table, and that's non-negotiable.

Pulling away, I ignore her slighted state. "I've been thinking."

"What about?" she asks, slight making way for worry.

"About how dramatic our married life has been." Dramatic? That feels like a bit of an understatement.

"Okay," she replies slowly, obviously bracing herself for where this is leading. Surely, after literally being run off the road yesterday, she's expecting this. We haven't even talked about what happened. I need to find things out, and I'm not comfortable with Ava being in the city with all these question marks hanging over us. I can't have Ava in danger again. And I don't want her to worry. Stress. It might be a tall order, but I'll do my best.

"Let me take you away," I say in a rush, making my eyes big, round, adorable and, hopefully, irresistible. "Just us two on our own." The police will have to wait to interview her, but it doesn't mean I can't give Steve all the information they need to start investigating this.

Ava smiles, and it's not what I expected at all. "We'll never be alone ever again," she says quietly, prompting me to glance down at her tummy. Never alone again. How wonderful does that sound?

I shift and quickly kiss her belly, then get back to convincing Ava we need a break. Her eyes when I return mine to them are sparkling with happiness. Acceptance. "Let me love you," I whisper. "Let me have you to myself for a few days."

"What about my job?" she asks, immediately throwing an obstruction in our way.

"Ava," I say softly, forcing myself not to stamp down my authority. "You were in a car accident yesterday." *Please don't make a battle of this. I need to keep my family safe.*

"I know." Her body softens beneath me, the fight leaving her. "But I have appointments and Patrick is—"

"I'll sort Patrick." Problem solved. "He'll deal with your appointments."

"Sort Patrick or trample Patrick?" she asks, full of suspicion.

"I'll speak to Patrick." Pay him well, and the old money grabber will accept keenly.

"Delicately." Her hands push into my shoulders, her face expectant.

"...ish," I say around a smile.

"No, Ward." Shaking her head, she becomes as stern as I've ever seen her. "No... ish about it. Delicately. End of."

Maybe. Depends if he takes the money quietly. "Is that a yes?" Without a sense fuck? I'm staggered. Not that she'd get a sense fuck in her condition. Which means I need to start getting better at *talking* sense into her. Like now.

"Yes," she breathes, as if exasperated by me. Who is she trying to kid? She wants some alone time as much as I do. It's a big win. Her job isn't a priority right now, and that feels good. "Where are we going?"

Good question. Subconsciously, I didn't think she'd agree, therefore I didn't plan that far ahead. I get up off the bed. There's no time to waste. She might realize she's being reasonable and retract. "Anywhere, I don't care." Where the fuck am I going to take her?

"I do," she blurts. "I'm not skiing."

I watch as she shoots up from the bed, looking alarmed at the prospect. Is she fucking high? Skiing? While she's pregnant? "Don't be stupid, woman," I mutter, fetching a suitcase from the dressing room. "You're carrying my babies in there. You're lucky I'm not chaining you to the bed for the rest of this pregnancy." I lay the suitcase on the floor, watching a slow formation of a crafty smile spread across her face.

She lifts her hands to the headboard. "You can if you like. I won't complain."

It takes everything in me to disregard her blatant tactics. "You're a temptress, Mrs. Ward. Come pack." I force my eyes away and take myself back into the dressing room, hearing her mutter indignantly.

I grab a few T-shirts, various shorts, some boxers, dropping them in a pile. And my book. I quickly retrieve it from the drawer I slipped it in last night before I climbed back into bed with Ava.

"Where are we going?" she asks, reminding me that I've still got some thinking to do.

"I don't know." Scotland? Too cold. The Peak District? "I'll make a few calls." I start putting my clothes into the case. "Aren't you going to pack?" I ask, keeping my eyes on her face and not the rest of her nakedness.

"Well"—she shrugs—"I don't know where I'm going. Hot, cold? Car, plane?"

"Car. You can't fly."

"What do you mean, I can't fly?"

"I don't know." I've read something somewhere, amid all the things I read, about flying while pregnant. Problem is, I can't remember exactly what it said. Do? Don't? So I won't take any chances. "Cabin pressure. It might squish the babies."

She lets out an over-the-top bark of laughter. "Tell me you're joking."

Joking? Her face when I look at her is somewhere between amusement and concern. "I don't joke when it comes to you, Ava. You should know that."

Reality hits her with a bang. It doesn't bode well. I can see the end of her equanimity looming. It was good while it lasted. "Cabin pressure won't squish our babies, Jesse," she says, a little high-pitched. "If you're taking me away, you're taking me on a plane."

For fuck's sake, if I'd have told her she couldn't go on a boat, she'd demand to go on a fucking cruise to prove her point, whatever the fuck that is. Fuck it. I should have said she can't go on a boat. I should never have sold the yacht. But would the babies get seasick? "It's not safe for pregnant women to fly." She won't listen to me, so perhaps she'll listen to the book. "I've read about it."

She looks shocked. "Where have you read about it?"

"In here," I say quietly, holding up the book, scuffing my bare feet on the carpet awkwardly. "You should also be taking folic acid." The silence is unbearable. I can feel her disbelief. What I don't know is if that's disbelief that I'm reading a book about pregnancy, or disbelief about the information I'm giving her. She can see the book, so I'll go with the information. God damn it, she's going to make me prove it? I randomly start fingering through the pages, searching for the passages I've marked. "Here, look," I say, showing her. "The Department of Health recommends that women should take a daily supplement of four hundred micrograms of folic acid while they are trying to conceive, and should continue taking this dose for the first twelve weeks of pregnancy when the baby's spine is developing." But what it doesn't state is if that dose changes should the woman be pregnant with multiple babies, like my wife. "But we have two babies," I muse. "So maybe you should take eight hundred micrograms." I make a mental note to check that as I flick farther through the book to find the bit I read about flying.

"I love you," Ava says.

"I know. The flying bit is here somewhere." Was it no flying at all, or flying to a certain point in the pregnancy? "Just—" I flinch when her hand smacks the book and it drops to the carpet with a slap. *What the fuck*? I toss Ava a scowl. She's grinning. What's so fucking funny?

Then, eyes on me, she throws a foot out and kicks my book a few feet away. Still fucking grinning. Totally uncalled for. "Pick the book up." She can defy me. But the book?

"Stupid book." She kicks it again.

"Pick the book up, Ava," I warn.

"No."

I realize what she's doing. Everything before me is screaming for attention. And who am I to disappoint? Like I said, I'm here to serve... "Three," I say calmly, holding up three fingers. Her grin confirms my suspicions. *Greedy*.

"Two," she retorts, surprising me.

"One," I say around a smile.

"Zero, baby," she breathes, her body preparing for my attack. I swoop in and lift her onto my shoulder, rolling my eyes when she squeals like she wasn't expecting it. Her laugh goes straight to my dick as I carry her to the bed and lower her most of the way before dropping her the last few feet. *Compromise*.

I lay myself on top of her and get my face close to hers. "Lady, when will you learn?"

"Never."

"I hope you don't," I admit, my eyes on her lips. "Kiss me."

"What if I don't?"

My God, she's a case. Yes, no, start, stop, do, don't. I hold her hip and apply just enough pressure to have her stilling on a sharp inhale. "We both know you're going to kiss me, Ava. Let's not waste valuable time when I could be losing myself in you." I drag my eyes across her face to her wet lips. "Kiss me now."

I dip, and she lifts, and we come together on a collective moan and equal power. She instantly writhes beneath me, rubbing me in all the right places. "It didn't really say I can't fly, did it?" she asks around our kiss.

"It's logical."

"No, it's neurotic. Pregnant women fly all of the time, so you are taking me on a plane to somewhere hot, and you're going to let my feast on you the whole time." She bites at my lip, before kissing me some more. "Constant contact." Another nibble. "I want constant contact."

Oh, how she pleases me. Is she finally understanding what makes me tick, or is she simply accepting it? Pregnancy is bringing out the best in my wife. I might have to make sure she's permanently pregnant.

"I can't fucking wait," I admit, getting up. "Come on, then. We're wasting valuable feasting time." I return to the dressing room and throw the rest of my things into the case, making sure Ava's is laid out ready for her to pack. Then I head downstairs with my bag and check the calendar on my phone, just to make sure my dates are correct. Amalie's wedding is this weekend in Seville, which means my parents are out of town. It's safe. I scroll through the contacts to a number I haven't called for a long, long time.

Ava wins.

The international ringing tone makes me close my eyes and inhale quietly.

"Mr. Ward?" Jose says, his Spanish accent as thick as I remember.

"Yes, Jose, how are you?"

"Very good, sir, very good. It's good to hear from you. How can I help you?"

I walk circles around the kitchen island. "How quickly can you have Paradise ready for me?" I wince, trying to mentally calculate how long it's been since I've been there. Years. For the first time, I wonder why Carmichael bought a villa in the place his brother moved to. Dad had nothing but contempt for Carmichael, and eventually me too. Was it a not-so subtle way of making sure Dad could never forget he had a brother, or how successful he was? Did Carmichael buy Paradise out of spite?

"It will need a bit of airing," Jose says. "It's not been rented since the renovations completed a year ago, but I stop in every few weeks to make sure everything is in order."

"Of course," I murmur. "So how long?"

"I will see if I can get the cleaning team there in the morning."

"Thank you, Jose. Add it to the management bill."

"Will you require staff?"

I look over my shoulder, smiling to myself. "No staff, but a delivery of groceries would be helpful. Some ingredients for meals, breakfast, some fruit and vegetables."

"No problem, Mr. Ward."

"Thank you. I'll be in touch tomorrow." I hang up and call to arrange a flight for tomorrow, then rummage through the boxes that Ava is yet to unpack, remembering seeing her passport in one of them. I email both of our details over to the charter company, then call Peterson.

"Hello, Rococo Union, this is Sally speaking, how can I help you?" the girl in the office answers, and she sounds about ready to call it quits on life. *Jesus.*

"Peterson, please."

"Who's calling?"

"Jesse Ward."

"He's out at meetings."

"Can I get his mobile number?"

"I'm afraid I'm not permitted to disclose Mr. Peterson's mobile number," she drones, monotone.

I take a breath of patience. "Can you kindly get him to call me? It's about Ava."

"What about Ava?"

"She was involved in a car accident yesterday."

"Oh my God!" That ignited a bit of passion in her voice.

"Indeed. She won't be in work today." Or tomorrow. Or the next day. Or...ever?

"I'll have him call you, Mr. Ward."

"Thanks." I hang up and find Elizabeth's number. It's time to face the in-laws. Break the news. I grin.

"Jesse?" she answers, sounding anxious. "Is everything okay?"

"Yes, perfect. I'm taking Ava away tomorrow."

"Ooh, lovely. Where?"

"Paradise," I say quietly, smiling fondly.

"And where is Paradise?"

"Costa del Sol. But it's a surprise. Anyway, we fly tomorrow from

Bristol. I was thinking of bringing her down to see you before we go."

"That would be wonderful!"

"Great. We're leaving soon, so should be with you late afternoon." I look down at my Rolex.

"We'll go out for dinner! Joseph, Ava and Jesse are visiting!"

I can't bloody wait to tell them we're expecting. "I'll let you know if we hit any traffic," I say, my phone beeping to tell me another call is coming in. "Gotta go." I switch the call. "Peterson."

"Mr. Ward. Sally mentioned a car accident. Is Ava okay?"

"A little shaken up."

"Any injuries?"

I squint, thinking. "A few cuts and bruises. She won't be in work today. In fact, she needs some time off."

"How much time?"

I don't like this. Bargaining for my pregnant wife's recovery time and well-being. "I'm taking her out of town." *Out of the country, actually.* "To get away from the chaos of London to recover."

"Oh, well. Okay. She'll be back on Monday?"

"Tuesday." I quickly hang up, calling Peterson a few choice names. I'm done with him. With his company. I need to somehow convince Ava she does *not* need the pressure of a boss. Not when she has a husband. She can't be trailing round houses and developments while she's expecting, especially not with twins. She'll grow faster. Be more uncomfortable. Every side effect of pregnancy will be doubled. Yet I can't tell her to quit. That would be a mistake. But I've bought myself some time with this mini break, and I'm praying we can find a compromise to this problem called a career. I quickly drop a text to Cathy letting her know we're out of town for a few days, and then message Kate, just in case Sam's forgotten to mention it. The phone on the wall rings, and I answer to Casey.

"I have delivery for you, Mr. Ward. Looks like wallpaper."

"Store it. I have decorators coming tomorrow. Cathy will be here to let them in."

"Yes, sir."

I hang up and text Cathy again, letting her know about the decorators coming, then stand and wonder…who else do I need to tell we're going away?

A distant, consistent thud comes from upstairs and, curious, I make my way to the stairs, finding Ava wrestling her suitcase down them. *What the hell?*

"Hey." Is she out of her fucking mind? She startles, and my heart nearly falls out of my chest when she wobbles. *Shit, no.* I fly up the stairs like a rocket. "What the fuck are you doing, woman?" I bark, incensed, steadying her.

"For fuck's sake, Jesse," she yells, and I flinch. "Fucking hell." Double flinch. "That was your fucking fault," she snaps.

I start twitching like I've been hit with high voltage. "Will you watch your fucking mouth?" I shout, ensuring her stability before I wrench the suitcase up. "Wait there." I stomp down the stairs, infuriated. "Absolutely zero sense," I mumble. "Fucking ridiculous. And she thinks working is an option? No. She can't be trusted to be sensible." I dump the case and make my way back up, picking her up. "You'll break your fucking neck, you stupid woman."

"I was carrying a case." She scowls at me. "It was *you* who made me jump."

"You shouldn't be carrying anything, except my babies."

"*Our* babies."

"That's what I fucking said." I get to the bottom and lower her, checking the footwear situation. Flats. That's one wise choice she's made. "No doing stupid shit, lady."

"How is carrying a case stupid?" she asks, fixing her clothes.

How? Did she miss the breaking news? "Because you're pregnant." Lord, send me strength and patience before I explode.

"You'd better rein it in, Ward," she hisses, wagging an accusing finger. Rein *what* in? Do I have to read her the list on what pregnant women *need* from their husbands? Love. Patience. I huff. Why can't she be—"Cornwall!" she barks.

I chuckle, and Ava frowns. "How many times are you going to threaten me with fucking Cornwall?" There's not much in this world I'm certain of, except my love for this woman and the hard fact that she would *never* voluntarily move back in with her mother.

"I'll go now," she yells, the volume of her voice making her shake. And perhaps the level of her frustration. She has no idea. It seems I got ahead of myself when I concluded she's finally accepted my level of commitment to her safety. And now my babies' safety too.

"Come on then," I say, serious, collecting her case. "I'll take you." I head for the door, smiling to myself. I can't hear her following. "Are you coming?" I look back, finding her stock-still, eyes a little wide before she corrects it.

"Have you called Patrick?"

"Yes. You need to be back in work by Tuesday." *But I plan on convincing you while we're away to never return.*

She watches me punch in the code for the elevator, and I dial John as the doors close. "I can't believe you used the countdown as the new code," she mumbles.

I ignore her. She absolutely can believe it. "Anything?" I ask when he answers.

"Not really. I finally got into the system and checked all the footage. Except the ones that still don't work near the garages. Fucking security company. Whoever got in came over one of the boundary walls."

I guide Ava out of the elevator when the doors open. "Let's get Steve Cook on it." My eyes narrow when I see the new concierge smile from ear to ear. And it's not because he's happy to see *me*.

"Hi, Ava," he chirps.

"Mrs. Ward," I correct him.

"Did you call the police?" John asks.

"Yeah," I say quietly as Ava starts getting into conversation with the concierge. "They want to take statements."

"But you want Cook involved?"

"He'll work faster. Plus, I can talk to him while we're away."

"Where are you going?"

"I'm taking Ava to Cornwall to see her parents." I tug her on, and she cranes her neck back, not letting me stop her having a nice morning chitchat with the concierge. "We're flying to Malaga after we've been to tell her parents we're pregnant." Silence. To be expected, I suppose. I come to a stop outside the doors of Lusso, smiling at the gleaming Aston waiting for me. "I'm taking her to Paradise," I add, in case he thought he misheard me.

"I think that's a nice idea," he says softly. Approvingly.

"Where are you?" It sounds like he's in his car.

"She's not answering my calls," he says flatly. "Just checking on her."

"For fuck's sake," I breathe, biting down on my back teeth, as if I can stop myself saying the forbidden. Like…offer Sarah her job back. "Let me know."

"I will. Enjoy it, okay?"

"Yeah, thanks, big guy." I swallow and open the boot, putting the cases in.

"What's this?" Ava asks.

"I think it might be a car."

"Sarcasm doesn't suit you, god," she huffs. "I mean, where has it come from?"

"It came from a garage to replace mine until it's located." I lead her to the passenger side and put her in the seat.

"They've still not found your car?"

"No."

"What's Steve doing?"

"Nothing," I say quickly, not liking her expectant eyes on me as I fasten her seatbelt. "He's looking into a few things for me." I adjust the part across her tummy, making sure she has room.

"Will you just stop?" She brushes me off and pushes me away, shutting the door quickly. I was definitely getting ahead of myself. This woman doesn't know how to be reasonable. I didn't give her the information she wanted, so she's not going to give me compliance. Very mature. I walk slowly around the front of the car, eyes burning a hole through the windscreen as she follows my path.

I get in, my body bunched behind the wheel. "For fuck's sake," I grumble, adjusting the seat and steering wheel.

"Why didn't we just take my car?" Ava asks, making me falter as I recline the back rest.

"You can't drive too far."

"No, but you could."

What's her point? "Yes, I could, but I have this now." I slide my hands onto the wheel, smiling as the engine purrs. I press my foot on the gas and get the usual thrill when the engine yells its eagerness to get going. "Listen to that." *Glorious.*

"Where are you taking me, then?"

"I told you, your mother's."

"Okay," she says, exasperated, fiddling with her mobile.

"Give me your phone." There will be no one else on our break with us, including people on phones.

"I need to call Kate."

"I've called everyone who needs to know we're going away," I say, plucking it from her grasp. "Including Kate. Unravel your knickers, lady." I'm more than surprised that she doesn't argue. I pull out of the gates, shifting in my seat, readjusting the back rest again.

"I'm excited," she muses.

I huff a sardonic puff of laughter. "To stay with your mother?"

"Stop it. I know you'd never accept separation while I'm pregnant."

Or separation *ever*. "Then why threaten it?"

"Because you drive me crazy."

I reach across and take her hand, squeezing. "How do you feel?"

"Tired."

"Then go to sleep."

"Maybe," she says, and I smile.

She's a goner before we make it out of the city.

Chapter 27

The long drive and Ava's lack of consciousness offers me plenty of time to deal with a few things. I called Cook. He happily took on the case. In fact, he didn't sound too confident in his colleague when he asked who I'd spoken to. His willingness was received gratefully. I gave him everything he asked for to get the case moving. I just hope he comes up with some answers before I have to take my family back to London. Disturbingly, the more I think about everything, the more I doubt Mikael is responsible. He might be a womanizing slime bag, but a criminal? I hate to admit it, but I think I was barking up the wrong tree. So…Sarah? I shouldn't put anything past her. But, again, she's many things—devious, hurtful, brazen—but capable of drugging Ava? Running her off the road? But she *does* know how to access my car.

I growl under my breath in frustration, feeling like I'm hitting dead end after dead end. And yet that horrible, niggling feeling persists. I go to my mobile and dial the medical practice in Scotland again, glancing across at Ava. She's still conked out, but I disconnect my phone from Bluetooth anyway and take it to my ear. "Hi, yes, my name's Jesse Ward. I've called numerous times about a doctor that used to work there. I'm yet to hear back."

"Ah, Mr. Ward, yes, you spoke to me. I passed your message and number over to the practice manager."

"Well, they've not returned my call."

"She's very busy."

"I appreciate that." I grit my teeth, tell myself I'll get nowhere throwing my weight around. Especially when I'm not there in person. "Listen, this is really quite important." *Like a matter of sanity.*

There's a brief pause before a light sigh. "Bear with me."

I deflate in my seat, despite there not being a positive outcome yet, as I tap the wheel, eyes between Ava and the motorway.

"Hello, this is Gloria Day speaking, practice manager. How can I help you, Mr. Ward?"

I sit up straight in my seat. "Ms. Day, thank you for taking my call."

"Yes, well, you caught me between appointments."

Get on with it. "I'm looking for a friend who used to work there. Dr. Alan Pierce."

"I'm afraid data protection prevents me from discussing former collogues."

"So he *did* used to work there?"

"Yes, Dr. Pierce is a former doctor here."

I squint at the windscreen, trying to calculate how old Lauren's father would be now. "Former as in no longer there, or former as in no longer a doctor at all?" Retired? Or is he dead?

"Mr. Ward—"

"Retired?"

"I'm—"

"Moved on to another practice?"

She exhales her irritation. "Alan left a few years ago, Mr. Ward. I haven't heard from him since."

"Do you have an address?"

"Mr. Ward, come on, you know I can't divulge that information," she says tiredly.

"So you *do* have an address?"

"Yes, but even if I could disclose that information, it would be pointless because he moved away from the area."

My mind races, trying to build a picture. I glance across to Ava. "And you've not heard from him since?"

"No, but I'm not surprised."

I raise my brows. "Why?"

Silence. She's said too much.

"I'm an old friend," I go on. "I was close to the Pierces when they lost their granddaughter."

"Oh," she breathes. "Yes, very tragic."

I wince.

"Look, Mr. Ward, all I will say is this." My ears prick. "Dr. Pierce was a very troubled man. He lost his granddaughter *and* his daughter, and his wife was ill and required full-time care."

I stare at the road ahead. "Lauren's dead?"

"Yes, you didn't know that?"

"Yes, of course," I blurt, feeling every muscle in me relax. A weight lifted. And isn't that terrible? She's dead?

"Now, I really need to get back to my patients."

"Thanks," I murmur, cutting the call before Ms. Day. "Fucking hell." I dial John, checking Ava again. "Lauren's dead," I say on a whisper as soon as he answers. "I got through to the surgery where her father worked, and they told me she's dead."

John doesn't whoop his joy, and neither do I. But, again, I will ashamedly admit that I'm relieved. "Do you think—"

I blow out my cheeks, hearing him. "She was ill, John." And her doctor father struggled to accept that. Perhaps he thought he could fix her. Who knows.

"I don't know what to say."

"Me neither," I admit, as Ava stirs in her seat. "Is everything okay at The Manor?"

"S'all good. Call me when you arrive in Spain." He hangs up before me, and I drop my phone into my lap, taking the wheel with both hands.

Shaking.

Because the question remains.

Who?

• • •

I'm staggered that she's still sleeping by the time I pull into her parents' street. "What a spot," I muse, crawling along, seeing wet-suited bodies on the beach in the distance running into the water, boards under their arms. It's sunny but gusty, the waves reliable for the surfers. I frown when we pass a quaint graveyard. "Interesting."

Craning my neck to see the numbers on the walls outside the houses, I slow to a stop when I reach number twelve, a tidy semi by the sea. The perfect retirement home. And now I need to load up on patience to get me through the evening and into tomorrow morning before I can whisk Ava away to Paradise.

I reach for Ava's knee and give her a gentle nudge, smiling when she yawns, stretches, and blinks. I unclip her seatbelt. "Where are we?" she asks, squinting at me.

"Cornwall."

"Stop it." She wriggles in her seat to wake up her muscles. "I need a wee." Her hand reaches for the handle but stills, and I see realization fall into her as she takes in the surroundings. "You weren't kidding?" she breathes, injured. "You're dumping me on my mum?"

I laugh on the inside as I pull her face toward me. "Don't threaten me with Cornwall."

And she bursts into tears all over me, sobbing uncontrollably. *Whoa!* "Baby, I'm joking," I say quickly. "Anyone would have to slice their way through me to get to you. You know that." Jesus Christ, is this pregnancy? Will it make her forget who I am, what I stand for, what I need? I tug her across the center console, and she's quick to hide in my chest, wetting my T-shirt with her tears.

I feel fucking awful. "Ava, look at me," I demand softly, trying to encourage her out. My heart melts and breaks all at once at the sight of her dejection.

"I'm going to be so fat," she says over a snivel. "*Massive.*" A sniff. "Twins, Jesse!"

Oh my God, what is she saying? She'll be even more beautiful.

"You won't…" She swallows, looking away.

Oh no, she's not seriously thinking *that*? "Desire you?" I say in disbelief, and she nods jerkily. "Baby, that will never happen." I only have to touch her and my dick pings to attention. That will never change.

"You don't know that," she sobs, her face bunched. "You don't know how you'll feel when I've got swollen ankles and I'm walking like I've got a melon wedged between my thighs."

Laughter rises fast and falls out loudly. "Is that how it'll be?"

She pouts. "Probably."

"Let me tell you, lady," I begin, holding her face, making sure she has my serious eyes. "I desire you more with every day that passes, and I believe you've been carrying my babies for quite a few weeks." I gaze at her stomach on a fond smile, circling my palm there.

"I'm not fat yet."

"You're not going to be fat, Ava. You're pregnant, and the thought of you keeping a piece of me and you warm and safe makes me fucking deliriously happy, and—" I still, feeling blood drop into my dick. *Oh, no.* See? One touch, I lose all control. It swells in my boxers, becoming quickly uncomfortable wedged between us. Not ideal when we're parked outside her parents' house. "It makes me desire you even fucking more. Now, shut up and kiss me, wife." *Stupid!* But can I control it? My hips shoot up on instinct, and Ava launches her attack, eating me alive, hungry and determined. Fucking hell, all she wants to do is sleep and ravish me. *Amazing*.

I hum. "There's my girl." How could she ever think I wouldn't want her? "Shit, Ava, I would *love* to rip those lace knickers off and fuck you stupid right now, but I don't want an audience." What am I saying? I refuse to *fuck* her.

"I don't care." She lets me take a quick breath before coming at me again, kissing me wildly. Jesus, what is this torture?

"Ava," I gasp, trying to free my mouth from hers as she pins me to the seat. "Cut it out or I won't be responsible for my actions."

"I won't hold you responsible," she breathes, relentless, thrusting onto me, grappling at my T-shirt. I growl, bite down on my teeth, close my eyes, try to talk reason into myself. Not here. Not now.

My dick doesn't agree.

Here.

Now.

"Fucking hell, woman." I'm a fool to think I can say no. Look at her, begging for me. *Wonderful*.

Rap, rap, rap.

Ava gasps, shooting back, and I look out of the window, breathless, finding a copper on the pavement with impressively high brows. Ava's quickly dying on my lap, her face beetroot. "That'll teach you," I whisper, putting her back in the passenger seat and releasing the window. "Sorry about that. Pregnant. Hormones. Can't keep her hands off me." I laugh when she wallops me, but wince at my dick still throbbing behind my fly. "See?"

"Yes...well...urm...public place. Move on, please."

"We're visiting." I give Ava my attention, smiling madly as she looks at me all wide-eyed. "Ready?"

"I thought you were taking me on a plane?"

"I am," I say, getting out and rearranging myself. "After we've told my delightful mother-in-law that she's going to be a grandmother." I close the door on her mouth hanging open and circle the car, pleased with myself. "Out you get."

"Why are you doing this to me?" She remains in her seat, eyes closed, trying to find some courage.

"They need to know."

"No," she grumbles as I help her out. "You just can't wait to advise my forty-seven-year-old mother that she's going to be a gran."

Absolutely. "Not at all." I walk her up the path, feeling her resistance between our extended arms.

"How did you know where to come?"

"I called and asked for the address." I nod to the Mercedes. "And I believe that's your father's car. Am I right?"

"Yes."

I reach into my pocket and pull out some cuffs, lifting her hand and kissing it.

She smiles. It falls the moment I secure the cuffs over our wrists. "What are you doing?" she gasps, wriggling her hand. "Jesse!"

I don't have a chance to explain, not that I need to. Elizabeth appears, delighted to welcome us. "My girl's home!"

"Hi, *Mum*," I say cheerfully, waving at her with my cuffed hand, dragging Ava's heavy arm up with it. Her face. It's another I'd like to box and unwrap when I need a laugh.

"Get those cuffs off my daughter, you menace," she hisses, hauling us inside while checking the street for witnesses.

I chuckle when Ava rolls her eyes and shoves me playfully. Okay, I'm done. Time to play the perfect son-in-law. So I remove the cuffs and rub life back into Ava's wrist.

"Happy?"

"Yes." I'm pushed aside by Elizabeth. "It's so good to see you, darling," she sings, hugging Ava fiercely. "I've got the spare room ready for you."

"We're staying?" Ava frowns over her mother's shoulder at me.

"We fly out in the morning. I thought we'd run a visit in before your mum starts thinking that I'm keeping you from her."

I'm surprised when Elizabeth gives up her daughter for me, hugging me hard. "Thank you for bringing her to visit."

"Make the most of it," I say, embracing her love for me. She might change her mind when she hears our news. "Because I'm kidnapping her in the morning."

"Yes, yes, I know. Joseph," she screeches in my ear. I wince, breaking away. "They're here! I'll make tea."

Ava leads me into the kitchen, where Joseph is at the table. "Hi, Dad." Ava leaves me to greet her father, and I take a seat.

"Ava, how are you?" He accepts her affection, albeit with a mild cringe, before offering me his hand. "Is she keeping you on your toes?"

I laugh on the inside. "Of course."

"I need a wee," Ava says, scooting off, leaving me with Joseph and Elizabeth.

"So how's married life?" Joseph asks, pushing his newspaper aside and relaxing back in his chair.

I smile up at Elizabeth when she slides a cup of tea in front of me. "Blissful," I say, taking a sip, smiling.

"And you two are okay?"

I smile wider around the rim of my mug. "All okay."

All *four* of us.

Chapter 28

Elizabeth suggested a local pub for dinner. Fine by me. I honestly don't mind where we tell them they're going to be grandparents, so why not over a nice steak? Well-done.

I make sure Ava's comfortable in a soft chair and get everyone's drink orders, predicting Elizabeth's wine and Joseph's beer.

"No wine?" Elizabeth asks, surprised when Ava asks for a water.

I push Ava's chair closer to the table, sneaking a look at Elizabeth, willing her not to make a big deal of it. Ava's parents probably think their daughter is being sensitive, given my apparent drinking problem. "No, we need to get away early," Ava says, perusing the menu, playing it surprisingly cool. Even more surprisingly, Elizabeth pipes down, but I get the feeling she's thinking as she returns her attention to the menu.

I dip into Ava's neck. "I love you," I whisper, smiling when her hand feels me out as I push my lips onto her cheek.

"I know."

Happy, I leave them and head to the bar, ordering and paying before making my way back, tray in hand.

"What are you having, then?" Elizabeth asks. "I think I'll go for the seafood platter."

Seafood? I sit and scoop up the menu, scanning the endless choices, many of which were on the list of foods to be avoided. Christ, it's like a minefield of unsuitable options. And I bet my wife fancies one of them.

Feeling her lean into me, I take her hand from my knee and kiss her knuckles, checking the steak choices. Rump, sirloin, T-bone. No fillet. I huff to myself. It's certainly not The Manor. At The Manor, I can guarantee my wife's go-to, so I don't have to stress about her picking from a list. "What would you like, baby?" I ask, silently begging her to choose steak.

"I'm not sure."

Fuck it.

"I'm having the mussels in garlic," Joseph says. I glance up, seeing him virtually dribbling at a blackboard on the wall. Seafood. And more seafood. "Bloody delicious," he adds.

That may be, but definitely not fit for pregnant women. So why the fuck is my wife checking out the blackboard, because there's no steak listed on there?

"I can't decide," Ava muses, deep in thought.

"Tell me what you're thinking, and I'll help you." I'll steer her toward steak. Problem solved.

"Mussels or the seafood platter."

"Neither," I say quickly. Impulsively. *Here we go*.

"Why?" Ava asks, a monster frown coming my way. Then… realization. "Oh, come on, Jesse."

Absolutely not. "No way, lady," I say, laughing. "Not a chance. There's some sort of mercury in fish that can damage an unborn baby's nervous system." This is non-negotiable. She needs to read the fucking book. "Don't even try to defy me on this one."

"Are you going to let me eat anything?" she asks.

"Yes." What does she think I am, the food police? "Chicken, steak. Both are high in protein, and that's good for our babies." I point to the steaks and the chicken, not that she notices. She's too busy sulking into her water. Neither has she noticed the fact that her parents are staring at us with mouths hanging open.

Bollocks.

Now, if she'd have just ordered steak…

"Do it in style, Ava." I take a deep breath and release it, waiting for the fireworks, because by the look on Elizabeth's face, there are definitely going to be some explosions. This is *not* how I wanted this to go.

"You're pregnant?" she breathes, eyes jumping between us. Ava's accusing glare is pointed my way, like this is somehow my fault. But rather than glare back, I look at the menu on the table in front of me, silent.

"Ava?" Joseph says.

"Surprise," she murmurs.

"But you've been married for five minutes." Elizabeth voice gets higher with every word she speaks, and I reach for my forehead, trying to rub the looming stressed headache away. "Five minutes!"

Slight exaggeration. But of course she'd be dramatic—this is Ava's mother. What did I expect?

"It was a shotgun wedding, wasn't it?" she blurts, attention all on me. "You married her because you had to."

I cough over nothing, locking down every muscle before I shoot up and take the table with me. What a fucking insult after what I went through with my ex-wife—not that she or Ava know. *That* was shotgun. *That* was toxic. A fucking nightmare.

"Thanks," Ava huffs sardonically, obviously as insulted as I am. Good. Then she won't mind if I have a little trample.

"Elizabeth," I say calmly, sensing Ava preparing to hold me back. "You know better than that."

She laughs. Oh, she's pushing me. Thank God Joseph steps in before I'm forced to sew my dear mother-in-law's mouth shut. "So you didn't know at the wedding?" he asks, forcing Elizabeth to back down, though her eyes are waiting keenly for an answer.

"No," Ava blurts.

I stare at her accusingly. She knew. I suspected. What the fuck does it matter now? And why the hell am I sitting here like an errant child being forced to explain myself? This is ridiculous; my patience is fading by the second. I reach for my forehead and rub again, as Ava gives me an apologetic, sheepish smile. Steak. It was a simple choice. Why the fuck did I bring her here?

"I see," Joseph says. What does he see? Nothing, because they're both blind to the endless triggers being thrown my way.

Don't explode.

Elizabeth exhales as dramatically as I would expect. "I can't believe it. A pregnant bride suggests only one thing."

"Then don't bloody tell anyone," Ava hisses angrily, getting herself worked up. No. I'm not having this. Pregnant women shouldn't get stressed. I grab her hand and start rubbing some calmness into her. Easier said than done when I'm fucking reeling myself.

"Elizabeth," I say more softly than she deserves. "I'm not an eighteen-year-old lad being forced to do the right thing after a quick fuck about with a girl." Been there, done that, and I've paid dearly for it. I feel Ava squeeze my hand, her worried eyes on me. God, if she knew. "I'm thirty-eight years old. Ava is my *wife*, and I am not having her worked up or upset, so you can accept it and give us your blessing, or you can carry on like this and I'll take my girl home now."

Elizabeth's looks like I've just slapped her. God, strike me down, I wish I fucking could, if only to knock the prissiness out of her.

"Now, let's all just calm down a little, shall we?" Joseph says. I don't miss the single look he gives his wife. Like…let me handle this. *Thank you, Joseph. And* please *do a better job than your wife.* "Ava." His tone is gentle and his face soft. "How do you feel about this?"

"Fine."

I can't hide my shock. She can't think of a better word?

"Perfect," she blurts. "Couldn't be happier."

Much better.

"Well, then," Joseph says, relaxing back in his chair, satisfied. "They're married, financially stable…" He chuckles. I think it's for my benefit. "And they're bloody adults, Elizabeth. Get a grip." He flashes her a rare smile. "You're going to be a granny."

I snort, hiding my smile before Elizabeth lays me out. She looks like someone's just told her I've pissed in her wine. My God, she's painfully exasperating.

"I will not be a granny," she says, outraged. "I'm forty-seven years old."

She just can't help herself.

"I could be a nana, though."

"You can be whatever you like, Elizabeth," I breathe, done with my testing mother-in-law for the day. Or the year. One night, I tell myself. Just get through this one night.

"And you should watch your language, Jesse Ward," she mutters, smacking the top of my menu. "Wait!"

"For what?" Joseph asks.

Yes, what drama has she thought up now?

"You said babies, plural," she says, her usually arched brows straight from her frown.

Oh.

"You said our *babies.*"

"Twins." I find Ava's belly and rub it, smiling. "Two babies. Two grandchildren."

Joseph laughs. "Well, I'll be damned. Now, that really is very special. Congratulations!"

Agree, Joseph. Really special. And Ava's smiling, *finally.*

"Twins?" Elizabeth gasps. I watch is disappointment as my wife's smile fades. "Oh, Ava, darling, you are going to be exhausted. What—"

"No, she won't," I snap before she gets going again. "She's got me. End of."

Elizabeth takes the warning, backing off. Have we finally reached an understanding? *Take the opportunity, Elizabeth. Make it count.*

She softens, her body *and* her face. "And you have us, darling. I'm so sorry. It's just a bit of a shock. You'll always have us," she says, reaching for Ava and taking her hand.

Smiling fondly, I watch mother and daughter come together, but I can see the wave of uncertainty ripple across Ava's face. *God damn you, Elizabeth.*

I get her attention and move in closer, holding her hand tight. Never to be let go. "You have me." I will be there day and night, be hands-on, do all the things. She'll never feel lonely, she'll never feel unappreciated. Everything I am and have will be put into our future. I'll probably drive her crazy. *Standard.* And she'll undoubtedly continue to push my buttons. It's who we are. What we do.

"Have you decided?" a waitress asks.

I return her enthusiastic smile, feeling Ava's palm find its way onto my leg. "I'll have the steak, please," she says. I look at Ava, who's forcing a smile at the waitress. I look at the waitress, who's *not* forcing a smile at me. It's a natural smile. Coy.

Oh.

I sink into my chair, looking between them, bracing myself.

"I'll have the steak," Ava says again, slow and clearly. "Medium."

I glance at the waitress briefly, mentally yelling at her not to poke the bear.

"Pardon?"

"The steak," Ava grates. "Medium. Would you like me to write it down for you?"

I laugh under my breath, despite myself. I shouldn't love it when she gets all possessive. But I do.

"Oh, of course." The waitress snaps out of her daze. "And for you?"

"Mussels for me." Joseph raises his brows at me, and I shrug, remembering one of the first things he said to me as his eyes climbed my body. *You're an impressive human, aren't you?* What can I say?

Elizabeth places her menu down, giving me a similar interested look. I shrug at her too. "The seafood platter for me. And I'll have another wine."

"And for you, sir?" the waitress asks, still writing. And smiling at me again.

Shouldn't. I really shouldn't. But…"What would you recommend?" I ask.

"The lamb is good."

"He'll have the same as me," Ava snaps, snatching the menus up and thrusting them at her. I chuckle. "Medium."

"The wife has spoken," I muse, pulling Ava closer. "I do as I'm told, so it looks like I'm having the steak."

Ava jerks in my hold, and I look at her fondly as her parents laugh at our shenanigans. "You're impossible," she mumbles while I dedicate a bit of time to her throat with my lips. "And since when do you do what you're told?"

"Ava, that was really quite rude. Jesse can make his own meal choices," Elizabeth says. And she loves me again.

"It's okay." I don't come up for air. "She knows what I like."

"You like to be impossible."

"I love watching you in trampling action." I nip at her ear, smiling when she shudders. "I could bend you over this table and fuck you really hard." And my mother-in-law would hate me again. Do I care?

Ava gathers herself and turns the tables. "Stop saying the word *fuck*, unless you're going to fuck me," she whispers.

"Watch your mouth."

"No."

"Cheeky."

"Let's raise a toast!" Joseph sings, forcing me away from mauling Ava's cheek. "To twins."

"To twins," Elizabeth says, prompting me to lift my glass of water. Ava's smiling again. I scrunch my nose, squeeze her knee, and hit my glass with the others. "Excuse me, I need the men's," I say, getting up and leaving the table. I feel Ava's eyes follow me, so I look back, finding her dark gaze on my arse. She's asking for it. And I know she's going to ask for it at her parents' house. And I know she's going to want it hard.

I ponder how I might handle that while I search for the waitress to tell her to make sure Ava's steak is well-done. But to tell her it's medium when it's served.

Chapter 29

As I expected, she threw her temptress skills at me left and right when we got back to her parents' last night. So I gagged her and fucked her as delicately as I could.

And the Quiet Fuck was born.

I can't wait to get her to Paradise so she can scream to her heart's content. Not that'll I'll fuck her hard. Nope. Gently does it.

We left the in-laws early and got on the road, just Ava and me, and that's how it'll be for the next few days. Blissful.

"Shit," Ava says out of the blue, jarring me, as I head for the private hangar.

Blissful? Maybe if I wash her mouth out with soap and water. "Ava, mouth," I grumble, looking across at her as she dives into her handbag. "What's up?"

She reaches for the door as I take a left, throwing me a scowl. "Will you take it easy?"

"There's no place you're safer than in a car with me." I scan the road ahead for the turning, slowing. "What's the matter?"

"My passport. I've left my passport in my box of junk." She continues to scratch through her bag. Don't know why. She just said herself it's in her box of junk. So it's a damn good thing I'm the organized one in this marriage.

"No, you haven't," I say, retrieving it from the safety of the glovebox. "But you *have* forgotten to get your name changed, *Miss O'Shea*."

She smiles and takes it. "So I'm traveling a single?"

"Shut up, Ava." Why does she choose words she knows will rub me up the wrong way? *Because she wouldn't be Ava otherwise.* I ignore her brief chuckle and pull to a stop, slipping out and looking at the jet over my shades as I round the car, smiling.

"Mr. Ward, welcome," Vincent says, appearing from the hangar with the captain, paperwork in his hands.

"Morning, Vincent. Good to see you." I nod to the captain, who politely nods back as I open the car door. "Come on." I take Ava's passport and hand it over with mine, giving Vincent a signature before popping the boot so our luggage can be carried on.

When I return to Ava, she's still in the car appearing bewildered. "Are you going to sit there all day, lady?" I ask, helping her out.

"What's that?" She frowns past me, and I look back on an unsure smile.

"That's a plane," I say, leading on and taking the steps up, smiling at the flight attendant—her name escapes me. But I've seen her around the rooms of The Manor, along with the captain. *Seen her in my bed.* Best not mention that to Ava.

I can already feel resistance between our joined hands. Is she afraid of flying? "Ava?" I ask when she stops outside the jet.

"I'm not getting on that thing."

I notice her chest is pumping. She is. She's afraid. I don't recall her ever saying she has a fear of flying. In fact, I distinctly remember her demanding I take her somewhere hot *and* on a plane.

"Of course you are." I try to encourage her onward, but she's firm in her stance, her eyes full of fear. Not a fan. I'm forced to step back out of the plane when she retreats. "Ava, you've never said you're scared of flying."

"I'm not," she says, only confusing me more. "I like big planes. Why are we not going on a big plane? Why can't we go on one of those?" she asks, pointing to a commercial aircraft.

"Because they're probably not going where we need them to." I go to her, crowding her body, which is smaller than it usually is, her uncertainty seeming to shrink her. "It's perfectly safe." I turn her face back to me so she can see my reassurance.

"It doesn't look safe." She eyes the jet. "It looks too small."

"Ava." I soften my voice. My eyes. My face. "This is me, your possessive, unreasonable, over-protective control freak." I'm humoring her, obviously. "Do you really think I'd willingly put you in danger?" I drop a pacifying kiss on her face.

"I feel a little nervous."

No shit. "Answer my question."

"No," she sighs. "I don't."

"Good," I say, taking her shoulders and guiding her on. "You'll love it, trust me."

"Good morning," the attendant says, her eyes interested. She'll have heard. Everyone will have heard. *Married. Pregnant.* Hopefully those two significant things will deter any inappropriate behavior that may have my hormonal wife throwing the attendant out of the jet without a parachute.

I walk Ava to one of the chairs and help her down, fixing her seatbelt. Lowering to the chair opposite, I sit and rest Ava's feet to my lap. Swollen ankles are a real thing. I'll have to rub her feet the entire flight.

"Champagne, sir?"

Kimberly. Her name is Kimberly. And by the look on her face, marriage and babies isn't an issue. But of course. She's a member of my fine manor. And, really, I wouldn't have the first idea of her relationship status, although I suspect the captain features somewhere in her life, and not in a professional capacity.

"Just water." I flick her a stoic face. A warning face. I think she gets the message if her prompt escape and falling smile are a measure. I remove Ava's shoes and start rubbing her feet. "Okay?"

"Not really." Surprisingly, she appears oblivious to Kimberly's obvious friendliness, her attention pointed out of the window. "There were regular flights available, weren't there?"

"I don't know, I didn't check," I admit. "We don't do commercial, Ava."

"*You* don't. I do," she mutters. "I haven't got swollen feet yet, you know."

Prevention is better than cure. "Close your eyes," I order, seeing Kimberly on her way back with our water. Ava sighs and settles, her petite body sinking into the huge leather seat, my thumbs rubbing firm circles in the soles of her feet. I nod at the table, prompting Kimberly to set the drinks down without a word, then I focus on Ava, watching a small smile creep onto her face. She's thinking of me. I'm not being presumptuous.

I get comfortable, hearing the door being closed, but I don't take my attention off Ava. I love watching her. I love wondering what's running through her mind. I love rubbing her feet, seeing her lashes flutter. Her breathing deepen. Her chest rise and fall. I know she's out for the count when her chin drops slightly.

My gaze falls to her stomach, the corner of my mouth twitching.

Watching her belly grow with our babies is going to be incredible. My future will be filled with nothing but amazing things. And my past is full of horror.

Don't look back.

"Don't look back," I whisper, sinking deeper into the seat. She's with me, and London is far behind us. Our troubles are far behind us.

For now.

The jet starts moving smoothly toward the runway, and we're soon speeding down it, the glorious weightless feeling coming over me. She doesn't stir once. Dreaming. Sleeping for fucking England again. I just can't see how work is an option for her at the moment. It seems the second she sits or lies down, she dozes off. I pull the camera up on my phone and snap a picture of her sleeping.

"Can I get you anything, Mr. Ward?" Kimberley asks, hovering over my seat.

"Just more water, thanks," I reply, and she's soon placing two glasses down. "There will be nothing else." This will be the easiest flight she's worked on. I want nothing. Just peace.

I lift Ava's foot to my lips and lick her instep, chuckling when she shifts in her seat, eyes still closed. My tongue drags across to her toe. Her leg stiffens and one eye opens.

"Dreaming?"

"Of you," she breathes, settling again. "Tell me when we take off so I can put my head between my legs."

"I'll put *my* head between your legs." I nip her toe, feeling her tremble.

"Just tell me."

"Look out the window, baby," I say softly, watching as she leans up and checks. She gasps lightly and looks around. "Why didn't you tell me?"

"And miss the sounds and looks you were making?" I kiss her toes and place her feet back down. There's too much space between us. "Come here." Reaching for her, I undo her belt and help her across to me, getting her comfortable on my lap. "Go back to sleep and dream of me, lady."

She settles, and I relax back, my head falling to the side to look out of the window. Paradise. It's been years since I've been. The risk of bumping into people I didn't want to see was too high. I never dared take a break at my villa. It would have been too lonely on my own. Too secluded. *No sex.*

Now? Seclusion is just what we need.

I fasten the belt around us and rest my head on her, closing my eyes, feeling content and settled. There's something special about falling asleep together. The closeness. The equal vulnerability.

And now as we fly away from the UK to another country, I can say, hand on heart, I feel the most relaxed I've ever felt.

It's going to be a hard feeling to let go of.

Chapter 30

My ears pop, telling me we're descending, and a quick check out of the window confirms it. "Mr. Ward, we're landing." Kimberly looks at Ava curled up in my arms, and I nod to the seat belt around both of us. I know she could put her foot down. I know I could be met by the police when we land if I refuse to adhere to safety instructions. But...

I smile and Kimberly deflates, wandering to her own seat and buckling up. The landing is as smooth as takeoff, as it always is with Captain. Which has been demonstrated by Ava's lack of stirring.

Kimberly approaches again as the plane rolls to a stop by the private hangar. "You'll get me fired," she says, waving a finger at my head.

"What?"

She closes in, her reaching hand coming closer, and my head retracts, moving away. "You have something," she says.

"I've got it." I rake a hand through my hair roughly. "Thanks."

"Honeymoon?"

"Kind of," I reply, looking down at Ava, wondering if she's going to wake up any time soon.

"It was quite a surprise," she goes on quietly. I don't need to ask what she's talking about.

"I'm sure it was." I feel Ava stir, peeling her way out of my chest. I smile at her hair stuck to the side of her face as she looks up at Kimberly, squinting.

"Welcome to Malaga, Mrs. Ward," Kimberly chirps.

"Thank you." She looks disorientated, confused, still so bloody tired. Is this normal?

"My beautiful girl's back," I muse, pushing the hair from her cheek and kissing it. "Enjoy your flight?"

She blinks at me, eyes on my head. "Do I yank your hair in my sleep?"

"You do a lot in your sleep," I say, letting her pat it down, looking out the corner of my eye to Kimberly. She's watching. *Brash.* "I could watch you forever."

"I need to stretch." She tries to stand, pulling the belt across our laps taut.

I unclip us, freeing her. "I needed to belt you in."

Her top lifts when she stretches. "Aren't I supposed to be belted into my own seat for landing, with my seat in the upright position, my table stowed away, and all of my belongings tucked neatly under the seat in front?"

"Yes. I very nearly had to trample the lovely lady." Jesus. My body creaks and yells as I stand, and I reach to pull Ava's top down as she groans, still stretching. "Done?"

"Yes."

Great. Let's go. I take her hand and walk us off the plane, and the sunshine and heat that greets us makes me instantly smile. As I descend the steps, I turn my mobile back on, watching as a few missed calls land. One from Dan. And a message asking why I didn't tell him we're out of the country. Like I owe him that information? I'll deal with him later. I also have a message from John to call him when I land. *And* I'm alone. I slip my mobile into my pocket, uneasy about what he might have to tell me, then take the keys being handed to me, giving the guy a scribble.

"Really?" Ava says, taking in the Aston. "We couldn't have taken a taxi?"

"I don't do public transport, Ava."

"You should." She laughs. "It'll save you a fortune."

I can't expect her to comprehend my wealth because she's only seen some of my bank statements. But money is something she definitely doesn't need to worry about. And hopefully one day, she'll get comfortable with that.

I put her in the car, get behind the wheel, and slip my shades on. "Are you ready to be binged on for the next three days?"

"No," she says, smiling coyly. "Take me home." Leaning across the car, she plants a kiss on me. Easy affection. Perfect.

"Not a chance, lady. You're all mine, and I'm going to make the most of it." My tongue has a mind of its own and plunges into her mouth, and before I know it, we're in the midst of a passionate, full-blown kiss.

"I'm always yours," she practically moans.

"Correct. Get used to it." Ripping my mouth away before I rip her clothes off—gently—I get the car into gear and pull off as soon as I hear the boot close, our luggage onboard.

"I am used to it," she sighs, getting comfortable.

I put some music on and reach for her hand, squeezing, feeling annoyed. Because my focus isn't now on me, Ava, and this much-needed mini break.

It's on why John needs me to call him—*when I'm alone.*

Chapter 31

I sensed her anticlimactic state as I rolled carefully down the bumpy, dusty track toward the villa. The grass outside the boundary was scorched and the trees looked sad, but the smell of honeysuckle? It brought Paradise back to me with a vengeance.

When I finally pulled through the gates, the scenery changed completely, as did Ava's face—transforming from disappointment to disbelief. I smiled as I watched her get out of the car and explore the front of the villa, her mouth constantly open, her sounds of awe satisfying. It's good to be here. Amazing, actually. Because I'm here with Ava.

Not lonely.

I knew she'd love it. "What's my beautiful girl thinking?" I ask from my place perched on the bonnet of the Aston.

"I'm thinking I've just officially arrived on Central Jesse Cloud Nine," she says, smelling the honeysuckle over the veranda.

"Where?" I ask on a light laugh, but she doesn't feed my interest and instead runs at me, her face a picture of excitement and appreciation. Mine's gotta match. I catch her in my arms and accept her kiss.

"It's my most favorite place in the world," she mumbles around my lips. Removing my shades, she gazes down at me, scanning my face with such concentration, it could be the first time she's looked at me.

"Are you happy?" I ask. This is what any man should live for. This look on his wife, this feeling of serenity and calm.

"Delirious.'"

"Then my work here is done." But it'll never be done. I have a quick nibble of her hot neck before I put her down, excited to show her the inside and the showstopper view of the Med.

I fetch the bags, Ava fetches her handbag, and I let us inside, dumping the cases down. "Wait here," I say, leaving her in the dusky darkness as I go back outside and work my way around the veranda, opening all of the shutters. By the time I get back inside, she's nowhere to be seen. Exploring. I take a quick gaze around, familiarizing myself with the inside, as I haven't seen it since the renovations were completed.

They did a great job. But what a fucking waste that it's been sitting here empty for so long. I can fix that. I wander around searching for Ava, opening and closing doors, going to the kitchen. I go to the glass doors, spotting her on the grass by the pool, looking out to the sea. The view. Fucking incredible, today especially so. And the sunset here is one of the best I've ever seen, the sun literally sinking into the sea. I smile, retrieve the key from the hook by the door, and wander out, breathing in the fresh air. No pollution. No sound of traffic. Just the gentle rush of waves. I glance up and down the deserted beach, a mile each way of absolutely nothing. And there never will be, because I own the land.

I follow Ava past the pool to the gate that leads to the beach, reaching past her and slipping the key into the lock, pushing it open for her.

She tiptoes across the wooden steps and arrives on the sand, and I watch her taking it all in. Feeling the peace and happiness radiating off her. I move in behind her and circle my arms around her upper body, pulling her back into my chest. "Still on Central Jesse Cloud Nine?" I ask quietly, her hair whipping my face in the breeze.

"I am," she sighs, content. "Where are you?"

"Me?" Moving my hands to her stomach, stroking, and kissing her cheek, I breathe out. "Baby," I whisper, wondering how I ever dared think to sell this place. "I'm in paradise." And it's never been as blissful as it is now. How I would have loved to have brought Rosie here. Taught her to swim in the sea, build sandcastles, let her run free for miles. It never happened. Couldn't. She never had a passport, and if she did, I would never have been granted that privilege.

As soon as the twins are old enough to fly, we'll be bringing them here. I'll get past the demons that keep me from Paradise by then, I have to, because my kids can't ever miss out on this place. And now Ava's seen it, briefly experienced it? She'll want to come back too, guaranteed. Which means I may have to swallow my fear of judgment and shame and share that last piece of crucial information from my past. "Come," I say, linking our hands on her belly, nuzzling her neck. "We have food being delivered and I need to give you a tour." I turn her but remain behind her, walking us back to the villa.

"It's wonderful," she says wistfully. But she has so much more on her mind, I know that.

"Agree." We make it back inside, and I show her around, taking in the renovations myself too. She's impressed. I'm impressed. How could we not be? It's something else. I show her to the master bedroom, laugh when she flops back on the giant bed, and grin when she eyes the huge walk-in shower, her smile coy and suggestive. "Nice shower," she muses, dragging her fingers across the glass screen as she wanders around.

"It is."

She stops at the sink and looks into the mirror, reaching for her hair and tucking a stray strand behind her ear. "Nice mirror," she says softly.

"Oh, it is." I move in and take her hips, crowding her from behind, getting my face close to hers. "Nice reflection." It will be better when she's naked and bent over, and I'm taking her from behind. Softly.

"Oh, it is," she breathes, giving me a teasing push of her arse into my groin.

I fail to suppress my groan, feeling activity behind my fly. "God, woman, you kill me."

"Shame," she says, turning quickly and tackling my mouth. "It's been far too long since you've been inside me, husband."

Boom.

My insides explode, and my tongue duels with hers, my hands reaching for her top to rip off. Gently.

But I'm stopped when the doorbell chimes. "Oh my God," Ava gasps, her flushed face pointing toward the door. "Who's that?"

I grin, tampering down the want. For now. "Grocery delivery." I readjust my groin, in physical pain, and take her hand. "Come on."

She groans her annoyance but lets me pull her back to the kitchen. I leave her at the island poking in and out of drawers, familiarizing herself with the space, as I answer the door. Three crates are on the veranda, another being carried from the van by a bearded, old Spanish man. "Gracias," I say, picking up the first and hauling it inside, slipping it onto the counter. "Three more," I say, heading back out.

After getting them all inside, I tip the man, and shut out the world, returning to the kitchen. She's started to unpack, inspecting all of the groceries, so I unload the crates onto the counter and then stack them by the door. "You okay while I sort the cases?" I ask, picking them up.

"Wonderful," she breathes, inspecting a pack of lamb.

I smile and leave my wife feeling wonderful, heading to the

bedroom. I lay Ava's case on the bed for her and open it, ready for her to unpack, and put mine in the corner for now. I need to call John.

I step outside and wander down to the beach again, looking back to the villa when he answers. "How's Paradise?"

"You'll have to come out and see for yourself."

"I'm kind of busy," he grunts. It's not a very subtle hint that he's alone and dealing with everything, including not being able to find a damn thing.

"Ava sorted some of the filing," I say.

"She sorted the bank statements and some invoices. The mountain has multiplied since. The accountants are still waiting for various paperwork, I have suppliers chasing payments, and I can't even access the bank accounts to pay them."

"Did you see Sarah?"

"I saw Sarah."

"And?"

"Drunk."

My hand rubs at my forehead, my exhale long and loud. It's not the worst-case scenario, but it's a step toward it. "And now?"

"Now I'm waiting for you to do the right thing and tell me she can come back, not only for her well-being, but for yours and mine too. Jesse, we're in a fucking mess here, boy."

"Jesus, John," I whisper, the pull inside real and fucking horrid. Another death on my hands. I can't. Ava *must* understand that. I haven't got time to even consider trying to come to grips with The Manor's filing system. I breathe in and brace myself to say the forbidden words. "Get her back," I say, closing my eyes. Sweating. "I'll talk to Ava." Not looking forward to that.

"She'll understand, I'm sure."

"Yeah," I say, not convinced. But perhaps when I've reminded her that I can't run The Manor *and* be there for her twenty-four seven, she may see Sarah's return as a blessing. I pray. "Make sure Sarah understands the conditions."

"Understood." Naturally, he doesn't need to ask what those conditions are.

"And if Ava says she's out, she's out."

"Understood. Heard from Steve?"

"No." I'll give him some grace since I'm out of town with Ava. *Safe*. "He can have the weekend." And I'm sure he'll call if he digs something up.

"I've got to go. The installation team from the new security firm need me. Try to relax, yeah?"

"Yeah," I breathe, staring down at my feet. "Call me if you need me." I turn my face up to the sun as I hang up and close my eyes, trying to push everything into a box while we're here. Enjoy this time.

My mobile rings as I'm walking back into the villa, and my heart misses a few beats. *Shit*. One last attempt from Amalie to convince me to go to her wedding? "I'm sorry, darling," I whisper, sending her call to voicemail. I'm pretty sure my family would be so thankful for Ava being in my life. I'm certain they'd love her and be over the moon that we're expecting. But I think of my parents, and I'm jarred. Angry. They're a trigger, something that always sent me to the bottle. They made me marry Lauren. And to try to make amends with them would be to risk what I have with Ava now. They're the key to the last skeletons in my cupboard. And I'm not ready to open that door.

Chapter 32

I've watched her all day fall in and out of daydreams and thoughts. I've asked her questions, sometimes three times before I've gotten an answer. She loves it here, who wouldn't? But bringing her here has spiked many more curiosities in her. Her mind's spinning at a hundred miles an hour, I can see it. I've taken endless pictures of her, smiled as I've looked back through the album on my phone to the very beginning. The first picture of her walking away from my manor. Did I imagine back then that I would be here now? Not in a month of Sundays.

"Would you like something to eat?" I ask, knocking her out of one of her many daydreams.

"Are you going to cook for me?" she asks, taken aback.

I scarcely hold in my snort of amusement. Me? Cook? "I could've had staff, but I wanted you to myself." I might earn myself a slap with what I'm about to say next, and my barely hidden cheeky grin is evidence. "I think you should look after your husband and fulfil your obligation as my wife."

Her face. Another for my files. "When you married me," she says, doing well to keep her tone even and calm, "you knew I hated cooking."

Yes, maybe, but the difference is, she *can* cook. She just doesn't like it. And if we're having kids, she's going to have to feed them. Good, healthy, nutritious food. "And when you married me, you knew I *couldn't* cook."

"But you have Cathy."

"In England I have Cathy to feed me, which is a good job as my wife doesn't." I fight to keep my amusement at bay, reeling her in. "In Spain I have my wife, and she's going to make me something to eat. You did a good job with the chicken." It was lovely.

Her indignance is brief, and I'm more than surprised when she stands up. "Okay, I'll fulfil my obligation."

I've challenged her. "Oh good. It's about time you did what you're told." *Take the bait, baby.* "Get to it, then." Should I duck?

"Don't push it, Ward." She goes to the fridge and opens it, pondering the contents while I watch in amusement, not quite believing she's taken the challenge. I mean, there are a million restaurants within a few miles that serve spectacular food, but that would mean leaving the villa.

She takes some things out and puts them on the counter, then gets to work while I sit happily at the table, drinking my water, watching my wife cook for me. In our villa. In Spain. Miles away from home. Whatever she's got planned for the menu, it smells bloody good.

I snap a few pictures of her before I get up, my arse becoming numb, and wander over to see if I can help. I suppose I should. "You're doing a great job, lady," I say as she faffs with some bell peppers.

"Don't patronize me," she retorts, pointing at me with the knife.

I retreat fast.

She doesn't plunge the knife deeply enough. She doesn't lunge and stab, she swipes and drags, and I'm powerless to stop her, completely paralyzed by the pure, unmistakable intent in her eyes. I've always thought she was unstable. Always questioned if there were issues that she needed help with. Even before our daughter died.

"Don't fucking wave knives around, Ava!" I yell, instinctively swiping it from her grasp with little care and even less accuracy. Jesus, I could have taken a finger off, grabbed the blade instead of the handle. Or, worse, slipped and cut Ava.

My stomach turns as she blurts her startled, urgent apology, my hand slowly lowering the knife down to the counter. I'm hot. My heart is racing. "It's okay," I breathe. "Forget about it." I can't tell myself to control my reactions to knives. It's instinctive, fueled by fear. And now the atmosphere is excruciating, and I take no pleasure in silencing my wife or making her feel so terrible.

Because she doesn't fucking know.

"Do you want to lay the table?" she asks meekly.

God damn me. "Sure." I turn away, my face screwing up, annoyed with myself for putting a dampener on our day. There she is again. Hitting me in my present. *She's dead.* I get some cutlery, fresh water, and lower to the chair, checking Ava in the kitchen. Quiet. She *and* I. Tension so thick and unbearable. She doesn't look at me either, probably so I don't see the tears in her eyes. I'm a cunt.

Fuck it.

When she puts my plate down, I quickly take her hand, and she finally looks at me. "I overreacted," I say, feeling awful.

"No, it's fine," she says, shaking her head and waving me off, like it's nothing. "I shouldn't be so careless."

True, but I shouldn't be so triggered. Not by Ava. But it wasn't Ava. It was Lauren. I encourage Ava down to the chair, determined to get us back onto...what does she call it? Jesse Cloud Nine? "We're missing something," I say, taking myself to the lounge and collecting a candle from the surround by the wood burner and the remote control for the music system from the coffee table.

I set the candle on the table, light it, and put a bit of Simply Red on.

"Mick Hucknall?" Ava says, smiling.

"Or God." Absolute legend. "Either will do."

"You're willing to share your title?"

I sit, happy we seemed to have kicked the awkwardness aside. "He's worthy. This looks good. Eat up."

She tucks in, and I discreetly lean over to check the meat situation. How well it's cooked. Jesus, it's sacrilege, really. Everyone knows beef and lamb are ruined if they're overdone. Anything past medium is overdone. But it's also safe.

Ava pauses, her knife and fork still on the plate, looking up at me, catching me in the act. Then turns her cut of lamb toward me. I hardly conceal my recoil; it looks cremated. How hard will I need to chew to get through it? It would have been insensitive to ask for my meat rare when Ava can't.

"May I?" Ava asks, her fork at her mouth, a piece of burnt lamb on the prongs.

"You may." No chance of any blood being in that, really, is there? And now I have to lie through my teeth. I take a piece, chew, and swallow. "You can cook, wife," I say. Shame on me.

"I've never said I can't," she says, happily chewing her way through her first bite. We might be awhile. "I just don't like doing it."

"Not even for me?" *Please say no.* Maybe I can fly Cathy in.

"I don't mind."

"I like you cooking for me." That's not a lie. I do. But maybe not lamb in future. "It's kind of normal."

"Normal?"

"Yes, normal. Like what normal married people do."

"Normal, like the wife cooks and the husband eats?" she asks, interested. She's trying to corner me. Prove something? "That's a bit chauvinistic."

There she is, putting words in my mouth. But I won't bite. Well, I will. Through this lamb with some effort. "Isn't this normal?" I ask.

"You mean having dinner together?"

"Yes."

"Yes," she says, casual. "This is normal."

And Ava and I aren't normal. Never will be. Normal people don't love like we love. Normal people don't connect like we do. Normal people don't need each other to survive. Constant contact. Various forms of fucking. I smile to myself, but it falters when I consider the arrival of the babies. Two babies. Not one, but two. A true blessing. But…wherever, whenever will be a struggle. "What about if I spread you on this table during dinner and fuck you?" I ask, nonchalant. "Would that be normal?" No. And there will be no spreading Ava on anything in front of the kids. Which means I'll have to choose my moments. And then maybe she'll be exhausted, because…twins. Maybe I'll be exhausted too. I mean, I have stamina, but…twins. *Fuck.*

Ava's chews falter, as does her cutlery on the plate, and her lip definitely twitches a fraction, evidence the lust has been stimulated. I shift in my seat, making room for my own stimulation. But can I control it? No. And that may be a major fucking issue when the babies are around.

"Our normal is you taking what you want, when you want," she says, composed, accepting. *Correct.* "You can chuck in a meal cooked by your wife, if you like."

No, thanks. "Good." I smile to myself and return to my dinner, avoiding the lamb. I'll always take what I want, when I want.

You deluded idiot.

Twins.

"I like our normal," I mutter.

"Is something worrying you?" she asks, studying me.

"No."

"Yes, there is. Are you suddenly considering the possibility of no *wherever and whenever* with two babies around?"

Fuck, how did she know? "Not at all."

"Look at me," she orders shortly, pulling my surprised eyes her way. "You are, aren't you?"

"Wherever, whenever," I growl like a chump, my grip of the cutlery firming, my dick dying down. This is terrible. The dynamics of our relationship will change completely.

"Not with two babies around."

Is she holding back a laugh? This is funny? Need I remind my wife that the physical side of our marriage is as essential for her as it is for me?

"They'll need a lot of my attention," she goes on, casual, munching her way through her dinner.

Funnily enough, my appetite has run for the hills, and it's nothing to do with the cremated lamb. It pisses me off that she's taking such delight in this realization. "Yes, your primary role will be the care of our children," I say, stern. She should punch me. I deserve it. "But a close second, and I mean a *very* close second, will be for my indulgence." *And yours, lady.* "Wherever, whenever, Ava. I might need to control my craving for you to a certain extent"—*Christ, Lord, and all that's holy, help me*—"but don't think I'm going to sacrifice devoting my life to consuming you. Constant contact. Wherever, whenever. That's not going to change, just because we have babies." You see it all the time in couples. *Normal* couples. The babies arrive, the sex leaves. That will *not* happen to us, because we're not normal. I fill my mouth with food before I add to my rant and get myself a slap.

"Even if I'm knackered from night feeds?"

What? I recoil. See, I knew it. "Too tired for me to take you?" We will *never* be too tired for each other.

"Yes."

"We'll get a nanny." Twins, for Christ's sake. A nanny would be reasonable.

"But I've got *you*."

Fucking hell, I'm getting a bit sweaty. We're going to have our hands full. "You do," I say on a sigh, setting down my knife and fork and applying a bit of pressure on my temples, pushing the headache back. "You do have me, and you always will." We'll be knackered *together*. Taking her hand on the table, I squeeze, smiling softly. Is this how it's going to be for the next seven months? Both of us seesawing between highs and complete meltdowns? "Promise me you'll never say *I'm too tired* or *I'm not in the mood*."

"You're the one who tells me I'm too tired." She laughs, but the outrage is there. "It's okay for *you* to knock *me* back."

"That's because I have the power." And it might be okay, but it's never easy. "Promise me," I order, squeezing her hand more.

"You want me to promise you that I'm here for you to take as and when you please?"

Hmm, well, I suppose that's the long and the short of it. Here's me praying that desire wins over exhaustion. I mean, it has in the past. There have been times when she's utterly beat and has insisted she's capable when she clearly isn't. The point is, I'm in control. Always will be in that department. "Yes." Listen to me. Just fucking listen to me.

She's frowning so hard. "What if I don't?"

Is she really going to play *that* game? I chuckle, pulling my T-shirt off and relaxing back, watching in satisfaction as my wife loses all focus, mesmerized by my chest. "You'll never resist this."

It's comical watching her gather herself. "I'm used to it," she says, going back to her dinner. "It kind of gets the same old after a while."

How she thrills me. Begs for me. Same *old*? I get up fast, grab her wrist, and take her quickly but gently down to the floor. She gasps, blinking up at me in surprise, her hair a wild mess around her face. "You're a shit liar, baby."

"I know," she breathes, the words wisps of air loaded with lust.

"Let's see how *used* to it you are, shall we?" Shifting her arms, I tuck them down by her sides and hold them there with my knees.

"Jesse," she says, stiff as a board beneath me. "Please don't."

"What? You're used to it."

I raise my brows as I lift to my knees, tackling the fly of my jeans under her wide-eyed gaze. Her chest is pumping, her cheeks a beautiful shade of lust.

"Jesse, let me up," she demands through her teeth, frustrated.

"No, Ava," I whisper, easing my jeans down a teasing fraction. Her eyes are nailed to my groin.

"Please," she murmurs.

Forgive me, but I need a little confidence boost. A reminder that we're *not* normal. As does Ava. I suck in air as I lower my boxers more, brushing across my raging hard-on.

"Oh God," she cries, slamming her eyes shut as I pull my dick out on a low, suppressed grunt, that one first stroke sending me dizzy. Her mouth is calling for me, her wet lips parted and inviting. I walk on my knees up her body and hold my breath as I guide the swollen head of my arousal to her mouth. *Jesus.* I wedge a fist into the floor to prop me up, as I guide my cock from side to side across her open mouth, bracing myself to push inside. Her eyes open. They sparkle, her heavy lids darkening her eyes more, as she stares at my cock.

Then she inhales and her eyes climb my body to my face. The look on her right now could be enough to tip me over the edge, have me coming hard.

"Mouth," she says, virtually licking her lips for me.

"What do I do to you, Ava?" I slip myself across her bottom lip again, pulling away when she opens her mouth to take me.

Rage mixes with the lust. "You fucking cripple me," she shouts, bucking beneath me.

As soon as she's settled again, accepting she's going nowhere, I start thrusting my fist up and down my shaft. "Watch your fucking mouth." Fuck, this feels good.

"Please," she begs. That turns me on too.

"Are you used to me?" I ask.

"No."

Fuck, I love this game. Love proving she can't control her want for me. "And you never will be," I say. "*This* is our normal, baby. Get used to this." I give her what she's begging for, slipping my dick into her waiting, eager mouth, locking down every muscle when she groans around my flesh, sending shots of pleasure racing through me. Her pace increases, her head lifting and retreating, greed and excitement taking over.

"Keep it gentle, Ava," I warn, forcing her back to steady and slow, deep and firm. "I love your fucking mouth, woman." My hips start moving, the blood simmering, the throb hard. She bites down lightly. I hiss over a curse, my thighs aching. My heart starts to race in anticipation of my release, my skin burning. It's coming. It's coming.

Her mouth becomes more aggressive.

Coming.

"Jesus fucking Christ," I bark, jerking violently, withdrawing from her mouth and circling myself. I start to thrust as Ava pants beneath me, her wild, excited eyes watching me pleasure myself. Sweat drips down my temples, my forehead, forcing me to sweep it away. Ava whimpers. Bites her lips. Licks them. It's my ruin. I position myself just right, thrust her tank up, yank the cups of her bra down, and rest my throbbing dick between her tits. I come like a freight train. "Jesus," I spit, watching my cock spurt cum all over her chest, both of us panting violently. My sensitive dick screams its protest when I rub it across Ava's chest, spreading myself far and wide.

"Wherever, whenever, baby." I fall to my elbows and catch her mouth, kissing her with purpose and conviction, as my dick throbs. "Fucking perfect."

She hums, accepting, embracing, and completely unbothered by the animal in me. I think I've proved my point. For now. I've no doubt I'll need to prove it again at some point.

"Come here." Getting us up off the floor, I tuck myself away and sort Ava out, putting her back at the table to finish her dinner.

"I didn't throw up," she muses, sounding impressed.

"Well done."

"Why didn't you come in my mouth?"

Easy. *Because I wanted to come all over her tits and rub it in with my cock.* "Might poison the babies," I say, smiling as I fasten my fly and take my seat.

"What?" She laughs, and then melts in her chair when I tell her I'm joking with a cheeky wink.

"Eat your dinner, lady."

"What are we doing tomorrow?" she asks.

"Well, I don't know about you, but I'm bingeing."

"You're keeping me locked up in Paradise all weekend?"

One hundred percent, yes. "I wasn't going to, but locks can be arranged." I try the peppers, apprehensive. Thank God, they're actually all right. So I'll eat the peppers, leave the lamb.

Ava grins at me, happy, and that is all I need. My wife's happiness. Her contentment. Her acceptance of our normal.

"God, I love that fucking grin," I muse. "Show me."

Turning her face directly to me, she nearly floors me with the power of her smile. "Happy?" she asks.

"Fucking delirious." A whole weekend of this? It doesn't get much better. Except an eternity of this. I'm working on it. "You done?" I ask, nodding at her plate.

"Yes, I'm stuffed." Hands on her belly, she falls back in her chair.

"I'll clean up." I stand, clearing the table and getting everything in the dishwasher before wiping the sides down. "What do you want to do?" I ask, setting the cloth on the sink. She's still in the chair. Still rubbing her belly.

"Well," she says, pouting, pondering, thinking. "You owe me."

My grin in instant. "Thought you were stuffed?"

"I am." She turns on her chair toward me, spreading her thighs a little. Inviting. *Temptress.* "But you didn't eat as much as I did, so maybe you can manage a nibble."

Fuck. I round the counter, pushing her chair back more, giving me space, and drop to my knees before her. Her hands go into my hair, her eyes bursting with desire. "Lift," I order, taking the sides of her skirt and pushing it up her thighs. Lace greets me, and I lower my face, slipping a finger into the crotch of her knickers and easing them aside. I stare at her pulsing, wet, begging flesh. Flick my eyes up to her. Wince when she gives my hair a severe tug. I smile, push my mouth between her legs, and lick her from back to front.

Her moan echoes around the villa and beyond.

Paradise.

Fucking paradise.

Chapter 33

I'm going to struggle to leave. I knew it was a risk when I brought Ava away, no matter where I took her. If we were alone, peaceful, just with each other to please, it was always going to be hard. I never anticipated this level of serenity, though. I can leave her in bed in the morning and go for a run with no worries. She can wander around naked without the fear of someone barging in. There are no work commitments, no kicking my heels all day waiting for her to be done. Showers are intimate and often, walks on the shore slow and meandering, Ava's cooking—thank God—I've managed to limit to breakfast. It seems silly to waste the vast options of restaurants in the area. So, yeah, I trump her Jesse Cloud Nine with my very own Ava Cloud Nine.

I don't want to leave, and I can see Ava is having the same fleeting thoughts. But she will because of her job. And that fucking sucks.

On Friday, we ventured out for a few hours to grab lunch, had a minor, trivial chat about suitable levels of exposed flesh in public—hers, not mine—played cards when we got home, invented Sleepy Twilight Sex—a new favorite, which sucks harder because that can only happen in Paradise—and skinny-dipped in the Med. On Saturday, I had the pleasure of Ava in her bikini for most of the day, dipping in and out of the pool, sunbathing, just generally chilling out. Watching her looking so laid-back does something to me. As does tending to her in every way imaginable. Shower time, breakfast time, dressing, undressing, rubbing her sun lotion in, fetching her water, feeding her. Just looking after her. Being on call. Smothering her, and Ava accepting it. *Loving* it. Because that's all there is to do. Love each other.

Fuck, I really don't want to leave.

Standing in front of the mirror after a shower, I inspect the man before me. I've never seen him look so well. Content, calm, and fresh. The Paradise Effect. Work isn't on my mind. I haven't wanted to tell Ava—haven't wanted to burst this luxurious bubble—but Sarah's back and things are straight at The Manor once again. Lauren isn't playing on my mind like she was, although there's definitely an odd mix of relief and guilt lingering somewhere deep that I'm trying to keep buried.

Because what good will it do to let it surface? She was troubled. I spent years blaming myself, even though she hurt me. Physically with a knife, and emotionally with my daughter. But now that she's passed and I don't fear seeing her ever again, it's time to let go of some of that guilt. There's no room for Lauren in my pool of remorse.

I dry my body and leave the bathroom, rubbing the towel through my hair, but stop on the threshold of the bedroom when I find Ava on the bed concentrating on painting her toes. My olive-skinned girl is bronzed and beautiful. And her tummy is definitely rounder. Small, tidy, and tight. She's surrounded by clean, crisp white, the bedding messy around her, the white voile drapes billowing lightly at the doors onto the veranda. The sun is hazy through the material, the smell of the sea ripe. I pout to myself, disheartened that I have to take her back to London tomorrow.

She looks up, and her body deflates with her dreamy sigh. That right there? Gold. I wander over as she props herself up against the headboard, her eyes following my path to the bed, and then up it as I walk on my knees to her.

"Let me," I say, putting her feet on my lap over the towel.

"You want to paint my toes?" she asks, interested as I claim the pot of polish. A lovely pink that complements her tan gorgeously.

"I may as well get some practice in." She has the loveliest toes. Perfectly formed. "You won't be able to reach them soon."

She kicks me playfully, and I grunt through my laugh, getting her feet back in place on my lap. I need to concentrate. Show my wife that I can literally do anything if it involves taking care of her.

She's quiet, and not for the first time since we've been here, I hear her thinking. "I don't want to go home," she whispers, almost sadly. It's the first time she's spoken her thoughts, and it's so nice to hear her say that.

"Me either, baby." I start with her big toe, getting some practice in before I tackle the small, trickier toenails.

"When can we come back?"

"We can come back whenever you like. Just say the word and I'll put you on that plane." Shit, I got a bit on her skin. God damn me. I drag my thumb across the bottom of her toe and pull back, inspecting, nodding my happiness. "Have you had a nice time?" I ask, getting a hit of the bliss staring back at me when I look up.

"Paradise," she says wistfully. "Continue."

I bet she never dreamt she'd enjoy being crowded as much as this. I realize it's probably the Paradise Effect—no one else to please, no work to do, no drama around the corner—but she's loved our time here alone. "Yes, my lady."

"Good boy." She snuggles deep into the pillow, watching me color her toenails. "What happens when we get home?"

I hold back my disappointed sigh, concentrating on her feet and not fucking up my task. I knew the questions had started swirling, and they'll only increase the closer we get to London.

"What happens is that you'll go to work and finally fulfil your promise to enlighten Patrick about Mikael." Or, hopefully, given how much she's enjoyed being here, she'll see sense and quit.

"Do you think Mikael stole your car?"

"I have no fucking clue, Ava." It seems more unlikely by the day, the more I think about it. He's a smart man. "I'm dealing with it, so don't worry your pretty little head." I switch feet.

"How are you dealing with it?"

I turn steely eyes up to her, and she reads the look well, withdrawing. I'm not ruining our last night with talk of London. "End of." I return to her toes, arranging the tissue between them better so it doesn't brush any of her wet nails. I really have a knack for this, although the brush could be smaller and the handle a little larger for men with large hands and big fingers like me.

Her little toes—the smallest—require just one light stroke with the brush, and I'm finished. "You're done," I say, replacing the lid and inspecting my work. "I'm even amazing at this."

Ava pulls her feet close and has her own inspection. "Not bad," she muses quietly.

"Not bad?" I question, insulted. "I've done a better job than you'd ever do, lady." I smirk as I get up, seeing a sea of disgust rise. "You're so lucky to have me."

"Aren't *you* lucky?"

"I'm luckier." Her indignance vanishes, her appreciation back. "Come on, lady. Let's go exploring.

Chapter 34

The marina is alive when we pull up, every luxury car known to man parked in front of the port where an insane number of yachts and super yachts are docked.

"Fucking hell," Ava breathes, her wide eyes trying to take it all in.

"Ava, please, watch your fucking mouth." I cast her a disapproving glare, not that she notices. She's too busy gawking at the boats. I cut the engine and climb out, reminding myself of the marina as I round the car. It's been too long. The buzz, the smell, the clammy nighttime air. "Out you get."

"Please don't tell me you own one of those," she murmurs as she lets me help her out, eyes still on the boats.

"No," I muse, putting on my shades. "I sold it many years ago." And I almost wish I hadn't now. Ava and me sailing around the world? Fuck, being in the middle of the ocean really could keep our bubble intact.

She looks at me, alarmed. "So you *did* have one?"

"Yes, but I didn't have a fucking clue how to sail the stupid thing." I should have hired a captain—got them to teach me how to sail. I walk Ava along the front of the port, past the endless cars.

"Why did you buy it in the first place then?" she asks, curiosity rampant.

I don't want to talk about Carmichael. "Over there is Morocco," I say, pointing toward the horizon.

"Lovely," she drones, rolling her eyes.

"Sarcasm doesn't suit you, lady." I tuck her into me and bite her ear in warning. "What would you like to do?"

"Let's mooch about," she says, looking around us.

I smile, unsure. "Mooch?"

"Yes, mooch. Like browse, peruse, mooch about."

"Okay. I feel another Camden coming on."

"Yes," she sings, thrilled. "Exactly like Camden." A frown. "But no funny sex shops."

My laughter bursts out of me. Need I remind her that she was the only one between the two of us that actually bought something from the *funny* sex shop? "Oh, there are plenty of funny sex shops on the back streets," I tell her. "Want to see?"

"No, I don't." She falls into thought, and I'm not sure I'm keen if her semi scowl is a measure. "You didn't find that attractive, did you?" she asks, her voice quiet. Is she talking about the dancer that was there? The leather-clad, busty, brash one? The one who struck an alarming resemblance and aura to Sarah? Does she not know me at all?

"I've told you before," I say, taking her face, making sure she's looking at me. "There's only one thing that turns me on." I get closer to her, breathe across her face as she looks at me with hopeful eyes. Insecurity. I don't like it. But I've read that somewhere in my book too. Or was it on the internet? I can't remember, but it struck me. Lots of reassurance. Lots of validation. I'm here for it. "And I love her in lace."

I push my lips to her forehead, breathing her into me, hearing her whisper a quiet, "Good." I hate that she asked me that.

"Come on, Mrs. Ward. Let's mooch." Taking her hand, I walk us past a few restaurants and up through one of the side streets to the back of the marina. It's busy, people dipping in and out of stores, others wandering lazily armed with ice creams.

We pass an ice cream parlor, and I notice Ava craning her neck to see the various colorful tubs on display. "Want one?"

"Maybe after dinner," she says, moving closer into my side, lifting my arm and draping it around her. I dip and push my lips into her hair, holding them there as we wander on. We pass a few souvenir stores, all full of cheap tat, and some stalls selling handmade coasters, wine stoppers, and beaded bracelets. I frown as Ava directs us to one, and she browses across a pillow loaded with rings.

"Fifteen euro?" I ask, looking at the collection dubiously. "They can't be real silver for fifteen euro."

"Of course they're not," she says, plucking one from the display—a thick silver band with a few emeralds. "It's costume." She slips it onto her middle finger and inspects it, holding her hand out.

"It complements your platinum and diamond wedding rings perfectly," I mumble, making her look at me tiredly. "Just saying." I point to a display of beaded necklaces. "One of those will look amazing next to your sixty-grand diamond necklace too." I notice the stall owner has narrowed eyes on me. I smile, feeling Ava nudge me in the side.

"We'll take them," I say, rootling through my pocket and pulling out two twenty euro notes before pulling one of the necklaces off the stand. "The ring and the necklace." I hand over the cash.

"It's fifty," he says.

Fifty? "Fine." I dip back into my pocket and pull out another ten. "Here."

"You're supposed to haggle," Ava whispers, coming in closer. "Fifty is too much."

Of course it is. "Why would I stand there for five minutes haggling over a tenner?" I give her the necklace and get us moving. Christ, The Manor makes more than a tenner every second.

"Haggling is part of the fun. They never give their final price straight away."

I smile and get her back into my side, locking her neck in the crook of my arm and tugging her close. "We'll haggle when we get back to Paradise."

"Haggle for what?" she asks, coy, peeking up at me.

I raise my brows. "You're sex mad."

"Oh, please." She laughs, tucking her new purchases into her bag. "Says he who owned a sex manor."

Is she joking about The Manor? I never thought I'd see the day. There's just one thing, though. She said *owned*. I still own the sex manor. Naturally, Owen Cutler comes to mind, and I wonder if John is right. Will they come back with a sweeter, less insulting offer? It's not about the money. I have enough money. So what is it about? Have I subconsciously concluded it's priceless, therefore no amount of money could buy it? A defense tactic?

"Are you okay?" Ava asks, knocking me from my ponderings.

"Yeah." I give her a reassuring smile. "Let's look in here." I nod to the next store and immediately feel Ava's resistance.

"Oh no, Jesse, come on."

"What?"

She frowns at the store front of *Dior*, her lips straight. "It's not in my price range," she says through her teeth, well aware of what response she'll get.

I growl. "When will you ever get your head around *us*, not you and me?" Little Miss Independent needs to remember that she's married, as well as who she's married to. Me. Lord of The Sex Manor. *Rich* Lord of The Sex Manor. Her *price range* has shifted up the scale since she met me.

"It's not the point."

"What's the point?" I need enlightening. "Do you want to go halves on everything?" I ask. "Like Lusso, cars, jets?"

She stares at me, annoyed, while I wait for her to come back at me. Nothing.

I sigh. What the hell are we doing arguing over this kind of stuff still? It's old fucking news. "Baby, I'm very rich, and until now I've never had anyone to spoil." Only myself with women and alcohol. And I was lavish with both, although the women didn't cost me a penny. "Please humor me." It's like Harrods all over again. I jut my bottom lip out, give her wide, hopeful eyes. I know I've got her when her shoulders lower. She's softening.

"You can buy me one thing," she breathes. "Just one."

I smile, chuffed. We both know one thing means limitless things. Like I said, Harrods again. "Come." I collect her hand and tug her into Dior. "Mooch to your heart's content," I say, releasing her and lowering to a cream chair.

She eyes the rails, chewing her lip. "Can I help you?" an assistant asks.

"No, I'm just brow—"

"Yes, she needs help," I say, blasting the assistant back with a megawatt smile. "The budget is *really* offensive."

Ava's mouth drops open, and the assistant suddenly looks curious, her eyes passing back and forth between us. Shit, did I just pull a *Pretty Woman* on my wife?

"Oh, she's not a hooker," I say, laughing nervously, wary of the incredulous expression on Ava's face. "We're married. I was just trying to say, you know, look after her. There's no budget."

"Oh my God," Ava says, closing her eyes, hiding from the doubt on the assistant's face.

"No, really," I say, seeing the doubt too. "She's pregnant. It's twins."

"Jesse?" Ava breathes.

"What?"

"Shut up."

I recline back in my seat. Stung. "Okay," I murmur, biting at my lip, watching the assistant flick uncertain eyes between us. But I do as I'm told and shut up. *She's my wife!* God damn me.

Pulling my phone out, I lose myself in that before I dig myself deeper, leaving Ava to mooch. A message from John greets me, telling me to call him when I can. "I can now," I say quietly, dialing. "All right?" I ask when he answers.

"Owen Cutler has come back and requested another meeting."

My eyebrows nearly hit the ceiling of *Dior*. "Weird. I was literally just thinking about him," I say, watching Ava being directed down a rail of leisure wear.

"I'm assuming they've done some homework and they'll come back with a serious offer."

My stomach flips, and I start to fidget in the chair. *It doesn't hurt to talk.* And we talked. *Priceless.* What's the point in meeting again?

"Do you want me to set something up?"

"No," I blurt without much thought, leaving John silent. "I mean, I need to think." For the first time, the whole situation feels real. Serious. I look at Ava's stomach as she's directed toward the display of handbags. Babies. Life as we know will change forever. But life as I knew it already changed forever the moment Ava walked into my office.

"Okay," John eventually says. "Should I leave it with you?"

Ava looks over to me, her head tilting in question. I must look as uneasy as I feel. I pull myself together and sit up straighter, looking at the handbag the assistant has just collected off the display and is showing Ava. I give the bag a thumbs up. Ava looks at it and dismisses it. "Yeah, leave it with me. How's Sarah getting on?"

"Like a duck to water, springs to mind. In the office *and* in the rooms."

I laugh sardonically. I bet. Fuck, I am not looking forward to breaking that news to Ava. *Wouldn't have to if I sell The Manor.*

"Have you heard from Steve Cook?" he asks.

"No." He's got until tomorrow to bring me *something*. "Listen, John, we're back tomorrow and there's still been no news on Van der Haus or my stolen car. Ava's going to want to go back to work." I'm a realist. "Can—"

"I'll drive her," he says, and I deflate, relieved. He hears me. "And the new security system is up and running."

"Good," I say quietly. "Thanks."

"Safe journey home."

I get up and wander over to Ava, ignoring the toothy, red-lipped beam of the assistant as I approach. "I like it," I say, as Ava holds up a cream sweater. "We'll take it."

"Of course." The assistant takes it from Ava's hand, her attention now on me. Still smiling.

Ava gives her a sideway glare. "There's no point, I won't fit into it soon."

"Then we'll take the next size up too," I say, prompting the assistant to flick through the hangers and pull out the sweater in the next size up.

"We also have this design in black," she says.

"We'll take black too."

"Jesse," Ava moans.

"What?" I laugh. "You said you'd let me spoil you."

Her forehead becomes a mass of lines. "I never said that."

"It was to that effect." I look through the hangers. "They have the trousers to match," I say, holding up some lovely wide-legged pants. "And they have a stretchy waist." I grin over the top of the hanger, and Ava's hand instinctively goes to her stomach. It's beautiful.

"The matching pants too, sir?" The assistant takes the hanger, her hand laying over mine, her smile getting wider by the second.

I snatch it away. "Yeah." She's walking a thin line. My wife's possessiveness is wild lately.

"I'll get it all wrapped." She pouts, backing away, her eyes taking a not-so subtle jaunt down my frame before she pivots and saunters off. Ava's eyes are narrowed slits on the assistant's back as she distractedly looks through another rail.

"We'll take that too," I say, reaching for the linen shirt Ava's paused on. "Come, sit," I say, walking her to the chair, rather than to the counter where she's closer to the assistant. "Your ankles are getting puffy."

"Fuck off," she snaps, and I laugh, crowding her in the chair, my arms braced on each arm, my face close.

"You need to stop swearing in front of the children."

She snorts. "Are you joking?"

"What?" I ask. "I don't swear anywhere near as much as you do."

"Oh my God, you're deluded."

I dip and slam a kiss on her mouth. "I'll go pay," I say, wrinkling my nose at her exasperated face as I push off, going to the counter.

"Make sure it's just for the clothes," she calls.

I stop halfway and turn a scowl back at her, and she smiles sweetly, her hand back on her stomach, circling.

My scowl disappears.

"Keep going, and I might break the rules and give you a Retribution Fuck."

Her arms are instantly held out in front of her, her wrists together. "I dare you."

I laugh, fucking delighted, and go to the counter.

Chapter 35

I think we're both sick of mooching a few hours later. The newfound feeling of hunger is stirring in my stomach as I put Ava's purchases in the car and assess the restaurant options on the front of the marina. "God, I've missed you," I say, seizing her, finally able to get both my hands on her now they're free of bags. I swallow her yelp as I kiss her, my lips slipping across hers. "Hmm, you taste good."

"If you want to wear ladies' lipstick, do it properly." She attacks me with her lipstick, beaming up at me. "Better. You're even more handsome with shimmery lips."

"Probably." But what color is it? "Come on, I need to feed my wife and peanuts." Standing her up, I wipe my mouth with the back of my hand, checking. No color, just shimmer. "These need tightening," I say, noticing the top of her dress getting lower on her boobs, the straps lengthening.

She slaps my hands away and walks off, and I recoil, injured, insulted, and everything in between. "That was uncalled for, wasn't it?" So fixing straps doesn't fall under acceptable levels of fussing? But painting toenails does? *Help me out, someone, please.* "I was only trying to help."

"Where are you feeding me?" she calls back.

And feeding does too? I'm so confused. And annoyed. Her terms. Always her terms. I reach for Ava's wrist and pull her to a stop. "Don't walk away from me," I grumble, turning her to face me again, confused by her smirk. She's playing? "And you can wipe that grin off your face." I move in and take it upon myself to do what I originally intended. Fix her fucking straps. "You're fucking intolerable sometimes," I mutter, moving to the other side. "I know you only do it to get a rise out of me." I check each strap. Double-check. "Better," I conclude. "Ridiculous dress." Had I known the straps weren't reliable, she wouldn't have left the villa in it. "Why do you insist on being so difficult?"

"Because I know it drives you crazy."

And there it is. An admission. Proof, not that I needed it. "You just enjoy reducing me to a crazy madman."

"You make *yourself* a crazy madman. You need no help in that department, Jesse. I've told you before; you do not dictate my wardrobe."

Maybe not, but I buy the clothes, that earns me *some* rights. "You drive me crazy," I mutter for the sake of it, reinforcing it.

"What are you going to do?" She's still fucking grinning. Why am I taking the bait? "Divorce me?"

I beg your pardon? "Watch your fucking mouth," I snap, stunned.

"I didn't even swear," she says, laughing.

"Yes, you fucking did." I scowl at a man who passes, his eyes on Ava for slightly longer than is acceptable. And *no* time at all is the only acceptable amount of time. "The worse word," I confirm, watching him quickly correcting himself when I catch him in the act, admiring my hysterical wife. "In fact. I forbid you to say it."

"You forbid me?" she asks, her laughing ramping up.

"Yes, I forbid you."

"Divorce."

For God's sake. "Now you're just being childish."

"...ish," she whispers, her lips puckered delightfully, ready for me to kiss. How she drives me wild. "Feed me."

"I should fucking starve you and reward you with food when you do what you're fucking told," I mumble, turning her toward the restaurant nearby. "I'll feed you here."

"Looks lovely," she says as I guide her with my hands on her shoulders.

"I love you," I whisper in her ear, feeling her body tense and her face push to mine.

"I know."

"Table for two, please," I say to the host. "Outside if you have it."

"Certainly, sir." He plucks two menus from the stand and shows us the way. "Drinks?"

"Water, thank you." I help Ava into her seat, pushing her close to the table. My smile is huge. Her chair will get farther away each week. "The tapas are sublime," I say, handing her a menu.

"You pick," she says, not bothering to look at the options. "I'm sure you'll make a suitable choice." Is she being sarcastic?

"Thank you," I say, unsure.

"You're welcome." Definitely sarcastic. She pours water and drinks a whole glass.

"Thirsty?" I ask, eyes wide as she glugs down another. "Be careful, you might drown the babies."

She snorts, spraying some water, and I smile as she wipes herself up. "Will you stop with that?"

"What?" I ask, injured. "I'm just showing some fatherly concern." The atmosphere suddenly goes from playful to tense, and I watch, confused, as Ava studies me, thinking. What?

"You don't think I can look after our babies," she says, her voice small. "Do you?"

What? Where's that come from? "Yes, I do." Although, admittedly, I'm concerned that she's relying on me to share all the dos and don'ts of pregnancy. Which, annoyingly, is the catalyst for many of our current disagreements. *If she would only read the book.* I know she wants this, has come to terms with it, is happy about it, but my life would be a lot less stressful if I didn't have to worry about what she's eating and whether it could be harmful to the babies. Am I being over the top? I don't think I am. Only a father who's lost a child might understand.

Which is why Ava never will.

"What the hell do you think I'm going to do?" she asks, her tone somewhere between scathing and wounded. More the former. I glance at her in question. Wait. What does she think I think she's going to do? I'm talking about food choices. Being careful. Taking it easy. Putting all the necessary things in place to make this risk-free and ensure both Ava's and the babies health and safety. What the hell does she think I—

Oh no.

"Don't," she whispers, her eyes flooding with tears. Shit, and now I've made her cry.

I move across to the seat next to her, pulling her in for a hug. "I'm sorry," I say, my voice soft and quiet. "Don't get upset, please."

"I'm okay." She snivels, wiping her nose. "I said, I'm fine." She breaks free, her expression fierce as she swipes up her water. She's angry. And I know she's not angry with me. She's mad with herself, reflecting on her fleeting, desperate, actions.

I've got over it, got past it. I realize what she was doing and why she did it. She needs to forgive herself. "Ava," I say gently. "Look at me." Her annoyed glower remains in place, her eyes on the back of the restaurant rather than me. For Christ's sake, it's our last night together here. This is not how I planned for it to be. Fuck, I need to ease up on the baby talk. "Three." So we'll go for some Jesse talk. I don't appreciate the roll of her eyes, nor the fact she's still refusing to look at me. Fine. She doesn't think I'll act on zero? She really has forgotten who I am. "Two," I go on, and she sighs, looking at her water as she sets it down, firm in her stubborn stance. "One." Another sigh. *Fuck this.* "Zero, baby." I pull her off the chair and tackle her to the floor with gentle ease, pinning her there, hearing a chorus of collective gasps from diners around us. Ava's big brown eyes are as wide as I've ever seen them as she stares up at my serious face. She can't believe me? Well, here she in on the floor, and here I am pinning her there. In a crowded restaurant. *Wherever, whenever.*

"Jesse," she breathes, motionless, looking positively shell-shocked. "Let me up."

"I did warn you, baby." My smile breaks. "Wherever, whenever." I guarantee my wife will do what I ask in future.

She starts wriggling when I make no attempt to release her. "Yes, okay. You've made your point."

"I don't think I have." I dip, my face close to hers. Her cheeks are a glorious shade of embarrassed. "I love you."

"I know, let me up."

"No."

"Please," she whispers, her gaze pleading.

"Tell me you love me," I demand.

"I love you."

I sag. "Say it like you mean it, Ava." *Not like you're desperate to get all attention off us.* Fat chance. Everyone is still silent, all listening. I'm quite surprised there's been no intervention, though. Lucky for them.

"I love you," she says again, this time gently, and I study her for a second, before relenting and helping her up off the floor. I remain on my knees before her. I'm not done.

"Get up," she orders, cautiously glancing around the restaurant.

She cares too much. I don't. I get close, slipping my palms onto her arse and looking up at her. "Ava Ward, my beautiful, defiant girl," I whisper, making her eyes widen again. *Yes, baby. A public declaration of love.* I have no shame when it comes to this woman. "You make me the happiest man on this fucking planet," I go on. "You married me, and now you're blessing me with twin babies." The crowd sings their sigh as I kiss her belly. "I love you so fucking much," I say with grit. "You're going to be an incredible mummy to my babies." Getting to my feet, dropping kisses on her body on my way up, I finish in her neck. "Don't try to stop me from loving you. It makes me sad."

"Sad or crazy?" she asks, a nervous tinge to her voice.

"Sad," I confirm, taking her cheeks, nose to nose. "Kiss me, wife."

There's a mild, disbelieving shake of her head before she plants one on me, and the crowd starts clapping. I break our kiss and look around, seeing people standing. Women swooning. Men undoubtedly considering upping their romantic game. Ava dying. Okay, I've made a big enough spectacle of us both. Time to eat. "I love her," I say one last time, sitting us down.

"Twins!" the waiter says, excited as he bursts through the tables. "You must celebrate." I flinch when the cork pops, flying across the restaurant, and he laughs, happy as he pours two glasses.

Ava stares at the glasses, her embarrassment now gone and awkwardness creeping up the back. "Thank you," she says politely. "That's very kind."

I reach for her knee under the table a squeeze, dragging her attention from the back of the restaurant to me. "I cannot *believe* you did that." She shakes her head as I remove the champagne, pushing it out of smelling distance.

"Why?"

She doesn't reply, her attention on the back of the restaurant again. She's distracted. "Do you know that woman?" she asks.

"What woman?" I follow her gaze.

"There." She nods her head, making me crane mine more. "The woman with the pale blue cardigan. Can you see?"

Pale blue cardigan? I can't see a pale blue cardigan. I start to turn back toward the table, but someone a few tables away gets up from their chair, clearing the way to the next table at the back of the restaurant.

All air drains from my lungs so fast, I jolt. And when I try to inhale, nothing happens. I can't breathe as I stare into her eyes.

My mother.

I return to face the table, my body turning cold. *Act normal.* I try to stop my hands from shaking, clenching my fists. I try to push back the stressed sweat. I try to blink my dry eyes. I'm incapable. It's been years since I've seen her. Seen any of them. What the hell is she doing here? It's Amalie's wedding weekend in Seville. *She shouldn't be here!*

"What's the matter?" Ava's palm comes at me, and I move back in my chair, trying to avoid it before she feels how cold and clammy I am. "Jesse?" she presses, the worry in her voice forcing me to shake my head clear, and hopefully the haunted expression from my face too. "Jesse, what's wrong?" I blink my focus back, my eyes scratchy, and find Ava staring at me, worried.

I look down at the table. *Play it down.* But my hands are still shaking, and there is nothing I can do to stop them. "We're leaving." *Escape.* My hand catches a glass as I get up from my chair, my trembling body failing me. Ava looks up at me, her face a picture of concern as I yell at myself to pull it together, rootling through my pocket for my wallet. I drop some money on the table and Ava allows me to pull her perplexed form up from the chair and guide her through the tables with no protest. When we make it outside, I take the lead, urgency ruling me. I steer her toward the car, starting to feel some resistance. *Fuck.*

"What's wrong with you?" she asks with panic. I aim the fob at my car and yank the passenger door open. She's unmoving before me, looking up at me in question. *Get in, please, baby. I need you to get in the car.* But I can't speak the words. I've lost my voice, but I haven't lost my sight.

My mother hurries out of the restaurant pulling her blue cardigan in, looking up and down the street. I pull in air, my heart beating wildly. In desperation, I take Ava's arm, trying to get her in the car. Mum sees me. I try harder to move Ava, but she's rigid.

"Jesse?" Mum says, hurrying over but slowing as she nears. As if approaching a volatile animal. Coaxing it into trusting her. Ava turns to face her, and Mum's eyes move between Ava, her stomach, and me. *Jesus.*

"Ava, baby," I say, quiet but shaky. Her expression isn't one I'd like to archive. Utter shock. She knows who this is. "We're going."

"Jesse, son," Mum whispers, her eyes unbearably cloudy.

Son? I'm her son? Then why the fuck did she treat me differently to her other *son*? "You don't get to call me that," I grate, trying to get

Ava moving. "Ava, get in the car."

Thank God, she finally moves, walking straight to the open door and lowering to the seat. Closing the door, I stride around the back, avoiding Mum at the front, but she meets me at the driver's door, blocking it.

Fuck.

"Jesse, please," she begs. My face bunches, so many painful memories assaulting me. I can't take it. "Please, I beg you, let's talk." She reaches for my arm, touching me. Holding me. Her eyes are beseeching. Sad. Desperate. Eyes that are older than I remember. "It never had to be like this."

"You and Dad made it like this." I pull myself free of her hold and back off, unwilling to push past her or move her. She looks so frail.

"We only ever wanted what was best for you."

By forcing me into marriage? Deciding my future? Reminding me every day that Jake was gone and it was entirely my fault?

Did they, Jesse? Isn't that what you *told yourself?*

I growl, physically pushing Jake's voice away with my hand on my head, turning away from my mother, unable to see her looking so distressed. The floodgates of my past have burst, and the memories are fucking relentless.

"Please." Ava's voice invades my chaos, and I turn to find she's got out of the car and put herself between me and Mum. A shield. A barrier. "I'm asking you to move," she says calmly.

"You shouldn't be here," I say to Mum tightly. I can't cope with the feelings she provokes. Any of them. It's exactly why I've avoided Amalie for so many years too. "Why are you here? It's Amalie's wedding weekend in Seville. Why are you here?"

Mum's eyes bounce between Ava and me constantly. "It's your father," she says, her hands now starting to play nervously. "The wedding, it got postponed because your father had a heart attack." I withdraw, shocked. A heart attack? Is he okay? "Amalie tried to get in touch after you never replied to her wedding invite."

Is that what she told them? That she couldn't get in touch with me? Easier than telling them I declined. My sister wanted to save their feelings. God damn her. "Tell me why Amalie tried to contact me? Why not you?"

"I thought you would answer your sister." She moves forward, and I move back. "I was hoping you would answer you sister's calls."

"Well, you were wrong," I yell, frustration getting the better of me. "You don't get to do this to me." I'm in a better place. *Finally*, I'm in a better place, and seeing her now, listening to her, having all of these unwanted feelings, is no good for anyone. "No more, Mum," I say, resolute. "Your influence already fucked my life up, and now I'm making it right all on my own."

Denials.

Throwing blame.

Oh, Jesse. All these years you've blamed yourself, and now it's Mum and Dad's fault?

Mum withdraws like she's been stung. "Twins?" she says quietly. I study her, taken aback by the pain in her eyes. Seeping from her old skin. It's emblazoned on every inch of her. So much fucking pain.

"Ava," I whisper, my throat thick and tight, my eyes still on my mother. "Please, get me out of here."

She comes to life before me, as Mum goes back to looking between us, panic rising. Her chance to make things right slipping. "I'm asking you nicely," Ava says, her tone stern. "Please, move."

"It's another chance, Jesse." Mum crumbles before me, and suddenly the agony inside worsens. The memories hit harder. My heart breaks all over again.

"Come on,'" Ava says, leading me around the car, away from my mother. She doesn't take her tearful eyes off me. Her mouth opens and closes repeatedly, her mind racing to find the right words, the words that will stop me walking away.

Ava guides me down to the seat, and I stare out of the windscreen, numb.

It's another chance.

For whom?

Them?

Or me?

Chapter 36

"Come with us, Jesse."

I stand on the steps of The Manor staring at my mum, frozen. Hungover.

Carmichael is behind me, silent, and Dad remains by his car by the fountain, unwilling to come closer.

"This isn't the life for you," she goes on, taking one step closer, looking past me. To Carmichael. He won't say anything. He won't intervene. "We'll help you. Please, son, don't waste your life. I can't face losing you too."

My eyes move to Dad, and he quickly drops his stare to the gravel. Unable to look at me. Ashamed? "I can't," I say, resolute. "This is my home now." I turn and walk back up the steps into The Manor, passing Carmichael. My head is banging. There's only one cure. "Vodka, please, Mario," I say, ignoring the fact that he's just glanced at the clock. He looks past me rather than gets me my drink, and I crane my neck to see Uncle Carmichael in the doorway. "What did she think would happen?" I ask, turning away from his expressionless face. "I'd pack my bags, all forgiven, and hop on a plane to Spain with them? Why the hell are they going to Spain, anyway?"

"Too many bad memories here for them, perhaps," he says.

I wince. Bad memories that I created. I'm just one huge disappointment. Why the fuck would they even want me to go? No, this is for the best. They can plough all of their love and energy into Amalie.

I look at Mario. He's still not getting me my drink. And I realize...

I face Carmichael, tilting my head. "It's not even ten," he says. "I'm all for you letting your hair down, Jesse, but you will always control your compulsions." He leaves the bar and me to mull over his words. "Control is imperative. And you have a child on the way."

"So do you," I yell, not appreciating the reminder.

"And I control my compulsions," he calls back.

I slam my fist down on the bar, looking at Mario. He shakes his head and gets back to his stocktake. Fuck him. Fuck Lauren. Fuck her for trapping me. Fuck my parents for forcing me to marry her. Fuck

Carmichael for not defending me just then. And more than anything,
fuck me for being such a fucking letdown.

"*I hope you're happy in Spain,*" *I mutter.* "*Thanks for abandoning*
me."

My eyes open to darkness, my skin cool. I'm in bed? I squint, my
eyes adjusting to the moonlight streaming through the window, casting
shadows across the bedroom. And...

I can smell her.

Ava.

I turn my head on the pillow and see her silhouette curled up next
to me. I don't remember the drive back to the villa. I don't recall getting
undressed. Getting into bed. But running into Mum? I remember every
torturous second of that. Every feeling. Every word.

And my heart hurts all over again.

I ease off the bed and find my clothes in a pile on the floor. I crouch
and get my mobile, wondering what the hell I'm doing. It's there as I
knew it would be. A missed call from Amalie. I close my eyes and push
my phone into my forehead, jumping when it beeps.

They've never blamed you.

I huff, dropping it back on my clothes and rising, raking a hand
through my hair. It's my past. I can't look back, only forward. I cast
my eyes toward the bed.

Where my future lies, sleeping.

I go to her, easing her onto her back and snuggling up close to her
warm body. Always so warm. *Safe*.

She is my home.

My future.

Everything I live and breathe for.

I won't risk anything ruining us.

Never.

* * *

I wake up slowly, feeling her fingers combing through my hair. The
warm air of my breath bounces off her neck back into my face. My
thoughts are calm. My body relaxed. Ava knew who she was looking
at last night before I spoke. She knew.

And she got me away.

"I would never have brought you here if I'd known," I whisper, so full of regret. It's been blissful, what we both needed. And now, it's tarnished. "I never wanted my life with you to be stained by my past." And hasn't that been the whole fucking point? Protect Ava and at the same time protect myself. Keep this wild, pure, amazing thing we have exactly that.

"It hasn't affected us," she replies. "So please don't let it."

"They have no place in my life, Ava. Not before, and even less now." *It's a second chance.*

She nods slowly, understanding. But how could she ever? "You don't need to explain anything to me," she says, resolute. It hurts. Her devotion and commitment. "You and me."

My smile is halfhearted as I fall to my back, pulling Ava onto me. "This place was Carmichael's," I say quietly. "It was part of his estate, as was the boat." I don't know why I'm telling her this. What does it matter now? We can never come back here, and the boat was sold years ago.

"I know," she breathes, making me shudder as she follows the line of my scar with the tip of her finger. Lightly. Delicately. Precisely. It's uncomfortably symbolic.

"How did you know?" I ask, looking down my body, resisting telling her to stop.

"Why else would you have a villa so close to where your parents live?" she asks. So she's thought about this?

"My beautiful girl is frightening me," I say quietly.

"Why?"

"Because she's usually so demanding for information."

"There can't be anything else you could tell me that would convince me to run away from you again."

Thank God she's not looking at me right now, because my face must be pained. Naturally, I don't want to talk about Lauren or Rosie. *It's another chance.* But there is one thing we do need to talk about. Sarah. We're going home today. I don't want to lie to her. "I'm glad you've said that." I feel Ava's finger stop moving and her body stiffen. "Ava?"

There's a beat of silence. "What?"

"I need to tell you something." And I know she's not going to like it. This is Sarah, after all, but she must let me explain. Hear me out. *Understand.* And to achieve that, I need to ensure she can't walk away. I fight with her to move her onto her back, and she doesn't go easily. Sitting on her thighs, I hold her hands, wondering how to start as she looks up at me like a deer caught in the headlights.

"I've had Sarah at The Manor while we've been gone." I blurt it all out fast and immediately wished I hadn't. Her face is irate. Disbelieving. Fuck, I should have given some context first.

"What?" Her voice is harsh. As livid as her face.

Explain! "She's dealing with things while I'm gone," I rush on. "John can't do it on his own, Ava."

"But Sarah?" she asks. "You said she was gone, end of. Why, after everything she's done, would you allow that?" She violently yanks her hands out of mine. "Get off."

"Ava," I sigh. "Will you calm down?" Her blood pressure must have just jumped into the danger zone if her red cheeks are a measure.

"Why?" Her lip curls. "Worried I might injure your babies?"

Yes, actually. And herself. "Don't talk fucking shit," I fume, snatching her hands and pinning them down before she clouts me one.

"You think it. Your constant monitoring and overprotectiveness tells me all I need to know."

Wait. I thought we were talking about Sarah? And I'm not monitoring; I'm being attentive. Sensible. Doing things right. *It's a second chance.* "I've always been overprotective," I hiss. "So don't brandish that card, lady."

"She goes, or I do."

For fuck's sake. Freeing her from beneath me before she does any of us damage, I watch her stomp away, an angry mist rising from her skin. Jesus, I totally underestimated the level on pissed off I'd get back. "I was in a mess, Ava," I explain, getting to the context side of this conversation. A bit late by the looks of things. "You refuse to work for me, and I need someone who knows what they're doing."

"So she's working for you again?" she screeches, spinning to face me.

That's what I said, didn't I? I growl and go to her, stopping, surprised, when she holds a hand up.

"Stop where you are, Ward," she seethes. "Don't try to placate me or convince me that this is all fine, because it fucking isn't."

Convince her? The chance would be a fine fucking thing. I can't get a word in edgeways. But she'll hear this..."Watch your fucking mouth."

"No," she snaps. I recoil, stunned. "She's in love with you. Do you know that? Everything she has done really is because she wants to take you away from me, so don't even *think* about trying to convince me that this is a good idea."

"I know," I say, quickly and easily. Of course I fucking know.

Ava could be looking at a monster right now. "What do you mean, you know?"

"I know she's in love with me."

Her forehead crinkles. "You do?"

"Of course I do, Ava." I have to force myself not to laugh. Did she think Sarah acted out of hate? "I'm not fucking stupid."

"You obviously are." She snorts. "You'll trample anyone who tries to take me away from you, yet right under your nose, she's doing the best job, and you're choosing to ignore it."

Ignoring it? Jesus. Context is wasted, because she will *never* get it. Maybe because the context stands for shit. It's the wrong context.

Ava disappears out of the room, and my heavy, pounding head drops back, my eyes on the ceiling. "Advice, anyone?" I ask seriously, waiting, listening. But no. I'm on my own. "Thanks a bunch, bro." I sigh. "I didn't just let it go unsaid, Ava," I say, following her to the kitchen. "I had it out with her and she admitted and regretted it all."

Her eyes widen as she downs some water. "Of course she regrets it." She swipes the back of her hand across her mouth, and a drop of water falls to her breast as a result. My eyes fall there. "She failed! She's probably regretting not doing a better job!" I jump when a loud bang sounds. Her glass hitting the counter. How the fuck did that not smash? "And you may as well have let it go unsaid," she rants on. "Did you offer burial or cremation?"

And now we're talking about funerals? "What?"

Her hand flaps between our naked bodies. "The usual option you give people who hurt me. Did you offer it to Sarah?"

This is too much. What a fucking shitter of an end to our wonderful break in Paradise. "No," I breathe, exhausted. "I offered her a job in return for her word that she'll never interfere again." How can I pull this back? Make Ava see I'm thinking of her too. It's mainly her. She's going to need me, and I can't very well be there twenty-four seven if I have to run The Manor. Not that I could run The Manor if I had all the time in the fucking world. I'm hopeless. "I told her that if you say so, she's out."

"I say so," she yells, going so red in the face, I'm sure she might pop. "I say she's out!"

"But she hasn't done anything."

"She's not done anything?" Disbelief. Yikes.

"I mean, she's not done anything since I reinstated her," I say calmly, trying to dial down the high energy before it ends in tears. "And you rewarded her with a tidy crack to the jaw for the stuff that came before."

"Why are you doing this?" she asks, now calm too. "You know how I feel, Jesse."

Fuck, yes, I do. And I understand. But this isn't only about us. There's more to be considered. Like a life. And I know Ava could never be so cruel to disregard a life, no matter whose life it is. "Because she's desperate, Ava. She has no life past The Manor."

"You feel sorry for her?"

This isn't just a simple case of feeling sorry for her. God, there's so much more to it. And yet...context. "Ava," I beg, as she refills her glass. I'm not surprised, her throat must be really fucking dry and really fucking sore. "First of all, I want you to calm down because it's not good for you or the babies."

"I am calm!" she screams, now going blue in the face.

Oh, enough is enough. She's going to burst a fucking blood vessel. I swipe the glass from her hand, ignoring her gasp of shock, and slam it down before lifting her onto the worktop. Taking her jaw in my grip, mine rolls, my glare as real as hers.

"Sarah has nothing," I explain. "I kicked her out when she came clean and thought no more of it." Fuck, I didn't want to share this. I hoped Ava was comfortable enough with the reassurance that Sarah will stay away from her. "Until John spoke with her and she was saying all kinds of fucked-up shit," I go on, loosening my hold of her jaw when she withdraws, her scowl turning into questioning. "The most worrying part mentioning death being better than living her life without me."

"Attention seeker," she fires, her scowl back.

Of course her mind would go there. But can I blame her? "I thought so too," I admit. "But John wasn't so sure. He found her. She'd slashed her wrists and taken a pile of painkillers." She loses all animosity in a heartbeat and, I can't lie, I'm really fucking relieved. "It was no cry for help, Ava. There was no attention seeking about it. John only just got her to the hospital in time. She wanted to die."

She's been shocked into silence, just staring at me in disbelief.

"I don't want another death on my conscience, baby," I whisper. "I live with Jake's every single day. I can't do it."

"She came to see me," Ava says quietly.

"She told me, but I'm surprised you never mentioned this before."

"I didn't think it was important." Her shoulders lift on a little shrug, and my previous thoughts are ignited. Was it that meeting between them that had Ava rushing to The Manor and confessing about the pregnancy?

It's possible, but I won't push that. And since we're putting some cards on the table..."It was Sarah who told Matt about my drinking."

Oh, her scowl. "Is that how you knew I was collecting my clothes from Matt's too?"

"She said she'd overheard you on the phone, telling someone you were intending on picking your stuff up. I was too mad to piece it together. I saw red, acted on impulse, and asked questions later."

"She said she couldn't work for you anymore, so how come she is?"

"I asked her." Not fucking true but, again, a small white lie for the sake of my wife's contentment. "I'll never find someone else to do the job, which means I'll have to do it, and I'm not prepared to give up my time with you. And you should know, she only accepted on the condition that you were okay with it." What the fuck am I saying? Bending truths just a bit. But, again, I don't need Ava to hate Sarah more for pretty much forcing me into a corner. *No more death.*

"You're not giving me much of a choice," she mutters.

It's not about having a choice. It's about having compassion.

"I'll tell her it's a no-go," I say, taking her cheeks. Did I completely underestimate the level of hatred I'm dealing with?

Yes. Tell her about Rebecca.

"I'm not prepared to see you so unhappy."

Her entire being folds before me, the reasonable woman I know, fighting past the emotional, unreasonable firecracker. "No," she sighs.

"I want you with me more than I want her gone."

And there it is. The end game. Us, together, all the fucking time. She wants me around all the time. "You do?"

"Of course I do." Her nose wrinkles, and I smile, because I know she knows she might regret saying that. "But you have to promise me something."

"Anything. You know that."

"When the babies arrive," she says, as I coat her forehead in kisses. "You won't be at The Manor day and night. You'll be with me as often as you can." Oh, my heart sings its happiness. The end of this trip is turning out better than I hoped, considering where we were last night. I pull away, holding her face, scanning her worried eyes. "I don't know if I can do this," she whispers.

She can do anything, and so can I, because I have her. "Ava, you'll have to bury me six feet under before I have it any other way. You can do it because you have me." I pull her into my chest, hugging the shit out of her as she wraps every limb around my upper body. Clinging on. Suddenly, all I can see is Owen Cutler, and all I can think about is the meeting he wants. "We're going to be okay."

"I know."

What would Ava say if I told her about Cutler? Should I tell her? "Let's not fight." I press my lips into her temple. "It makes my heart split in pain, and I don't want you stressing out. We have to watch your blood pressure." I must get a machine and educate myself on the safe levels so I can check every day. Maybe twice a day. Depending on how many disagreements we have.

Sliding her butt off the counter, I cup it with both hands and carry her back into the bedroom. "I'm confiscating that book," she mumbles into my shoulder.

"That's *my* book, and I'm keeping it."

"We need to make friends."

Oh? I eye her as she looks at me, doing a terrible job of hiding her cheeky grin. And suddenly her boob is in my face. "Did you read the part of the book that says a husband should service his wife as she demands?"

I latch onto her flesh and suck, and she's putty in my hold, but then I look at the clock on the bedside, groaning. No time. "I did, but our plane is scheduled for take-off in two hours. I need more time, so I'll service you when we get home. Deal?"

"No deal. I want to stay in Paradise."

"You're incorrigible, and I love it." I put her on the bed, ignoring her slighted face. "We need to catch that flight." *Before my parents turn up here.*

"I need you," she purrs, pulling out the big guns and seizing my dick in her hand. *Fuck.*

I resist and pull away. It's unheard of. "Ava, when I have you, I like to take my time." I take no joy from her look of disbelief. I try to kiss it away. And fail. "Pack."

Leaving her on the bed, I go to the bathroom, checking my phone on the way, contemplating texting John.

Thank God that's done. Although, actually, was the whole conversation around Sarah wasted breath? Because soon there might be no manor at all.

I laugh under my breath, uncomfortable.

No manor? It seems incomprehensible.

And yet, so did happiness and redemption only a few months ago.

Chapter 37

There was a heavy sense of regret the entire journey home. Regret we're leaving Paradise. Regret it ended on a bit of a low. Regret London is waiting for us. And for me, there's a whole host of issues that need resolving. I had thought my list of things to tackle was reducing. Somehow over the past few days, it's grown. Seeing my mum has knocked me sideways, I admit it. Historically, such an encounter would've had me diving for a bottle to wash down the remorse and anger, and my lucidity and feelings right now are also why I would reach for the vodka. I can't say I'm all too fond of the regret I'm feeling, or the worry, or the compassion. Mum looked so old. And Dad? How is he?

My knee jumps repeatedly as I stare down at my mobile. The kitchen is quiet, Cathy's not here yet, and Ava's upstairs getting ready for work. Can I? Should I?

I place my coffee down and snatch up my phone, dialing, standing, and walking around the island in circles. "Jesse?" Amalie says, unsure.

"Yeah, it's me." My sister inhales, while I fight the compulsion to yank at my recently knotted tie. "I saw Mum."

"I know."

I stop pacing. Of course she knows. "It didn't go too well." I roll my eyes to myself. "I mean—"

"You're married," Amalie says quietly.

"Yeah, I'm married." To someone I actually *want* to be married to. "We're expecting. I mean, she's expecting. Two. Babies, I mean. Twins. It's twins." I look up at the ceiling. "Ava's expecting twins."

"That's so amazing, Jesse."

"Thanks." Amazing is right. And obviously a massive surprise to them. "I'm sorry your wedding was canceled," I go on. "How's Dad?" My face bunches, and I don't fucking know why.

"You didn't see him? He was with Mum at the restaurant, Jesse."

"He was?"

"Yes."

"He didn't…" What? Say hi? Come shake my hand? Congratulate me?

"Come to you?" she asks. "For you to yell at him?"

"I didn't—" I pinch the bridge of my nose, taking air into my lungs. I did yell at him. Always. Usually drunk. "So he's okay?"

"They're monitoring him," she says, and I nod.

"That's good. Very good."

"So your wife..."

"What about my wife?"

"She's..." Amalie hums, and I show the ceiling my rolling eyes again.

"Younger than me, yes," I confirm, knowing Amalie would have wanted every small detail from Mum. "By nearly a whole twelve years, if you must know."

"And she knows about The Manor?"

"Yes."

"What's inside The Manor?"

"Yes."

"She knows about Jake?"

"Yes."

"Your drinking?"

"Yes," I grate.

"Rosie?"

My inhale is so sharp and deep, my entire body lifts. It also gives Amalie my answer. "Did you just take my call to remind me of all the shitty things that have happened in my life?"

"I'll take that as a no."

"Take it as you will," I snap.

"And here he goes, being all defensive as usual," she muses. My mouth opens, ready to launch, but no words materialize. I have nothing to say to that. Why? Because no alcohol is involved? Because I'm lucid?

Sober?

Have I suddenly realized that I've played a significant part in my estrangement from my family too?

A small silence falls between us, Amalie waiting for my scathing counter, me wondering what to say. "Are you still drinking?" she asks, her question soft and loaded with anticipation.

My knee-jerk reaction is to bellow a resounding, angry, insulted *no*. As I always have. But I don't have that right, and I can't be mad with Amalie for asking. "I haven't had a drink since I met Ava." Not strictly true, but sharing my four-day absence will serve no purpose here. "She's pregnant, Amalie. I—"

"You drank throughout Lauren's pregnancy."

"I didn't love Lauren," I say tightly, and again, I can't be mad. My family never saw me when I was sober while Rosie was alive. They just saw the broken man I was when she died. And by then, I was beyond hope. There was no point wasting their time. They couldn't fix me. "Listen, I didn't call to debate my fuck-ups."

"Then why did you call?'" she asks, making me scowl. *Smart-arse.*

"To see how Dad is."

"Do you care?"

"Well, clearly I fucking do, Amalie, because here I am on the end of the phone asking."

"So what's changed?"

My God, I suddenly remember how exhausting she is. Testing. Takes no shit. "I don't know, Amalie." I sigh and scrub my hand down my face. "Look, I've got to go."

"Wait," she blurts, now urgent. "Does this mean there's a chance?"

I don't need to ask what she means. And I can't bring myself to say no. Forgiveness is a medicine I'm yet to try. I hang up and before I can even think to call John, Amalie texts me.

I'm going to take that as a yes. Don't push me away again. And it just occurred to me…I'm older than your wife. Weird.

And there go my eyes again. I have a fucking headache. A knock sounds, taking me to the front door. I swing it open and find Clive holding up a tube. "Morning, Mr. Ward, a delivery for you."

"Thanks, Clive." I take it, close the door on his smiling face, and rush to my office, slipping the wallpaper behind the door for the decorator. I look at the wall. Fucking amazing. But it was absent some really important pictures I took recently, so I hopped onto the suppliers website while Ava was swimming on Saturday and added them to the design, got express shipping, and called the decorators back in. This wall's cost a small fortune. But, again, fucking amazing.

When I'm back in the kitchen, I call John and lower to a stool. "Morning," I sigh, hearing the sound of Ava's hairdryer in the distance.

"Sounds like you need a holiday."

"Ha," I quip, droll. "Are you still okay to pick Ava up for work?"

"Indeed. I'm on my way. Does she know?"

My lips roll as I stand and go to the fridge, collecting my peanut butter.

Better than vodka, bro. Well done.

With my phone wedged to my ear, I start dipping. "I didn't think I'd push my luck after telling her Sarah's at The Manor."

He laughs. "Probably wise. How did she take it?"

"As you would expect."

"So, it's down to me to advise your wife that she has a chaperone for the time being. Is that what we're getting to? Because, you know, you could advise her now."

Could. Won't. "You have permission to use extreme but gentle force." I suck the end of my finger, humming my happiness.

"Great."

"Anything on anything?" I ask around my mouthful.

"Nothing."

"On anything?" I ask, surprised.

"That's what I said, motherfucker. Welcome back." He hangs up, and I slowly slip my mobile into my inside pocket but pull it straight back out when it dings with a message. Ava's brother. Asking if I'm free today. "Nope," I say, leaving the message unanswered and returning my jar to the fridge, hearing the front door open and close.

"Morning, boy. Welcome home." Cathy dumps her bag on the island and immediately swipes up my coffee cup. "How was your holiday?"

"Wonderful." Slight exaggeration. "Would you make Ava some breakfast?"

"Yes, must keep that tummy full of good, healthy food!"

"Thanks, Cathy. Oh, and a decorator will be here around nine to repaper my office wall."

"It was just done on Friday."

Yes, well, Paradise shone the best light on my girl. "Just a few tweaks."

Weirdo.

"Fuck off," I grunt, leaving Cathy in the kitchen and heading upstairs.

Ava's sitting on the carpet in front of the mirror in lace when I walk into the bedroom. Hell, I should have woken her up earlier. But did

I hope she'd sleep in and get reprimanded by her boss? I can neither confirm nor deny. My smile is wide as I watch her beautifully lingerie-clad body move as she works her hands through her hair, blasting it dry.

"Morning," I say happily when I catch her admiring me in the mirror. She's right. I look hot today. I'm glad she's noticed. The appreciation stops there, though, from both sides. My smile falls when her face contorts into something resembling annoyance. What have I done now?

The dryer is dropped to the carpet, and she paces to the dressing room. "Wow," I breathe. I'm very glad I passed the baton to John where her transport is concerned. I know neither of us are particularly delighted to be back from Paradise, but is that my fault?

I quickly check the nightstand, making sure she's taken her folic acid. She has. That's one argument averted. My chin drops to my chest, my sigh weighed with impatience, my hands slipping into my pockets to stop me finding her and pinning her to the nearest wall.

Ava appears from the dressing room a few moments later, and I can't hold back my amusement as she marches across the bedroom to the bathroom, her boobs bouncing just enough for my eyes, but way too much for any other man's. And her legs? I can see the start of her thighs. So she's playing dirty, is she? My God, how she tests me. Usually with non-existent dresses. They're like a loaded gun for my wife.

I go to the dressing room and look through the rails to find something more suitable, settling on a lovely black number. Maybe it's a little tighter than I'd like, but that's my compromise. "Drives me fucking crazy," I mutter. "What did I even fucking do?"

I go to the bathroom door and watch her applying her mascara, refusing to look at me. So I get closer. She flicks her eyes to mine. "What do you think you're doing?" I ask.

"I'm putting my makeup on."

"Let me rephrase that," I breathe out, losing my amusement and finding some patience. "What do you think you're wearing?" It's getting shredded as soon as it's off.

"A dress."

"Let's not start the day on a bad note, lady." I present the alternative. "Put the dress on." To my utter surprise, she doesn't object, taking the dress and leaving, albeit on a huff. And she continues with the sounds of bother as she gets out of her choice of dress and puts on mine, fiddling with the zipper.

"Will you zip me up, please?"

I can tell it pains her to ask me. I can also tell I'll be getting nothing more than the pleasure of zipping her up. I need to snap her out of this unprovoked, foul mood. And maybe find out what the hell has put her in it? "Of course." I press my body to hers, make sure my breathing is heavy and my mouth's close to her face, and take in her freshly washed and blow-dried hair, moving it over her shoulder. The evidence of her bodily response presents itself to me in the form of a satisfying shudder. Well, satisfying for me, probably annoying for my wife.

Finding the zip, I slowly, seductively, pull it up, homing in on her cheek with my lips and—

I frown, the zip getting jammed, forcing me to abandon breathing my desire all over her face and checking it. The zip's fine. It's the gap between each side of the dress that's the problem. I bite my lip, furiously fighting to restrain my grin, knowing it's more than my life is worth to show my delight. Didn't I tell her she had a tummy? And did she believe me? "Oh dear," I whisper. Not at the dress, fuck the dress, but because this is not going to improve Ava's mood. But at least she'll have a reason for her sulks. Funny, isn't it? The cause for her bad mood will be the reason for my amazing mood. The babies are growing.

"What?" She looks over her shoulder, craning her neck to see. "Is it broken?"

"Ummmm…" I give it one more wiggle for the sake of it, if only to demonstrate it won't budge. "No, baby. I think you may have grown out of it."

She stills for a split second, taking that information onboard, before rushing to the nearest mirror on a burst of incredulous air. I watch as she scans her back, willing her to see this as a blessing. To be excited. I get it, she's young, has a banging figure—tight, tidy, and divine. She's worried about it changing. *Keep it together, baby. We've got this.*

"Can I put my other dress on now?" she murmurs solemnly.

I can't and won't enforce a different dress. She looks too overcome by the old news that she's going to…expand. *More to love.* So I sweep up the short number—*I'll cut you up another day*—and shake it out, being attentive and helpful as she switches back. The zip goes up with ease. This dress definitely has more give. That doesn't make it acceptable. We should go shopping. "Beautiful." I look her up and down, wondering if I could convince her to wear a knee-length sweater over the top. Too optimistic? "I need to scram," I tell her, checking my Rolex. "Cathy's downstairs and she's made you breakfast. Please eat it."

"I will."

Wow. Ummm…"Thank you?"

"You don't have to thank me for eating." She leaves the bedroom, her mood still in the gutter.

"I feel like I should thank you for everything you do without arguing with me about it," I mumble to myself as I follow her.

"If you were still fucking sense into me, I *would* argue."

"Are you pissed because I didn't service you this morning?" Is that the crux of her shitty mood? No sex?

"Yes."

"Thought so." So she feels neglected? Poor thing. Let's fix that. I yank her into my body and catch her mouth with mine, kissing the daylights out of her, feeling her leaning into me for support. "Have a nice day, baby," I say, sending her toward the island with a tap of her bottom, my eyes narrowed on the dress. *Snip, snip.* "Make sure my wife eats her breakfast, Cathy."

"I will, boy."

"I'll see you later. And don't forget to speak with Patrick," I remind her, making a call to Cook on my way out. "Anything?" I ask, closing the front door behind me.

"I was just about to call you."

I stop, staring at the elevator doors. I don't like the sound of that. "Oh?"

"Can you meet?" he asks.

Definitely don't like this. "I'm heading to The Manor."

"See you there."

Chapter 38

As the gates to The Manor open, I take the longest breath, my grip of the steering wheel tightening of its own volition. I can't put my finger on why. Because I know Sarah is here? Because Steve is on his way? Or simply...it's The Manor.

I drive slowly through the line of trees, counting them as I go. Fifty. Twenty-five on each side, all evenly spaced. All hundreds of years old.

Rounding the fountain, I pull into my usual spot and turn off the engine, leaning forward in my seat and removing my shades, looking up the front of the grand, majestic mansion. It's like I'm seeing it more clearly each day. Feeling like I need to take the time to absorb it and appreciate it. Or...what? Make the most of it while I have it?

I get out of the Aston and take the steps, slipping my keys into my pocket as I push my way in. I hear crockery clanging from the kitchens, activity of staff from the bar—all noises that are usually drowned out by the sounds of member's chatter and laughs. The flowers on the circular table catch my eye. They're callas. Seven, tall, elegant, white calla lilies. I trace my finger down the side of the vase, frowning. Then I pull out six of the stems and lay them on the table, leaving only one.

"Mr. Ward," Pete says, passing with a tray of silver salt and pepper pots. "Welcome back."

"Thanks, Pete." I check the time and dial John as I wander through the summer room, stopping at the French doors and looking across the grounds to the tennis courts.

"Just dropped her off at the office," he says in answer.

"Steve Cook is on his way."

"He's found something?"

"I assume so," I say, weaving my way through the couches. "How quick can you be here?"

"On my way."

I push into my office and come to a jarring stop when I find someone behind my desk. She looks up, smiles, and stands, revealing her body in all of its leather-clad glory. Except this outfit has long sleeves. I don't mention it's a bit early for the dominatrix. Or the fact that she probably shouldn't be thrashing a whip after what she's done to herself. I'm still stuck on the smile on her face. Have I ever seen a genuine smile on Sarah before? I don't think so. Weird. So weird. "Morning," I say, averting my eyes, taking in my office. Tidy. No paperwork piled high anywhere. She's been busy.

"Morning." Sarah comes out from behind my desk, letting me take my chair. I pull my jacket tails out and lower, scanning the surface. A pot of pens. A box of Kleenex. My laptop. "This is the contract for the new security system," she says, slipping a document in front of me. "Your tax liabilities for the last financial year, along with various tax forms that need signing." Another sheet. "This is the company incorporation renewal, and here's your bank details should you ever need to log in yourself and send any payments." A Post-it is placed on top of the papers. "I recommend storing it somewhere protected in your phone." A few rustles. "An updated list of members whose health assessments are overdue, a list of members who have given their months' notice, and the building inspector needs to come check the extension before signing off." More papers are placed down. "These are the registration documents for your wife's new car, her Mini has been released from the police investigation—let me know if I can give them the nod to scrap it—your bike has been delivered and put in the garage, and your driver's license is about to expire, so you'll need to renew it. You can do that online. I'll send you the link. And lastly, the estimate to repair the damage on your Ducati."

I blink up at her as she tilts her head, her face straight. "Thanks."

"No problem." She motions to the papers. "I've tabbed where I need your signature." Then she pivots and leaves.

Like nothing has happened. She was all business but with…a smile on her face. No scowls or derision in her expression. Does she really like organizing me and The Manor that much?

My attention falls back to the mass of paperwork before me, and I grimace, pulling it closer. It's something to do while I wait for John and Cook. And at least I know what I'm doing. *Thanks to Sarah.* So I get to work, signing where indicated, filtering through all of the papers, before stacking them to the side for her. Easy as that. I pick up and scan the spreadsheets. Sam and Drew are both still on the overdue medical list. "Fucking pains," I mutter, texting them both to remind them.

And then…I'm redundant. I rest back in my chair, pouting, looking around my office. This is what I wanted. No work stress. Time. Great, except my wife still has a boss and a job. I get up and go for a stroll, opening and closing doors, taking in every room, before heading upstairs and doing the same, visiting the extension last. Our suite. But I don't take in the interior. I go to the window and take in the view, resting my shoulder on the frame and counting the trees again, only reaching thirty before I can't see any farther. John's Range Rover emerges on the horizon, rolling slowly down the driveway. Can he even comprehend not driving through those gates ever again? It's been his life for longer than mine, and yet he's never succumbed to the lure of the rooms. He's never had a relationship either. His life's work has been as a solid friend, first to Carmichael, then to me. He needs freedom as much as I do.

I back away from the window and leave, pausing at the stained-glass window at the bottom of the stairs, glancing up to the communal room. And suddenly, I'm climbing the stairs, my heart, weirdly, beating that little bit faster. I push through the doors and slip my hands in my pockets, glancing around. How many mornings did the cleaners find me on one of the beds, naked? How many women have I fucked in here? In my own suite? It seems like madness now, that I would even entertain such hedonism. *Husband and Daddy.*

I slowly wander around, spotting pieces of the new furniture amid the originals. All things I would have tried. Not now.

A noise behind me pulls my body around. John cocks his head, and I smile mildly. "I feel a bit detached," I admit. "Like I'm looking at a past life." I run my fingers lightly over the top of a highly polished cabinet that's stuffed full of toys. "Like the heartbeat is dulling." I look at John, and he nods in understanding. The communal room. The heartbeat of The Manor.

I laugh to myself, the sound low and nervous. John's silence isn't helping.

"You saw Beatrice," he says, out of the blue, removing his glasses.

"Ava told you." How much has she told him? Out of pure habit and nothing more, I pull at my collar. I don't feel stifled. I don't feel hot. My heart is beating a little faster, I guess. "Can you believe of all the restaurants I could've chosen, I chose the one they were in." You couldn't fucking write it. "Ava noticed someone staring at us. It was… tense."

"Hmmm," he hums, and I frown.

"What does that mean?"

"I didn't say anything."

"No, you hummed."

"A man can't hum? Why didn't you tell me?" he asks.

"I've not spoken to you."

"You spoke to me on the phone this morning."

"I had other things on my mind this morning." Speaking of which, where the hell is Cook? I scowl down at my watch.

"So how did it go? With your mum, I mean."

I glance at John. "As you would expect."

"You've been drunk for the best part of sixteen years, motherfucker. If you ever saw your parents during that time, you were already drunk. You acted out. Then made a grab for more vodka. So that's what I would expect. Except, that didn't happen this time. So, again, how did it go?"

I pout like a scorned, challenged child. *It was unbearable. Seeing how old Mum looked. Learning Dad was unwell. Hearing her pleas and not being able to block them out with alcohol.* "It hurt," I admit, looking away.

"But you didn't drink."

"No, I didn't drink," I say, heading out of the communal room, suddenly feeling stifled.

"That's good." John follows me, falling into line beside me as we take the stairs.

"Yes, that's good. When did you become a therapist?"

"So, what now?" he asks, ignoring my sarcasm.

We round the landing and descend the staircase to the entrance hall. "What do you mean, what now?"

"Is there a chance?"

My eyes fall to my feet, watching my steps. Amalie asked the exact same question.

Is there?

"John, I don't really have the headspace right now to answer these questions," I say.

He nods, accepting, and diverts toward the bar. "I understand."

"Where are you going?"

"I have a feeling it's going to be a long day, so I'm getting caffeine."

No headspace? Then why can't I get Mum's sadness out of my fucking mind? I come to a stop by the round table. The lilies have been put back in the vase. I sigh, plucking them back out and laying them on the table, leaving that one single calla on display.

Understated elegance.

Where it all began.

I reach into my inside pocket and pull out the image of the babies.

Twins.

It's another chance.

And again, I wonder who Mum was talking about.

Them? Or just me?

Chapter 39

John's right. It feels like it's going to be a long day. So I follow his lead and stock up on coffee, except I don't join him on one of the couches in the summer room to drink it. Instead, I have mine poured into a takeout cup and go for another walk, lapping the grounds, mulling things over. So many things. I feel weirdly vacant, and it's beginning to piss me off. My head's scrambled, so when I see Cook *finally* pull through the gates, I'm grateful, despite knowing my attention is likely to be focused on something unpleasant.

I call John to let him know he's here and that I'm on my way, jumping when someone honks their horn at me. Sam pulls up, his window down. "What are you doing?" he asks, a monster frown on his face as he flanks me.

"Walking."

"From where?"

"Just walking." I give him an accusing look. "Did you get my text?"

"Yeah, I got your text."

"Get it sorted?"

"No need." He inhales and looks down the driveway toward The Manor. "I'm quitting."

I try and fail to contain my surprise. "You're quitting?"

"Me and Kate are…" His head tilts one way, then the other, as if he's pondering how to explain.

"Going to try a normal relationship?"

"Normal?" he asks, and I smile. "What the fuck is normal? We're going to try a relationship with no sex manor."

"Good for you," I murmur, looking up at the stained-glass window again. *The heartbeat's getting duller.*

"But for the sake of old times." Sam grins at me. "Mind if we have one more play?"

"Keep it between the two of you."

"Of course. It's like a farewell thing," he says wistfully, eyes back on The Manor in the distance. "She's been a part of my life forever."

"Yeah," I whisper, studying *her*. Imposing. Magnificent. Full of pleasure-filled promises.

And tragedy.

I feel like I'm subconsciously trying to come to terms with the end of an era. Is that what this odd feeling I have is? Or just the aftermath of seeing my mum? Or both?

"How was your break?" Sam asks.

I breathe in and exhale, finishing my coffee. "Nice while it lasted."

"Well, welcome home. I'll catch you later." Sam races off, and I carry on walking, finding the picture of the twins again. My eyes remain on the little undistinguishable blobs all the way back to my office.

I walk in and find Cook and John on a couch each. "It wasn't Van Der Haus who drugged Ava." Cook gets straight to business, stalling my arse midway to the couch opposite him. I look at John. He's removed his shades for this meeting. "He also didn't steal your car."

"Right," I say slowly, lowering to the couch next to John, hoping Cook's going to give me more than his baseless conclusions. He tosses some papers on the table between us. "What are they?" I ask, leaving them where they are.

"Passenger records for flights from Heathrow to Copenhagen in the past few months."

"You're going to tell me he was in Denmark on both occasions, aren't you?" I scrub a hand down my face, breathing out my frustration. Cook doesn't answer. He doesn't need to. "Fuck."

"I started a deeper dive into his finances before I had it confirmed he was out of the country, therefore out of the frame."

"And?"

"And I found out his credit records have been looked into recently, along with his business accounts. Requests to Companies House being made, things like that."

"Who's looking into his finances?" John asks. "And why?"

"The who is easy." Cook pulls his phone out and shows me the screen. "Haskett and Sandler. They're specialists and advisors in selling small to medium-sized businesses. The why?" He shakes his head, putting his phone away. "I'm working on the why."

"Is he selling up?" And fucking off back to Denmark, because that would be perfect?

"No, it looks like he's buying."

"Buying what?"

"That goes with the why, Ward. I don't know."

I huff, sinking back into my seat, thinking.

"So, if it wasn't him in the bar, or who stole your car," Cook says. "Surely you can forget about Van Der Haus."

"He still wants my wife." My voice is low, a bit like my mood. I mean, yes, it would have been convenient if it was Van Der Haus, but I think I knew deep down that he's not capable. So the question remains—who is?

Cook nods slowly, thoughtful. "Because you and Freja—"

"Yes."

"Well, he's been seeing someone, so perhaps he's moved on."

"Seeing someone?" I ask, shocked.

"Yes, it's somewhere here," he says, riffling through some more papers. "He met her for dinner. Petite, young, blonde."

I glance at John, seeing his curious expression. "Interesting."

"When was the last time you heard from him?" Cook asks as I rub at my forehead, trying to remember. I can't. It's been weeks. He hasn't called Ava—not that I'm aware of. Have I been worrying over nothing? Has Van Der Haus slithered off under his rock with his young, petite blonde, never to bother us again? I can't imagine so. He still has one big fat juicy detail I'm certain he wants to share with my wife about *his* wife briefly being on the end of my dick during my four-day meltdown. "I don't recall," I admit. I should be forgiven. A *lot* has been going on.

"I think you're barking up the wrong tree, Ward," Cook goes on, saying what I'm slowly accepting myself. "From what I can see, he's clean, respected, and he has an alibi on both of the occasions Ava was targeted."

Targeted. Jesus, it sounds so much more sinister when he says it like that. I look at John. He knows what I'm thinking. *Lockdown*. I'll have to explain to Ava, and she will have to accept that she won't be stepping foot anywhere without John or me.

Welcome fucking home.

"Before I go." Steve hands something to John, and both men ignore my questioning frown. "Listen, Ward, I understand your concern, naturally, but you really should have let the police deal with this from the start."

I'm beginning to wish I had. I thought it was cut and dry. I just needed to prove it and send that fucker out of the country with a threat and a mangled face that *no* woman would ever find attractive again. "Thanks for your help."

"No problem. When's Ava available to give a statement? We've been talking to the other drivers, but she's obviously a key witness."

"I'll ask her to call you."

"Thanks. Let me know if you need anything else." He walks to the door and takes the handle, looking back. "And there's no one springing to mind? Bitter exes, men you've stolen wives from?"

I lift my tired eyes but not my head, and Cook nods, reading between the lines, before he leaves, closing the door quietly behind him.

I turn to John and show the ceiling my palms. "What now?" I ask, getting up and starting to pace. "And what the fuck is that Cook gave to you?"

John unfolds the paper, and his eyebrows lift.

"What, for God's sake?" I press, going back to the couch and lowering, craning my neck to see.

"I had Steve look into Ava's brother," he says, holding the paper up.

"To see if he had a criminal record?"

"Well, yes, that, but also his financial situation."

"How the fuck would Cook—" It occurs to me. His wife. Juliette. *That's* how he got Mikael's financial situation too. He got his wife to look, because she would have access to credit reports and records.

"He's skint," John grunts, tossing the paper on my lap. "Brassic, broke, potless."

I scan the paper, seeing bank account records, credit reports, defaults on credit cards, loans, and car finance. "Fuck," I breathe. "What a mess."

"So that's why he's not going back to Australia."

"He can't afford the airfare," I say, suddenly parched. I get up and grab some water, swigging as I pace around the office. "So how did he afford his airfare here, and why the fuck would he come back to the UK to that mess?" Surely, he'd want to duck and dive around that financial shitshow.

"No idea," John says. "I've got to go collaborate the new system and sync the settings—make sure everything is still running smoothly before we sign off on the contract."

"That's it?" I ask, watching him leave. "You're going?"

"What do you want me to do, sit and brainstorm with you for an eternity? There's shit to do. I'll think while I do it. And by the way…"

"What?"

"Sarah doesn't know it's twins."

I groan and drop my head back. "Great."

John pulls the door open and bumps into Sam. "What the fuck are you doing here?" he grunts. "You're barred until you produce valid, clean medicals."

Sam slaps his shoulder and passes him. "I'm no longer a member, big man." Dumping himself on the couch, he puts his feet up, all comfy. "I've been thinking."

"Oh dear," John quips, leaving us.

"What about?" I ask, laughing at the filthy look Sam chucks back at John.

"I think I may have been a bit hasty."

I put myself on the other couch. "I already said you can play one more time—no medical necessary." For old time's sake.

"Yes, and Kate will be here soon. It's not that."

"Then what?"

"Well, the food's great."

"I know."

"And the spa facilities the best in the area. Probably the whole of the south."

"I know."

"And I love hitting a ball over the net every now and then."

"Cause what else will you do while your girlfriend works and you… don't?"

He smirks, not offended. Kate won't need to work either, but she will. And her cakes really are masterpieces. "Girlfriend," Sam muses, rolling the word over his tongue, falling into a brief daydream as I study him, amused, grateful for the respite from my troubles. "Weird." He shakes his head, sitting up on the couch. "And my mates are here," he adds, smiling.

For now, yes. My thoughts jar me. "What are you saying?" I ask, frowning to myself.

"Can I have a reduced mate's rate for use of the facilities, minus…" He points to the ceiling.

"Sure." And that is that. Talking of mates. "Drew coming by later?" I ask.

"I don't know." Sam gets up and gets on his way. "He's been weird since—" He stops halfway across my office, his body still.

"Weird since what?" I ask, slowly rising too, certain I don't like his persona. "Is he okay?"

"Yeah, he's fine." Sam nearly knocks me out with the width of his smile. "He's got a lot of pressure at work. I didn't see him much this weekend."

"He'll put himself in an early grave."

"Yeah, anyway, I'll see you later."

"Yeah," I say, absentminded again, slowly lowering to the couch. I need some fucking answers.

Chapter 40

I spend the rest of my day avoiding Sarah. *Compulsory.* And checking the verdict on rougher than average sex during pregnancy. Also, according to my wife, compulsory. And, damn it, no harm can be done to babies through sex. *But no one fucks like Jesse Ward.*

I'm on my way out to collect Ava from work when Sarah appears from nowhere, blocking my path to the Aston. My eyes move to the gravel as I take a wide berth around her. "You can hardly look at me," she says, but I don't stop, can't stop. She's right, I can't look at her. She's here, like she begged, and that's all I can offer her. "See you tomorrow," I say over my shoulder.

"Jesse, come on, can't it be like old times?"

Old times.

Pain, alcohol, ignorance.

Old. Times.

"She's trouble, son. I'm just telling you to be careful."

Be careful? Is that some kind of backward code for "do as you're told and expected"?

"But I'm trouble too, aren't I?" I retort on a slur. *Even drunk I could tell my dad I wouldn't go there with Carmichael's girlfriend, not even with a stick. But I won't. Why would I pacify him? I'm everything he predicted and dreaded, so no one wins.*

"Your wife is pregnant, Jesse, for Christ's sake."

"She won't be my wife soon." I take backward steps, retreating back into The Manor. Into my haven. *"Because I never wanted to marry her."*

"But she'll still be the mother of your child." He waves a hand up and down my drunk form. *"Look at you. Is this how you'll parent? Drunk?"* Then his hand is waving at The Manor. *"In this...this...sordid sex haven?"*

"I'll be a good father," I say, repeating Carmichael's words. *"I don't have to be married to be a good father."*

"No, but you need to be sober!" he bellows, his emotions getting the better of him. *"For Christ's sake, Jesse. Think of your mother. Hasn't she been through enough?"*

I stop in my tracks. "You mean losing Jake?"

"Yes, I mean losing Jake!"

"I lost him too!" I scream, nearly falling to my arse, stumbling with the help of alcohol and emotion. Dad recoils, shocked. Good. Perhaps he appreciates my agony now, because it sure doesn't look like he's feeling any himself. "I lost him too," I say more calmly.

"We can't watch you do this to yourself anymore, Jesse. We can't fix you."

I laugh, and it's demented. "Then you shouldn't have fucking broken me in the first place."

I turn and walk back into my sanctuary. Where no one judges me. Where I'm loved, appreciated. Where the pressures and consequences of life don't exist.

Or, more significantly, the consequences of my life don't exist.

I stop in my tracks and look back at Sarah. "Why did you tell my dad that we slept together?"

It's only one subtle step, but she definitely backs up, wary. "What?"

"Why did you tell my dad that we slept together?" I ask again, this time clearer, slowly, turning my body fully toward her.

"I didn't." She laughs. It's nervous. Pray do tell me she's not going to deny it? "I didn't tell him, Jesse. Maybe he overheard."

"Overheard you telling who?"

"I…well…" She stutters and stammers all over her words, withdrawing. "I don't know."

"You talked about it, did you? You talked about me and you in bed fucking after what happened to our daughters?"

She swallows. "Jesse—"

"Don't." I hold a halting hand up. Why I'm asking this after all these years, I don't know. I knew Sarah was the reason my parents knew what happened in the lead up to Rosie's death. After all, they called it. They warned me to stay away from her. And I didn't. But I didn't care that they knew because it gave them a reason to hate me. It gave them a reason to step away and leave me alone to waste the fuck away and slowly kill myself. No more confrontations. No more begging and pleading with me to be a better son.

They never asked you to be a better son, bro.

"Fuck," I bellow, kicking the gravel, making Sarah flinch. Stones ricochet off the paintwork of the Aston, the pinging sound pretty.

They asked you not to throw your life away. It was you who told yourself you were to blame. You who thought you were lesser than me. You who told yourself Mum and Dad didn't love you.

"Fuck, fuck, fuck!" I kick the side of the car, resting my hands on the roof and leaning in. I feel so fucking lucid. Seeing the world with new eyes, remembering the past differently. Sarah told them in an attempt to sever my relationship with them completely. So I would never leave The Manor. And it worked. I think I always knew it, but I never dared let my mind go there. Because I helped her achieve what she wanted and what I thought I needed. And she nearly achieved the same thing with Ava. Destroyed that relationship too. Why does she think that's love? *Fuck.* Will she *ever* let me go? "We're having twins," I say to the roof of the Aston. "Ava and I are having twins." *Another chance.* "You can be here, Sarah. Take what you need from The Manor, but me and you are done." I swing the door open, but before I can slip into the seat, a taxi pulls up around the fountain.

"It's Ava's brother," Sarah says, her voice undeniably wobbly. "I didn't have a chance to let you know I'd let him in." She walks off as Dan gets out of the cab. *The fucker.* I'm in no mood for him. And given he's broke, a taxi from the city is a bit extravagant. In fact, it screams desperation.

"And how are you going to pay for that?" I ask, making him stall as he pulls a card out of his pocket, his eyes studying me.

"With a credit card."

What am I doing? I haven't got time for this. I have somewhere I need to be. "I'm late," I say, getting behind the wheel.

"Wait, Jesse." Dan's soon by the passenger door, his face uncharacteristically pleading. I look up at him, and he sighs. "I'm fucked, okay? Totally fucking fucked."

"You want money from me?" I ask, astounded.

"I *need* money."

The fucking bastard. He treats me like scum and then has the audacity to come begging. *Lord, please, give me permission to lay the cheeky fucker out.* "You disrespect me, try to come between me and my *wife*, then you have the nerve to come here to my manor and ask me for money?"

"They want paying," he breathes quietly.

"Who?"

"The loan sharks."

I slowly get out of my car as I look at my wrist, conscious of the time. So it's not just legitimate borrowing he's defaulted on? "Dan, look at my face."

His eyes lift. Pathetic.

"Does it look like a face that gives a fuck?" I drop down to my seat and start the engine, revving it, taking my anger out on the Aston rather than Dan.

"They'll kill me," he says in between revs and, fuck my life, he has my attention. I look at him. Like, *really* look at him. I've seen desperation on a man before. Usually in the mirror.

I turn off the engine and get out. "Is that why you're here? In England?"

He nods.

"Do they know you're here?"

Another nod.

"Fuck." I pull my phone out and call John. "I need you to go get Ava from work. Her brother's turned up. He's"—I look at him, knowing it's with disdain—"in a spot of bother with some loan sharks."

"I've got a feeling this is going to be expensive," John rumbles, with zero humor. "I'm not far from her office."

"Thanks. Bring her here." I walk back into The Manor, Dan on my heels. "This way," I say over my shoulder, showing Dan to my office."

"It really is a stunning hotel."

"Yeah, let's not get into pointless small talk," I grunt, opening the door for him and letting him enter before I do. "Take a seat." I point to the chair opposite my desk and take my own. "How much?" I ask, cursing when my phone rings. I wouldn't answer, but it's Cook. "Give me a minute," I say, checking the desk is clear of anything Dan might see that could lead him to concluding my hotel isn't a hotel. "I've got to take this. Make yourself comfortable." I answer my mobile, leaving the room. "Cook?"

"Your car's been found."

"Where?"

"Abandoned at a waste site in the East End."

I keep walking, my mind in overdrive. I need some more fucking coffee. "So what happens now?" I make it to the bar and point to the coffee machine, and Mario gets straight on it.

"In light of the Van Der Haus news—"

"You mean the fact it couldn't be him." *Who the fuck was it?*

"The tracker's been deactivated. It's not had the license plates changed, been sold. Just abandoned. A two hundred grand car, abandoned."

My coffee slides toward me, and I pick it up, blowing off the steam. "I hear you, Cook," I breathe.

"This is someone with a vendetta."

"Right." I test my coffee and knock it back.

"I'll need all of the paperwork for your car. Registration, proof of purchase, insurance." *Which means I need to talk to Sarah.* "Today, please. Ava hasn't called me yet."

"She's at work."

"Can I suggest a bit of personal protection?"

I laugh to myself. That's been happening since I met her. "John's picking her up."

"I'm getting your car recovered. I'll get forensics on it. When can you do a statement?"

"I don't know. Tomorrow?"

"I'll come over in the morning. And Ava?"

"I'll see if she's free after work tomorrow." I place my phone down, along with my cup. *Fuck.*

"All right?"

I turn, surprised to see Drew. "Dandy," I mutter, waving a dismissive hand. "Are you? Sam said you're being weird." I mean, honestly, Drew's always a little bit weird.

I see his defences rise immediately, a scowl marring his perfect face. And then a hand rakes through his perfect hair. Have I touched a nerve? "I'm fine," he snaps, leaving the bar. Going off upstairs to fuck? I think it would possibly be Drew who'd suffer the most if I sold this place. The most after Sarah, anyway.

If I sold this place?

I grab my phone and go on the hunt for Sarah. "Hey, Pete, have you seen Sarah?" I ask, passing him in the hall. His eyes point up the stairs. But of course. It's past her working hours.

"Fucking hell," I mutter, calling her. No answer. So I climb the stairs, rounding the landing, looking at each and every door as I pass, hearing the sounds from inside. But she won't be in any of them. I reach the bottom of the next flight, looking up at the communal room doors. Take a breath.

I climb the steps with purpose and push my way in, and the familiar scent hits me now it's not empty. Sex. Drew's across the room, his shirt off, a woman with her legs open lying on a fur rug. He frowns at me in question. I wave him off and search the space. I don't see her first. I hear her. Or the thrash of her whip.

The salacious grin on her face as she inflicts immeasurable pain on the guy before her hits me hard. *Sadist.*

And I lose my breath for a second when something hits me.

Every man she's ever hurt...does she see me?

Me, for not loving her?

I swallow, feeling stifled, hot, uncomfortable. *Get what I need and get out.* I go over and interrupt her thrashing session, and she looks me up and down, twirling her whip. "Come back for more before you settle into daddy duties?" she purrs.

My nostrils flare. "I need something," I say, turning and walking straight back out.

I don't check to see if she's coming. I hear the heels of her leather thigh-highs following. I make it down the first flight. "The documents for my car, where will I find them?"

"In the wooden filing cabinet in the storeroom off the kitchen."

"Thanks." Carrying on down to the storeroom, I find four wooden filing cabinets and start rummaging through the first, pulling out files, papers, scanning them. Nothing vehicle related. I move onto the next, scratching through every tab, searching for anything to indicate I'm on the right track. Nothing.

Not long later, all four cabinets are empty, all the papers at my feet. "For fuck's sake."

"What the hell?" Sarah appears at the door. "Jesus, Jesse, I just sorted all of that out."

"Go back upstairs," I order shortly. "Ava's brother's in my office, and the last thing I need is him seeing you dressed like that." Or, God help me, Ava turning up and seeing her. "And Ava will be here soon, so you need to fuck off."

She huffs her disbelief, remaining at the door.

"I can't fucking find them," I grate, pointing to the chaos on the floor. Sarah shakes her head in exasperation and starts cleaning up the mess I've made, then she hands me what I'm looking for. I know it would have only been seconds had I not gone in like a bull. "I need these scanning and emailing to me." I shove them back into her leather-clad chest and leave. "Do it when I've gone home," I mutter, getting back to dealing with Ava's brother. The news of his imminent, potential death changes things slightly. I might think he's a first-class cunt, but my wife loves the rogue. Which leaves me no choice but to help him.

I walk in and find him sitting on the couch browsing through one of the magazines. "Superbikes," he says. "Do you ride?"

"How much?" I ask, lowering to the couch, making Dan slowly close the magazine, well aware I'm not into any chitchat.

"One fifty."

"I assume we're not talking in hundreds."

He shakes his head. "One hundred and fifty thousand."

"Is that including all of the outstanding debts here in the UK?"

"You've been looking into me?"

"Yes, I looked into you, Dan. Credit cards, loans, car finance. You changed your attitude toward me like the wind. Suddenly, you want to be all pally? Suddenly, the Australian dream is being forgotten so you can kick your heels around London with endless debt collecting agencies chasing you?"

"How did you get that information?"

And now he's hostile again? *Prick*. I won't expose Cook. "How much? Total."

"The loan shark is one hundred," he breathes, relenting. "The other fifty is for my debts here."

"One hundred grand? No wonder they want to kill you." Wish I could fucking let them. I shake my head, exhaling. "How the fuck does a man get into that level of debt?"

He sighs, rubbing at his forehead. Oh, he's stressed? "It was an opportunity I couldn't miss."

"To be turned over?" I ask, laughing.

"The surf school," he grates, unimpressed. Oh, he'd better be massively impressed with me right now. Forevermore, in fact.

"Go on."

"Carlos had the money he needed to get the equipment, the licences, the staff, and building. But I wanted in. It was a no-brainer. But I was kind of at the end of my rope with handouts from Mum and Dad, *and* credit. I met a guy in a bar one night. An investor. He gave me the number of somewhere to get cash fast with little questions." He smiles meekly, obviously embarrassed. "They asked no questions. Neither did I."

"Like payment terms," I say quietly. The dumb fuck. "Or interest rates."

"I handed the money over to Carlos."

"In cash?" I ask, astounded, and he nods, albeit reluctantly. "Jesus Christ."

"And that was the last I saw of him."

"I've met some stupid men in my time," I say, getting up and fetching some water. "But you, Dan, win the award for superior stupidity." Fuck me, I'm staggered. So he wasn't living the dream in Australia at all. He was actually living a fucking nightmare.

"I need to pay them," he says, pulling my alert attention his way.

Pay them before they find him. Or maybe they'll find Ava. And suddenly, I'm wondering—

Fuck, do I need to be thinking along those lines? No, it couldn't be. If they stole my car, they would have kept it. It would *more* than cover his debt. "How do they want paying?" I ask.

"An offshore account." He pulls out his phone, some cheap pay-as-you-go crap, and starts firing numbers my way.

"Hold up," I say, going to my desk and plucking a pen out of the pot before pulling open the drawers to find a pad. "Go again," I say, jotting down the details of the offshore account. "And your details?" I ask, noting them down as he reels off his bank details. "So one hundred to the sharks, fifty to your personal account?"

"Yeah," he says, quiet.

I drop the pen and look at him. "I'm adding another fifty thousand."

He recoils. "Why?"

"Because you're going to get on that plane and fuck off back to

428 This Woman Forever

Australia and do what you've told your family you've been doing. Because *that* will make your sister happy. And if your sister is happy, so am I." I quickly send a text to John telling him to take Ava to the bar—the last thing I need is her storming my office. I don't want to throw her brother under the bus. I just want him gone.

"Thanks," he says, holding his hand over the desk.

I look at it. Don't take it. "I'm going to assume your arsehole behavior and attitude toward me since the day we've met was because of the stresses you've been dealing with in your life." I know I'm wrong. He was born an arsehole. I don't know how. His parents are decent, and Ava's...placid? I laugh to myself. Hardly. But she's got a good heart. Being the better man, I accept his offered hand. "Please stay out of our marriage."

He nods, letting me do all the shaking. "Understood."

"And I might grant you the grace of being in our kids' lives." *Here's your first test, O'Shea. Don't fail—the money's not in the bank yet.* I need fucking Sarah for that.

His lips become straight, his eyes narrowed but questioning. "Are you planning on having kids?"

"She's pregnant." I rest back in my seat. "It's twins."

Poor fuck looks like he's gonna fall off his chair. I can see the endless retorts swirling around in his head, the accusations, the judgments. Question is, will he voice them? "Congratulations," he says quietly, without any sincerity.

"Thanks. We're thrilled, as you can imagine." I glance at my watch. "You can go now." Ava will be here soon, and I have no faith she'll listen to John when he tells her to wait in the bar. Plus, it's getting busy out there. "I'll call you a cab," I say, putting a call in, hoping there's one nearby that'll get him out of my face pronto. I'm in luck. "Ten minutes. I'll walk you out." I don't even get a chance to engage my muscles to stand. The door swings open and there she is, my wife, her dark eyes batting back and forth between her brother and me. *Fuck it.* I slap on a smile and throw Dan a warning look. She can't know anything, and I'm sure Dan agrees.

"Dan?" she says, as he slowly rids his face of any hostility and beams from ear to ear, turning in his chair. "What are you doing here?"

"Hey, kiddo." He's up fast and embracing her. "Congratulations."

Her eyes widen over his shoulder, before narrowing on me. "I might get to tell someone myself soon."

"I love you," I mouth, and she rolls her eyes.

"So what are you doing here?" She's asking Dan, but her accusing eyes are asking me. Won't tell. So I shrug, blasé, acting as surprised as she is that her brother is standing in my office in my sex club. And that there is part of her concern. No need. Dan's leaving, and I'm pretty sure he's not coming back anytime soon.

"Making amends," Dan says, and I nod, impressed. "I didn't want to go home without sorting this out."

"So you're friends?" she says, asking Dan again, but looking at me.

"Something like that," he replies. I laugh under my breath. *Nothing* like that. "Anyway, I need to shoot." *Yes, fuck off.* "I'm meeting Harvey up west." Leaving his sister still looking a bit bemused, he nods his appreciation. I can tell it kills him. "Thanks."

"No problem."

"When are you heading back?" Ava asks, dragging her markedly accusing glare from me and softening it when she's facing her brother. Of course, I'm the villain.

"I'm not sure. Depends on flights. I'll call you, okay?" He doesn't hang around, skirting past Ava after giving her a chaste kiss. He encounters John outside the door. The big man doesn't look happy as Dan edges past his imposing body.

"What was all that about?" Of course, Ava's on my case the moment the door closes.

"What?" I ask, quickly texting John to let him know a taxi is on its way.

"Look at me," she demands shortly, pulling my astounded gaze up as I click send and set my phone down. Superb. So her brother's a cunt, and I'm picking up the wrap *and* the bill. "Why was Dan here?"

"He apologized."

She laughs, condescending as fuck, as I swipe up my phone when it lights up with a text. The new wall is finished. Great. "I don't believe you."

I stand. Let's get out of here. "That makes me sad, baby." It really does. Why does she push? She'll be distraught if she knew what actually went down. I wish she'd trust me. "Now, tell me," I say, sweeping in with a swift change of subject. "What did Patrick say?" Van Der Haus may be out of that frame but, again, I'm wary. And I suddenly remember the last contact I had with him. I told him to back off.

Now why would I do that?

Exactly.

So I will continue to be cautious where Van Der Haus is concerned. Ava's quickly uncomfortable as I wait for an answer.

"You've not told him, have you?" I ask. How many times has she promised to sever all work ties with the Danish prick and not followed through? What, is she scared? Worried she'll upset her boss? Worried he'll fire her? "Ava?"

"He wasn't in the office," she rushes to explain, her hand fiddling madly. "But he will be tomorrow, so I'll speak to him then."

Nope. She's had endless opportunities. I've held back. Time is up. "Too late, lady. You've had your chance. Again and again and again."

"That's not fair. I told Mikael I won't be working with him anymore, so you can't say I'm not trying to resolve this."

Wait. "You did what?" She's spoken to Van Der Haus?

"I don't think he drugged me, Jesse," she says, hurrying over her words. "He said he wanted me, so why would he hurt me?"

I gape at her, stunned. He told her, actually *told* her, that he wants her? "What the fucking hell are you doing talking to him?" My fists ball, my body leaning forward of its own volition.

"He knows that you've..." Her lips twitch, she bites the bottom corner, then she has her hand at her mouth, getting more nervous by the second. She knows. She knows talking to Van Der Haus was a mistake. "Entertained other women while we've been together."

The fuckhead. There's only one way Van Der Haus would know I'd betrayed Ava, and I'm hoping Ava doesn't click. "We agreed never to speak of that again." Could this day get any worse?

A steely façade falls across her face, telling me things are about to get spiky. "It's hard when people keep reminding me of it," she retorts. "How does he know?"

Fuck. My mind circles, frantically searching for a viable answer as she studies me, waiting.

Slowly figuring out for herself that Van Der Haus's ex-wife was one of the women during those horrendous four days.

"She was one of them, wasn't she?" she eventually says, so calm.

God damn it. God damn Freja. God damn me. I take a moment, scrambling for air and reason as she stands up. She's leaving? Holding my breath, I get ready to seize her, stop her, go after her. But she comes closer, leaning over the desk toward me. "You said months," she grates. "You said you hadn't been with her for *months*, that you didn't understand why she was suddenly sniffing around. You've slept with her more than once too." She states it all as the facts she knows them to be, and I wilt, beaten.

"I didn't want to upset you," I growl, mentally doubling the pain I'm going to put Van Der Haus through.

She huffs mildly, a sneer on her lip. "Tell me," she says, her words steady and strong. "Did you call them up and have them make a queue outside your door?"

"No, they hear I'm on the drink and they're like flies around shit." Sarah was the one who let them in.

"I hate you," she seethes, and I flinch, injured.

"No, you don't," I say softly.

"Yes," she counters. "I do."

And I fucking hate me too, baby. "Don't make my heart crack, Ava. Does it matter who it was?"

"No, what matters is that you lied to me."

"I was protecting you."

"And it's hilarious that every single time you do that, you end up hurting me."

I wouldn't say hilarious. More tragic. "I know."

"So, have you learnt?" she asks, head tilted.

Learnt to be honest about *everything*? Not lie? There's only one answer. Even if it's the wrong answer. "Every fucking day." I reach for her jaw, squeezing so her lips pucker. "I'm sorry." For that, and for what's to come. Always fucking sorry.

"Good," she says, her eyes falling to my mouth. She's read my mind. I wet my lips, skating my eyes over her face. Fuck, after the day I've had, all I can think about is getting inside her and finding some peace and clarity.

"How did this happen?" she whispers, her eyes alive.

"Because, my beautiful girl," I say quietly, my heart throbbing, along with my dick, "we're meant to be stuck together. Constant contact. Kiss me."

"I've accepted that you're an arsehole, so there's no need to try and get me submitting to your touch now."

I smile secretly. "I missed you, baby."

She takes the quickest route to me, and that's over my desk. Fine by me. I help her, feeling at home with every one of her limbs wrapped around me, her lips on mine, kissing me hard. It's a familiar kiss. It's the same kiss she gave me on the night of the anniversary party after she'd overheard some ladies of The Manor discussing my bedroom skills. *Possessive. Ownership.* My wife's giving me a run for my money these days. "I wish you were pure and untouched," she whispers, sadness tinging the words, her mouth relentless.

I lower to the chair, breaking away from her attack with some effort. "I am." I smile at her flushed cheeks, taking her hands, feeling her rings. "The most important part of me is untouched." I put her palm on my chest and let it absorb the pounds. *Life.* "Or it was until you stepped into my office." That day. I wish I could relive it. The instant shift in my chest, my eyes opening for what felt like the first time in years. "Now it's being stamped all over and is exploding with pure love for *you.*" *Only you, baby. Never doubt that.*

She exhales, satisfied, watching her hand stroke my chest. "I like feeling it beating," she whispers, wistful. Her head is soon on my chest, and I smile down at her. "I like hearing it too."

I relax, content with her close, but a little uncomfortable in the groin area. "How was your day?" I ask.

"Crap," she answers quickly. "I want Paradise."

That's sweet. "I'm in Paradise whenever I'm with you," I say, stroking her hair, kissing it, over and over. "I don't need a villa." Just peace.

"You were more relaxed in Paradise."

"I'm relaxed now."

"Yes, that is because I'm sitting on your lap, coated in you," she quips. She's right. But I still poke her tickle spot, and she laughs, breaking out of my hold, grinning at me as she turns herself around on my lap. And once again, I'm amazed by her grace. I should have told her who was involved during that four-day absence. There are many things I *should* have done. And shouldn't have.

"How was *your* day?" she asks, leaning back so I can settle my face close to hers.

"Long." I won't bore her—or worry her—with the never-ending details. I need to figure out how I handle the coming days while Cook investigates. I also need to have a *word* with Van Der Haus. "How are my peanuts?"

"Fine."

Good. Let's get her home so I can share my new office feature wall and then fix the persistent problem behind my trousers. I engage to lift us from the chair. "Why's my brother's name written down there?"

I freeze, every muscle tensing. *Shit.* I see her reach for the pad on my desk, and out of impulse—and stupidity—I snatch it away, stuffing it in the drawer and slamming it shut. *Shit, shit, shit.* "Daniel Joseph O'Shea?" she asks. "Why have you got Dan's bank account number written down?"

"I haven't." *Idiot.*

Ava quickly stands, drilling accusing holes into me. "I'm giving you three seconds, Ward."

"The countdown is mine," I snap, at a loss.

"Three." She holds up her middle fingers in front of me. What, does she think I can't count? "Two," she says, dropping one finger, confirming it. I mentally roll my eyes. For fuck's sake. "You're giving him money," she gasps, her hand dropping.

Fuck. "No." Bollocks, why the hell did I leave that pad right there for her to see?

"You're a shit liar too, Ward," Ava hisses, bolting, catching me on the back foot.

"Ava!" I yell, scrambling up and running round my desk. "Ava, wait." I make it to the corridor and see her disappear through the summer room, her hair wafting as she runs full pelt. "Jesus," I breathe, going after her, hoping John's got Dan in that taxi already. I pull out my phone to text her brother—just to give him the heads-up, because she *will* call him—but I'm too late. Dan's still in the hallway, looking around.

Interested.

Fuck.

I lift Ava from her feet and turn her to face me, needing her to see my aggravation. "For fuck's sake, woman, you'll give the babies brain damage. No running."

"Get a grip," she snaps, fighting me off.

I don't like what I'm looking at. John, awkward. Dan, curious.

"If this is a hotel," he says, focusing on me. "Then where's the reception area?"

"What?" I snap, throwing him all the warning I can muster, willing him to be wise and fuck off.

"Where do your guests pick up the keys to their rooms?" he asks, turning his eyes onto John. "And why the need to have a gorilla escorting me everywhere?"

A gorilla? The dirty, insolent prick. Every modicum of my being is demanding I pound his arse and then let John have a go too. But, give me strength, I can't do that to Ava. So I motion back toward my office, urging Dan to take this away from the public areas of The Manor.

But Dan isn't looking at me to catch my gesture. His eyes are on the stairs, and Ava has become stiff under my hand on her back. And then I realize why.

Oh…Jesus.

Sam and Kate descend the stairs, wrapped up in each other—literally—laughing, touching, kissing. They're clearly not done, so why the fuck didn't they stay behind closed doors?

I feel Ava nudge me, and I look down at her as she stares up the stairs in horror. What does she expect me to do? Press rewind?

"I think we need to invest in one of those dildos," Sam says, feeling out Kate's arse, his face in her neck.

"Oh!" Kate giggles as they reach the bottom, still oblivious. My mate slips his hand between Kate's legs. *Fuck my life.* "Sam!" Kate throws her head back as Sam flings her over his arm, and then she sees us. Me first. I smile, eyebrows raised, as John grunts and Ava remains stock-still, in a state of shock and dread. These two. They're like a walking fucking advertisement for The Manor.

Kate's eyes finally find Dan. Widen. Then she shoots up and makes a pathetic, pointless attempt to compose herself.

"Hotel?" Dan asks, looking Kate up and down, before his eyes drift up the stairs. I can hear the background noise from some of the rooms. The odd whip. A distant scream. "Do you often let your friends carry on like this in your establishment?"

"Dan," Ava says, moving away from me. Oh no. I pull her straight back. She is *not* pacifying this fuckhead.

"I think you should come back to my office," I say, pointing back.

"No, thanks." He snorts, his full attention on Kate. I silently will him not to turn this into something nasty. "You're whoring it up at a brothel?"

"What the fuck?" Sam yells. "Who the fuck do you think you're talking to?"

"This is no brothel," Kate says, pulling Sam back. "And I'm no whore."

Enough. Has this prick forgotten I've just saved his skin? Would be a shame if I had to kill him ten minutes later. I go to Dan, my lip definitely curled, and move in close, placing a firm palm on his neck, applying just enough pressure to make him wonder if I could snap it. "Get your sorry, pathetic arse in my office," I whisper in his ear, feeling him stiffen. "Or I'll call the sharks myself and let them know where the fishes are swimming."

I step back, head tilted, and Dan wisely walks away, me following. I stall when I hear the telltale signs of Ava's heels on the marble. "Wait for me in the bar, baby," I say, pointing her in the right direction.

"I'd like to come," she says, but I can tell from her tone she knows she's trying her luck.

"You'll stay put." I pick her up, take her to the bar, and place her on a stool, pressing a pacifying kiss on her cheek before leaving her, fucking fuming as I pace to my office. Like I need Dan and his fucking dramas at my door. "Sit," I order, when I stride into my office, finding Dan in the middle of the room.

"I can't be—"

"It's not your turn to talk, Dan," I say, pulling my tails out aggressively and dumping my arse down, my hands on the desk. "This is The Manor, the most elite sex sanctuary in the country. There are over one and half thousand members, from all walks of life, but with one thing in common. They're loaded. Have to be to afford the forty-five-grand-a-year membership fee." He can't contain his shock. "Add the bar takings and restaurant, I have myself quite the tidy business here." *A business that's paying off your colossal debts.* "Throw in the building, my penthouse on St. Katherine Docks, and my villa in Spain, your sister and your soon-to-be-born nieces or nephews are going to be *well* looked after. But my money and how I've made it is fucking irrelevant, because what's most important to me is your sister's health and happiness. Don't fuck with her happiness, Dan, I'm warning you." He blinks, a little stunned, a little indignant. "And I'm sure you'll agree, this doesn't need to be mentioned to Elizabeth and Joseph. It would be a shame if the sharks turned up, jaws snapping."

"I think you've made your point."

"Good. I'll get the money transferred to the relevant accounts."

Ava flies into the room, and I sink into my chair. "Why are you taking money from Jesse?" she demands, furious, as Dan stares at me across the desk. I make sure he sees the message in my cool expression. "Are you going to answer me?"

"Ava, I told you to stay put." I sigh.

"I'm not talking to you."

I snort, as Dan's eyebrows fly up. "Well, I'm talking to you."

"Shut up," she hisses, nudging Dan in the back. "You're keeping quiet. Have you nothing to say?"

"See what I have to deal with?" I mutter, absorbing the impact of her fierce scowl.

"Speak," she orders, smacking Dan's shoulder. "What's going on?"

I don't know why he's looking at me. I can't save him, and after his obnoxious performance out there, I don't want to. *Have at him, baby.* "I'm broke," he grates, jaw rolling, his pride taking another hit. "Jesse's agreed to help me out."

"You asked?"

"No, he offered," he says, eyes still on me. That's a slight stretch of the truth, but I expect he'd happily share the fact that I told him to fuck off back to Australia and never come back—making this money more of a bribe—so I let him have it. "And there were no strings attached. Until ten minutes ago."

"You're bribing my brother?" Ava gasps. "You've paid him to keep quiet?"

"No," I breathe. "I've lent him some money and added a little clause to the contract at a later date."

"What about the surf school?" she asks, making Dan shrink and me laugh under my breath. "And why haven't you asked Mum and Dad? They would've lent you some money."

I look at my wife, sympathetic. I like Joseph a lot, respect him, but we all know the level of Dan's fuck-ups are way past his ability to fix.

"We're not talking a few quid, Ava." Dan drops his gaze, shame creeping up. "I'm up to my eyeballs. I've got myself a massive loan to fund my share of the business and my partner did a runner with it. I'm fucked."

"Why didn't you say anything?"

"Why do you think? I was turned over, Ava. I have nothing left."

She looks at me, her eyes sad and full of concern. Which is exactly why I wanted her away from this mess. "How much?" she asks. *Fuck.* "Five thousand? Ten thousand?" *Jesus fucking Christ.* "Tell me."

"Just a few," Dan blurts.

He's fucking hoping. She wants specifics. "Jesse?" she questions.

"I'm sorry, Dan," I breathe, pushing my fingertips into my temples. He may not believe it, but I truly am. Not for him. Only for Ava. "I'm not lying to her. Two hundred, baby."

Her head recoils, her body jerks, and she starts to wobble before my eyes. I'm out of my chair like a bullet. "Damn it, Ava," I hiss, steadying her. "Are you okay? Are you dizzy?" She looks dizzy. "Do you want to sit down?"

"Two hundred thousand?" she gasps. "What sort of bank lends two hundred thousand?" Color rises in her face, and despite knowing it's rage, I'm glad to see it. Color draining might mean passing out. "I'm fine," she barks, her cheeks flaming red, her hands fighting me off.

"Don't push me away, Ava," I warn, guiding her to a chair and getting her arse on it. She might not look like she's going to faint, but she's not heard the whole tale yet. "Don't be getting your knickers in a twist, lady," I snap, throwing Dan a dark look. "It's not healthy."

"My blood pressure is fine. Two hundred thousand? No bank in their right mind would lend that sort of money for a surf school."

"No, you're right," Dan's mutters. "A loan shark would, though."

"Oh my God." She covers her face with her hands. "What were you thinking?"

"I wasn't thinking, Ava."

"Is that the only reason you came home?" she asks, a certain edge of hurt in her words. Her older brother, her hero, her friend. He's let her down.

So it's a damn good job I'm in her life. And Dan's for that matter, or he'd be dead.

"They're looking for me. You don't get away with non-payment with these types."

"You said you were doing well," she says in disbelief. "Just stay here. Don't go back."

I knew she'd say that.

Dan's face softens. It's a new look on him, and only for his sister. "Ava, if I don't go back, they will come here. I've already been warned, and I believe it. I'm not putting Mum, Dad or you at risk a—"

I cough on nothing. Is he for real? He's already put them at risk, just by coming home. Dan looks at me, awkward. *Yes, be ashamed.* "These people are dangerous, Ava."

I work my hand into Ava's back, trying to loosen the tightness. It works, and she looks up at me. I fucking hate the despair and disappointment I see. "You can't just deposit that kind of money into a bank account," she says quietly, as if she doesn't want her brother to hear her concern for me. "Isn't it laundering? I don't want you involved, Jesse."

"Do you honestly think I'd do anything to put you and my babies at risk? I'm transferring enough money into Dan's account to get him back to Australia." *And a little extra to keep him there.* "I have the details of an offshore account where I'll transfer the two hundred." I'm not breaking this down for her. I'm not telling her I'm giving him more than he owes to keep him away from us. "They won't know where the money has come from, baby. I wouldn't do it otherwise."

"Really?" she asks, uncertain.

"Really. There are ways. Trust me."

"Okay." She accepts my kiss, relaxing for the first time since she stormed my office. "Thank you."

"Don't thank me."

"Have *you* thanked my husband?" she asks Dan, hostile.

"Of course. I never asked, Ava." How many times is he going to say that? Like it might save him from disgrace if he believes his family thinks he didn't ask me to get him out of the shit. "Your husband's been doing some digging." And then he throws *me* under the bus?

"Has he?" Ava asks, looking at me. "Have you?"

"I know a man in the shit, Ava," I say, insulted. If he fires one more bullet, I'm out. He can go it alone.

"Oh." She looks knackered all of a sudden. I'm with her. "Can we go home?"

"I'm sorry. I've neglected you." I glare at Dan as I get Ava up, making sure he knows I hold him responsible.

"I'm fine, just tired." She goes to her brother and gives him a hug he doesn't deserve. "When are you leaving?"

"Tonight. They'll be on their way over if I'm not back by Thursday," he says, rising from his chair. "So I guess this is goodbye for a while."

"You weren't going to tell me you were leaving?"

"I would have called you, kiddo." Dan looks at me, his expression impassive. "I'm not your favorite man anymore."

Damn right you're not.

"Now, fuck off," I breathe to myself, moving in and collecting Ava.

"Take care," she says.

"Can I?" Dan points to my arms around Ava's belly, locking her to my body.

No. "Sure." I hand her over with great reluctance and let them have their moment.

"Look after her," Dan says, his eyes on me as he presses his lips to Ava's forehead. And he still plays the fucking game.

I take my wife back, confirm I'll send the payment, and warn him not to kick off when he leaves.

And he goes, his walk as cocky as I know him to be, even now. I hold on to Ava for a few more minutes, let her have a moment, before coaxing her around in my arms. "Ready to go home?" I ask, brushing her hair back from her face with both hands and holding her cheeks as I kiss her nose.

"Yeah," she says quietly, deflated. I hope I can improve her mood when I show her my surprise. It's been a bad day for both of us, and there's only one cure.

The bubble.

Or Ava Cloud Nine.

"Come." I take her hand, collect her bag, and walk us out. John gives me the nod as I pass, and Sarah looks up from her gin at the bar. "I need a word with Sarah," I say to Ava.

"I'll wait in the car."

"No, you don't have to wait in the car," I explain, seeing her throw a contemptuous scowl Sarah's way.

"Yes, I really do," Ava replies, taking her bag from my hand and leaving. I watch her go, contemplative. I don't want to say all of our problems will disappear with the absence of The Manor from our lives, but a good chunk of them would. I breathe out, backing up to the bar.

"How did it go with Ava's brother?" Sarah asks.

"There's some bank details and instructions on the pad in my top right drawer," I say, keeping it business only. "Let me know when the funds are transferred. And email the paperwork I've requested ASAP."

"Of course."

"Thanks." I leave Sarah, everything heavy as I walk out of the bar.

"Jesse?" she calls, prompting me to look back. The moment I see her expression, I know I won't like what she's going to say. So I don't give her a chance to say it, carrying on my way, following Ava.

Sarah is my past.

Ava is my forever.

I'll always follow Ava.

Chapter 41

"You won't be able to carry me soon." She sounds sullen. Tired. I'll soon wake her up.

"Don't worry, lady." She's stuck to my front like glue as I walk us into my office. My stomach's doing flips. Will she like it? Think it's totally fucking weird. Because, I mean, it's a lot of Ava. "I've already increased the weights I'm lifting in preparation."

"Hey," she grumbles as I lower her, hanging on to my hair, ensuring I can't straighten back up. At her mercy. *Always*.

"You're a savage." I chuckle. "Are you going to let go?"

"Say sorry," she demands.

"Sorry. I'm sorry. Let go." My hair is freed, and she kicks her shoes off, breathing out her tiredness.

"Why are we in your office?"

"I wanted to show you something."

"What?" Eyeing me, she tilts her head, my fidgeting obvious. I look at the wall again. A *lot* of Ava. "What's up with you?"

"Turn around," I order before I bottle it, stepping back and bracing myself for my wife's reaction to my homage to her. Christ, it really is a lot.

She turns away from me, I start chewing my lip, and the moment her shoulders lift and she steps back, I step forward so she meets my chest.

Surprise, I think, releasing my lip when I bite down a little too hard. What does she think?

I watch her, pensive, as her head slowly turns from one side to the other, taking in the entire expanse of wallpaper. It looks incredible. Just as I imagined. If she doesn't like it, then she shouldn't have left the wall blank when she did the designs on this place. It was so obviously meant to be full of her. And besides, it's my office, so my rules.

She walks toward one of my favorite pictures. And, if I'm realistic, probably one of *the* weirdest. "That was the first one I took," I say, biting back down on my lip. "It became a bit of an obsession after that." Just like she did. She faces me briefly, her face a picture of...what is that?

Shock? Amazement? Horror?

Shit, I don't know. I back up to my desk and pluck a marker out of a pot as Ava walks the length of the wall, taking it all in. I'm sure she agrees. A *lot*. "Here," I say, winning her attention. "I want you to sign it."

She frowns down at the pen in my hand, tentatively reaching to take it. "Sign it with my name?" she asks, curiously amused.

"Yes, wherever."

She laughs, and it's a light wispy sound of utter disbelief. But she moves in, removing the lid and lifting the pen to the wall, homing in on the first picture I ever took of her. She writes, stands back for a few moments, and then searches out another image, moving in on that. Curious, I get closer to the wall so I can read her words. I breathe in. She's not signed it. It's so much more than that.

Today I met you.
This day was the beginning of the rest of my life.
From this moment, I was your Ava x

Fuck. I swallow down the lump in my throat, reaching for my neck and rubbing there, as Ava finishes writing on her second picture. The one I took on the docks the night she stopped fighting it.

Today I realized how in deep I was.

Jesus, I don't think I'll ever truly comprehend how deep I'm in. It's fucking bottomless. Every time I think I couldn't love her more, I wake up, and…I do.

And I wanted to be so much deeper with you.

I sniff discreetly, smiling to myself. There it is in black and white. A confession. She *wanted* to be in deep. I won't ask her why the fuck she resisted for so long. We're here now. Married. Pregnant.

Ava moves onto another picture, and I move with her, reading the one she's just written on. This is fun. Way more fun than I thought it was going to be and, thank God, my wife doesn't think I'm a weirdo.

Today I learnt that you can dance.

Yeah, baby, I can dance.

I also admitted to myself that I was in love with you, and I think I might have told you too.

Yep, she did. It was one of the most frustrating times in our relationship, especially the days that followed. She was absolutely legless.

Next.

Today I found out that I'm just for your eyes.

I snort quietly. Where is that jumper? I haven't seen it since I forced Ava into it. I hitch a brow. Did she cut it up? I move close to one of Ava's naked back, inhaling. That day. Fuck, it was intense.

Today I learnt that I'm for your touch and for your pleasure only.

Correct.

But my favorite part of today was when you told me that you love me.

I liked that part too. But my favorite was when I fucked a confession of love from her. Ava moves onto a picture of her in the Ritz, and I read the words by the picture of her handcuffed to the bed. The Retribution Fuck. A firm favorite, although shelved for the foreseeable.

Today I found out how old you are...

I scowl at the back of her head. What a horrific day.

... and that you don't like being handcuffed.

Positively hate it. Onto the next. I breathe in when she moves in on an image of her on the veranda in Paradise, and she's there a while, thinking, lifting the pen away, taking it back to the wall. Then, eventually, she moves back, clicking the lid back on.

Today I decided that you're right. We will be okay.
And yes, I do have a bump...ish, and I love you for giving it to me.
I'll always love you.
End of.

This is like my therapy wall. Everything I need to keep me going, and a massively useful tool to support me through my withdrawals when she might not be around. I start reading them again, storing them to memory, our own small love story emblazoned across my office wall.

Small story?

Epic story.

"I'm done," she says.

I come out of my daze and find her looking up at me, a small smile on her face as she holds up the pen. I eye it, thinking. Then take it and move in on the first picture.

Today my heart started beating again, I write, feeling it now, hammering in my chest. *Today you became mine.*

I move away, not looking at Ava. Can't. This wall has gone from being a lovely, decorative—slightly obsession-taming—showpiece, to our life in pictures and words. I scan the photographs, wishing I could add more now, even though there are dozens. Maybe I'll have the wall behind my desk done too. I spot another favorite of her in her wedding dress, sitting on the lawn. I smile and move in, my teeth sinking into my lip as I draw a perfect halo-shaped circle over her head.

I refrain from adding two horns too.

My girl is definitely a perfect blend of angelic and devilish, but somehow, I don't think she'll agree.

My beautiful girl.
My defiant temptress.
My lady.
My angel.
My Ava.

I slip the end of the pen into my mouth, chewing, looking across the rest of the photographs, wondering what else will be added to this wall over the years. If we move, it's coming. I'll have it preserved. Whatever it takes. It's my new favorite thing. Aside from my wife and babies, of course. Today has been a shitter. It's improved immensely.

It's not how you start. It's how you finish.

The pen is suddenly missing from between my teeth, courtesy of Ava, and she attaches herself to my front. "Ava," I breathe, clenching her bum cheeks in my palms, "today has been the longest fucking day of my life."

She must take those words as code for *rip my clothes off,* because my jacket is suddenly halfway down my arms and she's kissing me like she might not ever get the chance again.

"Easy," I say, helping her get it off, still managing to hold her in my arms. "What's the rush?"

"It's been too long," she murmurs around my lips. Fuck, it's been way too long. My dick punches against the fly of my trousers as I pry Ava from my body to set her down, ripping my tie off and dipping to get out of my shoes. "Take your dress off."

It's on the floor in a heartbeat—she's not fucking about—but she doesn't come at me, instead feeling her tummy, caught in a moment of wonder.

I rest my hand over hers. "Incredible, isn't it?" I dip and slip my hands under her bum, and her thighs split, scissoring my waist.

"Just like you." Her eyes are fixed on my mouth, watering.

"And you."

"Show me how incredible you are," she whispers huskily, pushing her body into mine. "I've forgotten." Her lips hover teasingly over mine, and I catch them, moaning, dropping my head back, blindly walking us out of my office to the sofa and laying her over the arm so her hips are high, allowing me to stand or kneel between her legs. I drop my trousers, kick them off with my boxers, and watch in satisfaction as her eyes drop to my arousal. I kneel, peeling her knickers off. Oh God. My mouth waters, my eyes flicking up to see her back bowing on the couch, anticipating my first kiss on her flesh. I start on her thigh, then the other, firm, long kisses, working my way up.

She breathes my name, squirms, her legs kick, her arms flail, trying to grip something that isn't there. She settles on my head, pushing me into her, wanting more friction.

"Have you remembered how incredible I am?" I breathe across her pulsing pussy, as she cries out repeatedly. Here we go. I lick my lips, place my palms on the insides of her thighs and push her legs apart, moving in, flicking my tongue teasingly.

"Shit!"

"Mouth, Ava," I warn, licking from back to front in one firm lash.

"Oh my God!"

I push my tongue deeply inside her, circle, hum.

"Jesse!"

She's getting frantic, her movements uncontrolled and chaotic. "Incredible?" I ask, my ears drowned by the sounds of her pleasure. "Tell me how it feels, baby." I wince when she yanks my hair, then slip my fingers through my mouth and into her pussy, and her body arches, her hands diving into her own hair and pulling. I work her with my fingers and mouth, looking up her body, wondering if there's a vision better than watching my wife come. I don't think there is.

But then she props herself up and watches me working her and, suddenly, there's a better vision. "Tell me," I press, wiping my mouth on her thigh, pushing a palm onto her stomach to keep her down.

"It feels like you were made to fit me."

Correct. Standing, I take her under her thighs, smiling when she props herself up with her palms wedged into the couch behind her. She wants to see this. My hand wraps around my girth, the pulse against my palm strong, and I brush the very tip across her sodden flesh, bracing myself to enter her. Her legs hooked around my waist try to bring me closer, her breathing becoming more strained as I tease us both. The parted lips of her pussy give me perfect sight to her swollen clit, the small piece of flesh thrumming, her opening pulsing too.

"Shall we try penetration?" I ask, mesmerized by the vision before me.

"If you like," she whispers, her words blasé, but her tone full of lust. Of desperation.

"If I like?" I ask, slipping inside a fraction, suppressing my grunt, the muscles of her walls tempting me in farther, squeezing me. "What about if *you* like?" I raise a brow, fascinated by the pumping of her chest, the shaking of her arms, the sheen of desire coating her face. *Ravenous.* One more inch. *Jesus Christ.* I reach for the lace cups of her bra and pull them down, and her boobs pop free, calling for some time. Each one gets a firm tweak, bringing her nipples to solid points, and Ava growls deep in her throat, her lips pressed together to stop her yelling. "My beautiful girl is trying to play it cool." She's so stubborn. *Scream for me, baby.* I get myself into position. "It's a shame she's shit at feigning casualness." I drive in to the hilt, and her head flops back, the moans she's been restraining leaving her body. "That's more like it." I hit her deep and hold still, taking a precious moment to gather myself. "Show a bit of appreciation, Ava." A bolt of pleasure catches me off guard, and my hips shoot forward of their own volition, hitting her deep and high.

"Again," she moans, thrusting her tits up, every inch of her begging. I love it when she begs. "Again."

"That depends."

"On what?" she asks. "You said it doesn't always need to be hard." She's right, I did. But it's been a while since it's been a little rough, and now I'm happy with the information I've sourced, I can relax a little. Just a little. "Then you do this to me. Have you finally read the part of the book that confirms you won't hurt the babies?"

I smile. She knows me too well. "Yes." I withdraw and thrust hard, forcing her to fall to her back on a delighted cry. "It's a good book."

"It's a good book now," she pants.

"It was always a good book, but it did say you must listen to your body." I'm in my stride now, driving in and out, the pleasure divine.

"I'm listening," she gasps, writhing. "And it's saying harder."

Oh? "The babies are protected." The buzz in my cock works its way down to my toes, making them curl. "I read that." Deep, controlled breaths. "And I can spank you, apparently." I strike her just perfectly on her backside.

"You've already spanked me."

"But I didn't think you were pregnant then." I spank her again, punishment for fooling me into giving it to her hard. "Good?"

"Yes." She looks at my chest, prompting me to look too, and I see what she sees. Strained muscles. Our bodies connected. My cock slipping in and out. "You look amazing," she whispers.

"I know," I say around gritted teeth, grinding my hips, absorbing the pleasure.

"Oh God!"

"I know." Jesus, I can feel it crawling through my body painfully slowly, getting ready to explode and take me out. "I fucking know."

"Jesse," she pants, panic setting in. "I'm going to come."

"I'm not," I hiss, engrossed in the vision of us, clinging to the incredible sensations. "Are you listening to your body, Ava?"

"Yes!" she yells, slamming a fist into the couch, her eyes moving from my dick entering her, to my chest, then my strained face on a loop. "And it's telling me I need to come."

Oh, smart-arse? How about *sore* arse? I spank her again, and the sound alone increases the urgency. "Don't be fucking smart." I drive deep, circle hard, watching as her flesh throbs before my eyes and her arms and legs become stiff. Oh no. I slip out, give it just a second for her impending explosion to simmer the fuck down, before I slide the entire length of my solid, engorged cock up the center of her pussy. Her back bows, my legs start to shake.

"Fuck, I need to be all over you." I get her from the couch to the rug in the blink of an eye, and push into her on collective moans, feeling her hands slipping across my wet back.

"Kiss me."

My mouth is on hers fast, my tongue exploring as I thrust steadily into her, and she's mad for it, mad for me, her kiss passionate and hungry, her nails in my arse, pushing me on.

Now feels like the perfect time to broach a lingering bone of contention, and given today's revelations, I'm even more passionate about it.

"I think"—I don't stop driving into her. Her pleasure is the key here—"you should"—thrust, lick, kiss, whisper. Attack all of her senses—"quit your job."

"No," she moans, easy as that.

"But I want to spend every day doing this." I circle my hips, nuzzle her neck, thrust smoothly. "Give me back your mouth."

No protests on that. "You'll have to wait until I get home," she breathes, rolling her hips into every advance I make.

"Wherever, whenever," I remind her, nibbling her lip.

"Except when I'm at work," she groans. "Deeper."

"Oh, so she can make the demands, then?" But I can't? *I'll go deeper, baby, if you quit your job.*

"I'm not quitting my job."

"And how do you expect to look after my babies if you're working?" I ask, exhaling shakily, not losing my pace.

"But you want me at home to do this, not to look after your babies."

"Now you're just being awkward." Breaking our kiss, I dip and suck her nipple into my mouth, and she stiffens as I clamp my teeth down in warning, before kissing my way back up her body. Her face. Fuck, it's my favorite look on her. Wild, post climax. "Deeper?"

"Please."

I drive in slowly, firmly, watching her absorb every inch of me on a hum before I kiss her hard. "Do you see?" I ask. "I'm giving you what you want." Totally beside the point that it's what I want too. Totally. "You should show your gratitude." I prop myself up on my arms. "Don't you think?" I pull out of her, slowly revealing my cock. It's dripping in her pleasure. Absolutely dripping. "Look at that. Just fucking perfect." I need to end this. For both of us. "She's beginning to pant." I lower my chest to hers, my forearms on the rug to hold me up. I need to see her face. "She's trembling all over." I'm lost in her dark eyes, my body absorbing every shudder. "I think she wants to come." Her hands plunge into my hair and yank as she starts to shake her head, holding her breath, and my drives become less measured, clumsier. "She definitely wants to come." As do I. "Fuck." My control slips, and I thrust deep and fast a few times, and Ava yells, violently yanking on my hair and biting me. The pain shoots straight down to my dick. "Fuck, fuck, fuck." All control is lost. I'm mindless on the pleasure. Every muscle screaming, my cock burning, my body dripping, my heart hammering. *Gone.* I just muster the energy and sense to tell her I'm there, and I feel her go too, her body snapping into a tense board before she starts vibrating, and then she goes soft.

Breathless.

I flop down on top of her, fucked. Panting. So wet, I could have just climbed out of the tub. "Please quit," I implore, knowing I'm wasting breath I haven't got right now. "Then we really can stay like this forever."

She says nothing, is probably incapable of speech. But she hugs me instead. Pacifying?

"Was that a yes?" I ask, dragging my mouth across her skin to her mouth. "Say yes."

"No."

"Stubborn woman," I mutter, hooking an arm under her waist and pulling her with me as I roll to my back, grateful for the cool blast of air to my front as she wedges her palms into my pecs and sits up. The shift of her body has me biting down on my teeth to sustain the friction on my sensitive, softening cock. I look up at her, smiling, rubbing her belly, pouting at her lovely boobs, which are going to get even lovelier as they get fuller. "We need to renew our vows," I say, hitching a brow at her confused face.

"We've not even been married a month."

"Yes." I make a play for her hip, feeling her jolt. But I'm distracted from my grievance when I consider the small bump. Incredible. "Only a month and you've already forgotten a significant part of your promise."

"You can take your *obey* and swivel on it," she says seriously, leaning down and circling my neck with her palms.

I grin and follow her lead, except my big hands overlap around her neck. We're nose to nose. "Who'd win?"

"You."

"Correct. I'm thirsty." Ava narrows her eyes playfully as she throttles me, and I laugh.

"I'll get some water," she says, catching my not-so-subtle hint.

"You can't pick and choose when you fulfil your wifely duties," I quip, helping her up and swinging for her arse as she wanders off gloriously naked, catching her sweetly with a satisfying slap. "Water, wench," I say around my grin.

"Don't push it, Ward."

"Don't even think about coming back in here until I can see your breasts again, lady," I call as she fixes her bra. Arms and legs splayed to get as much air to my body as possible, I take a deep breath. And sigh. What will tomorrow bring? I grimace. I don't want to worry Ava, but I don't want her to go to work. Van Der Haus is out of the frame, but has she got any thoughts on who it *could* be? Should I ask her?

Coral keeps floating around in the back of my mind, as does Freja, but…no. There's delusion and there's obsession. Fuck it, I'm at a loss, so I can only hope Cook comes up with some answers fast. And there's another something. Statements.

The sound of Ava coming back from the kitchen pulls my eyes from the ceiling. "Didn't you hear me?" I ask, nodding to her bra, which is still covering her boobs.

"I heard you," she retorts, facing me, one hand behind her back, the other holding two bottles of water. She blindly lets them drop to the couch, her eyes sparkling delightedly. Hmmm. What's she up to?

"My wife has a crafty look on her beautiful face," I say, pushing myself up and leaning back against the couch. I crane my neck, trying to see what she's concealing. "And she's hiding something from me." I raise my brows as I help myself to some water.

"Crafty…ish," she muses, nonchalant, taking a seat on my lap. I lose the water in favor of her bottom, cupping a cheek with each hand and pulling her closer.

"There's no… ish about it." I slap her arse and free her boobs again.

"What are you hiding?"

"Something," she muses, leaning back when I try to get a look. "No."

Hmmm. *Who has the power?* Stupid fucking question. So I wait as she drags out the whole affair, patient but not, until she slowly reveals what she's hiding from me.

"I'm in control," she says, understandably thrilled.

"Oh no." I laugh, not in humor, at my jar of Sun-Pat. "Not where that's concerned." I shake my head. "Forget it, no way, never." I try to seize my vice, but she's fast, removing it from my reach. I obviously haven't worn her out enough.

"Relax," she breathes, as I stare at the jar and her finger disappearing into it. A big dip. Disgust invades her face as she pulls her finger out.

"Don't tease me with it, baby," I plead, my mouth watering.

And then she does something I never expected. She wipes it across her boob. *Oh my God.* Peanut butter-dipped boobs. Could this be the best gift ever? I look at her, breathless with anticipation.

"Oops," she whispers around a satisfied grin.

Oops indeed. I lick my lips as I move in, smelling it mixed with the natural scent of my sexed-up wife, and it smells fucking delicious. "Holy fucking shit," I mumble around her boob, as she giggles, the sound orgasmic. My soft cock starts to fill with blood again. My God, it's never tasted so good, not the butter or her breast. "I didn't think it could taste any better," I say, moving back, checking I've got it all. "More."

She obliges, scooping out some more. "Would sir like the right breast or the left breast?"

"I don't have time to waste. Slap it on both."

She bursts into fits of giggles, and I nearly come on the spot as she coats herself. I practically shove her hand aside to make way, sucking her flesh into my mouth, humming constantly. "Unravel you boxers, god," she whispers into my hair as I feast on her. I finish with a bite of her nipple. "Ouch."

"Sarcasm, lady," I grunt. Fuck, that was good. A new way to eat my vice. And another reason why she needs to be readily available to me. I check both boobs again, seeing I've missed a blob.

"Tasty?" she asks.

"I'm never eating it any other way." I get that last little bit. "So now you *do* have to quit work because I need you to be available to lick when I please." I lean back on the couch, licking my lips, and Ava dips, licking my nose. I'm surprised. "I thought you hated peanut butter?"

"I do, but I love your nose." Her wrinkles as she pecks mine. "Will you do something for me?" she asks. Naturally, I'm cautious. I'll give her anything I can. I'm just worried one day she's going to ask me for something that I *can't* give her.

"What do you want, baby?"

She considers me for a moment, perhaps getting her request straight in her head. "I want you to say yes before I ask."

"You've been trying to butter me up," I quip, flexing my hands on her hips as she places the jar down.

"That's a crap joke."

"Pick the jar back up, lady. We're not done yet."

She does as she's bid and goes a little extra, putting some more on her boob. "Happy?"

"Ecstatic." I move and lick her clean. "Now, tell me what you want."

"You have to say yes."

Absolutely not. She could ask me for anything. A new Mini. My blessing to work up to full term in her pregnancy. To take no time off at all, just pop the babies out and return to her precious job straight from the hospital. No. "Ava, I'm not agreeing to anything without knowing what I'm agreeing to. End of."

"Please?" she says, taking on an unfair tactic, slipping her finger into my mouth.

"You're adorable when you sulk." I clean her finger. "Just tell me."

"I want you to revoke Sam's and Kate's memberships to The Manor." She hurries over her words, retreating on my lap, watching me, waiting. God love her.

"Okay," I agree easily, dipping myself and spreading some more of my vice on her chest.

Her frown is epic. "What?"

"I said okay." Opening my mouth, I lower and indulge some more. Jesus, finger dipping just isn't going to cut it anymore.

"It is?"

I lift my face and take her cheeks in my hands. I could be a fucker and use this as a bargaining chip. Tell her I'll cancel if she quits work. But…that would be pointless. She won't quit. "Sam already canceled."

Her mouth falls open. "I thought you were finally doing as you're told."

What's she on about? "I always do as I'm told. Come here." I help her up and get us on the couch, my belly full, my heart full. "Snuggle," I breathe, as she crawls onto my chest and settles, her sigh in my neck deep. How long before she can't lie front down on my chest? I pout. I'll miss that. How long before I can't get my arm around her stomach when we spoon? "Are you warm enough?" I ask, weaving my legs with hers, smiling at her sleepy hum. "I love you, lady," I whisper. Another hum. "You're going to be the best mummy."

"And you the best daddy," she murmurs, her hand stroking the area around my scar. "Thank you for my wall."

I smile sadly. "It's my wall, actually. So thank *you*."

"Welcome. But it's a little bit weird, all those pictures you took when I didn't know."

I chuckle. "I have an unhealthy obsession with you, baby," I say, dropping a kiss into her hair, tightening my arms. "It's old news."

"I know," she breathes. "I know."

"Tell me what your diary is like tomorrow."

"Well Mikael isn't in it," she quips, earning a nudge from me. *Definitely* not funny. "I have a lunchtime meeting with Ruth Quinn."

"Oh, the awkward one?"

"Yeah, her. She seemed quite normal at first, friendly, you know? But she's become a bit demanding. She called in the office repeatedly while we were away, was almost indignant that I didn't tell her I wouldn't be at work. I just need to get her job finished, get payment, and never work for her again."

I don't understand it. She doesn't have to deal with these people. She could pick and choose her clients, do what she wants, *when* she wants. She likes her boss, I get it. But even Ava would have to admit, Peterson has definitely become a little less easygoing the past few weeks. In fact, since he found out about *me*. I sense he's not all too happy about sharing Ava with a life outside her job. It's a common problem. Bosses hiring young, single, child-free people. People with no responsibilities other than working and earning. Full commitment to the job.

Yeah, she's trying. Half succeeding. But when the babies come, they will be the most important thing in our life. Nothing will come before them.

    My mind wanders. Could we move out of the city? Would Ava consider that? I don't want to raise our kids in this chaos. I want green land, clean air.

    And sanity.

Chapter 42

I feel her naked warmth all over my front, her soft boobs and belly pressed tight. I hum, happy, the peaceful sense of half slumber too glorious to leave just yet. Her soft voice in the distance is encouraging me to wake up. My dick hears her too, and my hands skate down her bare back to her bottom, my palms cupping her cheeks. Her breath on my face tells me her mouth is close. "If I open my eyes, I'm going to see big chocolate fuck-me ones, aren't I?"

"No, you're going to see big, wide, disturbed ones. Open your eyes."

I squint, peeking at her. She's right. Her eyes are, indeed, wide and worried. Then she flicks her head, and I catch sight of her problem. My dear, old housekeeper is standing at the foot of the couch, her face silently amused. "Oh," I murmur. "Morning, Cathy."

"You too love birds need to buy some pajamas." Pajamas? Not a chance. "Or at least keep your underwear on." Nope. "I'll be in the kitchen preparing breakfast."

I laugh, feeling Ava's mortification. "Morning, baby." Now Cathy's not got direct line of sight to between my legs, I open them, getting Ava nestled comfortably. "Let me see your face."

She burrows deeper into my neck, trying to disappear.

"She's all bashful." While I'm not. Cathy's copped a load of my fine form more than is acceptable for a housekeeper. "Shall we get you upstairs?"

"Yes." Ava pushes herself up and looks around, as I use my stomach muscles to lift and peek over the top of the couch to the kitchen. Ava snorts, laughing loudly, all embarrassment lost.

"What's tickled you?"

"You look like a meerkat." She collapses to her back and pulls her bra into place, semi gaining her dignity. "Wind your neck in." She snorts.

What the hell is she talking about? I fight my legs free from under hers and gather her up from the couch, lifting her onto my shoulder. "Where I'm from, that means something entirely different," I say, giving her bum a sharp slap as I carry her up the stairs, smiling, remembering last night. It was the perfect end to a shitty day. But today is a new day.

"It is *you* who needs to be doing the winding."

"I know what it means," she says, sighing. "I was being ironic. And there will be no winding of necks here."

"A man can live in hope." I carry her into the bathroom and put her down, turning the shower on. "There. In you get."

"I hope you're going to lock your office door now."

"Only for our eyes, baby." I laugh, although Cathy's not a prude. "I have a key and I've hidden one among the piles of lace in your underwear drawer, okay?"

Her eyes darken, a certain sign of mischief appearing. My semi-hard-on is in her hand a second later. "Ava," I whisper, wondering why she's not yet flown into a flat-out panic over the time. Surely she's realized that with Cathy's arrival, it's close to eight, which means she's late for work. Maybe she doesn't care? I withdraw, if only to test my theory, but rather than escape, I get a long, firm stroke of her hand down my shaft, bringing it to full hardness. *Fuck.* I slap my hands on my cheeks, hiding from the temptress's inviting gaze. "If I don't take you now," I say, "my cock is going to be aching all day long."

"Take me."

Oh? She'd rather morning sex than getting to work on time? She might get fired at this rate. I lower my hand as she steps into me, her head tilted, her smile small and demure. *Take me.* That's a demand. "Oh, I will." I lift her and sit her on the vanity unit, and a whole heap of memories flood my mind. Look at us then. Look at us now. "You can't escape now," I whisper, trapping her with my arms braced either side.

"I don't want to," she replies easily.

"Good." I kiss her gently, my body temperature rising. "I like your dress."

"I'm not wearing one, so we can't lose it."

"Fond memories?" I say quietly, breaking our kiss and looking at her closely. *Mine.*

"Very." The lust in her voice, how I love it. "Can you pin me against the wall now?"

I move in slowly, extending the anticipation, breathing hard, eyes darting across her face, everything inside singing.

"Oh my God, no!" Cathy's distraught yell hits my ears, stopping my mouth just shy of Ava's. *What the fuck?*

I bolt out of the bathroom, grabbing some boxers off the chair, and race downstairs, my hand holding my dick to stop it swinging around. Cathy has her back against the door, like a human barricade pushing it shut, but there's a foot wedged between the door and the frame stopping it. "Cathy," I say, stepping into my boxers and pulling them up.

She sees me and loses focus, and the door jolts behind her. Is someone actually trying to fight their way in? "It's that piece of work," she hisses, slamming her back into the door again. "I told her, I said, no, not today, and she tried to force her way in! She turned up while you were in Spain too. I warned her, Jesse. I told her to stay away."

I don't have a moment to wonder who *she* is.

"I need to talk to him."

I stare at the wood, my mouth open. "Coral?" I breathe in disbelief. *Fuck, no.*

"Yes, it's me, and I really need to talk to you."

I look back at the stairs, dread overcoming me. "Fucking hell," I mutter, going to the door. Ava will be here any minute to find out what had me dashing away as we were about to reenact our first sexual encounter.

"I thought it was Clive," Cathy says, red in the face, a mixture of exhaustion and anger. I wedge a palm into the door to hold it while encouraging Cathy to the side, out of the way of any flying wood.

"I'll deal with it."

"Who the hell does she think she is?" she snaps, yanking at her skew-whiff apron as Coral hammers her fist on the other side.

"Please, Cathy." I'm breaking out in a fucking sweat here, waiting for the bombs to go off inside the penthouse as well as outside. What the fuck is Coral thinking? And what the fuck does she want? "Go and sort out some breakfast for Ava." The second I say her name, she appears at the bottom of the stairs, buttoning up one of my shirts, her face an uncomfortable shade of impassive.

"What's going on?" She looks between my raging, uncomfortable form to the door, as Coral—fuck that woman—persistently hammers on the wood. She's lost her fucking mind.

"Nothing, baby," I say, calm but breathless, completely backed into a corner, as Ava stares at the door, wondering who I'm trying to keep out. "Cathy's making your breakfast. Go." I jerk my head toward the kitchen. I'm a fucking joke, but I live in hope that my wife might one day actually listen to me and do what she's told. I don't need her stressed. Yesterday was bad enough, what with the shitshow her brother brought to the mix. This is not how I wanted today to start.

"I'm not hungry."

"Ava," I breathe, feeling my patience fraying. Not with her, but with the fucking nutter on the other side of this door who is hellbent of making my life a fucking misery. "You didn't eat last night," I point out. "Go and have some breakfast."

"I said, I'm not hungry."

Coral continues to try and push her way in, and Ava continues to stand her ground. God, send me strength, I think as I glance at the ceiling, telling myself to keep my cool. "Ava, why the fuck can't you do what you're told?" I ask. "Go. And. Get. Your. Breakfast."

"No." She comes at me, eyes on the door, and tries to open it while I keep my back pressed against the wood. "Jesse, let go of the fucking door."

God damn her. "Watch your—"

"Fuck off!" She goes all out demonic on the door, fighting to get it open.

"Ava," I hiss, outraged, using one hand to try and pull her back before she does herself some damage.

"Jesse, we need to talk," Coral yells, silencing us both, as well as halting our physical tussle. Oh, Jesus.

Ava stares at the wood briefly before moving an incensed gaze my way. "What the hell is *she* doing here?" she asks, catching me by surprise and yanking the door open. "What the hell are *you* doing here?"

Coral hardly gives Ava the time of day, ignoring my wife and focusing on me. This is *not* going to go down well. "I need to speak to you," she says, throwing a death glare Ava's way. "Alone."

Ava's amused snort fills me with dread. I've seen the aftermath of her losing her rag. Coral's on rocky ground. "You've got more chance of having tea with the Queen. What do you want?"

I move in closer to Ava, getting ready to hold her back. Her cheeks are flushed, and it isn't because I was a heartbeat away from getting my dick inside her.

"I asked you a question," she presses, her body buzzing with anger and disbelief.

"Ava," I say softly, nervously. "Calm yourself down, baby."

"I'm calm," she snaps, very uncalmly, removing my hand from her back. "I won't ask you again." What the hell is she doing? I'm stepping in before Ava blows a gasket. So I move around her and hold a warning arm out, daring her to pass the line I've just drawn.

"Coral, I've told you before," I say, calmly—not feeling it—not looking her in the eye. I thought she was gone for dust. One less problem to deal with. But she's been showing up while we were away? And Cathy didn't mention it? How many other times has she shown up, and why hasn't she called me? Because she knew I wouldn't answer. Or, perhaps, because she wanted Ava to see her. This isn't feeling good. But I haven't got time for her deluded romantic notions. "It's never going to happen. You need to fuck off and find someone else to stalk." Don't tell me I need to get Cook to sort a restraining order too?

"Have it your way," she says, cocky. That's confusing. Have *what* my way? I sincerely hate the look on her face. Enough to want to slap it off, and I'm quite certain Ava feels the same.

Coral produces a small scrap of paper. "What the fuck is that?" I ask, nervous but way angrier.

"Take a look for yourself."

I whip it from her fingers on a snarl, at the same time keeping Ava back when I feel her pressing into the boundary line that is my arm. The moment I look at the paper, my stomach drops. *Oh, fucking hell, no.*

"What is it?" Ava asks as I stare, my eyes glazed and burning.

"That is a scan picture of his baby," Coral declares proudly, and suddenly Ava's not pushing into my arm anymore.

"Fucking hell," I hiss, catching her as she wobbles, seeing every bit of color drain from her face. Her dark eyes are wide, her lips parted. "Shit, Ava." I fucking knew this would happen. She mustn't get stressed! I pick her up and take her to the couch, sitting her down, looking up over her head when Cathy appears at the kitchen doorway. I hold up a hand, signaling we're good. "Breathe, baby," I order softly, pushing her head down between her legs. *My* head's about to spin off my neck. "Just breathe." How the fucking hell did this happen? I've always been so careful. *Always.* I hiss, stroking Ava's back, as I try to recall the times I ended up in bed with Coral. Mostly drunk. Can I be sure there were no accidents? A split condom, maybe one slipping off. Or maybe she took advantage of my inebriated state? It wouldn't be the first time. But…it's been months since I've been there. My eyes narrow, turning Coral's way. Why the fuck does she look so damn pleased with herself? *Because she's about to fuck your marriage and life up.* "What the fuck are you playing at, you stupid fucking woman," I growl. "I've not slept with you for months."

"Four months, and I'm four months gone." Her smile. She's happy. "Do the math."

"You can't be," I hiss. *She can't be!* "Fuck." My head falls into my hands, and I silently will myself to wake up from this nightmare. I have not one fucking clue what to say, what to do. Proof. I want proof. I stare at the scan picture on the floor, getting hotter, sweatier. I have the fucking proof. *Shit.*

Ava's hand appears in my downcast vision, picking up the picture. "Ava, what are you doing?"

"Yes, what are you doing?" Coral asks, coming forward. Like what? What is she planning to do? I hold a halting hand up, daring her to take one more step. My eyes drop to her stomach. Oh God, it's Lauren all over again. How didn't I see this coming? Once bitten, twice shy. But she's got me.

Wait, no. She hasn't *got* me. Does she think this changes things, that I'll leave my wife? Or is she banking on my wife leaving me? My heart turns in my chest, forcing my fist there to press into my flesh and ease the pain. This is my penance for trapping Ava. But, again, Coral doesn't get me. The baby, though? Will Ava accept it?

"I'm just trying to figure out," Ava says, studying the image. "Whether you're four or five weeks pregnant. I'm guessing just four."

Weeks? Wait, Ava's not seriously insinuating I slept with Coral four or five weeks ago? We were planning our wedding!

"I'm four *months*," Coral says. "Not weeks."

"No, you're not," Ava says, so calmly. I'm not sure I like this. "When was the last time you slept with her?" she asks, and I become all kinds of uncomfortable.

"Four, five months," I say. Maybe it was three. I don't know, but it definitely wasn't four to five *weeks* ago. "Ava, I can't think that far back. I didn't exist before you." Jesus, please tell me she doesn't believe

I betrayed her again. "I always used a condom, you know that."

"I know," she says, smiling a little. I don't deserve her trust, not really. "Was she one of the…" She inhales, looking for some bravery that I wish she didn't need. "Did you—"

"No," I say, resting a hand on her shoulder, squeezing some reassurance into her before rubbing at her nape. "Look at me." I need her to see the sincerity in my eyes. I'm no saint, I know that. I don't deserve this woman's faith or trust, but I have *not* slept with Coral since I've been with Ava, and that is a fact. "No," I reiterate, hating the relief I see fill her. If this baby is mine, it happened pre-Ava, and that's my only saving grace. I just hope she can accept that. And the child. But never Coral. She's a deceptive, immoral witch. But, again, that's not the baby's fault. Just like it wasn't Rosie's fault that her mother trapped me.

Then tried to kill me.

"You're going to stay with him when he's having a baby with another woman?" Coral says. "Where's your self-respect?" My God, I wish I could do the unthinkable and slap her out of this apartment.

"I'm going to trample now," Ava says quietly. It pulls an inappropriate smile from me.

"Knock yourself out, baby," I say, pressing my lips to her cheek. "But please, let's just make this one a verbal trample." And, sadly, that's not only because Ava's expecting my babies. I turn and face Coral. This witch is too. *Good God.*

"What are you two talking about?" Coral asks.

"Get me your picture," Ava says, looking at me.

"What picture?"

"The one that you carry everywhere," she says. "I'm not stupid. Where is it?"

My scan picture? Why the hell does she want that? "In my suit jacket."

"Go and get it."

Is she mad? "No, I'm not leaving you with her." Fuck knows what will go down in my absence.

"Her?" Coral asks, insulted. "Is that the way you're going to speak to the mother of your child?"

"You are not the fucking mother of my child, you deluded freak!" I will only ever see her as a smear on my life. And now one that can't be rubbed away. Ever. *Fuck!*

Ava walks away, so fucking calm, leaving me with Coral. "I can't believe you've done this to me," I hiss. "This is low, Coral. So fucking low."

"I didn't plan this, Jesse," she says, moving closer. "It was obviously meant to be."

"What, like we were meant to be?" I ask on a laugh. "Then why the fuck did I marry another woman, Coral?" She's fucking loo-la, I swear it.

"We had something special."

I practically dive from her outstretched hand. No. She'll never touch me again.

"Special?" *Someone, knock some sense into her, please.* "I screwed you for a while," I remind her for what feels like the millionth time. "I fucked you and then kicked you out. How the fuck is that special?"

"You came back for more. That has to mean something. You made me need you."

"No, you made *yourself* need me." There was no worshipping, no devotion, no love, not even any fucking smiles. She's fabricated a relationship that never happened, and that is on her head, not mine. "I barely even spoke to you when I was screwing you," I go on. "You were a piece of meat that was handy to have on call." *Before Ava O'Shea arrived in my life and everything except her was irrelevant.* "You're just like the rest of them, but even more desperate." I sneer, my contempt rife. "Get a good seeing to and you think your life depends on it. What the hell makes you think that I'd leave my wife for you?" I ask, looking her up and down.

"Because I'm having your baby."

"You're lying." If I keep saying it, it might come true. If she didn't have that proof, I would laugh her out of my penthouse with a boot up her arse. But she's come armed with evidence, and that changes everything. God damn it, how did I let this happen?

"She *is* lying," Ava says quietly.

What?

I feel something inside lift as I look back at her. Again, so calm. Too calm for a woman who's just found out her husband is fathering a child with another woman.

"I'm not," Coral says, indicating the picture. "You have the proof there."

"Yes, I do." Ava shows her the picture. Wait. I frown. That's *my* picture. It's tatty, the edges worn from me holding it so much. "This is a six-week scan picture," Ava says.

"No, it's a four-*month* scan picture."

"This isn't your baby, Coral."

"Whose is it then?"

Oh my God, is what I think's happening actually happening? *Coral doesn't know Ava's expecting?*

Ava gazes down at the scan picture. *My* scan picture. *My* scan picture with *my* babies on it. "This is my baby," Ava muses, almost wistful. "And Jesse's."

"What?" Coral asks, unsure.

"Well, I say baby," she goes on. "What I actually meant was *babies*. You see, we're having twins, and I know you're trying to pull a fast one because this really is a six-week scan picture. And there are two peanuts here, smaller than your one blob, I know, but I can get a feel for it. I don't know. Maybe it's motherly instinct." She smiles, while I stare at her, mouth agape. "Is that all?" she asks.

I'm speechless, wanting to grab the pictures and compare them. Or maybe I'll just take her word for it. Is she right? Has Coral got herself pregnant and is trying to pass it off as mine?

"Unless you can miraculously produce this missing strip that'll confirm your dates," Ava says, pointing at the photo. "I think we're done." The picture gets tossed on the floor at Coral's feet. "Now fuck off and go find the real father of your spawn."

I flinch on Coral's behalf, certain I'm not stepping in right now. Jesus, Ava looks on the verge of exploding, although, surprisingly, she's keeping control of it.

"Are you leaving?" she asks when Coral doesn't budge. "Or do I have to drag you out?"

Now, I absolutely will step in then. But I don't need to. Coral grabs her scan picture and scuttles out quietly, and Ava makes a meal of slamming the door, her body heaving. Adrenaline? Fuck, I don't even know what to say as she turns toward me. She looks so mad. Fuck me, can I put this woman through any more stress?

"Av—"

She walks past me without a word, leaving me standing by the door, feeling lost and ashamed. Dropping my head back, I curse quietly to the heavens. I hate that there was even room for doubt. *Fuck*. Exhausted, I perch on the arm of the couch, shaking my head in disbelief. Nothing should surprise me anymore, and yet here I am, constantly fucking surprised.

"You okay, boy?" Cathy asks quietly from the kitchen entrance.

"Had better mornings, Cathy," I say, my body heavy.

"Coffee?"

Alcohol.

I shake the fleeting thought away, struggling to my feet. "No, thanks. I've got some serious sucking up to do." I trudge off, having to use the handrail to help me up the stairs, hearing the shower. She's under the spray washing her hair when I make it to the bathroom, and I hover at the door, anxious. I can't leave her on bad terms today. I already know it's going to be stressful, waiting on information on who the fuck stole my car, not to mention the fact that it's been confirmed Van Der Haus is still sniffing around my wife, waiting for me to fuck it all up so he can sweep on in and sweep her off her feet. I'm probably being dramatic—she'll never fall into that Danish arsehole's arms. But still. I'm feeling uncertain, and particularly shitty for ruining her day before it's gotten started.

I don't usually need any courage or push to try and improve my wife's mood with a potent, underhanded hit of her godly husband, but today feels different. Ava seems...tired.

Of me?

Of our life?

Fuck, Paradise feels like eons ago. Pushing my boxers down, I step out of them and into the stall behind her, seeing her shoulder blades pull in, a sign that she knows I'm close. Defensive? Preparing to brush me off? I take the sponge off the shelf and wet it, moving in and starting to wash her. She pulls away immediately, and my heart sinks in disappointment.

"I'm not in the mood."

Oh God, the fatal words. I've really fucking done it this time. God damn me. Pouting, I try one more time to bring her around, slipping my hand onto her stomach. Skin on skin. It's what I've always depended on.

"I said I'm not in the mood." She dips out of the shower, escaping me, and this time I know it's not because she's worried she'll cave in to my form of making friends.

"You promised you'd never say that," I whisper as she dries herself. Her hands stall briefly before she wraps herself in the towel and tucks the top in, looking up at me. I know my eyes are full of apologies. Hers are full of hopelessness.

"I'm late," she murmurs, leaving, and my aching heart cracks painfully as I watch her go.

"Fuck it," I breathe, running my hands through my hair, wetting it, finding some energy to wash. I can't, however, find the energy to dress once I've dried off and scrubbed my teeth. Instead, I sit on the bed while Ava gets herself ready for work, ignoring me, my mind circling on loop with millions of apologies, trying to figure out how to voice them.

And then she's ready and leaving. *Fuck*. I dive up and put myself in the doorway, stopping her. But not touching her. "Baby, my heart's splitting," I say, willing her to forgive yet something else from my shitty past that's infiltrating our lives. "I hate fighting with you."

"We're not fighting." She can't even look at me. "You need to get the code on the elevator changed," she says, cold and harshly. "And find out how she got up here too." That's a good point. Why the fuck would Clive do that?

She's past me before I know it, and I'm instinctively going after her. Instinct. Shit, I'm back to depending on that. I reach for her and catch her wrist, stopping her from making her escape. "I will," I assure her. I'll also be tearing Clive a new arsehole, but for now I have more important matters to contend with. And I'm rooting for instinct. "We need to make friends."

"I'm dressed," she sighs. "We are not making friends now."

I smile, loving that's where her mind goes. "Not properly, no," I say, making her face me. "But don't make me spend all day knowing that you're not talking to me," I beg, getting on my knees. "The days are long enough already."

She looks down at my sorry form on a sigh. "I'm talking to you."

"Then why are you sulking?" I ask.

"Because a woman has just invaded our home and tried to stake a claim on you, Jesse," she says, irritable, like I'm asking a dumb question. Which I know I am. "*That* is why I'm sulking."

"Come here," I order, not giving her a chance to protest, pulling her down and cuddling her. She doesn't fight me. I'm taking that as a good sign. "I love it when you trample."

"It's tiring," she mumbles. "I really need to go."

"Okay." I'll take that. "Tell me we're friends," I order, holding her face. God, she does look tired. I decide here and now that I'm picking her up from work on Friday and taking her back to Paradise. No arguments.

"We're friends," she breathes, exasperated.

"Good girl." I beam at her, happy, but I am mentally plotting the demise of Coral for causing this shitshow. "We'll make friends properly later. Go get your breakfast. I'll be two minutes."

"I need to go, it's eight thirty already."

"Two minutes," I say, standing us up. "You'll wait for me."

"Hurry up then," she snaps, pushing me on. I quickly find my phone and answer John's missed calls on my way to the dressing room.

"Morning," I say, holding my phone to my ear as I drop my towel and pull on some boxers. "What's up?"

"Did I just see Coral leaving?"

"Yes, you won't believe the fucking morning I've had."

He laughs. "I bet I will."

He couldn't possibly. "We're coming." I hang up and rush into my suit, trying to call Sam, just needing to vent. But the fucker doesn't answer. So I try Drew. Nothing. "Where are your fucking friends when you need them?" I mutter, stuffing my feet into my brogues and pulling a tie off the rack, fixing it as I head back down.

"Here he is," Cathy sings. "And he's dressed." She wrinkles her nose, a cheeky glint in her old eyes.

"I'm dressed." I chuckle. "As is my beautiful wife." And doesn't she look beautiful today?.

"Can I go to work now?" she asks on a roll of her eyes.

"Have you taken your folic acid?" I ask, sorting my collar, aware that despite being grumpy with me, she's still admiring me.

"Yes."

"Have you had your breakfast?" I ask, and she indicates a bag. I can't put my foot down. If she feels anything like me, this morning has chased away any appetite. "You better eat that." I seize her hand. "Say goodbye to Cathy."

They sing their goodbyes and we leave, ready for another day. But not.

"Morning, Ava," Clive says, happy as fucking Larry. Not for long. "Mr. Ward."

"Clive," I say, reminding myself that he's an old boy, "how the hell did a woman make it past you and up to the penthouse?"

"Mr. Ward," he says, laughing. "I've just come on shift."

"Just?" Don't tell me that young, good-looking fucker is responsible for this. I'll have him fired.

"Yes, I relieved the new boy only ten minutes ago," Clive confirms as he checks the time.

"When's he back on shift?"

"I finish at four. Did he do something wrong, Mr. Ward? I have advised him of protocol."

Protocol? "For what fucking use it's done," I mumble, leading a quiet Ava outside. "John's taking you to work."

"When do I get my Mini back?"

"You're not. It's a write-off."

"Oh," she whispers, becoming even more despondent. "Well, when do I get to drive myself to work, then?"

"When I find out who stole my car." I'm honest as I pull the Range Rover door open, helping her into the passenger seat and getting her seatbelt on.

"Why aren't *you* taking me to work?"

"I have a few meetings at The Manor." I kiss her scowl away.

"Then why did you make me wait for you?"

"So I could put you in John's car and remind you to speak with Patrick."

"You're impossible."

"You're beautiful. Have a good day." I close the door and give John a look, not that I need to. He won't let Ava out of his sight, and I'm not resting until I have some answers.

Slipping into the Aston, I pull out of Lusso and drive to The Manor to meet Cook. I order two coffees with Pete and take a seat in the bar rather than my office, knowing Sarah will be in there. I settle and open a message from John, raising my brows.

Peterson is in the office today.

"So let me hear you tell me otherwise, baby," I muse, dialing John, but I know deep down Ava telling her boss doesn't really make any difference. If Van Der Haus wants to reach my wife, there are plenty of options for him to take. Unfortunately for him, he has no shit on me now. No bullets to fire. Will that make a difference? I laugh under my breath as John answers.

"How did she seem?" I ask.

"Quiet. What's happened?"

"Coral showed up this morning with a scan image of a baby. Told us it's mine." There's silence. I can only imagine John's face. "It's not mine."

"You're sure?"

"I wasn't, no, because Coral said she was four months gone. Ava worked out from the scan picture she was lying. Things got a little tense."

"So it's not yours?"

"Definitely not mine." Thank the fucking gods, but it's some poor fucker's and I'm seriously feeling sorry for that man. "Ava does passive-aggressive well."

"She's got a good teacher."

"Ha ha," I drone. "Talk later." I hang up and scroll through my phone, searching for Van Der Haus's number and dialing. He answers promptly.

"Mr. Ward," he says, sounding subtly surprised. "How lovely to hear from you."

"I'm sure," I say, not offering the same courtesy. "Don't make me resort to intervention." I make a mental note to ask Cook whether a restraining order is possible. It's harassment, after all.

"Ohh, sounds ominous."

"Leave my wife alone."

"Our relationship is of a professional capacity, Mr. Ward."

"Don't bullshit me. You called her yesterday."

The small delay tells me he's surprised. "Work related."

I laugh, and there's an undeniable shred of psycho looming in the sound. "She knows about Freja." Let's just put it out there and put this to bed. Hopefully.

"Oh, I know Ava knows about your sordid liaisons with my wife at your seedy sex club *before* you met, but does she know—"

"She knows, Van Der Haus," I grate. "She knows *everything*." There's another beat of silence, and I roll my shoulders, wetting my mouth with my coffee. "My brief encounter with Freja post Ava was a grave misjudgment on my part, and I will live with that regret for the rest of my life, but Ava, in all her grace and glory, has forgiven me." I reach for my collar and pull it, feeling hot. "That's the beauty of true love." And something he's obviously yet to learn, because Freja couldn't forgive him for betraying her, and she absolutely shouldn't. He persistently and without a scrap of remorse, cheated on her. "Forgiveness is a gift it offers." More coffee. "So, again, stay away from my wife."

He hums, mulling over my warning. "I might find that impossible."

"Impossible isn't an option." I hang up, uncomfortable, wondering where the fuck he gets his kicks. Even without me in the picture to threaten death, Ava's not interested. I check my Rolex and start typing out a text Cook, asking how long he'll be, feeling uncomfortable this far away from Ava, but Amalie's name shines on my screen, stopping me.

I'm very aware of the kick of my heart. My deep inhale. And yet, this time, I don't even consider ignoring her. "Hey, everything okay?" I ask, tense. "Dad? Is he okay?"

"He's okay," she says, and I breathe a sigh of relief. "Have you had time to think?"

I laugh. I haven't had time to piss in the past day. "What am I thinking about?"

"You know, Jesse," she breathes. She's right, I do. But it's been quite an action-packed twenty-four hours. "Is there a chance?"

I sink deeper into the soft, cushioned seat, rubbing my hand across my forehead. I'm being held back by one thing. Exposure. I can't make amends with my parents without revealing the final skeleton in my closet. The biggest skeleton. The one that really could destroy us. "Fuck," I breathe, feeling stifled. Torn. "Amalie, I'm scared," I admit.

"What of?"

"I'm scared she'll leave me if she finds out about Rosie and what happened to her." I swallow, clearing my throat, checking the vicinity. I'm alone, just the staff coming and going, not paying attention to me in the corner.

"God damn it, Jesse, will you stop fucking blaming yourself?"

I frown. "Watch your bloody mouth."

She huffs. "If anyone is to blame, it's Uncle Carmichael."

"What?" How did she conclude that?

"He took Rosie, Jesse. He took her to punish you for something he basically orchestrated. He knew what would happen if he took you to that manor of his. He knew if he shoved you under the nose of that viper, twisted, money-grabbing girlfriend of his you might have caved at a weak moment. He. Took. Rosie. He put her in that car and drove away feeling unwarrantedly injured and betrayed."

They're really fucking hard words to hear. And, of course, not true. "He did nothing but be there for me," I say quietly, uncomfortable. Because Carmichael's character is being blackened? Or because what she's saying could be true?

"He took you away from us, Jesse," she goes on. "He enabled a teenager to rebel when he should have been supporting Dad while you had your teenage strops and placed blame for your attitude and hang-ups at everyone's door except yours. Yours and Jake's. You *never* blamed Jake."

I inhale. Jake? Why would I blame Jake?

"And do you know what?"

She's not done? I don't know if I can take any more. I look at the top shelf behind the bar. My go-to when I can't face the world. And it all makes fucking sense.

Escape.

"What?" I murmur, making myself listen.

"You couldn't blame Jake because Jake was basically you. You without the chip on his shoulder."

Ouch. I reach for my shoulder, as if looking for that chip. "Are you done?" I ask softly.

"Yes," she sighs. "Except for one thing."

"I don't know if I can take much more, Amalie," I confess. "I'm feeling quite fucking shit right now."

"I've never seen Dad more broken than when you ran away to that manor."

I wince, wanting to crawl into my coffee cup. "Amalie, please."

"He loves you, Jesse. Always has. As much as Jake and as much as me." Her voice starts to break, and that finishes me too. I roughly wipe my face, checking around me. "Why didn't you ever see that?"

Because I was a bratty teenager with, as Amalie said, a chip on my shoulder. And then I was too bitter or too drunk. *Fuck.* "I have to go," I say, needing some air.

"Tell me there's a chance."

I stand, swallowing. *There's a chance.* "I don't know," I whisper, the ache inside, the pain in my heart, rampant.

Have I been ignorant? Not only blind drunk, but simply blind? *I've been hiding.* Arrogant. I inhale, my chest tightening. I feel so mad. Not with myself, but, and it's a first, with Carmichael. He didn't mean for something so terrible to happen. But in that moment as he walked away from me and Sarah with Rosie and Rebecca, he was punishing us. And then...tragedy.

He enabled a teenager to rebel when he should have been supporting Dad while you had your teenage strops and placed blame for your attitude and hang-ups at everyone's door except yours. Yours and Jake's.

Something clicks.

My parents are the key to complete my happily ever after. I blow out my cheeks, my head beginning to pound. "Fucking hell," I whisper, stressed, heading for the changing rooms and throwing some running kit on. I sprint out of The Manor and straight down the driveway, my legs like pistons.

I've never seen Dad more broken than when you ran away to that manor.

I grit my teeth, running faster.

He loves you, Jesse. Always has. As much as Jake and as much as me.

Faster.

Why didn't you see that?

Because I was lost in my own hang-ups. Drunk. Angry.

Lost.

"Fuck," I breath, slowing to a jog, drenched and hardly able to form a sentence, so when Sam calls, I answer with a weary, wheezy grunt.

"I need to see you," he says urgently. "Now."

Chapter 43

Steve confirmed he's been called in on a raid and can't meet me until later, so I quickly showered, changed back into my suit, and drove back into the city, my head fucking spinning. I meet Sam in a café around the corner from Drew's office, and he looks fucking shook when I walk in. Totally spooked. I lower to the chair opposite him, wary, helping myself to the coffee he's ordered. "What's up?" I swear to God, if Dan's not on a plane back to Australia and is still here causing shit, I can't promise I won't break the fucker's legs. "Kate told me about your little visitor this morning."

I sag in my seat. "Is that it? You want a debrief on the soap opera happening in my apartment this morning?" I roll my eyes, sighing loudly. So Ava's told Kate. No surprises there. "Coral tried to pass off her unborn baby as mine, it didn't work, the end." I help myself to some water as Sam sits forward, hands on the table.

"Coral's five weeks," he says.

"According to Ava."

"It's definite?"

"Well, she's no expert, Sam, but what I do know is the picture she saw definitely wasn't of a four-month pregnancy." And that's all I care about. It's not mine. Thank fuck.

"So we're definitely talking weeks. Maybe five, maybe six?"

"Four, five, six," I breathe, exasperated. Only Coral knows exactly how many weeks. "Is this leading somewhere?"

"How long ago was The Manor's anniversary party?"

I frown, casting my mind back, trying to work back through the weeks. It's hard when my brain is mush, thank you, Amalie. "Sam, I'm not exactly operating at full capacity at the moment."

"Let me help you out."

"Please."

"It was five weeks ago."

Pausing, taking some water, I look at him over the glass, not liking where I think this might be heading. I place my water down. "Mate, to be clear," I say, my voice tight, "when Coral showed up at The Manor that night, I didn't go anywhere fucking near her." The outrage and anger catches up with me, and I stand, fuming. "What kind of arsehole do you think I am?" Should I be asking that?

"Sit down," he snaps, reaching for my arm and yanking me back down into my seat. "For fuck's sake, get a grip."

"You get a grip! Sitting here accusing me of fucking behind my wife's back."

He hitches a brow. I don't appreciate it. "I'm not accusing you of anything."

"Then—"

"Shut up."

I recoil.

"Do you remember Drew disappearing?"

"N—" I snap my mouth shut. "Yeah, he left early. Right after you three had finished whatever it was you did." It's me raising my brow now. I won't ask. Don't care. What's the fucking point of this?

"I couldn't get hold of him the next morning. So after I left The Manor, I stopped by his place, and what did I find?"

I do not have the energy or brain power to play this game. "I don't know Sam, what did you find?"

"Coral."

I shoot back in my chair. "Excuse me?"

"I found Coral slipping out of his front door."

I stare at Sam, mouth open. "Five weeks ago," I murmur, and he nods. "Fuck, that's why he was being all weird. And you fucking knew!" I stand, again, outraged. *Again*.

"Sit the hell down."

I do, plonking my arse in the seat. "Fuck," I gasp.

"Yeah." Sam laughs, nervous. "Fuck indeed."

I rake a hand through my hair. I can't believe this. "And she, the fucker, tried to pass it off as mine?"

"Fucked up, man. Really fucked up."

"Wait," I say, something coming to me. "You know Coral turned up at Lusso this morning because Ava told Kate?"

"Yes."

"And does Kate know about you finding Coral sneaking out of Drew's?"

He nods. "I had to tell someone, man."

He looks panicked. He shouldn't be. Ava knows it's Drew's baby. But she hasn't called. I huff. Because she's busy. With her job. "It's fine," I say. It's one less thing for me to tell her, I suppose.

"Can we get to the more important matter?"

"More important than some crazed bitch trying to trick me into believing she's pregnant with my child when she's actually pregnant with my best mate's?" I gawk at Sam, suddenly catching his drift. "Drew," I breathe. "Oh my God, he's going to flip the fuck out." He hates Coral. "Wait." I hold up a halting hand. "I put her up in a hotel that night."

Sam laughs. "Yeah. She didn't sleep there."

My head feels like it could pop. "What the hell was he thinking?"

"I don't think he was thinking, Jesse. He must have been absolutely obliterated, because when I turned up in the morning, he couldn't recall a thing. I asked about Coral. He looked at me like I was stupid."

"She preyed on him," I breathe. Fuck me, was this completely orchestrated to try and trap me? I wince for my best mate, seriously not looking forward to breaking *any* of this to him. "And our wedding," I go on. Things are coming back to me. "Coral showed up, and suddenly Drew disappeared." Every time I've asked him what's up, he's got arsey.

"He didn't want to be anywhere near her." Sam looks as disturbed as I'm feeling, and a silence falls as we both try to process this.

I'm struggling. I wouldn't put much past Coral, but this? I'd like to say it's beyond my comprehension, but...Lauren. I come over a little sweaty, my collar choking me, forcing me to tug at it. Lauren was ill. Violent. Erratic. And now I'm sitting here running back over all of my encounters with Coral trying to figure out of she's in the same bracket because, Christ, I wouldn't wish a Lauren on my worst enemy. I pause for thought. Maybe Van Der Haus. And definitely the fucker who's tried to hurt Ava. It brings me back to Coral. Was it her? The drugs, the car. I shift on my seat, feeling extremely unnerved.

"We've got to tell him." Sam breaks the silence and interrupts my thoughts, waving the waitress away when she comes to ask if we'd like anything else. *Vodka?*

"Of course we've got to tell him," I say, downing my coffee. "I'm just not looking forward to it." I stand. "Let's get it over with."

"Now?"

"Can you think of a better time?" I walk out of the café, texting Cook on my way.

Look into Coral Seymour

Cook will know Coral. In fact, I'm sure he's been there. And then I wonder, thinking back to the whole messy scene outside The Manor when Ava showed up unexpectedly and discovered it wasn't a hotel. Mike, his reaction, his delight. Right before I smashed his face in.

Look into Mike Seymour too

I'm leaving no stone unturned. "I *can* think of a better time, actually." Sam joins me on the pavement, his cheeks ballooning. "When I've learned some self-defense."

I huff, starting the walk to Drew's office nearby, contemplating calling him. I've never been in Drew's office. Never just turned up. He'll know something's up.

We arrive and stand on the pavement outside, looking through the glass at the desks, all with bodies sitting at them. "He might not even be here," Sam says as I take the handle.

"He'll be here." He's either at work or at The Manor, and he's not at The Manor right now. Pushing my way in, I'm greeted with numerous sets of eyes when everyone looks up. I smile. "Is Drew around?"

A lady stands, coming out from behind her desk, looking between us. "Can I tell him who's asking?"

"Jesse," I say. "A friend. And Sam."

Realization pops into her eyes, and she smiles. "Well, what a pleasure to finally meet you both." Her hand comes toward me, and I shake before she offers it to Sam. "I've heard a lot about you."

I raise my brows, casting an interested look to Sam. "He talks about us?"

"All the time."

"How sweet."

"I'm Andrea."

"Lovely to meet you, Andrea." I crane my neck, trying to see past her. She's a lovely lady, but we're on an urgent mission. "So, where is he?"

"Give me a moment." She wanders off, leaving us standing like two plums by the door, every single one of Drew's employees—all women—staring at us, twiddling pens, straightening backs.

"Feeling scrutinized?" Sam asks quietly. "Fucking hell, I'm being mentally undressed."

"Uncomfortable?" I laugh to myself. He's used to being *actually* undressed. By various women, in one of the various rooms at The Manor.

Drew appears, suited, a massive fucking frown on his face. "What the hell are you two doing here?"

We both smile like chumps. "Missing your face, my man," Sam chimes, and I roll my eyes.

"Your office is that way?" I ask, indicating to the door as I pass him, his confused face following me.

"Come on in," he muses.

I take a seat at his desk, pushing the other chair out for Sam, gazing around. "Fucking hell, it's a pristine as you." Not one thing out of place, his desk an organized surface, with one posh pen in the pen pot and one file to the side.

"What's going on?" he asks, lowering cautiously to his huge leather chair, eyes bouncing between us.

Fuck, where do I start? "I had a situation this morning."

"A situation? What?"

Sam's shrinking in his seat, happy to let me take the lead. A million words are rolling around in my head—bitch, pregnant, liar, trapped—but I'm struggling to know where to start. "Sam told me about the night of the anniversary party."

Drew's instantly hostile, glaring at Sam. "You've been gossiping? I told you to keep your fat mouth shut."

"It wasn't like that," Sam says, a little high-pitched.

"Then what was it like?"

"He told me out of necessity."

"I hardly even fucking remember," Drew hisses, jaw rolling, eyes icy. "It was a grave mistake, and to be clear, I don't particularly like the woman."

A grave mistake? Oh, he has no idea.

"I know she's been an issue for you," he goes on, raking a hand through his hair, "And to be honest, I've never been so drunk in my life. I can't believe I went there, even when I was pretty much unconscious."

Poor guy is sweating. Jesus Christ, I need to just get it out there. This is painful. "I'm sorry if you feel like I've—"

"She's pregnant."

Drew's whole body jumps in his seat, like he's received a physical punch. "What?" His eyes move from me to Sam, then back again, back and forth, as we remain in our chairs, unmoving, unspeaking, and expressionless. A smile breaks the corner of his mouth, slowly stretching across his face. "You're fucking with me." He breathes out, sagging in his chair. "Fucking hell, you cunt. You had me there."

I press my lips together, slowly shaking my head, as Drew's smile fades.

"We're not joking, mate," Sam says quietly. "Jesse's seen the scan picture. It all lines up to the night of the anniversary party."

Drew stares across at us, lost, and I see him mentally calculating the timeframe in his mind. Then he frowns. "How come you've seen the scan picture?"

Ah. I shift in my chair, all kinds of uneasy, and Sam must see my struggle because he speaks up so I don't have to. "Coral showed up at Jesse and Ava's place this morning. She told Jesse the baby was his."

"What?" Drew blurts. "Wait. Is it?"

I glare at him in disbelief, and he notes my reaction, lucky for him, and backs down. "No, it isn't," I confirm for the sake of it. "It's been months since I went there."

"Coral told Ava she was four months pregnant," Sam pipes in, his hand resting on my forearm, a signal to cool it. "Obviously to place Jesse in the frame. Ava only realized she was bullshitting when she looked at the scan picture. There were details missing, and the fetus is like…smaller than a peanut or something." He shrugs. "Coral couldn't double down because Ava showed her a scan picture of the twins."

"Fuck," Drew breathes.

"And all of this has left me wondering if maybe Coral could be responsible for drugging Ava and running her off the road," I add.

"Christ, are you telling me my baby momma is an A-rated psycho?" He stands and starts to walk circles around his office, and Sam looks at me nervously, seeing me fighting to absorb the sting. Drew stops. Looks at me. "Sorry, mate, I wasn't thinking."

"Don't worry about it."

"Fuck!" He punches the filing cabinet, his hair coming out of place, and for the first time in a long time, I see Drew Davies looking something less than perfect. "I fucking hate her. I hated her before this, and now I fucking hate her more." He kicks the filing cabinet. "The lying, deceitful bitch." Dumping his arse in a chair, he drops his head in his hands. "What the fuck am I going to do?"

Sam and I remain silent, because *that* I don't have the answer to. Drew's never talked about having kids. Christ, he's never even talked about settling down. He's a fuck and work machine. Women serve only one purpose. To relax. And Coral is probably the furthest away from relaxed a man can get. "We're here for you, mate," I say as he emerges from hiding in his hands and flops back in his chair on a tired exhale. He takes a moment. A few breaths. Stares at his mobile. "I haven't got her number." Then he looks at me.

I huff at the irony and text it to him. "Listen, she won't know you know."

He huffs. "Oh, she'll know I know." His teeth grit. "When I bellow down the phone at her."

"We'll give you a moment," I say, not wanting to hear this conversation.

Sam stands with me, and we leave Drew to make the call. "It went better than I expected," Sam says quietly as we walk through the desks, all eyes back on us.

"What, because he punched the filing cabinet and not one of us?" I pull the door open and step out onto the street, checking the time. A message from John lands, telling me he's just dropped Ava off for an appointment at Lansdowne Crescent. That's where I followed Ava to on the Tuesday after she left me. So it was sticky Ruth Quinn's home. He's waiting outside. Good man. "I'm just checking in with Ava," I say, dialing her.

"Jesse," she answers, whispering. "I'm in a meeting. Can I call you back?"

In a meeting. With that testing client. "I'm having Ava withdrawals. Are you having Jesse withdrawals?"

"Is there a cure?" Her playful tone is a balm to my pounding headache.

"Yes," I murmur. "It's called constant contact. What time are you finishing work?" When do I get to lose myself in her and forget the shitty world I'm dealing with?

"I'm not sure," she says, and I frown. "I have a meeting at two with Patrick."

"Oh good. You're finally going to see through on your promise to talk with him."

"Yes." She sounds thrilled. Whatever. I bet it won't be as awkward as the conversation Drew is having with Coral right now. Speaking of which, I wait for her to mention the breaking news. She doesn't.

"Well," I say, looking at my watch. "It won't take *that* long, will it?"

"No, probably not, but it doesn't matter because John will be waiting for me, won't he?"

I smile. "He will." *And you'll never know how grateful I am that you're not making a big deal about it.* "How are my babies, lady?"

"*Our* babies are fine," she says, widening my smile. It's all I need. Ava and my babies. But…is it? I shy away from the mental image of Mum's face during our encounter. Shy away from the pain. But it's getting harder to evade it. Amalie's words are a constant buzz in my brain. "Jesse," Ava says, back to whispering. "I need to get back. I'll see you later."

"What am I supposed to do until later?" Steve's on a raid, unable to answer any questions, and Drew's in a full-blown meltdown. Maybe Sam and I can take him for some lunch. If he still has an appetite.

"Go for a run."

"I already did that. Maybe I'll go shopping."

"Yes, go shopping," she chirps. "I love you."

"I know."

"Bye." She hangs up, and I breathe out, looking over my shoulder. Sam's on the phone, probably filling Kate in on the events of this morning. I'm still surprised Ava hasn't mentioned Coral and Drew. I can only conclude that she's just relieved Drew's been nailed and not me. Although it could have turned out *very* differently.

Drew appears at the door of his office, looking like he's been to war. I expect the filing cabinet has taken a beating again. I can relate. Coral brought that kind of urge out in me too. "I need a drink," he barks, stuffing his hands in his pockets and marching past. "I'm going to The Manor."

The Manor. His sanctuary.

Drink.

Escape.

I wince. Again, I can relate. Fuck, he didn't ask for this. Poor fucker. Sam hangs up to Kate and looks at me, and I shrug, heading for my car, Sam to his.

And this will be my afternoon. Watching over my friend while he gets wasted and drowns in his sorrows.

I'm here for him. But I will be monitoring the levels of consumption. And yet I know I don't have to. Drew's got way more self-control than I had.

Except, of course, for when he let Coral into his bed.

What a fucking mess.

Chapter 44

I order two beers and a water, settling down at the bar on one side of Drew, Sam on the other. He's quiet, staring into his beer. Coming to terms with his fate. After a few minutes, he swipes up the pint and necks it, slamming it down and ordering another.

Three pints in, we've not moved, and Drew's doing some serious venting. Coral's been called every name under the sun. She didn't even deny it, and although Drew's well aware he's firmly in the frame, he still wants a test when the kid's born. Wise. I don't blame him.

"So there's no chance of a proposal, then," Sam says in jest. It's not appreciated, Drew slowly turning a dark glare his way. I laugh and get up when John calls, excusing myself and stepping away.

"Where are you?" he asks when I answer.

"Consoling Drew."

"Why?"

"Coral's baby. It's his."

"Jesus Christ."

"Indeed. What's up?"

"Okay." He drags the word out, like he's psyching himself up. It's odd.

"John?"

"Don't lose your shit."

I still, staring at my shoes, my muscles becoming uncomfortably tense. All early warning signs that one is at risk of losing one's shit. "Is that a request or a demand?"

"A request."

"Spit it out, John."

"Ava's received some anonymous warnings."

My lungs deflate on the spot, draining. "What?" I wheeze, eyes darting.

"When I took her to a meeting, a courier was outside her office. On a bike. He or she gave her an envelope. Inside was a message."

"What message?"

"It alluded to the previous warning to stay away from you and some shit about Ava not knowing who you are. It got delivered with some dead flowers."

"Jesus Christ," I breathe, moving on unsteady legs to a nearby chair and dropping to the seat. "She had a warning to stay away from me? When?"

"I don't know when she got the other one. She tore it up."

I growl in disbelief. "She did what?"

"I said *don't* lose your shit," John warns.

"I'm not losing my fucking shit. Send me a picture of it," I demand, hanging up and dialing Cook, standing, needing to feel my legs. Not so much the burn in my gut. She tore it up? And why the fuck didn't she tell me? Cook doesn't answer, so I try again. And again. And again.

He eventually picks up on a hushed, impatient hiss. "I'm in an operation debrief."

"It's important. I just found out Ava's been getting threats. She didn't tell me, tore the first up, but I have the second."

"What did they say?"

"I don't know exactly. Some rubbish about her not knowing who I am." Fuck, she *didn't* know who I was. "They told her to leave me. You need to talk to Coral Seymour." It's her—it's got to be. It's another dimension of shit for Drew to deal with too, but so be it. If he's unlucky, his kid will be born in jail. If he's lucky, he'll get full custody so Coral will be out of his life.

"I'm nearly done here," Cook says, sounding thoughtful. "I'll head over to The Manor. You said you have the message?"

"I have a picture of the message. I'll send it. John has the original."

"I bet his hands have been all over it already, right?"

"Yeah."

"Call him and tell him not to touch it again."

"Okay." I hang up and text John rather than call him, just as the boys clock me sweating pure stress nearby. Both turn on their bar stools, ready to come check on me. I hold a hand up, keeping them back from the blast that might happen. I dial Ava.

Breathe, breathe, breathe.

It rings and rings, and I see her in my mind's eye plucking up the courage to answer.

Breathe, breathe, breathe.

"Please don't shout at me," she cries when she answers.

Breathing has *not* worked. "What the fucking hell were you thinking?" I ask, seeing Sam and Drew lean back on their stools, eyes widening. "You stupid, stupid woman!" I get up and start pacing, up and down, arms flailing. "I've been pulling my fucking hair out trying to work with Steve Cook and figure this shit out, and all along you had a handwritten threat? And you tore it up? Evidence, Ava. Fucking evidence." I gasp for some air, hearing her quiet, emotional apology, willing myself to calm the fuck down before I send the bar up in smoke. Or burst my wife's eardrums. *She shouldn't be stressed. Her blood pressure can't get high.* "Fuck," I whisper, mentally punching myself in the face. "Tell me you're not leaving that office this afternoon."

"I have a meeting with Patrick," she rushes to remind me. Yes. At two. It's nearly two. "I'll speak to him about Mikael."

I move to a nearby table and rest a palm on the wood, leaning into it, my head hanging, my eyes closed. So now she's keen? Now she appreciates the danger? "This isn't the work of Mikael, Ava." She said it herself yesterday. "Steve confirmed Mikael has been back and forth to London over the last few weeks, but completely legit." Maybe I should have shared this news as soon as I learned it. I didn't because *maybe* I thought that would be the excuse Ava needed to never tell Peterson she can't work with Mikael. "He couldn't have drugged you and he couldn't have been driving my car because both of those times he was in Denmark."

There's a beat of silence. "What about the man in the CCTV footage?"

And that's a point. It was *definitely* a man. Definitely *not* Coral. But did I see the suited guy who looked like Van Der Haus actually put anything in Ava's glass? No. I just assumed it was him because he resembled Van Der Haus. It could have been anyone in that bar. Even Coral. My head banging, I rise and rub at my temple. Sarah's standing on the threshold of the bar observing me having a meltdown. I turn my back on her, uncomfortable. "I don't know, Ava. My car was found yesterday. Steve's looking into it. The tracker's been deactivated."

"Should I come to The Manor after work?" she asks quietly, so willing.

"No," I say, as Sarah passes me, settling with some gents on a table in front of me, now able to see my face again. I turn and walk out of the bar. I'm not surprised when Sam and Drew follow me and meet me on the steps, both concerned. "John will take you home as soon as you've spoken to Patrick," I say. "I'll meet you there. Given this new information I've *just* found out, I've got Steve swinging by. Don't leave that office, and once John's taken you home, you stay put. Do you understand me?"

"I understand," she says quietly.

"Good girl." Fuck, I shouldn't have yelled at her. "I'll speak with Steve, but I'm out of here the second I'm done." She needs a hug. *I* need a hug.

"I love you," she blurts in a panic.

"I know you do, baby." I look to the heavens, praying for some answers soon. I can't say I will ever relax completely when it comes to Ava and the babies, won't bother even trying to convince myself I will, but knowing who's responsible for all this shit will obviously take the edge off. "We'll have a bath when I'm home. Deal?"

She agrees, and I hang up. Sam's on my left, Drew's on my right. All of us staring down the driveway. "Ava's been getting threats," I say, almost robotically, like drama is all I have to give today. It is.

"Coral said she didn't drug Ava," Drew murmurs. "Or run her off the road."

I look at him, shocked. "You asked her?"

"In the heat of the moment, yes." He rolls his shoulder, pouting moodily. "I wasn't thinking straight, I'm sorry."

Don't lose your shit.

"What did you expect her to say?" Sam asks, laughing. "Oh, yes, baby daddy," he squeaks in a pathetic female tone. "It was me, it was me."

"For fuck's sake, Drew."

"I'm sorry." He shrugs. "Is it bad I want to fuck?"

"Why would you think it's bad? It's your go-to."

"But I'm possibly going to be a dad." He flinches at the very words. "Best-case, it was Coral, mystery solved, she gets banged up, and I get the kid," Drew says.

"Best-case?" Sam asks.

"I'll get a nanny. It'll be fine." He puffs out his chest. "How hard can it be?"

"You won't be able to fuck willy-nilly," I say.

"Who's willy-nilly?" Sam asks, and Drew and I burst into laughter, bending at the waist. "What?" Sam asks. "What did I say?"

"Nothing." I chuckle, the laughter feeling good. A brief reprieve from the nightmare. But…back to the nightmare.

I sigh, turning and heading back inside. "Jesus, who would have thought, eh? Me, married with twins on the way, Sam settling down and departing from The Manor, and Drew being used as a sperm donor."

"I'm not changing," Drew grunts. "It's who I am. What I do."

I believe it. I poke my head around the bar door, seeing Sarah still holding court with the table of guys, so I head to my office and wait for Cook, calling John.

"You didn't listen to me, did you?" he grumbles. "I could see Ava from across the road at her desk trembling."

I grimace. I'm not proud. "Cook's coming over now. Ava's in a meeting with Peterson, then she's leaving. Can you take her home? I won't be far behind."

"Sure. Listen, I took her to that meeting earlier."

"At Lansdowne Crescent?"

"That's it. A woman."

"Ruth Quinn?"

"I don't know. Ava mentioned something about being admired."

Fuck me, don't tell me I've got to fend off women as well as men? I've known John a long time. He doesn't make somethings out of nothings. He's not wired that way. Ava's mentioned this Ruth Quinn is hard work, but she never mentioned she might have the hots for her. "Do you think I need to step in?" My wife's going to have no clients left at all.

"Look, she was familiar. And I got chills. I haven't had chills for years. Not since…"

I frown. "Not since what?"

"Since Lauren was in your life," he says softly.

I laugh, a little uncomfortable. "Lauren?"

"Yeah."

"But she's dead."

"Yeah." He huffs, slightly amused, slightly uncomfortable. "I'm just. I don't know. She looked like Lauren."

"I've seen women on the street before who looked like Lauren." I stopped one. She was understandably startled. "And I got chills too." I get it.

John hums his agreement. "I think maybe you ought to step in."

Yes, Lauren's dead but, like I've said, John doesn't make somethings out of nothings. So I will be stepping in. "I hear you," I say, as another call comes in. A quick glance tells me it's Cook. "I've gotta go, Cook's calling." Walking to the couch, I lower. "Steve."

"Hey, so here's one for you," he says. "I'm on my way, by the way."

"Hit me." What's he found out?

"I have a friend of a friend of a friend who got hold of Haskett and Sandler's inventory. Clients, businesses they're valuing and selling, that kind of thing."

"And?"

"They've recently valued the company Ava works for."

"Rococo Union?"

"Yeah."

My brain is clearly on the lag. "Peterson's selling?"

"And the company he's using to sell have been checking Van Der Haus's financial records."

It hits me like a brick to the face. "Fuck, no," I breathe, rising slowly up from the couch. "He's—"

Stay away from my wife.

I might find that impossible.

"Oh my fucking God." I feel like I'm in a flat-out panic, not able to get anything to work. "Are you saying Ava's boss is selling to Van Der Haus?"

"I'm saying the information I have certainly points to it, but I can't confirm."

My phone dings, announcing another call. I ignore it. "She's in a meeting with her boss." I inhale. Is Peterson telling them he's selling up? "Fuck!"

"Could he also be introducing them to the new owner?" Steve asks.

I freeze. Hell, no. My phone dings at my ear again, and this time I look. It's John, and I have a horrible feeling I know what he's going to say. I quickly switch the calls. "John?"

"Van Der Haus just went into Ava's office. What do you want me to do?"

I snatch my keys off the desk and head out, nearly taking Drew and Sam off their feet as I steam past them, the floor shaking under my feet. "I think he's bought Rococo Union," I gasp, out of breath, not that I'm running. I'm just…breathless.

"What?"

"I think Van Der Haus has bought the company my wife works for." I swing the door of the Aston open and fall into my seat.

"What?" Drew and Sam yell in unison, both of them in the way so I can't close my door.

"Move," I bark.

"No." Drew shakes his head. "Never, no way. You'll fucking kill yourself driving in this state." He points to my hand on the door handle. It's vibrating so much, it's almost a blur. "You need to calm down."

"Calm down?" I ask.

"Tell me what's going on," Drew demands. "How do you know this? Where's Ava? And Van Der Haus, where's he?"

I look at him, feeling spaced out, trying to remember every question he just threw my way. Can't.

"Fucking hell." He snatches my phone from my hand, looking at the screen. "John," he says, walking a few paces away while Sam keeps guard of me and the car door. "It's Drew. He's losing his mind. What's the deal?" Drew listens, looking my way, as I try and fail to cool the rage. "You need to get her out before Jesse spins on in there like a Tasmanian Devil and leaves irreparable damage in his wake." Drew nods, hanging up, and hands me my phone. "Take a few deep breaths before you make your next move."

I listen to him, breathing in and out, while Sam cups my shoulder and rubs firmly and I clutch the steering wheel. "I'm calm." I can't be shouting my mouth off again to Ava. "I'm calm," I reiterate, holding my hand out for my mobile. I dial Ava. She doesn't answer. I don't try again, not prepared to waste any time, calling John back instead.

"She's not answering," I breathe. "Are you in there?"

"She's fine," John says, a little breathless too. He's acted. Gone in there to check.

Then suddenly I hear Ava down the line, sounding small and

unsure. "Jesse?"

"What the *fuck* is he doing there?" I ask, feeling Drew's and Sam's disappointed eyes on me. The *fuck* was really quite unnecessary, and the very reason Drew's right. Keep me away. But the question? Totally necessary. I need to know if Steve's hunch was right.

"He's bought the company," Ava says, all so matter of fact.

Lord, hold me back. "Get your bag," I hiss, raging. "Get John, and leave." I release my grip of the wheel, my hand sweating. "Do you hear me?"

"Yes."

"Do it now while I'm on the phone."

"Okay."

I hear Peterson's questioning voice. Then Ava's assertive one. She sounds so together. It's more than I am.

"I'm sorry, Patrick," she says, a rustling sound coming down the line. Packing her bags? "I can't work for Rococo Union anymore."

She's right. She can't. And I don't have the capacity or sense to be happy about that right now. Yes, I wanted her to be a lady of leisure, to enjoy her life, not graft for someone else's gain. Yes, I pushed it. But I never pushed her out. Van Der Haus has pushed her out.

Peterson starts a confused babble of words, pressing Ava for sense and reason. "Mikael has assured me that you'll be made a profit-sharing director."

My jaw goes lax, and I look at the boys. "The cunt's trying to buy my wife."

"Serious?" Sam asks.

"Fucking lowlife," Drew mutters, as I get back to listening, hoping John's ready to step in if necessary. Van Der Haus would be buried in the plaster of a wall if I were there. No doubt.

"Sal," Ava says, her voice getting quieter by the second. I'm struggling to hear her. "He's been using you to keep tabs on me. I'm sorry."

And there goes my jaw again. The woman he was with? It was Sally? Ava's work colleague? My God, is there anything he wouldn't do?

"What now?" Sam asks.

"He was dating Ava's work friend to keep track of Ava."

Both boys mirror my disbelief.

"Are you so desperate that you'd destroy someone as sweet as Sally?" Ava asks, still quiet, but I detect the edge of disgust. "Are you so desperate to get revenge on—" I lose her, and I squint, listening harder, pushing the phone into my ear.

"Revenge on that womanizer is just an advantage." Mikael's distant, grainy voice takes me from disbelief to borderline psycho. "I've wanted you from day one." *I fucking knew it.* Of course he'd want her. Who wouldn't? "He doesn't deserve you."

I inhale, flinching at the reality of hearing someone else say what I've known all along. I don't deserve Ava. I don't deserve happiness. I don't deserve another chance. Amalie's words stamp all over my mind. *It's not your fault.* So many people have said it to me. But for the first time today, I considered believing it.

"I'm sorry, Patrick," Ava says, and I hear footsteps past the rustle of her mobile rubbing with her bag, her clothes. I don't know. She's leaving. I sink into the leather of my seat, swallowing.

"Ava?" Van Der Haus says, gentle.

Hearing him call her name hardens every muscle again. I stare at the steering wheel, waiting for what he might say next. It's nothing Ava won't know, but can I relax?

"He fucked other women when he was with you, Ava," he says, and I cough. "He doesn't deserve you."

"He does deserve me!" Ava shouts, sounding deranged, the volume and sheer distress making me jump in my seat. I look at Sam and Drew, who are still standing by, waiting for updates or to stop me leaving. "No one gets to pass judgment on him," she goes on, not letting up. "Except me. He's mine!"

The words ring in my ear, reverberating and sinking deep. I'm hers. She owns me. Only her judgments matter. Only Ava's feelings matter. How she cares for me, loves me, sees me—that's all that matters.

"Did you drug me?" she asks.

"Ava, I would never hurt you." Van Der Haus's voice is so soft. So pacifying. It just reaffirms what I always feared. He truly wants her, not just for revenge, but because she's beautiful, talented, spirited, and driven. "I've bought this company for you."

"You're consumed with the need for vengeance. You don't even know me. We've shared no intimacy, connection, or special moments.

What's wrong with you?"

"I know a good thing when I see it, and I'm prepared to fight for it."

Fight? Can't he see it's over? Is he going to hang around for me to fuck up again, hoping Ava sees the light and leaves me?

"You'll be fighting in vain," Ava says. "And even if you succeed in your attempts to break us, which you never will, you couldn't have me afterward."

"Why?"

"Because without him, I'm dead."

I release the breath I've been holding and feel my heart thrash in my chest. Not anxiety. Not fear.

Life.

The doors of John's Range Rover shut. Has she forgotten I'm here on the end of the phone?

"Jesse?"

What do I say to her? I don't know, so I leave the line quiet for a while. Stunned. "I don't deserve you, he's right." I clench my chin in my hand, for the first time uncertain whether I agree with myself. "But I'm too selfish to give you up to someone who does." And that someone isn't Mikael. But it might be me soon. *If I can accept myself.* Forgive myself. "We'll never be broken." My fucking voice is cracking, God damn me. "And you'll never be without me, so you'll be living forever, baby."

"Deal," she murmurs, sounding emotional, tired, but at the same, I sense relief.

"I'll see you in the bath."

"Deal," she says again.

I hang up, start the car, and look at the boys. "I'm fine, and I need to get home."

They both nod, and I buckle up, send Steve a message to let him know I'll call him later, pulling away calmly to demonstrate my stability. I've never felt so stable and, weirdly, a desire to kill Van Der Haus isn't dominating my emotions.

I pull out of the gates of The Manor, letting the window down, and A Man's, Man's, Man's World comes through the speakers. I laugh lightly at the irony. "True," I muse, thinking, reaching into my pocket and pulling out my picture of the babies. I smile, setting it on the dashboard so I can look at it often, driving sensibly through the country roads on my way back to the city. Calm. Thoughtful. She's left her job, she's all mine, and I will make sure she's content and fulfilled. Whatever she wants, she can have it. Ironic that after spending the best part of my relationship and marriage to Ava trying to convince her she doesn't need to work, it's the fucker who tried to ruin me who made it happen. A weight feels like it's left my shoulders, despite learning about the threats Ava's received. She won't be leaving my sight, and now she doesn't need to.

My phone starts ringing, cutting the music, and an unknown number illuminates the screen.

Scotland?

I frown and tentatively accept the call. "Jesse Ward."

"It's Alan."

I stare at the road, at a loss. "Alan…?"

"Pierce."

"Oh," I breathe, my stomach turning. "Alan."

"I heard you've been trying to get hold of me."

I wonder how, but I don't ask. "Yeah, um—" Shit, how the fuck do I explain that? I thought I saw his dead daughter. I thought I'd check with him to see if she's still incarcerated. Miles away from me and my new wife. "I'm sorry for your loss, Alan."

There's a beat too long of silence. "My loss?"

I falter, his genuine confused reaction to my statement confusing *me*. "Lauren."

"Yes, I'm sorry too," he says, his words a tired exhale. "I'm sorry I ever thought I could fix her."

I wince. The site of my scar twinges. Could I have fixed her by loving her? "Can I ask…" I stall. *Fuck*. "Can I ask how?" Why do I want to know? It's warped and, actually, will do me no favors in my own recovery process. Could bring on more guilt, more stress.

"How what?" Alan asks, the confusion back.

And now I'm with him. "How she died?"

"Lauren's not dead, Jesse," he says, so clinically. Detached.

The fuck? An underlying panic rises. "You told—"

"I told people I'd lost my daughter, because I did."

Every scrap of air leaves my lungs. "What?"

"She's not dead, Jesse. She was in a psychiatric hospital for years. They released her. They shouldn't have. Her mother and I had to step away before she killed us, whether that be in a fit of rage or because she made us ill."

Ice creeps into my bloodstream.

"I'm just sorry..." He's clearly struggling. I'm with him. But for me, it's my breathing. It's diminished. "I'm very sorry about what she did to you, son."

I stare at the road disappearing under the wheels of the car.

Paralyzed.

Chapter 45

I texted John to tell him in as few words as possible about Alan's call, to sweep the penthouse, and call me the minute he's out of Ava's earshot. By the time I'm at Lansdowne Crescent, he's still not called, so *I* call *him*, stressed, panicked, out of my fucking mind.

"Yes," he snaps in answer, sounding really fucking grumpy.

"Are you home?"

"We're here now. Cathy's already left, but I'll stay until you arrive."

"I'm at Lansdowne Crescent." But I can't remember exactly which house Ava went in. "Can you recall a door number?"

"It's a blue door. Needs painting."

I spot a blue door, and my eyes remain on it, lasers. "Lansdowne Crescent," I muse, turning off my engine.

"Yes, Lansdowne Crescent." John says, pensive.

"And you think it was Lauren?"

"I can't be sure. I only got a glimpse, but if it's not her, it's her doppelganger."

I'm praying it's the latter. "We could be overreacting, right?" I ask, not wanting to insinuate that John might have been seeing things. "Making something out of nothing?" I'm clutching at straws, I know I am. This is not fucking good.

"I really fucking hope so," John whispers.

I get out and walk up the path to the house, going to the window and cupping the glass, looking inside. "I don't think anyone's home," I say, the glass steaming under my breath. I just need to see who lives here. See if we're off the mark.

"There's no one there?"

"The client you took her to see, it was definitely Ruth Quinn?"

"Yes, Ruth Quinn. I already told you. I know my eyesight ain't as good as it used to be, but I'd put my life on it."

Put his life on it that he thinks he saw Lauren? "*Now* you're putting your life on it?"

"You need to call the police," John hisses. "Not go looking for her, you crazy motherfucker."

"I'm not leaving this house until I see with my own eyes who lives here." I go to the door and knock.

"Jesse," John goes on, sounding insultingly soothing. "You need to get your arse back here. Leave it for the police to deal with."

"No, John," I shout, hitting the door a little harder, my temper and fear getting the better of me. *I'd put my life on it.* All I can hear are Ava's words about this client. She's testing, demanding, always fucking calling or dropping by her office. *Fuck.* Every time I've thought I've seen Lauren, it's been around the area where Ava's office is. Every single fucking time. "Just tell Ava I've got caught up in traffic. I don't want her to know about this. It could be nothing." I'm praying it's nothing. *Praying.*

"It's too late," John sighs, defeated. "She's standing right here. You'd better come home."

"Fuck!" I smash my fists into the door, probably raising the dead as well as the whole of London. "Answer the fucking door!" I shove myself away and rake a hand through my hair, looking to the clouds and forcing myself into some calm breathing. I'm a joke. "Can you put her on the phone?" I ask. My time dodging that final, crucifying piece of my past is up. Because even if we're wrong, Ava's heard too much.

"Who is she?" It's the first thing she says, her voice strong.

I stalk to the end of the pavement and look up at the house, searching the windows. "I'm not sure."

"What do you mean?" she yells, her composure lost, fear fueling her.

"I'm on my way home." I give up; there's no one home, and if there is, they're not going to answer. "We'll talk."

"No," she snaps. "Tell me."

"Ava," I wheeze, getting in my car, exhausted by my emotions. "I didn't want to say anything until I was sure it's her." A Ford honks me when I pull out in front of it. *Take it easy.* "I'll explain when I can sit you down."

"I'm not going to like this, am I?"

"Baby, please, I need to see you." Hold her hands. Hold her *down.*

"You didn't answer my question. What else could you possibly have to tell me, Jesse?"

"I'll be home soon," I murmur quietly, putting my foot down when I reach the main road.

"Will it make me run?"

"I'll be home soon," I say again, on auto pilot. I disconnect the call and grip the steering wheel hard, along with my teeth. Try in vain to get my head on straight. Then I dial Steve.

"Everything okay?" he asks warily, sensing my stress.

"I have another name for you. Two actually. Lauren Pierce and Ruth Quinn."

"Right," he says slowly, waiting for more.

"They could be the same person. Lauren Pierce is—" I breathe in, fighting the words forward. "She's my ex-wife." Steve doesn't react. He just listens. "She was unwell. Mentally, I mean. She was in hospital for many years, and I'd heard she'd passed away. I've just found out she's not dead."

"Tell me more," he says, calm and patient. Professional. No judgment, no show of surprise, although I'm sure he feels it.

"Ruth Quinn is a client of Ava's. A difficult one. I don't know a lot on that front. But John took Ava to an appointment this afternoon and caught a glimpse of this Ruth Quinn. He thought she looked familiar."

"Familiar as in, like your ex-wife?"

"Yes."

"How long has it been since John's seen her?"

"Sixteen years, maybe seventeen."

"And you?"

"Same."

"That's a long time, Jesse."

"I know," I grate. I hear him. Why now? "I've been to the address of Ava's client. There's no one there. It could be nothing"—fuck, I hope it's nothing—"but it could be something, Steve, and I really need to know."

"I've got you. I'll check out the names now and come back to you. What's the address of this client?"

"Twelve Lansdowne Crescent."

"I'm on it. You shouldn't have gone there. Where's Ava?"

"At home with John."

"Listen, try to relax, okay? I'm sure there's nothing in it, but it's wise to check it out. Are you comfortable with me coming to your home to take these statements?"

"Yeah, sure. We're in the penthouse at the new Lusso building on

Katherine Docks."

"I'll call you when I'm on my way."

I hang up and repeat his words over and over. It's nothing. It's been over sixteen years. Why would she decide to haunt me now? I'm so strung, I jump when another call comes in. "John?" I say, tense.

"The concierge has mentioned someone loitering around outside so I'm going down to check it out."

"A woman?" I ask instinctively, my heart missing a few too many beats.

"No, a guy. By the bins."

I sigh, loosening up. "It's probably the homeless dude," I say. "I took his trolly out a few weeks back. He sneaks in when the gates are open and rootles through the bins."

"I'll go check," he says. "Ava's upstairs. I locked the door."

"Is she okay?"

"Worried."

I hear the front door close down the line. "I'm five minutes away." I hang up and focus on the road, trying to make some sense out of all this. But I can't. I don't know whether it's because I simply don't have the capacity or if it simply can't make sense.

Three more calls come in before I make it to Lusso—Sam, Drew, and Kate. I don't answer, my energy levels zapped. And now I have to explain to Ava why I was trying to break down her client's door. I park up and scan the car park for the homeless guy, but don't see any sign of him. I bet John saw him off. Probably with a few quid in his pocket.

I walk into the lobby, scanning the desk area for Clive or the new concierge. There's no one. I glance down at my watch, walking on, the sound of my shoes hitting the marble echoing around the lobby.

As I approach the lift, I lift a hand, ready to hit the call button.

Stop dead in my tracks when I see John.

Unconscious on the floor.

"No," I whisper, immobilized for a few precious seconds, my eyes nailed to his big body lying on the marble, half concealed behind the concierge's desk. What the fuck is happening? "John?" My legs come to life, and I run to him, checking him over, my hands all over his big body. "John, can you hear me?"

He stirs, grumbles, his eyes opening and closing, hissing in pain.

I see the blood around his head.

"Fuck," I hiss. "John, what happened?"

His hand pats around on the floor, feeling, until he finds my forearm and squeezes. "Go," he wheezes, finding my eyes. "Go."

I withdraw, every inch of me turning cold.

"Go!" he coughs.

I look up above the elevator. It's at the penthouse. "Oh my God," I breathe, standing and sinking my fist into the doors. "Fuck, fuck, fuck!" I turn and run to the stairwell door, smashing in the code and yanking it open. I fly up the stairs like a tornado, adrenaline and fear fueling me.

Terrified.

I push through the last door and emerge into the foyer outside the penthouse, stalking toward the front door. I don't feel for my keys, my head telling me to get the fuck in there fast. So I shoulder barge it, and the second I right my bent body, I see Ava, folded over, holding her tummy.

And I know.

I. Just. Fucking. Know.

"No," I whisper, catching sight of someone disappearing into the kitchen. *Fuck, no!* There are clatters and bangs, but...Ava. What the hell has she done to her?

Ava's eyes meet mine. Tears are streaming, yet her sobs are quiet. My God, I'll fucking *kill* her. Rage breaks through my terror, so fast and fierce, I start to quake where I stand, consumed by it. It goes against everything inside me, but I leave Ava where she is and go to the kitchen. The minute I see her, nausea rises.

My blood turns to ice.

She's not really changed that much. There's still crazy in her eyes.

A knife in her hand.

A sick smirk curving her lips.

"Here we are, me and you, as it should be," she whispers, out of breath, as I move around the island, making sure I keep something between us. I don't correct her. I realize I have to choose my words carefully. Be cautious, wise. Try not to poke her. I've seen many versions of Lauren. This one in front of me? It's the worst. The most dangerous and damaging.

I stare at her, trying to catch my breath. "Put the knife down,

Lauren," I say calmly, silently willing Ava to stay away. Hoping she's been sensible and got her and our babies the fuck out of here *and* called the police.

My hope is dashed when I hear a thud and Lauren's eyes move to the doorway. *Fuck*. Ava's standing on the threshold, looking the most petrified I've ever seen her. *God damn her.*

"Oh my God," she whispers, her eyes nailed to the blade in Lauren's hand.

"Nice to see you, Jesse," Lauren muses, a nasty, sinister edge to her voice, causing many horrific memories to come flooding back.

"No," I whisper, so tense my body hurts. "It's not. Why are you here?" Why now, after all these years, has she chosen to invade my life?

"I was happy to let you wallow in misery," she says, making me pull in air, my questions being answered with that one scathing statement. It's Ava. Happiness. Peace. That's why she's here. "Drink your life away," she goes on, the knife swaying. "And try to fill the void that *you* created by mindlessly fucking about." And there it is. She was happy that I was miserable. Hollow. In constant pain. "But then you went and fell in love." She smiles, and it's loaded with nothing but hatred. My God, how long has she been hovering on the sidelines of my life, watching me slowly dying? "I can't let you have happiness when you've destroyed mine."

"I've paid tenfold for my mistakes, Lauren," I whisper, catching a glimpse of Ava. Her horrified face, her disbelieving, watery gaze. It crushes me. Absolutely fucking crushes me. It's been Lauren all along. The drugs, the car, the threats. I wasn't seeing things. I wasn't going fucking crazy. "I deserve this," I murmur, not sounding very convincing.

"No, you don't," she muses, like it's a foregone conclusion. "You took my happiness, so I'll take yours." Her knife is pointing at Ava. My happiness. And Lauren's happiness? That was me. It wasn't Rosie. It was me. She's here because I took *me* away from her.

"I didn't take your happiness." I was *never* going to be her happiness.

"Yes!" She explodes, her face flashing red, and I flinch. "You married me, and then left me."

The sound of complete shock that bursts from Ava was expected. Doesn't make it easier to hear. I want to explain, tell her the full story, build the picture, before Lauren gets to where I know she's heading.

Rosie.

"You didn't know?" Lauren says, seeing Ava's reaction. "Well, there's a surprise. It might also explain why you've stuck around."

Jesus Christ, what the fuck am I going to do? Trying to pacify her won't work. I've dealt with her enough to know what I'm dealing with, and I'm dealing with the same woman who lost her mind and gunned for me. If it were just me standing here, I'd take my chances. But it's not just me. And I don't like the crazed looks she keeps turning Ava's way.

To Lauren, my wife's the problem.

"Nothing can break us," Ava whispers shakily, and I swallow, my heart turning. I want to believe it.

The sick feeling in my gut worsens as Ava gazes at me, scared, her head shaking mildly. I did this. Caused this. I walked her into the middle of this, and I don't know if I can get her out unharmed. Get our babies away from this psychotic madwoman who has every intention of doing irrevocable damage.

"I'm so sorry." How did I let this happen? What kind of man am I? "I should have told you." Should have given her every detail, made her aware so she could at least recognize the signs.

"It doesn't matter," she says desperately.

"It *does* matter," Lauren hisses. "She knows nothing, does she?"

I stare at Ava, wishing and hoping, wishing and hoping, my head shaking.

"She doesn't know about our daughter?"

A sense of calm finality comes over me, my eyes closing briefly as I exhale, needing to escape the shock. But I catch Ava jerk and instinct has me moving toward her.

"Stay where you are!" Lauren screams, halting me, my breath held, my eyes set on my pregnant wife as she gasps for breath, feeling for something that isn't there to steady herself.

"Ava," I yell, startling her.

"Yes, we were married," Lauren declares, proud. "And he left me when I was pregnant."

What? No. She does not get to spin her tale. She does not get to be economical with the truth. "I was forced to marry you *because* you were pregnant," I seethe, trying to keep a lid on the inevitable anger, pushing back visions of me walking on numb legs down the aisle.

Walking toward my tragic fate. "I didn't want to, and you knew it. We were seventeen years old, Lauren. We fooled around *one* time." And she tricked me. Got me plastered. Helped me escape. *Fuck!*

"Don't blame your decision on your parents."

My parents? No. I blame *her*. "I was trying to right my wrongs. I was trying to make them happy." And it was all wasted. I only made things worse. *More* tragic. "I—" I see Ava backing away in my side vision, but I don't look her way. I keep Lauren's eyes on me. *Yes, get away. Run.*

"Don't move," Lauren barks. "Don't even think about trying to leave, because this knife will be in him before you make it out the door." I'm sure Ava's realized by now that the scar on my stomach wasn't caused in a car accident. So she'll know Lauren is serious. Deadly serious. "You've not even heard the best part." Lauren flashes me a satisfied smile, enjoying this as much as only a psycho would. Performing. Shooting for the most shocking, the most extreme reactions. "So it would be nice if you stick around to hear me out."

"Lauren," I say, my voice low. What the fuck is she expecting from this? That Ava will hear her, leave me, and we'll live happily ever after?

"What? You don't want me to tell your young, pregnant wife that you killed our daughter?"

It hits Ava like a boulder. Fuck, she's going to pass out. The stress, the pressure, the emotions. But if I move?

I look at Lauren. "No," I yell, seeing her moving toward Ava, the knife poised. *My God, no.*

I fly across the kitchen like a bull, catching Ava, blocking Lauren's path to her. "Fuck," I hiss, my vision blurring as pain radiates through my body and an awful sound invades my ears, like a squelch. I still for a moment, paralyzed. And then I feel the knife in my side. I breath out on a rush and start to shake, adrenaline kicking in. Urgency. I haven't got long.

I spin, grab her, and smash her to the ground, and Lauren's hands grip my wrists as I straddle her, heaving, the pain getting worse, the feeling of warm wetness creeping across my shirt. I blink, over and over, trying to clear my vision. And when I do, she smiles. She's fucking stabbed me. *Again.* But she was aiming for Ava. For our babies.

I roar, losing all control, and punch her in the face. Only Lauren would laugh. "I didn't kill my daughter," I bellow, drawing back and going again, sinking my fist into her face, the sounds of her laughing unbearable. How can she laugh when we're talking about Rosie. How?

"You did," she sings, delighted, her hands hitting at my chest, catching me in my side. The pain flares. "The moment she got in that car, you sent her to her death."

"It wasn't my fault!" I grunt, feeling dizzy, the flow of blood leaving my body so fast I can actually feel it pouring out of me.

"Carmichael should never have taken our daughter," she screams, laughing. "You should've been watching her!" She spits out some blood, baring red-stained teeth. "I spent five years in a padded cell. I've spent twenty years wishing I'd never let you see her." She spits at me, scratching at my sleeves. "You left me without you, then you killed the only piece of you I had left! I'll never let you replace her," she screams. "No one else gets a piece of you!"

Deranged and desperate, black dots now hampering my vision, I swing aimlessly, feeling and hearing bones crunch against my fist.

And then...silence.

No more tormenting words.

No more laughing.

The adrenaline leaves me, and suddenly air isn't so easy to find. I gasp, my lungs burning, as I raise my hands and hold them in front of me, trying to focus on them. "Fuck," I whisper, looking down at my shirt.

"Nothing will break us."

Ava?

I search for her, finding her on her knees. I have to get to her. I have to get her out of here. Struggling to my feet, I wobble, trying so hard to shake the dizziness away. And isn't it incredible that now, when I can't see a fucking thing, I still see Ava. So clearly. But I don't like it. The mess of her face, the tragic despair in her eyes. "I'm so, *so* sorry." I barely get the words past the lump in my throat, my steps heavy and clumsy. I feel so weak, my heart racing.

"It doesn't matter. Nothing matters."

I put one foot in front of the other, but I don't seem to be going anywhere. *She stabbed me.* I swallow, trying to wet my mouth, suddenly unable to talk. *Ava, call an ambulance.* My legs start to give, my body becoming too heavy to hold me up, and I drop to a knee, gasping. There's no air to be found. Ava's bewildered. My breathing becomes short and sharp, anything deeper causing slicing pain in my stomach.

Help me.

I sway on my knee, my uncoordinated hand reaching for my jacket and shoving it back, showing Ava the knife wedged in my side.

"No!"

I lose my balance and strength, collapsing to my back, my head hitting the kitchen floor with a smack. My eyelids feel so heavy, my body so fucking cold.

"Oh God, Jesse!"

Don't panic, baby.

"Oh God, no no no no no. Please no!"

Come on, Ava. I need you to pull it together.

"Don't close your eyes, Jesse."

I'm trying, baby, but I'm tired. So fucking tired.

"Baby, keep your eyes open," she snaps. "Look at me."

Breathing is getting harder with each painful breath, even the lightest of inhales causing untold pain. "Ava…" *Call an ambulance.* "Ava…"

She hushes me, her tears falling and sinking into my shirt as she starts feeling around in my pocket. She pulls out my mobile, juggling it in her hands.

Calm down, Ava. Just calm down.

Fuck, I can't keep my eyes open. But I can't close them.

Because I'm terrified I'll never see her again.

"I need an ambulance," she yells, her panic making her words almost indecipherable. "Please, my husband's been stabbed." Her hand meets my chest, her eyes now just dark blurry dots. I'm losing her. "The penthouse. The code for the elevator is 3210. It's the Lusso building on St. Katherine Docks. Please, he's losing consciousness. He can't talk. The blood, there's so much." Her voice cracks, and my heavy lids win, my eyes closing. "Please. Jesse, open your eyes," Ava snaps, but for all the will in world, I don't have the strength. "Don't you dare leave me," she yells, sobbing. "I'll be crazy mad if you leave me."

I can't breathe. "I can't b—" A wave of pain radiates through me, and I try to harden my body to stem it. Focus on breathing. *I must keep breathing.*

"Jesse!"

I fight with everything I have, use energy I can't afford to lose, to open my eyes. She's blurry but clear. And isn't that the poignancy of our story? Would it be too much to ask my body to grace me with one more touch too?

Yes.

Is this it? Have I had my time? My happiness? My moment? My love?

It would seem unfair if it wasn't so symbolic.

It was me or Ava. And it was always meant to be me.

I stare at her, hearing her talking but not understanding what she's saying, hearing music but not really knowing what it is. Something I recognize. "Unbreakable," I wheeze, getting heavier and heavier.

I'm done.

I close my eyes and freefall into my darkness, feeling an odd sense of peace filling my broken body.

Because I can leave this world knowing my wife and children will be safe from my tragedies.

Chapter 46

"Stand back, coming through!"

Who the fuck is that?

"We have a thirty-eight-year-old white male, knife wound to his upper stomach, knife still lodged, lost a lot of blood, BP forty-five over thirty."

I frown.

"We need to get him on the table. Stat. Prep surgery." I feel hands on me, my body becoming light momentarily. Then I'm gaging, choking, something blocking my throat. Then beeps. Yells. Panic.

And then—

Nothing.

Chapter 47

I inhale and take in my surroundings. Trees, grass, shrubs, water. I recognize it. The sun is blazing up above, the sky a vivid blue, a few fluffy clouds dotted around. No city noise, just tweeting birds and branches swaying in the gentle breeze.

It's a perfect day.

I smile as I trudge down to the small barrier between the lake and the path, looking across the water to the island. Ducks, hundreds of them, bob on the surface, weaving perfect paths through the water, cute ducklings following them. It's spring. My favorite season of the year. It's the season I met my wife.

It's just past seven in the evening. What the hell am I doing in the park at this time? She'll be at home waiting for me.

I start walking up the path but slow to a gradual stop when I realize I don't know where my car's parked. "Fuck," I curse, reaching into my pocket for my mobile. No phone. And as I gaze around the park, I realize it's empty. At seven o'clock in the evening on a beautiful spring day?

I frown, my eyes dropping down my suited front, and some unknown, higher power has me reaching for my jacket. I pull back one side. "What the fuck?" I whisper, staring at the knife plunged in my side. I turn on the spot, my eyes darting, panic rising. But where's the pain? There's blood, so much fucking blood, but where's the pain? I stagger a few paces forward, and then I see someone in the distance. A man with a child on his shoulders. They're blurry, but definitely there. *Help me.*

But as they get closer, I realize he's not a man.

He's a young lad.

My brother.

"Jake?" I breathe, not nearly loud enough for him to hear me, but he hears, smiling back at me, getting closer while I stand stock-still, mesmerized by the sight of him. His floppy hair, the cheeky twinkle in his eye. I follow his arms up to the hands he's holding either side of his face. Small, chubby hands. "Oh my God," I whisper, meeting Rosie's eyes.

"Daddy," she sings, jumping up and down on Jake's shoulders, making him laugh.

"Steady, girl, my shoulders aren't as big as your dad's."

Confused as fuck, I look at my shoulders. Wide shoulders in an expensive suit. Older shoulders. What the hell is going on? Looking up at my girl, I stare, transfixed. Awed. I just want to grab her down and squeeze her. And Jake too. "Where are we?" I ask. "What is this?" I move forward and nearly knock myself out when I crash into something invisible. "The fuck?" I blurt, ricocheting back.

"Watch your mouth, Daddy."

I recoil, surprised, as Jake laughs his adolescent nuts off and Rosie chuckles, the sound squeaky and completely adorable. "Watch your mouth, bro." Jake smirks.

I tentatively reach forward with my hand, feeling for the glass blocking my way to them. Could I smash it?

"No," Jake says. "I wouldn't even try."

"I don't understand."

"We're in heaven, Daddy!"

"We are?" I look around, so fucking confused. "It looks like St. James's Park to me."

"Heaven is wherever you want it to be," Jake says. "We chose here, didn't we, Rosie?"

"Quack, quack, quack."

I laugh lightly, but it's tinged with nerves. "Heaven," I muse, looking down at my stomach. At the knife.

"You're not in heaven," Jake says, winning my attention.

"Where am I then?"

"Well, you're kind of in-between."

"What? In-between where and where?" Shit, am I going down instead of up?

"It's not your time yet, Jesse," Jake says, smiling, backing up. Where's he going? I'm not done.

"Wait," I yell, my hands on the invisible barrier between us, my eyes bouncing between my brother and daughter, desperate to go with them. But—

"Ava," I whisper. *It's not my time.*

"You're going to have a girl and a boy!" Rosie sings.

"What?"

"You better name the boy after me," Jake says, chuckling. "And let me tell you, if you think the past twenty years have been a punishment, wait until you meet your little girl." He's getting farther and farther away, fading.

"Jake, wait," I call, my palms feeling across the barrier, my face pushed up close. "Please don't go." *Don't leave me.*

"You're needed, bro." His smile is like a balm, but I see the sadness in his green eyes. He misses me. "We're good."

"You're good," I murmur.

"And Daddy?" Rosie says, palms on the top of Jake's head, leaning closer as he continues to back away.

"What, baby girl?" I whisper, taking her in, every beautiful inch of her, refreshing all the memories I have of her. "Take the money."

"The money?" I frown. "What money? I have money."

"See you soon, Daddy."

"It's not that soon, my girl." Jake laughs, eyes on me. "You're never alone, Jesse." He smiles. "Even when you're alone." Jake looks past me, and then I hear her.

"Jesse, please, open your eyes."

I look back over my shoulder.

"Why isn't he waking up? It's been too long."

"Ava?" I question, searching for her in the blankness.

"Go to her," Jake calls.

"But what about you?" I ask, my panic rising again. Am I supposed to choose? "I should be with you." It should have always been me.

I face the glass again, feel it. Search the space beyond.

They're gone.

And my heart breaks all over again.

Chapter 48

It's the strangest feeling. I can't open my eyes, can't talk, can't feel, can't move a fucking muscle. I've tried. Endlessly. I'm trapped in a body that's refusing to work.

But I can hear. I can't respond, but I can hear, and I can think. I'm not in a good way, I know that. I've heard the lowdown, the details of my surgery, what everyone's expectations are. It's a waiting game for them. For me, it's just a matter of when I have the strength to open my fucking eyes. *It's not your time, Jesse.*

"Wake up," I hear Ava say for the thousandth time.

I'm trying, baby.

"You stubborn man."

You have a nerve, Ava Ward.

"Why won't he wake up, Mum?"

"He's healing, darling. He needs to heal."

Oh great. My adorable mother-in-law is in town. I might just stay exactly where I am, silent and still, until she fucks off.

"It's been too long. I need him to wake up. I miss him." The bed jolts beneath me, and then I hear her cries.

No, baby, no more tears. I can't stand it.

"Oh, Ava, darling, you need to eat," Elizabeth says.

Yes, she does. Someone, feed this woman immediately.

"I'm not hungry," Ava snaps.

Give me strength.

"I'm making a list of your disobediences, and I'll be telling Jesse about each and every one of them when he comes round."

No need, Elizabeth. I've made my own notes, and I can tell you your daughter is lined up to receive twelve Sense Fucks, eight Retribution Fucks, and five Apology Fucks. I'd leave town if I were you.

"Beatrice and Henry have just arrived, darling."

What the fuck? My mum and dad?

"Can they come in?"

No, don't let them in. Don't let them see me like this. Jesus fucking Christ, I'm not at full strength. I can't take that kind of stress.

Make amends.

What?

"Just for a few minutes," Ava says, and a few moments later, the atmosphere shifts. Tense. And I can't escape it. Can't move. Can't hide.

Can't drink myself away from the pain.

"How has he been?"

Dad?

I feel something on my face, tickling. *Fuck, that's annoying.* I try to disregard it, try to listen.

"And what about you, Ava? You need to be taking care of yourself."

Yes, Dad, tell her. You tell her to look after herself or it'll be thirteen Sense Fucks.

"I'm fine."

See? Do you see the level of stubbornness I have to contend with?

"Will you let us take you for something to eat? Not far, just down to the hospital restaurant."

You go, Ava Ward, or so help me God.

"I'm not leaving him. He might wake up, and I won't be here."

For fuck's sake, woman.

"I understand."

You shouldn't. She needs to eat.

"Perhaps we can bring you something, then?"

"No, thank you."

For the love of God!

"Ava, please."

Amalie? Amalie, is that you?

My arm is suddenly moving, not because I made it move, but because I'm about to be prodded at again for the thousandth time.

"Good evening," the nurse says.

Evening.

"How is this fine specimen of a man today?"

Yes, that's me. Fit as fuck.

"Let's see what's going on." I'm pulled here, pushed there, something is stuck in my ear. And won't someone stop that irritating beeping sound? "Just the same. You have a strong, determined man, sweetheart."

And a pissed off one too.

I try to lift a hand and fail. Deciding I might be trying for too much, I try to lift a finger, focus really hard, put everything I have into it. *Fuck*. Everything hurts. But then…

I breathe in. Oh my God, I moved it. My finger definitely moved.

"I know," Ava sighs.

I focus on my finger again, trying to make it move, to make them see I'm here. Hearing. Listening. Come on, come on, come o—

What the fuck?

I stop trying to move, distracted.

What is that?

Something's tugging on the end of my dick, and I suddenly need a pee. And I can't get up.

Shit.

I need the toilet!

I try to hold it. I really try. But…I groan to myself as I let it happen, relief and mortification mixing.

"We'll leave you in peace. You have my number."

Dad?

Make amends.

No, Dad, don't go, please.

"You good, girl?"

John?

"I'm not staying."

Why, you just fucking got here?

"I just wanted you to know that they both appeared in court today and both have been remanded."

Both?

"Okay," Ava says.

Wait, someone please elaborate. Both?

"I don't mean to be rude," Ava goes on. "But I don't have the en—"

Then get some damn sleep, Ava, for Christ's sake. God, you're getting it. When I can move more than my little finger.

"Ava, go home, have a shower and get some sleep."

Kate. Listen to Kate.

"We'll stay. If he wakes, I'll call you immediately. I promise."

No need to stay. Unless you want to witness a thirty-eight-year-old god piss himself constantly.

"Come on, Ava."

Drew? Fuck me, is the whole world and their dog here?

"There, see? We'll stay and Drew can take you home for a while."

I roll my eyes at the sound of Sam. Not actually, of course. Because I can't. I try my finger again. It moves again, but even that's exhausting. The concentration.

"No," Ava snaps, stroppy. "I'm not fucking leaving, so just stop it."

Watch your fucking mouth!

"Wake up!"

Not until you watch your damn mouth.

"Please eat, Ava."

And eat. I'll wake up if you eat.

"I've eaten some salad."

Something more than a few leaves.

"I don't know what else to do," Kate says hopelessly.

I do. Drag her. Kicking and screaming if you have to. Just mind the babies.

"We'll go," John says.

How's your head, motherfucker?

Another dip of the mattress beneath me, and then...silence.

No. I need noise. With no noise, there's only my thoughts, and my thoughts take me back to the kitchen. To Lauren. *Fuck.*

I strain, certain I must be shaking with the effort to move just a finger. Just a little fucking finger.

Fuck it.

I stop trying, and I let my mind wander to where it will go, inevitably dreading where that might be. I've been back in that kitchen every time I've partially come round. Watched from the edge of my life as I stepped in front of Ava and blocked her from Lauren. Watched as the knife plunged in and she dragged it, slicing me, before I knocked her away and she lost her grip. This knife was sharper than the knife she used sixteen years ago. I hardly knew I'd been stabbed, only felt an odd pressure in my side, before the pain kicked in and the blood started flowing. I've watched as I collapsed. I've watched as comprehension found my distraught wife. I've watched as she sobbed and demanded me to open my eyes. To not die.

It's not your time, Jesse.

Watch your mouth, Daddy.

Pain slices me, and I jolt.
Fuck.
And then, as if my mind is protecting me, it shuts down.
And all I see is darkness.

Chapter 49

My eyelids twitch, the muscles coming to life, and light blinds me, forcing me to slam them shut again. Fuck, did I just open my eyes? I breathe in, hope crashing into me. I squeeze my lids shut and release them, cautiously peeling one open. My eyes hurt. My face muscles hurt. Suddenly everything fucking hurts. I look around the room, still as can be, not only because I'm incapacitated, but because if my whole head is in agony by just opening my eyes, I can't begin to imagine the level of pain waiting for me if I actually move.

I drop my eyes, and I'm greeted by a mass of messy brown hair. I exhale lightly, wary, and suddenly all I can feel is my heart beating. *Ava.* I'm mesmerized as I stare down at her sleeping, her head resting on the bed, her body hunched over.

"How old are you?" she mumbles. I'm unable to stop my small smile. I sustain the pain, swallowing too, trying to push some words past my lips.

"Thirty-eight," I whisper groggily, amazed when I hear my own voice. "I'm thirty…eight, baby."

I hear her hum and mumble, her head moving as she rubs her face into the sheets.

"My beautiful…girl is…dreaming."

And that's me done for the day, my eyes closing again, the effort to keep them open way too much. Christ, will I ever be able to move again? I'm fucking drained. Heavy. Hurting.

I feel the bed move. She's woken up? God damn it, I missed her. I focus, concentrating on moving my finger again, anything to tell her I'm here. Anything to stop her worrying. *Fuck.*

An unbearable, screechy sound attacks my ears. *God, make it stop.*

"Jesse?"

I still, not that I'm actually moving, and listen. Did she say my name? *Ava?*

There's suddenly a pressure on my shoulders, and my upper body is moving. Fuck, that's agony, the pain starting at my neck and radiating down to my toes.

"Jesse?" Ava cries.

Beep!

"Jesse?"

Beep!

My whole body starts shaking involuntarily, and I can't fucking stop it. What the hell is she doing, trying to kill me? *Stop, Ava.* The pain is excruciating. As is the noise.

"Too...loud."

"Jesse?" she gasps.

"What?" My arm suddenly has life, moving up, my body going into protection mode, trying to block the pain and noise. I hold my head, feeling like it could fall off.

"Open your eyes," she shouts. *Fuck, why all the shouting?* She's panicking. I don't need panic, I need calm.

"No," I grunt. "It fucking...hurts."

"Oh God." Her words are a desperate gasp. "Try." A plea.

If it will quieten her down, I'll do anything. My face bunches, my eyes squeezed so tightly shut, that's causing pain too. *Relax.* I let the tiniest bit of light past my lids, trying to get used to the invasion again. "Fucking hell," I mumble, not only because I'm in fucking agony here. The sight of her through my grainy vision shocks me. Her face is blotchy, her hair matted, her eyes sunken. Jesus Christ, she's not been looking after herself. Why has no one force-fed her? She's wasting away. God damn it, I want to enforce some rules, but I can't fucking move.

On a wracked sob, Ava comes at me, and I don't have the time or capacity to stop her. My eyes are suddenly wide open as she smothers my face with her lips. Pain. Shit, aren't they giving me anything to help with that?

"Sorry," she screeches, breaking away.

"Fucking hell, Ava." I don't recognize my voice. I try swallowing, the scratch painful too. Everything's painful. I succumb to it and let my heavy lids fall again.

"Open your eyes."

Fuck me.

I drag them open. "Then stop inflicting fucking...pain on me, woman."

Her lip wobbles, her red nose sniveling. "I thought I'd lost you." She hides her face in her hands, her body quaking with the force of her sobs, and there's nothing I can do to comfort her.

"Baby," I breathe, damning my broken body to hell and back. "Please don't cry…when there's…fuck all I can do about…it." I try to turn my torso a little so I can reach for her. "Fucking hell," I gasp, holding my breath, tensing. "Fuck." No, not happening.

"Stop moving," she says, stern.

Fine by me. God, what day is it? How long have I been here? I fight past the fog, trying to recall…anything. I feel like I've been pulsing in and out of an alternate universe, reliving each day, forgetting it, starting again. Right now, I can't remember a damn thing.

I lift my arm and look down at the line into it. Glance around the room. That's right. I'm in hospital. Half dead because—

The onslaught of memories hit me again, the scene from the kitchen ready for another replay. "She hurt you." I instinctively try to sit up, and I pay for it, the pain diabolically intense, but my panic is fiercer. *Fuck.* "The babies."

"We're okay." Ava is soon standing over me, working against me. "Jesse, we're all okay." She doesn't let me win, forcing me to the bed. "Lie down."

"You're okay?" I ask, reaching for her tired face. She doesn't look okay. She looks wrecked. "Please tell me you're okay."

"I'm fine."

"And the babies?"

"I've had two scans," she says. Oh, that's good. Very good. I let my body sink into the bed again, needing to close my eyes. "I should call the nurse."

"No, please," I whisper, dragging my heavy hand to her neck. "Let me wake up before…they start poking…me about." I inject some power into my arm and pull her closer.

"I don't want to hurt you." She doesn't? Too late for that. I put up some resistance when she tries to pull away, gritting my teeth. I don't win because I'm stronger. I win because she gives in. "Jesse."

"Contact. Do what you're told."

She does, which is a welcome result, because there wouldn't be much I could do about it if she didn't. "Are you in much pain?"

This isn't pain. I don't know what this is but it's fucking unbearable. "Agony."

"I need to get the nurse," she whispers, her volume now at a tolerable level.

"Soon." I sigh. "I'm comfy."

"No, you're not."

True. But I suppose I ought to get used to uncomfortable. I need some painkillers. Where's the fucking nurses around here? I frown at myself.

"I'm glad you're still here." I turn my head and pucker my lips, kissing her. "I'd have given up if I didn't constantly hear your defiant voice."

"You could hear me?"

"Yes, it was strange and fucking annoying when"—fuck, get me some painkillers—"I couldn't tell you off. Will you ever do what you're told?"

"No."

"Thought not." Why change the habit of a lifetime? But my habit? Keeping secrets I shouldn't keep? I have to change that habit. I have to get comfortable talking about my past. "I have some explaining to do."

"No, you don't." She's suddenly scrambling away, and she catches me in my side as she does. Doesn't stop me from holding on to her, though. *Idiot.*

"Fuck." Lord, help me. "Fucking, fuck, fuck, fuck," I grunt, holding her close, and she eventually relents, thank God. "Just stay put and listen. You're not going anywhere until…I've told you about"—Deep breath—"Rosie." I don't think I've said her name out loud since she died, and hearing it in my voice, albeit gravelly and dry, brings on a whole new facet of pain.

You can do it, Daddy.

Shit. I can do it.

Can I?

"Lauren was the daughter of my mum and dad's good friends," I begin, starting to tell the story I should have told long ago, fighting against the discomfort to speak clearly. "I'm sure you can imagine the type," I battle on. "Well-bred, rich, and highly respected in the snotty community that we…were forced to tolerate." God, how I hated them.

"We fooled around once and she ended up pregnant." Planned by her, not me. "We were seventeen, young and stupid." Me more so. How did I not see what she was doing that night she appeared in my bedroom with a bottle of vodka—a means to escape my grief if only for a short while? "Can you imagine the scandal? I'd really done it this time." I'm not sure what's more painful—talking or moving. "Fuck," I hiss, testing myself. Definitely moving.

Ava's quiet. Listening. So I shouldn't stop. Get it all out.

Deep breaths.

"Emergency meetings were called between Lauren's family and my own." I remember sitting there, numb and mute, listening to my future being meticulously planned. Lauren was smiling. Happy. "Her father demanded I...marry her before word got out and ruined both of our families. Jake..." I fade off briefly to take a breath. "Jake had not long died. I went along with it, hoping my compliance might build some bridges with my parents." I feel Ava's hand squeeze mine, and I swallow a few times, trying to moisten my dry mouth so I can continue. "The joint effort of both families did an amazing job of convincing the community that we were hopelessly in love."

"She was," Ava says, quite matter of fact.

"And I wasn't." If anything, I was terrified. I take a few more breaths, fighting through the pain to continue. I'm not stopping until this is done. "I was married off and moved into her parents' country estate within a month. Everyone was happy, except...me. Carmichael gave me an escape, and I...I finally...plucked up the courage to call a halt on the whole diabolical farce." *Breathe.* "But when Rosie arrived, I was..."—A hard swallow—"determined to be a dad. That little girl was the only person on the planet who loved me for me, no expectations or pressure, she just accepted me in her innocence. It didn't matter that she was a baby." I smile on the inside. "She was a real daddy's girl. I could do no wrong, and I knew I never would in her eyes. That was enough to make me evaluate the lifestyle I'd slipped into while Lauren was pregnant." I can't get her fucking face out of my head, and it's pissing me off. "Carmichael got the best solicitor involved to try and gain me full custody because he knew that she was my redeemer, but Lauren's family dug up every dirty little secret, from Jake, to The Manor, to my brief lifestyle, from when I left Lauren until Rosie was born. I didn't have a hope."

"And your parents had moved to Spain by now?"

I laugh. I don't know why. Because it fucking hurts. "Yeah, they escaped the shame I'd brought on the family." What kind of delusional idiot am I? Still telling myself things, but to what end?

"They abandoned you," Ava says quietly, with no judgment.

"They wanted me to go with them. Mum begged, but I couldn't leave Rosie full-time with that family. She'd be frowned upon as an illegitimate child, even though she had me. Not an option."

"So then what?"

Here we go. "Rosie was three and I made the worst mistake of my life." Ava knows the next bit of the puzzle, but she would never have pieced it together. Why would she? She only had minimal facts. "I slept with Sarah."

"Sarah?"

"Carmichael and Sarah were together."

Up she comes, so fast I don't have a chance to stop her. "They were?" Her face. Expected, I guess. "Sarah and Carmichael?" she questions. "But I thought he was a playboy."

"He was." A terrible, hedonistic flirt. "With a girlfriend." *Tell her everything.* "And a child."

"What?" Eyes wide, she stares at me, and I see she's trying so hard to hold on to her shock and control her rampant curiosity. "Go on."

Fuck, this story is long. "Carmichael walked in on me and Sarah," I say, shaking away the look of sheer disappointment on his face. "He hit the roof, got the girls, and left."

"The girls?"

"Rosie and Rebecca."

"Your Rosie and their Rebecca," she whispers. "The car accident?"

I nod, exhausted, needing to close my eyes for a few moments. Hide. "I didn't just kill my uncle and my daughter," I whisper. "I killed Sarah's girl too." Strangely, Sarah's never thrown that accusation at me. Never.

"No," Ava whispers. "That can't be your fault."

"I think you'll find that my poor decisions have been the cause for everything, Ava. I've fucked up on so many levels so many times, and I've paid for it, but I can't pay anymore, not now I have you. What if I make a bad decision again? What if I screw up again? What if I'm not done paying?" My body sinks into the mattress as all air leaves my lungs with my panicked words.

Ava bites into her lip, stunned, clearly trying to wrap her mind around the barrage of information. "You are more than done paying," she says quietly, turning her eyes to my torso. "When did she hurt you before?"

"After Rosie died, she tried so hard to make me see that we needed each other. She had always been a little unpredictable." That could be the most under-egged statement ever made. "But when I continually rebuffed her advances, she really started behaving erratically. We're talking full-on bunny-boiler style."

"Did she get pregnant on purpose?"

"Probably." What am I saying? *Definitely*. But I can't regret Rosie.

"And she stabbed you?"

"Yes."

"Did she go to prison?"

I shake my head. "No."

"Why?"

"Her family got her help and kept her away from me in exchange for my silence." Poor Alan. He only ever wanted to fix his daughter while at the same time ignoring the obvious issues she had.

"But look at the mess she made of you," Ava whispers. "How did you pass that off?"

"It's pretty superficial. She did a better job this time." Yeah, she got me good, and to think she was aiming for Ava? My blood runs cold, and Ava flinches and pales a little.

"You didn't even go to hospital, did you?" she says, and I shake my head. "Who stitched you up?"

"Her dad. He was a doctor."

"Oh my God." She lowers to a chair, stunned. "And where were your parents whilst all of this was going on?"

"They'd already returned to Spain." *And I ignored any attempt of contact. Drunk. Ashamed.*

"Jesse." She thinks really hard, as if she's not sure she should say what she wants to. "Your mum in Spain. Second chance?"

I smile sadly. "You really do know everything now," I whisper. "Are you leaving me?" She doesn't answer, and I stare at the ceiling, waiting.

Hoping. Could I blame her? No. Could I stop her? No.

"Look at me."

Fuck, I don't know if I can. I feel my eyes welling up, my throat closing. It's going to really hurt if I let my emotions out. But everyone knows the more you try to suppress a good cry, the more body-wracking it'll be when you let it claim you.

Facing her, I let go, struggling to see her past the blur.

"Unbreakable," she says, the word shaky but resolute, and I exhale my gratitude, the pain suddenly bearable.

"Hold me." She's seen me at my absolute worst, and now my weakest. No man wants to show their vulnerability. I don't plan on making a habit of it, but the reassurance radiating off her is fuel to my broken body.

She comes to me carefully, awkwardly trying to position herself around me. "Jesse, be careful."

"It hurts more if I'm not touching you." I tilt her face up to mine and study her, letting her touch me, feel me.

"I love you," she whispers, pushing her mouth to my dry lips.

"I'm glad." So glad.

"Don't stay that. I don't want you to say that."

Why does this anger her? "But I am."

"That's not what you usually say," she protests, feeling my hair, then pulling it.

Oh, I see. I smile to myself. "Tell me you love me."

"I love you," she replies quickly.

"I know." I instigate the next kiss, riding the pain while trying to hide my discomfort. It's probably the feeblest kiss I've ever given her.

"I'm getting the nurse now. You need some painkillers."

"I need you. You're my cure."

"Then why are you still tensing and hissing in discomfort?" she asks, holding my face.

"Because it fucking hurts." Get me those painkillers pronto.

She smiles, stealing one more kiss, and gets up off the bed carefully. And I feel…light. So fucking light. *It's not your time yet, Jesse.* Because I have a job to do here.

I watch Ava as she faffs around my bed, fixing the sheets. "What are you smiling about?" I ask.

"Nothing."

"You're going to love this, aren't you?" I say, lifting my head so she can plump my pillow.

"I have the power," she whispers playfully as I grimace.

"Don't get used to it."

"Oh," the nurse sings when she whirls in. "Oh my." Going to the monitor beside my bed, she presses a few buttons. "Welcome back, Jesse."

"Thanks," I grumble, bracing myself for the onslaught of poking.

"Feeling groggy?"

"Shit." Was she expecting cartwheels? "When can I go home?"

"Let's not get ahead of ourselves." She chuckles. "Eyes, please." She shines a light in my eyes, making me squint. "Your wife has told me all about these eyes." Oh? "They really are quite something."

You bet your arse they are. "Is that all she told you about, nurse?"

"No." She smiles wickedly. "She's told me about that roguish grin too." Roguish? "Bed bath?"

What? "No, I'll shower," I mutter, hearing Ava chuckling.

"No can do, young man," the nurse says, raining on my parade. "Not until the doctor checks you over and we remove your catheter."

I have a piss bag? Oh, please tell me I don't have a piss bag. The nurse holds up a piss bag. "For fuck's sake." How long have I got to stay here?

"I'll call the doctor."

Yes, please do. Hopefully he'll be a little more reasonable and will compromise. I find Ava, happy to see some color back in her cheeks. "Get me out of here, baby."

"No way, Ward." She offers me a straw. "Drink."

"Is it bottled?"

"I doubt it. Stop being a water snob and drink."

Don't have much choice, do I? "Don't let that nurse give me a bed bath."

"Why not? It's her job, Jesse, and she's been doing it very well for the past two weeks."

Wait, what? "Two weeks?" How the hell is that possible? "I've been out for two weeks?"

"Yes." She flinches. "But it felt more like two hundred years."

Has she eaten *anything* in those two weeks? Showered at all? Two fucking weeks? Ava sits on the edge of the bed and plays with my ring. "Don't ever complain to me about having a long day again."

"Okay." Two weeks? My God, how many times have I relived the nightmare in those two weeks? "She hasn't really been sponging me down, has she?"

"No, I have," Ava declares, and that makes me feel so much better. She's been looking after me. She hasn't left my side. If I needed any kind of confirmation that she's committed, I suppose I have it.

"So while I was naked and unconscious," I say, restraining my smile. "You were…" How do I put it? "Fondling me?"

"No," she says slowly. "I was washing you."

"And you didn't have a sneaky touch?"

"Of course." She comes close, and my smile widens. "I needed to lift your limp dick to get to your saggy balls."

I feel instantly sick. "I'm in hell. Fucking hell on earth. Get me a doctor. I'm going home."

"You're going nowhere," she says over her delighted chuckle, kissing me, like that might pacify me. It won't. I'll discharge myself.

"I need to pee."

I frown down my body as Ava slips into the attached bathroom, feeling a brief urge to pee too, and then…nothing. Because, the bag of piss. "God," I grunt, letting my head sink into my recently plumped pillow. I shift a little, grumbling in pain. This bed is lumpy. I'll be far more comfortable at home, in my own bed, with my favorite nursemaid.

How can I convince them?

The door opens, and a middle-aged man in chinos and a white shirt—sleeves rolled up—wanders in. "Jesse," he says, going straight to the machinery and checking things over.

"Doctor?" I ask.

"Trauma surgeon. Mr. Emerson. I specialize in knife-related injuries. How are you feeling?"

"Like I've been stabbed."

He laughs, motioning to the sheets over my stomach. "May I?"

"Help yourself."

He pulls them back and looks over the dressing covering half of my side. "You've been through the mill." He picks up my notes and starts looking through. "We removed the knife during surgery. We hoped the damage was limited to a deep puncture, but it seems the blade was moved once it had penetrated."

I look at the ceiling, blinking back a flashback. Her eyes. "She lost her grip when I shoved her away."

"That undoubtedly saved your life. If she'd pulled the knife free, it would have been a very different story."

I nod, closing my eyes. "Are you saying I'd be dead?" I squint into my darkness at the blurry silhouette of a very tall man in the distance.

"In a nutshell. Your lung collapsed while you were in theater, and you'd lost an exceptional amount of blood. The internal injuries were extensive. Your body went into preservation to heal, hence you've been out for a while."

I realize it's not a tall man, but a kid on someone's shoulders. I frown, opening my eyes. "Two weeks," I say.

He smiles. "How's the pain?"

"Awful."

Ava appears from the bathroom and puts herself out of the way, smiling to the surgeon when he nods his hello. "I'll have Nurse get you some more morphine." He goes to the wall and yanks some gloves out of a dispenser, pulling them on. "Let's have a look," he says, picking at the edge of the dressing, easing it off, humming.

I wince and look down at the raw wound. "Fucking hell," I breathe.

"You're very lucky."

I flick my eyes to Ava, seeing her arms folded, listening. I give her a small smile. She doesn't return it. *Lucky.* "And the bag?" I ask, nodding in the general vicinity of my bed, where it's hanging on the side.

"The bag needs to stay for now."

"I can make it to the bathroom, Doctor."

"I think you're a little optimistic."

"But—"

"There's really no buts about it, Jesse. The bag stays. Maybe tomorrow. We'll see if you're up for a little walkabout tomorrow." He collects some things from a wall cabinet. "You've just come round."

"What about this, then?" I ask, holding up my arm. He looks over his shoulder, smiling as he shakes his head.

Defeated, I sigh, letting him redress my stomach as Ava watches, her concentration fierce. "Everything looks fine," he says, pulling off the gloves and dropping them in the bin. "I'll have Nurse fix you up with that morphine. I'm on the ward tomorrow morning, so we'll see if you're up for a little walk then."

"I will be."

"We'll see." He looks at Ava. "I'm putting you in charge," he says around an ironic smile. Ava laughs, and I snort.

"Don't feed the beast, Doc," I grumble, making him chuckle his way out of my room.

I watch Ava move to the high-backed chair and sit. "The more you cooperate, the sooner you'll be released."

There's the problem. Cooperate. Whenever has she known me to be good at that? "You look tired. Are you eating?"

"Yes."

"Ava. Go now and get something to eat."

"My mum fed me a salad." A fucking salad. "I'm not hungry."

Give me strength. And then it occurs to me. "What have you told them?"

"Everything," she says, simple and easy. "Except for your four-day absence."

"Okay," I whisper, feeling heavier on the bed. *Everything.* "Go and get something to eat."

"I'm not hun—"

"Don't make me tell you again, lady," I snap, done. She will not use my inability to walk to her advantage. "Piss bag or not, I'll march you down to that fucking restaurant myself and shove some food down your throat."

She recoils, injured, and I feel utterly shit about it. *Fuck.* They know everything. All of my horrid secrets and fuckups. "I'll get you something too," she says quietly.

"I'm not hungry," I reply, hearing the door close behind her. I drop my eyes and stare at the wood, just as it opens again. Nurse has a bag of fluid in her hands. She chitchats happily, while I lie back, letting her change the bag and inject something into the canula on the back of my hand, sending freezing cold liquid up my arm.

"Twins," she says, washing her hands at the sink. "How exciting. You better hurry up and recover."

"I will as soon as they let me out of bed."

She chuckles. "Slowly but surely. You'll fall flat on your face if you stand up too soon."

"Right," I say, watching her leave. I shouldn't have snapped at Ava. I sigh and close my eyes, feeling like I'm running the gauntlet of flashbacks and memories. In my body, out of my body, struggling to straighten everything out, figure out what's real and what was dreamt. Her parents are here. I squint in my darkness, pulling something from the back of my mind. Elizabeth. I heard her. Yes, she was trying to get Ava to eat. She settled for a salad. It's something, and I'm grateful. Did I hear the big man? I breathe in when it comes to me. John on the floor. He was hurt. They were remanded. Both of them. *Both?* My brain begins to ache, and then the floodgates open again, another mishmash of recollections hitting me. I hear my dad.

I still, willing that particular memory forward. Were they here?

And I deflate.

Why would they be?

A light knock on the door sounds, and I snap my eyes open. Did I imagine hearing Dad? Did it happen? I get frustrated with myself, not knowing what's real, what's not, what was a dream, a memory, a flashback. All I know right now is Ava is real, she's pregnant, I'm really fucking broken, my in-laws are here, and they know everything.

The door opens, and a head appears around it.

Who it is sends me into an instant spin. "Sarah?" I gasp, trying to sit up, cursing and giving up, falling back to my back on a hiss. "You can't be here." I'm ambushed by every shitty thing she's done to us, panic overtaking me. She tried to break us up. She tried to chase Ava away. She whipped me, told Ava's ex I'm an alcoholic, fed him shit on me.

Ava will lose her mind. I've put her through enough since I came round, offloaded the past I tried to bury, and now Sarah's here? No. "Please, you have to go."

"Ava knows I'm here," she says, slipping in and closing the door.

"What?" I can't imagine that's true. Why would I believe her? She's lied persistently and callously since I met Ava. I reach for my aching head, feeling information overload.

"She's outside." She stands at the end of my bed, pulling her bag onto her shoulder. I catch sight of a bandage on her wrist. And another memory comes to me.

"You tried—"

She shifts uncomfortably, rearranging her sleeves to cover the evidence. "How do you feel?"

"Terrible."

She nods, not asking to take a seat, and I don't offer her one either. I'm uncomfortable. Why is she here? "Jesse—"

"I can't forgive you, Sarah," I say, making her step back. "I can feel sorry for you, but I can't forgive you for trying to ruin the best thing that's happened to me since Rosie."

Her eyes drop, shame emanating from her feeble form. "I didn't want you to be happy without me."

It's a horrible punch in the gut. Horrible. "Why?"

"Because I'm in love with you," she whispers, finally saying it out loud. "I've been in love with you since we were seventeen, Jesse. I stayed with Carmichael so I could stay with you. Got pregnant to keep my place in his life. *Your* life. I whipped people and imagined it was you. Punishment for not loving me back."

I flinch, looking away from her. And I see a vision of her thrashing a man's back, the look on her face. Enjoying herself.

"I hate Ava," she goes on, on a roll, her voice now breaking, the tears flowing, "And I hate you for loving her. I've spent my entire adult life trying to make you see me, then *she* walks into your office and within a second, you saw her."

"You have to leave."

"I know." She sniffs, wiping her nose. "You won't see me again." She walks forward tentatively, coming close, taking advantage of my incapacitated state. I close my eyes as she slowly dips and pushes a kiss to my cheek, lingering. I hold my breath, feeling her lips quivering. Smell her. "Goodbye," she whispers, finally breaking away. I open my eyes and watch as she walks to the door, and when she reaches it, she looks back. "I love you."

I turn my face away from her, the pain doubling. As does the anger. The door closes, and I bite down on my teeth, clenching my fists. She couldn't even apologize? She couldn't be sorry? She didn't even acknowledge the fucking state I'm in here. And yet, I don't feel like I have the right to be mad. If that's her way of letting me go, what the fuck do I care if she does or doesn't care?

"You vindictive bitch!"

My eyes shoot toward the door. "Mum?" I whisper.

No.

But then...

Yes.

I'm ambushed by my mother's sad face, her old hands pulling in her pale blue cardigan. Very quickly, I'm not thinking of the pain—physical or emotional. I throw the sheets back and heave my legs off the bed, cursing to high heaven. Okay, physical pain isn't fucking off anytime soon. "Bastard," I mutter, standing, the sheets slipping to my waist. I grab the tall metal stand beside my bed, not only for support, but because I can't go anywhere without it. "Shit." I take one unsteady step, holding the sheet around me. Then another. "Fuck!" My eyes bulge when something pulls on my insides, and I look back to see a tube trailing from the bed to my groin. "Fucking hell." My cheeks balloon, sickness rising, blood draining from my head. I reverse my steps clumsily, pull the bag off the side of the bed, and re-hook it onto the frame with the other fluids, then stagger to the door, throwing it open.

I'm met with a chorus of gasps as I take in the scene.

"Jesse, for God's sake," Ava yells, coming at me.

"Mum?" I come over a little lightheaded—shock, no doubt.

"Oh Jesse, you stupid man." I can see two of her. And Amalie. And Ava. Fuck, is that Sarah? "Get back in bed now."

"Give me five minutes, Beatrice," Ava says. She has two faces. Both full of scorn. I blink, my hazy, double vision screwing me over. How does Ava know my mother's name?

Her palms meet my chest, easing me back a step, and the door closes. "What do you think you're playing at?" she snaps, furious. "Get in bed."

Does she fancy changing her tone? And her fucking volume? "Ca—" *Whoa.* Black dots start to creep into my vision, Ava's two faces become four.

"Oh shit," she yelps, as I try to close one eye, gain some focus, feeling my body go as light as my head. "Shit, shit, shit." I'm suddenly tipping backward, freefalling, and my arse hits the lumpy mattress on a grunt, my back soon after, my legs hanging over the side. Fuck, that hurts. "You're an idiot, Ward." For once, I agree. I've got room spin. Feel sick. What the hell was I thinking? "Why can't you do what you're bloody told?" Ava works around me, and my legs are soon rising.

"I feel pissed." Fuck, someone stop the room spin. I cover my face with my forearm, clenching my eyes closed.

"You got up too quickly."

No shit. "What are they doing here, Ava? I don't want to see them." I look weak, pathetic, everything they thought I was. This isn't how it was supposed to be.

Her hand wraps around my arm and pulls it away, and I open one, cautious eye. I haven't got the energy to deal with this. *Or the drink on hand.*

"You have me," she says softly, her face and tone telling me I'm about to be appeased. Can I be? "And I'm all you need, I know that, but this is a chance to put everything in your life right." Her eyes are imploring, the kind of gaze from my wife I could never disregard. And, really, would I ever want to? They're here.

Is there a chance?

They came to be by my bedside. And because I was unconscious, I couldn't push them away. And now, too, because I'm sober. "Just give them a few minutes," she pleads, hopeful. "I'm here forever, no matter what, but I can't let you pass up an opportunity to find peace in this part of your life, Jesse."

Well, doesn't that make so much sense. "I don't want anything to ruin what I have." What if they tell Ava about all of the hideous things I said? Fuck, I said some awful things. Bratty, unforgiveable things. I close my eyes, ashamed.

"Listen to me." My cheeks are squeezed, and I obey her silent order, opening my eyes. "After everything we have been through, do you really think there is anything else that could possibly fracture what we have?" She has a point. "It'll be done on your terms. We'll take it slow, and they will accept it."

My terms? God, I deserve the least grace in this situation. "I only need you," I grumble, very aware I'm simply being a coward. I reach for her tummy and stroke gently. "Just you and our babies."

"You don't have to want something to need it, Jesse." She sighs, holding on to her patience, holding my hand on her belly too. "We're having twins. I know we have each other, but we'll need our families too." I know she's making sense. The ache inside is as real now as it was twenty years ago. There's a void that can't be filled by anyone other than my mum and dad. That's a fact. "And I'd like our children to have two sets of grandparents," she adds, not that she needs to. I realize there are endless reasons for us to make amends. "We're not normal, but we should make our children's lives as normal as possible. It won't change us or what we have together." She squeezes my hand, reinforcing her words, as I scramble for the courage I need to tackle the final piece of my past. She's so reasonable. I'd never say it out loud. I'm so fucking lucky to have her. I force her down to hug me. "Tell me you love me," I order.

"I love you." It's not a sigh, but it's close.

"Tell me you need me."

"I need you."

I breathe in as deeply as I can without it killing me. "Okay." I let go of Ava and point to my head. "Plump my pillow, wife." I grin. It's so forced and fake. "I need to be comfy for this."

She doesn't slap me, but it's only because she can't. "I'm going to give you some privacy."

"You're not staying?" I ask, alarmed. Alone with my parents?

"No, I don't need to. You'll be fine." And without giving me a chance to plead my case, she disappears out of the door, leaving me alone.

I'll be fine.

Will I?

My heart starts beating double time, and there is fuck all I can do to stop it. My fingers twiddle. Then I frown, feeling at my jaw. What the fuck is that. I roll my eyes, exasperated. Over two weeks' worth of growth. I hardly look the part for a reunion. I must look like a Yeti. For fuck's sake. Naked, wounded, hairy, pasty, dry lips, things dangling out of my body, and a fucking piss bag.

My chaotic trail of thoughts grind to a startled stop when the door opens. My chest expands. My heart picks up speed again. "Fuck, fuck, fuck," I whisper.

And then Dad appears.

And I lose it.

Composure is gone, and I shake my head, my throat closing up on me, my eyes burning. "Oh, my boy," he whispers, losing it with me.

Fuck.

I roughly wipe at my face, feeling so fucking pathetic, and then Mum appears, and I'm gone again, face streaming, shame and regret joining me at one of the most vulnerable points in my life. I can't run. I can't hide.

Can't drink.

And I don't want to.

"I'm so sorry," I croak. "So, so fucking sorry. I didn't mean the things I said. I didn't hate you. I hated myself."

Amalie, crying silently, holds on to Mum as Dad hurries over to my bed and takes me in his arms. Hugs me so hard, I can hardly breathe. But while it really fucking hurts, I need him more than I need the pain to fuck off.

"Son, no. It's me who's sorry," he sobs.

"But—"

"No, no buts. We've had years agonizing over losing you. We just wanted to—" He sniffs. Mum weeps. "Love you, my boy. Have missed you so much."

We've lost years. Fucking years.

They love me.

They've missed me.

His words? Words I never, ever thought I'd hear? They're what I needed to hear. I never thought I'd feel their hugs again in my life. But they're here. For me.

Something breezes through my body—not pain, not discomfort—but something I've never felt before.

Forgiveness.

Mum joins us, hugging Dad as Dad hugs me. All three of us a mess of snot and tears and sobs. And Amalie stands at the end of the bed watching us. Smiling mildly through her tears.

I've never really known her as a woman, only a little girl. And that's really fucking tragic. I can tell she's going to bust my balls often.

Fucking hell, what have I let myself in for?

Mum and Dad ease away gently, and Dad lowers to the chair next to my bed, close, both of his hands taking one of mine. Mum perches on the bed. Amalie comes round the side and punches me in my bicep, grinning.

I look between them, wondering where the fuck we start. "So the wedding," Amalie, chirps, sitting too. "Now Dad's getting better, and Jesse's pulled his head out his arse, I was thinking the next few months."

"Wonderful," Mum says, starting to faff with my sheets, flattening them.

"Wonderful," Dad murmurs, not taking his eyes off me. It's as if he can't believe he's touching me. Looking at me.

"All right?" I ask softly.

"I'm perfect, son," he whispers, his lip quivering again. "Perfect."

Perfect.

I didn't think the word truly existed until I met Ava. Not that she's perfect, she's far from it. I laugh on the inside. Really far from it. But us together?

It's pretty fucking close.

And despite everything that's happened, the only reason my mum and dad are sitting here now is because of her.

Because she made me brave.

She brought me to life.

She made a man worthy of love.

She made this man.

Chapter 50

It's the next day. If anyone tries to stop me getting out of this bed, they'll be faced with force. I'm getting bedsores. My arse is dead. I want to go home.

"Your blood pressure is a little on the low side," Nurse says, making a note of it.

I can feel Ava's high brows aimed at me. "Makes a change," she muses. "It's usually high enough to blow his head off his shoulders."

Casting an unimpressed look her way, I snarl quietly. Her lips twitch.

"A bit hotheaded, are you, Jesse?" Nurse chuckles, and Ava laughs.

Yes. Hilarious. "I'm going for a walk," I grumble, pushing my fist into the mattress to get up.

"Ah, ah, ah," Nurse warns, coming to the bed. Like she could stop me. "Mr. Emerson would like to see you first."

I slump back down, exasperated, slamming my head on the pillow. Ava's face appears, those eyebrows looking annoyingly high still. She's finally showered. Finally eaten a stable meal. I made sure of it. After I apologized for being short with her. She looks so much better. I smile, reaching for her face and stroking her smooth, makeup-free cheek. "How's my wife and babies this morning?"

"Perfect," she muses, dropping a pacifying kiss on my lips. Good. I need it. "Here." She produces a ChapStick and smothers my lips, puckering her own as she does. "Better. I got you something."

"What?" I ask as she produces a jar on Sun-Pat. "Oh, thank God." I don't know what the shit was she brought yesterday, but it tasted like sand. "Load up, baby."

She laughs, dunking her finger, and bringing it to my lips. I don't take it. "What's up?" she asks.

I nod to her chest, and she snorts. "I told you," I say. "I won't eat it any other way."

She rolls her eyes and pulls away, forcing me to reach and grab her wrist on a chuckle, taking the blob off her finger. I hum and settle, as Nurse grimaces and Mr. Emerson strolls in, smiling.

"Morning," he says, taking the files out of Nurse's hand.

"His blood pressure is a little low," she tells him.

"It is?"

"But I feel okay," I say. "Great, actually."

"Maybe we should hold off for another day."

"Agree," Nurse says.

"Absolutely not." I push the covers back and shift my legs, and Ava quickly discards the jar, cursing at me. "Watch your mouth," I wheeze, fighting through the pain to get my legs off the side of the bed.

"Jesse, for Christ's sake."

"I'm fine." And the sooner I demonstrate it, the sooner they'll release me from this hell hole.

"Doctor, please."

"Jesse, I don't think you're ready," Mr. Emerson says gently. "What's the rush?"

The rush? The rush is I've wasted nearly two decades of my life being wasted, ignorant, and empty. I need to crack on with life. "I'm fine," I reiterate, letting my feet meet the floor, padding them gently. "Just a little stroll to the café or something."

Mr. Emerson shakes his head, with no faith in my capabilities. I'll show him. Ava faffs by my side, while the Nurse joins Mr. Emerson, shaking her head. "Please, Jesse," Ava begs. "You'll do yourself more damage and then be here longer."

I ease my arse up, slowly rising, remembering the crazy headrush I got yesterday when I shot out of bed. Not showing how much it fucking hurts through my face is a task. "See?" I say, finally upright, Ava holding on to my elbow. "I'm fine." I take one step, and the impact of my foot meeting the floor sends a wave of pain rippling up through my body. *Fuck.* "Totally fine," I grate, taking another step. The door seems to get farther away, and I close one eye, squinting, when it turns into two doors. *Oh fuck.*

"Jesse!"

My body becomes weightless, a cold sweat breaking, and the sound of urgent words are muffled.

And then.

Black.

I open my eyes. Look around. I'm on my back. "After three," someone says. "One, two, three. Up!" Then I'm floating.

"What happened?" I ask groggily, bobbing up and down, seeing two men at my feet I don't recognize.

"You passed out."

Ava?

I look up over my head and see her behind me, following us, quite the epic scowl on her face. I come to rest on the bed. Mr. Emerson appears, his expression saying a whole lot of *I told you so*. But he doesn't say a thing, getting to checking my wound.

I slam my head back, frustrated. "Give it time," Ava says, pulling one side of my boxers up a little. "What's the rush?"

My shoulders drop, and I hiss when Mr. Emerson peels back my dressing. "Fuck."

"Sorry," he says gently. "It's looking good."

"But I can't go home," I grunt. "What if I swear not to leave my bed?"

He laughs. "Jesse, I don't know you very well, but something tells me you're not very good at doing what you're told."

I snort. "You're getting me confused with my wife."

Ava lightly smacks my bicep before pouring some water, and I watch her faff some more, wondering how long it'll be before she gets bored of looking at me lying in a bed.

"Your lung collapsed, Jesse. The internal injuries were extensive. If anything unexpected arises, I need you close to the operating table in case I need to go back in."

I grimace. "Like what?"

"Infection, stitches popping or, worst-case, internal bleeding."

"Internal bleeding?"

"Which would be most likely caused by impact. Such as hitting the deck from passing out." His eyebrows jump up, and I roll my eyes so hard, *that* might even cause internal bleeding.

"Fine, I hear you."

"Good." Mr. Emerson finishes up, tells me he'll be back tomorrow, and leaves with Nurse.

"So what are we doing today?" I quip, bored out of my mind already.

"Well, you could read," Ava says, pulling a book out of her bag. My pregnancy book. I smile as she sets it on my thighs. "And your mum and dad would love to come visit if that's okay."

I nod, drifting off into thought. I don't know what happens next. But I do know I'm not dreading it, and that's the best place I could be. "How's Drew?" I ask.

"Surprisingly calm."

I bet he's just very fucking relieved Coral wasn't responsible for all of the shit going down in my life. I shudder, just at the thought of Ava being alone with Lauren all those times. "Have you heard from Van Der Haus?" I ask, a little reluctantly. That little flashback came to me in the night when I woke up sweating. It's never ending—all the various puzzle pieces slowly coming together to give me the whole picture. The whole picture before Lauren stabbed me.

He doesn't deserve you.

Van Der Haus tried to take my happiness too.

"No," Ava says easily, making me wonder if she's simply protecting me from the stress. "He's pulled out of the deal to buy Rococo."

Oh? I bet Peterson is reeling. There goes his retirement plans. But then I also wonder, with dread, I admit, if this means Ava will return to the company? Oh no, will Peterson sweeten the deal for her? Offer her directorship? I flinch when a sharp pain hits my lip, releasing it from between my teeth.

"Okay?" Ava asks.

"Yeah."

The door knocks, and Steve Cook pokes his head round. I know this has to happen. "I suppose you have some questions, huh?"

"I'll go get us some breakfast," Ava says, keen to escape.

"I'll need to talk to you again too, Ava," Steve says. "When you're ready."

She nods and wastes no time leaving us, and I can't say I'm sorry. I don't want her to hear the horrors of my past again. Steve settles on a chair, pad in hand. "We'll have to do this more officially when you're well enough," he says. "But for now, we're building the picture."

"Where is she?" I ask.

"On remand at a psychiatric facility. Casey Grand is on remand too, albeit at a Category B."

"Casey?" I ask, confused. *Both are on remand.*

"The new concierge at Lusso," Steve explains. "Your ex-wife's lover. He copied the keys to the apartment, and that's how she gained access."

Fucking hell. "I gave him the code for the elevator. Handed my car keys over to him."

"Which is how he stole your car."

"He stole it?" I ask, and Steve nods. "Has she talked?"

"A whole lot of fucking crazy, Jesse." He laughs, in disbelief, I think. "Why the fuck didn't we know about her?"

I flinch. "I don't know, Steve."

"She's been watching you for a long time." He goes to his pad. "There were many pictures of you. And of Ava. She rented a room in a house in Lansdowne Crescent."

"It wasn't her house?" I ask, and Steve shakes his head. *Fucking hell.*

"It was rented under Casey Grand's name. From what we can establish thus far, she contacted Rococo Union around the time you started dating Ava."

Jesus Christ. All these years she was happy I was obliterated…but the minute I met Ava, she was in Lauren's demented scope. And dating? Ava would call it stalking. I rub at my forehead, feeling nauseous. Then something comes to me. "John."

"Took quite a wallop to the head. He's fine. Angry with himself more than anything. He mentioned you thought you'd seen Lauren Pierce a few times."

I nod and take a breath, starting to explain to Steve, going into every detail.

Making sure she's locked up for a very long time.

Chapter 51

"I'm not using a wheelchair," I grunt. "End of."

The porter turns right back around and wheels it out, and a collection of exasperated sighs fill the room. I give each of them a moment of my eyes—Ava, Sam, Kate, Drew, *and* John. "It's not happening." I need to walk. *Have* to. I won't admit it aloud, but I'm nervous to go home. I'm still in so much fucking pain, can't walk ten paces without being out of breath, and I'm worried I'll pass out again. I could fall on Ava, knock her on my way down, because I know for certain she'll try to catch me.

So I'm walking. If I make it to the car on my feet, I'll feel more confident. If I don't? Well, then I'll be passed out, and I expect they'll put me straight back in the hospital bed for a while longer.

I look down my front as I sit on the edge of the bed while Nurse arms Ava with endless dressings and pills. My T-shirt is hanging off me. I've never been so small. Or tired. Fuck me, I'm constantly exhausted.

"Ready?" John asks, knocking me from my daydream.

"Ready." I wedge my fists into the mattress and ease myself up slowly, breathing steadily. It's easy to hold my breath to try and stem the pain, but holding my breath results in a blackout. So yes, I must breathe.

"Okay?" Ava asks, joining my side, like she can hold me up. "Why don't you just let me push you in the chair?"

"God damn it, Ava, you are not wheeling me out of this hospital," I snap. Even that drains me. Fuck. "I'm sorry," I mumble, reaching for her hand on my arm and patting. "Ignore me."

She remains patient and silent, not leaving my side, as I make my way through the hospital, slowly but surely, taking regular rest stops. The others hang back, ready to step in and catch me. It's a miracle, but I make it to John's car.

And fall asleep on the way home.

...

Clive is painfully attentive when we get to Lusso, flanking my dragging body, declaring all kinds of disgust and outrage. If I had the strength and any cash on me, I'd slip him some notes to shut the fuck up.

The stairs are the first thing I note when I step inside the penthouse. Yeah, not happening. "The couch," Ava declares, leaving John to hold me up as she hurries to the sofa, sorts the pillows, and gets a throw. "There."

John tries to get me moving, but I gravitate toward the kitchen. "Just give me a sec," I say, gently breaking away from him and walking slowly toward the entrance. The floor is spotless. Sparkling. Whenever I used to stand here, I'd see Ava on the launch night of Lusso in her red dress. I'd see her in her lace underwear sitting on the island. I'd see her pressed up against the wall, me buried deep inside her.

Now all I see is Lauren wielding a blade.

We can't live here. I turn and find Ava behind me, her face pensive. She knows what I'm thinking. But it's a conversation for another day. A day when I've got the energy to give. "Come," she says, leading me to the couch and getting me comfortable, straining to lift my legs. "I'll get you some water."

I smile my thanks and watch her go to the kitchen, hating how much she's having to do because I'm an invalid.

John pulls his black suit jacket out and lowers to the nearby armchair, looking to the kitchen. Making sure Ava's out of earshot, I expect. "I've pondered whether to mention this," he says, his deep voice quiet.

"What?"

"Cutler's been in touch again. A week ago."

I frown, thinking. "Cutler?" Am I supposed to know who that is?

John smiles, only mildly, but I still get a flash of his gold tooth. "He represents the leisure company who wants to buy The Manor. You were considering entertaining another meeting."

I frown, looking out the window across the skyline. I was in talks with someone who wants to buy my manor? Surely not. But then...new eyes. It all comes back to me. The insulting meeting, my walks around the grounds, the odd and jarring thoughts I had. "Is it a serious offer this time?"

"That I don't know. I stalled him, obviously. But given your reaction in our last meeting, I can't imagine he'll willingly put himself up for another dressing-down."

I inhale, reaching for my stomach and holding it.

Take the money, Daddy.

I stare out of the window, my eyes burning, the words coming from nowhere. "Take the money," I whisper.

"You don't know how much they're offering yet." John laughs.

"Then let's find out." I look at him so he can see the resolution in my eyes.

"I'll call him."

I nod, smiling mildly. "Thanks."

The door of the apartment opens, and Kate and Sam stroll in, weighed down with Waitrose bags. Then Drew. "You going to close the door?" I call when he leaves it open.

"No."

Elizabeth follows in behind, clocks me on the couch, and slaps her hand on her heart. I brace myself for a strong dose of my mother-in-law. "Jesse Ward, my wonderful son-in-law." She comes at me, making me want to shield myself. "Look at you." Her hand meets my forehead. "How do you feel?"

"Harassed."

She tsks and goes to the kitchen as Joseph puts himself on the other chair near John. "I tried to tell her to back off."

"It's fine," I breathe, smiling. After everything they've learned about me, it's a relief they're even here. Accepting me. And I'm wonderful.

Amalie bowls in, a man I've never met with her. This must be the groom. She's being tactical. I'm in no fit state to dish out warnings. "Afternoon," I say as she comes at me too, dropping a kiss on my forehead. I reach for her hand, giving it a little squeeze. Mum, Dad, and Amalie have been at the hospital every day. Just a few minutes here and there, breaking us all in slowly, but they haven't missed one visit. "Are Mum and Dad here?" I ask as she drags her fiancé over.

"Yes, on their way up. This is Dr. David."

I lift a hand. "Should I call you Dr. David?"

"David will do," he says on a laugh. "Pleasure to meet you, Jesse."

I smile, feeling overwhelmed, my home becoming more and more full. "Make yourself at home," I mumble. "Everyone else has." My eyes are getting heavy, but when Mum walks in with Dad, I forget all tiredness. *Life*.

Dad does what Dad's done every day since I came round and comes to me, dipping to hug me. And I find the energy to hug him right back. Always. "You all right?" I ask.

"I just came from the cardiologist."

"Why, what's up?"

"Nothing's up, son," he says, perching on the arm on the couch next to me. He just can't be any farther than a few feet away when we're together. "I missed a checkup back home, so they referred me to a colleague here. I'm fine." He taps his chest. "The ticker is fine."

"Hello, darling," Mum says, her turn to have a fuss. "Are you hungry? Thirsty? Had your meds? The dressing, it's clean, isn't it?"

"I'm fine," I assure her. "Ava's in the kitchen with Elizabeth."

Off she goes, knowing exactly where the kitchen is. And then Dad excuses himself to use the bathroom, and he heads off in the right direction too. They've been here while I've been in hospital? I peek up when Ava appears in front of me with a glass of water, bending to place it on the table.

I reach out and place my hand over hers on the glass before she can remove it, and she flicks her eyes to mine. She doesn't snatch her hand away. She doesn't retract. I smile mildly, hoping she sees my deep appreciation. I take her hand and push my lips to the back of it.

"I'll be leaving then," John says, excusing himself, giving me a nod. I nod back, and Ava looks between us, curious.

"What was that?" she asks.

"Nothing." I pull her down to the couch, so she's sitting on the edge. "Ava, baby, why is every single person we know in our home?"

She smiles. "Because I invited them." Leaning down, she drops a kiss on my lips. "And, My Lord, because they love you dearly."

They love me.

Accept me.

I fall into a daydream, the hustle and bustle of our home melting into the background. My bachelor pad full of...my family. The thought of my parents anywhere near Ava would have filled me with dread only a few weeks ago—knowing they were spending time with her without me knowing or even around. What they could have told her.

Now?

Ease.

Because of you.

I grab Ava, riding the pain, and smother her with my mouth, silently thanking her for bringing me back to life. And for bringing me back to my family. "We're going away as soon as I can drive again," I tell her.

"Where?"

"To Paradise, baby."

Chapter 52

"Congratulations, Mr. Ward."

"Thanks." I hang up, feeling an odd sense of loss and gain. Sadness and happiness. Guilt and inculpability. That's it. It's gone. The contracts signed, no going back. I blow out my cheeks and stand, the creak of my bones and pull on my muscles still there, but now milder.

I walk to the bedroom, standing on the threshold, just watching her for a while. There's definitely a belly now. And she's more beautiful by the day. I leave her to sleep, going to the kitchen. I pull the paperwork from the drawer and set it on the counter, answering a call as I go to the fridge. "Dad," I say, pulling out a basket of strawberries.

"My boy, we're at the marina. Do you need me to collect anything before we come over later?"

"I've got it all covered, thanks, Dad," I say, biting into a strawberry and going out onto the veranda, seeing a few people on the beach getting things ready. "Is Mum okay?"

"She's wonderful," he says, sounding blissful, and I smile, but it's sad. My mum's come back to life with me. Her eyes don't look so old, her face is somehow lighter. The guilt remains. "Have you told Ava yet?" Dad asks.

"Not yet. I just took the call. Contracts are signed." Which means my bank balance will soon explode. "I'll tell her when she wakes up." I wander back into the kitchen, finishing my strawberry.

Dad chuckles. "I remember when your mother was expecting you and Jake," he says, and I stop, resting my arse on the counter. "She was asleep ninety percent of her day."

I smile.

"And then awake for ninety percent when you both arrived."

I laugh lightly. "It's going to be full-on."

"Oh, you'll be okay. Besides, you have me and your mother, and Ava's parents too. And friends and John."

My heart swells. "We do," I agree. "Listen, Dad, I've had some money sent to your account."

"What?"

I can sense it, the unease. But he and Mum should be enjoying their later years, doing whatever the fuck they want, and I have more money than I know what to do with. More on the way. "I've sent some money—"

"I don't want any money, Jesse," he says, sounding stern.

I roll my eyes. "Tough." He doesn't see it as my money. He sees it as Carmichael's. "It's nonnegotiable, and I'll be pissed if you don't blow it on extravagant, really unnecessary luxuries."

He sighs.

"Dad, I've made more money in the last sixteen years than I could spend in ten lifetimes. Something good has to come out of everything that's happened."

"You have," he says. "You've come back to us."

"I have. And I became really rich while I was gone."

He chuckles, and an easy silence falls between us. "You know, Jesse, I don't know what it was that drove me and my brother apart," he says quietly. "But it wasn't that place. It was difficult even before The Manor."

I nod to myself, taking another strawberry. I feel like Dad and Carmichael's relationship may have been similar to Jake's and mine. One golden boy and one rebel. Dad and Jake were the golden boys, Carmichael and I were the rebels. And that wasn't on Dad and Jake. That was on us. We chose our paths. I'm just so fucking grateful mine eventually led back to my family. Carmichael's path led him to an early, tragic death. But I've finally accepted that that's not solely on my head. I have to let go of the guilt. And now, I can finally start. "Go buy Mum something nice, Dad," I say. "Can't wait to see you later."

"You too," he replies gently. "Love you, son."

He can't say it enough. I know how he feels. The desperation for someone to know how much they mean to another. I know how much I mean to him. *Finally.* I hang up and sigh, a happy, contented sigh, as I put the strawberries back in the fridge and head for the bathroom to take a shower, taking my phone with me in case someone else rings and Ava gets suspicious. She's still sleeping when I pass through the bedroom. I slip the paperwork into the bedside table and go to the bathroom, flipping the shower on. My mobile rings as I'm placing it down by the sink, and I still, staring at the Scotland number.

I breathe in, staring at it ringing. Can I?

I bite my lip, answering. "Alan," I say, hiding the surprise and trepidation from my voice.

"Jesse," he breathes. "How are you?"

I look down at my stomach. "I'm well," I answer, not feeling the need to inflict anymore anguish and guilt on him. "How are you?"

"Well," he replies, not achieving what I have. He sounds completely overcome. "I…" An uncomfortable silence descends, and it's absolutely not what I want or need. "I'm—"

"Alan, you don't need to—"

"She's—"

"I don't want to talk about Lauren," I say, feeling harsh, but he doesn't need to call me to justify or tell me where she is or what's happened to her. I know. I listened. And then I pushed it out of my mind and went back to my wife to carry on with my life. "Are you okay?" I ask. I only care how they are.

"I am," he breathes, almost in relief. He thought he owed me more than he does. "I'm okay."

"I'm glad."

There's an awkward silence again, and I honestly don't know what else to say. So I say nothing and hope he does.

"I'm glad you've found happiness, Jesse," he says softly. "You deserve to be happy."

"That means a lot, Alan," I reply, hiding my surprise well. "Thank you."

"Well, I'll be going then."

"Take care."

"You too."

I hang up and lower to the toilet seat. I deserve to be happy. I think I'm slowly getting my head around that.

Chapter 53

I rub the towel through my hair, standing at the bathroom door watching her. She's awake now. Relaxed, stretched out, peaceful. "Comfy?" I ask, winning her attention. I swear, I have never seen Ava looking more perfect. *Glowing.*

"No," she says. "Because you're not in here with me." She indicates for me to join her and, of course, I do, kneeling on the end of the bed and working my way up until I can half lie on her, my chin on her belly.

"Good morning, my beautiful girl," I whisper, as her hand slips into my hair.

"Good morning." She sighs. "What are we doing today?"

Oh, she will *love* it. "I have it all planned out." But there wasn't much actual planning, to be honest. This time, it's not about scale. It's about us. Us and the people who love us. "You will do what you're told," I say, looking up at her as I kiss her belly. I'm counting the kisses needed to cover her bump. More are needed each week.

"Does it involve cards?" she asks, coy.

"No." I smile, remembering our last game of cards in Paradise. It ended in Sleepy Twilight Sex.

"Does it involve Twilight Sleepy Sex?"

"Maybe later." When my family aren't around.

"Then I'll do whatever you want."

Of course she won't. "Your day starts right now, Mrs. Ward." I finish coating her belly with my kisses and move, sitting myself on her hips. I reach for the bedside cabinet and grab the paperwork—Ava's wedding present, *my* wedding present—and hand it to her. "Here."

"What's this?" She warily accepts the paperwork that details the sale of The Manor. *Fucking hell, it's gone.*

"Just open it."

She looks utterly terrified as she works the envelope open, her eyes jumping from me to her working hands. She pulls out the paper and reads, the lines on her head increasing the farther she gets down the page. I bite at my lip, waiting.

"You've bought another house?" she eventually asks.

"No." I smile. "I've sold The Manor." *My God, I've sold The Manor.* That's the first time I've said it out loud. It's feels surreal.

"You've what?" she breathes, lifting beneath me, trying to sit herself up. She looks completely stunned. Expected, I suppose. In the end, it wasn't such a hard decision. I've outgrown the grand, magnificent building. It no longer has a place in my life. Besides, as I noted on my various walks around the grounds, it's wasted. Now, it'll be an incredible golf course and thousands of people will get to enjoy what I have these past few months. The gardens.

I encourage Ava back down to the bed. "I've sold The Manor." I shift and spread myself all over her, cupping her face with my palms.

"I heard you," she whispers, scanning my face. "Why?"

Why? She doesn't need to ask. The Manor no longer gives me purpose and reason. John first told me that weeks ago. I know Ava's often thought it, but she would never have enforced such a monumental ask. I kiss her instead, and our lips coming together suck us into the usual vortex of passion.

The Manor is gone.

My life is here ready to be lived.

I hum, happy. "You taste heavenly, lady."

"Why?" she repeats, her limbs coiling around my body, locking me to her. She wants *something.* So I'll give her one of the many reasons she won't have considered.

"You know when you're a kid?" I say. "At primary school, I mean."

She smiles through her frown. "Yeah."

"Well." How do I explain this? "What the hell would I do if the babies asked me to go in for one of those open days these schools have?"

Her curiosity is dying and her humor growing. She knows where this is heading. But she'll still make me say it. "Open day?"

"You know, when daddies stand up and tell their kids' classmates they're a fireman or a copper." I knew she'd find this funny. I roll my eyes to myself. "What would I say?"

"You'd tell them you're The Lord of The Sex Manor." She giggles, and the sound is life. But still, she's mocking me. This was a very real worry. I grab her hip and tickle her. "Stop!"

"Sarcasm doesn't suit you, lady."

"Please stop!"

I do, only because I don't want her peeing on me. "You would tell them that you own a hotel," she says, her breathing labored as she gathers herself, her grin massive. "Just like we'd tell the babies."

Just like that. But I've been there. It was fucking stressful. Besides, like I said, that's not the only reason. *New beginnings.* I lift off her and drop to my back, knowing she'll soon be straddling me. And she is, being careful to avoid the site of my wound, hands on my bare chest, her belly directly in my sights. "I don't want it anymore," I say, holding her thighs.

"But it was Carmichael's baby," she whispers. "You wouldn't sell it when your mum and dad demanded it, so why now?"

And there's the thing—they never actually *demanded* it. They begged, and there's a huge difference. I should have sold it when Mum and Dad begged me to. But, again, I wouldn't have met Ava, and that seems like an impossible something to accept. "Because I have you three," I whisper, my eyes dropping to her tummy. All I feel is complete wonder whenever I look at her belly.

"You'll always have us three, anyway."

"I want you three and nothing to complicate that. I don't want to lie to our babies about my job. I would never allow them to spend any time there, which means my time with you and the babies would be limited. The Manor was an obstruction. I don't want any obstructions." And that is that. "I have a history"—*a painful, complicated history*—"and The Manor should be part of it."

I watch as she absorbs the words. She wants to smile but feels guilty. I wish she'd smile. There's nothing to feel guilty about. "So I get you all day every day?"

"If you'll have me," I counter, slightly shy, also confident, especially when I see her relent and let loose that smile.

She attacks me, thrilled, and it's the best response, but just as I'm about to indulge, she shoots back up, all delight gone, worry replacing it. "What about John and Mario? And Sarah? What about Sarah?"

I don't want to talk about Sarah. I still can't believe how blind I was. How I let guilt get in the way of my own happiness. And Ava's. "I've spoken to them." Or John and Mario, anyway. I've not seen Sarah, but John's told me what her plans are. I half listened. Pretended to care. I don't think I'll ever forgive her for what she did. And *tried* to do. "Sarah's taking up an opportunity in the US and John and Mario are more than ready for retirement." I've made sure retirement will be comfortable, and the golf resort will reemploy most of the other staff. It was part of the deal. The very sweet deal, just as John said it would be.

"Oh. And will the members renew under the new owners?"

"Yes." I laugh. "If they like playing golf."

"Golf?"

"The grounds are being converted into an eighteen-hole golf course."

"Wow. What about the sports facilities?"

"They're all staying. It'll be pretty impressive." The plans to be submitted to planning were something else. Almost made me want to take up golf. But, I won't. I know I can never step foot through those gates ever again. "Not much different to my setup, except the private suites really will be hotel rooms and the communal room will serve as a conference room for businesses." I had to laugh when I was shown those particular plans. The communal room. No longer packed full of naked, sexually adventurous, hedonistic professionals, but now packed full of…well, they might be hedonistic. But they'll be dressed. And at work.

"So that's it, then?" she asks.

"That's it." No more talk of The Manor. "Now, I need to get you ready for the rest of your day." I try to get up and go nowhere.

"I need to freshen up my mark," she says, eyeing my pec. "And you need to work on mine too."

Fuck, I'd love to, but I just heard a car coming down the driveway, which means people are arriving. "We'll do it later, baby." I quickly get up, which isn't so quickly these days, my insides tugging, and set Ava aside. "Go take a shower." I look over my shoulder to the windows as I spank her arse, directing her toward the bathroom. She goes with ease, thank God, and I quickly wrap a towel around my waist and go out the doors, spotting Drew, barefoot, wading through the sand at the end of the garden. "Hey," I whisper-shout. "You're early."

"Fucking sand everywhere," he mutters, flapping the front of his shirt.

"My man!" Sam sings, dragging a cooler box with him.

"Shhhh," I hiss.

"Where is she?" Kate calls.

I slap a palm on my forehead. "My God," I breathe, shooing them off, pointing down the beach. They all look. All hunch their shoulders, realizing, holding their fingers to their lips like, yes, okay, we can be quiet. Off they go, just as Amalie rounds the corner, Dr. David in tow. "Where's Mum and Dad?" I call quietly.

"Dad disappeared for half an hour," Amalie yells, and I show the sky my palms, exasperated, hoping the shower is blocking out the noise for Ava. "He came back with a diamond bracelet for Mum. You should see her face."

My eyebrows jump up. And I smile. Spoiling her. I'm happy.

"You know," Amalie goes on, her volume still too high, "the replanning of our wedding is costing slightly more than we anticipated."

I laugh. "Yeah, I bet."

She gives me an impish grin. "Love you, brother."

"Yeah, I bet," I mumble, backing up. "Go."

I go to the wardrobe and pick out a dress for Ava. Lace. A bit short, perhaps, but I'll deal with it. Then I pull some shorts on. White. Will she cotton on?

My finger touches my new wound, tracing the length of it. No tingles. I bite at my lip as I move my finger to the old wound. Trace that too. No tingles. I smile and go to the kitchen, looking out of the window, seeing Joseph and Elizabeth getting out of a cab. I hardly suppress my groan when Dan appears too. I inwardly call him every name under the sun as I nip out the front to direct them round the back. Elizabeth squeals when she spots me, but soon shuts up when I raise a finger to my lips, looking back into the villa nervously. My God, does everyone we know not understand the element of surprise? Ava's parents creep off, but Dan remains, hands in his pockets watching them go. What's he hanging back for? "All right?" I ask.

As soon as Elizabeth and Joseph are out of range, he comes to me, holding his hand out. I don't miss the brief drop of his eyes to my stomach. I swear, if he mentions anything about what happened, I can't promise I'll hold back. I take his hand tentatively and let him do all the shaking. "Take care of her," he says.

What can I say? Tell him not to insult me? There have been numerous nights I've woken up in a cold sweat from a nightmare. It's always the same dream. Or more reliving one of the most terrifying moments of my life. Walking into the penthouse and seeing Ava bent over, hysterical, and seeing my ex-wife wielding a knife. I shudder on the spot, pushing it back. My lack of honesty put Ava in that situation, and I will never forgive myself for that. "I'll take care of her," I murmur, breaking our hands. "Thanks for coming." I had no choice but to invite him. *And pay for his airfare.* "And, Dan," I say, as I back away. "Stay away from Kate and Sam."

He nods, accepting, and goes after his parents as mine pull up, John driving them. The big man gets out, and I'm surprised to see him in some linen trousers and a shirt. Both cream.

"Nice," I muse as he looks over his glasses at me.

"Motherfucker," he breathes, and I laugh, walking on bare feet to the car and opening the door for Mum, helping her out.

She gives me an accusing eye. "Your father's been splashing some cash."

"He has?" I ask, innocent, as she holds out her wrist. "Ooh, fancy." I take in the delicate piece. "You look lovely, Mum."

"And you look...not ready." She takes in my white shorts as John chuckles.

"I'm ready," I assure her.

"For what, a swim?"

"Maybe," I muse.

Confused and perhaps a little exasperated by me, she hands over the flower as Dad moves in for a hug.

"Hey, Dad."

"Ready, son?"

"For Ava?" I ask. "Never."

He laughs and releases me, holding the tops of my arms, looking at me. Studying me. I let him have his moment as John leads Mum around the side of the villa toward the beach. Dad doesn't say anything else. He inhales, squeezes my arms, then moves in and kisses my forehead. "Good luck, son." Releasing me, he wanders off, and I watch him go until he rounds the corner.

A deep breath.

Complete.

I go inside and trim the stem of the flower, tucking it in the back of my shorts, then fetch Ava's dress, my timing perfect. She's at the wardrobe when I enter the bedroom. "I've picked something."

She looks back, taking me in first before the dress. Her hands move away from the rails. "It's a bit short, isn't it?"

"I'll make an exception," I say nonchalantly, going to her and helping her into it. I zip her up and take her in. "Cute." I look out past the billowing voile drapes, hoping everyone is in place as I claim Ava's hand.

"I need shoes." She laughs as I pull her to the doors.

"We're paddling," I say over my shoulder, walking us around the pool to the gate that leads to the beach. I see everyone in the distance and look back at Ava to see if she's spotted them. No. Her eyes are on me.

"Can we paddle on our backs?" she asks.

"Pregnancy does wonderful things to you, Mrs. Ward."

"I always want you this much."

"I know you do." I stop us at the gate and spend a short while taking her in. Glorious. "You're missing something." I pull the calla from the back of my shorts and tuck it behind her ear, fixing her air around it. "Much better."

She smiles as I lean in and kiss her cheek before walking us on. "Watch that piece of splintered wood," I warn, stepping across the old sleepers. "Careful."

"You should have let me put some shoes on, then." She leaps across the wooden planks.

"Ava, no jumping," I yell. "You'll shake the babies up."

She laughs, totally ignoring me, and leaps the rest of the way down to the sand. "Come on," she calls, breaking out into a jog but soon slowing again. I smile as she comes to a gradual stop, taking in the row of people before her. All smiling. Our family. All people who love us.

It's a delayed reaction, but she gasps and faces me. "What are they doing here?"

"They're here to witness me marrying you."

"But we're already married." A huge frown creeps onto her forehead. "We are, aren't we?"

I laugh. "Yes, we are." I look up to Mum and Dad. Old, glassy eyes look back at me. Yes, this is for Ava. But it's mostly for me and for them. I don't mind admitting that. And, bonus, I get to marry my wife again. With all of my family. Just how it should have been.

That's one lesson I've learned.

It's not too late to do things the right way.

"But my mum and dad missed our day," I say, giving my attention back to Ava before I let my emotions take over. "And we should have done it this way before."

I walk us through our family to the registrar by the shore, and turn Ava to face me, holding her hands with both of mine.

"We are gathered here today," the registrar begins as Ava looks up at me, a small smile on her face, her bewilderment clear. I hold her hands tighter, watching her mouth move, her eyes shine.

"Will you love him, cherish him, honor, and obey him?" she's asked, "for as long as you both shall live?"

I raise my brows as Ava's smile becomes knowing. "Well?" I ask.

"I will," she says quietly as I move in closer, bringing her hands to my mouth. And now it's my turn.

"I love you," I say quietly, tilting my head when she tilts hers. Watching her closely. I thought I'd known peace. Ava's trampled all over that. "An eternity with you wouldn't be enough, Ava." I smile as her lip begins to tremble, feel my throat getting thicker. "From the moment I saw you, I knew things would change for me." She breathes in, and I definitely hear a collection of emotional whimpers from the crowd. I can't look, especially at Mum and Dad.

Don't, bro. They're a wreck.

You're never alone.

I breathe in. "I plan on devoting every second of my life to worshipping you, adoring you, indulging in you, and I plan on making up for empty years without you." My voice wobbles terribly. *It's another chance.* And I'm grabbing it with both hands and never letting go. "I'm taking you to Paradise, baby." Or Jesse Cloud Nine. Either will do. I lift her up to me, holding her to my front. "Are you ready?"

She nods as she speaks. "Yes," she whispers, but her words are strong and assertive. Everything I need. "Take me."

"Oh, I took you long ago, Mrs. Ward," I say, as she pulls at my hair. "But right now is where it really begins." I slam our mouths together and kiss her with purpose. "No more digging to get beneath me," I mumble around her mouth. "You know everything there is to know."

Freedom from my demons. "And no more confessions, because I have nothing left to tell."

"I think you have," she says, snuggling into my neck.

"I do?"

"You do." She nibbles at my cheek as I walk into the sea. "Tell me you love me."

Except that, of course. And I will tell her every day for the rest of our lives.

I find her eyes, those dark, beautiful eyes. Eyes I've been lost in since the first moment I looked into them.

She's real.

And she's mine.

"I love you so fucking much, baby."

I wade into the sea, looking up at her as she turns her face toward the sky. "I know," she yells to the clouds.

And I laugh and sink us both into the water, completely wrapped in Ava, her mouth adoring mine.

This smart, beautiful, patient, sexy, graceful woman.

Mine.

Forever.

Epilogue

SOME MONTHS LATER

"Make it stop," she sobs. "I can't take any more."

Her hands are fisting anything she can lay them on, and she currently has my hair in them. My head jars from her yanking. "One last try, baby." I turn my face into her to find her lips, kissing her softly. There are no sparks of desire, just pure, raw love. "Together, okay?"

She nods against me and resumes nuzzling into my neck. Then I feel her body tense, her mouth open against my throat, and her grip of my hair crosses the line into violence. She screams, her teeth sinking into my flesh, one hand pulling my hair, the other digging into my bicep. I blank it out, all of the pain she's inflicting on me, because it's nothing compared to what I've experienced. *Nothing.* I clench my teeth. Fucking hell, seeing her like this, the pain, her tears. Fucking awful. I burrow deeper into her neck, squeezing her hand in both of mine. *Come on, baby.* I kiss her wet skin, nibble her neck, let her feel me there, silently encouraging her. How long will they let this go on before they intervene?

"That's it, Ava," the midwife shouts before calling for her colleague's assistance. "Yes, it's coming. Harder, Ava. Push harder."

Ava's face is beetroot, her eyes clenched, her head thrown forward. "Come on, Ava!"

The scream that fills the delivery suite is piercing.

"Oh my, we have a girl."

And then there's a moment of silence, everything falling into slow motion.

Am I in the real world, or is this a dream?

"Oh my God," Ava gasps, pulsing on the bed against me. "A girl."

A girl.

And let me tell you, if you think the past twenty years have been a punishment, wait until you meet your little girl.

I breathe in, stunned into stillness, my heart hammering. I'm almost scared to look. But I can hear, and damn, she has some lungs on her. I let out a choked sob as I lift my head.

"Mr. Ward, we're going to cut the cord, okay? We have another baby coming, and it's coming fast."

I just about manage to nod. A girl. I have a baby girl.

I bite at my lip to stop it wobbling, looking down at Ava's soaked, red face. Her eyes are closed. Her chest pumping. Jesus, she's exhausted.

"We need another push, Ava," the midwife says, her head back between Ava's legs, cheering her on.

"No more," Ava cries, turning her face into mine, her wet cheeks slipping over my bristle. "Please."

My heart clenches. "Come on, baby," I whisper. "You've got this."

"I'm too tired."

"Look at me," I demand, squeezing her hand.

Her eyes slowly drag open. Glassy. Her dark orbs pale. I'm so fucking proud of her. How she's handled this pregnancy. How she's faced her fears and marched on determined and strong. I stroke her wet cheek, dragging my thumb across her rosy lips as she looks at me, waiting for my words of encouragement and love. *Depends* on them. "How loud do you think you'll scream?" I ask, and she laughs over a sob as she begins to stiffen again, a sign another contraction is on the way.

She looks at me in panic. "Really fucking loud," she starts to pant.

I smile, squeezing her hand. "We've got a girl, baby."

"A girl." She strains the words out. "You have a girl again."

Fuck. "Yeah, I do." I dip and kiss her forehead as she builds to the next push, her hold of me getting tighter. "Ready?" I ask, feeling her nod, her breath held. I brace myself, squeezing my eyes shut, and she bellows out an angry yell, the sound echoing around the room as the midwife cheers her on and I take the brunt of her strength. Then she slumps into the bed again, exhaling.

And there's another cry.

"A boy!"

What?

We have a boy. One of each?

Somewhere, in the back of my mind, I knew it. *I fucking knew it.*

Rosie.

I drop my head onto Ava's shoulder, unable to stop the tears. My exhausted heart is showing no sign of letting up, and I know it probably won't for the rest of my life. I haven't even looked at them yet. I haven't smelt them, felt them, or told them how much I love them. "Well done, baby," I whisper, finding Ava's face and smothering her with kisses. She doesn't respond. It's probably one of the only times in our relationship that she can't.

"Mr. Ward?"

"Are they okay?" I ask.

"They're perfect. Congratulations."

I burrow back into Ava's neck as the midwives work, and she finds the strength to hold me, sighing, gently stroking my hair and dropping small kisses on my skin every now and then. No words need to be spoken—not for a very long while. It's Ava comforting me now. And I need it.

She eventually finds the strength to pull away, searching out my clouded eyes, and as soon as hers land on mine, reality is confirmed. *My* reality. "Go and meet your babies," Ava says, smoothing her small palm down my rough cheek. "It was twenty-six years before I found you. Don't make them wait for you a moment longer than they have to." She pecks my lips and then looks over my shoulder, and I muster up the courage to turn and finally introduce myself to my babies, walking slowly across the room.

I gaze into the cribs, utterly astonished. The love is instant. So intense, it physically hurts. There are only two other moments in my life when I've felt this level of awe and hope.

Rosie.

And when their mother walked into my office for the first time.

How? How did I create these two beautiful creatures? They look so small. So fragile. Christ, they will literally fit in the palm of my hand. "They look tiny," I say quietly. "Too small."

"They're both a good weight for twins," one of the midwives says, smiling.

I can't take my eyes off them as she wraps them up and pops little hats on their heads.

"Are you ready to hold them?"

I look at her in alarm. "What?"

"Hold them, Mr. Ward," she says over a laugh.

"Hold them?" But they look too small. I hold up my hands, turning them over in front of me, as if to demonstrate the size of me against them.

"Skin on skin." The midwife dips into my baby girl's crib and lifts her out, carrying her over to Ava and holding her with one hand as she helps Ava pull her gown down, exposing her chest. She lays our little girl front down on Ava's skin, covering her back with the blanket. I watch in awe as Ava buries her face in the top of her head on a sigh. "Mr. Ward?"

"Yeah?"

She nods at my T-shirt-covered body and, without thinking, I reach down and pull it up over my head, moving to the chair by Ava's bed, lowering, unable to take my eyes off her. Ava smirks at my bare chest as the midwife carries my little boy to me and sets him down. *Fuck.* The moment he comes to rest on my skin, my heart kicks. It beats harder and faster.

More purpose.

He looks even smaller on me. I cup his micro arse with my big palm, letting the midwife fix the blanket around us, and I stare down in wonder as my baby boy's little cheek rests on my flesh, his eyes closed.

"Do we have names?" the midwife asks.

I look back at Ava. She looks so sleepy. She nods, and I bite at my lip to stop it trembling. *Fuck.*

You're going to have a girl, Daddy.

"Maddie," I say quietly, my voice tight, as I watch Ava stroke her head. She smiles softly at me, nodding to my boy in my arms. I look down at his head, stroking over the fine hairs. Dark blond hair.

You better name the boy after me.

I breathe in, my chest expanding, my boy rising with it. "And this is Jacob." I rest my lips on his head and breathe him into me. "After my brother."

Peaceful.

This isn't real.

But as I look up into my wife's eyes, my unbelievable reality sinks in. And the tears come again.

Do I deserve this?

Yes.

Yes, I do.

• • •

<small>THREE YEARS LATER...</small>

The water sparkles under the spring sunshine, like millions of diamonds are floating on the surface of the lake, the ducks weaving through the water with grace and efficiency. Everything seems so vividly clear. The blades of grass. The detailed patterns of bark on the trees. The faces of the people around me. I can smell the spring air. Every sense is heightened.

It's seven thirty. What am I doing here? I'm sitting. I look beside me to the wood. I'm on a bench? Glancing around, I see runners, walkers, strollers, dog-walkers. The park is busy, as you would expect on a beautiful spring evening. But, again, what the hell am I doing here? I rise to my feet, noticing I'm wearing a suit.

A suit. I haven't worn a suit since I sold The Manor. No need for any armor anymore.

Weird.

I dip into my pocket to get my keys. No keys. I pat my body down. No keys, no phone. "The fuck?" I breathe, circling on the spot, trying to pull anything from my brain that would explain why the fuck I'm in St James's Park. Alone. With no keys and no phone.

In a suit.

I still for a moment, thinking, memories floating on the edge of my mind. I breathe in when a shooting pain hits my stomach, and I pull my suit jacket back, my heart missing too many beats. I look down at my shirt.

White.

No blood, no knife.

What's going on? I take a few steps on the path and come to a sharp stop when something down by the water catches my eye. "What?" I whisper, rushing toward the railings that keep people away from the edge of the lake. I take hold of the top, eyes unwavering from the side of the water, and kick my leg over. I walk down to the edge, my eyes burning, not daring to blink, watching as her little chubby hands fumble with the bag of bird seed. The bag splits, and the seed scatters at her feet.

"Oopsie daisy," I whisper, my heart climbing up into my throat.

She spots me, her green eyes widening. "Daddy!" And she runs my way.

I breathe in sharply, searching for the invisible wall, waiting for her to crash into it. "Rosie, no!"

She doesn't.

She throws herself at me, and I catch her, amazed, feeling the impact of our bodies coming together. The force robs me of every bit of air in my lungs. Her little backside rests on my forearm, her thighs wrapped around my torso. Then her palms slap against my cheeks and squeeze. "Oopsie daisy," she says, giggling.

I'm rendered stupid, just staring into her green eyes, taking in her dark blond hair. She's wearing her little pink T-shirt with a rainbow heart on. The last thing she was wearing when Carmichael carried her away from me. "Hey, baby girl," I whisper over the lump wedged in my throat.

She laughs, pointing to the water. "Quack, quack, Daddy."

"You want to feed the ducks?" I ask, carrying her down to the edge of the water, soon getting caught up in the swarms of ducks flapping around, greedy for the seeds she's dropped. She laughs her little arse off, delighted. I can't take my eyes off her.

Heaven is where you want it to be.

I breathe in, turning when I hear footsteps behind me.

Jake.

"There you are," he says.

"I found Daddy," Rosie replies, wriggling out of my hold. I reluctantly lower her to her feet and watch, stunned, as she starts clapping her hands, stomping through the crowd of ducks.

Jake passes me, chasing after her. "Come on, Rosie, we have to go."

Go?

"Where?" I call, following Jake down to the water. "I just got here." I reach for my chest, pressing my hand into it. Beating. Hard. Jake passes me, now with Rosie on his shoulders. "Jake, wait," I call, and he turns, walking backward, Rosie's little palms resting on his forehead, her legs dangling down his front. And he doesn't say a word.

They're fading.

No.

Fading.

Please, no.

Then, the very second before they disappear, he smiles. "Love you, bro," he calls.

And Rosie waves, yelling, "Bye, Daddy!"

Fuck. "Love you both," I whisper over my devastation, going after them, but as I reach the railings, something emerges from the haze where Rosie and Jacob just vanished.

Ava.

I come to an alarmed stop, my heart going wild in my chest as she walks toward me, her smile falling when she spots me. I must look like I've seen a ghost. I rake a hand through my hair, hot, clammy. She's holding Maddie in one hand, Jacob in the other.

"Daddy!" they yell, trying to come at me, but Ava holds onto them as I let out another whimper, and this time it's one of relief as I take in my wife and kids.

"What are you doing on that side of the railing?" Ava asks, frowning as she takes me in from top to toe, worried.

"I..." I exhale, laughing under my breath, looking back to the edge of the water. There's a mad feeding frenzy happening, the ground littered with seed. I look down at my hand clasping the empty packet of bird feed. "I was feeding the ducks," I say quietly, returning my attention to Ava. She looks charmed. Maybe a little knowing.

I put myself on the right side of the fence and crouch, collecting the kids up, one in each arm. I look between them. Miracles. "Ready to go home?" I ask.

It's a Daddy Sandwich as they both hug my head and I go to Ava, seeing she's quietly curious still. I bend, letting her drop a kiss on my lips. "Your keys and phone," she says, pulling them out of her handbag. "You left them on the table in the restaurant."

I did?

"You did," she muses, as we start walking out of the park. "What happened?" she asks, eyes on me as Maddie and Jacob slap my cheeks in time to my steps.

"Nothing happened," I assure her, lowering the kids to their feet, smiling when they go bombing off across the grass. I put my arm around Ava, bringing her close, watching the twins chasing each other as we wander along behind them.

I look over my shoulder. "Just saying goodbye to someone," I whisper.

Two someones who have talked me off the ledge and walked alongside me. Helped me get to where I am today. My *new* normal. My *daily* happiness.

No more self-loathing and torture.

I look down at Ava tucked into my side, as she looks up at me, smiling her understanding. "I love you," I whisper, pushing my lips into her hair, breathing in deeply.

"I know," she murmurs, resting her hand on my chest as we follow the kids. "It's been a lovely day."

"Pure bliss, baby," I reply, smiling.

Forever.

All because of this woman.

Acknowledgments

To my readers, I hope you've enjoyed your time inside the Lord's mind. It's been an exhilarating but exhausting ride. I absolutely adore him, as I know many of you do too. He's my first. And the very reason I get to say this to you over and over again... Thank you. Thank you for reading and thank you so bloody much for supporting me and my words. May I bring you many, many more. And a special shoutout to Lisa and Katherine. We've been together so long, I've forgotten how we met! Thanks for all of your help over the years. I appreciate you both so much and couldn't do it without you. JEM xxx

About the Author

Jodi Ellen Malpas was born and raised in England, where she lives with her husband, boys, and Theo the Doberman. She is a self-professed daydreamer and has a terrible weak spot for alpha males. Writing powerful love stories with addictive characters has become her passion—a passion she now shares with her devoted readers. She's a proud #1 *New York Times* bestselling author and *Sunday Times* bestseller, and her work is published in over twenty-seven languages around the world.

jodiellenmalpas.co.uk

Don't miss the exciting new books
Entangled has to offer.

Follow us!

 @EntangledPublishing

@Entangled_Publishing

@EntangledPub

an imprint of Entangled Publishing LLC